Praise for *Fortunes of France*

"Modern-day Dumas finally crosses the channel" *Observer*

"An enjoyable read, distinguished by its author's
erudition and wit" *Sunday Times*

"Swashbuckling historical fiction… For all its philosophical
depth [*The Brethren*] is a hugely entertaining romp… The
comparisons with Dumas seem both natural and deserved and
the next 12 instalments [are] a thrilling prospect" *Guardian*

"Historical fiction at its very best… This fast paced and
heady brew is colourfully leavened with love and sex and
a great deal of humour and wit. The second instalment
cannot be published too soon" *We Love This Book*

"A highly anticipated tome that's been described as
Game of Thrones meets *The Three Musketeers*" Mariella
Frostrup on BBC Radio 4's *Open Book*

"A vivid novel by France's modern Dumas… [there is]
plenty of evidence in the rich characterisation and vivid
historical detail that a reader's long-term commitment
will be amply rewarded" *Sunday Times*

"A sprawling, earthy tale of peril, love, lust,
death, dazzling philosophical debate and political
intrigue… an engrossing saga" *Gransnet*

"A master of the historical novel" *Guardian*

"So rich in historical detail… the characters
are engaging" *Sunday Express*

Born in 1908, ROBERT MERLE was originally an English teacher before serving as an interpreter with the British army during the Second World War, which led to his capture by the German army at Dunkirk. He published his hugely popular *Fortunes of France* series over four decades, from 1977 to 2003, the final instalment appearing just a year before his death in 2004. *The Brethren* is the first book in the series, followed by *City of Wisdom and Blood*, *Heretic Dawn* and *League of Spies*.

Heretic Dawn

ROBERT MERLE

PUSHKIN PRESS

Pushkin Press
71–75 Shelton Street
London WC2H 9JQ

Original text © 2016 Estate of Robert Merle
English translation © 2016 T. Jefferson Kline

Heretic Dawn first published in French as
Paris, ma bonne ville in 1980

First published by Pushkin Press in 2016
This edition first published in 2018

1 3 5 7 9 8 6 4 2

ISBN 13: 978-1-78227-509-1

Designed and typeset by Tetragon, London
Printed and bound by CPI Group (UK) Ltd, Croydon, CR0 4YY

www.pushkinpress.com

HERETIC
DAWN

1

THERE'S ONE THING I'M CERTAIN OF. We're just like the sea—tranquillity is merely a surface impression. Beneath, everything is motion, tumult and undercurrents. So a man should never consider his happiness assured or his soul in peace at last. Once we believe we're content, we discover something else that sets our appetites on edge.

As I rode away from Monsieur de Montcalm's chateau, glad as I was to be reunited with my father, looking so hale and happy, and as delighted as I felt that we were on our way to Sarlat, my beloved Mespech and all its dear inhabitants, my joy was far from unalloyed. Every now and again I felt a sudden stab at my heart at the thought of leaving Angelina de Montcalm behind, and of the uncertain happiness we'd vowed to each other, betokened by the pledge I wore on the little finger of my left hand: the gold ring studded with an azure stone that she'd given me in the little turret that flanked the east wall of Barbentane.

"Ha!" I thought. "I'm a Huguenot heretic and a penniless little brother with no inheritance! How dare I tempt Fortune by asking for her hand, even if it's for her future hand? Given Monsieur de Montcalm's obvious distaste for me, will she really consent to wait so long, especially given all the studies I must complete and the years of hard work necessary to earn a doctorate and set up practice as a physician? I'll never have enough bread in my basket to offer her the life to which her rank entitles her—or mine entitles me, for that matter!

"Haven of grace! How I love her! And how forbidding and horrible the idea of losing her! But however much I trust her word, shouldn't I fear her father's tyranny, her mother's intrusiveness, the girl's own apprehension about growing old while she languishes interminably, never fully certain of her future, in these precarious times, when a man's life—especially a Huguenot's—weighs no more in the balance than that of a chicken?"

And yet, in the midst of these worries that so knotted my throat, I derived enormous comfort from recalling her slow, languid and gracious step, the tender light in her doe's eyes and the marvellous benevolence of her soul. "No indeed," I mused. "Whatever may befall me, I know I've not made the wrong choice! Were I to search the whole world over, I'd never find a woman who joined so much heart to so much beauty."

My father had decided that we'd go by way of the Cévennes in order to reach Périgord by the mountainous road, rather than take the easier and prettier route through Carcassonne and Toulouse. After the surprise attack on Meaux, where the leaders of the reformed religion, Condé and Coligny, had nearly seized the king himself, the war between Catholics and Huguenots had suddenly spread throughout the kingdom, and since the two cities I mentioned were now in the hands of the papists, it would have been extremely dangerous for us to stop there, no matter how well armed we were. Certainly, with my father, my two Siorac cousins, myself, my half-brother Samson, our valet Miroul, our Gascon Cabusse and our mason Jonas, we were only a party of eight—enough to defend ourselves against any ambushes by highwaymen we might encounter in the mountains, but not enough to confront a royal militia.

In Sarlat and throughout the surrounding region, we were well respected by the papists themselves (except for some of the most bloodthirsty of them) because my father was a loyalist Huguenot and had never taken up arms against his king, but also because he had supplied the city with food during the plague and then, afterwards, rid the town of the butcher-baron of la Lendrevie and his rascals. But in Carcassonne and Toulouse, no one knew us, and we knew that Huguenots were all assumed to be rebels, so that if we were taken, we'd be immediately condemned and put to the sword.

As soon as the mountain roads became too steep to maintain a brisk trot, we slowed our sweating horses to a walk, and my father, pulling up alongside me, and seeing me all dreamy and lost in "malancholy" (as my poor Fontanette would say in her southern dialect), bade me tell him all about my life as a medical student in Montpellier, expanding on what I'd been able to write in my letters, and without embellishments or omissions of any kind.

"Oh, Father," I laughed. "If you really want the unvarnished and sincere version, we'd better ride on ahead of the others. I wouldn't want the more shameful parts of my story to be overheard by my cousins or by our men—and certainly not by my beloved Samson, whose dove-like innocence would no doubt be sullied by my account."

At this my father burst out laughing, and immediately gave spur to his horse in order to put some distance between us and the others. And so I told him everything: my life, my labours, my loves, the incredible setbacks, joys and perils I'd experienced in Montpellier and in Nîmes—though I confess I omitted the piteous demise of my poor Fontanette, not because I wanted to hide it from him, but because I was sure, in the telling of it, to burst into tears, as I had already done at Barbentane, sitting at my Angelina's knees.

"My son," said my father when I'd done with my story, "you're lively, valiant, quick to forgive and quick to anger as well. You take many risks. You always want to right any wrongs you witness, which is a noble but perilous instinct. And though you always seem to be clear-headed in your actions, you seem not always to reflect before you act. Listen well to what I have to say: caution, prudence and patience are the teats of adventure. If you want to live a long time in this cruel century, imbibe their milk above all. Husband Fortune carefully and she will care for you. *Nosse haec omnia, salus est adolescentis.*"*

As he spoke these words, I looked at my father, overcome with tenderness that he should finish his speech, as I would have expected, with a quotation from Cicero. This hero of the battles of Ceresole and Calais was as proud of his prowess in Latin as he was of his knowledge of medicine, which was his first vocation, as you may perhaps remember, dear reader. Handsome and lithe in his physical presence, without a trace of fat, sitting straight as an "I" on his horse, his eyes a brilliant blue, his hair only slightly grey despite his more than fifty years, he had not changed a whit in all the years I had known him.

"My father," I replied, "you're right and I thank you for your wise counsel. I will try to correct my lack of prudence. But," I continued with a wry smile, "would you be a baron if you hadn't wagered everything on your first duel, which forced you to abandon your study of medicine to become a soldier?"

"Pierre de Siorac," frowned my father, "honour dictated my actions, and honour must come first in everything we do. I doubt you could claim the same motive in all the risks that you've run. Firstly, isn't it patently evident that you risk the hooligan's knife when you frequent rich ladies of the night?"

"That rascal got the worst of it!"

---

* "The safety of our young depends on knowing these things."

"By a stroke of luck! And didn't you break every law known to man when you went digging up two dead men in the Saint-Denis cemetery in order to dissect them?"

"So did the great Vesalius!"

"And risked his life doing so! And, by the way, was it to further the work of dissection that you fornicated with a bewitching sorceress on the tomb of the Grand Inquisitor?"

"But I absolutely *had* to get her away from where we were exhuming the bodies!"

"To get away from her?" replied Jean de Siorac, pretending that he had misheard what I'd said. "To get away from her by having your way with her? That's a strange way of getting away from someone!"

Here he laughed at his little joke, and I along with him, though I was pretty certain he would have done the same thing in my place, since, to my knowledge, he'd never been able to resist a petticoat, diabolical or otherwise.

"And thirdly, my son," he continued, still frowning, "where on earth did you get the idea that you should shoot the atheist abbot Cabassus on his gibbet?"

"I did it out of compassion. He was suffering terribly."

"And it was your compassion, I'll warrant, that led you to save Bishop Bernard d'Elbène of Nîmes?"

"Naturally!"

"And in that case you did the right thing: your sense of honour dictated that you save an honest enemy from vile murder. But for the grave-robbing, the arquebus shot and the fornication, no excuse. In none of that do I see any attention to the law, reason or prudence. You acted like a madman."

I had no answer to give him on that score, though I still held my head high, humility not being one of my strong points.

"My son," Jean de Siorac continued in the gravest tone and turning to look me in the eye, "I have decided that you may not return to Montpellier until our war with the papists has ended."

"But Father!" I cried, with inexpressible sadness and bitterness. "What about my medical studies and all the time I have devoted to them?"

"You will work at Mespech, diligently studying your books and helping me with dissection."

Not knowing how to answer this, I fell silent, and, though in my heart of hearts I loved life at Mespech, I couldn't help feeling bitterly disappointed at having to remain far from Montpellier for such a long time—and, in truth, far from Barbentane as well.

"Pierre, my son," said Jean de Siorac, who, having guessed my thoughts, considerably softened his tone, "don't despair. Great love is but fortified by absence. If it should die from such a separation, well, then it wasn't great enough."

Which, however true it may have been, wasn't much consolation.

"For me, your safety must come first," he reflected, "and that's why I must pull you away from the troubles in Montpellier as long as papists and Huguenots continue to cut each other's throats in the name of Christ. François is my eldest son," he continued, not without a hint of sadness, "and he will inherit Mespech. And François," he added with a sigh, "is what he is and what you know him to be. But you, my younger son, shine with such valour and talent that I have no doubt that it is in your stars to add great lustre to the name you bear. On the other hand, you are impetuous, imprudent and high-handed. So, God willing, I intend to keep you alive, for you have but one life and I wouldn't want it to be nipped in the bud, as that would turn my old age into bitterness and pain. For, my son, I shall tell you my true feelings: I value you infinitely more than all my wealth and titles."

Although exceedingly touched by his words, I could not speak, so tight was the knot in my throat, and tears flowed down my cheeks, for my father had never before told me how much he loved me, no matter how easily he expressed his feelings—being, like me and like the person he had made me, a spontaneous man who always spoke his mind and hid nothing, except from his enemies.

Oh, reader! As used as I was to Mespech (where we arrived by forced march a mere fifteen days after leaving Barbentane), I was very happy to be there again, a prince in this chateau, loved and adored by all, masters and servants alike, and loving all of them in return, right down to the last valet, and, what's more, rediscovering the sweet embrace of my good old nursemaid Barberine, whose arms wrapped me happily into her bosom that first night at home, while my father reviewed his correspondence. I didn't fail to ask permission to read the dispatches arriving from the north concerning our religious troubles (for news travelled fast from Huguenot to Huguenot), and pored over them, hoping for news of the victory of our side—naturally desiring, out of love of humanity and the kingdom, an end to this bloody struggle, but also looking for news that would assure my rapid return to Montpellier and to my Angelina.

The fortunes of war seemed, at least momentarily, to smile on us. Having scarcely 2,000 soldiers, Condé and Coligny, with astonishing fearlessness, had been able to isolate in Paris—an immense city entirely won over to the papists—the 20,000 soldiers of the constable, Montmorency.

It was marvellous! The fly was putting the elephant to flight! And worse than that, was starving it to death. Pillaging the villages (except for Saint-Denis, Saint-Ouen and Aubervilliers, which they were occupying), the Huguenots had emptied the barns, burnt the mills and stopped all carts trying to enter Paris. Gonesse bread no longer reached the capital. The Saint-Cloud market was empty: neither butter nor meat could get through from Normandy.

The 300,000 Parisians, gnawed by hunger and even more by the hatred stirred up by their strident prelates, dreamt of attacking this handful of insolent reformists, who had the temerity to make fools of their enemies. But Montmorency temporized. He didn't want to unsheathe his sword yet—not, as some suggested nastily, because he wanted to spare Condé and Coligny, who were his nephews (a perfect example of this fratricidal war!), but because, being as he was excessively cautious and lacking in nerve, he preferred to await the arrival of Spanish reinforcements before attacking.

However, the Parisians' unruliness forced his hand, and so Montmorency, to punish their disobedience, set up as his avant-garde a ragged bunch of volunteers, hiding their fat bourgeois paunches beneath their costly, shining armour, who marched out of the city gates in front of the paid Swiss guards. Coligny and his poor meagre devils, dressed all in white, fell upon them, routed them and put them to flight. As they fled, these portly merchants ran full pelt into the Swiss, throwing their ranks into disorder—a turn of events that Montmorency, a man of limited imagination, had not foreseen.

The Turkish ambassador, watching this action from the hillside of the little village of Montmartre, was agape at the daring and courage of our white cassocks. "If His Highness had these whites," he was reported to have said, "he could circle the entire earth, for nothing could withstand their advance!"

And, indeed, nothing could withstand Condé's attack, who, at the head of his horsemen, pushed his assault directly at Montmorency. One of Condé's lieutenants, the Scotsman Robert Stuart, who'd earlier been cruelly tortured by the papists, sought out Montmorency and broke his back with a single pistol shot.

The head of the royal armies now dead, our little army, too small to carry off a victory, withdrew, undefeated, to Montereau, where it sought to increase the size of its ranks, while, within the capital, the Parisians licked their Huguenot wounds, and worked to augment their own numbers. And so a sort of truce was established that lasted pretty much the entire winter, each side working to fortify itself for the decisive battle. And how interminable this winter seemed to me, isolated in my little crenellated nest! I suffered, too, from the frost and snow in Périgord, after the sweet warmth of the Montpellier skies. I wrote to my doctor-father, Chancellor Saporta, to Maître Sanche and to Fogacer. I wrote on every one of God's days to my Angelina. And I wrote once a month to Madame de Joyeuse and to Thomassine.

I must confess that my body missed these last two as much as my heart missed Angelina. You must understand that it isn't that I didn't wish to remain faithful to my sweet angel, but how could I be condemned for such a long time to the gall and bitterness of chastity, I who so appreciated the delicacies of the female body? To be able to manage that, our animal natures, born of those imperious organs (each one of which pushes so hard to accomplish its mission), would have to stop forcing their way into our brain canals! But when these daily pleasures are no longer available, the resulting abstinence cries out to those lively spirits in great number and we are tyrannized in our leisure moments during the day and especially at night when we need to be sleeping. And so, when my daydreams turned to dreams of love, I couldn't help remembering the pleasures I'd indulged in from time to time at the needle shop and at the Joyeuse residence in Montpellier—thoughts which unsettled me when I wanted to think only of the pleasures that awaited me in Angelina's arms. Alas, the Périgordian proverb is right: you can't eat the smell of roast meat; and the bouquet of future loves cannot replace the humble crust of bread whose merit is to be there when our stomachs are growling and our mouth is watering.

At the present moment, to tell the truth, I had nothing—neither the celestial ambrosia nor the earthly crust—being stuck in Mespech like a prisoner, forbidden to visit Sarlat or any of our villages, since the Brethren (my father and Sauveterre) feared for our safety in these troubled times.

I had found Uncle Sauveterre much greyed, his neck even thinner in his Huguenot collar, and dragging his wounded leg behind him. Nor had his perpetually sour temperament improved—he spoke scarcely three words a day (of which two were quotations from the Bible), constantly frowning and muttering about Jean de Siorac's weakness for Franchou, my late mother's former chambermaid, though my uncle seemed to dote on the bastard my father had sired, who was already a year old and whom they'd named David.

Franchou, who was nursing him, was already pregnant again, and happy that my father had let her know he'd be content to have a daughter, since at Mespech, he said, with Jacquou and Annet (my milk brothers, Barberine's sons) there were plenty of males, and he wanted a pretty sweetling to brighten up our old walls. Having heard this, Franchou was able to abandon herself unreservedly to the pleasures of being with child, assured that the fruit of her loins would be well received, for, as much as my father wanted a girl, no one has ever seen a man turn up his nose at the birth of a son.

That winter, despite the cold and snow, we had wonderful Sunday dinners at Mespech, when Cabusse would come from le Breuil with Cathau; our stonemason Jonas from his cave house with Sarrazine; and Coulondre Iron-arm from the les Beunes mill with Jacotte—the three wenches looking so fresh and pretty in their Sunday dress, their lace bonnets perched on their heads, and each carrying a baby in her arms—not to mention Franchou, who was proudest of all of them, since her baby boy was the son of a baron. We never left the table without at least one of the four undoing her bodice and pulling her lily-white breast to nurse her babe—except Cathau, who always turned away while she breastfed since Cabusse was so jealous. But there was certainly enough, with the three others, to satisfy our eyes and soften our hearts, and my father, in his place at the head of the table, would silence Sauveterre's sardonic sermons with a wave of his hand, so that he could quietly savour the beauty of these nursings, which he never tired of, so much did he love life. Sauveterre, for his part, kept his eyes lowered in his belief that woman is nothing but trickery and the source of eternal damnation—at best an ephemeral pleasure followed by a life of worry. And yet even he was overjoyed at the idea that Mespech's community of little Huguenots was multiplying, and would carry forward the torch, after we were gone, of the only true religion in this world.

On one particular evening, I noticed Barberine watching Jacotte suckle her little Emmanuel, who, unlike his taciturn father Coulondre Iron-arm, was as noisy a little one as we'd ever had in this house. "Oh, my time has come and gone," she sighed. "Now that Madame has departed this world," she whispered, dropping her voice so as not to sadden the baron with her memories, "what am I doing here? What good am I, since all I know how to do is to give milk like a poor cow in the barn? At least when Madame was here, as soon as she knew she was pregnant, I'd get pregnant by my husband so that Madame only needed a part-time nurse at the beginning until I could deliver and provide both babes all the milk they needed. But now what good am I? It breaks my heart to see these strong young wenches giving suck to their babes just as I used to do for the baron's children. And now look at me! What good am I any more? I don't even know how to cook a roast like Maligou or run the household like Alazaïs!"

"Barberine," I replied, "are you saying it was nothing to have nursed François de Siorac, who will be the next Baron de Mespech? Am I myself not going to be a great doctor in the city someday?

And my beautiful little sister Catherine, who will someday marry a great lord?"

At that, Catherine blushed with pleasure, lowered her azure eyes and, in her confusion, took her two braids in her mouth. She was approaching adulthood with Little Sissy (the daughter la Maligou claimed to have had by a Gypsy captain, who, through sorcery, had forced himself on her fifteen times in her barn). I remembered how my jealous little Catherine would rage in mute fury when she was three years old and saw me carrying Little Sissy on my shoulders—Little Sissy who was now a grown woman, while Catherine was still a child, having no other beauty than her marvellous face, all pink and white, with her sky-blue eyes, golden hair, full red lips and cute little nose. But as for her body, she hadn't yet fleshed out, so her legs were long and thin, her derrière and bosom as flat as my hand.

I couldn't help noticing this difference the next morning, when, strolling from room to room, I entered, full of my own thoughts, the room in the east tower my father called "the baths" because there was a huge oak tub in front of the open fire, which Alazaïs, la Maligou and Barberine had filled with pails of hot water brought from the kitchen.

"Hey, Pierre!" cried Barberine. "Be off with you, my pretty boy! An honest lad doesn't go peeping at the girls while they're in their bath!"

"What?" I countered. "Isn't Catherine my sister? And Little Sissy practically the same? Haven't I already seen them naked a hundred times when they were little?"

So saying, hands on my hips, I stepped up to the tub, enjoying the sight of these fresh flowers in their natural state. Catherine, blushing crimson, sank down up to her neck in the soapy water, but Little Sissy, devil that she was, suddenly exclaimed, "I'm clean enough, Barberine!" and stepped out of the tub, naked as she was, and had the effrontery to go and stand in front of the fire, turning this way and that to dry herself, batting her eyelashes coyly as she did so, her large, jade-black eyes glancing slyly at me. There was no need for me walk around her to caress her with my eyes: her efforts to dry all her parts exposed her golden Saracen skin to the light of the fire, displaying her graceful arms and her high, apple-like breasts, and, below one of the finest waists you ever saw, her thighs and buttocks nicely rounded, neither too skinny nor too corpulent.

"Oh, you vile strumpet!" cried little Catherine, her blue eyes suddenly filling with bitterness. "You beastly creature! Shameless hussy! Cover yourself, Gypsy witch! You wicked prune! Don't you know it's a capital and deadly sin to let a man see what you're showing him?"

"There, there, my little pearl!" laughed Barberine. "There's no sin in looking, only in doing. Looking's not the same as licking! And tasting isn't taking. But of course, one often leads to the other, as we know all too well. Eh, my little rooster?" she said, turning to me. "I've already told you, get a hold of yourself! I know not what designs your master has for this pretty lass, but it's not for you to go turning her head with your hungry looks before we know what he has in mind for her!"

"Dear Barberine," I cooed, giving her a peck on the cheek (and on her voluminous bosom, as much for my own pleasure as to pacify her), "I meant no harm, as you know very well!"

"I know you meant exactly the opposite, you rascal!" returned Barberine, half in jest and half in earnest. "You're breathing fire like a stallion in a field of mares! What a pity you can't pass on some of this ardour to your brother François, who's as cold as a herring in a barrel of brine."

"Oh, he's not as cold as you think," I retorted. "He goes about dreaming of his Diane de Fontenac."

"Dreaming is like meat without sauce," replied Barberine, "if there's no touching that comes of it! And how's François supposed to marry the daughter of the sworn enemy of Mespech?"

Her words immediately brought my Angelina to mind and the obstacle that her parents' religion put in the way of our cherished project—despite the fact that they liked me well enough—and, suddenly filled with melancholy, I left the women and their bath. But wishing to rid myself of these dark thoughts, I headed towards the hall where Cabusse was giving a fencing lesson to François, who greeted me with a wave of his épée, but nary a smile or a trace of any light in his eyes as he felt very little love for me. What a difference from my beautiful, strong, innocent angel, Samson, who, as soon as he caught sight of me, leapt from his stool, threw his arms around me and gave me a dozen kisses on both cheeks. Still holding his hand, I sat down by his side and watched François, who, to tell the truth, was not a bad-looking fellow, neither weak not awkward in body, able to shoot accurately with both hands, as good a horseman as any and far from ignorant. But he was unbearably withdrawn, tight-lipped, rigid, secretive and infinitely bitter, all too conscious of his rank and of his future barony, haughty with our servants, and, while little Hélix was still alive, haughtily disdainful of my affection for her, clearly preferring his own inaccessible and noble loves.

And there was no doubt about their inaccessibility, for the robber Baron de Fontenac, whose lands bordered our own, dreamt of and breathed and lived only for our destruction, covering his wickedness under the mantle of the papist religion. It's true that his wife did not resemble him in the least, being of sweet temper and Christian virtues, and in this her daughter, thank God, took after her mother. But these poor women had no leverage against this angry wild boar, who swore vengeance against the Brethren for having had his father banished for his crimes and for managing to get their hands on our beautiful domain, an acquisition which made them not only his closest neighbour but kept him from becoming the most powerful baron in the whole Sarlat region.

Of course, during the time we were ministering to his daughter, Diane, while she was infected with the plague, we'd hoped for some reconciliation since no other doctor in Sarlat would have consented to go near the Fontenac castle and the baron had been obliged to ask my father for help. Jean de Siorac consented only on condition that she be brought to Mespech and quarantined in one of our tower rooms, where he'd managed to cure her—the only lasting impairment from her confinement being the incurable longing that spread to François's heart.

Alas, this dog of a baron didn't even have the gratitude of a cur: as soon as the internecine wars that raged among the subjects of the same king recommenced, we learnt that he'd urged several other Catholic noblemen of the Sarlat region to join him in a surprise attack on Mespech in order to destroy this "nest of heretics". Their scheme was greeted with cold stares from virtually every one of our neighbours, given how much respect the Brethren had inspired in the region, and how little this wicked baron. Puymartin (who, though a papist, was a good friend of ours, having fought with us against the butcher-baron of la Lendrevie) was the first to warn us of Fontenac's machinations, and urged us to be careful since, having failed to mount a direct attack on us, the rascal might use stealth or ambush instead.

This warning, brought by a horseman on 16th February, redoubled our vigilance and limited our excursions beyond Mespech's walls. When we did venture out, we went in a well-armed troop with helmets, halberds and pistols, preceded by the Siorac brothers, both great hunters whose sharp eyes and ears were alert to any danger.

At nightfall, our household and livestock were carefully secured behind our walls, all our doors bolted; the massive oak doors of the entry tower were locked and secured on the inside by iron bars, and the portcullis lowered. When it wasn't raining, we'd put torches in sockets at regular intervals in the chateau's walls which could be lit at the first alarm and which would allow us to see the number and position of our assailants. To Escorgol, who normally guarded the main entrance, the Brethren added my valet, Miroul ("Miroul's got bright eyes! Oh yes, but / One is blue, and the other's chestnut", little Hélix would sing when feeling some relief from her long agony), so that at the first suspicious sound, Escorgol could dispatch him to us to quietly spread the alarm, since he was so fast and agile.

My father took Samson and me on a tour of the underground passage that had been dug while we were away in Montpellier, and that now linked the chateau with the mill at les Beunes, which was the weak point in our defences. Our mason Jonas had reinforced it with small loopholes in the walls, but it was only a one-storey structure with but a wooden stockade to protect it, and could not have sustained an attack by twenty resolute ruffians with only Coulondre and his Jacotte to defend it. They were brave enough, but Coulondre had only one arm and Jacotte a nursling to attend to.

The mill was an attractive target, for, year in year out, it was full of sacks of grain, since the entire valley brought their harvest to be ground there—not only grains for their flour but walnuts for their oil, and our many swine and Coulondre's were kept there to enjoy the rich spillage from it—extraordinary treasures in these times of famine, and all too likely to tempt the palates of the bands of beggars afoot in the region. We well remembered that in 1557 (when I was only six) Fontenac took advantage of my father's absence at the siege of Calais to finance and dispatch a large band of Gypsies to attack Mespech. They'd come very close to taking the chateau, and Uncle Sauveterre had managed to avert disaster only by paying them a large ransom to get them to withdraw.

"But Father," I protested, "if this underground passage allows us to send help to the mill, couldn't it also, if the mill were taken, permit our enemy to invade the chateau?"

"Pierre, my son," he replied, "remember, first of all, that the passage leads to just inside the outer walls of our fortress, and from there you'd still have to cross the moat surrounding our walls, which could only be managed by taking the two drawbridges, the one that links the bridge with the island and the second which connects the island to our lodgings. Secondly, the opening of the passage is secured by a metal grille which can only be opened from outside. What's more, twenty yards behind this opening another metal grille can be lowered which would trap our assailants in a cage and put them at our mercy."

"But how would that put them at our merthy?" asked Samson, his azure eyes widening in wonderment while he lisped the word "mercy", as was his wont.

"By this trapdoor that you see here," my father explained, "we can creep down to the roof of the passageway that covers the section between the two grilles and hit our trapped enemies from above with lances and pikes and, if they're wearing armour, with arquebuses."

"What a pity," sighed Samson, "to have to kill so many people."

"True enough," agreed Jean de Siorac, "but, dear Samson, can you imagine what they would do to us if they were to take Mespech? And to the women of our household?"

This said, he worked the grilles in their casings to make sure he could raise and lower them at will.

During the night of 24th February, scarcely a week after Puymartin's warning, my father entered my room, lantern in hand, and told me in a calm voice to get up and arm myself for battle, as he feared a surprise attack, since Escorgol had heard some men moving about near the les Beunes mill, and noticed a fire burning in the woods nearby. I obeyed immediately, arming myself, and went down to the courtyard. The night was clear and frosty and I found there, gathered in the most ghostly silence, all of the men of Mespech, wearing helmets and cuirasses, and each armed with a pike or an arquebus.

My father, lantern in hand, had two pistols stuck in his belt. "My brother," he said to Sauveterre, "I'll take Pierre, my cousins and Miroul to assure the defence of the ramparts near the lake. You'll have Faujanet, François and Petremol to guard the ramparts nearest the lodgings. Don't light the torches set in the ramparts and not a word out of anyone! We're going to give these villains a nasty welcome! There's no worse surprise than to be surprised when you believe you're going to blindside your enemy!"

I was very glad to remain with my father, convinced that, at his side, I'd see some action and earn his praise—all the more so since, once we'd passed the drawbridge, he sent Samson and the Siorac cousins off to patrol the catwalk on the ramparts, keeping only Miroul and me with him, which made me feel even more important. Lantern in hand, though it was hardly of use since the moon was so bright, my father headed immediately towards the exit from the underground passage, but once there, instead of raising the first grille as I thought he would do, he lowered the second.

"What, Father?" I whispered. "Aren't we going to take the passage and head to the mill to give a hand to Coulondre and Jacotte?"

"Is that what you'd do if you were me?"

"Assuredly!"

He smiled and in the light of the moon his eyes were shining from beneath the visor of his helmet. "Well, you'd be wrong. How do you know the enemy isn't already in the passage at the other end?"

Of course, at this I fell silent, ashamed of my stupidity. And I was more astonished yet when I saw him, lantern in hand, raise the grille at our end of the tunnel. "Pierre, my boy, once I'm inside, lower the grille again but don't raise the second one yet—wait until I give my express command to do so."

"But Father," I gasped in fear, "what are you going to do, caught in this trap?"

"Hide in a niche in the wall that's farther up on the right and is just big enough to hide a man, cover my lantern and wait."

"Wait for what?"

"Jacotte."

"So, Father, what must I do in the meantime?"

"Stand ready to raise the grille at the exit. Miroul should be ready to raise and lower the second one. Don't show yourself. The moon is up."

I knelt out of sight at a right angle to the grille, straining to see into the inky darkness into which my father had disappeared, crouching in his niche like a fox in its den. His lantern, though covered, emitted a little light, but he knew how to keep marvellously quiet—so quiet that, listen as intently as I might, I couldn't hear his breathing. On the other hand, I had no trouble hearing the clatter of wooden shoes as Jacotte hurried through the tunnel.

"Who goes there?" hissed my father, without emerging the least bit from his hiding place and without showing his lantern.

"Jacotte."

"Alone?"

"With my sweetling."

My father then said something that would have astonished me if I hadn't understood from the way he pronounced the words that they were a code they'd agreed on long before: "Is the babe well, Jacotte?"

"Well indeed."

Which doubtless meant that no one was standing behind her with a knife in her ribs, for my father uncovered his lantern and held it out at arm's length, but without yet showing the rest of his body. I could now see that Jacotte was standing behind the second grille, breathing hard from her run through the passage, looking pale and terrified. She was, indeed, alone.

"Miroul! The grille!" said my father.

And immediately the grille was raised and as soon as Jacotte passed beneath it, it was lowered after her.

"Pierre! The grille!" ordered my father.

I raised the grille blocking the exit and my father, leading the good wench by the arm, emerged with her from the passage.

Jacotte was a tall, robust and resolute lass, who, with the little knife she wore in her belt, had killed a highwayman two years before when he and three others had tried to rape her behind a hedgerow in the fields. Coulondre Iron-arm, who luckily happened on the scene, dispatched the three others—one of the reasons that she'd married him, though he was twice her age. And yet as strong and courageous as she was, she was trembling like a bitch before a wolf, not for herself, but for her husband, who'd ordered her to leave him at the mill.

"How many are they?" whispered my father.

"At least a dozen but not more than two score."

"Do they have firearms?"

"Oh, yes, but didn't shoot. And, respecting your orders, Coulondre didn't fire either. But the poor man," she continued, her voice trembling, "won't be able to hold out for long. The rascals have piled some sticks in front of the door and lit them, and oak though it may be, the door's going to burn."

"It'll burn all right, but those villains won't piss any straighter because of it. Miroul! Go fetch Alazaïs! On the double, my lad, on the double!"

Miroul was off like he'd been shot from a crossbow and, for the few minutes that he was gone, my father, frowning, pinched his nose as he meditated on what he'd do next—and I wasn't about to interrupt him!

Alazaïs, who, as my father put it, "had the strength of two grown men, not counting her considerable moral strength" (being a severe and implacable Huguenot), appeared, wearing a cuirass with a brace of pistols and a cutlass tucked in her belt.

"Alazaïs," my father said, "hie thee quick as a bird and warn Cabusse at the le Breuil farm and Jonas in the quarry to arm themselves and be on guard. They may be attacked too!"

"I'm off!" she panted.

"And tell Escorgol to send me Samson and the Siorac brothers. We're going to lend a hand to Coulondre Iron-arm!"

"Ah, Monsieur!" breathed Jacotte in relief, but couldn't get another word out through the tears that choked her.

"Jacotte," replied my father, tapping her shoulder, "go tell Sauveterre where I'm headed, and tell him not to budge until I return. And as for you, take your babe to Barberine and then hurry back and close the grille after we've gone."

Which she did. And so we headed into the passageway, running like madmen, with Samson, Miroul and the Siorac brothers following me and my father, who, despite his fifty-three years, was bounding along like a hare, his lantern extended in front of him. It's true that the passage ran steeply downhill since Mespech, as its name indicates, is set on a hill and the les Beunes mill is down in the valley.

Coulondre was immensely relieved to see us appear at his mill, though his long, sad, Lenten face gave no sign of it and he breathed not a word nor a sigh. The room which the tunnel opened into was quite large and on our left was the door the assailants were trying to set fire to, and we could hear the flames crackling through the thick oak. On our right was a latticed enclosure that opened onto the pigsty where the sows, piglets and hogs were squealing in panic at the smell of the fire.

"Monsieur," hissed Coulondre, "shall we save the animals and push them into the tunnel?"

"No," said my father as he studied the burning door, "there's not enough time and we have more urgent things to do. My friends, let's

27

pile the bags of grain to create a rampart that will protect us when they come in, and with the door to the tunnel behind us, we'll be able to escape if need be. Make a thick pile, shoulder high, so we can hide behind it as they come in."

We did as he ordered and he pitched in, working as hard and as fast as any of us, his face radiant with the excitement of the work and the impending battle.

All our labours no doubt made some noise, but I guessed that the ruffians outside couldn't hear us, partly because our entire porcine population was squealing loud enough to break one's eardrums. Our wall of grain now a yard thick and chest high, with gaps here and there to allow us to see our assailants, we all crouched down behind it. Having lit the wicks of our arquebuses and primed our pistols, we waited feverishly, our hearts pounding, yet secure in the knowledge that we had the underground passageway behind us.

"My brave lads," my father said, "when I shout 'God with us!' stand, make a terrible din and fire!"

"'Tis certain," growled Coulondre Iron-arm, "I'll shoot straight at 'em and aim to kill! When I think these villains are burning my oak door with my own firewood!" He said this with heaviness in his voice, but then Coulondre always sounded sad, being so taciturn by nature and lugubrious of tone—despite the fact that he'd done all right for himself, was well paid for keeping our mill and our swine, and, though already grey, married to a strong and handsome young woman who took good care of him.

"Don't worry, Coulondre," soothed my father, who held him in great affection. "Don't worry! Don't cry over your door. At Mespech I've got plenty of seasoned oak and finely cut! I'll tell Faujanet to make you a new door, even stronger than this one and braced with iron!"

"Thank God and thank you, my master!" replied Coulondre, who'd only complained so that he'd be promised a new door. And however much his grey eyes retained their usual sad expression, I thought I could see a hint of a smile behind them. And I felt secretly happy as well, not only to be here, however much my heart was pounding, beside my father and my brother Samson, not just because it recalled our struggle in la Lendrevie when we took on the butcher-baron, but because this battle looked to be ours, since the villains thought the mill was unguarded and that the miller was, as he always was on Sunday nights, away at Mespech, Coulondre having been careful to make no sound when they had begun their attack.

"Pierre," my father whispered, "I know how brave you are but don't be foolhardy. When you've fired your pistols, I want you to duck out of sight. There's no shame in taking cover."

"Father," I replied, deeply touched by his great love, "don't worry! I've learnt my lesson. Caution, prudence and patience are the teats of adventure."

My father laughed at this, but his laugh was as silent as a carp and I, having received such excellent advice, decided that the best thing I could do would be to pass along some good advice to my brother. I elbowed him softly and whispered:

"My brother, remember, I beg you, not to be so slow in firing as you were in the battle in la Lendrevie and when we fought the highwaymen in the Corbières."

"I promith, Pierre," he lisped, and as he spoke the door of the mill burst into flames, illuminating his beautiful face, and I couldn't resist throwing my arms about him and embracing him, which elicited a bit of a smile from my father.

"What an incredible force, two brothers who love each other as you do!" he said quietly, his eyes still fixed on the door in flames. "It's the same with Sauveterre and me: no one has ever been able to defeat us, and no less so, as you'll soon see, than this dog Fontenac! My brothers in arms, God keep you! Here we go, I believe!"

When you think about how long it takes a beautiful oak to grow, it's a pity that it can burn as quickly as this poor door did—and all the more pity that it took so much careful artistry to fashion it. My Huguenot heart bled to see such a waste of this handsome and well-crafted portal—not to mention the massacre these villains would have wreaked on our pigs, our grains and our mill if they'd been able. The bitterness of these thoughts sharpened my anger against these miscreants and eradicated any compassion I might have felt. Clutching my pistols in both hands, I wanted only to dispatch them quickly.

Meanwhile, the fire burned so hot that the iron hinges gave way and a few blows from a sledgehammer and a battering ram finished it off. They'd soon dragged it outside and now had their way clear. And clear they no doubt believed it was, and the house empty, for they crowded inside, as one might say, as grains into a mill, torches in hand, as if they wanted to set fire to everything inside, and our pigs set up an even more deafening wail of squealing.

"God with us!" shouted my father in a stentorian voice. And rushing out from behind our sacks we let out screams that would have unstopped a deaf man's ears, and the highwaymen were frozen in their tracks and stood open-mouthed in disbelief, changed into pillars of salt like Lot's wife. We shot them like pigeons, and except for one among them who thought to throw himself on the ground, we mortally wounded or killed all of them. Coulondre Iron-arm leapt forward to dispatch the sole survivor, but my father prevented him from this, and, hoping to interrogate him, ordered that his hands be tied and that he be brought back through the tunnel to Mespech.

This was a good-looking fellow, about thirty years of age, black of hair and of skin like a Saracen, with fiery eyes and a proud mien, and well spoken, it appeared.

We threw him down on the ground in the great hall of Mespech, and my father, standing over him, hands on hips, said with his usual jolly and playful manner, "Your name, you rascal!"

"Captain Bouillac, Monsieur," the fellow answered proudly, his black eyes emitting sparks.

"Captain!" replied Jean de Siorac. "Some sort of captain you are!"

"At your service, Monsieur."

"You serve me ill, villain! I intend to hang you."

"Monsieur!" answered Bouillac without dropping his proud manner. "May I not buy my freedom?"

"What?" spat my father. "Take stolen money from a blackguard?"

"How now? All money is good when given," returned Bouillac. "What's more, this money's honest wages. I was paid for my services."

"I think," said Sauveterre, stepping forward into the hall with a furled brow and his usual limp, causing all our people to give way to his dark humours, "I think we should hang this blackguard straightaway."

"But wait!" replied my father. "None among us was killed or wounded."

"I still think we should hang the bastard."

"But wait! Bouillac, where did you get this money?"

"I'll be glad to tell you, Monsieur, if you accept my offer."

"You'll tell all once I put you on the rack!" answered Sauveterre, his eyes burning with anger.

"True enough," said Bouillac without losing his haughty demeanour, "but torture takes time and you're very pressed for time. As for me, since I'm destined for the noose in any case, I have an eternity to kill!"

At this flash of wit, which was not without its salt, aftertaste or piquancy, my father broke out laughing in admiration of the bravery of this rascal, and very interested in what he still might learn from him.

"Bouillac," said he, "let's talk frankly. How much will you offer us for your life?"

"One hundred écus."

We all fell silent and looked at each other, so struck were we that a highwayman should have such a hoard. But at the sound of these coins, Sauveterre changed his expression and said, with a cutting tone, "Two hundred."

"For shame, Monsieur!" said Bouillac. "Bargaining with a beggar!"

"A good Huguenot always bargains!" laughed my father.

"Two hundred," repeated Sauveterre.

"Oh, Monsieur, you're strangling me!"

"Perhaps you'd prefer another kind of strangling!"

"Agreed! Agreed!" confessed Bouillac with a huge sigh. "My neck will have it no other way."

"We have a bargain!" crowed my father. "But now we have a battle against time!"

"Monsieur, while we were preparing to kill your swine and burn your mill, Captain Belves's band was heading to le Breuil to massacre your sheep."

"By the belly of St Vitus!" cried my father. "I thought so! How many are they?"

"Seven, with Belves."

"I thank you, Bouillac. I'm going to head off this attack."

Rushing from the room, my father ordered Miroul, Faujanet, Petremol and the two Siorac brothers to saddle up immediately and gallop to help Cabusse, who luckily wasn't alone since he had the Herculean Jonas with him and possibly Alazaïs as well, if she'd been able to reach the sheepfold, which I calculated she would have since she was a crafty wench.

"Bouillac," said my father on re-entering the hall, "who paid for and planned all this?"

"A brigand who robs and steals without ever leaving the comfort of his chateau or dirtying his hands."

"Fontenac?"

Bouillac nodded but said not a word, and my father well understood the reason for his reticence, merely looking Bouillac in the eye.

"Monsieur," said the highwayman, "am I free to go?"

"Certainly, once your ransom's paid."

"I'm off to get it," said Bouillac, "as long as you'll return my horse to me, and my pistols, sword and dagger, which are the tools of my trade and without which I'm unable to exercise my particular talents."

"I'm afraid not," said Sauveterre. "We'll release you unarmed. If you want your tools, it'll cost you another fifty écus."

"Ah, Monsieur," returned Bouillac, "you're feeding me poisoned fruit!"

"Fifty écus… or nothing," ventured my father.

"Nothing?" said Bouillac, frowning.

"Nothing, on condition that you formally bear witness against Fontenac before Ricou, the magistrate."

Bouillac fell silent and thought about this for several minutes before finally giving in. But little did his testimony matter in the long run, for 'twas in vain that the Brethren brought his evidence to the parliament in Bordeaux, since the papist judges were so inflamed against the Huguenots that nothing ever came of our complaint.

But I'm getting ahead of myself. Scarcely an hour after we captured Bouillac, Michel Siorac (who could now be distinguished from his brother by the deep scar on his left cheek from the battle in la Lendrevie) appeared in front of the chateau gate at Mespech on his frothy-mouthed gelding and shouted to Escorgol that they'd killed all the intruders at the le Breuil farm or put them to flight. My father and Sauveterre put their heads together and decided that, after having dispatched the wounded men, they'd pile the bodies on a cart and, in the dark of night, take the dead from the two bands and dump them on Fontenac's drawbridge.

"Let him bury them," snarled Sauveterre, "since he paid them!"

But before dispatching the funeral wagon to its intended destination, my father picked out one of the thinnest men killed at les Beunes for us to dissect before rigor mortis set in. Alazaïs carried the cadaver on her back up to the library of Mespech, where, having laid him out on the large table, she shamelessly undressed him without batting an eye. She made no more of a naked man than of a flea and put all her love in the Lord, directing her entire appetite to the Eternal.

Miroul started a roaring fire in the hearth and lit a large number of candles, and, still sweaty from combat, our helmets and cuirasses scarcely removed, my father set about the prosection. He had no compunction about this, even though it was a task which, at the school of medicine in Montpellier, no ordinary doctors would have stooped to, considering themselves too elevated for such work, according to some vainglorious belief that to touch a body would lower them to the level of the labourer, who is considered inferior by the learned physician. The sad consequence of this practice is that the prosector, normally a barber surgeon, ends up knowing a great deal more about the human anatomy than the doctor, since he has delved in with his hands (which no eye can replace) and discovered the physics of the relationships of the organs within the body.

And so it was, by the light of a candelabrum that Miroul held high above his head, that my father, in the silence of our exhausted household (Sauveterre himself having long since gone to bed, hunched, broken and dragging his lame leg behind him like an old crow), cut into the chest of this poor devil, who that very morning had been alive and sure of victory, while I sponged away his blood, to get a better view of his insides.

"This churl had a lot of blood," I said. "It's gushing like a cataract!"

"Hah!" agreed my father. "You're right about that! It flows. And that's the great mystery of life. Blood flows through our bodies. But

34

why? But how? What force makes it flow upwards when we're standing? Notice that if blood flowed like the water through the les Beunes mill or the Dordogne or any of our earth's rivers, our brains would naturally empty of blood and our heels fill up with it the minute we got up in the morning. But that's not what happens. So blood must possess some mysterious property that moves and circulates it through the body. But what is this property?"

"Do we know what this property is, Father?"

"We don't yet know completely, but perhaps we're on our way to discovering it. Miroul, bring your candelabrum nearer. Look at his heart, Pierre. Do you see these little doors? Sylvius in Paris and Acquapendente in Padua have described them in great detail. They're doors, no doubt about it, or sluices, which, opening and closing by turns, admit or refuse the flow of blood. Is the heart the motor we're looking for? Servetus thought so, for he wrote about the 'attraction' the heart exerts on blood."

"Servetus? Michael Servetus whom Calvin burned at the stake in Geneva?"

"He burned him for heresy, not because of his medical theories, both of which, to tell the truth, Servetus included in his book *Christianismi restitutio*, all the copies of which were set on fire and reduced, like their author, to ashes."

"All of them, Father?" I gasped through the knot in my throat that practically stifled my voice as I remembered the atheist abbot, Cabassus, who was burnt alive on the public square in Montpellier along with his treatise, *Nego*.

"All but one," replied my father. "All but one that luckily fell away from the pyre a little singed by the fire, but still intact.* I bought it

---

* This copy can be found today in the National Library of France in Paris. [Author's note.]

35

from a little Jewish bookseller in Geneva on one of my trips there. I still have it."

And, laying his knife on the cadaver, my father went to look for Servetus's treatise on the shelves in his library, and, his eyes shining with a strange light, he opened it to a page bookmarked by a ribbon. I'm not ashamed to say that I caught my breath, so possessed was I from head to heel by such a burning desire for learning that it made my heart nearly leap out of my chest.

"Here's the magnum opus," he said, his hands trembling feverishly. "My son, I abhor the theology that is set out in these pages, but I treasure the medical knowledge they hold, above all my other possessions, for Servetus has provided a luminous explanation of the function of our noblest organs. Listen, Pierre, open your ears to what I'm going to read to you, for this is the ultimate and unsurpassable *summum** of the medical knowledge of our times.

> "The mass of blood flows through the lungs, and there receives
> the benefits of purification, eliminating all impurities and
> fatty humours, after which it is recalled by the attraction of
> the heart."

"Oh, Father!" I exclaimed, trembling like a leaf in April. "Read it again, I beg you! What a sublime passage! I feel illuminated by its beauty!"

And so my father, his voice trembling, reread the passage that I've just written here in a pen as shaky as his voice was, for I was careful to memorize it word for word, to seal it for ever in the storehouse of my mind. It's still there, entire, intact and untouched like the most glorious banner ever planted on the shores of a new land by this peaceful explorer of the human anatomy.

---

* "Summit."

"How can it be, Father, that our minds are so suddenly illuminated by the striking clarity of this text? Why is it that we immediately believe it to be true?"

"Because it lines up perfectly," my father replied joyfully, "with the reason God gave us to recognize evidence of the truth. You haven't forgotten what was famously written about the heart by Aristotle—whom the papists have made an idol and whose every word is held sacred by them—that it is a hot organ, and since it risks overheating, the lungs are bellows that provide fresh air to keep it cool. What nonsense!" cried my father, holding high Servetus's *Christianismi restitutio*. "Nonsense and totally obvious absurdities! Fallacies and tomfoolery! Idiocy masquerading as science! Isn't it flagrantly evident that in the heat of summer, the lungs breathe in hot air, which couldn't possibly cool the heart! Quite the contrary! And Michael Servetus has produced irrefutable evidence in the passage I just read. For what possible purpose could the lungs bring in air if not to nourish and purify the blood, and how would the blood leave the lungs if it weren't *recalled*—note this word, please!—if it weren't *recalled* by the heart?"

"Agreed!" I cried, feeling as though inebriated from drinking from this cup of knowledge. "It's the truth, you can sense it; it is the marvellous truth, the secret of all palpitating life in one sentence! For there is no life without the blood that flows, winds and branches out throughout our body. But, Father, why did this brilliant mind have to perish in flames?"

"Oh, Pierre," replied Jean de Siorac, his face suddenly full of sadness, "I cannot entirely fault Calvin; Michael Servetus in his crazy audacity had dared to deny this other irrefutable truth: the mystery of the Holy Trinity."

I certainly did not wish to argue with my father, for fear of increasing his distress, but it did seem to me, in my heart of hearts, that these two kinds of evidence, the medical and the theological, were of very different orders, the first being based on our observation of nature, and the second, I mean the Holy Trinity, being based on the authority of a sacred text, and therefore sacred but not intelligible to our human understanding, so that we had to swallow it without chewing it, our eyes closed tight; which meant that I for one swallowed it as I would an apothecary's pill, without looking at it or tasting it, and without the divine illumination that I found in Servetus's truth.

My father, having washed his hands in vinegar after his dissection, and finally feeling the fatigue of all the rushing around we'd done, suggested we take some refreshment before going to bed. I acquiesced with the greatest enthusiasm since, being in the bloom of my youth, my stomach was insatiable. Miroul lit our way to the great hall and served us up some victuals, then sat down with us to devour them. Which we did, at least for a few moments, in silence, our mouths watering and working our jaws like ravenous bulls in a pasture, very happy to be there, safe and sound, the wicked who'd tried to kill us now dead, and all of our goods intact—save for one oaken door.

'Sblood! How good it was to feel the solid walls of Mespech around us, its vast lake and its outer walls. And stretching out beyond our well-managed domain, which provided for all our worldly needs. For nothing was brought to our table that was not raised on our land: the ham from our pigs at les Beunes, the butter from our milch cows, our bread from the wheat of our fields and our red wine from our own vineyard—even the table was made of oak from one of our trees. I'd come upon it in the woods one evening after the wind had toppled it, lying there waiting to be sawed.

Among all the innumerable marvels of nature that God in His goodness has provided, we must not forget our food, which is not only a pleasure to the palate but our best defence against contagion: a truth I learnt from my father, who'd read it in Ambroise Paré's learned treatise on the plague. Paré teaches us that a well-nourished body is like a well-defended fortress, with moats, walls and drawbridge. For if our veins and arteries are not well provided with food, they will allow the poisons in the air to enter the body, and principally the heart, the lungs and the genitals.

And so, I reasoned, as I heaped the fruits of our harvest on my plate, I was fortifying myself, and could almost feel the bread, wine and meat running through the subterranean canals of my system, like brave little soldiers, ready to kick out any evil intruders that contagion might have brought to the gates of my bodily castle. And, stretching out my legs in front of me, sipping an excellent glass of wine, with my beloved father on my right and Miroul on my left, able to speak our minds in confidence and friendship, I felt a deep contentment—my spleen and liver healthy and happy as well.

"Father," I asked, in the midst of such good feeling, "may I ask what plans you have for Little Sissy?"

At this my father's eyebrows arched in surprise and an amused glint appeared in his eye. "Well, only that she should continue as she is. Isn't she your chambermaid?"

"Certainly."

And since I said no more, my father continued with as innocent a tone as he could manage, but his left eyebrow arched quizzically, "So, do you think she should have other duties?"

Hearing which, I decided to hold nothing back: "Well, yes!"

"Yes? Which ones?"

"Well, I think…" I replied, but was too ashamed to continue.

"You think what?"

"I think…" But I still couldn't get any further.

"Aha!" laughed my father. "What good is thought without speech? If your mind is pregnant with an idea, for goodness' sake give birth to it!"

"Well," I ventured, my throat so tight I could hardly speak, "my thought is that Little Sissy, beautiful as she is, is probably better at unmaking beds than making them."

My father burst out laughing so hard I thought the buttons would pop off his shirt, while on my other side Miroul, who could not afford to smile, kept his blue eye cold as ice while his brown eye glinted with mirth.

"So, my son! You've a taste for this little serpent and her little apples? Well, proceed! For never was there a prettier, more buxom little wench in all Sarlat. Sad to say, speaking frankly and plainly, I would have wished that your older brother, François, might take a fancy to enter these pretty lists to break his first lance. But he turns up his nose at having anything to do with our people and wants to try his luck with some noblewoman, which, since I'm not the king, it's not in my power to grant. So here he is, at his age, a virgin and wetter behind the ears than a newly hatched chick whose shell is still sticking to her behind."

I made no answer to this, since I could see that my father, for all his joking, was saddened by the fact that his firstborn was so slow to become a man and produce an heir, even if an illegitimate one. After all, his father had recognized his own bastard children (which was fairly common in Périgord, especially among the nobles of the region), and treated them all as his legitimate sons, and even Sauveterre treated them as his nephews, for if my uncle thought profligacy was a sin, fecundity in such a threatened community he considered a virtue. This was another reason Fontenac was so despised in our family: he had respect neither for his own blood nor for the blood of others, and banished from his walls all the children he'd conceived out of wedlock.

"But Father," I said, partly to end the long silence that ensued after his words, "did you ever tell François your feelings about Little Sissy? Perhaps he believed you were reserving her for yourself? Fruit forbidden to your sons?"

My father looked me in the eye and burst out laughing again. "Now there's a question, my dear Pierre, that I would term both clever and cutting, and that has, quite effectively, as they say, killed two birds with one stone."

But he never did answer my question, and, rising in an abrupt and military manner, he made a sign to Miroul to take up the candelabrum and light our way. "My son," he said curtly, "to bed!"

I followed him, quite crestfallen, since nothing appeared to have been resolved, neither for the present nor for the foreseeable future, as to the bitterness of my solitude. However, as we approached the room where the Baron de Mespech slept with Franchou, he suddenly turned around and, with a saucy light in his eyes, gave me a huge hug, planted big kisses on both my cheeks and whispered in my ear, "*Vale, mi fili; et sicut pater tuus, ne sit ancillae formosae amor pudori.*"*

"Oh, Father!" I cried, but not a word more, I was so choked with emotion.

The door closed on Jean de Siorac, I embraced my gentle Miroul, who, as sleepy as he was, smiled at me, letting me know that he had understood what my father said, however little he understood Latin. He wanted to give me the candelabrum, but I refused, as I wished to keep both hands free and to enjoy the light of the moon, which was flooding through the windows. Once Miroul was gone, I headed towards Barberine's chambers in the west tower, which she shared with Annet, Jacquou and Little Sissy, who slept together in a bed on the opposite side of the room. Naked though she was, I picked the last of these up in my arms, careful not to wake her, carried her into my room, placed her on my bed and climbed in next to her. She continued to sleep soundly, her breathing peaceful and regular.

---

* "Be well, my son; and, like your father, don't be ashamed to love a beautiful serving girl."

So, holding myself back, though it was terribly hard, I forced myself to wait for daybreak, when she would open her eyes of her own accord. I held her close in my arms, her body so svelte, her skin so soft, her flesh so ripe, her innocent face bathed in moonlight, and so it was a long, sleepy, dreamy wait, which I remember vividly to this day; even more vividly do I remember what followed, so strident is our appetite for such fruit and such devotion.

And certainly it was a cardinal sin, as Alazaïs's mutterings, Sauveterre's frowns and my father's rakish smile all attested. But isn't it hypocrisy to repent one's sins without discontinuing them? And how can I ask forgiveness of my Creator when I never stop being happy that He granted the first man this sweet and seductive companion in the Garden of Eden?

The ardent desires I felt for my Angelina, the suffering her absence caused me, had in no way abated and I thought of Mespech, which kept us so far apart, as a kind of jail, but it was a jail I could now more easily accept. Not that I felt the kind of tender friendship for Little Sissy that I'd felt for little Hélix when I was younger. But I enjoyed and liked this "Gypsy" girl, who was very demonstrative with her feelings, quick to anger, to bite or to scratch, yet ferociously proud, it seemed, to be my wench. She was mischievous, impish, more stubborn than docile, and yet she preferred to lie about than to exercise, and, in the housework, she avoided the hard tasks, dreamt a lot and focused little, was sassy and rebellious with Alazaïs and confronted this mountain of a woman like a hissing little snake, and never wholly gave in however many slaps she got. With men (except Sauveterre) she was prickly and at the least provocation reacted with a dirty look or a shrug of the shoulders. With women (except Barberine, whom she liked) she stung like a wasp. With everyone she could be execrably malicious. Otherwise she had a pretty good heart.

*

The spring of 1568 was as beautiful as the winter had been hard. There was enough gentle rain to nourish the soil and enough sun to swell every living thing with sap. Flowers made their appearance in mid-March, their first buds glazed and shining. Sadly the spring didn't just bring a renewal of life; it also revived the war that had been hibernating in the limitless mud of winter. Our Huguenot army was no longer a force of 2,000 ragtag adventurers who'd been so afraid when they laid siege to Paris. To these had been added 10,000 reiters and lansquenets dispatched by the Elector of the Palatinate, as well as significant reinforcements from Rouergue, Quercy and the Dauphiné, so that the entire army had now swelled to some 30,000 men. Condé and Coligny had decided to direct their attack on Chartres, the breadbasket of the capital.

Since the constable was dead, Catherine de' Medici had entrusted her entire army to her cherished son, her sweetling, the Duc d'Anjou, who was just my age. And if the Huguenots took Chartres, who knows what would become of the beautiful wheat fields of Beauce? Catherine was a good mother, but only to one of her children. She disliked her eldest, Charles IX, but since she loved what he brought her, the governance of the kingdom, she had no intention of risking everything—especially the life and reputation of Anjou—in such a hazardous roll of the dice as this uncertain battle. So she proposed a treaty, and Condé, who hadn't a sol to pay his German reiters, agreed to sign the Peace of Longjumeau, which was as counterfeit a treaty as ever was signed. The ink on this agreement was scarcely dry before persecutions against the Huguenots started again all over the kingdom. The Peace of Longjumeau was signed on 23rd March and we learnt of it on 8th April, so fast did this news travel from Huguenot to Huguenot in the Sarlat region during these troubled times.

"What say you, Father?" I said bursting into his library. "May it please you to give Samson and me permission, now that the war has ended, to return to Montpellier?"

"And what would you do there?" asked Jean de Siorac. "The lectures ended at Easter."

"Lectures at the college, to be sure, but not the private courses that Chancellor Saporta and Dean Bazin offer for money. Moreover, if I arrive in time, my doctor-father Saporta will perhaps allow me to sit for the baccalaureate in medicine, so I could visit the sick and deliver prescriptions to help cure their ills."

"Ah!" sighed my father. "That's all well and good, but what about all the risks and perils in Montpellier?"

"My dear father, the risks there aren't any greater than they are here, where we hardly dare stick our noses out of doors for fear of some rebuff as long as that dog Fontenac goes unpunished. What's more, if I can believe what Madame de Joyeuse has written, the papists in Montpellier have considerably lessened their ill feeling for me after what I did to save the bishop of Nîmes."

"But do you really believe what she says?" sighed my father. "I rather think this noble lady is very hungry to see you again."

He argued the point with me for two days, and was very sorry to let Samson and me go since we had such happiness together throughout our winter in Mespech, but still! We had to go to take our exams and Samson had to return to finish his work in Maître Sanche's pharmacy, else he'd never be able to become an apothecary. Ultimately resigning himself reluctantly to our departure—as did Uncle Sauveterre with no less chagrin, though he hid it under his frowns—my father resolved to accompany us there with Cabusse and Petremol.

Poor father! And poor us! He left us in Montpellier on 28th April 1568 and didn't see us again in Mespech until September 1570, two and a half years later. The war between the Huguenots and the royalists had not failed to rekindle, Catherine de' Medici having tried to capture and kill Condé and Coligny at Noyers. And as the war was once again ravaging the whole country, it became almost impossible to travel the major roads of France without risking a hostile encounter with the papists.

When I returned to Mespech in 1570, the first thing my father did was to have me read dispatches he'd received during these troubles from two dear friends, one named Rouffignac, who was fighting in the Huguenot army, and the second none other than the Vicomte d'Argence, a captain in the royal armies, the very man who captured Condé in the battle of Jarnac. I read these missives with the greatest of interest, and since they were never published and both of their authors have since been called by their Maker, I'm going to provide my readers with the marrow of their contents for their instruction.

Although he admired Admiral de Coligny, Rouffignac did not hide his belief that the admiral had committed an incredible error on this occasion. When Tavannes (who was the de facto leader of Anjou's royal army) appeared on the right bank of the Charente river, and the Châteauneuf bridge, Condé was occupying Bassac and Coligny Jarnac. And the admiral, rather than immediately falling back to join Condé's troops, lost an incredible amount of time calling his scouts back, and when finally he was forced to fight, Tavannes pressed him so hard that he came within a hair's breadth of being overrun, and appealed to Condé for reinforcements. Rouffignac wrote:

> Destiny would have it that, as the Prince de Condé put foot to stirrup, La Rochefoucauld's horse stepped on his foot and broke his leg so badly that the bone was sticking through his boot. He nevertheless insisted on joining the battle, and, grimacing terribly, painfully pulled himself into his saddle.

"Messieurs," he said to the gentlemen surrounding him (among whom was La Rochefoucauld, who, in tears, was savagely whipping his horse), "see in what state the Prince de Bourbon enters the fight for Christ and country!" This said, he charged with his customary impetuosity an enemy that was ten times greater than his forces.

We all know what followed. Coligny attempted to bring relief, but before they could reach him, Condé was surrounded by a mass of royal troops, his horse killed beneath him. He leant up against a tree, threw his useless pistols from him, drew sword and dagger and continued to fight tooth and nail. "I recognized him," wrote d'Argence,

> and ran to his side. "Monseigneur," I said, as I commanded the soldiers surrounding us to lower their swords, "my name is d'Argence and I'm at your service. May it please your highness to surrender to me. You can no longer fight since your leg bone is sticking out of your boot." And as he did not answer, I repeated, "For pity's sake, Monseigneur! Surrender! I swear I will guarantee you safe passage."
>
> "Then I am your prisoner," groaned Condé most bitterly, and threw down his sword and dagger.
>
> As he said this, I saw the Duc d'Anjou's guards galloping towards us, all aflame in their bright-red capes.
>
> "Aha," said Condé, without batting an eye and despite his terrible pain, "here come the red crows to pick my bones."
>
> "Monseigneur," I said, "now indeed you are in great peril! Hide your face so they won't recognize you!"
>
> But he wouldn't consent to do so, since such a masquerade was beneath his dignity.
>
> "Ah, d'Argence," he sighed, "you won't be able to save me now!"
>
> And, indeed, no sooner had Montesquiou, the captain of Anjou's guards, heard the name of the prisoner, he cried, "Kill him, by God! Kill him!"

I ran to his side as he dismounted and told him that the prince was my prisoner, and that I'd guaranteed him safe passage, but Montesquiou strode over to Condé armed with his pistol and, without a word, stepped behind him and shot him in the head, so that one eye was blown out of its socket by the bullet.

"Ah, Montesquiou," I cried, "an unarmed man! A prince by blood! This is villainy!"

"'Tis villainy indeed," agreed Montesquiou, and, looking down at the dying prince, tears streaming down his tanned face, he added, "As you know all too well, I'm not the one who ordered this done."

I did indeed know that the order to dispatch forthwith all of the captured Huguenot captains—and especially Condé and Coligny—if they fell into our hands, had come directly from the Duc d'Anjou, who had also ordered that the body of Condé be brought to him, not on a horse, as would have befitted his nobility, but—as the ultimate insult and degradation—on an ass, his head and legs dangling on either side—an indignity that caused more than one of his royal captains to blame him privately, since Condé had been such a valiant warrior.

My father was rereading this letter over my shoulder while I was seated at the table in his library, so I said, "Is this not an odious murder?"

"Odious! And what's more a huge mistake! For it would have been easier for the king to come to terms with Condé than with Coligny. I don't remember who it was who said of Condé,

> *"This little prince, as handsome as a king*
> *Would always laugh and always sing.*

"By the belly of St Anthony, that's him all right! The prince was valiant in combat, decisive, high-handed, scrupulous, quick to anger and, it must be said, perhaps too easy-going. Having a head more passionate than political, he twice signed treaties with the Medicis that were most disadvantageous to our side. But read what Rouffignac said about Coligny."

The admiral, I must confess here, was not always wise in his conduct of battles, as we saw at Jarnac. But he was a man of faith and of trust, tenacious, untouched by despair and anchored in the belief that no single battle could lose the war. He was exceptionally crafty in retreat. And in this case, withdrawing his army under the cover of night after the sad day at Jarnac, he was able to save it and find a safe place to encamp. The queen of Navarre joined him there. Oh, my friend, what a fearless and unflinching Huguenot we have there! She introduced to the soldiers Condé, the son of the slain leader, and her own son, Henri de Navarre, who was then just sixteen years old.

"Ah, Father," I sighed in envy of the young prince, "isn't it a pity? Navarre is two years younger than I but has already taken the field of battle!"

"My son," replied my father, raising his eyebrows in jest, "what are you telling me? Are you a Bourbon? Are you a blooded prince? Are you in line to inherit the throne of France should the three sons of Catherine de' Medici die childless? Let Navarre jockey for his own position in history, and as for you, continue your work here. That's the wisest course."

Thus chided and put in my place, but more as a pleasantry than as a corrective, I continued Rouffignac's letter.

If the admiral lost the battle of Jarnac because of the error I've just described, he lost the battle of Moncontour because of the mistakes of his German reiters. The moment they occupied the strongholds that Coligny had designated for them, our Germans threw down their arms and demanded their pay! "No money," they shouted in their gibberish, "no combat!" Ah, my friend, what a fix! What a reversal! And what a fatal delay—which was fatal to none more than themselves. For surprised in the flatlands while they were arguing, the Duc d'Anjou's Swiss guards surrounded them, fell upon them and, due to the longstanding jealousy between these two groups of mercenaries, slaughtered them all down to the last man. And that was the only salary they ever would receive in this life, the poor beggars!

As for us, after Jarnac, we lost the battle of Moncontour to the greater glory of the Duc d'Anjou (even though he did nothing, for it was Tavannes who did it all), which delighted the old bitch Medici, charmed that her favourite son was carving out a reputation for himself greater than that of his brother the king. But do you think that this reversal brought down Coligny, all wounded as he was, one cheek pierced by a bullet and four teeth broken? Not a bit of it. At Moncontour the remains of our army began a long, unbelievable and twisting march that you've probably heard echoes of.

Listen! From Saintes, to which we'd retreated, we succeeded in getting to Aiguillon, where we took and pillaged the chateau—abandoning along our way the horses we'd exhausted—and from thence to Montauban where we were reunited with the army of the seven vicomtes. Thus fortified and reinforced, we devastated the countryside around Toulouse, to punish this fat, ignorant town for the murder of Rapin. From there, on to Carcassonne, which we were careful not to attack, having no appetite to break our teeth on its ramparts. Then to Narbonne, which we also refrained from attacking, instead sacking the inland countryside, our trumpets sounding "Papau! Papau!" to mock the papists there. Then, heading south, we crossed—believe it or not!—into Roussillon, to thumb our noses at Felipe II, this white tombstone of a Spanish king, and prove that all the Huguenots hadn't died at Moncontour!

There we did some pilfering and, returning through Montpellier (where your two handsome scholars were living), we refrained from attacking this silly town but contented ourselves with pillaging the surrounding villages. But at Nîmes we settled in for a while since this town was now loyal to the Huguenot cause.

From Nîmes, we travelled north through the Rhône valley and reached Saint-Étienne and then la Charité, which is also loyal to us, as you know, and where we were able to recruit some more soldiers and collect arms, cannon and money.

But listen carefully! Almost every time we confronted the royal garrisons in this winding valley, we were beaten, and yet, each time, we vanished only to reappear somewhere else, burning and pillaging, like the wolf who, instead of letting himself be trapped, bites and flees: and so it is that without winning a single battle, Coligny won a war of attrition on his enemies.

"My father," I said, amazed, "so Coligny won the war by a tactic of retreating?"

"Rouffignac," laughed my father, "is a Gascon, a braggart and of a bellicose temper. And yet what he says is at least half-true. You should read d'Argence if you want to understand the other half."

And so saying, he handed me the page that d'Argence had filled with a hand as tiny and careful as Rouffignac's was large and untutored, though, out of an innate prudence, he'd never signed it.

My friend, what a strange world the court is, where, to belong, you must turn your back on everyone: brother, mother, sister and friend! After Moncontour, the Duc d'Anjou's laurels are causing the king to lose sleep and bite his nails. He wants by hook or by crook to take control of the army but instead of overrunning Coligny in his lair, he's bogged down at the siege of Saint-Jean-d'Angély. Guise, whose glory has been overshadowed in this army, is also becoming increasingly bitter at the Duc d'Anjou's current fame. He's written to Felipe II that the king's brother is secretly plotting with Coligny. So from the depths of his Escorial, Felipe has decided to believe him and has refused us any of the gold he gets from the Americas. Not a sol in 1570 to help end the war! But Guise has done worse than this: he's making eyes at Margot, the king's sister. This flint is sure to spark a fire on such a torch.

She's as hot—nay, in as great heat—as ever, since she was broken in by her brothers at a very tender age, and unzipped the duc in a trice and tucked him into her bed. The king's got wind of this profligacy. He ordered Margot to appear at dawn, and scarcely was she in his presence before he and Catherine leapt on her like furious fishmongers, and hit and kicked her, scratching and bruising her, and ripping her chemise. When Guise learnt of this the next day, he naturally feared assassination by the king's henchmen, so he fled and got himself married. But now he's in disgrace for having aimed at the throne by the whiteness of her thighs, and all the most zealous papists who were supporting him have fallen out of favour as well.

Catherine has other reasons to be angry with the leaders of the Catholic party. Felipe II, now a widower since the death of her daughter, Elizabeth, refuses to consider Margot, whom Catherine is pressing on him, since he's doubtless afraid the girl's flames make a bad match for his own icy nature. And right from under Medici's nose, he's stealing the older of the Austrian archduchesses, whom she was planning to marry to Charles IX, leaving the younger one for the French king. What's even better, this haughty Spanish sovereign insists that the marriage contract of his cousin, Charles, be signed a quarter of an hour after his own! Ah, my friend! This younger sister and this quarter-hour, how heavy they weigh on our hearts! So she's very tempted to get revenge on the presumptuous Spanish monarch and on Guise by making peace with Coligny, who, though always beaten, keeps rising from his own ashes like the phoenix. And so they've wrapped up and signed the Peace of Saint-Germain, which I'll warrant is good for your side as long as both sides respect it.

"So, Father," I asked, "is d'Argence right? Is this peace good for the Huguenots?"

"Not in the least," sighed my father as he stood behind me, leaning both hands on my shoulders. "In no way, Pierre. Freedom of conscience has been granted, but freedom to worship is restricted to the chateaux and to two cities by region. What is freedom of conscience if freedom to worship is not full and entire? That's why this Peace of Saint-Germain doesn't augur well: the war with the papists cannot fail to flare up again."

2

I T WAS NEVERTHELESS A WELCOME RESPITE, which lasted two years. I hope the reader will forgive me for galloping roughshod over this period in order to get to the incredible setback and immense peril that led me to travel to Paris to seek the king's pardon.

My beloved Samson was named "master apothecary" in August of 1571, a promotion I cannot remember without recalling the famous onion market that was held in Montpellier on the same day, while my brother was creating, at considerable expense to us, a therapeutic solution composed of more than twenty-seven different elements, a potion so secret that none, not even physicians, were allowed to see it, the vision of these mysteries being reserved solely for the use of master apothecaries, who, because of their rank, were granted access to them.

While he was busy concocting this famous medicine, whose properties are sovereign in the treatment of a number of diseases, I found myself wandering through the winding streets of Montpellier under a sun hot enough to bake flies (even though reed mats had been hung from house to house over the streets to lessen the heat). I happened onto the place de la Canourgue and there encountered a most astonishing sight, the likes of which I've never seen anywhere else: an entire city constructed entirely of onions.

These bulbs are sold by the batch in the Sarlat region, but here the farmers braid them very artistically, and these braids are piled up carefully so as to create ramparts ten feet high, between which narrow passages are effected in such a way that the entire square becomes a city in which one can walk to the right or to the left between these odiferous walls. There are so many of these passageways that you could lose yourself in their labyrinthine network. I was thoroughly delighted with this spectacle, never having seen such a prodigious quantity of the vegetable which, in the south of France, raw or cooked, is so much a staple of the cuisine that the people of Montpellier will, on this single day, buy enough to last the entire year. But even more than by the quantity of the bulbs, I was amazed by the variety that was displayed here: there were onions of every size, consistency and colour, some yellow, some red, some as big as your fist, others the size of an apricot and others still tiny, white and quite sweet to the taste.

I stayed there for at least two hours, so amused was I—almost as pleased as Anne de Joyeuse had been when I'd presented him with the army of wooden soldiers. I also enjoyed the spectacle of the mass of people who'd gathered in and around this city of onions, both girls and housewives who'd come for their annual purchase and the workers and gapers, who'd come simply to dawdle. For they all seemed to be having the time of their lives, walking through the maze of onions, laughing and chattering to each other, enjoying the soothing perfume of this healthy and comforting vegetable, so good for the heart, for the liver and for the genitals, certainly medicinal in many different ways. This great multitude also rejoiced, no doubt, to see piled before them an immense quantity of food sprung from the rich earth of the region, out of the goodness and mercy of the Creator, so that all, even the poorest among them, could be assured of food for the coming winter. For a braid of these onions costs but two sols, and, with a crust of bread and a single bulb of these good fruits, any beggar will have enough for a decent meal.

At every corner of these castles of fruit, each man standing with his wench, the labourers who'd sown and harvested these onions were singing out in Provençal: "Beautiful onions. Beautiful onions!" Or else: "Eat an onion—it's good medicine!" Or yet again: "Eat an onion and live a long life!" Or again: "Who eats his onions in goodly measure / Will work his wench with greater pleasure!"

These salesmen, so happy to be raking in such piles of money to recompense them for their hard work, nevertheless kept their eyes peeled and a long rod in their hands to rap the knuckles of anyone who tried to steal any of their produce as they walked by. But they flailed these petty thieves without malice, shouts or frowns, somehow maintaining the general good humour of the labourers of this region.

This onion market is held every 24th August, the feast of St Bartholomew, a saint who, for us Huguenots, is no different from any of the other papist saints whom we'd dismissed, belonging more to a cult of superstition than to faith, but he was a saint whose name we would hold in infinite execration for ever, after the events of exactly one year later, as I will relate.

My gentle Samson so loved his work that he was transported with pleasure to have been promoted to master apothecary after his years of hard toil. Following this triumph, as was the custom, he was paraded on horseback through the city. Given his beauty, both of visage and of body, I heard several onlookers opine that it was a pity he was a Huguenot, given how much he looked like the Archangel Michael, just stepped out from a stained-glass window.

I leave you to guess the effect he had on the young women of the city, who came running en masse, devouring him with their eyes. But although the women of Montpellier might be, by common consent, the most beautiful wenches in the kingdom, my innocent Samson was entirely oblivious to the eager glances and blushing hot cheeks that he provoked, having amorous thoughts only for Dame

55

Gertrude du Luc. Indeed, scarcely had we returned to our lodgings before he begged me to compose a missive describing in detail the *actus triumphalis* of which he'd been the hero—not that he didn't know how to write, but because his style was so dry and curt it read like a prescription. I grudgingly acceded to his request, though I still felt some bitterness towards the lady, who'd not been content to float in the azure of Samson's presence while here, but had wished to wallow in manure with another. To debauch herself with one of Monsieur de Joyeuse's captains after leaving Samson's arms! Is that faithful? Is it reasonable? Is it virtuous? Ha! I could have killed the wench for this infidelity!—although I thank God that my beloved Samson never learnt any of this, and that I was able to hide it from him, to keep from wounding his noble heart.

I myself was promoted to the rank of doctor on 14th April in the year of Our Lord 1572. To tell the truth, I was nervous enough to bite my nails nearly off before taking my *triduanes*, exams so named because they last three full days, during which, from morning till night, I had to defend my theses and argue in Latin not only with the four royal professors, but with other ordinary doctors, some of whom prepared insidious ambushes for such occasions, hoping to shine at the expense of the candidate.

However, having worked so diligently, devoured all my books, performed dissections and taken care of a good number of patients for my doctor-father Saporta, I was not without a good deal of confidence in my knowledge of medicine. And yet I worried terribly—not just about passing my *triduanes*, but about my inability, given my lack of funds, due to the immense expenses of medical school, to offer a grand dinner for all my friends. Of course, I could have written to my father, but I hated to cost him so many beautiful écus, and after turning this over in my mind for quite some time, I resolved to reveal my concerns to Madame de Joyeuse, while we were catching our breath together one afternoon after a session of our "school for sighs" behind her blue bed curtains.

"What?" cried this noble lady. "What are you telling me? That you need money? Why didn't you say so! Shouldn't my little cousin be enabled to live according to his rank as well as anyone else? Aglaé de Mérol will disburse 100 écus as you leave."

"Ah, Madame!" I cried. "How grateful I am for your marvellous benevolence. You are as beautiful as you are generous, and I will be grateful to you with all my heart and with all my body for ever!"

Having said this, I lavished kisses on her pretty fingers, which were so suave, so smooth, so perfumed and more expert in caresses than any woman's hand in the entire kingdom.

"Ah, my sweet little man!" replied Madame de Joyeuse, who loved lively people and who watched the effects of advancing age arrive with abject terror. "Don't thank me; it's nothing but a little gold and costs me so little since my father was so well-to-do. But you, my Pierre, you give me infinitely more than I could ever give you, so old and decrepit as I am."

"Old, Madame! Decrepit!"

And in truth she was neither one nor the other but very bewitching in her mature and luscious beauty, as I was prompt to tell her, and with such persuasive force that, in the end, melting into my arms, inflamed and sighing, she whispered in my ear, with sweet tyranny, "My sweet, do that thing I like!" Oh, I so loved her then, for her infinite goodness and for the power she gave me over her!

When those 100 écus joyously tintinnabulated their way from her money box into my purse, beautiful Aglaé de Mérol, who was counting them out in the salon, suddenly burst out, in the petulant and lively way she enjoyed teasing me, "What's this? Another gift? You're costing us dearly, I think! Almost as much as Monsieur de Joyeuse! Though it's true, you're much better to us than he is!"

"Oh, Madame!"

"No 'oh'! Our master has the unhappy habit of never being here, running after all the rustic petticoats in his jurisdiction. And you, venerable doctor, you're here all the time and not afraid to administer your excellent cures!"

"Madame, I'm aghast! Is this any way for a virgin to talk?"

"Monsieur," she replied, "I am a virgin, as you know, only reluctantly, since I can marry only a man who possesses 50,000 livres of income, and the three or four men in our region who qualify do not appeal to me in the least."

"Madame," I answered, pursuing our little banter, "haven't I already explained to you that I'll marry you as soon as I have 50,000 livres of income?"

"But you'll never have them!" she laughed, for she loved our badinage. "Moreover, I very well know that you're madly in love with your Angelina, and as constant in your love as you are inconstant in your body, sowing your seed to the winds."

"I, Madame?"

"Don't deny it! Whom are these coins destined for if not some chambermaid?"

"This chambermaid, as you call her, is named 'doctor of medicine'."

"How now? It costs you 100 écus to be promoted to doctor?"

"One hundred and thirty! I still need to find the other thirty! A candidate's expenses are infinite!"

"If it's thirty écus you need, I can give them to you out of my own purse here and now."

"Oh, Madame!" I cried. "You're the most beautiful angel on this earth, but I'd be ashamed to accept them."

"What?" she exclaimed, her eye suddenly darkening with anger. "You would refuse my money because I can't enrol in your 'school

58

of sighs'? Do we have to get to that point in our relationship before you consider me your friend?"

So I had to accept. She would have been angry, I'll warrant, given that the sweet sex are so infinitely giving once their hearts have been touched, if only in friendship. For there had been no intimacies between us, other than a few pecks on her dimples and nothing but a very rapid little kiss on her lips but with both hands behind my back, which is how she'd ordered it. So I left the Joyeuse residence greatly burdened by gold coins, but unburdened of my worries and overcome with gratitude for these two wenches. However, now that my purse was filled, I had to empty it straightaway, however much it cost. I had to bring my doctor-father Chancellor Saporta his due, that is, thirty francs' honorarium, for it was he who would preside over my *triduanes*. I was very hungry as I did so to catch sight of Typhème, the beautiful young bride of this greybeard, but of the sweetling there was not a trace. Saporta was a veritable Turk, and kept his wife closed in his room for fear that someone might steal her away—or even steal a look at her—so that I went away with nothing to show for my thirty écus, not even the pleasure of seeing her or even a word of thanks.

Dean Bazin—whom my schoolfellow Merdanson had named "the foetus" since he was so small, emaciated, puny and sickly; what's more, he was venomous in look and speech—greeted me even less warmly. Since I was the "son" of Chancellor Saporta he hated me as much as he did my "father".

Moreover, since his plan to preside over my *triduanes* had been undercut by Saporta, he felt cheated out of the thirty-écu honorarium, being as miserly and snivelling as any mother's son in Provence. Which tells you with what grimaces and gnashing of teeth he pocketed my two écus and ten sols, predicting in his whistling voice what a stormy and vexatious time I'd have of it at my *triduanes*.

Dr Feynes, the only Catholic among the four royal professors, received my offering with his customary beneficence. Wan and pale, he was even more than usually self-effacing, feeling himself to be a timid little papist mouse who'd wandered into a Huguenot hole. I could expect no vexations from him, but no help either: he scarcely opened his muzzle and weighed but little in our disputations.

As for Dr Salomon d'Assas, whom I'd saved for last, he lavished more thanks for his two écus, ten sols than if I'd laid at his feet all the treasures of the king whose name he bore (though of course he had dropped this name in favour of d'Assas, the name of his lands in Frontignan). He received me once again under the leafy boughs of his garden and offered me some of the delicious nectar he drew from his vines along with some pastries baked by his chambermaid Zara, who looked so languidly graceful that I could have swallowed her whole after tasting her pies. But that was impossible and would have been downright felonious, given how much Dr d'Assas loved her and trusted in my friendship.

"Ah, Pierre de Siorac!" he warned. "Watch out! The man who's predicted stormy and vexatious times for you has set innumerable pitfalls for you. Every one of his questions will be a trap! You can't escape it."

"But what can I do? How can I get around it?"

"Listen! Here's what you must do," continued d'Assas, who was round and benign from head to foot. Saying this, however, he opened his mouth, but suddenly fell silent.

"Venerable doctor, for heaven's sake, tell me!"

"I don't know," he said, looking me over with his dark eyes, so mild yet so cunning. "Should I tell you?"

"Tell me, I beg you!"

"Promise me you'll tell no one."

"I swear!"

"It's my belief, Pierre, that to pose a series of insidious questions to the candidate—questions on the most difficult, debatable and obscure points—is a nasty trick. Do you agree?"

"Of course!"

"Then, Pierre, the best defence against a ruse is a better one, yes?"

"Naturally!"

"Pierre, listen up! The man in question pretends to know Greek, but in fact never mastered it. He quotes things but all awry. So, my friend, between now and tomorrow you must memorize the passages from Hippocrates and Galen in your text, and when this so-and-so asks you a trick question, just answer calmly in Greek and with the casual air of a player taking a pawn."

"But what if the Greek text has no relation to the question?"

"Ah, but that's the beauty of it! Rabelais used this same trick with his most sticky debaters! And if they knew Greek, he'd stump them with his Hebrew!"

"Aha!" I laughed. "What an excellent trick and hilarious joke!"

And, looking at each other knowingly over our goblets of his delicious wine, we suddenly burst out in an uncontrollable belly laugh.

Later that same day I visited the doctors Pinarelle, Pennedepié and La Vérune, who were not members of the Royal College of Medicine, but ordinary doctors who gave occasional lectures at the school and were admitted to judging panels as a courtesy by Dr Saporta, though I would happily have done without their attendance, since they cost me six écus, thirty sols, which brought the honoraria paid to my judges to forty-three écus.

But that was not sufficient. On the eve of my *triduanes* I had gifts brought to the lodgings of each of the seven doctors that had been prescribed by an immemorial custom as to both quantity and quality:

1. A block of marzipan weighing at least four pounds, well iced with almond paste and stuffed with dried fruits.
2. Two pounds of sugared almonds.
3. Two candles made of good and sweet-smelling wax of at least a thumb's thickness.
4. A pair of gloves.

These offerings were delivered to the seven lodgings by the beadle Figairasse, to whom I paid a commission of two écus, twenty sols, both for the delivery and for his role in introducing and seating the visitors at my exams—as well as for, to my greater glory, sounding the college's bells when I had been proclaimed a doctor, and finally for preceding me through the streets of Montpellier, dressed in full armour, to announce throughout the city my triumph.

And in further obedience to ancient customs, I hired four musicians to play the fife, drum, trumpet and viol, and I brought them at sundown on the eve of my *triduanes* to serenade the doctors I've mentioned. Almost all of them condescended to open their windows and throw a few sols to the musicians (whom I'd paid handsomely), and acknowledge my deep bow while their wives clapped courteously. However, at Saporta's house, Typhème, no doubt on orders from her husband, did not show herself. And as for the lodgings of Dean Bazin, they remained as closed as the heart of a miser, the dean no doubt wishing to make it clear just how detestable he found me. As I took my leave of the musicians, I reminded them to be at my parade three days thence, for when the beadle went before me, they were supposed to precede him playing happy tunes as would befit a triumph.

You must not imagine, dear reader, that with these offerings I'd completed my expenses, no matter how hard my heart ached at having to waste so much on these sumptuous superfluities. And isn't it a great pity and a scandalous abuse that so much money was necessary when all that should have been required was knowledge? Well now, listen to this! During the three days that my exams lasted, custom required that I serve wine and cakes not just to the judging panel but to all the assistants who crowded into the examination hall to hear me, and who were rewarded with food and drink for having to sit through so many hours of tedium. And so I had to ask the innkeeper at the Three Kings to help me out during my *triduanes*, to which she consented graciously on condition that she be paid handsomely. Throughout the three days, she circulated through the hall with pitchers of wine, goblets, little pies and marzipans, aided by two sprightly chambermaids, who were pawed at by more than one member of the audience, including even the ordinary doctors, as these girls passed by, their two hands burdened with refreshments.

These expenses were heavy, but, sadly, necessary to keep my judges and assistants in good and benign humour, failing which the first would have turned me on the spit and the second would have jeered and taunted instead of applauding me as they did vociferously at every response I made, given how full their stomachs were and their spleens well doused and dilated with wine.

As expected, Bazin did his best to throw me to the winds, hog-tied, but at the first insidious question he posed, I answered with a long citation in Greek from Hippocrates, delivered distinctly and proudly, head held high and chest puffed out, and the audience, believing that I had turned the tables on the dean and put a stake through his heart, applauded wildly. At this, Dr d'Assas, bobbing his head, and baritoning from his nether parts, smiled angelically, while Chancellor Saporta, who knew Greek far too well to be a dupe to my hypocritical ruse, nevertheless remained mute and even stared scornfully at his dean, who sat down crestfallen, abashed and undone, and nearly choking on his own venom. To see the dean so thoroughly annihilated, the ordinary doctors thought twice before attempting to set any traps for me. However, Dr Pennedepié, who nourished a mortal hatred of Dr Pinarelle because he'd stolen one of his patients, wanted to use me to get revenge on his enemy, and asked me whether, in my opinion, a woman's uterus was simple or bifurcated. The question couldn't fail to embarrass me since I knew that Dr Pinarelle held, against all reason and evidence, Galen's authority on this to be absolute and that his statement on St Luke's day that he preferred "to be mistaken with Galen than be right with Vesalius" had made him the laughing stock of the entire town. So of course, Pennedepié was using me to embarrass his enemy. But since Bazin's hatred was enough for a lifetime, I did not want to have either of these two doctors on my back. So I resolved to test the waters with the prudence of a cat, and replied in Latin very quietly and modestly:

"Venerable Dr Pennedepié, *haec est vexata questio*.* On the one hand, the great Galen, having dissected the uterus of a rabbit and found it bifurcated, asserted that the uterus of a woman must also be so constructed. And, no doubt, his opinion has considerable weight, given the authority of the doctor, who is universally venerated as one of the masters of Greek medicine. But, on the other hand, our contemporary Vesalius, a bold and able medical doctor, who was a student in our college, dissected a woman, and not a rabbit, and found that her uterus was univalve."

Having said this, I remained silent.

"And you yourself, what do *you* believe? Univalve or bifurcated?" insisted the good Dr Pennedepié, pressing his advantage.

"Venerable Dr Pennedepié," I replied, my face glowing with humility. "There are in this hall so many people more knowledgeable than I, and I would rather they decide this question."

---

* "The question is very debatable."

"And yet," said Dr Pennedepié, "we must attempt to cure the illnesses of our women patients. So if you had a patient who had pain in her uterus, you would have to decide what to do."

"In which case, venerable doctor, having always found the uterus in my dissections to be one, I would decide in favour of unicity, without in any way deprecating the great and venerable Galen, who judged according to the evidence available to him in his time."

A dreadful silence fell on the assembly which would have done me in had not d'Assas suddenly raised his hands and cried in a loud voice:

"He has answered well and with enviable modesty for a candidate of his age!"

I thought I'd escaped relatively well from this ambush, but, as it turned out, not as well as I'd hoped. When the jury came to deliberate, Dr Pinarelle was opposed to awarding me the highest honours since I had, "in my presumptuous insolence, dared to confront the authority of the divine Galen". As luck would have it, since he was but an ordinary doctor, he could voice his opinion but had no vote. What considerably surprised me was that Dr Bazin, who, as a royal professor, did have a deliberative vote, immediately voted for high honours, being too intelligent not to mask his defeat with the appearance of benevolence. He was a man who, even in the face of imminent death, put his career above all, so when he saw Madame de Joyeuse and her ladies-in-waiting appear at the final session of my *triduanes* and, all decked out in their most seductive finery, take up seats in the first row, the venomous looks he'd darted at me throughout the proceedings became quite suddenly and surprisingly benign.

Oh reader! You can well imagine that my heart was beating a fanfare of drums and trumpets to wake the dead when my doctor-father, Chancellor Saporta, commanded me to climb to the platform where the jury had just decided my fate, and then declared me doctor of medicine, with high honours, asked me to repeat the Hippocratic oath, and then handed me, one by one, and with the customary solemnity and gravity required for such occasions, the symbols of my new estate, to wit:

1. A square doctor's bonnet, all black except for a crimson silk cord that hung from the top, and which I doffed immediately.
2. A golden sash, three inches wide, which I immediately fastened around my waist.
3. A heavy gold ring engraved with my initials that I put on the ring finger of my left hand, where it nestled with the little ring Angelina had given me.
4. An edition of Hippocrates's *Aphorisms* beautifully bound in calfskin.

Thus hatted, sashed and ringed, and holding my copy of Hippocrates's magnum opus, I gave a speech of thanks in seven different languages: in French (with a low bow to Madame de Joyeuse), in Latin (bowing to the ordinary doctors), in Greek (bowing to the royal professors, with a special reverence in the direction of Dr d'Assas, who had translated this speech for me), in Hebrew (with a bow to Maître Sanche, to whom I owed my knowledge of that language), in German (bowing to my fellow students from Basle), in Italian (simply because I knew a bit of this admirable language), and finally, to the surprise of all, given that it is an idiom that is considered rustic and uneducated, in the local Provençal dialect used in Montpellier. After a moment of surprise, there was a deafening roar of applause from the entire hall in appreciation of my friendship, in gratitude for the love I expressed for this city, its people and its language.

This done, Chancellor Saporta rose and embraced me warmly, rubbing his rough beard against my cheek, and bade me sit down at his right hand while the beadle Figairasse, striding out of the hall, went to ring peals of the college bells in my honour. He wasn't stingy in his effort and I got my money's worth out of those two écus and twenty sols. It was a din loud enough to deafen for ever those who heard it.

This racket finally over, the royal professors, the ordinary doctors and the assistants processed out through the streets of Montpellier to the Three Kings inn, where I hosted, as was the custom, a banquet which cost every sol I had. At least this was my last outlay but it was the most monstrous. Happily all those who stuffed and nearly drowned themselves at my expense didn't share my financial worries.

Madame de Joyeuse was good enough to have her carriage bring her to the inn and, once there, had herself placed in a private room from which she sent for me. Managing to sneak away from the crowd, I hastened to her side and found her comfortably settled with Aglaé de Mérol at her side. Both of them were in their finest silks and satins, fully made-up with pearls in their hair and smelling of all the perfumes in Araby.

"Well now, my little cousin!" cried Madame de Joyeuse. "A kiss for you! You were perfect! Not that I understand a word of Latin, mind you, but you looked as beautiful and graceful as a cat, though a cat with sharp claws under its velvet paws. And best of all, there wasn't a trace of the crusty old pedant in your tone or your appearance. Kiss me again! You were sublime! Aglaé, tell him how wonderful he was!"

"Monsieur," Aglaé conceded with a glint in her eye and a trace of a pout, "you were admirable in every way!"

I bowed to Madame de Joyeuse and happily kissed her lips.

"Greet Aglaé as well!" she proclaimed when I'd finished my embrace—certainly a more pleasing one than Saporta's rough beard.

"But Madame, I don't believe I dare!"

"Monsieur!" she snorted. "Do you think I don't know all the trouble you give her, virgin though she may be? Is there no end to your impertinence, you monster? So, since you've ordered the wine, drink it!"

"Madame! What a betrayal! You've repeated all my compliments?"

"Every one, Monsieur!" laughed Aglaé, while I obediently kissed her, though not with too much ardour, so that Madame de Joyeuse wouldn't begin her usual refrain about her advanced age.

"So, my sweet," said the lady, "come and see me tomorrow as soon as you've finished your triumphal procession though the city."

"But Madame, I'll be all sweaty and dusty!"

"Well, then! We'll just have to clean you up in my bathtub!" At which they both giggled like schoolgirls and looked at me with so conspiratorial an air I didn't know what to think. But I've learnt that when you don't understand something, it's best to treat it light-heartedly in the heat of the moment.

"Mesdames," I laughed, "is this not strange? Now that I'm a doctor, it's you who wish to cure me!"

Whereupon I kissed their smooth cheeks and tender hands. Oh, the gentler sex can be so sweet and enveloping! How I would have missed them if God had forgotten to create them! And with what ardour I watched them as they departed, laughing and babbling in their gold-embroidered bodices.

The crowd was so dense in the main dining room of the Three Kings and everyone so busy gorging themselves at my expense—while our hostess went from one person to the next, her eyes shining as she calculated how much their sharp teeth and dry throats would come to on her slate, which I'd have to settle tomorrow—that no one noticed my brief absence. When I caught sight of my beloved Samson, with Miroul at his side, I noticed that he was deep in conversation with a well-proportioned lass wearing a black mask that completely covered her face, but whom I nevertheless immediately identified thanks to a particular trait, which I'll explain. She only appeared to be a lady for, despite her rich attire, she was but a commoner, as her Provençal dialect and Cévennes accent made all to evident. She now lived discreetly in comfortable profligacy, very highly esteemed by a few wealthy bourgeois, a handsome canon of Notre-Dame des Tables and Captain Cossolat, for among her other qualities (such as an expertise in frolicking and lewd games) she was faithful in her friendships, more of a good girl than an angel, although her sex, unlike that of angels, was absolutely indubitable.

Making my way through the crowds, I approached her and whispered in her ear, "Ah, my good Thomassine, here you are! If you weren't wearing a mask, I'd give you a kiss!"

"What!" she gasped. "You recognized me?"

"Of course!"

"But how?"

"By your figure! There's not a more shapely or fetching body in all of Provence!"

"You rascal!" she laughed. "You have such a way with words! And not just with the ladies, it seems, but also with these bigwig doctors!"

"My dear Thomassine, what on earth were you doing at my boring *triduanes*?"

"By m'faith! What gibberish! Was that French you were speaking?"

"No, it was Latin."

"Oh, mercy! What strange twaddle! I couldn't understand a word of it! But I could easily see that you're as silver-tongued as they come and there wasn't one among those berobed bigwigs that could get the better of you!"

I took leave of her to fetch a goblet of wine and a Bigorre sausage, and holding the latter between my thumb and my index finger as Barberine had taught me—rather than, as that pig the Baron de Caudebec did, in my fist—I used my left hand to fill my goblet, and was returning to Thomassine's side when I heard a great commotion over by the door, and headed that way. There I beheld Captain Cossolat struggling with a tall, thin, dark-haired devil, quite badly dressed in a ragged doublet but wearing at his side both sword and dagger. Cossolat was attempting to arrest this fellow because he was not a doctor, a student or a known citizen of the town, and so he'd collared him and was accusing him of having come in to gorge himself at my expense and, who knows, pick a few pockets.

"Monthieur," lisped this great spindleshanks with an offended air, "how dare you lay a hand on me! I am a perthon of quality. My name is Giacomi and I'm a mathter-at-armth."

"A likely fable!" cried Cossolat. "There's not a master-at-arms in Montpellier that I haven't met, since arms are my profession! Tell me, knave, who knows you here?"

"I do!" I replied, stepping forward, since I liked this fellow's demeanour and his lisp, which reminded me of my beloved Samson.

"What, Pierre? You know this rascal?"

"I do!" I lied, my cheeks swelling with this happy falsehood. "His name is Giacomi, and I invited him here."

"I've only been here three days," said our guest quickly, "which is why the captain here hadn't met me yet."

"Pierre," growled Cossolat, releasing him, but looking askance at me, "do you really answer for this fellow?"

"Indeed I do," I laughed, "as much as I answer for myself!"

At this, Cossolat, who was a full head shorter than Giacomi, but very stocky, with broad shoulders and well-muscled arms, looked the man up and down with a most unfriendly air and said, "Italian, remember this well: I don't like it when a fellow of your aspect walks around my town wearing a sword and dagger when he's not got a sol in his purse." Having said which, he turned on his heels and marched off stiffly, clearly irritated.

"Monsieur doctor," said Giacomi greeting me, "what thanks and good wishes I owe—"

"Bah," I said, interrupting him, "forget it! It's nothing. I simply didn't want you to be locked up for stealing a sausage on the day I received my promotion."

"Especially, honoured doctor," he replied squinting with such a piteous and dainty air at the sausage I was holding in my right hand, "since I haven't eaten anything yet."

At this, I burst out laughing.

"Well then, eat, my friend!" I said, handing him goblet and sausage. "Eat your fill and drink up. It's not going to empty my wallet on a day like this!" And shoving him into the little room that Madame de Joyeuse and Aglaé had just vacated, I had our hostess feed him his fill and promised him I'd come back to talk to him as soon as my guests had left.

Scarcely, however, had I entered the grand hall before one of the pretty chambermaids who had been so pawed over during my *triduanes* approached me with a mysterious smile and told me that there was a masked and veiled "woman of noble bearing" asking for me at the entrance to the inn.

I hurried out and found a tall, very well-dressed and bejewelled woman wearing a mask, and, over the mask, a black lace veil, which she removed when she saw me, revealing a head of strawberry-blonde hair. She was none other than Dame Gertrude du Luc.

"Ah, Madame! You, here! So far from your beloved Normandy! How happy Samson will be to see you!"

"And what about you, my brother," cooed Dame Gertrude, in her Norman French, "aren't you happy as well?"

"But of course, Madame," I answered, already impatient with her coquetry and suddenly remembering her affair with Cossolat; and, without missing a beat, but with a sudden coldness, I went on: "…if indeed you are as faithful to him as he is to you."

"What? Could you doubt it?" cried the little hypocrite, happy that her mask could hide her shame, if shame she could feel. "But my brother," she continued, "aren't you surprised to see me here?"

"Of course!"

"I am," she said placing her hand on my arm so that I could see the large ring on her gloved finger, "on a second pilgrimage to Rome, having derived such great spiritual profit from the first one."

"Ah, Madame," I replied with honeyed piety, "this is very edifying indeed, as long as you don't use up all the indulgences you earned in the papal city just getting there."

"You wicked Huguenot," she hissed with feigned anger, "you're making sport of me! Do you feel so little pity for the foibles of a poor papist?" And so saying, she threw her arms around me and held me tightly, pressing the full length of her body against mine; and, I confess, she was so soft, so mellow, so undulating, that I felt my mouth suddenly turn dry and words fail me—though these certainly wouldn't have been necessary if we'd followed the path down which this Circe was leading me. Nor could I withhold pity for her weaknesses when she was exposing my own with such art! What a lesson for me—and one that reminded me I should never judge my neighbour!

And yet I didn't want to give in any further when I thought about my beloved Samson; so, taking Dame Gertrude by the shoulders and pushing her back from me, I whispered in her ear:

"Madame, this time I will serve you, but no Cossolat! Or I'll lose my temper!"

Breathing very hard behind her mask, she remained as mute as a carp, giving sufficient proof of her bewitching power to retreat, if indeed that was what she was doing, for I clearly understood, as I watched her pant, that this Norman ogress had appetite enough to cast the three of us together into the furnace of her desire—Samson, Cossolat and me—and the Devil knows who else.

"My brother," she said in a dying voice, as if she were out of breath, "I know Thomassine is here—and Samson. Go, I beg you, and summon them. I've got a carriage waiting outside the door to take them to the needle shop where I hope the good Thomassine will give me a room, but please! Hurry! I can't wait any longer! I feel like I'm on fire!"

Oh Lord! The power of a woman! What a hold it has on us! How men grovel before it—men who in their pride and pomp are stupid enough to think they control everything! The minx had so overwhelmed, troubled and mollified me that I hurried to obey her, crazed as I was! But not as crazed as Samson, who almost fainted when he beheld her suddenly standing there, lifting her mask to reveal her irresistible smile.

In a trice, he was hers, and he stepped, as if tied hand and foot, into her carriage, throwing his Huguenot conscience to the winds, while at his side Thomassine was secretly lamenting that such a great love was planted in such risky terrain. I remained standing there in the doorway of the inn, feeling sorry for Samson's simplicity, at the same time thinking—and knowing exactly why I was having such a thought—how much I would have enjoyed being in his place.

When I went back into the inn, I was congratulated on all sides for the superb way in which I'd defended myself on my *triduanes*: compliments that I listened to politely and happily enough, and yet my mind was elsewhere, as if in a fog of that melancholy that often follows our greatest joys and successes. To tell the truth, I was also feeling the immense fatigue that three days of aggressive disputations had produced, and, since night had long since fallen and one by one my guests were taking their leave, my responses became less and less effusive. The only exception was d'Assas, whom I held back for last in order to express my great thanks. Ah, what a good man he was! And so fat! And so lively! And so benign!

"Pierre," he said as he embraced me warmly (as much as he was able, for his great paunch prevented him from hugging me), "here you are, a doctor at the tender age of twenty-one. Now that you have your plumage, you must leave the nest! You know how much I shall miss your zeal for knowledge and your zest for life! Of all the students I've had in the last five years, you were the one I loved best and I would have given you anything—except," he said with a wicked smile, "my chambermaid Zara and my Frontignan vineyard, both of which attracted you—if not the first, then most certainly the second. Now a word about medicine, Pierre. As you depart from the Royal College, you must also leave behind this scholarly rubbish: the contentious disputations, the pompous pedantries, the Latin and"—he smiled broadly—"even the Greek, which you haven't learnt! All this silliness! This hollowness! *Crede mihi experto Roberto!** Three-quarters of what you were taught here isn't worth a dead horse's fart! Practise your dissections! There's where the truth lies! Under the knife! Before your eyes! Under your fingers! And read only those teachers who have experience with cutting! Michael Servetus! The great Vesalius! Ambroise Paré! Throw away into the deepest dungeon the Pinarelles and Pennedepiés and all the pompous asses who worship Aristotle, Hippocrates and Galen as if they were gods and daily exclaim: *Vetera extollimus recentium incuriosi.*"† Just remember, Pierre, that he who speaks by the authority of the ancients offers only unprofitable dust. We Huguenots, who reject the authority of the Pope, popular superstitions, the saints and all the golden idols, must also be Huguenots in medicine! We must rediscover the naked truth of nature beneath all the age-old errors! An ass wearing a doctor's bonnet is still an ass! Let it bray for its ancient oats! Let Pinarelle believe in his bifurcated uterus!

---

* "Trust me, for I have the requisite experience!"

† "We raise to the heavens ancient wisdom and turn our backs on what is modern."

And let Pennedepié enjoy his nasty tricks! Pinarelle and Pennedepié! Pennedepié and Pinarelle! Pierre, my friend, remember these two ridiculous and senile pedants as the alpha and omega of ignorance. And don't they just look the part?—as long and unhappy as two days in Lent! Oh, Pierre! The truth is naked and science is gay!"

Whereupon, choking down a sob, I thought, he embraced me warmly. I walked him to the door, where his cart was waiting, and as he leapt into it with an agility that I wouldn't have expected of someone so portly, I watched him whip his horse into a lively trot, and was surprised to feel suddenly small and sombre, as though, somehow, he were taking with him my youthful years of study in Montpellier. And indeed, they had come to an end! The straw beaten, the grains in the sack, all that remained on the field was the stubble of harvests reaped. Certain it is that we must harvest food for the winter, but who doesn't shed a tear to see the beautiful standing wheat fall before the scythe?

I returned to the great hall, where the tables were now piled with the remains of my repast. From the other side of the room, the hostess bustled over with a huge smile on her face to tell me that she'd present me with the bill the next morning. Hardly able to answer, my heart suddenly heavy, I called to Miroul, who was sitting on a stool chatting with one of the chambermaids. According to which side of his face he turned her way, he gazed at her either with his blue or with his brown eye, and under such an assault the lass was melting like butter in the sun, but then it was her job to melt, since the poor girl was but one of the commodities offered by the inn. I ordered Miroul to fetch me my sword, dagger and pistols—which I'd left at the inn that morning since it was forbidden to carry arms at the Royal College of Medicine—and while waiting for them I began to think about my large bed, when all of a sudden I remembered that I'd left Giacomi in the little room off the hall. And it was a very lucky thing, as we will see, that I didn't forget him.

His feast devoured, the Italian was sleeping like a log, his elbows flat on the table and his cheek on his elbows, with the air of blessed felicity that you see on the faces of the chosen in stained-glass windows in papist churches. I tapped him on the shoulder.

"Ah, Monsieur doctor!" he stammered, blinking in the candle-light like a bat in the sun. "You've done wonders for me by filling my stomach! I dreamt I was in heaven!"

"Giacomi," I replied gravely, but not with a frown, "so what are you? A pickpocket? A hired assassin?"

"Not a bit of it, Monthieur doctor!" he replied, raising his head and speaking with his Italian lisp. "I was, as I said, a master-at-arms in Genoa and well respected for my talents. But having killed in an honourable dual a gentleman who had provoked me, I had to flee my country to save my skin. And so hurriedly, that I left without any money."

I looked him over. He had a very curious face: it was oval, quite thin, with well-tanned skin, or rather dark-brown, and features that communicated irrepressible joy—the edges of his eyelids, the corners of his lips and his nose, which bent oddly heavenward. His jet-black eyes protruded from their sockets, revealing lots of white, and were constantly moving this way and that, like little ferrets, but absent of any malice or trickery. He was tall and thin, with long arms and legs and something so quick in his movements that he reminded me of a bird. From his frank and open face, I decided that he must be telling the truth. Moreover, he seemed well enough educated and not without book-learning, and spoke French reasonably correctly.

"But Giacomi," I ventured, "can't you have money sent from Genoa?"

"Alas, no! When I left, the hussy I was living with ran off with my purse, my jewellery and my furniture. Ah, Monsieur doctor, I was left, as you see me here, with nothing to my name. But I'm not going to dwell on it. *Nessun maggior dolore che ricordarsi del tempo felice nella miseria.*"*

I was delighted to hear him quote Dante, whom I ranked above all the poets of his time, and whether 'twas the configuration of his features that give him a naturally happy face or whether he carried within him an inexhaustible source of gaiety, he looked joyous even when quoting these sad verses.

"So, not a sol to your name?"

"Not one!"

"And where will you sleep tonight?"

"Same as last night: under a buttress at the church of Saint-Firmin, with one eye open, and dagger in hand, since this town is crawling with hooligans who wouldn't think twice about dispatching a fellow just to steal his worn-out doublet."

This set me to thinking and finally I said, "Giacomi, how would you like to sleep in Miroul's room tonight? He's a good companion."

"Ah, Monsieur doctor!" he cried, raising his arms heavenward, a gesture that reminded me of Fogacer (who, I'd heard, was now living in Paris, having fled his native city, as I had, but for very different reasons).

"Well, do you want to?"

"Yes, of course!" replied Giacomi, but not without a trace of reticence, which I couldn't help but notice. "Better a roof than the cold sky, and better an honest servant than a robber."

At this point, with a quick knock on the door, Miroul entered, bearing my arms. In response, Giacomi stood up with a most gracious smile and asked, less in the manner of a servant than in that of an *écuyer*, if I'd give him permission to inspect my sword. I agreed, unsheathed it

---

* "There is no greater grief than to remember good times in the midst of unhappiness."

and handed to him. Taking it in his long hands, which seemed very nervous and delicate, and, it seemed, quite clean—proof that he'd asked our hostess to allow him to wash them before his repast—he held it up to his wrinkled nose as if to smell it, his protruding black eye scrutinizing the length of steel. After which he placed the blade on his left index finger about three inches from the hilt and balanced it so that it tipped neither towards the hilt nor towards the point.

"Monsieur doctor," he now asked, "may I test its flexion?"

Upon my assent, he held the point up to the wooden door and, his arm flexed, thrust forward, while bending his knee, and the blade bent into a perfect semicircle so that the point was no more than a foot or so from the hilt. After which Giacomi relaxed his arm and the blade immediately straightened, without the least trace of the flexion it had undergone. But, as yet unsatisfied, Giacomi pulled from his boot a small key, with which he tapped little blows on the blade every inch or so of its length while holding his ear to the steel to listen to the sound, as if he were tuning the strings of a viol.

This done, he pronounced with a pompous air—but still with the lisp which seemed to rob his words of their seriousness: "Monthieur doctor, I observe, first of all, that your blade is not flat like some vulgar battle sword made for slashing but not for thrusting. It's triangular, and thins gradually from hilt to point. I see no black stains: so there are no weaknesses in the metal that might cause it to break. As the point is slightly broken, I can see that the interior of the blade is grey and not white, thank God. Moreover, when I flexed it, the blade did not bend at the point but along its entire length in a perfect semicircle, and, as soon as I relaxed the pressure, it regained its original straightness vibrantly, an obvious sign that it was properly dipped, which was confirmed when I tapped it with my key. Lastly, the sword is beautifully balanced from the pommel to the point, which means it's light in the hand and will be prompt to strike, as long as its wielder's brain is. In short, Monsieur, it's my judgement that you have here a good friend and one who, as it's not a woman, will not betray you. *La donna è mobile qual piuma al vento*,* but this friend here is faithful and shines with a solid and irrefragable virtue."

"Ah, Giacomi," I laughed, "don't you think it's true than men are also *mobile qual piuma al vento*? You're still licking your wounds from your wench in Genoa! *Ab una non disce omnes*."†

As I said this, I thought of my Angelina, who'd been waiting five years without ever wavering in her resolution, as steadfast in her great love as a storm-battered rock. "Oh, Angelina," I thought, "as soon as Samson has been liberated from his flesh trap, I will joyfully throw at your feet the ornaments of my new title, by whose virtue I shall be able to enrich myself enough to marry you!"

"Monsieur doctor, are you listening?" said Giacomi. Emerging from my trance, I watched as he lined the sword up, point downward, next to my leg. "Aha! Just as I thought! It should have been a good inch longer since there is an ideal proportion between the length of the sword and the height of the swordsman—a rule that your sword-maker must not have known, however good an artisan he was."

"An inch!" I countered. "Who cares about an inch?"

"Ah, Monsieur doctor," corrected Giacomi, "there are times when an inch can make all the difference between life and death." And though he spoke of death, his face appeared happy and full of mirth. But perhaps it was only his upturned nose that gave me this impression.

While Giacomi, his gentle lisp echoing my brother Samson's, continued to hold forth in melodious French in his precise and elegant manner, accompanied by very gracious gestures—though one could

---

* "Woman is as fickle as a feather in the wind."
† "From one example we cannot claim to know all of them."

sense, beneath this offhandedness, reserves of strength—Miroul, who understood the language of the north passably well, was listening open-mouthed to the Italian. Seeing which, Giacomi turned to him and said with great gentility:

"*Compagno*, I see that you wear you sword on your right hip. I surmise, then, that you're left-handed."

"That I am."

"*Eccellente!*" replied Giacomi. "*Eccellentissimo! È tutto a tuo vantaggio.** And what's even better, you have eyes that don't match, a sign of great agility and skill."

"I hold my sword in my left hand," replied Miroul, delighted to be thus praised, "but throw my dagger with my right."

"And where do you hide your short sword, *compagno*?"

"In my boot leg."

"Just one?"

"Just one."

"Seeing as you have two legs, you must have two short swords," smiled Giacomi, and the corners of his mouth were lifted towards his enormous ears so contagiously that Miroul and I couldn't help mirroring his joyful mien.

Our hostess interrupted Giacomi's lessons to bring Miroul a torch and tossed a few unenthusiastic civilities my way before she headed off to bed to fill her head with visions of the day's takings, like a pregnant woman her fruit.

I'm not sure the Three Kings is still there in Montpellier, but, at the time, it faced the tower of the same name that rises between the Lattes gate and the Babote tower. This last is a round, fairly wide structure facing south-west that overlooks, both to the right and to the left, the city wall. From the Three Kings, it wasn't more than a

---

* "Excellent! Most excellent! It's all to your advantage!"

fifteen-minute walk to the place des Cévennes, where I lodged with Maître Sanche, the famous apothecary. But at night we had to take some precautions on this route.

Miroul, unsheathed sword in his left hand, held a torch aloft in the other and walked three paces in front of us to light our way. But Giacomi suggested that, since Miroul was left-handed, he should walk on my left to protect me, so I did as the Italian suggested, and Giacomi walked on my right, sword in hand. It was a moonless night and not a sound could be heard around us except our footsteps, which we muffled as much as possible to enable us to hear as we walked along the left facade of Notre-Dame des Tables—or rather what's left of it after the damage our side stupidly wreaked on it after we took the city from the papists during the troubles a few years previously. Once past Notre-Dame, we left the rue de la Mazellerie du Porc, which is straight and fairly wide, and headed down the rue de la Caussalerie, which is a narrow, winding alley that opens on the place des Cévennes, where I lodged. But scarcely had we entered this street before Giacomi whispered:

"Monsieur doctor, we're about to be attacked. I can feel it in a little muscle in the palm of my right hand. If it happens, we three need to fight back to back so we can all protect each other. And, Monsieur doctor, may I borrow one of your pistols?"

I gave it to him without saying a word, and he stuck it in his belt, and with his left hand drew an impressively long dagger from his boot. I drew mine as well and rolled my cape around the arm that held it, my heart beating wildly, and even though a moment before I was ready to drop from fatigue, I now felt as light and sprightly as a hare.

"Monsieur," hissed Miroul on my left, "I think I hear something brushing the walls of the nearest houses."

"Hm," I said, "I think we're going to have to fight it out. I can sense it too."

The next ten steps we took were on cat's paws, our feet scarcely touching the paving stones, our legs tensed and our ears straining for the tiniest sound. Despite the fact that the dancing light of the torch lit the way ahead, we still couldn't see a living soul.

"Back to back, Monsieur doctor!" whispered Giacomi.

The rue de la Caussalerie and the rue de l'Herberie (so named because all the hay the city needed for its 20,000 horses was stored there) were not at right angles to each other, and it was in this turning that the attack was launched.

"Kill! Kill!" cried a loud voice, ripping through the silence of the night, and suddenly a cloud of derelicts, bursting from the darkness like so many rats from a sewer, engulfed us, weapons in their fists and emitting strange howls, without any thought of the nightwatchmen, believing they'd overrun us in a trice before the gendarmes could arrive.

We closed ranks, back to back, or rather thigh to thigh since there were three of us, and, without a word, or even a cry for help since we knew that no inhabitant of the city would dare open his door to shelter us, we put cold steel on these ragamuffins, whose most potent weapon might have been their stench, which nearly had us fainting from nausea. At their first rush, Giacomi dropped two of them at his feet by doing nothing more than extending his arm with an unbelievable quickness, while with his dagger parried the blows they threw at him. But the storm was now buffeting me and all I could see were sword points threatening me, although I was less concerned by these than by a long pike that was aimed at my chest but still too far away for me to deflect it. However, having dropped two or three of these brigands in their tracks, I had the time to slip my dagger between my teeth, seize my pistol and fire it at the pikeman. His weapon fell into the street and, returning my pistol to my belt, I grabbed it with my left hand and used it to keep at bay the attackers on my left, whom I could not reach with my sword. I couldn't see what Miroul was doing while I was so occupied, but when the first assault fell back, I saw two bodies lying before him in the street, proof that his labours had not been in vain.

Although our attackers did not launch another attack, neither did they withdraw, but took counsel among themselves in a strange dialect I couldn't make out. Certainly the wounded and dying that lay around us must have given them pause, especially as it was now more difficult to have at us since those they had lost now served as a rampart that protected us!

"Monsieur doctor," hissed Giacomi, "forget the pike, it's just getting in your way. Recharge your pistol. It'll serve you well when these ruffians come back to bite us."

I did as he bade me, but while I did, I wanted to make contact with these rascals, which, lacking other advantages, would at least gain us some time.

"You there!" I cried in the street slang of Montpellier. "Wouldn't it be better to come to terms? What would you rather have, my purse or the blood of my heart?"

"Since we saw you treat all your friends to a feast at the Three Kings, we'd prefer the former," yelled a large, muscular brigand who wore a black patch over one eye, "but now we want your blood as well! You've killed too many of our honest comrades!"

"No, no, my good fellows," I cried, "it wasn't malice! We've got a right to defend ourselves! So how many of you are going to die on the street before I spill my guts for you? Don't you think it'd be better that I give you my wallet in exchange for free passage?"

"Not on your life!" cried the man with the patch. "We'll get the money anyway when we kill you! I want you three bled dry like chickens on a spit! My honour demands it!"

"Giacomi!" I whispered. "Did you hear that? Is honour a gold ring in the snout of a pig?"

"Well, we'll make him understand that it's not!" cried Giacomi with a little laugh.

Scarcely had he spoken before, with a shout of "Kill, 'sblood! Kill!" the brigands hurled themselves on us again but without the fire or bravado they'd shown the first time, some of them stumbling on their own dead that surrounded us, and their weapons meeting the points of our swords at every thrust. And yet, as they advanced in more orderly fashion, they endured fewer losses, and I realized that, following the orders of their one-eyed leader, they were now just trying to wear us down—a tactic that would likely succeed if the nightwatchmen didn't arrive. But I knew, as everyone in Montpellier did, that unless Cossolat's guards backed them up, the watch would be in no hurry to help us, being more fearful of the brigands than the brigands were of them, since their soldiers were neither young, skilled in arms nor particularly valiant.

"Giacomi," I whispered, "I don't see their 'honourable' leader. Do you!"

"No, Monsieur doctor," said the Italian, who, even in the teeth of death, remained suavely polite. "He's way over there, giving commands, but he's not attacking. His honour forbids it."

"I see him!" said Miroul.

"Is he within range of your knife?"

"Yes!"

"Give me your torch to free up your right hand," I said, placing my dagger between my teeth and reaching towards him with my left hand.

This movement almost cost me dearly, a sword tip glancing off my forearm, which would have pierced right through had I not been covering it with my cape, which was fastened by a copper pin and which the blade glanced off, as I determined the next morning, leaving only a scratch that I hadn't even felt.

I seized the torch and held it aloft, truly amazed that Miroul could fight so well in such an awkward posture, and feeling badly exposed myself with my dagger in my left hand. I kept my eyes glued on the sword tips that threatened my chest like so many mortal wasp stings, so I saw only out of the corner of my eye the gesture Miroul made of seizing his knife from his boot and throwing it. But I definitely heard, over the strident clashing of swords, the grunt of the one-eyed man as the knife lodged in his chest, and then the shouts of the rabble: "Old dead-eye's croaked!"

And at this we sensed a hesitation among our assailants that we quickly took advantage of, having at them with our good blades a good deal more effectively than they ever would have wished. Some of the rascals fled the engagement, melting back into the shadows whence they'd emerged, while others, as if enraged, redoubled their attack, shouting vengeance and death, and so savage was their impetuosity that this time we laid out a good half-dozen of them on the cold ground before their bellicose fire was extinguished.

In the calm that followed, Miroul reclaimed his torch and Giacomi whispered, "Monsieur doctor, are your lodgings far from here?"

"Forty paces."

"And you've got the key?"

"I have it."

"Monsieur doctor, throw them a handful of écus and couronnes! We'll run for our lives. Dagger in mouth. Sword and pistol at the ready."

Oh reader, you can imagine how hard it was for a Huguenot heart like mine to toss a handful of coins to the winds! How it hurt to hear the tintinnabulation of these coins sown on the paving stones with no hope of any harvest! So, as the beggars threw themselves on the coins as they rolled here and there, we set off at a run, bounding like madmen, and met no more than four of them in our path, two of whom we shot like pigeons at a fair, the other two immediately ceding us the right of passage.

However, the rest of the bunch, having regained their courage, pursued us, and we had barely reached Maître Sanche's door before they were at our heels. To keep from being cut down from behind, we had to turn on them suddenly, our swords flashing. It was their final assault and their most furious, and I had to marvel at the crazy courage of these desperate rascals, who, having harvested my money, now sought to take my life at the risk of their own, in the name of this bizarre and very particular notion of honour, which, among the least of men as among the most powerful, makes war an inevitable condition of our species. Giacomi and Miroul, feeling more at ease in defending this narrow gateway in which they no longer had to worry about being attacked from behind, relished the chance to dispatch what remained of this horde.

Having opened the door behind them, I had to call them twice before they would consent to take shelter, whereupon Miroul with a great curse (and he a good Huguenot!) hurled his torch in their faces.

Once inside and the door bolted, Balsa, Maitre Sanche's one-eyed assistant, appeared, lantern in hand, looking quite terrified. "Ah, venerable doctor, you're bleeding!" he cried.

And, indeed, as I caught sight of myself in a small mirror that hung in the entryway, I saw that the left side of my scalp had a gash two inches long. The wound was neither deep nor serious, but it was pissing blood like a cow in a meadow, and my cheek, neck and collar were all crimsoned. "Ah, Miroul," I exclaimed, suddenly realizing what was missing, "I've lost my handsome doctor's bonnet all festooned with gold braid! It must have fallen off when I received this wound!"

I nearly went back to look for it, so mortified was I that, on the very day I'd received high honours at the Royal College from Chancellor Saporta, those ruffians had stripped me of my trophy. But instead, I needed to clean and dress my wound and bandage Miroul, who'd been slashed in the shoulder—Giacomi alone having escaped injury, so excellent was his skill in battle, his sword point sharp, his reach long and his thrust lightning fast.

We hadn't yet gone off to bed when an archer came to ask after us on behalf of Cossolat, who, finally appearing at the place des Cévennes—since the night watch had been beaten earlier in the evening in another part of town—had arrested the rascals we'd wounded and, without even taking them to jail, had sent them with their boots on to the gallows. ("With their boots on" is, of course, just an expression, since none of these beggars could afford a decent pair of shoes, much less boots.)

I sent the archer back to Cossolat to ask him if he would mind looking for my doctor's square bonnet, which I desperately needed for my triumphal parade the next day. However, the next morning, having received no news of it, I sent a town crier through all the neighbour-hoods of the city promising a reward to two écus (the only money I had left) for anyone who would return it to me. But this promise of a reward was to no avail, other than to spread the news among the workers and inhabitants of the city of our previous night's clash in la Caussalerie, which Cossolat's guards (who, of course, had not seen it) recounted everywhere they went, embellishing the numbers of our assailants with each retelling so that, in the end, we three were reputed to have killed or wounded at least a hundred brigands in one night.

Meanwhile, the loss of my doctor's bonnet bothered me no end and so I wrote a letter to my doctor-father Saporta, which Miroul delivered. The chancellor replied quite reasonably that, since I'd received a nasty scalp wound, I couldn't wear a bonnet and so would be dispensed from having to wear one in my triumphal procession.

And what a triumph it was! I was acclaimed throughout the city by large crowds—not, of course, because I'd been promoted to doctor, since there were a dozen or so of these parades each year, but because I and my two companions had so stoutly manhandled an army of

87

bandits, who were the terror and scourge of the good people of the entire city, and who nightly committed horrible excesses, stoving in the doors of houses, killing noblemen and rich merchants indiscriminately, and raping their wives and daughters.

My mare Accla's black coat shone with all its mirroring light after Miroul brushed her down that morning, despite his wound, though luckily it was only to his right shoulder. With infinite patience he had braided her mane and her tail, weaving ribbons of red silk at every tuft and fitting a crimson blanket under the shiny pigskin saddle that Petremol had made for me. In this finery, preceded by the beadle Figairasse and my musicians playing happy tunes, and followed by the royal professors and the ordinary doctors, the assistants and medical students, all in their academic robes and some mounted on horses, others on mules, I rode through the most beautiful streets of Montpellier amid a crowd of people applauding me vociferously as if I'd just slain the dragon that was terrorizing them. You might well imagine that being so appreciated by the people—in the same city where I'd been a public enemy after having shortened the suffering of the atheist abbot Cabassus—I felt like a peacock on my beautiful Accla, though I was careful not to let it show, but maintained an inscrutably serene expression throughout, except, here and there, to give a wink to some of the beauties who were applauding me from their windows decorated with flowers.

My parade complete, I hurried to the Joyeuse residence, but of what happened there I shall say not a word, having offended some of the ladies who read the previous volume of my memoirs and were shocked by some of the descriptions of our love-making. And though I believe that these same ladies have much more reason to be offended by what's going on around them in their daily lives than by the spiciest of tales they read in books, I set too much store by their friendship to risk wounding them further.

Isn't it amazing how like the teeth of a saw is a man's destiny! Promoted to the rank of doctor with high honours after my *triduanes*, I was nearly brought low the next day by the knives of a group of brigands. And, barely having escaped these assassins, the following day I find myself acclaimed as an angel and a hero by this sheepfold of a populace. And that very evening, I receive the laurel wreath from the hands of the most suave, beautiful and noble woman in Montpellier, who, having heard of my losses, rushes to compensate and comfort me. Ah! Life is but a dream! I have come to see that the fatal Tarpeian Rock lies but a stone's throw from the Capitol's glory, and that 'tis Fortune's whim to send us scuttling back and forth between them.

The only thing missing from my present happiness was my beloved Samson, who was being held tightly in the arms of his Circe at the needle shop and was unable to escape the hungry ogress's charms for the entire five days she spent in Montpellier on her pilgrimage to Rome—and during these five days, they left their bed only for the dining table, and the dining table only for their bed. Of course there was another, much higher pleasure, which I longed for, and whose marvels I continued to hope for in my heart of hearts. But of that, more later.

My purse brimming over, I left the Joyeuse residence, overcome with gratitude for the woman who resided there, and returned at a gallop to my lodgings, with Miroul and Giacomi riding at my sides with swords unsheathed, since Cossolat had advised me not to walk the city's streets at night, fearing that the brigands, thirsty for revenge, would ambush me.

As soon as I was back in my room, there came a knock at my door.

"Ah, Giacomi! Come in!" I smiled. "Did you ask Balsa whether anyone has returned my bonnet?"

"Alas, Monsieur doctor," sighed Giacomi, "no one has come! I'm sorry for you, both for the loss and for the augury."

"Augury, Giacomi?"

"But don't you see?" replied Giacomi, standing at attention before me. "It couldn't be clearer! If your bonnet has disappeared on the day you obtained it, then fate has decreed that you will never exercise your calling!"

"Giacomi!" I replied, very put out. "That's nothing but superstition! Fortune does not provide signs that allow us to foretell the future. I dearly love my new profession and I'll practise it with or without the bonnet! It's not the bonnet that matters, but the head beneath it, and this one I've done my best to fashion so that it can cure—God willing!—man's diseases."

"Monsieur doctor," Giacomi replied without giving me one of his usual Italian bows, which, however low, never communicated baseness but rather high breeding, "whether the augury is good or bad we cannot know! *Che sarà, sarà!** I would be very unhappy to have offended you in any way, especially when I have to take my leave of you."

"Take your leave, Giacomi? To go where?" I gasped.

"In truth, I know not," he replied, his visage radiant as usual, as if the uncertainty of his future were a laughing matter.

"Then why must you leave me?" I said with some heat. "Without you, Giacomi, without your marvellous swordsmanship and your wise counsel in the face of danger, I would certainly have died."

"Without you, Monsieur doctor," answered Giacomi, his black eyes protruding out of his smiling face, "I would be locked in a jail. But…" he continued with an elegant gesture of his long arms, at the end of which he fell silent.

"But, Giacomi?"

"Monsieur doctor, I would not wish you to think that I do not like Miroul, whom I hold, on the contrary, as one of the best fellows in all creation."

---

* "What will be, will be."

"But, Giacomi?"

"But I'm not completely comfortable sharing a bed with a servant. Monsieur doctor, do not, I beg you, think I'm arrogant. In Italy, only gentlemen of good breeding may become masters-at-arms and I'm held by everyone in the town where I was born to be a noble man if not exactly a nobleman."

"Ah, *maestro!*" I replied. "I confess I wasn't exactly sure of your condition, though I've heard tell that master swordsmen from Italy, whether in the king's or the Duc d'Anjou's service, are considered gentlemen at the French court. Here, as you know, a master-at-arms is considered only a soldier, expert in the exercise of his skills, but not necessarily in the knowledge of his art, limited in his understanding, rustic in his manners. I place you, *maestro*, well above the best of them, and if this is so important to you, instead of Miroul, I shall invite you to share my own quarters for lack of separate chambers in which to lodge you."

"Ah, Monsieur doctor!" cried Giacomi. "How grateful I am for your amiable, courteous and infinite beneficence, but again, I beg you not to think that I'm acting out of pride or silly posturing. It's not so much for myself that I want respect, but rather for my sword, which is, for me, at once a rank, an art, a profession and a philosophy." This said, he placed his long, delicate hand nervously on its sheath. "And if you would condescend to one more thing, Monsieur doctor, and, out of your goodness, address me with the polite form *vous* rather than the familiar form *tu*, you would complete my happiness."

"*Maestro!*" I laughed. "If that's all it takes to keep you, I'll call you *vous* from matins to vespers! In my arms, my friend! Give me a hug!" And pulling him towards me, I gave him a hug and kissed both his cheeks, though he had to lean over a bit so I could reach them; but he returned my kisses frankly, then stepped back and patted my shoulders and back with his long hands.

"Monsieur doctor," he said when we'd finished our endearments (which, I noticed, brought tears to his shining, black eyes), "I believe that you are of the religion?"

"I am."

"I am Catholic, myself," he said gravely, though he couldn't, for all that, keep his face from looking happy, "and though I am aware of all the terrible abuses that have corrupted the mother Church, I have to tell you that I have no intention of leaving her, since I feel like the best of bad sons, not very happy in her lap, but less happy outside it."

"That's fine," I smiled, looking him in the eye, "a lukewarm papist and a not very zealous Huguenot: each of us can accommodate the truths of the other."

"Or the errors," added Giacomi, returning my smile. "But, Monsieur doctor, what shall my daily duties be?"

"*Maestro*, you shall teach me the finer points of your art. I do not fence very well, as you've observed."

"Not true! As far as I could tell by the light of the torch, you attacked in the French manner, that is to say, furiously, with ardour and without a moment's hesitation, covering your mistakes by damnable bodily feints and using your whole torso where a turn of the wrist would have sufficed."

"Well, *maestro*," I cried, "you've made me out to be as gross and untutored a swordsman as if I were a cook in a fight with only his spit to defend him! But just wait! I'll be a very serious student!"

"And I, Monsieur doctor, shall be your vassal," returned Giacomi, with one of his deepest and most graceful bows, and added, quoting Dante, in his beautiful and expressive Italian, "*Tu duce, tu signore e tu maestro!*"*

---

* "You will be my leader, my lord and my master."

"*E tu maestro!*" I cried. "But Giacomi, you're using the *tu* form with me!"

"It's the poetic *tu*," he answered, though his contrition seemed a bit feigned, since he was the most self-assured man I'd ever encountered.

"Giacomi," I continued, as though I'd momentarily forgotten myself in the emotion of this exchange, and liking this *maestro* already more than I could say, "I have a younger brother whom I hold very dear and an older brother whom I care little for. Would you consider becoming my older brother, by choice if not by blood?"

At this, Giacomi fell silent and, though he smiled in gratitude, I felt as though he was taken aback by my French impetuousness and I blushed and couldn't speak.

Seeing this, the *maestro*, guessing my confusion, took my two hands in his and said with courteous gravity: "With all my heart, Monsieur doctor, if you really believe I am worthy of such an honour."

Ah, Giacomi! I still feel a rush of emotion as I write these lines, so many years having withered and been blown to the winds since that day. And though I seemed to be fishing impulsively and without due consideration of the consequences of my offer, I now feel, after much reflection, given the mettle you displayed in the first test of our friendship, I was right to bind my soul to yours with grappling hooks of the strongest steel!

My other brother, after his five days spent in that ardent furnace, returned thinner and dreamy, and slept for twenty-four hours straight, after which he abandoned himself to despair for sinning against Our Lord's law, having fornicated outside the sacrament of marriage, at one moment berating himself mercilessly, at the next talking endlessly of his sorceress, with a light in his azure eyes in which we could read the delights that had devoured him so completely without, however, satisfying him. Indeed, for some people the abyss of ardent pleasures has no end and, once plunged therein, they can never climb back out.

"Ah, Monsieur doctor!" Giacomi opined with a sly smile. "When I hear you talk about your brother Samson, it occurs to me that this Norman wench has a lot in common with my wench from Genoa, and of the pair we'd do well to quote the divine Dante, who said of hell: '*Lasciate ogni speranza, voi ch'entrate.*'"*

Meanwhile, after the sanctimonious lady had left for Rome, whinnying after the indulgences that they were selling like a mare after her oats, I recounted to Samson our battle in the rue de la Caussalerie.

"Oh, Pierre!" he moaned in shame. "While you out were risking your life, I was holed up, wallowing in sin. If those rascals had killed you I could never have forgiven myself!"

"But here I am, alive, my brother! And you'll be with me when we go to Barbentane to see my Angelina, accompanied by Miroul and my brother Giacomi."

"Your brother, my brother?" wondered Samson, his azure eyes suddenly clouded, whether in confusion or pain I couldn't tell. He looked at me quizzically for a moment and then came right to the point like an arrow shot from a crossbow, his transparent eyes staring at me with such candid innocence "Do you love him more than me?"

"Of course not, my Samson!" I cried, rising from my stool and embracing him; holding him tight, I said, overflowing with emotion, "Samson, you are the summit and cloudy peak of my fraternal love and no one can ever replace you there!"

He brushed away his tears with the back of his right hand and, not being one of those jealous hearts that never trust anyone, he believed me without hesitation and was immediately and for evermore satisfied.

The next morning I received a letter from Angelina that plunged me into despair. Monsieur de Montcalm, it seemed, had been embroiled

---

* "Abandon all hope, ye who enter here."

for months in a lawsuit concerning a mill he owned in Gonesse, and had now decided that it would be most advantageous for his suit to go to Paris and plead with the judges there.

As he could not bear to be separated from them even for a day, he was taking his wife and daughter with him.

"Oh, Monsieur," wrote Angelina,

what a nasty turn of events. I shall already be arrived in the capital when you receive this and very vexed, I assure you, to be there, as I was looking forward with such joy to seeing you at Barbentane after your *triduanes*! And I haven't any idea how soon we will return to Provence, since this sort of lawsuit can drag on as slowly as a slug on a lettuce leaf and create so much slime you completely lose your way in it! Oh, Monsieur, I'm all the more furious since I've heard Monsieur de Montcalm tell my mother that he intends to marry me off in Paris, and he will be very surprised to discover that, as I love no one, nor anything as much as you, I am firmly and obstinately opposed to such a plan. For I have pledged my love to you till death one day part us—an alternative, may God be my witness, I do not wish for, desiring only the inexpressible happiness of one day being wholly and entirely yours.

Ah, dear reader, has anyone ever received a more innocent, touching and naive letter? And can you imagine the mix of bitterness and joy these adorable lines produced, since Angelina was both so near to my heart and yet so far away, there being no way I could possibly join her in Paris were she to remain there for a long time? How could I get to the capital? With what money? And under what pretext could I possibly persuade my father to allow me to make such a perilous and expensive journey?

Throwing myself on my bed, I kissed this letter as I would have kissed the hand of the woman who'd written it, and bathed it with the tears I simply couldn't hold back. Try as I might, I couldn't stop the sobs that wracked me, so cruel was this wound, and all the more so since it would have only been a week's forced march to reach Barbentane, and I was already imagining how warm and sweet her body would feel in my arms when suddenly she'd been snatched away and sequestered in an inaccessible place on the other side of the kingdom. Now the many months that separated us felt like the ocean that stretches limitless away in front of a shipwrecked man on a raft. What an arid desert my life now seemed! After this reversal, everything seemed vain, dry, rocky, uninteresting, absent of any comfort whatsoever—not even my recent appointment as a venerable doctor of medicine, which now seemed like a hollow victory in the teeth of my suffering.

Oh the folly, the dreams, the fond insatiability of a lover! I held Angelina's letter close to my heart and, but a minute later, wiping away my tears, pulled it from my doublet and wanted more than anything to reread it. What a haven of grace! I reread it more than a hundred times, each time comforted by the sound of her voice (since her letter was as lively and as petulant), and I believed I could see her standing there, looking at me with her infinitely tender doe's eyes. But alas! What a high price I paid for these imaginary pleasures, since the more they made her present to me, the more they rendered her absence acutely painful.

For three days I almost never left my left my room, but lay on my bed suffering a thousand deaths, crying and groaning, descending to the great hall only to eat a few morsels of the stingy repasts at Maître Sanche's table. In the end, Madame de Joyeuse sent her valet to enquire after me and I sent him back with the message that I had taken to my bed and had, for the nonce, to remain there. Would you believe it? This noble lady, as crazy as I was, but for a different reason, had the audacity to come to visit me at nightfall, it's true, and in a rented carriage so that no one would see her coat of arms outside my lodgings, and, in addition, wearing a mask, veil and dress that she thought would look bourgeois (but which, in my view, were hardly that).

She stayed three long hours, locked in my room, consoling me (since I told her all about Angelina) and gradually her comforts slipped, by insensible degrees, onto an emotional slope that gradually brought me to comfort her. Which I did out of gratitude and good breeding, and, yes, because the seclusion of the past three days had done nothing to temper my vigour, a fact I observed with astonishment, having believed myself dead to the world.

In any case, the next morning I felt well enough to begin my fencing lessons with Giacomi, though not for very long this first time, yet long enough for me to realize that I had to unlearn everything I'd learnt with Cabusse, since, without moving his body at all, or even, it seemed his arm, Giacomi managed to keep my point from ever touching him, whereas his, if he'd wanted to, could have opened buttonholes in all my vital parts.

I can still see my Giacomi at this first lesson (Miroul sitting on a stool, not missing a single detail), standing so tall and graceful in his precise and perfect positions, seeming to be a spider in the physical distribution of his body and a bird in his vivacity, his black eyes protruding, on his face an expression of courteous civility, while ceremoniously he parried my awkward thrusts and touched me, but held back just as his blade made the touch.

"Pierre," he said, finally taking two steps back as lightly as if he were dancing, "hold on tight! I'm going to have the honour of disarming you!"

So saying, he lowered his sword in an ample and noble salute. I couldn't believe that I was hearing such quiet assurance, but before

I could react, my right hand was empty, my sword leaping from its grasp and hurtling itself to the other end of the room.

"Ah! My brother!" I cried. "What magic is this?"

"Magic?" cried Giacomi, who seemed insulted by this word. "Say, rather, art! Art and knowledge! A technique honed through study and mastered through unceasing practice!"

The next day I received a letter from my father, which ordered me, since I'd received my promotion to doctor, and Samson had been promoted to master apothecary a year ago already, to say farewell to Montpellier and return to Mespech where, though we were not "prodigal sons", he would kill the fatted calf for us and in honour of Giacomi, who had saved my life, and of Miroul, whom he respected well above his condition.

I gave myself a week to say goodbye to Thomassine, to Cossolat and to Madame de Joyeuse, who wept to break my heart and held me so tight I thought she'd never let go. She made me swear to come back as soon as I could without offending the Brethren, and out of her incredible generosity gave me enough money to allow us to buy new clothes—not just Samson and me, but also Giacomi, whose doublet was on its last stitches, and even Miroul, so that he would be dressed as befitted a servant of my father's barony.

3

A FTER THE EDICT OF SAINT-GERMAIN, a kind of uneasy peace reigned in France between papists and Huguenots, much like those that had preceded it, begrudging and unstable—especially since the offences against our side were so frequent here and there that we hadn't returned to the throne the fortresses that the edict had specifically obliged us to surrender. In any case, I decided that we could risk taking the easy, longer route home through Carcassonne, Toulouse and Montauban rather than ride through the mountains of Cévennes and Auvergne, which would have slowed and fatigued our horses.

It turned out to be the right decision, for we encountered no attacks or ambushes by the highwaymen of this region and had no adventures save for the non-warlike kind that one comes across in the inns along the way, where the chambermaids are required to see to the needs of their male clientele. But I did not abuse this privilege as the Baron de Caudebec was wont to do, remaining in each hostel only the time required to rest our horses. During each stay, Samson reasserted his inflexible virtue in Dame Gertrude de Luc's absence, of course, but had no influence over mine, as you would guess, nor over Miroul's or my brother Giacomi's, decked out as he was in a scarlet velveteen doublet that I'd had sewn for him by Martinez, my tailor, before our departure.

With the money Madame de Joyeuse had given me, I bought him a beautiful stallion (necessarily taller than our mares, since, given Giacomi's height, his feet would have been dragging along the ground if he'd had to ride Accla). And thus ensconced in his saddle on this warhorse, being our senior by five or six years and a good head taller than any of the three of us, he looked like nothing so much as Mentor, keeping watch over Telemachus.

When, after three weeks on the road, we arrived in Sarlat without any delay or misfortune of any kind, and believing we'd already reached our haven—Mespech being no more than five leagues hence—I asked the innkeeper of the Three Sheep to furnish us with a room where, divesting ourselves of our cuirasses and helmets, we donned our doublets so as to appear in all our finery when we greeted the Brethren and all our people in Mespech. This was pure vanity and Giacomi said as much—advising us not to disarm before we were safely within our walls.

But I refused to heed his warning, thinking there was little risk, since I knew the road between Sarlat and Mespech so well I could have told you who tilled this field or that, or owned such and such a farm or hut.

I decided we should take the les Beunes road, which would be the least tiring for our weary mounts, though not the safest for us since it followed the river through a narrow dale, which was flanked on both sides by high slopes too steep for a horse to climb. Giacomi, immediately unhappy with the lay of the land, pointed out that we were entering a funnel trap that offered no escape other than by retracing our steps if we were attacked by a large group, and that put us in danger of being fired on from behind. We followed his advice, and stopped to load our pistols and unsheathe our swords, which we dangled from straps from our wrists—a thoroughly unnecessary precaution in my view, especially since we were but five or six stones' throws from our mill at les Beunes, whose roof I could make out in the distance through the foliage.

However, when we passed the turn-off for Taniès, we saw four horsemen there, mute and immobile, but who spurred on their steeds as soon as we'd passed, and came trotting along behind us.

"Ah," I said, "I don't like this a bit!" remembering a similar situation we'd encountered in the battle in the Corbières. "Let's take pistols in hand and ask these rascals what they're up to."

"My brother," cautioned Giacomi, "listen to me! Let's take but one pistol in hand and hide the other between saddle and leg. The best tactic is to conceal from your adversary the weapon you intend to use as a last resort."

At my command, we turned our horses abruptly and confronted our adversaries face to face, pulling up short a dozen paces from them. Of course, they pulled up short, surprised at the sight of our pistols and caught off-guard, the hunters suddenly become the hunted; so there we were, facing each other with no idea what to do next.

The problem was that, though we were armed with pistols, we were not holding them at the ready, and though they looked like ruffians, they didn't seem to be highwaymen and were wearing a sort of livery, as if belonging to some gentleman's household.

"Who do you work for?" I shouted with as mean an expression as I could muster.

To this they made no reply, but looked at each other with the greatest discomfort. This forced me to repeat my question, but this time I drew my pistol and levelled it at the fellow opposite me, who looked like a Gypsy, with a lean and muscular body, lively, liquid eyes and his face dripping sweat as soon as he saw my weapon pointed at his heart.

"Monsieur, we are Baron de Fontenac's men."

"So! And do you know who I am?"

To which the Gypsy answered, after some hesitation and as if he were confused as to how to answer, that I was unknown to him.

"My brother," whispered Giacomi, "the man is lying."

"So I believe," I replied softly. "Shall we shoot them?"

"No," Giacomi counselled, "they're not armed. 'Twould be murder."

"Let's shoot them anyway!" said Miroul. "That'd make four fewer troublemakers for us to deal with."

"Oh, no! No, no!" Samson exclaimed, staring at us in all his azure innocence. "Are they not Christians, same as us?"

"I know the measure of these Christians!" snarled Miroul, whose whole family had had their throats cut by such ruffians as these.

"My good fellows," I called, "what were you doing on the Taniès path?"

"We were just returning from the village," said the Gypsy leader. And certain it was that he was lying again.

"So then why were you galloping up behind us?"

"Just wanted to pass you by."

And right away, my finger started itching most urgently to dispatch this fellow without any more ado, but I remembered that Fontenac controlled the judges in Sarlat (so completely that Bouillac's testimony about the raid on our les Beunes mill had gone unheeded) and I didn't want to give our scourge of a neighbour the excuse to drag the Baron de Siorac before the Présidial for the murder of his men, and so resolved to solve this situation peacefully.

"Well then, we'll let you pass us unharmed," I announced, "and may the God who judges us decided whether I've done the right thing."

"We thank you and thank God, Monsieur," answered the Gypsy, who opened his mouth wide to take in a lungful of air in evident relief. "I will find a way to pay you back should the occasion arise."

We pulled our horses aside on the edge of the path and they rode by, very relieved to be alive, and their backs, I'll wager, tingling with the fear of our bullets until they'd passed the bend in the road.

"My brother," Giacomi now asked, "where is Mespech?"

"Just beyond that bend, you take a path to the left, cross a little bridge over the les Beunes river leading to our mill, and from there another path leads to the chateau."

"Is there no other way to get directly to the mill?"

"I'm afraid not. The fields you see off to our left are too swampy to negotiate."

"Well then," said Giacomi, "instead of flying like starlings into the nets they've set for us, I think it'd be wiser to return to Sarlat."

I thought about this for a minute. "I don't agree. Our horses are exhausted. The Gypsies would surely catch up to us and then we'd be forced to fight far from Mespech without any hope of the help they'd surely be able to provide. What do you think, Samson?"

"But who says these good people want to attack us?" he asked, his blue eyes opened wide in innocence.

"Ah, Samson!" I said, smiling to mask the pain I felt at this impasse. "You really don't live in this world! You read too much of the Gospels and not enough of Machiavelli!"

"Too much of the Gospels? That's no way to talk!"

But before I could answer, Miroul said, "Monsieur, may I tell you what I think?"

"Speak, Miroul."

"Well then, *primo*, as you said at your *triduanes*, let's fire a shot into the air to alert Coulondre Iron-arm at the mill so he can send Jacotte through the underground passage to Mespech. *Secundo*, let's send one among us, and I volunteer to do it, to the bend in the road to reconnoitre."

"Miroul! You speak with a golden tongue! Only I'm going to flip your suggestion on end and put the *secundo* first. Go, Miroul, and see if you can see how many they are and what arms these good people are carrying."

And so Miroul, carefully hiding his pistol in his boot, dismounted in the blink of an eye, and throwing Giacomi his packhorse's lead, and to me his gelding's reins, he headed off, light as a feather, his feet barely touching the ground, to where the road turned, and there, instead of poking his head out by degrees to see what lay ahead, I saw him scale a steep rock that stood at the bend in the road, reach the top and creep along its crest so as to survey the length of the road ahead.

"What enviable agility!" remarked Giacomi in such quiet and serene tones that I couldn't help but admire his coolness in the heat of our present predicament. "With your permission, my brother," he added, "I'd like to instruct Miroul in my art. Although he is not of sufficient birth to warrant it, he has earned this consideration."

"I think so, too. And don't you think it's a pity that this honest fellow, as frank as an unbitten écu, valiant, loyal, possessed of good and unfettered intelligence and great dexterity and skill, cannot aspire to a state higher than valet simply because he happened to be born of lowly parents in a farmhouse?"

"He could advance to a higher position if he joined the Church, since he can read and write—or better yet seek his fortune through arms. But in either case he'd have to leave you and he'd never do that. He nurtures too great a love of you for that."

"And how could I bear it if he left me?" I replied with great feeling. "He's very dear to me, as well, valet though he may be."

However, while I was saying this, affecting a tranquil tone with Giacomi, despite the anxiety of the moment, which had, so to speak, sunk to some subterranean level in me, it didn't escape me that I had put my own convenience ahead of Miroul's advancement. This thought made me angry with myself, and as he was just then returning, I said to him, "You took a long time. What were you doing up that rock?"

"Monsieur," said Miroul (his brown eye growing sad while his blue eye remained cold as a sign that he was very hurt at my reproaches),

"I wanted to get high enough above them to see whether they had pistols stuck in their saddlebags, which, I must say, looked quite empty of any firearms. On the other hand, at the tail of this little band of no more than seven men, I saw two riderless horses, which may well mean that there are two rascals waiting to ambush us from atop the bluff at Taniès and pick us off like pigeons."

"I thank you, Miroul," I said, thoroughly ashamed at my impatience. "I couldn't have done so well. Did you see the traitor Fontenac?"

"Indeed I did!" he replied. "Wearing a crimson doublet and cap, and sitting very straight atop a proud white horse that's trying to make us believe that the soul of his master is of the same colour."

And although I didn't find this joke much to my liking, I laughed out loud at it to soothe the wounded feelings I'd inflicted on my gentle valet.

"Miroul," I said, "tie the packhorse to the bough of yonder fig tree that's growing out between the rocks of the bluff here, remount your horse and fire a shot into the air, as you suggested, and then reload."

While Miroul did as I ordered, Giacomi took his cape from his shoulders, and, having placed one of his pistols underneath his thigh, threw the cape over his knees.

"Samson," I cautioned, "don't be so dreamy and thoughtful. I know you're valiant—be quick and decisive. And remember to fire right away if fire you must. This Fontenac is the scourge of Mespech, as we've told you a hundred times."

"I'll remember," said Samson.

I then quietly recited the Our Father and the three others joined in, and having made the sign of the cross on my forehead, my lips and my heart, I exclaimed with happy confidence, as my father would have done had he been there, "Comrades, the day is ours! Let's go!"

We put spurs to horses, but gently, and set off with our swords dangling by their ties from our wrists, and with pistols in hand, our horses moving at a walk, their ears pricked; and as for us, our eyes were peeled, darting this way and that, and our hearts were pounding in our chests as you can well imagine, underneath our feigned calm. God knows how long it took to round the bend past Miroul's rock, and much longer it seemed to us. But suddenly, there we were and surprised to behold our enemies, even though we knew they'd be there. There weren't seven of them as Miroul had reported, but eight, and the eighth, leading the two riderless horses, was the priest of Marcuays, whom the farmers in the region called "Pincers", because of his debauchery, as I've recounted elsewhere.

"Hey, Monsieur priest," I cried, "what are you doing here?"

But he was unable to answer since our horses all began whinnying like crazy, probably because our mares smelt an uncut stallion in the opposite camp. The horses of our enemies also began a wild chorus in response, as well as a sudden chaos of croups, hooves and chests that we had to control and calm before human words could be heard. I said "words" and not "reason" since it's my belief that man is a less intelligent animal than his mount and a thousand times more cruel.

All this time, unable to hear a word in this din, we all looked each other over, and, for my part, with great curiosity, for though this Fontenac was the sworn enemy of my family (as his father was before him) I'd never laid eyes on him before, since the baron had never actively participated in any of the ambushes he'd set for us except the present one, which considerably surprised me and aroused my curiosity. And although he was the most egregious brigand in all of creation, I couldn't keep from admiring him as he sat stiff and upright on his white horse trying to control it. Physically he was handsome enough, a large and strong gentleman, tending towards corpulent, I judged. He had a haughty face, with curly hair and beard and intense eyes. However, his face betrayed, when he turned his head, too much of a resemblance to a bird of prey, with a nose shaped like a vulture's beak. Fontenac's clothing corresponded exactly with his aspect: he was superbly dressed in a crimson doublet with matching shoes and red satin slashes.

In the saddle next to his, on a heavy stallion, sat a large, broad-shouldered fellow, chest thrown out, short of leg and with so vile and bloodthirsty a visage that it made his master look positively virtuous by comparison. I recognized him (having caught sight of him in Sarlat, though he showed himself infrequently there, being in such bad odour) as being Fontenac's major-domo (and possibly the baron's bastard brother), but, unlike Samson, unrecognized as such, and he called himself the Sieur de Malvézie, though there was no land of this name in the Sarlat region. He was a man reputed for his dastardly deeds, and for having put his paws on all the shittiest enterprises that the baron, who had planned them, wouldn't have touched with the pinky of his gloved hand. For this baron was a two-faced devil, a zealous papist, assiduous in his attendance at Mass, ingratiating himself with the bishop, and well regarded by this prelate, since he did not skimp in his calculated largesse to the diocese.

When the horses had quieted down, Fontenac, who, for his part, had not failed to study me from head to toe, said gravely but not aggressively, "Monsieur, what are you doing here with pistols drawn and swords unsheathed on a road that belongs to my domain?"

I took a moment to answer him, surprised at the impudence of this brigand in claiming that the les Beunes road belonged to him. "My brother," whispered Giacomi, "this mountain of a man wants to provoke you into a duel and his priest is there as a witness. Be very measured in your answers."

"Monsieur," I replied, bowing, "I hadn't heard that this road belonged to you."

"Ah, but it does," Fontenac asserted without batting an eye, "by virtue of an ancient right that I am intending to advance."

"Monsieur," I said with all the calm I could muster, "such a claim would require the assent of the seneschal of Sarlat, which could not be given without a decision of the Présidial. In the meantime, and until you have such authority, do me the favour of letting me pass to return to my home."

"Monsieur," said Fontenac, "I cannot accede to a request that is made by an armed man."

"Monsieur," I countered, "we only bared our swords because four of your men chased us down from behind. But as soon as we knew they were your servants, we let them pass."

"But didn't resheathe your swords," snarled Fontenac, "and here you are addressing me with pistol in hand. This is an offence!"

To which, after a kick from Giacomi, I answered, "If there is an offence, Monsieur, I will end it. Monsieur the priest of Marcuays will bear witness to my goodwill in voluntarily disarming and in offering you our excuses."

This said, and immediately imitated by Samson, Giacomi and Miroul, I returned my pistol to its holster, happy to feel the other one still hidden under my left thigh.

At this, the Sieur de Malvézie, his ugly mug reddening with spite and his eyes flashing with violent hatred, cried with a thunderous voice, "Why bother with this silly chatter, let's be done with this rascal!"

Giacomi gave me another kick, so I forced myself to maintain a calm demeanour and pretended not to have heard Malvézie's insult so as not to have to answer it.

"Calm down, there, Malvézie!" cried Fontenac.

"Monsieur, now that I have put my arms aside, I make the same request as before: let us pass."

"I'll think about it," said Fontenac.

And during his silence, which was no doubt a way to figure out how to renew the provocation, I took a sideways glance at Giacomi, who was searching out of the corner of his eye the bushes on the hillside of Taniès to see if he could see the barrel of an arquebus. "Ah!" I thought. "Now I understand: a bullet for Samson, a sword thrust for me, and the two younger sons of the Baron de Mespech will be dead on the same day. What a glorious day for you, Fontenac! And who will ever know what really happened on this road since there's only one witness, the feckless priest of Marcuays?"

"Monsieur," Fontenac finally replied, "did you hear Malvézie's suggestion?"

"No, Monsieur, I heard nothing."

"Should I repeat it?"

"'Tis of no use. I wouldn't hear it any more clearly the second time."

Fontenac smiled and said with the most offensive sarcasm: "A coward who would protect his honour had better turn a deaf ear."

Again, Giacomi kicked my boot, so I replied, "Monsieur, let the Siorac family worry about their own honour."

"What, Monsieur!" teased the baron with feigned surprise. "You're a Siorac! Well then, you should know that I despise that family. They have done nothing but heap offences and iniquities on me and on my father before me."

"Well, then, you should challenge the Baron de Siorac to a duel, not his younger son."

"His younger son!" cried Fontenac with disdain. "Are you the same Pierre de Siorac who befouled his family name by going to study medicine in Montpellier?"

"Perhaps you will recall, Monsieur, that, six years ago, my father befouled *his* family name by curing your daughter of the plague."

This could not fail to bring the baron up short, and he glowered at me but said nothing. But I, rushing to take advantage of his lack of composure, said in an icy but polite voice: "Monsieur, I request in all civility and courtesy that you let us pass immediately on our way."

"Well Monsieur, you play with words well enough, but can your swordplay match your words?"

"What! You're challenging me to a duel? Ah, Monsieur, you're aiming way too low. I'm but small game for you! You should challenge someone equal to your own prowess, such as the hero of Ceresole and Calais!"

"This false hero," snapped Fontenac, grinding his teeth, "is but a knave. His father was a lackey."

Here, Giacomi gave me an extra hard kick, but this time I ignored his mutely urgent advice, and replied in a cutting voice, articulating clearly each of my words: "My grandfather was no lackey. He was an apothecary in Rouen. My father was a member of the legion in Normandy and was promoted to captain and then *écuyer*. He was awarded the title of chevalier for his valour on the field of battle at Ceresole by the Duc d'Enghien. King Henri II made him a baron after the siege of Calais. Monsieur de Fontenac, if you repeat the words you just spoke, this time I shall hear them."

"I repeat them," said Fontenac, with eyes aflame and crest at high mast.

"Monsieur, I call you to account. Name the place and time."

"Here and now!" cried Fontenac triumphantly. "Will this little clearing just down the hill do?"

I knew this field well for having belonged to a labourer named Faujanet, a cousin of our Faujanet, but who'd refused to sell his land to the Brethren and held out alone in this little enclave of well-watered, good farmland.

"Yes! It will do fine!"

"My brother," whispered Giacomi, "be careful not to drop the pistol you're hiding under your right thigh." I agreed with a nod and, unhooking my cape, I did as he suggested and secretly slipped the pistol into a saddlebag.

"My brother," said Giacomi quietly, "remove your doublet and ask the baron to do the same." Which I did, but the baron, shaking his head, refused without saying a word.

"Aha!" cautioned Giacomi. "I thought when I saw how straight he was sitting on his horse that he must be wearing chain mail under his doublet! Pierre, you'll have to strike him in the face or neck."

"My brother," said Samson looking ashen, eyes shining and teeth so clenched that he wasn't lisping, "should I shoot this felon right now, who dares against all the rules of honour to cover himself with mail while fighting a duel with an adversary in a shirt?"

"Don't you dare, Samson! The papists would cry murder!"

This said, I dismounted and, throwing the reins of my Accla to Samson (so that, with reins in both hands, he wouldn't be able to shoot anyone), I stood, head bowed, both hands on my saddle blanket.

"What are you doing?" cried the baron. "What's all the delay? Are you such a coward—"

"I'm praying to the Lord, Monsieur," I interrupted, "before joining battle with you."

But in truth, may God forgive me, I was not praying at this moment, but wanted to hear Giacomi's instructions. He understood and joined his hands next to mine on Accla's saddle and said very quietly: "My brother, this villain is more than forty years old. He's strong, but quite heavy and weighed down by his nasty armour. Run him out of breath! Keep breaking away and moving in circles around him like a fly on a lion! Harass him, then duck away! And be careful of his nasty tricks, like throwing his cape in your face to blind you. Keep ducking away, for the love of God! Don't grab him—he'd crush you! And again, keep breaking away! With all his pursuit of you, his legs will tire, his attacks slow down and his brain become confused. Moreover, by constant delay, you'll give the people at Mespech time to get here. As for you, *take no chances*—don't try any risky tricks. Attack only when it's a sure thing and aim at his face."

"Giacomi," I said, "now let me give you some advice. Don't get too caught up in watching the duel. Keep an eye on bushes on the Taniès hillside where you think these snipers may be hiding. I put Samson's life in your care. And Miroul's as well."

"Monsieur," shouted Fontenac, "this prayer is taking for ever! Is your soul so black that you need so much time to recommend it to God?"

"Monsieur," I replied in a strong voice, my eyes flashing, "it's not for my soul I'm praying, but for yours!"

I must say I was happy with this retort, and, wrapping my left forearm in my cape, I held my dagger in that hand and, with my sword in my right, I headed towards the field, wanting to remain several steps ahead of Fontenac so he couldn't strike me from behind before we got there. I bounded onto the field and turned to meet him, my blades at the ready. Fontenac was surprised by my vivacity, for I was already in position while he laboured to descend from the road to the pasture, taking small steps and being careful not to jump as I had. His laboured approach augured well for our duel, I thought.

I threw a quick look at our les Beunes mill, whence any help might come, but nary a soul or noise could be seen or heard there other that the barking of the dogs. And so I turned to meet my assailant, convinced I'd have to save myself or perish here.

Once on the field, the baron rushed at me, sword held high, with a speed that surprised me and gave me pause, for I wouldn't have expected it from the way he climbed down the hill. And when I saw this mountain of a man charging at me with a face that had lost any semblance of civility, shouting and grimacing like a demon, hurling foul and horrid insults at me with an ear-splitting fury, and slashing at me with such violence he would have severed a stone wall, my heart fell into my entrails—especially since, at the first clash of swords, he very nearly knocked my sword from my hands. And so I broke away, almost fled from him, while up on the road his henchmen, believing me already overwhelmed and killed, screamed their hatred and venom at the top of their lungs.

"Hey, you coward!" shouted the baron. "You're running away! Stand your ground, you chicken-hearted sissy! I'm going to make lace of your guts!"

And striking my sword, he hit it with such force that, again, he would have knocked it from my hands had the wrist strap not held. I broke away again, but this time to the side, and like a bull he charged straight ahead and I was able to land a point in his leg as I fell to the ground. Then, forgetting Giacomi's advice, I took a huge chance. As he rushed at me roaring like the seventy devils of hell, Fontenac would have pinned me to the ground, had I not rolled over several times on the grass and then leapt to my feet as nimbly as a cat. Again the baron charged, his ugly maw opening wide with the fury of the imprecations he was shrieking, but I noticed that he was dragging his left foot where my sword had left its mark. Again I jumped to the side, but instead of somersaulting away as I had so madly done before, I began circling around him, my sword point flying like a wasp around his head, but not yet hitting him. By now my initial terror was gone and my confidence growing and I remembered Giacomi's advice and engaged my sword with his, but so closely that he couldn't use his strength to slash at it as he'd done twice before. Of course, he made one more attempt at this, but missed, and so we stood engaging point to point, but I was able to parry all of his blows because his fury had robbed him of any accuracy.

I also remembered to pay close attention to his every move, fearing lest he try some felonious trick. And when I saw him grab his cape with the hand that held his dagger, I broke several steps away, expecting him to try to toss it in my face to blind me. But instead, having waved it high several times, he dropped it on the grass beside him, and it must have been some sort of signal, for immediately three or four pistol shots rang out which nearly cost me my life—as the baron must have planned—for, taking my eyes off him for but a second to look at my friends up on the road, he would certainly have run me through had Providence or instinct not inspired me to take a quick step to the right, so that his blade slipped between my left side and my arm, ripping my shirt, but missing its mark.

I broke away again and began spinning around the baron, attacking and retreating at will, and much reassured by what my quick glance at my brothers told me: that they were still up there on the road, mounted on their horses. And seeing that they were safe filled me with renewed joy, vigour and confidence and I went back on the attack. But, if it please you reader to abandon me for a moment, sword and dagger in my hands, facing this monstrous baron, as if immobilized in a painting, and return to the group on the road to see—as I only learnt later—what happened when the baron gave the signal to his snipers.

As I had expected, Samson was having a tough time holding both Accla's reins and those of his own horse, especially since his eyes were glued on the combat down the hill. My mare, sensing that he wasn't paying full attention to her and excited by the presence of an uncut stallion in the enemy's cavalcade, *and* being no doubt in heat, began moving back and forth, turning her rump this way and that and tossing her head, breathing fire and giving surreptitious kicks at Samson's gelding as if to reproach him for being cut.

And though the gelding was not fighting back, habituated as he was to living in fear of Accla, he didn't fail, having been kicked, to begin bucking, making it even harder for Samson to manage the two of them. And so Accla, feeling no longer properly held by Samson, and governed by my own presence, began bucking and pulling savagely on her reins as if to escape, standing up on her hind legs and pawing the air. It was at this moment that the baron gave his signal to the snipers in the bushes, just as Giacomi had guessed he would, and they both aimed and fired at Samson. But my poor Accla, at that very moment rearing even higher than before, was hit in the neck and the head by their bullets and immediately fell to the ground. Meanwhile, the smoke from the assassins' arquebuses had revealed their hiding place, and Giacomi immediately seized the pistol he'd hidden and shot one of them, and Miroul the other, and the two snipers rolled down the hill and ended up at the feet of the enemy's horses, and so they too started bucking in panic.

As for Samson, always a bit slow to grasp what was going on around him, he saw none of this, having eyes only for poor Accla and thinking only of my despair at losing her. But suddenly pricked with anger at this heinous act, he grabbed his own pistol and, pointing it at the Sieur de Malvézie, he cried with his delicious lisp: "Whath thith, Monthieur? You've killed our Accla!"

To which Malvézie, raising his two empty hands—on which the blood of his many victims had, alas, left no trace—and cried in the most piteous and hypocritical tones, so out of keeping with his ugly butcher of a face:

"Nay, Monsieur, I am unarmed, as you see!"

So Samson, having failed to see the ambush from which Accla had saved him, and always ready to believe others, no matter how vile their actions or intent, resolved not to open fire on this scoundrel—which was a most unfortunate decision, as we shall see. But he did continue to hold Malvézie in his sights, which gave Giacomi time to seize his other pistol from his saddlebag and to yell to Malvézie, "Monsieur, if one of your men moves even so much as his little pinky, you're dead."

But in truth none of our adversaries gave any thought to fighting since their two dead companions were lying at the feet of their horses and they could see that my duel with their master was not turning to his advantage.

For the baron was bleeding profusely now from the wound in his calf, breathing loudly, and seemed out of breath from all the effort he'd made to catch up with me, so that now, trying to catch his breath instead of wasting more of it, he'd stopped shouting insults and was quietly and angrily trying to figure out some new malfeasance he could practise on me to trip me up.

I could so clearly feel all this sly calculation going on in his pineal gland (which is supposed to be the seat of thought) that I watched him like a cat ready to pounce, tensing my muscles, all my nerves at the ready and taking no chances, my blade never losing contact with his for a second, and my eyes careful to keep track of what he was doing with his left hand—which was lucky. For suddenly drawing this hand behind him, he was going to throw his dagger at my face, I realized, and so I suddenly dropped to my knees, so that his weapon whistled over my head. Fontenac was so confused by my vivacity and so angry to have so futilely lost his dagger, with which he'd been parrying some of my blows, that he seemed to lose heart to the point of retreating several steps, lowering his sword and telling me in the most civil tone: "Monsieur, we're never going to resolve this combat, let's end it, I beg you."

"Monsieur," I replied, lowering my sword, "you've called my father a knave, my grandfather a lackey and me a coward. Do you withdraw all of these insults?"

"I withdraw them," conceded Fontenac in the most hypocritically noble tone. "I owe it to your bravery and to my mercy. And as for your right of passage on my road, I will be generous enough to concede you this as well. Put up your sword, I beg you."

I found myself confounded by such base impudence and all the more so as I could see perfectly well that this evasion was nothing but an ugly preface to the baron's next low blow, and found it so distasteful that I felt literally nauseated by it. I therefore stood my ground, picked up my sword and, deciding to push this villain's revolting comedy to a bloody conclusion, declared, "Monsieur, I thank you a thousand times for your generous offers, but I have decided not to accept them. I shall pass, instead, over your body."

Hearing this, without a word of response, and without giving me time to put myself on guard, he rushed at me like a madman, letting loose a terrible yell, sword extended. But I had anticipated this reaction, stood my ground and raised my point to the level of his face. He continued his mad assault and literally spitted himself on my sword point which penetrated two inches into his left eye and made such havoc in his brain that he collapsed all at once in a heap like a bull in a butchery under the expert knife thrust of the butcher.

I stood amazed at this thrust, which I hadn't planned, hesitant to take credit for it, unable even to believe that this man lying at my feet, sealed in his eternal death, this perennial enemy of my family, had died at my hand. I could hardly believe my eyes since, lying there, he seemed even taller than when standing, his face even more vile and wicked than at any time in our dispute, even when he was hurling his vicious insults at me.

And yet, when I saw he wasn't moving, I ran towards the road, where I was afraid the battle was raging between his henchmen and my brothers.

I have to give credit where credit is due: the Sieur de Malvézie, of all of Fontenac's rascals, was the first to take to his heels when he saw the baron fall, and disappeared without checking to see whether he was dead or not. He was off in a burst of speed, grabbing the priest's bridle and leading Pincers away with him while the others were drawing their swords and attempting to block our way and give no ground. Evidently they thought they were stronger, being five to our three, having forgotten that we had pistols. But, strangely, our side had also forgotten their firearms, and, unsheathing their swords in response, Giacomi, Miroul and Samson crossed steel with these villains.

Scarcely had I reached the road before I saw my poor Accla lying dead, and was so transfixed with grief that I was frozen to the spot—and would have been run through by one of Fontenac's men had not Giacomi deflected his sword at the last second with the pistol he was holding in his left hand but hadn't thought to fire.

"'Sblood!" I screamed, suddenly drunk with anger. "Shoot them!"

"What?" gasped Giacomi. "Fire on men who have only steel to oppose us!"

"Fire, Giacomi!" I cried. "Do we have to risk another life besides Accla's?"

And since neither Giacomi, nor my younger brother, nor Miroul, to my unbounded rage, would do what I told them, I seized a pistol from Samson's saddlebag and immediately dropped one of their men in his tracks. This was too much for the rest of them. Wheeling their horses away, they fled from us at a gallop.

"And Malvézie?" I cried. "What's happened to that scoundrel?"

"He fled," said Samson, turning his innocent face towards me all shining with happiness to see me safe at last.

But I couldn't bear the news of Malvézie. "How on earth could you let him escape?" I shouted. "Miroul, your horse!" And throwing myself in the saddle, I cried, "Friends, let's after him! We have to destroy this nest of hornets while we can if we ever want peace!"

I didn't wait for them, but put spur to horse and was off. But Miroul's gelding had lost a shoe and was galloping very gingerly on one leg, limping painfully over the rocky road, and so I was myself pained to see Samson pass me, then Giacomi, and even Miroul on the baggage horse he'd quickly unloaded. As I followed lamely behind, almost in tears of rage to see myself so relegated to the rearguard of my little army, I spied in the distance one of Fontenac's henchmen, who, separating himself from the others, had struck out across a large field near the les Beunes river, and so I urged my mount after him, thinking that she'd gallop more easily on the grass. And I was right. She regained her heart with every step and so I managed to catch up with the fellow before he reached the edge of the woods that bordered these fields.

"Ah, Monsieur!" he pleaded, seeing me swooping down on him. "Mercy! Don't kill me! I'm not one of the baron's soldiers, just his basket-maker."

"You would have killed me, however, basket-maker or not!"

"I was forced into it, Monsieur! The baron's orders! But I bear you no grudge, Monsieur, neither you nor your family, since I'm Little Sissy's father."

"What!" I cried, open-mouthed in surprise, and lowering my sword. "You were the captain of the Gypsies…"

"Well, Monsieur, not really the captain. I just pretended to be when I was with the sweetling and the sweetling was so credulous…"

That he should use the word sweetling to describe la Maligou, who was now so large of paunch, pendulous of breast and wide of posterior, struck me as so ludicrous that I burst out laughing so hard I nearly fell from my horse. The Gypsy derived great relief from seeing me laugh and laughed with me, realizing that I wasn't going to kill him. "But you know," I said through tears of laughter, "the sweetling you've described claims that you took her by force fifteen times that night in the barn!"

"Fifteen times!" gasped the Gypsy. "That's twelve too many! And of force there was but very little."

I broke out laughing again, and may the delicate ladies who are reading this please remember that the animal spirits in me that had been so constrained and repressed by the anxieties of battle needed just such a joyful occasion to let themselves go.

"Well, my Gypsy friend," I said finally, "you've entertained me too well! I'm going to pardon you."

"Can I run away?" asked the Gypsy.

"I'm afraid not. You're my prisoner. Rules of war. Throw down your sword and dagger. I'll have someone fetch them. Walk ahead of me to the road."

We reached the road just as Samson, Giacomi and Miroul were returning, somewhat abashed, I thought, to have been unable to catch up with Fontenac's henchmen before they barricaded themselves in his chateau, so that the upshot was that I, who was in the rear-guard, was the only one to bring home a captive—whose testimony, as you may imagine, was to be of great help and consequence in the future.

Since Miroul needed to fetch his baggage horse, we had to return to the field where we'd had our first confrontation with the baron, and once there, seeing my Accla lying dead on the road, I was seized with enormous regret that I'd laughed at the Gypsy's stories when I should have been weeping over the death of my poor mare.

Upon reflection, I ordered Miroul to leave the baggage horse there, and the captive with it, and to gallop to Mespech to notify the Brethren, who, with all of our household, must be out haying in one of the fields around Marcuays, since our mill was quite deserted—so that our pistol shots wouldn't have been heard by anyone, except by some of the labourers and inhabitants of Taniès, whose frightened faces we could see peering over the walls of the town, but who didn't dare come out into the road to find out what had happened, knowing that no good will come from a labourer who sticks his nose into barons' quarrels.

I also told Miroul to bring back a wagon to carry the bodies of the baron and his men since it wasn't right to leave them exposed at night to be pillaged by men and devoured by wild animals.

After Miroul galloped off, I sent Giacomi and Samson down to the field to ascertain whether Fontenac was indeed dead as I believed, and I remained alone with my Accla, sitting on the embankment above her body and drifting into a reverie, thinking about all the adventures we'd had together—ever since the day when Fontenac had given her to my father to thank him for having cured his daughter of the plague, and my father had given her to me and I'd become her master. But could I really say I was her master, since we were in some ways one body together and I only commanded her by obeying her innate horse's inclinations?

Accla had shared every one of the incredible perils that I'd known for these past seven years: in the battle of la Lendrevie after the plague in Sarlat, in the Corbières hills when we fought the highwaymen, in Nîmes on the terrible night of the "Michelade", and in the woods of Barbentane when we saved the Montcalms and Angelina from those bloodthirsty bandits. 'Tis true that she wasn't without her little mare's caprices, and was at times so stubborn and uncooperative it drove me crazy, biting and kicking other horses unbelievably hard and never allowing herself to be passed on the road, always needing to be first in everything: on a gallop, with her oat bag, at the water trough and at the smithy for shoeing. But she was as tender as a lover with her master and never felt my approach without a soft "pfft" from her nostrils, placing her long fine head on my shoulder, pushing me in the back with her muzzle to ask for treats which she never got enough of; so gracious and light-footed in her paces that it was a delight to see her trotting in the pasture, her mane waving in the wind like a girl's head of hair, touching the ground so lightly that you'd have thought she merely caressed it. She never failed me, no matter how perilous things got, as if she had an instinct for battle, responsive to every touch of the boot, so valiant that it left me breathless, fearing neither war cries nor the clashing of swords, nor even the explosions of the firearms, her ears seemingly attentive only to the sound of my voice, trusting me as if I were her God. Alas, my poor beauty, Accla, I'll never see your magnificent black eyes again, so bright yet so soft. If only I could have saved Samson without your having to suffer this terrible death from the bullets that were intended for him.

I was plunged in this melancholy when, hearing the sound of hoof beats and the sound of wagon wheels, I saw my father and a dozen of our people burst onto the road from the direction of the mill, cross the little bridge and head towards me at a gallop. I jumped to my feet as my father dismounted, and what a homecoming embrace we gave each other!

"Thank the Lord," he said in a voice choked with emotion, holding my head tight against his to hide his tears, "you're safe! And my Samson as well! And Miroul! And Giacomi! The traitor must have got wind of your arrival and posted a watchman in Sarlat to signal your arrival and prepare this nasty ambush. My two younger sons! What a devilish business! What a blow it would have been if he had succeeded!"

Samson arrived at this moment and we were both warmly welcomed by all the Mespech community, all of our servants wishing to hug and embrace us, overcome as they were with joy at seeing us safe and sound after the terrible fear they'd had at the thought of losing us while they were out haying. And that was only the men of our household. You can imagine what it was like when we reached the chateau and the wenches got involved! There were tears, cries, caresses, jokes and questions to last a lifetime! And after these expressions of love and welcome from all of them, my father pulled us away and led us to the library, where Sauveterre was ensconced, laid up for the past two days with terrible pain in his bad leg—and in a very bad mood, it appeared.

However, his severe black eyes (whose sudden wrath I so feared when I was younger) softened when he saw us, and he embraced us, albeit with dry eyes (though I thought I detected some trembling in his lower lip despite his implacable Huguenot austerity). He had to hear the whole story, which I recounted as clearly as I could and which he listened to very diligently. After this, he sighed deeply and said, "When you cut down a fig tree, you have to destroy its roots. Otherwise it will grow back again and leave a new tree in its place. You were well advised to kill Fontenac in a loyal duel, but, duel or no duel, you should have dispatched that dog Malvézie. My nephew, you fought well, but didn't kill anything. Our troubles are not over, quite the contrary."

On Sauveterre's advice, and so that no one could claim that his testimony had been extorted by torture, we did not keep the Gypsy at Mespech, but sent him off under careful escort to Monsieur de Puymartin, who was a papist but one of our good friends who had fought alongside my father against the rascals at la Lendrevie after the plague in Sarlat.

Puymartin consented to employ him as his basket-maker. The Gypsy had no desire to return to Malvézie at Fontenac's chateau after testifying before Ricou, the notary, about what he'd seen on the les Beunes road.

The day after the duel, Monsieur de La Porte, the police lieutenant in Sarlat, paid a visit to the Brethren at their request, bringing a clerk and a doctor, and examined at my father's behest the body of Fontenac. La Porte determined that, as Giacomi had suspected, the baron was wearing a coat of chain mail under his doublet, and, asking the doctor to examine the wound to his eye to discover whether it had been caused by bullet or sword, they concluded that it could only have been caused by a blade. My father then showed them the bodies of Fontenac's men who'd been killed in the encounter, as well as the two arquebuses they'd used to fire from the bushes and that bore, engraved in their stocks, the name of the artisan in Sarlat who'd made them. When presented with them, the man remembered having sold them to the brigand baron the previous Easter.

But Monsieur de La Porte was not yet satisfied, as he was extremely meticulous and prudent in these matters and he insisted on hearing, separately, one after the other, the witnesses and actors in this drama, namely, Samson, Giacomi, Miroul and myself. As he was concluding his investigation, Puymartin arrived with Ricou, the notary, and three of his men, and passed on to La Porte the testimony that the notary had written in Provençal under dictation from the Gypsy. But Monsieur de La Porte would accept Ricou's report only after it had been translated into French, since there was a royal ordinance that required that all evidence submitted in courts of justice be in the language of the north. So while the notary laboured over his translation, La Porte asked me to write down the details of my duel with the Baron de Fontenac. He waited till I'd finished my work and the notary had completed his before departing.

He took his leave very politely, as was his wont, his eyes always very glacial, without giving his opinion on anything or making any pronouncements, abiding scrupulously by the letter of his office. However, the way he smiled suddenly when he said goodbye to my father suggested that he considered his work done.

And so it was, but the same was not true of that of the judge, who, as Monsieur de La Porte had warned us, arrived a week later at sunset, without any escort (which might be explained by the fact that his country house was so near to Mespech). Samson and I and the Brethren were the only ones to speak with him. The five candles of the candelabrum, lit in honour of our host, despite our Huguenot economy, illuminated the honest, square, ruddy face of this Périgordian gentleman, sitting above his white ruff collar.

"Monsieur," he began, "I have not forgotten your valiant conduct during the outbreak of the plague in Sarlat and how, not content to provision the starving inhabitants with a huge side of beef, you were the only one, with Puymartin, to dare confront the butcher of la Lendrevie and to defeat his band of brigands. And so I have come here, not in my role as judge of the seneschalty, but in my own person, to warn you that a plot is being hatched against your house. Things are taking a very bad turn against your sons that I don't like at all!"

"What?" exclaimed my father. "The baron set up a dastardly ambush and now you're nitpicking over my sons' behaviour!"

"We're not talking about lice, my friend, but libel, and libel from you-know-who! They can't forgive Mespech for being a nest of heretics and although we've made peace with your side and Coligny is now received at the king's court and well ensconced, it would seem, in the royal favour, some Présidial judges, out of religious fervour, are inclined to place the blame on your sons."

"And on what evidence would these judges base such an iniquitous falsehood?" demanded Uncle Sauveterre.

"On the basis of the testimony of the priest of Marcuays, of course!"

"Pincers!" cried my father. "But is there anyone in Sarlat or in the entire region who doesn't despise this drunken scoundrel?"

"He's a priest," said Monsieur de La Porte, "and that's enough for his testimony, however full of inconsistencies it may be, to outweigh the Gypsy's."

"Full of inconsistencies?" asked my father.

"Infinitely so! When Pincers was in Malvézie's sway, he wrote a version of the incident that put all the blame on your sons. But when the seneschal demanded that Malvézie release him, I took Pincers from between his claws and set him back up in his church in Marcuays where he wrote in my presence a testimony that concurs pretty much with what I heard here."

"So we're safe!" said Sauveterre.

"I'm afraid not. You see, the minute I left, Pincers became terrified that Malvézie would come for him, so he put himself under the protection of the bishop of Sarlat, and there he wrote a third version of his testimony, which is unfortunately quite close to the first one."

"Well, that's testimony that must be disqualified because of its variations!"

"Not at all! The majority of the judges in the Présidial have declared the third version is the valid one since it was delivered in the presence of the bishop and consequently inspired by the Holy Spirit."

"The Holy Spirit!" cried my father, gnashing his teeth. "Would you listen to these hypocrites who advance their worldly affairs under the mantle of religion!"

"Monsieur," said Monsieur de La Porte—though I couldn't tell whether he was kidding or in earnest, "I am a Catholic and I respect my bishop."

"Monsieur," countered my father, "Huguenot though I be, I also respect your bishop, but not in his worldly dealings. The Holy Spirit blows where it wills, as John writes in chapter three, verse eight, but why would this wind not turn this weathercock around again? What does the latest wind say?"

"In a word: that your sons surprised the baron on the les Beunes road and fell upon him and killed him."

"That's a huge and shameful lie!" I cried.

"So I believe," said Monsieur de La Porte, "but I have only provided the evidence for the matter and cannot serve as judge in it. And all that stands between my arresting you and your brother and bringing you to the parliament in Bordeaux is a majority decision by the Présidial judges, who disagree with me."

"Can this really be?" gasped my father.

"It can," answered Monsieur de La Porte gravely.

At this, we four paled and fell silent and sat there trying not to let our distress and indignant anger explode in front of our visitor.

"Monsieur," said Jean de Siorac finally, "I thank God that you've come here in your own person to warn us. But may I push your goodness and indulgence a bit further and ask what you would decide to do if you were thrown into the predicament we are facing?"

"I'll wager," said Monsieur de La Porte, "that the king has invited you, Monsieur, along with all the other noblemen of Périgord of both the papist and the reformed persuasions, to come to the capital to attend the marriage of his sister Margot to Prince Henri de Navarre, which will be celebrated in August."

"Indeed, I have received the king's invitation."

"Well then, instead of going there yourself," suggested Monsieur de La Porte, rising and speaking very quietly as if he wanted to be only half heard, "send your two sons to Paris to represent you. Once there, they can use their visit to beseech the king's pardon in this matter." And he added, speaking in the same soft voice and out of one side of his mouth, his face turned away from us: "They must be gone by dawn tomorrow. I would be devastated to find them here at noon."

"At noon!" cried my father, leaping to his feet. "What? So soon?"

"Ah, did I say noon?" replied Monsieur de La Porte. "It must have escaped me! Oh, and also," he added, as if a detail of no importance had suddenly occurred to him, "they should not go through Périgueux, where I might pursue them, but through Bordeaux, making a most useful detour to the chateau of Michel de Montaigne, whom they should ask to compose their petition to the king, which Montaigne will assuredly do. He is a man of substance, who cannot abide partisan iniquity, and who has a very good opinion of you since you were such a faithful friend of Monsieur de La Boétie, whom he continues to mourn, and always will."

"Ah, Monsieur," cried my father, "How can I tell you—"

"Don't say anything," interrupted Monsieur de La Porte with a smile, "since I've said nothing to you, but came here just to chat about my haying, because with all my troubles, I'm probably not going to have enough for the winter."

And having said this, he bowed to Sauveterre, who, always crippled by his old wound, couldn't stand up to see him out, then embraced my father warmly and took his leave.

When Miroul came to wake me the next morning, well before daybreak, I was sleeping peacefully, my arms around Little Sissy, my nose buried in her long black hair, which always smelt so clean since she washed it every day and dried it in the sun whose rays, she hoped, would give it a slight shade of copper. I don't know which of the wenches in Mespech would have taught her this recipe, but it didn't really show, her hair remaining as deep and shadowy as before. As for me, loving the bluish darkness of her locks, I was always amazed at our sweet minxes' ways. God gave them a face and they want to make another one, either by make-up or by colouring their hair. They just seem to want to be different from what nature made them.

But don't mistake me. I don't blame them. I do the same with these memoirs when I cross out a word that seems too dry and put two words in its place that I find more to my liking. Am I any different in this than those Parisian ladies who, believing they're too bony in a certain place, will wear false rumps and fluffy petticoats to make them look bigger? The coquetry of our sweetlings—this dear and delicious half of humanity—is but art added to nature. We should admire them (quite the opposite of what the ministers preach to them) for the infinite care they take to look in the mirror. Otherwise we wouldn't love women for their femininity but for some stupid criteria imposed on them by monks and preachers.

By the light of the oil lamp that Miroul had brought, I arose, sprinkled my face and body with water and, wetting a corner of my towel, washed and scrubbed my teeth, which were naturally in excellent shape, and I wanted to keep them that way as long as I lived. Meanwhile, Miroul was waiting, shoes in hand, ready to give them to me, and, out of the corner of his eye, watching my Little Sissy, who, sitting naked on the bed without any sense of shame whatsoever, was caressing her firm, apple-shaped breasts; and then, pulling up her knees and resting her elbows on them, she placed her delicate hands on her temples and stretched her dark liquid eyes sideways to make them more almond-shaped, which she knew I liked. This done, she began to complain about my leaving:

"Ah, Pierre! You're scarcely here a week and now you're off again! And when will you return? What good is it being Pierre de Siorac's wench if I never get to see him? Poor, poor me! Did you ever see a pretty girl who got less loving than me?"

"Come off it, Little Sissy!" I scolded. "I should be the one to complain! I kill a felon in a duel and now I have to go into exile to keep my neck from the gibbet!"

"Ah, Monsieur!" said Miroul, handing me my shoes, his brown eye shining. "Our exile won't be so terrible. Monsieur your father has furnished us with plenty of money. Paris is the most beautiful city in the kingdom. And what's more, Madame Angelina will be living there."

"What?" shrieked Little Sissy. "Madame Angelina is in Paris? Oh, Pierre, I'm done for! You'll never come back again!"

"Go easy, there, silly girl!" I frowned. "Don't deafen me with your screams when I'm not even awake yet, still groggy and dreamy, hungry only for my bed—and for you!" (Hearing this she softened a bit.) "And now I've got so many leagues to go before I find a bed for the night. Of course I'll come back here, silly bewitched girl, as soon as I've obtained the king's pardon! My father's money won't last for ever. And isn't Mespech the nest where I was born?"

"Ha!" snorted Little Sissy. "If it were just Madame Angelina, who, being a virgin and all, you must respect, but there are all those Parisian harlots, so expert in their wiles and so rigged out that they'll have you jumping about them like a cat on hot bricks every day you're there!"

"Then I know a lot of Parisian girls in Périgord!" I laughed, and, pulling her to me, with cuirass and helmet already on, I said, "Come, Little Sissy, give me a kiss, my pretty! One last kiss for the road! Be a good girl, and polite, and work hard while I'm gone! Get up early! Don't lie around in the sheets! Don't run from difficulty! And don't argue with Alazaïs or with Barberine, who is so good to you!"

"Oh, my Pierre!" she cried, throwing her bare arms around my neck. "May it please God to have made me pregnant in the last week, so that I can laze about in bed and eat as much as I want and do nothing but dream about you, 'cause I hate housework and want only your love and to care for the baby I'll give you! Oh!" she said, pulling me close despite my rude chain mail. "I'm so proud to be your wench, and will be prouder to make you a little Siorac baby. That's the work I want, Pierre, and none other!"

"Little Sissy, my pretty, a kiss!" I said, keeping back my tears. "Another kiss! And be a good girl, behave! And if you do I'll bring you back something pretty from Paris!"

"Really? What?" she cried, her beautiful black Gypsy eyes lighting up, her hands pressed tightly as if in prayer.

"Oh, I don't know," I smiled, heading for the door, "maybe a ring, or a lace kerchief or a silk ribbon…"

"A ring!" she cried. "It's a ring I want! A gold ring not a silver one, so it'll look pretty on my brown skin!"

"A gold one then," I said, caught up in her pleasure, "on condition you don't argue with Alazaïs and that you do her bidding."

"I promise, Pierre!" she cried as I opened the door. "And may God watch over you!"

"Well, Monsieur," smiled Miroul, who was carrying my arms as we traversed the corridors of Mespech, "now you're in debt for a ring when you could have got off with a ribbon! The wench won that hand and handily so!"

And even though he said this as a joke, I could see that there was a barb to his words, and feeling this prick I replied:

"It's all right, Miroul, a master should be generous: didn't I buy you a new outfit in Montpellier?"

"I thank the Lord and I thank you, Monsieur, *and* Madame de Joyeuse... But as for her, she's not going to be in Paris to fatten your purse, so you'd better think about that."

"It's all right, I tell you, Miroul—Samson will think for both of us!"

"But this ring, Monsieur! And gold! We've scarcely left and we're already ruined! And for a wench who serves so poorly at Mespech."

"Yet she serves me well enough! And when you come right down to it, she's bewitched me!"

"Ah, Monsieur! Who doesn't bewitch you! You're made of such tender stuff when it comes to a petticoat."

"A frailty I inherited from you-know-who."

"Who, I'm sure, would never have promised a gold ring to a chambermaid who doesn't do two sols' worth of work in an entire year!"

"All right, Miroul, that's enough of that refrain! You'll get me really angry if you continue with it."

And, in truth, I was already angry, but at myself, and, although I wasn't going to show it, my Huguenot conscience was sorely pricking me for having played at being a rich grandee with Little Sissy.

Down in our great hall, my father was sitting alone, waiting for me and devouring a beautiful white bread, some ham and a bowl of milk. He looked serene, though I thought I detected some melancholy in his expression. After having gestured to me to have a seat and enjoy my breakfast, he rose and began pacing back and forth, his boots ringing on the stone floor; however, when I was in the midst of my meal, he cried, quite angrily and in stentorian tones:

"A week! I waited a year for you and Samson! A whole year! Providence is mighty stingy to give me only a week with you! A week and you're out on the road again! Outlaws! In mortal danger! Oh, how fatal Samson's delay to shoot that dog Malvézie! If he'd killed him we'd not be in this mess! Left alone, Madame de Fontenac wouldn't have tried to get back at us, given how grateful she is for having saved her daughter and because she knows better than anyone the evil committed by her husband, who, in his youth, kidnapped her, raped her and forced her to marry him! But this Malvézie never stops plotting, scheming and pushing! He wants to take over the Fontenac domain for himself! He'll do anything to acquire rights that he didn't inherit from his bastard birth. Diane and her mother are done for if he succeeds. Two women! What can they do against this monster?"

But then coming to a sudden halt, putting his hands on his hips, and his tone and expression altogether changed, Jean de Siorac said, "I heard you call *maestro* Giacomi your brother. Did you become brothers?"

"In word only, not by a notarized decree, since neither of us possesses any goods that he could settle on the other."

My father thought about this for a moment, smiled in his sly and humorous way and said, "You who were born in the second half of this century do things much faster and more precipitously than those of us born in the first. It took you two days to take Giacomi as your brother whereas Sauveterre and I took two years."

"But you loved Sauveterre straightaway!"

"Ah, yes! At first glance! At the first shot! In our first battle! As soon as I saw what kind of a man he was, of what nobly tempered steel he was made of!" But then he smiled and sat down opposite me and said: "As for *maestro* Giacomi, other than that I'm very reassured to have such a skilled swordsman accompany you, I must say I like him a lot. I don't care whether he's of noble birth or not: there's a natural nobility about him. In matters large and small he's a man of infinite elegance."

I was very happy to hear these words and, blushing with the pleasure he'd given me (though still worried about the question of the ring that Miroul had so stung me about), I said, "Do you think we'll have any trouble getting the king to pardon us?"

"I don't know. Coligny is reputed to be in great favour with Charles IX. Unfortunately, I don't have much confidence in this little king who lets himself be governed by his mother, and even less so in the woman herself. My Pierre, tread very carefully at court and be prepared to turn on your heels! Queen Medici is the soul of the state, she who has no soul! And to tell you the truth, this so-called favour granted to our side by the king frankly stinks! Paris hates us! Guise is forever plotting! The papist priests are screaming for our extermination! I would never have sent you hence, you and Samson, into this perilous Babylon, were it not absolutely necessary!"

"My father," I replied, full of trepidation from the sombre tableau he'd just painted, "I will return on the very day our pardon is granted."

Hearing this he looked me in the eyes and gave a great sigh of relief. "Oh, Pierre, your departure is making me feel very old! I'm already too sedate, too heavy, too ripe. To see you and Samson here in all your youthful vigour, such beautiful branches from my old trunk, keeps me young! When you're gone, my mind focuses on the number of years I have left and is constantly whispering how to grow old and die. A week! How little I've drunk from that fountain! Adieu, Pierre! Be well, keep yourself safe! And since they killed your Accla, take my beautiful Pompée from my stables. She's yours."

"What, Father? You're giving me your mare?"

"Take her! Take her! No thanks necessary! She now belongs to you."

I would actually have preferred it if he had not given her to me since it hurt me so much that, for my sake, he would deprive himself of something so dear, and I couldn't help seeing in this deprivation the kind of indifference to oneself which is sometimes found, along with miserliness, to be one of the effects of age—whose ravages were already so apparent in Uncle Sauveterre, so dried up and halting in his black clothes that he reminded me of a limping black crow in the bottom of a ravine. But my father, who still seemed so youthful and vigorous as he came and went, still enjoying his Franchou (as well, no doubt, as other passing petticoats in the farms around our chateau), seemed now to be showing some signs of heaviness, not of body, but of heart, and a kind of diminution of his usual gaiety of spirit.

My adieux bid to all this ageing family of Mespech (though 'twas true that there seemed to be no lack of children, my father assuring their continued arrival), I threw myself into Pompée's saddle—she seemed very surprised and, as lively mares often do, wanted to test my reactions and tried to throw me off. But I showed her immediately that my hand, my seat and my legs were as steady as my father's, but in no way scolded her for her petulant display, since I didn't want our marriage to begin with blows. When she had calmed down, though I was still trembling slightly from the combat she'd just waged, I caressed her neck, admiring how her golden coat and blonde mane shone in the early-morning light. And I whispered to her in a calm and caressing voice: "Hey, beautiful Pompée, I'm so happy you've shown such spirit, for we've got some good leagues to go before you get your oats in Montaigne, and many more leagues still before we get to Paris."

At some distance from the Château de Montaigne, I had our troop stop at a little inn that looked friendly enough, and sent Miroul on ahead to ask the lord of the manor if he would consent to welcome us, our difficulties having come on so suddenly that there'd been no way to give him earlier notice of our arrival. We dismounted and tied our horses in the shade, since the July sun was so strong even in the late afternoon. We sat down under an arbour covered with vines, and our hostess, who had little to recommend her physically, brought us a wine that was so strangely delicious that it would have been impolite to water it down, but we did anyway since we didn't wish to be light-headed when we met Monsieur de Montaigne. Our stomachs crying to be filled, we ordered some ham, butter, wheat biscuits and a beautiful melon. The entire meal, including seven measures of wine, cost but five sols. I thought that we should offer our hostess seven, but Samson, who controlled the purse, objected, and I didn't insist, Giacomi pointing out that it would be best not to do anything that would make us stand out in the memory of this good wench, who scratched around us like a mother hen in a barnyard, listening to everything we said, there being very little traffic on this road and doubtless little news to digest.

Miroul returned after an hour to inform us that Monsieur de Montaigne's secretary was waiting for us at a nearby crossroads. Remounting our horses we headed in that direction, and there, under the shadow of a grove of chestnut trees I saw a tall knave clothed in black mounted on a rather shabbily appointed workhorse, and who (I mean the knave) looked rather severe but greeted us civilly enough. He told me that he judged, by my demeanour and behaviour, that I was the leader of our little troop, and, if so, then I must be the younger son of the Baron de Mespech. He asked, therefore, if I could prove that this was so. I answered him that I was carrying a letter from my father to his master. He wanted to see it. I handed it to him. And, taking it, he broke the seal quickly and casually, and, even though it was not addressed to him, read its contents. After which, he dropped his suspicious airs and asked very politely if we would remove our helmets and cuirasses and put on our doublets. Monsieur de Montaigne, he explained, did not like people to appear before him in his peaceful retreat, armed for war as we were.

It must have been about six o'clock when we finally reached the chateau. The secretary led us, once we'd taken off our boots, to the tower where Monsieur de Montaigne had the library that he would later describe in his *Essais*, where he regretted that he hadn't designed a gallery where he could stroll, rather than a tower in which he was forced to walk in circles, as he was doing when we arrived. He greeted us with extreme civility, and having bid us be seated, read the letter that the secretary handed him already unsealed, shaking his head as he did and then rereading it once he'd finished, which gave me the opportunity to look at him, which I did with much curiosity, since he had—well before his pen had added to it—so great a reputation in the kingdom.

He was then thirty-nine years old, and already a year ago he had, as he put it, withdrawn into the bosom of the "learned virgins", by which he meant the Muses, wishing to consecrate "the sweet ancestral refuge of the Montaignes to his liberty, his tranquillity and his retirement". He struck me, from the way he welcomed us, as having very little of the courtier about him; or rather, he played at being a sort of counterfeit courtier, since he copied neither the manners nor the allure of the court, but wore a large ruff, and about his neck the medal of the order of Saint-Michel that the king had given him a year previously. For my part, I saw in him rather a clerk or a magistrate, for he displayed little physical grace, being short and rather stocky, with a pate so bald there was not a single hair on it. He was obviously more apt with the pen than with the sword, though he wore an épée at his side and, according to what I'd heard, loved to discuss warfare and battles—a tendency that our neighbour Brantôme scoffed at, so great and intractable is the prejudice of *la noblesse d'épée* against *la noblesse de robe*.*

I had a chance to study him further during our conversation. He had a high, rounded forehead and high cheekbones, a full but not fat face with a long, aquiline nose, large, black, Judaic eyes and a look that was sometimes gay and jocular, at others prudent and mistrustful, as though he were worried. His fleshy lips pointed downwards at the corners of his mouth, and his moustache accentuated and continued this slope, giving him a sad air—at least until his smile came into play, which then lit up his face in the most delicious way. In short his physiognomy seemed to be a balance between two equal forces: joviality and melancholy.

He was dressed with quiet elegance in a black velvet doublet with hose of the same colour and white slashes. He wore a sword at his belt, as I've said, even though he was at home. And as for his beard (which was greying) he trimmed it closely rather than letting it grow full as Rondelet and Saporta did. I couldn't tell if this style was a result of his belief that this was more appropriate for a nobleman, or because he tolerated a beard more than he liked growing one simply because he didn't like to shave. Though not as well tanned as my father, the Périgordian sun had not failed to give his face good colour and he seemed altogether healthy and vigorous.

"Monsieur," he said as he folded the letter and stuck it in his doublet, "I know your father through what my late friend Monsieur de La Boétie told me, that he is a man who works hard for the common good. I want you to tell me all about your affair at length and at your leisure. For the time being, I invite you to follow me into my chateau where I usually spend a few hours before dinner."

---

* "The nobles of the sword" [the feudal, knightly class of nobility]; "the nobles of the gown" [the judicial and administrative class of nobility].

"Ah, Monsieur de Montaigne," I exclaimed as I rose, "you have here a very beautiful library, which is much larger than the one at Mespech, which itself is already fairly substantial."

"My father began it before me, and since I became a man I have spared no effort or expense to round out this inheritance." As he pronounced the words "round out" he made a large gesture with his slender white hand and smiled as he displayed the shelves, which exactly followed the curve of the walls, since the room was perfectly round—except the part that held the winding staircase, which was enclosed in a small square tower adjoining the larger one. You might have said that this library, in its rotundity, was like the cocoon in which the worm encloses itself to weave its beautiful and protective envelope.

As we descended the stairs, my host paused to show us his bedroom, and next to it a small cabinet which communicated with the chapel beneath it by means of an opening in the wall, so that one could hear the words and music of the Mass without getting out of bed.

"Aha!" I smiled. "We have the same arrangement at Mespech! My father and Sauveterre had it constructed early on in their work on the chateau, so that, at a time when the Huguenots were still under heavy persecution by the papists, and didn't dare openly declare their faith, the Brethren could appear to be hearing Mass without actually doing so."

"Oh, but I really hear it!" said Montaigne. "I hear it! And in complete devotion and diligence! My mother," he continued with some emotion, "was a Sephardi and was forced to abandon the religion of her ancestors, since in Spain they resorted to torture and the stake to convert the 'heathen'. And so she embraced with great enthusiasm the reformed religion. My brother did the same but with a zeal that Monsieur de La Boétie condemned, I recall very well, on his deathbed. But for my part, Monsieur," he added, "putting peace and moderation above all things, I am of the same religion as the king."

He said this with such a wry smile and inner pleasure that he led me to believe that if the royal faith were to change, his own would not have too much trouble following it.

"All of which is to say," he added after a silence, "that I am Catholic and celebrate Mass."

"Monsieur de Montaigne," objected Samson, in his candour becoming much more audacious than either Giacomi or I would have dared to be, "you confess the Mass, but can you really say you go to Mass if you do not get out of bed?"

"Ah, yes, but I *hear* it!" said Montaigne with the faintest of smiles. "And isn't hearing Mass the first duty of a Catholic?"

Having said this, he continued on his way down the stairs, and crossing a vast and well-paved courtyard, he led us into the great hall of his chateau, which I found to be well appointed with furniture, rugs and paintings. Scarcely had we seated ourselves, however, than a chambermaid came to ask in Provençal if he would be willing to see Mademoiselle his daughter and her governess. He agreed, and when the maid had left, he said:

"I beg you to give me licence to interrupt our conversation by this visit, which is a daily ritual in our family. I lost three of four children in infancy, not without regret, but without great anger, so Léonor is the only child left to me, and I love her in proportion to those that I lost. You will see her and I beg you to pardon her excessive childishness. For although she's already at an age where the law will allow the most high-strung girls to marry, she is slow to develop, thin and soft, and has scarcely begun to emerge from childhood."

At this moment, Léonor entered, followed by an old woman appearing pinched, argumentative and nasty, who looked at us as if her pupil risked evil and perdition by even casting her eyes on us. Léonor went to offer her father her pale cheeks to kiss and then turned to us and, eyes lowered, made an awkward bow—since her body was so angular, her flesh so barely covering her bones and her breasts as flat as my hand. And yet her face, though thin, was quite beautiful and her eyes very luminous.

The governess, whose lips were barely visible they were pulled so far back in her mouth, which was missing part of her dentition, began a narrative of Léonor's activities of the day which struck me as more silly and childish than anything her pupil might have said in her most naive moments, all of which Montaigne listened to, or appeared to listen to, nodding his head, his eyes fixed tenderly on his daughter.

"Very good," he said at the end. "Please read me something, Léonor."

So the governess handed her a very large book, which Léonor laboriously placed on her lap, before beginning to read in a soft voice, stumbling and hesitating frequently since the book was in French—which, I'll wager, was both the interest and the difficulty of the exercise. If my memory serves me correctly, the text was entirely about plants, trees and bushes, and, as she read it, Léonor encountered the word "beech" which is, of course, the name of a tree, but which she mispronounced "bitch", whereupon the governess snapped rudely, "Madame, don't say this word! It is unacceptable in the mouth of a girl."

"So what should I do?" said Léonor naively. "The word appears twice in the sentence!"

"Read the sentence, but skip over the word."

"Really? Twice?" replied Léonor, who perhaps had more wit to her than it first appeared.

"Twice."

So, right away, Léonor reread the sentence as follows:

"Above the bushes that I've just described, could be seen the branches of a superb *ahem* and at the top of this *ahem* a nest of doves." After which, without Monsieur de Montaigne saying a word, or throwing her a wink, the reading having come to an end, Léonor received another kiss on each cheek from her father and followed the old hag out of the room, as sweetly mannered as she was inadequately filled out.

"There you have it!" cried Montaigne, when they had left. "This is how they are raising our daughters! The word 'beech' becomes a crime because it sounds like the word 'bitch'. So instead of saying it innocently, now it's been eliminated and we have no idea what it's all about."

"But Monsieur de Montaigne," I objected, "you could have intervened."

"Oh, no!" he cried, throwing both hands in the air. "I don't dare question the rules or get mixed up in her governance. The control of femininity is a mysterious business: it must be left to women. But, if I'm not mistaken, contact with twenty lackeys couldn't have more firmly impressed on Léonor's imagination the usage of these 'dirty' syllables as effectively as this good old woman has by her censorship."

I laughed at this, and Giacomi as well, but not Samson, who, if he'd had a daughter to raise, would have been every bit as implacable as this old ogre.

"Aha! Another visit!" said Montaigne as a grey-and-white-striped cat leapt onto his knees. It had very silky fur and was as long as a weasel, with a little triangular face and green eyes, and there was something so wild and feminine about her that it was a marvel to see her on Montaigne's lap, purring under his caress, at times pretending to claw, at other times feigning to bite him with such feline frolicking.

While he was scratching his cat between her ears, Montaigne looked at me with a smile spreading slowly across his face and his eyes shining brightly, an expression that I could only describe by saying that it had the effect of making you complicit and in agreement with what he was about to say before he opened his mouth. And so, though he was not handsome, you found yourself predisposed to agree with him before he spoke, and even when he said something that was entirely opposed to the common view of things, he managed to engage you with finesse rather than shock you with its novelty. Moreover, no subject was too insignificant or too small for him, which made his manner seem easy and open, and made you feel reassured and comfortable.

Pretending to attack his cat with his hand, and she pretending a counter-attack with her claws, Montaigne said with his slow smile: "I'm playing with my cat, but who knows whether she isn't playing with me? Who knows whether I'm not exactly for her what she is for me? Or if she believes she's amusing me more than I am her? We carry on with these reciprocal mimicries. I have my times when I like to play and she has hers."

Passing on to the subject of hunting, he said that his neighbours were all caught up in it, but that for him, he would hunt deer or boar on horseback, as his father had done before him, but that he considered it a violent pleasure, and didn't like hearing the squeal of a rabbit between the hounds' teeth. Nor, he said, could he see a chicken's throat cut without disgust.

"But we have to eat!" said Samson.

"Assuredly so!" replied Montaigne in his jocular tone and looking at my brother with his usual beneficence.

Meanwhile, his cat—whose name was Carima—unhappy that he'd interrupted their game, leapt to the floor from his knee, her tail proudly held high, and went off to mope in a far corner of the room, where there was a small rug that she immediately began to scratch, as if in revenge for having been so neglected.

And even though Montaigne, from what I could observe, didn't like her to damage his things, he nevertheless let her do it, having no appetite, it seemed to me, to chastise people or animals—no more Carima than the governess of his daughter.

"So let's talk about your affair," he said, shifting his gaze from his cat to me.

I told him everything, without embellishing or omitting anything: my duel with Fontenac, the inquest by Monsieur de La Porte, the partiality of the judges of the Présidial, our flight and our intention of asking the king to pardon us.

"Well!" he exclaimed after listening very diligently. "There's partisan impartiality for you! And what damage it does to the equilibrium of things in the kingdom! These judges accuse you, despite the flagrant evidence that's been presented, because of the report of a single witness as if they were ignorant of the old adage: *Testis unus, testis nullus*.* And as if they weren't aware that this pitiful witness changed his story not once but twice!"

Having said this, he did not add, as I would have expected, that he would draft a petition for me to the king, which my father had begged him to do in his letter. And though I was astonished at his silence on this subject, I did not despair, reasoning that, before giving it to me, he wanted to think about it some more—for the matter was not without some delicacy, in that it led him to defend the Huguenots against the most fanatical members of his own party.

A chambermaid came in to announce that dinner was awaiting her master's pleasure, and we went to table. Montaigne presented his wife's regrets for not attending as she was confined to her room with a headache, something that she seemed to get once a month and for but one day.

This meal presented certain surprising singularities that, even today, I can remember vividly. The bread was unsalted and the meat, by contrast, heavily salted. The wine arrived at the table cut by an equal amount of water and wasn't served in goblets, as at Mespech, but in glasses, since Montaigne wanted his eyes to enjoy it before his palate did. There were no spoons or forks, so we used our fingers,

---

* "If there's only one witness, there is no witness."

which seemed to be a disadvantage to the lord of the manor since he went at his food with such haste that he twice bit his fingers. Both meat and fish were served as we would serve pheasant, by letting it hang for a day or two, which produced a smell that turned my stomach, accustomed as I was at Mespech to eating fresh meat and fish. We ate without napkins, but at each different course a chambermaid brought us each a white napkin on which we wiped our hands—and Montaigne dirtied his rather dramatically since he ate greedily, excusing himself for his manners.

Towards the middle of the dinner, a little valet who was bringing a large platter tripped on an uneven tile and fell, the plate shattering into tiny pieces, spreading the meat he was carrying all over the floor. This made a great commotion, which silenced our conversation, and the little valet picked himself up all ashamed and terribly pale, scarcely daring to look at his master. But Montaigne said, with an even voice and without batting an eye, "Jacquou, please ask Margot to clean up this mess and bring us the next course."

After Jacquou left, infinitely relieved, I told Monsieur de Montaigne how much I admired his philosophical approach here, for even at Mespech, where we never whipped anyone, we didn't fail to scold those who stumbled in their work.

"Well," said Monsieur de Montaigne, "the people who serve us do it for a less advantageous salary than we give to our horses and dogs. We have to allow for some mistakes in our valets. If we have more than we need, we should be open to using some of it generously: the gleaner's portion."

His words brought to mind what Monsieur de La Boétie had said to my father about the harvest at Montaigne's estate, where, when some of the sheaves came apart in the wagon, Monsieur de Montaigne had said not to rebunch them, so that the extra grain falling in the field would increase the gleaners' provender. Likewise, Montaigne held rigorously to the ancient custom by which his fields, once harvested, should be opened to cattle of the poorest farmers—whereas at Mespech they were ploughed immediately, burying the stubble in the field to fertilize it. Of course, this method was more reasonable and profitable to the landowner, but it so antagonized the people in our villages that in the beginning we had some difficult moments with them.

But to return to our pleasant, copious and Périgordian meal, I can't remember how or why we got to talking about love and marriage, but Monsieur de Montaigne was remarkably open on this subject, loving, it's true, to talk endlessly about himself—not for small-minded, mediocre or egotistical reasons, but because it was the entire condition of man that he painted in talking about his own experiences and habits.

"When I was a young man," he said with his customary abandon, "I gave myself over as licentiously and inconsiderately as any other to the desires that governed me. And not without glory, though in a lasting and durable way rather than in quick sallies: *sex me vix memini sustinuisse vices*."*

"Six, Monsieur!" I exclaimed with a laugh. "I can't understand how anyone could be dissatisfied by such a number! As for me, I'd be very happy!"

"But I'm not," said Montaigne, "since voluptuousness is too often vicious and sudden—it makes love too rapid and precipitous. And I end up feeling like that fellow in antiquity who wanted to have a neck as long as a crane's in order to savour the food that traversed it for as long as possible."

At this I laughed heartily and Giacomi along with me, but not my poor Samson, who was secretly so uncomfortable with these wanton subjects that he kept his eyes lowered and his expression as pensive as possible to give the impression he hadn't heard them.

---

*   "I can barely remember managing it six times."

Montaigne then asked me, with his slow smile, how I treated the wenches I'd known once they were mine.

"Very well!" I said, caught off guard.

"Then you've done well," said Montaigne, "and unlike most men, for I believe that we should behave with them as conscientiously and as justly as in any other relationship. As for me, since I desire neither to fool them nor to cheat on them, I've never pretended to have feelings I didn't really have. I was so chary of making promises that I think I've kept more of them than I actually promised or owed. And finally, I've never broken with any woman out of scorn or hatred because the intimacies they've shared with one oblige one to some regard for them. Monsieur de Siorac," he continued with a smile, "I've heard that in Montpellier you were the protégé of a lady of high birth and means and that she even called you her 'little cousin', though you were hardly her cousin."

"I had," I confessed, with a respectful nod of my head, "this immense privilege."

"It was your luck and your privilege, Monsieur de Siorac," said Montaigne. "When I was your age, I had such an appetite for the honest women I might meet that I eschewed, shall we say, commercial opportunities, wishing to sharpen my pleasure by conquest. I was a little like the courtesan Flora, who would sleep with no one less than a dictator, consul or senator: I counted as my reward the dignity of my lovers."

"To tell the truth, Monsieur de Montaigne, it's not the case that I despise common love affairs. On the contrary, I've found them satisfying and sometimes emotionally very fulfilling!"

"I don't despise them either," said Montaigne, "especially since I could never be content, like the Spanish are, with a glance, a nod, a word or a sign. Who could ever dine, as our Périgordian proverb says, on the smoke of a roast? I need more fulfilling meats and more

146

substantial flesh. For I feel some emotion in love, and am not satisfied by dreams alone!"

"Well!" I thought. "There's the difference between this great man and me! For when I think about my Angelina, do I not feel such emotion as to lose my appetite for food, drink and very nearly for life? And in her absence do I not lose myself in the most amazing dreams?"

"I gather, Monsieur de Montaigne, that you're somewhat impatient with courtly love?"

"Oh, yes," he answered with a smile, "when it doesn't lead to anything. We must always keep our wits and our discretion in love. We want to enjoy ourselves but not forget ourselves. Love, Monsieur de Siorac, should not lead men to sighs and tears. In essence it's an awakening of lively and happy agitation. It is harmful only to fools. My idea of the best conduct of love is a healthy emotion, enabling us to lighten our minds and bodies. And as a doctor I would prescribe it to a man as willingly as any other to keep him healthy well into his old age."

"Well, he's certainly not wrong about that," I thought. "All you have to do is compare the way my father and Sauveterre have aged to see that my father has done much better by proliferating bastards than Sauveterre has by his implacable virtue."

As we had arrived at the fruit course, Jacquou served each of us a melon, which neither I nor either of my companions was able to finish because of its size, but I observed that Montaigne loved this fruit so much that he ordered and devoured a second that was just as big as the first.

"Marriage," Montaigne continued as he wiped his mouth, moustache and beard with the napkin the chambermaid had brought, "is meant to be a very dull pleasure with neither sting nor heat. And it's no longer love if it lacks arrows and fire."

"But," I protested, thinking of my Angelina, with whom I expected a great deal more than dull pleasures, "can't one teach one's wife the special delights which make voluptuousness so lively, acute and exciting?"

"Absolutely not!" cried Montaigne, raising both hands heavenward. "Be very careful not to introduce into this venerable estate the extravagances of amorous passion! You should be careful, as Aristotle advised, that you do not caress your wife to the point where pleasure makes her lose her mind! And if she must learn such rashness let it at least be at the hands of another!"

"Well," I thought, "our sage is, for once, not making sense, even though he's lined up Aristotle, the Church and common wisdom on his side. Gracious! I shouldn't instruct Angelina in the delicious caresses I've learnt? I shouldn't make sure her pleasure is as great as mine? I should wait for a rival to teach her how to enjoy love?"

However, I said nothing, not wishing to argue with this great mind, who, because he dared differ from what was considered common sense and dared envision deeply original approaches to every subject, abounded in new and exciting perspectives, and expressed these so beautifully, mixing into his French here a Latin maxim, there a Périgordian turn of phrase, that ultimately his combination of rustic and learned locutions provided music to your ears and fruit for your understanding.

I was in the midst of these reflections when Montaigne, gulping down his last slice of melon, suddenly cried out and clapped his hand on his mouth.

"Monsieur," I cried, "what's the matter?"

"Nothing," he groaned. "From wolfing down my melon, I ended up biting my tongue. But it's nothing, though it hurts terribly when I do it. And so now, Monsieur de Siorac, you're going to Paris. You will find great comforts there," he continued, as though he'd entirely forgotten the grave reason that drove me there, and the favour my father had asked of him: that he compose a request for my pardon. "And when will you set off?"

"I'm afraid it must be tomorrow, Monsieur."

"What! You would deprive me so soon of your youthful faces! You've scarcely arrived and how you're off again!"

"But, Monsieur, we cannot tarry here! We're outlaws and may be seized at any moment and thrown in jail!"

"Ah, 'tis true!" he sighed. "How I would have loved to ride alongside you on this trip, though I do travel quite a bit and was in Paris just two years ago, leaving the governance of my house to my wife—who, among her many other excellent virtues, knows how to run a household. Some people complain that travel interferes with one's marital duties. I don't believe it. The pleasure of seeing each other every day is trumped by the joy we derive from the emotion of parting from and returning to our loved ones. In any case, there is no agreement in marriage that we must always remain tethered like dogs. I believe that a wife should not be so greedily focused on her husband's front that she can't see his rear from time to time!"

I laughed at his witticism, and Giacomi as well, but not Samson, who kept his eyes rigidly fixed on his hands in his lap, wishing he were leagues away, so wounded was his modesty.

"Monsieur de Siorac," Montaigne continued, "I hope you will allow me to be silent for a while since I'm tired of talking on a full stomach. While I rest my voice, however, be so good as to tell me the story that has been attributed to you about a diabolical witch in a cemetery in Montpellier."

"Ah, Monsieur," I laughed, "although the wench was eventually burnt at the stake, she was no witch as I first believed, and the Devil was only metaphorically dwelling in her petticoat."

"So, tell me about it!" urged Montaigne, folding his hands over his stomach and looking at me intently, his eyes shining.

I obeyed, though I was ashamed to recount this affair in front of my beloved Samson, from whom I'd managed to hide it until this moment, and I watched with some distress as his blue eyes opened wide in amazement to hear of such mad goings-on—which is why I prefer to gloss over it here, not wishing, as I've already explained, to offend the delicate ears of the ladies who have objected to my liberties with the fair sex.

"As for witches," agreed Montaigne, when I'd finished my tale, "I am distressed to see that almost everyone believes in them—or pretends to—and Ambroise Paré is first among these believers, which doesn't shock me, since he was a great physician, but outside of medicine not a very learned man. In Bordeaux, some witches were put on trial. Everyone was crying 'Devils!' before the trial, the priests along with the crowds, but I didn't want to be influenced by this mob, so I went and talked to the poor women without threats or torture. I found them mad as hatters, to be sure, but there was no devil in them other than their imaginations, and their visions were more likely due to hallucinogens than to hemlock."

I was very glad to hear Monsieur de Montaigne's thoughts on this subject, since I'd found so few people in Montpellier who doubted what the judges and priests held as truth, when they sent to the stake so many of these unfortunates. In their warped minds, these poor creatures believed their accusers, attributed their deviations to the work of Satan and ended up convinced of the power of their rites, in which they mimicked the rites of the Church, but backwards.

Meanwhile, Monsieur de Montaigne, apparently no longer concerned that our discussion was detrimental to his digestion, returned to the subject of Paris. He had great admiration for the capital and eloquently sang its praises—a speech that was as diverting as it was enchanting since I still remembered Captain Cossolat's description of this sewer city, its stench, its difficulties, its buffeting crowds, the unbearable uproar of its carts and wagons, and the infinite arrogance of its inhabitants.

"Monsieur de Montaigne," I said, "your description has a very different ring from what I often heard in Montpellier."

"Pure prejudice!" replied my host. "As for me, when I'm most dissatisfied with our kingdom, I feel the most positive about Paris; she won my heart when I was young! The more I've visited beautiful cities, the more the beauty of this one has won my affection. I love her for herself, and not for her pomp and foreignness. I love her tenderly, including all her warts and stains: I am French only by my love of this great city, great in her people, great in her cuisine—but especially great and incomparable in the variety and diversity of her commodities. She is the glory of France and one of the most noble ornaments in the world."

At this speech, we three looked at each other with delight, inflamed with the beauty we'd be heading towards the next day as we took to the highways of the kingdom. So inflamed, indeed, that I almost forgot the purpose of our visit. And I only remembered it when, after this eloquent portrait of the capital, Monsieur de Montaigne rose and excused himself, explaining that there was a task he must perform before he went to bed, adding that, if we were indeed resolved to leave at dawn, we should bid our adieux now, since he was accustomed as an old married man to rising late. And, not knowing whether he had completely forgotten my request, or whether his silence on the matter was a sign that he refused to comply, I was trying to decide how to bring the subject to his attention when he concluded the evening by saying,

"Monsieur de Siorac, I am going now to dictate to my secretary your plea to the king. He will give it to you tomorrow morning as you leave. All you'll have to do is sign it."

"Oh, Monsieur," I cried, "what a debt of gratitude I owe you!"

"Not at all. Injustice committed against one man is an injustice to humanity. It is every man's duty to work for justice, lest he himself be unjust."

"Monsieur," I replied, "one last question. May I say that my request to the king was written by you?"

At this he frowned, and, his expression becoming quite circumspect, he seemed unsure as to whether he should say yes or no, but finally, his generosity overcoming his prudence, he decided on a compromise, and said with a smile, "If you're asked, and if you believe that it will be useful to the outcome you seek, yes. But otherwise, say nothing."

4

WE REACHED MONTFORT-L'AMAURY without incident towards evening on 1st August, and finding we were still a good day's ride from Paris, I decided we would spend the night in this beautiful market town, whose ancient towers stand at the edge of the forest of the same name. But the two inns of Montfort refused to open their doors to us since there was not a closet or even corner of either that was not filled, given the veritable tide of gentlemen from Normandy and Brittany who had been invited by the king to come to the capital for the marriage of Princesse Margot. So we would have been in the most extreme discomfort (being unable even to sleep in a field, since this 1st August was so rainy and cold), had not the hostess at the second inn, seeing us in such a fix (and, no doubt, swayed by our honest faces—and Samson's beauty), suggested that we go knock on the door of Maître Béqueret, the apothecary, whose shop stood just to the left of the church, and who, given the size of his house, would likely have room for us.

When we got there, his valet tried to slam the door in our faces, given the number of importunate people who had already tried this address, but I was so earnest and polite that he hesitated long enough for me to slip a few coins into his hand and finally agreed to fetch his master. This gentleman did not open the door of his house to us, but received us in his shop, which was as large as Maître Sanche's in

Montpellier and, in addition, so new and beautifully arranged that Samson was immediately bewitched. His wide blue eyes gazed with wonder at all the druggist's bottles, with their gold lettering, that filled his shelves from top to bottom.

Maître Béqueret, a tall, brown-haired, black-eyed man with a sympathetic face, listened courteously while I explained who we were and what we were asking. But when I'd done, he refused quite civilly but firmly my request, saying that, as the wealthiest master apothecary in the town, it was beneath his dignity to rent out rooms, even to the sons of the Baron de Mespech—though he was, he added, very honoured to meet us.

He bowed quite coldly and I returned his bow, but before giving up entirely, I said in as casual a way as I could manage that he ought to know that I was a doctor of medicine from the Royal College in Montpellier, hoping this would soften him a bit, but he refused to change his mind.

At that moment, the rain redoubled its force against the window-panes and my heart fell flat and my hair stood on end at the thought of spending a night at the mercy of this storm.

Defeated, however, I began to take my leave of Maître Béqueret, when Samson, who, lost in wondrous contemplation of the shop, hadn't heard a word of our conversation, suddenly burst out, "Oh, Maître Béqueret, what a beautiful display you have here! And what noble bodies and substances you have in your jars! It's quite clear that you spare no expense to provide the greatest quality in your medicines!"

"How can you tell, young man?" said Maître Béqueret archly.

"Because, for example, your senna is from Alexandria and not from Seyde, which, though less costly, Maître Sanche considered vile, dirty, full of mud and gravel and unworthy of feeding to an ass."

"What! You worked under the illustrious Maître Sanche in Montpellier?"

"For five years," replied Samson, "before I was promoted to master apothecary myself on 24th August 1571."

"Heavens!" gasped Béqueret. "You are a colleague! And the student of Maître Sanche! Why didn't you say so immediately instead of brandishing your titles of nobility? Make yourself at home, my dear colleague! And you too, venerable doctor of medicine," he added, looking my way, but with perhaps less warmth, since I was from a related family, but not of the same lineage as an apothecary.

And what a welcome the good apothecary provided I leave to your imagination, inviting the four of us to stay there, and stable our five horses in his barn for the entire month of August, since we would assuredly not find lodgings in Paris given the masses of guests who were flooding the capital for the wedding of Princesse Margot—"may the Blessed Virgin watch over her!" To which I said, "Amen!" and Giacomi as well, but Samson was visibly offended in his Huguenot rigour by such an idolatrous invocation. I thanked Maître Béqueret a thousand times for his invitation, but explained that I could not tarry in Montfort, but had to go immediately to Paris and would have to spend the entire month there—not just Margot's wedding day—since I needed to present to the king a plea, on which my entire future depended.

"Well then, Monsieur," interjected Dame Béqueret, who was, like her husband, dark-haired, with a pleasant face, though it was somewhat more pinched looking than his, "why not leave us your amiable colleague?"

"Oh, Madame! Samson, here for a whole month! It would be too great an expense for you, I fear!"

"Not at all!" said the lady. "No expense whatsoever, by my Norman faith!" (For she was from that province.) "Your brother would provide great help and service in my husband's shop, especially at a time when he's so overwhelmed by the demand, since there are so many people in Montfort this August."

Samson's eyes lit up, but how could I have consented to his holing himself up among these phials when Fortune had provided him a chance to visit the most beautiful city in the kingdom, or perhaps of the whole world, according to what Monsieur de Montaigne had said? And although my host was now as reluctant to see us leave as he had been but minutes before to provide us lodging, I decided that we would all leave the next morning. Hearing this, Miroul, who was helping their chambermaid to serve our table—a sweet and frisky little mare with whom he'd been flirting throughout our dinner—said, "But Monsieur, we can't do that! Your Pompée has lost both shoes on her forefeet! You can't possibly ride her until we get her shod!"

"Well, we'll take care of it tomorrow!" I answered with some annoyance.

"But we can't," he reminded me, with another amorous glace at the wench. "Tomorrow is Sunday. The smithy won't be available."

"What's more," said Maître Béqueret, "with all the gentlemen stopping here on their way to the wedding, he's got more business already than he can handle. I'd be surprised if he could shoe your horse before Wednesday!" At this, of course, Miroul's brown eye glowed with pleasure.

"Three nights we have to wait here," I groaned inwardly, "when Paris is so close!" And angered by this turn of events, I gave Miroul and then the maid each a nasty look, as if this whole delay were a ruse meant to accommodate them. But my valet, seeing this frown and realizing that, indeed, his own interests were secured in any case, gave me a big smile, and said in Italian, "*Il saggio sopporta pazientemente il suo dolore.*"*

"*È vero dio!*"† cried Maître Béqueret, who was proud of his Italian, which was now in vogue in Paris ever since the Florentine queen had taken the reins of the kingdom.

---

* "The wise man accepts his misfortune with patience."
† "'Tis God's truth!"

The next morning, as I was standing shirtless in my room, there was a knock at the door and Maître Béqueret entered, bowed politely and said, "Ah, Monsieur de Siorac, how comforted I am to see the medallion of the Blessed Virgin you are wearing! From certain signs I thought I detected yesterday, I was convinced you were Huguenots, and didn't know how to go about inviting you to join me at Mass this morning—it would be very dangerous for me and my family in Montfort were I to give shelter to heretics, since here, as in Paris, they are so furiously hated."

"Venerable Maître," I said, "you were right in your first guess: with the exception of Giacomi, we three, masters and valet, are of the reformed religion. And as for me, I wear this medallion only because it was my mother's dying request that I do so till the end of my life. However, Maître Béqueret, you have been so welcoming and so gracious that I would not wish to compromise or endanger your house, and so I will agree to accompany you to Mass."

"I thank God and you!" sighed Maître Béqueret. "This is a great weight off my chest! Although I am a sincere Catholic, I am not so zealous as to dream, like some in my religion, of disembowelling and burning those of the new religion. But you'll see, alas! in Paris, that there are many, many fanatics, and I'm very sorry to see you and your brother have to go and get embroiled in such hatred. You're risking your lives!"

"But venerable Maître, is it not true that our leader, Coligny, enjoys the king's favour at the moment?"

At this, Maître Béqueret frowned. "Yes, of course! But some people think that the king has only embraced Coligny the better to smother him, and with him all the Protestant nobles who have come to Paris for the wedding."

With this observation, which, the more I thought about it, weighed heavily on my heart, my host departed, very gratified by my compliance with his wishes. And since I was much less assured of Samson's compliance, I went immediately to his room to tell him of Maître Béqueret's invitation.

He had just awoken, and was so handsome and so vigorous, his visage so innocent, his eyes so azure, that I felt an immense joy just looking at him stretching lazily in his bed, running his fingers through his copper-coloured hair. But his eyes darkened when I told him about the invitation to Mass.

"I won't go!" he said emphatically.

"Samson," I explained, "we cannot put our gracious and welcoming host in such discomfort and danger."

"I won't go," he said, more rigid than Calvin himself.

I was suddenly so angry I could not restrain myself from shouting, "You *will* go! I command it!"

"Well," Samson said, visibly troubled and hurt, "so you're scolding me! Would you dare speak to me this way, Pierre, if I were not a bastard?"

"Samson," I moaned, taking him forcefully in my arms, and showering his cheeks with kisses, "that's crazy! Who's talking about birth here? Do we not have the same father? And as for the shepherdess who bore you, she must have been a worthy, good and beautiful wench, since you resemble her!"

Hearing me speak with such respect about the mother he'd never known, the poor girl having died of the plague when he was still in his infancy, my beloved brother burst into tears, and seeing him crying, I hugged him to me and again kissed his freckled face, saying, "I order you by the authority I have as your older brother, none other."

"Older brother? Whath thith?" he lisped charmingly. "Weren't we born in the thame month and year?"

"Yes, but I was a week earlier than you." At this he laughed through his tears, and seeing him brush them away with the back of his hand, and the sun coming out again after such a storm, I said,

"Samson, our father gave you authority over our purse, and to me he gave the command of our little troop since I'm better at negotiating our worldly paths. You must come, I beg this of you."

"Then I shall," he said, lowering his head like a ram, "but it does not please God that I shall be praying among all these idolaters."

"Well," I thought to myself, "what a noble zeal that leads to abstaining from prayer!"

"You must trust your conscience," I counselled him. "But just remember that the papists worship the same God that we do."

"But not in the same way!"

"Samson," I asked, "is it the way we pray that matters, or the love we owe to our Creator?"

To which, though not persuaded, he at least found no answer and so fell silent. And since this silence continued, I asked him if he would prefer to remain in the apothecary shop of Maître Béqueret for the month of August, as I'd been asked, and he answered yes with a huge sigh, since, as he explained, he loved his work so much that he was besotted with it and yet he understood that it was not his duty or even reasonable to do so. And then, as I was heading for the door, he said, very awkwardly and blushing to the roots of his copper-coloured hair:

"Did you know that Dame Béqueret is Norman and from the same village as Dame Gertrude du Luc? Do you think she knows her?"

"Oh, Samson," I thought, "so you're not implacable in everything!"

"Why don't you ask her?" I said, smiling to myself.

"Oh, I wouldn't dare!"

"Then perhaps you think I might dare?"

"Yes," he mumbled, lowering his eyes.

"I'll think about it," I said, enjoying this little game. "In the meantime, Samson, you should get dressed. Mass is at ten!"

*

As soon as he saw that he couldn't keep either me or Samson in Montfort-l'Amaury, Maître Béqueret put in a word for us with the farrier and the good smithy promised that my Pompée would be shod by dawn on Monday.

We thought that at this hour we'd be alone on the road, but as we approached the capital, we were amazed by the number of travellers: gentlemen on horseback or in carriages, innumerable carts loaded with hay, wood, milk, fresh meat, vegetables, barrels of wine or basketfuls of eggs that came from the villages surrounding Paris, to feed the Pantagruelian hunger of a city whose workers and inhabitants number more than 300,000, from what I'd been told—an immense and incredible number, I concede, but one which was confirmed by reliable sources.

As all of these good folk from the flat countryside moved very slowly, some pulled by workhorses, others by mules and others still even by oxen, we couldn't help passing them as we trotted along, looking at them and being looked at in return with astonishing effrontery, and yelled at in an amusing and often derisive way in French, which greatly surprised us since this language is entirely foreign to the peasants in Provence, and used only by well-educated people.

As I came alongside one of these open carts, full of jugs of milk and baskets of eggs, a comely milkmaid, a pretty bonnet on her head and her scarf revealing more than a little of her full bosom, round as the eggs in her baskets and whiter than the milk in her jugs, observed my hungry looks and cried out with a laugh:

"Handsome fellow, pretty eyes! So you like my wares?"

"Alas, my friend," I replied with a wink, "as the Périgordian proverb says, you can lick beauty, but you can't eat it!"

"Well, that's already a lot that you can lick it," replied the maid with a belly laugh, "whether you're in Paris or Périgord, if Périgord exists, for the Devil if I know where that place lies."

"It's in the south, my friend, below the Loire."

"I could tell from your accent it's in the south. So, good Monsieur, you're coming to the wedding?"

"I am!"

"I hope you enjoy it after all the expense that's been lavished on it! These royal weddings are such a splash! Kings don't fornicate any better than we do, and the husband can't piss straighter than my late husband, I can tell you! And so, pretty man, what are you? Rome or Geneva?"

I hesitated a bit before answering: "I'm of the same religion as the king."

"Nay!" said she with a wry smile, having seen me hesitate. "The king? Which king is that? The king of France or the king of Navarre? They don't have the same one. One goes to his service, the other to his Mass, even though one's marrying the sister of the other. There, there," she added, hearing no response, "it doesn't matter to me! It's for the nobles to fight over Churches. As for me, what my priest tells me goes in one ear and out the other, so that in these matters I have as much brain as a sucked egg."

"Oh, good woman," I laughed, "I don't believe you. There's nothing wrong with your brain!"

"Nor with yours! Though you speak French like a southerner. Oh, oh! I've upset you, Monsieur! No offence, I beg you!"

"I took none, I assure you!"

"Are you married?"

"My friend," I laughed, "if I'm not, will you have me?"

"Oh, no!" she giggled. "Widow I am and man will I have none! I'm better off since my late husband died. Marriage is a nasty business. Look at Navarre and Margot. He won't get a virgin for a wife. She was too taken with Guise. And she won't have him for herself: he's too fond of the petticoat. This wedding is a bad bargain."

"Ah, my friend, you have a lively tongue, I see."

But before she could answer, we were so pressed from the horsemen behind us, with imprecations that would make a bull blush, I had to spur on Pompée, and lost the milkmaid from view. I was surprised, however, how openly she dared gossip about the royal family, and with such impertinence. "Well," I thought, "if two leagues from Paris people are already so mutinous and rebellious, what will it be like in the capital?"

The five horsemen who had so bumped us from behind, and with such foul language and mean aspect, finally passed us, madly whipping on their malnourished mounts with sharp crops.

"I despise these profane and pitiless rascals," snarled Giacomi, who was usually so serene, "and if I hadn't restrained myself, I would have had at them with my sword." Hardly had he said this when these impatient ruffians, finding a horseman clothed all in black blocking their way, hurled a torrent of insults at him, and one of them knocked his hat off with his crop.

"*Bestia feroce!*"* cried Giacomi. "My brother, shall we have at them?"

"By all means!" I agreed, drawing my sword.

But when these scoundrels saw the four of us bearing down on them, swords flashing, they gave full rein and we were unable to give them more than a couple of sword swipes before they'd galloped away.

"Miroul," I said, "pick up that gentlemen's hat and dust if off for him."

"I thank God and I thank you," said the stranger, who had the appearance of a legal man, and he immediately asked my name, and told me his, which struck me as most poetic, for he was called Pierre de L'Étoile—though he did not look like a poet, neither in his dress nor in his appearance, nor yet in his speech, which seemed moralistic

---

*   "Savage beast!"

and morose and very bitter about the morality of our times. The rampant immorality surrounding us, he said with great indignation, surpassed anything he'd known in his youth, the population having been corrupted by the bad example set by the royal family, the civil wars, the fanaticism of the preachers and its own stupidity!

"The people of Paris," he complained, "are more ignorant and gullible than any other in the world, and insolent in proportion to their ignorance: *quo quisque stultior, eo magis insolescit.*"*

I looked at him as he rode by my side, all the while exhaling his angry wisdom. He had a long nose, lips curled in anger, and a deeply furrowed brow, and yet, when he turned towards me, his lively eyes sparkled with some beneficence in spite of his bile. I sensed in him a man of unshakeable honesty and character—and, as events were to prove, I was not wrong about this. I guessed as well from the rigour of his aspect and speech that he was a Huguenot, but he disabused me of this idea as soon as I told him I was for reform.

"Oh, Monsieur," he gasped, looking around with a terrified look, as if, despite the din of the wagons and horses on the stones of the road, someone might overhear us, "you mustn't talk so openly here, trusting the first person you meet. There is great peril in Paris not just in saying who you are, but in being what I am. I'm of the Roman Church to be sure, but not so fanatical that I prefer a Spanish Catholic to a French Huguenot. I suspect that who's really in charge of the kingdom now," he added, gnashing his teeth, "is a cabal of Catherine, who is Florentine, Guise, who is from Lorraine, the papal nuncio, who is Roman, and Felipe II, who is Iberian. By God, I hate it that foreigners have come to Paris to rule us and put knives in our hands to dispatch the Huguenots, who are, after all, our compatriots! *Nefas nocere vel malo fratri puta.*"†

---

*   "The more stupid a man is, the more insolent he becomes."

†   "It is a bad thing to slander even a bad brother!"

"So," I thought to myself, "if even for this good fellow I'm a 'bad' brother, I shudder to think what I will be for the Parisians!"

Meanwhile, Pierre de L'Étoile fell silent, struggling to regain control of his mood, which, without doubt, was bilious and sad, but isn't it a sign of good health to express one's anger this way? Isn't it better to drain the pus from an infection than to leave it under that skin to poison the blood?

"Monsieur de Siorac," he continued after catching his breath, and finding a more civil tone, "have you reserved a room in an inn in Paris?"

"I'm afraid not. We're trusting to good fortune."

"Which," said Pierre de L'Étoile, "will not smile on you. There isn't at present a single room, no matter how small or paltry—and I include the most piss-stained and infested in the city—that isn't so full you couldn't lodge a single cockroach."

"So what should be done?" I asked, very upset by this news.

"You must stay at the home of some worker or inhabitant of the city, which, in any case, would be much better for you."

"And why so?"

"Because," said Pierre, "all the innkeepers have been told by the provost of the Grand Châtelet to report all the names and origins of their guests, as well as a list of their horses and arms."

"Their arms!" I said quietly. "I don't like that one bit!"

"Nor do I!" agreed Pierre. "This Spanish Inquisition stinks!"

"But I don't know a living soul in Paris!"

"Monsieur de Siorac," said Pierre de L'Étoile, "I owe you a debt of gratitude for having chased off those insolent rascals whom, if I could, I would have gladly sent to the gallows." (And he grew angry all over again as he said this.) "And if you are willing, I will take you to the rue de la Ferronnerie, to the home of a dressmaker who, because I have somewhat straightened out his affairs, would gladly lodge you. His name is Maître Recroche, and he's more miserly than any Norman of Normandy, though he was born in Paris, as I was, and, like me, has never budged from here—except that I sometimes visit my land in Perche, whence I'm returning now. But Maître Recroche is a good enough fellow, though he likes money too well. And he won't report your names to the provost as long as you attend Mass, as I would advise you to do."

"Ah, Monsieur! I must go to Mass!"

"You must," said Pierre de L'Étoile. "It's the rule of rules, and one that must be obeyed here."

Whether it was the "rule of rules" I doubted, and still do. Some people say that disguising what one believes in the face of persecution is wisdom. Others call it cowardice. Who can decide in such grave circumstances? There's no doubt that rushing to offer yourself to the gibbet and disembowelment is madness. But if we never confess what we believe in this world, what kind of world would we have?

And so we went along, saddle to saddle, talking, Samson and Giacomi following us and trailing behind them, Miroul skilfully leading our packhorse. We could not proceed faster than a walk since the approach to Paris was now so encumbered by wagons that we occasionally had to stop altogether and wait for the tangle of horses to get sorted out. Ah, how interminable these last few leagues seemed in my fever to lay my eyes on this city I'd heard so much about and that Cossolat had execrated as entirely as Monsieur de Montaigne had lauded it to the skies.

We crossed the Seine at a little village called Saint-Cloud, and since the bridge was so narrow, and though it further slowed our progress, I had time to admire the sailboats taking advantage of a favourable wind to move upstream against the current. There were many of them, and large enough to carry various goods, some straw, others hay, since, as Pierre de L'Étoile told me, there were 100,000 horses in

Paris. Which, when you calculate it, makes one horse for every three inhabitants! Is that not amazing! I imagined that the carting of hay and straw must have been much less dear by river than by road. And yet, I also imagined from what I saw, that sailing required patience and allowance for delays when the wind refused to cooperate, especially given the many curves in the river. As for me, I found the sight of all of these sails quite beautiful, some coloured red, others blue, slipping languidly along the surface; and, in the opposite direction, a series of barges followed the rapid current with nothing but their oars to guide them.

Once past the pleasant little village of Saint-Cloud, on either side of the road the fields and pastures opened up again, and nested here and there in this verdure were little villages, whose labourers crowded on both sides of the road, selling their produce, which only added to the confusion of the traffic of carts and wagons. But what I found quite beautiful in the midst of all this confusion were the many windmills set up on the hills in the distance to the right and left of the road, their turning blades catching the last rays of the setting sun. I thought to myself that these mills had better not stop turning day or night if they wanted to grind enough flour to feed the vast population of this city.

Towards nightfall, we reached the Faubourg Saint-Germain, which didn't appeal to me in the least, being poor and run-down, its streets unpaved and the shadowy figures that haunted them dirty, clothed in rags and mean-looking, walking slowly in front of our horses and darting nasty looks at us as if they wanted to rob or kill us if they could.

We passed by the rich abbey of Saint-Germain-des-Prés, whose walls rose to impressive heights, as if the monks within had wanted to protect their treasures from the covetousness of the villains who swarmed at their feet. The entire abbey struck me as a city within a city, since it was surrounded on every side by so many beautiful buildings. Pierre de L'Étoile explained to me that on the other side of the abbey lay the clerks' meadow, which had been the cause of endless disputes between the monks and the students at the university who had disputed the ownership of these fields from time immemorial. If it hadn't been after six, he would have made a detour to show them to us, since it was in this meadow that the reformers in Paris had first gathered to sing their Psalms, a sign of the frightful persecutions they were later to endure.

Pierre de L'Étoile became so angrily indignant when he talked about these inquisitions that I began to think, despite what he had said earlier, that he harboured secret sympathies for the reformers. I found this very moving and it increased my affection for him more than anything he'd said or done up to that point.

As we talked, and Monsieur de L'Étoile pointed out various out-lying sections of the city he loved so much—even as he repeatedly pointed out its "warts and blemishes" (though I understood later that such a querulous love is shared by most Parisians)—we finally reached the city walls, which, to my great surprise, I found mediocre, paltry, dilapidated and badly maintained.

"Tell me, Monsieur," I gasped, "are these the walls of the great-est city in the kingdom? What a pity to see them in such disrepair! Carcassonne, by contrast, has superlative defences and Montpellier is also well protected by its common wall."

"God bless us! Monsieur de Siorac," hissed Pierre de L'Étoile, suddenly angry again, "you don't know how right you are! For this section of the wall, which runs from the Buccy gate to the Saint-Germain gate, isn't even the worst of it, as bad as it looks! If you only knew what a pitiful state the wall in the Saint-Martin section is, you'd blush, as I do, for the sorry state of the kingdom. Rabelais said of that part of the wall, that if a cow farted nearby, she would demolish an entire section of it! But do you think any effort was made since the divine Rabelais's death to restore this paltry mess? Not a bit of it! We spend much more on the foppish finery of our princes than on the security of their capital!"

We passed the drawbridge at the Buccy gate in a great press of carts and wagons and were obliged to present our safe-conduct passes, which, luckily, Cossolat had delivered to us in Montpellier before our departure from that city, for we had none from Sarlat since Monsieur de La Porte, who was the only one authorized to dispense them, was supposed to be hunting us to throw us in jail.

But the sergeant hardly even looked at them, doubtless because he was so exhausted from the press of humanity that had passed by him, hurrying like madmen to get into the city before they closed these gates for the night.

Oh, reader, what a disappointment! For even though the street we took once we passed through the Buccy gate was straight enough, the houses on either side were so high, so badly aligned, the paving stones so littered with garbage, filth and sewage water, and the air so putrid and dense, that I thought I'd entered a cesspool instead of a great capital.

But I kept my feelings to myself so as to avoid causing pain to my choleric companion, and, on the contrary, as we were passing the church of Saint-André-des-Arts I expressed my admiration for this structure, to which he replied sullenly, as if he were ashamed of the mud our horses were slogging through:

"Certainly it's a beautiful monument, but, like us, it's lodged in all of this filth and garbage. But this is better," he added, as we entered a wide street, lined on both sides by very alluring shops, which were surmounted by very beautiful new houses, all of equal height and all aligned and built of brick and stone. "You will notice, Monsieur de Siorac, how the pavement here has been washed clean: the merchants have kept it so, since they don't wish their customers to be put off by the bitter stench of the city's mud."

"So what's the name of this street?" I asked, amazed.

"It's not a street!" replied L'Étoile, "it's the Pont Saint-Michel!"

"A bridge?" I gasped, thinking he was joking. "But I can't see the Seine!"

"You can't see it since the houses on both sides are hiding it!"

"Well! I don't know what to admire the most," I mused after a moment, "the beautifully joined paving stones, the cleanliness of the gutters or the pink bricks of these houses!"

"In which I'd hate to live!" said L'Étoile, pouting.

"Why ever not, Monsieur?" I asked. "They're so beautiful!"

"Because it's dangerous living over a river that's as turbulent as this one! For the moment, the Seine is in a sweet mood, but in her fury she floods and spares nothing! There's not a bridge in Paris that she hasn't swept away at one time or another, drowning everyone on it. The Pont Notre-Dame was the most recent to go, and before that, the Meuniers! And this very bridge on which you're standing dates roughly from the time I was born, since the previous one collapsed under the water's furious assault some thirty years ago."

Since I didn't feel that the danger was imminent, and there was so much to see in these shops, whose windows were brightly illuminated already, well before nightfall, with candles, I would have been happy to dawdle here—especially since I observed that there were many fine young ladies crowding the pavement who were beautifully dressed and who wore elegant black masks, a sure sign of their noble rank.

"Monsieur de Siorac," cautioned L'Étoile in his most morose and moral tone, "if, as I fear, you have an appetite for the ladies, Huguenot though you may be, you'll have your hands full in this city, which is more corrupt than ancient Babylon, and enjoys such a monstrous reputation that it's enough for a wench from the Île-de-France to spend a few days here for the people of her village to believe that she's lost her virginity. But, I beg you, let us tarry no longer! The rue de la Ferronnerie lies at some distance and, come nightfall, the streets are no longer safe, for there are some streets and alleys in Paris where you'll get your throat cut as soon as the sun sets!"

"You mean the city has no lights?"

"It should. And, by law, they are supposed to be provided by its citizenry. But in Paris, laws often remain dead letters, since Parisians are, by nature, so oppositional. It's the same with the gutters: each house is required to wash the street before it with buckets of water, especially when they discharge their excrement."

"Oh, no! What's this? My head is all wet! It's raining!"

"It's nothing," said L'Étoile, "some housewife has just watered her potted plants. In truth, you'll see these flowerpots full of marjoram and rosemary everywhere in Paris, despite the fact that they're a great annoyance to passers-by and expressly forbidden by royal decree. So you have the choice, Monsieur de Siorac, when you're out walking: you can either walk in the middle of the street bathing your feet with sewage, or walk close to the houses and have your head sprinkled. And it's really not so bad when it's only water. But, I beg you, we must not tarry here! It's getting dark, we should hurry."

We set off at a trot, mostly to please him, since he needn't worry about the thieves of Paris, surrounded as he was by the four of us, all armed to the teeth and packing pistols in our belts. It's a fact, however, that as we were heading along the rue de la Barillerie, which goes by the palace, a monument I would have liked to stop and enjoy, even at dusk, the press of carts had thinned, and from every side I could see people hurrying as if they could think only of getting home and barricading themselves inside.

"What about the watch, Monsieur de L'Étoile?" I panted, surprised to see the Parisians prey to such anguish and terror at the approach of night. "Aren't there any nightwatchmen to protect the workers and inhabitants of the capital?"

"There are two groups," replied L'Étoile, grimacing with a bitter smile. "We're so well defended in this city! Two! One is a made up of bourgeois and artisans who patrol their neighbourhoods and are called 'the sitting guards'—and God knows, they sit! For these hardies spend their time under an archway, throwing dice by lantern light and emptying their flagons—and you can bet they're not going to get off their rears if they hear anyone calling for help. The other group, 'the royal watch', is made up of forty officers on foot and another twenty on horseback. This group can't be accused of sitting—they gallop, since throughout the night they ride around fully armed, always moving and forever useless since, as they are riding on paving stones, they make such a racket that any thieves who may be afoot hide until they've passed and then go back to their work like flies on sugared candy."

"Monsieur de L'Étoile," I said, "as soon as we've greeted Maître Recroche, and if he's indeed willing to lodge us, I plan to escort you immediately to your own house."

"Oh, Monsieur, a thousand thanks," sighed L'Étoile. "What a relief! My lodgings are in the rue Trouvevache but, as close as it is, it would be perilous for me to attempt to go there alone."

This said, we fell silent for a while. Once over the Pont au Change, we rode along the grand'rue Saint-Denis, which had enough mud and filth to fertilize a farm, so different from the rue de la Ferronnerie, where we turned left, another merchants' street whose paving stones were washed clean—although it was, according to L'Étoile, the worst aligned street in the capital, the houses on one side appearing to bump into each other in their attempt to stick out into the street, and with, on the opposite side, a series of shops built as lean-tos into the wall of the Cimetière des Innocents like warts on a hog's back, so that it was a miracle that you could make your way through all of these extravagant projections and protuberances. And I imagined it was even worse when the merchants set out their stalls in the street in front of their shops.

"You might think," said my guide, in the mournful tone that was habitual with him when he spoke of this city, which he cherished despite all its faults, "that you see here an abuse which cries out to be rehabilitated, but you should realize, my friend from Périgord, that in Paris, the more an abuse cries out for reform, the greater its chances of being perpetuated."

I laughed at this witticism, but soon fell silent again, since, out of the corner of my eye, I could see from his expression that he didn't think it was a bit funny and that I should take him seriously.

"What?" I gasped. "If the king says 'I wish it!' they wouldn't fix it?"

"Listen to this," replied L'Étoile bitterly. "Henri II, as he was riding in his royal coach from the Louvre to his house in Tournelles, passed, as always, by the rue de la Ferronnerie. Because of all these projections, warts and excrescences, he was caught up in a tangle of carts so impossible to clear that he was delayed there for an hour, swearing and ranting. When he finally arrived at Tournelles, still fuming, he made an ordinance that required that every structure in the rue de la Ferronnerie that exceeded the proper limit to be demolished within the month. So what do we see, Monsieur de Siorac? Eighteen years later, things are in exactly the same state they were that day."

"But, Monsieur de L'Étoile," I said, open-mouthed, "is this not amazing? Every Huguenot in the kingdom trembles at the very name of Henri II, yet Paris pays him no heed!"

"Well, that's just what I was telling you!" cried L'Étoile. "Paris is a rebel and a renegade and tolerates no restraint or law! She takes herself for the king himself and seeks only her own good pleasure, preferring disorder, tumults and fornication! To make her bend the knee before him, the king would have to twist 300,000 necks one by one!"

"May it not please God to do so!" I laughed. "I'd never want an unpopulated Paris!"

But I wouldn't have laughed if I'd been able to see the future:

Prudens futuri temporis exitum
Caliginosa nocte permit Deus. *

and all of these Parisian encumbrances which made our good L'Étoile gnash his teeth seemed mere fodder for a good laugh to my happy nature. Oh, my good reader! I'm writing this from the vantage of old age, and as I trace these lines thirty-eight—yes, thirty-eight!—years after my arrival in Paris I get a knot in my throat and tears spring to my eyes, since, two months ago, in this same rue de la Ferronnerie, which lack of respect for the royal ordinances left so tortuous and impassable, the royal coach was stopped not by the protuberance of the shops but by an encumbrance of wagons, and an assassin, armed by the zeal of the priests, pierced the noble heart of Henri IV. Ah, what a terrible blow! Oh, misfortune! In my immense grief I cannot imagine how France will ever recover from it!

Pierre de L'Étoile, once he'd dismounted, had to bang loudly on the door and shout Maître Recroche's name repeatedly before an eye appeared though the iron lattice of the peephole and the door was half-opened to admit L'Étoile and myself, but not a soul more, and, as soon as we had squeezed through, our host and Baragran, his assistant, both heavily armed, slammed the door closed in our companions' noses and immediately refastened all the chains and bolts.

"Maître Recroche," began L'Étoile, "I would be extremely grateful if you could provide lodging for these three gentlemen friends of mine and their valet and horses. Monsieur de Siorac is a medical doctor and the younger son of a baron from Périgord."

---

* "God in His wisdom hides under a mantle of darkness the events of the future."

To this, Maître Recroche shook his head, but answered not a word or a grunt. He appeared to me as much dwarf as full-grown man, with lustreless, dirty, greying hair and cheeks that were pale and pockmarked; he was adorned in a ragged greenish doublet, wore no ruff collar, but a dirty flat one, and had very long, spidery arms (short as he was) and a vulture's hooked nose.

Telling his assistant to hold the candle high, he silently looked me over, his little bright-blue eyes shining as if he were weighing us (my purse and me) to the nearest ounce.

"Maître Recroche, did you hear me?" asked L'Étoile.

"Quite well, Monsieur. But baba!" (And what he meant by this "baba", which he stuck in here and there, I could not fathom, and wonder if he himself knew, having the extravagance to invent words at will, and to use ten where one would have sufficed, perhaps consoling himself for his miserliness by this copious verbal expenditure.) "Baba, Monsieur, I don't offer chambers, it's beneath me."

"Of course! Of course!" said L'Étoile with more grace than I would have expected from his atrabilious nature. "But, on the other hand, you have chambers!"

"Baba, chambers! Chamber-ettes! Mini-chambers! Nothing that could accommodate this gallant gentleman!"

And here he tried to make a sort of bow to me, by lowering his head and making a sweeping gesture with his long arm, and that this salutation was done more out of pure form than civility I was convinced by L'Étoile, who knew the man, and I frowned angrily, but didn't give ground, and returned his bow with a like degree of stiffness.

"This gallant gentleman," returned L'Étoile, "has no place to sleep."

"Baba, that's different," conceded Maître Recroche, scratching his nose with a very dirty fingernail. "If the gentleman has no place to sleep and is, in addition, a friend of yours, we must accommodate him, must we not, even if it's with a micro-chamber. But can I do this? There's the rub!"

"I beseech you, Maître Recroche," said L'Étoile, who appeared to be working so hard at maintaining his patience that sweat was dripping from his brow. "I beg you! Decide! It's getting very late!"

"Decide!" stalled Maître Recroche. "Baba! That's sooner said than done! The chamber-ettes I'm referring to are only big enough for two and there are four of these gentlemen."

"Then we'll sleep two to a room," I conceded.

"Baba," returned Maître Recroche, "the thing is, the beds in these rooms are scarcely wide enough for one!"

"But we'll have to fit two in a bed," I said.

"Not on your life!" gasped Maître Recroche. "Two big men like yourselves would surely break these little bedlets!"

"Whatever is broken we'll pay for," I parried.

"Well said!" agreed Maître Recroche as if to himself, running his right index finger along his nose. "I can imagine things working out with this lodger, if I lodge him. However, Monsieur de Siorac," he countered, "the window is agonizingly small and is covered in oil paper rather than glass."

"Then I'll open it."

"Don't you dare! It overlooks the Cimetière des Innocents, whose soil gives off such poisonous vapours that they'll eat up your flesh within nine days! Why, the night air is so sulphurous and gaseous that it sets off will-o'-the-wisps!"

"Maître Recroche," I demanded, "name your price!"

"All right, if I must!" sighed Maître Recroche with a nasty glint in his little blue eyes. "Venerable medical doctor," because you are the friend of Monsieur de L'Étoile, I will charge you a mere three écus for the three of you for the month, whether you stay the month or not."

"Three écus for two chamber-ettes!" cried L'Étoile, raising his arms heavenward.

"Nay! Nay! You're mistaken!" corrected Recroche with a benign air. "I mean three écus per mini-chamber, and one sol per day for each horse, but you must pay for your own hay."

"Six écus!" cried L'Étoile. "That's highway robbery! Lower your price!"

"Baba!" replied Recroche. "Highway robbery? The problem is that there is a great demand for rooms in Paris now. What can I do? I have to live. My chamber-ettes are more in demand than palaces in Poland and I offer them to this gentleman only out of my great love for you!"

"I thank God and I thank you for your generous sentiments," said L'Étoile through closed lips.

"That's six écus in freshly minted coins, hard cash and paid in advance," said Maître Recroche, lowering his eyes humbly, yet speaking in very harsh tones.

We had to summon Samson, and push him very hard before he would consent to disburse such a sum for lodging and stables. This done, the assistant Baragran, carrying a bright lantern and riding pillion behind Miroul, accompanied us, while, with swords drawn, we took Pierre de L'Étoile to his lodgings and returned, dead tired, our arses aching from so many hours in the saddle. But the physical pain was nothing compared to the pain we felt at being so badly and dearly lodged ourselves.

"Maître Recroche," I enquired, once our horses were stabled and fed, "might you have some wine to offer us before we bed down?"

"Baba! Some wine?" simpered Recroche, raising his long arms. "You'll not find a drop of wine, vinegar or spirits of any kind in this house! Thank God, no one in this house imbibes! It's too costly a luxury!"

"Water, then!"

"Baba! Water! Do you think my water is like the air you breathe? It's not that vile water from the Seine that they serve in Parisian taverns, water tainted with enough offal, piss and all kinds of filth to give you diarrhoea that would kill you! My water is drawn from my well, pure of mud, gravel, sea salt or sulphur."

"In short, it's water. I assume we must pay for it, Maître Recroche?"

"But of course!" trumpeted Maître Recroche, rubbing his nose. "It will cost you one sol a day for the four of you and two sols for your horses."

"At that price, I assume you allow us to bathe!"

"Who do you take me for?" gulped Maître Recroche indignantly. "The Duc d'Anjou? We have no bathing basin in this house, nor any wood to heat one. You must go to the public bathhouses like everyone else in Paris."

Having said this, he led us into a large room, which he called his workshop, where, by the light of two candles, his assistant, Baragran, a maid of about my age and a boy of about fifteen were sitting in a circle sewing, the poor lad yawning to break his jawbones he was so sleepy.

"Wait for me here," said Recroche, "I'll fetch your water."

"What's this, friend?" I said to Baragran once the master had left. "You're working by candlelight?"

The assistant, who had a square face, broad shoulders and hands that looked like they could strangle a bull, at first said not a word in response, appearing to be entirely consumed by his efforts to thread a needle with his thick fingers. Which he succeeded in managing, to my great surprise, without a hitch.

"Gotta live," he mumbled at last.

"Listen to that!" mocked the girl, raising her nose. "This fat parrot stupidly repeats every word his master utters!"

"Go easy there, Alizon!" snarled Baragran.

This Alizon, who, since our entrance, had kept one eye on her work (she was sewing a bonnet) and one eye on us, was as lively, light and dark-skinned as a fly in hell and her speech seemed more concise and to the point than any I'd heard that day.

"Am I a fish that I shouldn't say what I think?" she continued. "I have only my mouth to comfort me in my distress!"

"Quiet down, silly hen! Who keeps you alive, if not our master?"

"That shit-for-brains," she hissed back. "It's we who keep him alive! I don't know whether I'm alive or dead I work so hard for him! It's all right to put needle to cloth from dawn to dusk! But at night! When am I supposed to sleep? Even his mule gets to sleep! Am I less than a mule?"

She said this as if convulsed in anger and yet she never missed a stitch, and it was marvellous to watch the agile velocity of her fingers as she spoke, all the while throwing looks at us that would have awoken the dead.

"'Sblood!" cried Baragran. "If the Baronne des Tourelles insists on having her bonnets ready at dawn before she leaves for the country, isn't it our job to satisfy her?"

"No! No! And No!" Alizon burst out, her black curls shaking furiously. "We should have refused to work at night! I told you, but you wouldn't listen, you big idiot!"

"You stupid ninny!" snapped Baragran. "Am I one of those saboteurs who band together, stop their work, ruin the master's business? D'you think I want to end up unemployed and without a crust of bread like I was before?"

"You've got no balls and fewer brains!" seethed Alizon, drawing herself up on her stool (to show off her figure, I guessed). "Our master is not so easily ruined, but you'll be dead long before he is!"

"I'm not afraid of work," said Baragran proudly, though his

reddened eyes and hollow cheeks seemed eloquent evidence of his adversary's point.

"Maybe not, but you've got nothing but bull's fat between your ears! What's life worth if it's spent on fattening up our master?"

As she was saying this, Maître Recroche returned, carrying two pots of water that were so small that I would have called them, in his particular parlance, potlets or mini-pots. 'Sblood, they economized even on water in this house, even though it was free and not produced though the sweat of other people.

"The master isn't so fat, you chatterbox!" he said in a way that made it clear he'd been listening at the door, though he said this more in jest than in anger.

"He's fat in coins," proclaimed Alizon, "and no one's going to take him down a peg! He gives little to those who serve him!"

"What!" cried Recroche, pretending to be offended. "Baragran, don't I give you six sols, ten deniers a day? Isn't that fair wages in Paris?"

"Yes, master," interjected Baragran.

"Aren't you happy!"

"Yes, master," conceded Baragran.

"Yes, master! Yes, master!" mimicked Alizon, her black eyes throwing flames. "Did you ever see such a ridiculous, flat-footed arse-kisser? What about me, Maître Recroche? I work every bit as much and as hard as this imbecilic lice-picker and I'm a trained bonnet-designer whereas he's only a cap-maker, so did you ask me if I'm happy with my three sols, five deniers? Ask me so I can tell you directly!"

"What can I do?" whined Maître Recroche, as he scratched his nose. "It's the custom to pay a wench half of what a man makes."

"That works out well for you!" sniffed Alizon.

"My friend," Recroche observed, "if I really wanted to accommodate myself, I'd lay off Baragran" (at which his assistant jerked up his head, eyes filled with fear) "and hire another wench."

"Ah, no you wouldn't! You'd be scared that the two wenches, having such stinking wages, would join together to protest against your miserliness and refuse to work!"

"Now, now, Alizon," said Maître Recroche, frowning, "let's have no talk of protests here, or I'll throw you out in the street! It's a crime forbidden by the doctors and lawyers!"

"And so is working all night by royal ordinance!"

"Baba! Royal ordinances!" sneered Recroche, with a shrug of his shoulders. "Hey, Coquillon, my friend!" he said, shaking the young apprentice. "Wake up and get that needle going! The baronne is expecting her bonnets at dawn!"

"Now here's one who likes to laze about," teased Baragran, "and have his work done by others!"

"That's because he's the son of a master," Alizon added bitterly, "and is so spoilt that, after three years as an apprentice, what does he know? Nothing! Couldn't make a man's hat, or a square bonnet in fine linen, nor yet a velvet professor's cap! And you can bet he'll be promoted to master by the guild with or without any creative work."

"Go to with your jealousy!" sneered Maître Recroche. "It's Providence who decides whether we'll be born rich or poor, and she must be respected. Good gentlemen," he continued, turning towards us, "please to follow me and I'll show you your micro-chambers."

Oh, reader! The miser wasn't lying, for whatever terms he used to describe his lodgings were all too generous given the two cramped bowels of chambers that awaited us, which each contained only the narrowest of beds, an uneven table, a tiny washbasin, a stool and nothing else. The floorboards were badly joined, and even more badly planed, squeaking loudly at the slightest step, and the walls and ceiling were so dirty and encrusted that you would have thought that a million flies had blackwashed them with their faeces. And for the "windowlet", roughly the size of a handkerchief, it opened not onto the cemetery, which at least would have assured us some peace and quiet, but onto the rue de la Ferronnerie and, beyond that, the tombs of the Innocents. I could see its crosses shining lugubriously, lit by the light of the moon, which was full and beautiful, and which illuminated right in front of the windowlet a hawthorn that had grown over the cemetery wall, thanks to the plentiful fertilizer provided by the fat of those buried therein. As for the air, it was hardly as noxious as Maître Recroche had claimed, but it was nevertheless bitter, verging on putrid.

"Don't go claiming I didn't warn you!" gloated Maître Recroche. "These little chamberlings are not palaces, after all! It used to be that I could provide free lodgings to my companions. But the judges and magistrates forbid these practices, yet didn't raise our prices for the other rooms, which caused us great penury! Messieurs," he said with a trace of a bow in which we could feel the scorn of the thief for his victims, "I wish you goodnight. You will be well sheltered here from the inclemency of the weather and the perils of the hooligans of Paris."

"Might you not," I observed as he withdrew, "allow us a bit of light?"

"Alas, I cannot," whined Recroche, "I do not offer candles to my lodgers."

"I'll pay you, then!"

"That will be two sols," murmured Recroche, his eyes modestly lowered.

"Two sols for a candle!" cried Samson, whom I'd never seen so heated and angry. "Two sols! That's robbery!"

"And so I'm a thief, am I?" snarled Recroche, spinning around as if he'd been stung by a wasp and sneering in derision. "In that case, I refuse to lodge you, Messieurs, and that's final. Prices correspond to need. Don't buy things if you think they're too costly, but I'll not tolerate these nasty and egregious accusations!"

"What a perfect scoundrel," I mused. "He not only wants to rob us, he demands respect for doing so!" However, I grabbed Samson forcibly by the arm, pulled him to one side and said, "Pay no attention to my younger brother. I'm the one who does the bargaining. The price named is the price we'll pay. Give me the candle, if you please. Here are your two sols. Maître Recroche, with all due respect, I bid you goodnight."

This said, I made him a bow as perfunctory as the one he'd given us, which had the desired chilling effect: he turned on his heels and went down the stairs without a word—and without light either, for I slammed the door behind him, leaving him in total darkness. 'Sblood! This candle was ours and we'd paid dearly for it, including the flame!

"Samson," I said, "you will share a room with *maestro* Giacomi and I with Miroul."

Samson's displeasure at this arrangement was quite evident, and seeing his reaction, Giacomi (who clearly understood the reason for my choice) hastened to announce in his exquisite Italian and with great delicacy, "I have already shared a bed with Miroul and will be happy to do so now."

"Not a bit of it! It shall be as I've decided."

And giving a warm embrace to my gentle Samson, I pushed him towards the other micro-chamber; seeing which, he asked with his inimitable lisp, "My brother, have I cauthed you thome dithpleathure?"

"Not at all!"

"Then why don't you share my bed?"

"Because Miroul is thinner than you."

This explanation seemed entirely to satisfy him, naive as he was. But seeing that Giacomi had not followed us and that we were alone, he whispered awkwardly, "Did you ask Dame Béqueret…"

"Of course!" I replied, secretly happy, and raising the candle the better to see his face.

"And what did she say?"

"That she knew her."

"Ah!" he sighed with a most delicious smile, which almost immediately gave way to a look of deepest chagrin. "These are sinful thoughts, are they not?"

"Then think them without thinking about them!" I laughed, and partly in jest and partly with deep emotion, I embraced him again. "Giacomi," I called, "your bedfellow is waiting for you!"

Giacomi gave me a big, friendly smile, but said not a word, so tired was he. Leaving him the candle, I went to lean on the windowsill of my micro-chamber and contemplate the Cimetière des Innocents bathed in moonlight. "Well," I thought, nearly dead from fatigue, and thoroughly disgusted by our lodgings, "is this where I'll end up at the conclusion of my earthly voyage, in one of these little tombs?"

My present shelter is hardly the smallest or darkest of all those I shall doubtless have to occupy.

"Monsieur," said Miroul, as though he could feel my melancholy, "don't let it eat away at you! You'll get to see Madame Angelina as soon as you've found out her address."

How he knew, before I even suspected it, that she was the reason for my deepest worries, I'll never know. But banishing this thought as soon as I understood it, I said goodnight to Samson, who, having undressed, was bringing me the candle. I undressed as well and was going to throw myself on my bed when there was a knock at the door. Thinking it was Maître Recroche again, I went to open it, naked as I was, with a candle in my hand.

"Oh! Good Monsieur! And handsome at that!" said Alizon, not a bit embarrassed to see me naked as Adam. "If you've done with the candle, might I beg it of you? If I have to work for three sols with but one I'll ruin my eyes."

"What? Your master didn't give you the other one?"

"No, he took the other to bed with him."

"Oh, you poor girl, he sold us your candle!"

"Nasty vulture!" hissed Alizon. "He'd shave an egg!"

At which I laughed, never having heard anything like it in Périgord.

"Begging your pardon, Monsieur. I wish you goodnight."

"What?" I gasped. "You don't want the candle?"

"No, Monsieur! Not if it's yours!"

"Alizon, it's yours. I don't need it to sleep by."

"But Monsieur, I'll burn it down to nothing and you'll have nothing to light you at dawn."

"Go ahead, take it! No need for ceremony."

"Oh, Monsieur, I thank you," gushed Alizon making a deep bow. "I'll remember this sweet gift. And if I dared at this time of night, I'd give you a kiss."

"Oh, go ahead, my friend!" I laughed, offering her my cheek, on which she deposited a chaste little kiss and then fled, candle in hand, down the stairs as nimbly as you please.

"Monsieur," smiled Miroul as soon as I'd closed the door, "you've made a new friend!"

"And you," I answered with some spite, "another in Montfort-l'Amaury."

"Ha! Monsieur, are you still upset about that?"

"Not at all," I lied, "now come to bed you rascal, enough tarrying! I'm exhausted."

"Monsieur, I shan't. As thin as I am, I'd take up too much room. I'll sleep on the floor."

"I wouldn't hear of it! It's all rough planking! Get in the bed! I order you!"

He obeyed, but towards the middle of the night when I had to get up to relieve myself, I saw by the light of the moon that he was sleeping on the floor as he'd told me he would.

*

I slept very fitfully on that hard bed, dreaming that I was being chased down the grand'rue Saint-Denis by a hoard of monks who, brandishing their cutlasses, were making ear-splitting cries: "Kill the heretic, kill him!"—while I struggled through the mud, my head the target of buckets of piss that the housewives were emptying into the street. When I opened my eyes, I was soaked in sweat, and through the open window I could see pink clouds announcing the new day. As I got up, I gave Miroul a tap with my foot and he immediately seized the knife in his belt (for he'd slept with his clothes on), and cried, "What's this? Who dares attack my master?"

His dream was so much the brother of mine that I couldn't help laughing, which helped chase away my phantoms and improve my spirits. And feeling refreshed and full of renewed energy, I went over to the washstand to tip the mini-pot into the washbasin which I had to call the micro-basin in Recroche's language, it was so small, and poured out enough of this expensive liquid to sprinkle my face, hands, armpits and chest. After which, donning my leggings, chemise and doublet, I said to Miroul, "Miroul, go saddle our horses. As we say in Périgord, he who rises early gets to piss where he wants. As the sun rises, we'll have the streets to ourselves and we can find an inn where we can eat some bread and meat, for I'm hungry as a bear!"

"And what about your brothers? Should I wake them as well?"

"No, no. *Bene dormit qui non sentit quam male dormiat.** Let's let these dormice laze about in their nest and we'll sally forth by ourselves. I'll wait for you in the workshop downstairs."

I went down and found Baragran, Alizon and Coquillon, all sitting on the floor, their arms and legs akimbo, all three deep in sleep—but my footsteps awakened Alizon, who opened one eye and only one quarter of her mouth when she spoke. There were no bonnets visible,

---

* "He sleeps well who isn't aware he's sleeping badly."

and so I surmised that Maître Recroche had gone to deliver them to the Baronne des Tourelles. As I looked around for my candle and found no evidence of it, I concluded that the miser had put it under lock and key before leaving.

"Oh, Monsieur," moaned Alizon, "is it you? I'm dead tired and my eyes are blurry. How would I have managed without your candle?"

"Go back to sleep, sweet Alizon," I soothed, "I'm going out to find something to eat, since I'm hungry as a dog who hasn't eaten for days. Where can I find something to eat around here?"

"There are several inns, but not one will be open yet," she said, looking out of the window. "It's too early. You might try one of the street vendors as you go along, since some will be selling leftovers, or a baker his pies, but for God's sake, Monsieur, be careful not to drink a drop of the Seine water that's hawked by these merchants! It's poison for anyone not from here, though for us Parisians from Paris, there's no danger." (And, exhausted as she was, you would have thought, to hear her claim with such pride that she was a "Parisian from Paris", that she was of noble birth.)

"I'm very grateful for the warning, Alizon!"

But her eyes had already closed and she fell back into a sleep that I knew, alas, would be interrupted by the return of Maître Recroche. I thought to myself how wonderful it would be if her master were to encounter some unfortunate accident that would delay his return until after the noon hour. Happily, as I learnt later, Providence had heard my prayer.

Once we were mounted and on our way, my valet asked me for the translation of the Latin phrase that I'd cited regarding my brothers' sleep. I provided it and he found the sentence so much to his liking that he repeated it over and over to himself until he'd learnt it by heart. My gentle Miroul was so enamoured of languages, whether Italian (he was constantly asking questions of Giacomi), French, which he spoke moderately well, or Cicero's tongue, with which he'd gained some familiarity from hearing me discuss medicine with my colleagues in Montpellier.

And from all these crumbs, which he gathered and put into piles, and from which he'd constructed a smattering of knowledge, my Miroul managed to understand some Latin phrases, such as the one my father used when he'd given me Little Sissy, saying, "*Ne sit ancillae formosae amor pudori.*"*

And so, reader, if you're wondering to what use he put these bits of language, I'd say that he used them in the same way—*mutatis mutandis*—that, as students of medicine, we used them to impress our patients. And so Miroul loved to strut his linguistic stuff in front of various chambermaids he was courting, hoping to appear well educated to advance his cause. I often enjoyed, at one inn or another, hearing one of the maids whisper in the corner angle of a staircase, "What, Miroul, you speak Latin?"

"It's my duty! Am I not the aide and assistant of a venerable doctor of medicine, or, so to speak, *il suo braccio destro*?"†

"What's that?"

"Italian."

"Oh, Miroul, you speak Italian too?"

"Passably well," Miroul would answer, with appropriate modesty, "and also a bit of Parisian French."

But this French would have served him only in Provence, for he could never have got away with it in Paris, where the girls would have mercilessly mocked his awkward attempts to speak their beautiful language. And yet he wasn't in the capital more than two weeks before he was impressing me, given the progress his ear for languages and

---

*   "Don't be ashamed to love a pretty serving girl."

†   "His right arm."

his ready tongue had made, with his remarkable successes with the fairer sex, bearing in mind how much sweet nothings open the way to more physical expressions of love.

But I would be unfair to my good valet if I led you to believe that his only interest in language was for the uses I've just mentioned. He was naturally given to learning, and possessed a ready mind that quickly absorbed both language and the rudiments of science and dissection.

But to continue my tale: as we left Maître Recroche's lodgings at daybreak, I had brought along a letter addressed to Monsieur de Nançay, captain of the royal guards, with whom my father had served at Calais under the Duc de Guise, requesting his help in gaining admission to the Louvre in order to present my petition to the king that had been drafted by Monsieur de Montaigne. But it was much too early in the morning to visit this gentleman, who lodged on the Île de la Cité and, since the cathedral of Notre-Dame was also situated on this island, I resolved, after breaking our fast, to go to visit this marvel.

And so we headed down towards the Seine on the grand'rue Saint-Denis, which, early as it was, was not yet encumbered by wagons, but was nevertheless as noisy as a carnival, for a countless number of peddlers went about, crying their wares in the grand'rue and the adjoining streets, wearing baskets at their waists that were suspended from their necks and contained all the necessities of their shops, each one chanting simple verses to attract the housewives who, still bleary-eyed from sleep, their hair barely done up, a wrap thrown hastily over their shoulders, were half-opening their doors to call to them. "Isn't it amazing," I mused, "that in Paris there's a whole range of commodities and in such plenty that you don't even need to go outside your house to buy them, but they're brought practically to your bedside, as if these common folk of Paris were so many princes that were being zealously served?"

For the entire month that I was in Paris, I heard these lively, babbling peddlers hawking water, milk, matches, scouring pads for your dishes, bottle brushes, boot polish, chalk to wash your linen, needles, brooms of holly, kettles, rat traps, flint and guns, salt, baskets, new almanacs (containing "good predictions"), "nice red wine", "beautiful glasses", straw, anise, wooden stools, kitchen knives, and, no doubt, anything that can be eaten on this wide earth—including large condiments for your too-small cucumber and whale blubber to enhance your potency, whose crier advertised prudently:

> *"Here's sweet meat for Lent,*
> *Helps love's merriment!"*

And on this morning, as giddy as I felt from all of these chants, which made such a great chorus on all sides, I was brought up short by the sight of a convoy approaching us, bearing a body to the Cimetière des Innocents, and led by a fellow dressed in black, who was called the "ringer of the bodies" in Paris, and went ahead of the priest, ringing his bell and crying:

> *"Now say your prayers, my friend,*
> *When you hear me ring my bell.*
> *This brother was most honourable*
> *Whose life has reached its end."*

Miroul and I both made the sign of the cross as they passed, very happy to feel so alive and so happy as we rode along on this Parisian morning. And yet I said sotto voce a paternoster for this "brother", however papistical he may have been in his blind life.

"Amen for this poor idolater," echoed Miroul when the convoy had passed, "and may God take pity on his errors. Monsieur, with your permission, I'm hungry! I have such a strident hunger that a mere crust would satisfy me! *Jejunus raro stomachus vulgaria temnet.*"*

"*Temnit*, Miroul."

"*Temnit*. Thank you, Monsieur, for correcting me. That's a very useful quotation. I can say it at least twice a day in our current lodgings!"

I laughed to have such a worthy valet, who was so silly and so diverting, but I had to keep my ears open to the various street cries so as not to miss a peddler of meat. Seeing me listening so attentively, a water carrier bearing a leathern bottle on his back and a collection of shining tin goblets attached to his belt, came up chanting:

> *"Who wants some water, who craves a sip?*
> *It's one of four elements you cannot pass by.*
> *No one can do without a drop or a drip!*
> *Believe me, for surely I dare not tell a lie!"*

"Good gentleman," said this exceptionally portly fellow, whose stomach stuck as far out in front as his water skin stretched out behind, "will you have some of my water? You can drink it without peril: I don't get it from the place Maubert or from the Pont Saint-Michel."

"And why not in either of those places?"

"Because there it's stagnant, foul and dank."

"So where do you get it?"

"Opposite the Île Louviers, which is to say outside of Paris and upstream from the city."

I suspect that he was lying, but even if he'd spoken the truth I would have refused. I excused myself by saying that I drank only wine, but for his poem I threw him a small coin, which he received with barely a word of thanks, so put out was he that I disdained his water.

---

* "An empty stomach rarely rejects vulgar food."

"Monsieur," cried Miroul, "here comes a more substantial meal!" And he pointed to a fellow emerging from the rue des Lavandières, who was wearing a white cap, from under which there protruded a head of flame-red hair, and who, opening a mouth as wide as an oven, cried:

> *"See me for it's the finest pastries I've got,*
> *For Gautier, Michaud or Guillaume;*
> *Every morning I'm out selling some,*
> *So get your pastries and your pies while they're hot!"*

"Friend," I cried, reining in Pompée, "come over here! For we're some of the patrons you're seeking, though we're not named Gautier, Michaud or Guillaume! But why these names, good man?"

"'Sfor the rhyme," said the peddler, heading over to us, but being unusually careful since on the flat basket that hung from a cord around his neck and was supported by both hands, he carried a stack of his merchandise covered by a clean napkin that he suddenly pulled away to reveal a bewitching assortment of golden baked pastries that were still smoking hot and smelt heavenly.

"'Sblood, Monsieur!" gushed Miroul. "I can scarcely keep from drooling!"

"Shush, Miroul!" I hissed in *langue d'oc*. "If you go talking about drooling, he'll charge us double."

"Noble gentleman," said our pieman, whose face was as round and golden from his oven fires as his wares, "if you are very hungry, as I guess you are from your looks, I'd like to recommend my hot pies."

"Well, I'm not Michaud, but how much?"

"Nor a Jew must you be, Monseigneur, for these are pork pies!"

"I am a Christian. How much is one of your pies for a poor Christian?"

"Three deniers."

"What! Three deniers for a meat pie?"

"No bargaining! Though you're from Provence, if my ear is right, I'm giving you the Parisian price."

"Nay! What would you say to four pies for eight deniers?"

"I'd say no! Fie, then, Monsieur! A gentleman bargaining like a Lombard!"

"And how do you know I'm a gentleman?"

"By your horse, Monsieur, who is very beautiful."

"You're mistaken, I'm on my way to sell it to buy some hay."

"Monsieur, you jest! But just to oblige you, I'll give you four pies for ten deniers. Take it, it's my last offer."

"Sold. Here are some nice clean coins."

"And here are your hot pies. Monseigneur, be careful that no one steals your horse while you're visiting Paris!"

"My valet will guard it for me!"

"He looks pretty skinny to me."

"I'll be less so," said Miroul, "when I've eaten your pies! By the belly of St Anthony, I'm drooling all over my doublet!"

I gave him two of the pies and began devouring two of the others, which had delicious thick crusts and whose succulent contents did very well at calming my vehement hunger.

"Well!" laughed the pieman. "Don't you have sharp teeth! Eat up! Eat up! You can only get pies like this in Paris and in Paris mine are the best! My good gentleman, I wish you good day with all my heart, and may the Blessed Virgin watch over you—unless, being from the south, you're a heretic."

"No more than you, good pieman!" I said as clearly as my full mouth would allow.

And off he went down the grand'rue Saint-Denis.

"No doubt," I said, trying not to devour too quickly but to taste all the hot unctuousness of the crust and innards of my pie, "no doubt I'm only one of thousands of hungry people served by this pieman, but Miroul, did you hear that scoundrel? Being from the south, we're immediately suspected of heresy and just as quickly scorned. 'Sblood! He's the heretic!"

"Monsieur," spluttered Miroul through his mouthfuls of pie, "the stronger and more numerous decide who's the heretic. Us in Nîmes, the papists in Paris."

"You speak with golden tongue, Miroul!" I joked. "I'll have you promoted to 'doctor of good sense'. Hail that buxom girl peddling milk I see over there. Call her! I've got no voice left!"

"Dairy maid!" yelled Miroul though a mouthful of pie. "Over here, I beg you!"

At which the blonde girl turned round and headed our way carrying her two pots, each hanging from a kind of yoke she bore, which forced her to stand very straight, a posture that was much to her advantage! She danced towards us, despite the shouldered dairy, with a light step, chanting in her warbling voice:

> *"Every morn, when light comes streaming,*
> *I cry out 'Milk!' for all the nurses*
> *Whose babes are now awake and screaming,*
> *Saying: 'Quick! Give 'em a pot, you nurses!'"*

And, on a higher note, she would repeat "Give 'em a pot!" her tremulous voice emphasizing the *o* in pot. The little chant wasn't very sophisticated, the poet finding only "nurses" to rhyme with "nurses", but I was enchanted both by the voice and by the maid.

"My friend," I called, "even though I'm no longer in swaddling clothes, will you give me some of your milk?"

"Good gentleman, I cannot," she replied, with a saucy eye, "I have pots but no goblets since I sell direct to people's lodgings and not to passers-by."

"Oh, good dairy maid, if only you were a young mother, I know where I'd get my milk!"

She laughed, pretending to be shocked, but couldn't help looking at her bosom with evident pride.

"Well, Monsieur," she answered, "clearly they'll take it hot or cold in the provinces where you come from, but here we behave like civilized folk!"

"I'd mind my manners better," I replied, "if I weren't so thirsty. But who wouldn't pardon an old drunk who drinks directly from his flask?"

Just then, someone hailed her from one of the nearby houses and off she went with her dancing step, balancing her shop on her shoulders, but she threw me a look that told me to wait and that she'd come back. I couldn't help admiring her beauty as she went, warbling her street cry in such pure and sweet tones: "Quick! Give 'em a pot, you nurses!"

"Monsieur," Miroul asked, "what did she mean by 'They'll take it hot or cold'?"

"That they don't fear anything or anyone, I suppose. These Parisians have their own jargon, just as we do."

"But it's very nice to listen to, coming from her! Monsieur, shall I ask her to meet us somewhere?"

"Wait a bit. You haven't seen anything yet, Miroul. *Quod coelom stellas, tot habet tua Roma puellas.*"*

Of course I translated this Latin verse for him, whose meaning and words pleased him enormously.

Meanwhile, our blonde milkmaid danced back to us, holding in her right hand a goblet she'd borrowed from one of her regulars, for which I offered my profuse thanks and compliments. I drank two servings, and Miroul as well, all of which cost only one denier. I gave her two, and with a smile she said, "My gentlemen, if you want to find me again, I'll be

---

* "Rome has as many girls as the sky has stars."

in this street every day at the same time." And, saying this, she was off again, chanting in her clear voice, "Quick! Give 'em a pot, you nurses!"

Ah, reader, I never saw this pretty country lass again, who so lightly danced along the muddy streets of Paris selling her milk for a few sols—a small profit for so long a trek from her village to our Babylon—but in my memory I can see her just as clearly and with the same pleasure as on that day: her bright eyes, her blonde curls, her pretty bosom and, more than anything, that marvellously delectable smile by which she seemed to open both body and soul to the unquenchable joy of being alive among the living. Indeed, I cannot think of Paris, which was to fix indelibly in my memory of those days of late August such gruesome impressions, without recalling that sweet milkmaid with her nimble step and her sunny smile.

Monsieur de Nançay lived in the rue des Sablons on the Île de la Cité, and though it was still too early to visit him, I asked directions from a Guillaume or a Gautier whom we happened to pass, to be sure to arrive there quickly after visiting Notre-Dame. This fellow, I deemed from his dress and his bumptious and stupid expression, must be a shop assistant, and he answered my request for directions with a yawn, and, though I was on horseback and he on foot, looked me up and down and said indignantly, "What, Monsieur! You don't know the rue des Sablons?"

"Would I be asking you if I did?"

"But, Monsieur, everyone knows where the rue des Sablons is!"

"Perhaps, but I've just arrived from Périgord."

"Périgord," he said even more haughtily. "Never heard of such a country."

"That's because it's not a country but a province of our kingdom."

"A province, Monsieur?" cried this brazen-faced Gautier, with utter disdain. "You live in the provinces? Oh, heaven! How does one live in the provinces?"

"Better than in Paris."

"But, Monsieur! That's not possible! Only an ass would be content to live in the country!"

"Monsieur," whispered Miroul in *langue d'oc*, "should I give this rascal a good kick?"

"What's that?" cried this Guillaume. "What's that gobbledygook you're babbling? What did he say?"

"He said," I replied archly, "that he's going to give you a good kick in the arse for your impertinence."

"Oh, Monsieur, no offence was intended!" the fellow cried, quite crestfallen. And he quickly added, "At the Grand Châtelet, turn to the left, and take the Port-au-Foin. Then cross the river on the Pont Notre-Dame and go straight on. The rue des Sablons will be on your left. You can't miss it. The Hôtel-Dieu is there, and Notre-Dame."

"Thank you, good peasant," I replied.

"What!" he cried, as though wounded to the quick. "Why do you call me a peasant?"

"Because," I answered, "you've never left your village and you know nothing of what's outside it."

Hearing this, and doubtless believing me to be some madman fallen from the moon, the fellow hurried off, casting terrified looks behind him. With a laugh, Miroul and I turned our horses in the direction he'd indicated and headed towards the Pont Notre-Dame.

When I'd got to know Paris better, I realized a strange and absurd thing about this city that is traversed by a wide river. The right bank was lined with a quay that runs uninterrupted from the Louvre to the Célestins convent. The left bank had no quay except at the Tour de Nesle and at the Pont Saint-Michel, and the latter was only a dozen or so years old and replaced a plantation of willow trees which ran right down to the water. Everywhere else the banks were earthworks that sloped down to the river, which meant that at high tide the river occasionally burst its banks so far that, in 1571 for example—according to what I've been told—you had to take a boat to cross the place Maubert.

As for the quay on the right bank along which we were riding, it was not much to behold. It was part masonry, part wood, but both parts looked to have been hastily and grossly thrown together, hardly worthy of the heavy traffic of hay, straw and wood that it supported. On the other hand, the Pont Notre-Dame, onto which we mounted, left me open-mouthed in admiration. It was so beautiful and so wide that three wagons could cross together, and it was lined, like the Pont Saint-Michel, with houses of matching heights, constructed of brick and stone, lined up evenly, and each having a number from one to sixty-eight, a novelty that should be extended throughout Paris since it's so difficult, even when you know the name of the street, to find a friend's particular lodging—especially at night, when everyone has withdrawn behind locked doors and is unwilling to open up or even to give directions. It's even worse for the delivery of letters, for addresses can look like the following:

MONSIEUR GUILLAUME DE MORMOULET
Nobleman
Rue de la Ferronnerie in Paris
The house is situated four houses to the right of a house with
hawthorn bushes opposite the Cimetière des Innocents.

Isn't it an incredible bore (and one that is a source of infinite indiscretions) to be obliged in broad daylight to ask a man's neighbours where his dwelling might be, thereby exposing oneself to the unbridled gossip of the Parisians?—as I was to experience that morning in the rue des Sablons, where, having dismounted, I knocked on the door of a beautiful mansion to ask where Monsieur de Nançay might be found.

A chambermaid opened the door, and, having heard my request, went straightaway to find a governess, who, having heard my query, disappeared in search of the daughter of the house, who, rather than answering any more than the first two, looked askance at me and said, "Monsieur, what strange French is this you're speaking? And where did you acquire this bizarre doublet you're wearing, which is so far from being in fashion here?"

"Madame, I am from Périgord, and my doublet, which, I regret, is not to your liking, was made in Montpellier by Monsieur de Joyeuse's tailor. Might I enquire, Madame, where I might find Monsieur de Nançay?"

"Montpellier?" she replied, opening her beautiful eyes wide in surprise. "Where is this mountain, then?"

"It's a city, Madame, near the Mediterranean."

And whether she'd heard of the Mediterranean to this day I remain in doubt, for, making a profound reverence (which was sure to please), she told me that before she could answer my question, she must ask her mother, who appeared soon after on the threshold, all decked out in a pale-blue morning dress, which was constructed to display, as best it could, her more than ample proportions. Her face was overly made up and her hair too blonde to be honest.

"Madame," I said, bowing almost as low as the cobblestones, "I am your humble and obedient servant. May I ask you—"

"Monsieur," she cooed importantly, inspecting me from head to toe, and appearing satisfied with her inquisition, "if, despite your strange accent, which tells me you're from the provinces, you are, as I believe, a gentleman, I'd like to know who you are."

"Madame," I said, secretly grinding my teeth, but outwardly maintaining my most suave and beneficent manners, "my name is Pierre de Siorac, and I'm the second son of the Baron de Mespech in Périgord."

"Good," she breathed in relief, "you're not just any Guillaume or Gautier. But, Monsieur, she said with extraordinary eagerness, what business have you with Monsieur de Nançay?"

"Madame," I replied, "with all the respect in the world, should I not reveal my affairs to Monsieur de Nançay himself?"

"Nay, Monsieur," she assured me without the least sign of annoyance, "I am one of Monsieur de Nançay's intimates, and I would be remiss if I allowed an intruder into our house."

"I am no intruder, Madame," I replied, feeling somewhat prickly. "My father knows Monsieur de Nançay. They fought together at Calais under the command of the Duc de Guise."

"The Duc de Guise!" she cried, overcome with emotion, her breasts heaving. "Your father served with the Duc de Guise! Ah, Monsieur! He is my hero! The greatest, the handsomest, the holiest of gentlemen in France! The saviour of the kingdom! The shield of the Catholic faith! The true king of Paris! Monsieur, for the love of the Duc de Guise, ask me anything! There's nothing I wouldn't do for you!"

"But Madame," I said, "I only want to know where Monsieur de Nançay lives."

"Ah, Monsieur, this is a very delicate question! I'm not at liberty to decide this by myself. I ask only your patience"—Holy God, I'd developed enough of that commodity to sell some off!—"and with your permission, I shall go straightaway to ask my husband."

And so off she went, and after so many repeated consultations, all Miroul could do was hide his head in Pompée's mane to hide his laughter. The daughter had returned, her mother gone, and stood on the threshold, silently observing us, as if we'd arrived from some other planet, which was all the more strange given the multitudes of Huguenots who had come to Paris from the farthest reaches of the kingdom to attend the wedding of Princesse Margot.

The husband, who at length made his appearance, was a portly, bald man, with piercing eyes—a rich merchant I supposed—clothed in an austere brown doublet and ruff. He, too, felt compelled to ask me an endless series of questions, so that, in the end, so as not to offend a man who claimed, as his wife had done, that he was "a close friend of Monsieur de Nançay" (both of them lying), I was forced to tell my entire story, to which he listened with the greatest interest; he then called his wife in order to repeat it in its entirety to her, embroidering considerably the details of the duels, a subject that appeared to be dear to his heart.

After this narrative, which lasted at least a quarter of an hour, he was willing to share with me the fact that Monsieur de Nançay lived in the house next to his. "Ah!" thought I. "If only I'd had the good fortune to knock on that door before this one!"

"But," he added, "you cannot visit Monsieur de Nançay now! It's much too early!"

"I thought so," I replied. "So, instead, I shall head for the cathedral of Notre-Dame and spend an hour or so there."

"Ah! Monsieur!" he gushed, believing of course that I was going to hear Mass. "I'm so relieved to meet a pious and devout young man like you, given the invasion in Paris—and in the very court of the king—of the satanic heresy of Calvin!"

Hearing this, I bowed silently and took my leave of the two of them—now three in number, since their daughter had returned with her mother, and was now throwing amorous looks in my direction, despite my unfashionable doublet—and mounted my horse. Miroul threw me such a mirthful look, with his brown eye shining, that it was all I could do to keep from laughing out loud in the faces of these good, though astonishingly annoying people.

As for Notre-Dame, I was amazed and astonished when I saw it, but I won't try to describe it here: you'd need an entire book. And although I was, in my Huguenot faith, repelled by so many idolatrous images, whether in stained glass or carved statues, I found them so beautiful that I would never have wanted them to be destroyed, as so many churches were by the most fanatical members of my party, but instead would have them preserved for the admiration of our children, though not as objects to be worshipped—which should be reserved for God alone. Moreover, if we were to consider them not as sacred objects, but as representations of man, it seemed to me we'd appreciate them more, the less we adored them.

The most marvellous of all these idols, or at least the one that I found most pleasing, was a statue of the Virgin by the door of the cloister. She had a pretty, oval face and a small, straight nose, and her eyes were widened in surprise. It was so lifelike that I thought the sculptor must have had a Parisienne for his model—or, perhaps, even to share his bed! And he must have loved her enough to want to "revirginize" her in stone and to have left her gracious image for future generations.

Miroul waited outside to guard our horses, and I was sorry that he couldn't share these treasures with me, and even more sorry that Giacomi wasn't here, who so loved the arts and spoke so knowledgeably about them. But I scarcely had time to look around a bit before a little dark-haired cleric, no more than seventeen years in age, I guessed, approached me and, looking at me with soft eyes, asked in fluting tones:

"Monsieur, would you like to climb to the top of the towers of Notre-Dame? You can see all of Paris, since the cathedral is the tallest monument in the city."

"Monsieur priest," I asked in the most benign tones, but inside feeling quite wary, having very little confidence in those who wore those robes, "I'd be interested if it's not too much money."

"Won't cost you much," replied the priest, with a forced smile. "Five sols for the diocese. Three sols for the beadle, who will give us the key. And two for me, who will guide you to the top."

He said this with such a suave and soft voice, and touched me so caressingly as he did so, and displayed such an engaging smile, that I couldn't tell whether my guide was a man or a woman. Zeus himself, if I dare invoke him in a Christian church, might have been mistaken, though such a mistake seemed of little consequence to him if I am to believe the rape of Ganymede.

"Monsieur priest, agreed," I said, backing away a bit with a cold look and without reaching for my purse.

"Well, then," said the little cleric, "let's see your money."

"Oh, no! I'll pay afterwards!"

"Oh, Monsieur!" he laughed. "I, Aymotin, am an honourable man!"

"Aymotin! That's your name?"

"Yes! But I'm not a priest yet! Monsieur, without money, the beadle won't give me the key."

"All right. Here are three sols for the beadle. The five sols for the diocese will be paid once we're at the top. And your two, Aymotin, when we're back down here."

"Oh, mercy, Monsieur, you bargain like a Jew, a Lombard or a Huguenot!"

"Which I'm not. Hurry, Aymotin, get me the key. I'll gambol about a bit while I'm waiting for you."

"Monsieur," said Aymotin with a sly smile, "in Paris we don't say 'gambol about', which is very *langue d'oc*—we say 'take a stroll'."

"So," I said, "you speak *langue d'oc* too?"

"No. I was born in Paris and have never left. But I have a very good friend who speaks with the same jargon as you, mixing *langue d'oc* and French."

And, giving me another of his sideways looks, and holding up his robe with both hands so as not to trip over it, he trotted off with surprising gracefulness.

He was so long in returning that I believed my three sols were lost and gone, but eventually he returned, though I wasn't sure whether his return was due to his probity or to the interest he'd taken in me.

"Monsieur," he said, "I have the key to the steps, but not the key to the bell tower: for that the beadle wanted three more sols."

"So we won't see the bells. Let's go!"

The door unbolted—I had to lend him a hand, given the enormous weight and size of the key and the slenderness of his wrists—he climbed nimbly up ahead of me, frequently glancing back over his shoulder to give me a smile or an encouraging look.

Oh, reader, how immense and beautiful is Paris when seen from the top of the towers of Notre-Dame! What a thrill to see it stretching out at my feet like a picture, the houses so tiny and the Seine curving gently through its middle.

Meanwhile, Aymotin had become so winded from climbing the stairs that it was a pity seeing him gasping for breath.

"Aymotin," I told him, "you climbed too quickly, and didn't allow your lungs to purify the blood coming to your heart."

"What?" cried Aymotin. "Are you a doctor too?"

"Too?" I asked, suddenly pricking up my ears. "You know another doctor?"

But Aymotin, reddening and shaking his black curls, replied evasively, "Oh, I know several doctors. There are no fewer than sixty-two doctors in Paris and you can see them from morning to night going to see their patients, wearing their square bonnets and astride their mules."

Then, turning away from me, he walked up to the balustrade and with a wide, very gracious gesture, showed me the capital, as if he were offering it to me as a gift. "Behold, Monsieur, the most beautiful city in the world!" And stretching out his arm, he showed me that the island we were on also housed the palace, and the Sainte-Chapelle; on the right bank were the wheat markets, the second-hand clothing markets, the sheet markets and, along the river, the Louvre, grandiose and almost menacing with its august white-marble exterior; just behind the Louvre was the wooden tower that marked the limit of the city, constructed as it was as part of the wall surrounding the capital. On the left bank there were numerous beautiful churches—too many to name; outside the walls was the abbey of Saint-Germain-des-Prés, whose three towers seemed so superb on this bright morning; within the walls, as if to mark the western edge of the city, the Tour de Nesle. Throughout the city we could see a web of turrets, clock towers, portcullises and gables that testified to the immeasurable riches of the lords and merchants who inhabit the capital. As I leant over, and while Aymotin continued his presentation, I could see below me on the place Notre-Dame the people walking, who looked like flies, and could even pick out my Pompée from her chestnut coat, though she looked no bigger than a mouse.

"As you see," said Aymotin, "Paris is divided into three cities by the Seine that flows through its middle. To the right, there is the most extensive part which is called la Ville…"

"Like that, *la ville*?" I asked. "And the others?"

"Ville with a capital *v*," replied Aymotin, "because that's where the king lives in his Louvre. But some call it the Saint-Denis quarter. Then there's the part where we are which is called, as you know, the Île de la Cité."

"And to the left?"

"That's called l'Université because of all the students who live and study there, who annoy the night watch, make mischief with the monks of Saint-Germain, bother the bourgeois and commit a thousand other pranks that I couldn't describe."

But Aymotin told me this without a trace of the morose severity that one would have expected of his robe, but rather with a somewhat malicious gleam in his eye.

"Some people call l'Université the Hulepoix quarter, just as they call la Ville the Saint-Denis quarter."

"Hulepoix!" I laughed. "What a bizarre name! Hulepoix! I like it! But what are the names of the two little islands so full of greenery that I see in front of the Île de la Cité and are parallel to each other?"

"The one on the right is called the Îlot du Patriarche, and the one on the left the Îlot du Passeur-aux-Vaches.* The king, to whom they belong, had the idea of connecting them and joining them to the Île de la Cité to sell them to builders, but the project died for lack of money. Behind you, Monsieur, there are three other little islands that you can't see, since they're hidden by the cathedral, and the king also wanted to join them into one and call it the Île Notre-Dame, but that project also fell into the dirty water of the Seine."

"Are there cows on Îlot du Passeur-aux-Vaches?"

"Of course, and there's no need for a cowherd, which is a great saving of money."

"Well," I mused, not knowing what to look at since I saw so many marvels, "how many people are there in this immense city?"

"Three hundred thousand."

"And streets?"

"Four hundred and thirteen."

"What! Someone counted them?"

"Naturally!" snorted Aymotin, his dander up, as if all of these streets belonged to him. "Listen to these verses that I learnt in school:

> *"Within the Île de la Cité you'll find*
> *Thirty-six streets that twist and wind,*
> *While over in Hulepoix quarter you'll see*
> *Enough streets to total eighty-three!*

---

* "Islet of the Patriarch"; "Islet of the Cows' Ferryman".

But over in Saint-Denis, you will discover
Six less than 300; so over
All the three quarters you'll have seen
No fewer streets than 413."

"Four hundred and thirteen!" I gasped. "How could you ever find someone you knew if you didn't know where they lived?"

At this, Aymotin looked at me curiously and asked if I was in the situation I'd just described, and I, not wishing to speak to him about my Angelina, the thought of whom was driving me to despair, simply said that I was looking for a friend, who, like me, was a doctor from the Royal College of Medicine in Montpellier (at which I noticed that he trembled slightly, although he still appeared to be on his guard, maintaining the perpetually gay, suave and attentive smile that he wore like a mask on his pretty face).

"His name is Fogacer," I said, "and though we are of different complexions, Fogacer being little interested in petticoats and I chasing them like mad, we get along well and have become great friends. Do you know him?"

"I'm afraid not," replied Aymotin rather too quickly, lowering his eyes and turning away.

"Aymotin," I said, not without considerable heat, "if you know him, it would be tragic if you didn't tell me how to find him; I need so much to see him."

Turning back to face me, and looking me in the eye, Aymotin took a step towards me and spoke in very grave tones that I never would have expected either from his age nor from the silly antics that he'd thus far exhibited to me.

"Monsieur," he announced, "I am, both as a cleric and by nature, discreet. And all the more so by my complexion, which is exactly what you have guessed it to be. My memory has therefore become a tomb. A face, a name, an address—everything falls into its depths and is buried there. I could never remember anything that might incriminate another."

Having reflected on this amazing declaration, I was more than ever convinced that Aymotin was a member of this great brotherhood, whose members, in the great appetite that they have for each other, have abolished all differences between them—of rank, of wealth, of knowledge and of religion, and live out, in this equality, their perilous passions, promising only to keep their mutual secret and knowing that there will be no quarter, for one or the other, if they are discovered.

"Aymotin," I said, "that's fine. I understand you. All I ask of you, then, is to remember a name and an address and to provide them to this doctor if Fortune were to lead you to cross paths. My name is Pierre de Siorac and I'm lodged in the rue de la Ferronnerie in the home of the bonnet-maker Maître Recroche. Here are the five sols for the cathedral chapter. And five more for you."

"Monsieur," said Aymotin, suddenly returning three of the sols I'd given him, "I've kept just two. And for what you've said, I would not ask for any payment. I will do what you ask if I can. I like to oblige good, honest and charitable people."

And thereupon, contemplating me like a hen sparrow might her mate, shaking his black curls from right to left and uttering a deep sigh, he gave me such a piteous look that I might have accommodated it if he had only been of the tender sex to which he wanted so much to belong. But, finding this thought somewhat embarrassing, I again leant over the balustrade to cast a last glance at the square below, where the tiny size of the people seen from so high above had so diverted me only minutes before.

And recognizing Pompée by her chestnut coat, I was suddenly speechless to see her at the centre of a great tumult, and four or five beggars trying to wrest her away from Miroul, who was desperately fighting them off with fists and kicks, and who was unable, finally, to avoid defeat by so many assailants.

"'Sblood, Aymotin!" I cried. "They're trying to take my mare!"

And running, I hurtled down the stairs of the tower, rushed out the door, past the portal and onto the cathedral court, and unsheathing, fell like lightning on these miscreants, making strange cries and having at them with the flat of my sword, careful not to pierce any of them—except one who pulled out a knife from his rags and would have stabbed me, for which I punished him by slashing his arm with my dagger. At this, he dropped his weapon, and ran away, crying that he'd been killed, the others following behind him, disappearing into the adjoining streets like cockroaches into their holes.

"Miroul!" I cried, once I'd won the field. "You're bleeding! Are you wounded?"

"It's just a bruise to my fist," replied Miroul, "and nothing serious. But Monsieur, look at your doublet! You can't go visiting Monsieur de Nançay looking like that! We'll have to sew you up first!"

Sadly, he was right! My blue satin doublet, which had been so carefully made by the Jewish tailor in Montpellier, was brand new and, I must say, very becoming and, if I do say so, very beautiful. And even though the frivolous lady in the rue des Sablons despised it as being "not in fashion", this doublet which I was so proud of and wore with such pride had suffered a two-inch rip on its front, and when I looked more closely, I confess, dear reader, that I was near tears. Oh, Lord! What a strange animal is man! When I should have been on my knees giving thanks to Providence for saving my life in this encounter in which the blade of my assailant had passed so close to my heart, I was broken-hearted at the damage to my clothing!

"Monsieur," said a fellow who, along with a good three dozen Guillaumes and Gautiers, had watched, open-mouthed, the attempted robbery of my horse without so much as lifting a finger or calling for help, "it's a fact that your doublet is badly torn!"

"And whose fault is that," I cried angrily, "if not those who stood around watching these villains do their business without a word or any effort to help my valet?"

"Well, Monsieur," cried a Gautier, "risk getting beaten up? And in a street fight? I'd be careful *not* to intervene, as much as I might pity the loss of your doublet!"

"And who says it's lost?" I screamed against all reason.

"Well, it's a fact, isn't it, that it's ruined," observed another, "and I can't see how even the best seamstress would be able to do much for it."

"Monsieur," said another, "take it to the used-clothes market. The Jews will buy it from you. Won't be much, but it's better than nothing."

"Wait, Monsieur!" cried Miroul, seeing me flushed with anger, and so out of control that I was on the verge of drawing my sword again. "I beg you! No need to get angry! You're safe! Your Pompée as well! Let's go back to our lodgings! Alizon will do wonders with your doublet!"

"Can you believe it, Miroul?" I said in *langue d'oc*. "In broad daylight! In front of Notre-Dame! In front of these gawking onlookers! 'Sblood! Why is Paris so famous? It's a cut-throat's heaven!"

5

MAÎTRE RECROCHE HAD NOT YET returned to the house when we got back, but Alizon, who was just waking up, had no sooner seen my torn doublet than she had taken it from me, threaded a needle with some blue silk thread, and undertaken to repair it. As her fingers flew, she listened wide-eyed to my story with eager ears and cries of "Amazing!" or other glosses on my tale.

"Ah, Monsieur," she said in her rapid and sharp Parisian accent, "it's a miracle you weren't killed! One valet to guard two horses? What were you thinking? There are more thieves in Paris than lice on the head of a monk! Blessed Virgin! They'd steal the king's carriage with the king inside it if his Swiss guards weren't there to fend them off!"

"Alizon," I replied, "you sew beautifully, but do you think the repairs will be visible?"

"Well, as for that," she sighed, stretching and pulling her shoulders back, either to rest a bit or to show her figure off (or both?), "it won't show as much as a man's member does in the middle of his body but more than the eyeliner on a woman's face. You can't repair clothing without leaving a scar, and especially silk. You could still go about in this doublet, but you certainly couldn't wear it to visit the king in his Louvre, if that's what you want to do. You'd have to order another one, my noble Monsieur, and all the more so since..."

"Since, Alizon?" I asked, since she wouldn't go on.

"Well, Monsieur," she said looking at me sweetly, "I don't want to wound your pride, as you are so nice, but this doublet I've just repaired is most assuredly *not* fashionable here. In Paris, a doublet has to be much more ample in the shoulders, and wider under the arms to include a pocket for your purse, and should finish up in a point at the fly, with some stuffing to inflate the stomach, especially since you're so thin. It's the Duc d'Anjou who wants it so, since he thinks a good stomach adds nobility to a man's silhouette."

"Another doublet, Alizon?" I cried. "How you talk! Samson will never give me the money for it, since he keeps so tight a watch on our purse! And as for me, I wouldn't go ordering a doublet with the little bit of money I've got left."

In response, Alizon threw me a glance, then another, and yet one more while she continued sewing with an unstoppable speed, and all I could think about was how dark she was, of skin, of eyes and of hair, sweet little fly from hell that she was, with her little body so slender, so shapely and so lively, with a waist you could enclose with your two hands like a child's.

"Well, Monsieur," she said after what seemed like a very long time, "what a pity! If I were a high and mighty noblewoman, living for my pleasure without a care in the world, I'd give you the money you need to make you as beautiful in your clothes as you are without."

I opened my mouth to thank her for such a sweet compliment when the door of the workshop flew open and Maître Recroche burst in with a package in his hand, all muddy and battered and in a such a bad humour it looked as though he could eat a bonnet. "Baba!" he cried in an angry voice and with his eyebrows raised. "What goes on in here when the master's away? Are you sleeping? Hey, Baragran! Coquillon! Get up! Get up!" he repeated, administering a hard kick in the kidneys. "You think you can laze about? Sleep all day?"

"And you all night, while we're working!" spit Alizon.

"Shut your little trap!" he said, raising his arm as if to slap her, but Alizon seized her scissors and held them so resolutely in front of her face, her black eyes blazing fire, that Recroche quickly put his hands behind his back and said, "What's this? A doublet? Are we making doublets here now?"

"Nothing but a repair," said Alizon, "and it's done. Monsieur de Siorac, here's your clothing."

"What?" cried Recroche, rubbing his vulture's beak with his index finger. "So you're doing work for someone else in my atelier? And during time that you owe to me? That's a felony! It's entirely against the rules of the guild!"

"Ah, yes! These rules! It was your colleagues and you who wrote them!" sneered Alizon.

"Maître Recroche," I intervened, "'tis I who asked Alizon to do this repair. And since she did it in your atelier, on your time—"

"Using my thread and my needles," snarled Recroche.

"And your *scissors*," observed Alizon bitterly.

"I'll pay you for it."

"That will be two sols," said Maître Recroche in the most modest tones and lowering his eyes.

"What?" shrieked Alizon, now abuzz like a bee whose hive has been hit. "What! Two sols for two minutes of my work when you pay me three sols, five deniers for an entire day!"

"Silly hen!" cried Maître Recroche with utter scorn. "The price of your labour and the price I demand for my goods are two different things. Without that, where would I get any profit? And this," he said, seizing my doublet, "is an exquisite repair, executed with the tiniest needlepoints, an example of the very high quality of work done in my atelier."

"Ah, Maître Recroche," I laughed through my anger, taking my clothing from him, "say no more, or you'll end up charging me double for my doublet! Not a word more! Here are your little coins. And thank you so much for the needle and the thread, the stool she sat on and for Alizon's marvellous work."

At this Alizon laughed out loud and even Baragran smiled, anxious as he was to remain in his master's good graces and not to be replaced by a wench worth only three sols, five deniers.

"All right! Back to work!" ordered Recroche, whose humour had softened a bit since my two sols were warming his wallet. "Monsieur de Siorac," he said, "please don't believe that everything is about profit in my work. I had to wait three long hours in the antechamber of the Baronne des Tourelles to deliver the bonnets she'd ordered to be sent no later than daybreak. Three hours! While the baronne was asleep! You hear? Asleep! And she is still sleeping, I'll warrant!"

At this point there came a knock on the door. Coquillon, at a sign from his master, ran to open and an insolent knave of a valet strutted in wearing an amaranth livery with flaps of gold, and sniffed in a very haughty tone, "Is there a Maître Recroche hereabouts?"

"There is!" answered Recroche, as amiable as the iron bands that reinforced his doors.

"My mistress," said the valet, nose in air, "the Baronne des Tourelles, desires a word with you."

"She would be most welcome!" replied Recroche curtly; after which, hands behind his back, he pretended to be studying the ceiling, finding this valet, I surmised, to be an insufferable buffoon. For his part, the valet looked at us one after the other as if we were so many piles of excrement by the side of the road, and sniffed as if he were afraid we might infect him with our breathing.

"I shall go," he said through pursed lips, "and inform my mistress."

And off he went. If one were to judge the mistress by the servant, one could only see in him a bad augury of what was to come, and I already imagined her with the traits of an angry gorgon. But, oh reader! What a mistake! I didn't have eyes enough to devour her when she came in, all a-sparkle in her pale-green satin gown, copied, as Alizon explained later, from ones that Princesse Margot had worn, which were the most ample petticoats in the entire kingdom, so ample indeed that the ladies who wore them could scarcely fit through a doorway. Above this sumptuous, flared dress, her bodice was laced tightly enough to accentuate and swell her breasts and make them appear so round and large that they seemed almost bare. Above these charms, her long, gracious neck was set off by a large round collar that extended up behind her neck like a lace tail of a peacock. This ornament was studded by pure oriental pearls, set in three rows, encircling her neck. Her hair was braided in coils in which glittering emeralds and golden combs could be seen. It was a marvel that such a structure could maintain its balance on this pretty head.

And what a beautiful sweet face she had! It resembled the face of the Virgin I'd seen in Notre-Dame: a fine, straight nose, a cherry-coloured mouth, eyes blacker than jade. But the Virgin was sculpted in marble, and this face was so lively and animated that you would have said it was that of a sweet baby robin, turning its beak this way and that, hopping from branch to branch.

This beauty was followed by a pretty, strong chambermaid (whom Miroul immediately engaged in a battle of seductive looks) who carried the lady's purse, her perfume bottle, her handkerchief and her mask; by a little valet carrying a fan; and by a heavy devil of a groom who was dragging at the end of a rope a plank which (as I saw later) he was to place on the sticky pavement outside the door so that his mistress wouldn't soil her dainty slippers when she got out of her carriage.

I was able to catch a glimpse of one of these dainty shoes under the vertiginous movement of the folds of her gown and saw that it was of a matching green satin with a gold buckle and a very high heel. Thus perched on one end atop her heels and on the other enlarged by three good inches by her majestic coiffure, the Baronne des Tourelles seemed taller than I, and more voluminous as well, but her middle seemed so thin that, in all, she resembled an hourglass.

"Well, Maître Recroche," she cried in a voice so rapid and abrupt that the words fairly crackled on your ear like the rain in a storm on your roof, "I bring you my sincerest apologies for having lingered in bed whilst you were waiting in my antechamber to deliver your bonnets! *It weighs on my conscience!* I had dined and stayed up so late the night before! And in such hilarious company! Oh, Recroche, *I should die of shame!* Recroche, Recroche, where are the bonnets? Let me have them immediately! This instant! Without delay, I beg you!"

"Without delay, Madame?" countered Recroche with a deep bow in which he expressed, it seemed to me, some secret disrespect, being of those Parisian merchants who like neither the nobles nor the princes and value no one and nothing more than themselves. "Delay, Madame? Didn't I 'delay' for three long hours in your antechamber? My atelier was, meanwhile, unoccupied. My companions without work! My business abandoned! Well and good, Madame, but that will cost you ten sols more, that delay."

"'Tis no matter!" cried Madame de Tourelles. "Recroche, those bonnets! Those bonnets, this instant! Ah," she added, "I'm suffocating! It's so hot this August! *I could die of it!*"

And putting her hands on her slim waist, as if to undo the corset that was oppressing her bosom, she cried, almost faint: "Corinne, my perfume! Nicotin, my fan!" Then, having breathed in the one and agitated the other, she was refreshed, and Recroche having unpacked the bonnets, she tried on each one over the structure of her hair arrangement while Alizon held a mirror for her, looking quite sullen.

I leave to your imagination the cries, the exclamations, the little faces, the chattering, the gracious turns of her neck, the swellings of her bosom and the "I could dies" that accompanied this fitting. When, at last, the baronne had finished, and asked Corinne for her purse to pay Recroche, she whispered a few words into his ear, which I couldn't hear, but whose meaning I guessed when Recroche turned to me and said, "Monsieur de Siorac, the Baronne des Tourelles requests the pleasure of being introduced to you."

"Madame," I said, stepping forward, "I am overcome both by your person and by your good and kind benevolence." And, so saying, I kissed—not her hand, but the tips of her fingers, as Madame de Joyeuse had taught me to do, as she didn't want me to be so greedy in these matters, saying, "My sweet, don't kiss the ladies' hands as if you wanted to swallow them! And as for the fire in your eyes, try to moderate it. An honest lady is not some chambermaid that in a single glance you can lay out on the grass! Leave her, for goodness' sake, some time to make up her mind!"

That Madame des Tourelles was satisfied with my ardent but respectful behaviour I believe, since she paid me a thousand little compliments, and with these compliments she mingled various adroit questions, posed in such a lively, prompt, imperious, yet simultaneously coaxing and coquettish manner that I was unable to resist so much suave authority, and in less than five minutes I told her almost everything about me.

"Monsieur," she said, "would you be good enough to accompany me to my carriage? My groom's plank is so narrow that I'm afraid I might fall onto the muddy pavement! *I could die of it!* Monsieur, your hand, I beg you!"

"Madame," said I, "it is yours, and with it, my arm and my sword!"

"Well, Monsieur," she laughed behind her fan, "you're very gallant in your Périgord! Your sword! I wasn't aiming so high!"

"Madame," I replied, taking a lighter tone, not allowing myself to be deterred by her offhandedness, "it's nevertheless true. Use me as you please, I'm yours."

"Monsieur de Siorac," she replied with a look that, had I taken it for what it clearly said, would have given me infinite rights with her—but then isn't that exactly the point? There is no look, whether it has a literal meaning or not, that can't subsequently be denied to have such a meaning. "Monsieur de Siorac," she said, but then fell silent, pretending to be confused.

"Madame," I said hanging on her vermilion lips, "speak, I'm listening."

"Monsieur de Siorac, will you climb into my carriage and ride a little way with me?"

"Certainly, Madame."

"Monsieur," she said, correcting her remonstration with a more amorous look, "we don't say 'certainly' in Paris. It's the language of the Huguenots. We say, 'assuredly'."

"Assuredly, Madame," I said with a bow, "I'm yours until the end of the road, and, if you wish, until the end of worlds known and unknown."

"Monsieur," she laughed, "you have an easy tongue, it seems. And if you're as vigorous as you are witty, we shall be great friends for a while. But climb in, I beg you!"

With great emotion, I found myself sitting beside this noble lady, or at least as close as her voluminous hoop skirt would allow, on a very well-padded seat in her closed carriage, which was, as far as I could tell, upholstered in pale-green satin, Corinne and her little valet sitting opposite us.

"Corinne," she said as soon as the carriage started up, "pull the curtain. You too, Nicotin. Monsieur," she said, "I can't bear it. *I'll die of it!* Give me a kiss, I beg you!"

Ah, what contortions, stretching and reaching of arms and torso I had to do to reach over the immense and rigid hoop skirt and kiss the lips she tendered me, which, in truth, were so soft and smooth as to damn all the papist saints whom she believed in. I had not tasted such a delicious repast since my departure from Mespech, and, forgetting the encumbrance of her clothing, found myself on fire.

"Monsieur," said Madame des Tourelles, pushing me away, "go easy! Be more gentle, I beg you! You're behaving like you're going to devour me!"

At this, Corinne, who hadn't missed a drop or a crumb of the spectacle we offered her in the blue shadows of the carriage, burst out laughing, and let go of little Nicotin, whom, the moment before, she'd been tickling and teasing, she being so strong and the little fellow so youthful that one might have guessed he were a girl in disguise. I couldn't doubt, as I watched these two disporting in a way that reminded me of my little Hélix, that the chambermaid and, perhaps, her mistress were well used to this kind of carrying-on with the little rascal.

Madame des Tourelles, after having had a laugh at her own wit (I wagered that she wouldn't fail to brag of her conceit later on that same day), immediately went at it again, but this time I was careful to remain suave enough to satisfy her, which gradually led her to unbutton my doublet and chemise and slide her right hand under them to stroke my chest, a caress I would have greatly enjoyed if, all of a sudden, she hadn't withdrawn her hand with as much horror as if she'd been burnt.

"What, Monsieur!" she gasped, pulling away. "You have hair on your chest?"

"But assuredly, Madame!"

"From top to bottom?"

"From bottom to top."

"Oh, heaven!" cried the baronne. "Corinne, did you hear that? Monsieur de Siorac has all his hair! Oh, gracious! How could anyone be *so* provincial?"

"But what can I do? It's nature that made me hairy!"

"*By my conscience!*" she cried, half-laughing, half-angry. "Corinne, did you hear? Monsieur," she continued, "did you really not know? For a long time, we haven't worn hair here! No doubt it's all right for an old greybeard! But I dare say that in Paris you won't find a single young gentleman who doesn't have all his hair removed before he offers his services to the honest ladies of the court!"

I might have answered that it wasn't I who offered these services, but that another had requested them. I preferred to remain silent, however, well aware that ladies can pardon anything in their lover except discourteous language, and I had learnt from Madame de Joyeuse that in commerce with women, you have to take it or leave it, slights along with caresses. Those of the tender sex often take revenge on their lovers for the injuries inflicted on them by their fathers or husbands. I've never found anything but advantages in letting myself be misused without complaint, for I've observed that most often my lover will treat me with great tenderness after wounding me, and that after the claws come the velvet paws, and these last in exquisite proportion to the former. So I said nothing, but looked at my beautiful companion wide-eyed, and as if I were terrified of having fallen from her good graces.

"Oh, Madame," cooed Corinne, who was the first to respond with sympathy to my predicament, "now he's all distressed and abashed! For heaven's sake, let's give him back our lips! Monsieur de Siorac has sinned only out of ignorance! It's a venial sin at worst, and quickly forgiven! In less than an hour, a good barber at the baths will make him as smooth and soft as Nicotin!"

"Well," I thought, "how you do go about it, Corinne! You have me already shaved and clipped! Sent right back to my beardless childhood! Don't I risk, like Samson in the Bible, losing my strength from all these Parisian refinements?"

"Monsieur," soothed Madame des Tourelles, taking my hand and mingling her fingers with mine in the most delicious way, "if you wish to serve me, as I believe you are so inclined, you must remedy these imperfections, and see to your doublet, which you must have inherited from some ancestor…"

"Oh, Madame!" cried Corinne.

"You must not wear a doublet which has been resewn in front. You'd be the laughing stock of the court!"

"Madame, we've arrived," said Corinne.

And indeed, the carriage pulled to a halt and Madame des Tourelles withdrew her fine, pretty, perfumed hand from mine and said with a caressing smile, "Monsieur de Siorac, I must leave you. Here we are in the rue Trouvevache. This little house with the blue shutters is mine. I come here when I'm tired of the setbacks, troubles and noise that I must bear in my mansion. Monsieur de Siorac, I shall be here towards six in the evening tomorrow and will receive you alone for supper."

"Madame," I replied, "I will be infinitely happy to accept."

"I hope so," she cautioned with a soupçon of haughtiness, "as long as you do everything I told you."

After this, I kissed her fingertips with the greatest respect and got out of the carriage as deftly as I could, as I did so giving a nod to Corinne, who, as far as I could tell, seemed unusually interested in me, though at the moment I could not foresee where this interest would lead us.

I walked quickly away so as not to be spattered by mud as the carriage started off, and in the quick motion I made to get out of its path, I found myself in a narrow doorway, and was surprised to feel the door opening behind me. Pierre de L'Étoile appeared, all dressed in black, his aquiline nose elongated by all the worries he had.

"Ah, Monsieur de L'Étoile!" I cried. "By what miracle have you appeared here like some *deus ex machina*?"

"No miracle, no mystery," replied L'Étoile. "This is my house. As is the one opposite which you've been looking at with such interest. I rented it out, at Recroche's request, to the person whose carriage you just stepped out of. There was a time," he mused in his morose and moralistic tones, while throwing me a half-scolding, half-amused look, "when it was only the lords of the court who kept such, ahem, little houses in Paris at some distance from their mansions. But now," he sighed, "the honourable ladies do as well."

"Indeed, Monsieur!" I said.

"Monsieur de Siorac," he continued, "I have business in the rue de la Ferronnerie. Shall I accompany you, while we chat?"

"The pleasure will be mine!"

"Mine as well. You are well aware, no doubt, that I fulminate against our present morality. Did you know what the late Jeanne d'Albret told me when she came to Paris to sign the marriage contract between Henri and Margot?"

"What did she say?" I replied politely.

"That in the royal court it's no longer the men who pursue the women, it's the women who pursue the men."

"Ah!"

"Please don't feign surprise, Monsieur de Siorac," he continued, lowering his voice. "You're a very strange sort of Huguenot. Scarcely are you in Paris one day before you've been hooked, and, what's worse, are all atremble at the end of your hook."

"Monsieur," I replied, more bitterly than politely, "do you see me 'all atremble'?"

"Oh, yes, decidedly. But we must hurry. I'm expected in the rue de la Ferronnerie."

And, saying this, he hurried his pace, his long, thin, stiff legs churning, his neck and shoulders held stiffly, but his curious, ferreting eyes darting this way and that with enviable insatiability.

221

"Monsieur," I said, taking great care not to name her, "so you know this lady?"

"Like the back of my hand. Except that my right hand isn't unaware of what my left is doing, whereas, at the Tourelles residence, they don't know what's going on in the little house in the rue Trouvevache. Monsieur de Siorac, I detect a weak smile. Did you believe you were the first?"

"Neither first not last. But, Monsieur, may I ask how it is that you know this lady?"

"Through Recroche, having learnt that the lady was interested in renting a little house near her bonnet-maker."

"And why so near?"

"Because of the extreme refinement of her coachman, who would rather wait for her outside the workshop of her bonnet-maker than in the rue Trouvevache."

"Aha! What a clever ruse!" I cried.

And this time I didn't laugh weakly, but out loud.

"Ah, what a relief!" said L'Étoile, with a bitter smile, but his eyes bright. "I was afraid our sorceress had snared your soul along with your body. Ah, Monsieur de Siorac, what shreds your tenderest feelings would have left on those thorns! Our Circes of the court have hearts as cold as their private parts are hot! Inside and outside, all is show and vanity. They'll throw you away as soon as you don't satisfy them any more."

"Yes, so I heard, as soon as her little heart has tired of this vast world."

"It won't ever tire! It's too hungry. Venerable doctor, I will take my leave of you here. Would you like to meet Ambroise Paré?"

"Oh, Monsieur! Nothing would make me happier!"

"I will try to make it happen then."

And while I stammered my gratitude and salutations, the honest L'Étoile went to knock on a door, leaving me enchanted with his prudence, his wisdom and his beneficence.

When I entered the workshop of Maître Recroche to ask about my brothers, I found Baragran and Alizon doing their needlework, and as they went about it, they had at each other in a furious argument.

"You can't deny, silly goose, that the baronne is as beautiful as the Holy Virgin!"

"Beautiful!" snarled Alizon. "Beautiful, the baronne! Most assuredly I deny it!"

"That's because you're jealous!" said Baragran.

"Jealous! Me? You fat idiot!" Alizon retorted bitterly with a half-pitying, half-derisive laugh. "That'll be the day! Jealous of a baronne? My noble Monsieur, did you hear this idiot? Jealous, me, of a baronne?"

"It's not so much about her nobility," countered Baragran, "but about the lady's beauty! For she *is* beautiful. Yes, I'm saying it and I'd say it again, even with a noose around my neck. And I'd add that it would take a hundred Alizons mixed together to make a wench as brilliant as the baronne."

"And what's she got that I haven't got, you poor impotent fool," cried Alizon, "except her plumage?"

"Her plumage?" scoffed Baragran. "But her feathers are hers!"

"Oh, no they're not! Pluck her, Baragran! And what will be left? Take off her bodice, her hoop skirts, her silk gown, her high heels, her pearls, her ridiculous coiffure, her false braids, her perfumes and the powders she pastes on her face! And what will you have left, Baragran, my sweet? A wench neither younger nor prettier than I, who's not made any different, who's got the same slit in her middle as I, and who doesn't give her men any more pleasure than I would!"

At this I laughed out loud, remembering what my little Hélix had said of Diane de Fontenac when that lady was convalescing from the plague at Mespech and sat in the window of our gatehouse, wearing her ermines, attracting my brother François's attention and my own like filings to a magnet. Well, I thought, this Parisian fly stings as hard as my little Périgordian wasp! And suddenly surprised to have thought about my poor little Hélix as if she were still alive, I felt a sadness so poignant that I had to turn away and look out the window onto the street, my eyes blurry and my throat in a knot.

Giacomi and my beautiful Samson awoke from their long sleep powerfully hungry, and, having but a faint memory of the two meat pies I'd swallowed earlier that morning, my first concern was to discover a restaurant with a table for four, and sit down to a flagon of wine and a roasted chicken, but this proved more difficult than I'd thought given the enormous crowds that had arrived in Paris for the marriage of Princesse Margot. However, on Baragran's recommendation we were able to find one in the rue de la Truanderie whose prices were clearly marked on a wooden pillar outside the door in conformity with a royal ordinance (which, I heard, was mostly ignored). Our host, a cousin of Baragran, received us quite civilly, though in his own inquisitive and talkative way, wanting to know the whys and the wherefores of our visit to the capital. But when I'd happily satisfied his curiosity, he repeated our story to his patrons and to his neighbours without the least malice, having the Parisian mania for always wanting to appear in the know about everything. And from that moment, liking us the better for it, he promised us a table morning and night in his cafe, which relieved us greatly, for the food was good and the prices modest, in comparison with what they were elsewhere in Paris, though three times what I would have paid in Sarlat.

I was careful to ensure his continued good graces by the stories I told him of my misadventures in the capital, and especially of the attempted theft of my horse directly in front of Notre-Dame, which furnished him with an entire day of gossip at my expense.

I'd be hard put to be able to describe him today since he had a very ordinary face, but I do remember his name, for he made a great deal of the fact that he was called Guillaume Gautier. He's no longer living, having tasted too many of his wines, but his son took over the management of the restaurant and will cook you up a good roast for a reasonable price. I dined there last Thursday, and if the reader would like to taste his simple fare, all he has to do is mention my name to Abel Gautier (the son) and he'll be received like a lord. The street is calm, with few wagons or other conveyances, and the serving girl is quite pretty.

After we left the restaurant, we headed down towards the river and entered the Île de la Cité on the rue des Sablons, where Monsieur de Nançay had his lodgings. There we met a very strange procession: it was led by a wicker mannequin which measured a good two toises tall, was dressed in the red uniform of the Swiss guards of the Louvre, and brandished a bloody dagger; its face was represented by a grimacing mask that seemed as if were borrowed from some hellish devil. Pinned to the chest of this miserable creature was a placard proclaiming, *urbi et orbi*,* that he was an "assassin and heretic". Behind this mannequin came a dozen priests in surplices, stoles and camails. They had their backs turned towards it and were walking backwards—which must not have been easy in these muddy streets—and so were facing a statue of the Virgin, carried on the shoulders of four powerful and moving caryatids who, considering their aprons and the knives in their belts, must have been butchers. On either side of the statue, little clerics were skipping along, swinging censers which created a constant odiferous cloud around it, but they seemed utterly unable to relieve the suffering of the good Virgin, whose face and breasts were mutilated and bloody, if the vermilion stains you could see lining Her

---

* "To the city and to the world."

body and filling the cracks in the statue, were, in fact, blood. "*Se non è vero, è bene trovato*,"* Giacomi whispered in my ear.

I found out later that the senseless attack on the statue that this parade was commemorating had happened 144 years previously: a Swiss guard, in the pay of the king, had lost his wages rolling dice, and, after leaving the tavern in the rue aux Ours where he'd been fleeced, angry and disappointed, and so drunk that he couldn't tell a white thread from a black one, threw himself on the statue of the Virgin that blessed the passers-by, and unsheathing his dagger tried his best to kill Her. He almost did, but as we saw, Mary bled abundantly and, after a century and a half, has continued to bleed, in particular during the procession during which they carry Her, preceded by Her assassin in wicker, throughout the streets of the Saint-Denis quarter, to Her pedestal where, after some chanting, prayers and incense, they burn the Swiss guard in effigy.

A fairly large crowd was following the statue and the mannequin, chanting praises of the Blessed Mother and damning Her murderer to the execration of all people and to the infinite torments of hell. These chants were shouted, rather than sung, and in a manner not so much devout as bellicose: the chanters' faces were inflamed and, a sight which completely stunned me, they brandished knives, hatchets, pikes here and there, with furious cries, promising to burn at the stake all atheists, Jews and Huguenots—these cries were accompanied by nasty and menacing looks at any passers-by, as if they suspected them of failing in their adoration of the martyred Virgin.

As this procession took up the entire width of the street, the four of us squeezed into a portico which gave onto two doors, a carriage gate and a pedestrian passageway, and thus we were able to let these fanatical papists and their bleeding icon pass by, and as I watched

---

* "If it's not true, it's well made."

them, I tried to separate from my observations the disdain I felt at this superstitious masquerade. But achieving some neutrality would not be enough, for Giacomi, elbowing me roughly, whispered in Italian,

"My brother, these rascals are giving us very suspicious looks. For goodness' sake, doff your cap and make the sign of the cross!"

I promptly obeyed, as did Miroul, but Samson remained as frozen as a block of ice, his body stiff, eyes blank and cap firmly on his head.

"Samson," I hissed in *langue d'oc* as vehemently as I could, "remove your cap! I command you!"

"Absolutely not," he replied, as hard as a diamond. "This is a matter of conscience. I shall not salute these idols."

"Samson," I cried, furious now, "once again—"

But I didn't have time to say any more, for about thirty of these inflamed churls encircled us—or rather gathered in a half-circle around us, for luckily we had our backs to the doors. This crowd began brandishing their weapons, red-faced and vociferous, gnashing their teeth, their eyes practically popping out of their sockets, shouting with ear-splitting cries: "Eviscerate these heretics, these stinking demons who dare insult the Blessed Virgin!" Shouting as loud as I could in this infernal uproar but unable to be heard, I finally unsheathed my sword, as did Giacomi and Miroul, but these maddened fanatics scarcely retreated a step before our sword flourishes, continuing to shout their terrible insults at my poor Samson, who never thought to draw his sword, but stood straight up, head held high, and cap firmly in place, and faced them without giving way or moving at all, hoping no doubt for the happiness of martyrdom in his unshakeable zeal.

"Samson!" I cried, beside myself. "This is madness! Are we going to die for a bonnet?"

But he answered not a word, his face illuminated by the prospect of his eternal happiness at the right hand of the Father. "Oh, heaven!" I thought in my rage. "He's as stupidly zealous as these idiots who are assaulting us!" And what was worse, I could see that his marvellous courage, far from impressing the populace, merely increased their hatred, since they preferred to see in my unfortunate brother's serenity the proof that he'd given himself body and soul to Beelzebub, from whom he drew this supernatural strength. And just then, one among them, who, as always in this sort of crowd, is crazy enough to believe God has inspired him, shouted:

"Kill! Kill! The Virgin tells us to! I've heard Her voice!"

At this the rest of the fanatics, taking up his cry, immediately rushed us, despite our threatening sword points, until, retreating slowly, our backs were almost against the doors.

"Ah, Monsieur!" cried Miroul. "What shall we do? Kill them?"

I shook my head without responding, seeing clearly that we were in a desperate predicament since we either had to kill them or let them kill us—but in either case, whether or not we spilt their blood, these rascals were so zealous to avenge the outrage to their Virgin that, sooner or later, their numbers would prevail. I was trying to decide if we should knock at the doors against which we were pinned in the barest hope that some charitable Christian lived there, when I saw, bursting through the crowd, a huge devil of a sergeant of the French Guards, who, being at least six foot four, was a head taller than anyone else there, with broad shoulders and a head so large, a complexion so rosy and eyes so fierce that he might have served as the signpost for a tavern! He simply waded through the mob as if it were butter, using his cane to open the way before him and demanding passage with a voice that must have dominated all the drums of his regiment.

And what a marvel it is that such a large body, a splendid uniform and a loud voice can have such an effect on a mutinous multitude! For as drunk as it was with the carnage it sought, the crowd parted in front of the sergeant like the Red Sea before Moses, so completely that, as he approached, he made a gesture that we should lower our swords and, with his cane, dispersing our assailants, he stepped up to Samson and demanded in a stentorian voice the reason for this tumult, which was disturbing the king's peace. As our enraged assailants withdrew and grew quiet, we rejoiced at the arrival of this gigantic French Guard, and I took advantage of this respite to take up a position on the sergeant's right, while Giacomi moved to his left, thereby creating a rampart of our three bodies that hid Samson from the crowd. And Miroul slipped quietly behind my brother, who was immobilized, mute, his brain still in the mists of his vision of martyrdom, and took his cap from his head without his even noticing. Miroul then hid the offending bonnet in his doublet, which he quickly rebuttoned. It was a subtle ruse that worked wonders, as we shall see, but at the moment I didn't see, my attention glued to the French Guard and the mob.

From among them, who were now growling like a mastiff on a leash, but afraid to come too close to the bewitched cane of the sergeant, there now emerged a fairly tall and strong fellow, whose blood-soaked apron and large knife identified him as one of the butchers, and I thought that his corporation must nourish a particular devotion for the Virgin, since I'd see four of his colleagues bearing the statue of Mary.

"These satanic monsters," cried the butcher, "these sacrilegious demons had the temerity not to remove their caps when the Blessed Virgin passed!"

"But they're all holding them in their hands," observed the sergeant.

And as he said this, Giacomi, Miroul and I brandished our hats so all could see them. Seeing this, the crowd began to shout:

"It's not them, it's the other one!"

"Which other one?" said the guard.

"Sergeant," I said, loud enough for the crowd to hear me, "sadly, they're talking about my brother, who's suffered from a cooling of the brain and has lost his mind."

"And where is this brother?"

229

"He's right behind us. He's too stupid even to run away!"

The sergeant turned around, saw Samson and, struck by his appearance, took him by the arm and led him over to the crowd, where Samson remained just as immobile as before, his azure eyes gazing with inexpressible sweetness on these fanatics, since, having no doubt that they were going to kill him, he imagined himself too close to eternal happiness not to pardon his executioners. In truth, he didn't look so stupid as he did simply absent from himself and the world, but it would have been easy to be mistaken about this, and the sergeant, very moved by his beauty and his uncanny calmness, didn't know what to think of this devil who looked so much like an angel. However, a moment later, as he gazed at Samson's copper-coloured hair shining in the August sun, he realized that my beloved brother's head was bare, and, turning to the crowd, he yelled, "What nonsense is this? The gentleman is in keeping with today's fashion: he has no hat."

At these words, complete silence fell over the street as the entire crowd gazed at Samson with the most extreme stupor, eyes wide, while Samson himself, touching his head with both hands, said:

"My hat! Where's my hat?"

And looking wildly all around him, he seemed completely lost. If he'd been play-acting, he couldn't have done any better, nor could I, nor Giacomi, who fell speechless at this miracle and began looking here and there, and soon the crowd themselves began looking around them as well. Things had almost reached the point where these fanatics would have helped us find the very hat that had symbolized the sacrilege that minutes earlier they wanted to avenge.

We were in the midst of this strange predicament when a woman in the crowd, whom I remember vividly even today since she was so large of bosom and of derrière that it looked like she was carrying two enormous sacks in front and two that had slipped down her back behind her, suddenly raised her eyes heavenward and cried in a loud voice:

"What are you looking for? By my faith, I tell you you'll not find a thing, you fat, silly men! It's not hard to figure out what's happened! One of God's beautiful angels who was passing by, troubled that this poor red-headed madman—for he is a redhead, you see, as madmen often are—forgot to take his hat off before Notre-Dame de la Carole, so he snatched it from his head and carried it off into heaven as an offering and a trophy to lay at the feet of the Blessed Virgin, and the Lord Her Blessed Son."

"Amen!" shouted the crowd with one voice, and yet I could tell that they were still in some doubt and hesitation, for these words had come from a mere wench, and according to popular opinion the only brains a woman had were between her legs. And so they stood there unmoving, uncertain as to whether they should kill Samson or let him go, yet still in a dangerous mood, in case someone else, in the name of the Virgin, should inspire them to further violence. And so I decided to seize on the rebound the heavy ball the woman had thrown, and to jump into the game of mystification and manipulation of these poor idolaters. To be sure, it would be lying, but shouldn't a wise man speak to men according to their particular folly when common sense is lacking and would be of no help?

So, climbing quickly onto one of the ledges of the doorway, I cried:

"Good people, I feel that this good woman has spoken the truth! The beautiful angel she spoke of could have burnt my brother alive and reduced him to ashes instead of taking his hat. And if this angel didn't, it was because he was so filled with pity for this poor lad, who, as I told the sergeant, is so afflicted with madness that he knows not what he says nor what he does, sometimes saying he's a Huguenot, at others a Jew and still others a Turk. How can we hold a madman's folly against him? Oh, good people, this innocent has a heart so pure that the Lord, having denied him his reason, gave him instead a face so beautiful and a body so vigorous that anyone could see that this poor fellow is himself an angel whom God will take right up into His Paradise when he dies."

At this, the sergeant of the French Guards, whether persuaded by my speech or simply because he wanted to put this tumult to rest, shouted, "Amen!"

But the crowd was still hesitating when one of the men—who only moments before was calling for the death of my brother—now hearing talk of angels, said that nothing was more certain, for he himself had seen with his own eyes a great light on Samson's head and, an instant later, his hat had vanished.

This testimony carried the day. The entire crowd was overcome with amazement at this miracle and began to see Samson with new eyes, some of them praising his angelic beauty, others bemoaning his poor clouded brain, and some of the women even came up to him and wanted to touch his shoulder or take a hair from his head (since red hair brings luck), and because Samson was so confused he simply let this all happen with the most edifying patience. They even brought him some milk and someone slipped some coins into his hand (which he didn't refuse), while others anointed him with musk and benzoin, my brother thanking each one profusely.

Believing in his simplicity that the scales had simply fallen from the eyes of these people and that they had renounced their idolatry, he called them "my brothers" and "my sisters" with his sweet voice, while his blue eyes looked at them with infinite beneficence. "Oh, Lord Jesus!" said one. "It's true the poor fellow is a lunatic! Would he love us if he hadn't lost his mind?" And he kissed his hand and his doublet. So touched were they by his candour and beauty and by the sweetness of his nature that I thought for a moment that they were going to take Samson on their shoulders and carry him through the streets in witness to this new miracle of the Blessed Virgin.

However, the priests, none of whom had been able to witness this scene, because it had all happened at the very tail of their procession, became worried, as I heard later, by the discovery that many of their following had dropped away, and sent some clerics to bring this little flock back into the fold, which the *missi dominici** did with marvellous speed—so great, alas! is the authority, in this papist city, that the clergy wields over its bloodthirsty sheep.

When the last of these had departed to help set fire to the wicker mannequin—a poor sacrificial victim, I concede, when they could have had my brother's beautiful red blood to avenge the blood that was spilt 144 years before by the martyred marble of their idol—I asked the sergeant of the French Guards if he'd do me the favour of having a drink with us to help settle our emotions. Though he hesitated, he consented, and with a thousand thanks, he led us to a nearby tavern, where he must have been a regular, since scarcely had he entered before a very forward wench brought him, with many smiles and glances, an excellent wine that, for once, I didn't have to order at Parisian prices.

The five of us finished the flagon in the blink of an eye, and out of courtesy I would have ordered a second had the sergeant not raised his hand and opposed it, saying that, as a master-at-arms at the Louvre, he drank little, and particularly not in the afternoon or before fencing lessons, wishing to conserve his wind and breath. I almost told him who Giacomi was, but changed my mind, observing that Giacomi himself said nothing and maintained an inscrutable expression, the *maestro* being very particular about the quality of people with whom he condescended to cross swords—not out of self-importance, as we'd seen, but because he so valued his art that he didn't want to lower it to the level of some unpolished swashbuckler. And yet, by almost

---

* "Emissaries of the Lord."

233

imperceptible signs, it seemed to me that he liked the sergeant well enough, who appeared to have manners and a bearing above his condition, and who was polite, quite reserved—reticent about himself, not inquisitive about others—and little inclined to parade his prowess, as one might have expected from his height and strength, which surpassed any I'd ever seen before. As deep as his voice was and, as we'd observed, capable of thunderous shouts when necessary, he spoke gently in company, gestured little, and maintained a serene expression.

I told him my name and whose son I was, which he found very interesting since his father, who'd preceded him in the military, as his grandfather and great-grandfather had done, had fought at Calais. It seemed that the word "Calais" untied his tongue, for he told me he was from Toulouse and that he was called Rabastens. Surprised that he was from the south, I asked him how it happened that he spoke French in the Parisian manner; he smiled and told me that he'd had to work very hard at it since the Parisians, in their arrogance, were quite intolerant of any accent but their own. We all laughed, and he along with us, knowing full well what we speakers of *langue d'oc* thought of this attitude.

After this we felt more at ease with each other, and noticing that he asked questions neither about the incident in the street nor about Samson (though he must have noticed that my handsome brother, on closer inspection, was not in the least demented), I decided that I could trust him completely, and told him that I was on my way to visit Monsieur de Nançay in the rue des Sablons, and why.

"Well," observed Rabastens, "you won't find him. He's not at home now. He's gone to play tennis at the Louvre."

"At the Louvre? Do you mean there are tennis courts at the Louvre?"

"There are two of them, not inside, but set against the surrounding walls and very conveniently placed to the right and to the left of the entrance on the rue d'Hostriche. The captain, who despite his age remains one of the most capable players of the court, prefers the court on the left because, he says, the ground is more solid, the light better and the balls more lively. They call this court the Five Virgins because the master there has five daughters who are awaiting husbands."

"Will they get them?"

"Assuredly so! The master is quite well-to-do since the king gives him his business."

"The king plays tennis?"

"Furiously!" replied Rabastens.

And that this word fit Charles IX perfectly I would soon discover for myself, for you couldn't set foot in the Louvre without people everywhere telling you with what *furia* the king blew his trumpets, brandished the hammer in his forge or shot the arquebus; or how he hunted like a madman, and leapt off his horse, knife in hand, to kill his quarry, loving the sight of blood spurting from its fuming entrails.

Rabastens very politely offered to take me to the Five Virgins to see Monsieur de Nançay, since he himself had to go to the Louvre for his fencing work. So we headed back to the rue de la Ferronnerie, and went as far as the grand'rue Saint-Honoré, which hardly deserves to be called "grand", although there are many beautiful nobles' houses there.

Since the names of the streets on our left, which had been carved in stone at eye level, had become illegible over time, Rabastens named them for us so that when we returned we'd remember the route we'd taken and not have to ask some insolent Guillaume. And so we passed the rue Tirechappe, then the rue de Bresse, next the rue des Poulies, and turned left into the rue de l'Hostriche, which was the most famous in Paris since it led to the Louvre.

"I call it rue de l'Hostriche," Rabastens said, "since that's what my father called it. But some Parisians call it l'Autruche, thinking it's named for the ostrich, and still others call it l'Autriche, thinking it's named for Austria. There's no way to know who's right and who's wrong, since the name has completely worn away."

"But isn't there a map of the city that would show it's real name?"

"I've heard there was one," Rabastens replied, "although few have ever seen it, and those that have claim that it was full of mistakes, both in the layout and in the names of streets."

"Well," I thought, "what a strange and anarchic city, where everything is so uncertain: the lighting, public safety, street names!" But I fell silent when I saw the Louvre, which filled me with a kind of silent awe and even fear, such as the subjects of a great and powerful monarch should feel in his presence. And though I'm not normally subject to such abject emotions, I nevertheless couldn't help feeling dwarfed by the immense city that surrounded me and by the prodigious building that commanded the kingdom.

Certainly it's no insignificant thing in Sarlat to be the younger son of the Baron de Mespech, lodged in a chateau with such beautiful ramparts, cousin of the Caumont brothers of Castelnau and Milandes, allied with Pierre de Bourdeille, the abbot of Brantôme, and friend of so many Huguenot and papist gentlemen in Périgord. But here, what was I? What did I matter? What was I worth in this capital city and at the foot of the Louvre, bristling with its towers? This was the seat of royal power, with its Swiss guards, its prisons, its cannon (a single one of which could have destroyed the walls of Mespech), and its sovereign, descended from a great line, absolute master of one of the great kingdoms of the universe, holding irrefutable sway over the lives and liberties of his subjects—and what's more, solemnly crowned, anointed by the holy chrism, ruling by a divine right that even the Huguenots wouldn't dare contest!

The wall surrounding the chateau began at the corner of the rue de l'Hostriche, but you couldn't see the three towers that were lined up along it, since the king had allowed houses to be built up against this wall, which considerably diminished its defensive value. But did the king really need this enclosure, these moats which ran along his formidable palace to protect him? Against whom? There were so many riches that flowed his way and so many gentlemen to protect them, who were so zealous to serve him that they would have given their souls to him if he'd asked for them.

The keeper of the tennis courts and five or six guards, poleaxes in hand, stopped us at the entryway into the Five Virgins, and wouldn't have let us pass had not Rabastens pushed us through ahead of him, including Miroul, for which I was very grateful since our valet had acted so quickly to save my Samson.

In truth, this tennis court wasn't any better than the one belonging to Chancellor Saporta in Montpellier, other than in its grandstands, which were so full of courtiers and noble ladies that there wouldn't have been room for a pin—this was doubtless the reason that Rabastens led us, by way of a small staircase, to a stand that was smaller but higher than the first one, and that occupied the back wall and was made of wood like the grandstand; the wall opposite this structure was made of closely joined stone bricks so that one could play, as they said in Paris, *à la bricole*, that is, one could make the ball ricochet against its surface to place it in the opponent's camp without its passing under the rope. But I express myself badly when I use this word, for the two opposing camps were separated by a rope, to be sure, but to it were attached a whole series of closely spaced fringes that extended to the ground: a refinement unknown in Montpellier, where occasionally there were very hot arguments about whether the ball had passed over or under the rope; here, however, the fringes impeded the ball's progress when it was launched too low, so that there were fewer disputes—or at least so I believed.

The smaller stands, to which Rabastens led us, were occupied only by a scorekeeper, who stood ready, a piece of white charcoal in hand, to mark the points of the match on a board placed at the front of the stand, and easily visible by the spectators in the grandstand that was at a right angle to ours. The scorekeeper's face had been sewn up with a scar across the top of his bald skull; he had a wooden left leg and the face of a veteran of several wars—which he must have been, for, initially unhappy about our arrival, he softened considerably when he saw Rabastens, and immediately placed on his shiny bald head a feathered hat of the kind worn by the foot guards twenty years previously, and then doffed it when he made a deep bow to the sergeant, who returned the gesture with great dignity.

"Monsieur," said the man, "if these gentlemen are with you they are welcome here. But they should sit at the back and shouldn't show themselves since these stands are reserved for the score."

"I understand completely," said Rabastens.

We four then bowed to the scorekeeper, who again put on his hat (which had as many feathers as a rooster's tail), and doffed it a second time as he bowed to us, though without as much pomp or so deep a genuflection as he'd made to the sergeant.

As for me, I only had eyes for the grandstand, never having seen an assemblage so richly attired in silks, brocades and pearls, and other precious stones, nor one so colourful, the courtiers, as well as the ladies, dressed in clothes of which not a sleeve or stocking was the same colour as any other item, so that you would have thought you were looking at a garden of a thousand different flowers displaying a thousand palettes of nature.

But I was distracted from this gay and gallant spectacle by a great commotion in the grandstand caused by the entrance of the queen mother, whom I recognized by her black clothing and by the retinue of ladies-in-waiting of such beauty as to stop your breath in your lungs. These ladies were in truth famous throughout the kingdom for their beauty, and gave the impression of flying around

Catherine de' Medici in their brilliant finery like so many brilliant pieces of the rainbow.

The queen mother took her place in the middle of the grand-stand under a canopy painted with the fleur-de-lis that I would have thought reserved for the king. But that she should casually usurp it did not surprise me, since d'Argence had written to my father that at Charles IX's entry into the city of Metz, three years previously, Catherine de' Medici had demanded that she enter the gates before the king her son—you heard me: before the king!—and with her own cortège of ladies and officers. Well, no doubt the Florentine needed revenge for all the slights and scorn she'd suffered, both in the court of François I and during the reign of her husband, Henri II, when, with Diane de Poitiers reigning, even in the conjugal bed, she had to accept her rival's supremacy.

It seemed as though, from that time on, she had only insults for names: "the shopkeeper" was the name the courtiers in the Louvre gave her when she arrived from Florence. "Jezebel" was what the Huguenots called her after the Meeting of Bayonne, at which she tried to bargain for French blood with the Duque de Alba, in an attempt to exchange the massacre of the Protestants for a Spanish marriage.

I could only see her from above and in profile, except when she turned her head to the right, which she did quite often, her large, dilated eyes paying close attention to everything that was going on around her. She seemed smaller and more obese than she'd been described to me, her cheeks round and puffy, her lower lip hanging loosely, and yet not at all languid in her movements, but, quite the contrary, lively and vigorous. She had a worried look in her eyes, which were veiled by heavy eyelids that gave her a somewhat toad-like appearance. Pierre de L'Étoile had told me that she had taken great umbrage at the fact that Coligny had Charles's ear, and was pushing the king to go to war in Flanders, believing that the favour

our leader enjoyed might threaten the great power she exercised in the state and force her into exile.

I cannot fathom how all those splendid ladies-in-waiting, with their beautiful hoop skirts, managed to squeeze in behind the queen mother on this grandstand, which was already so full, but I certainly wouldn't have minded to find myself in the middle of their ranks, with all the rustling of the petticoats, and I began to dream about it with great appetite given how much women's beauty holds sway over our thoughts without our even willing it to. But suddenly I remembered my unfortunate doublet, which, not content simply to be outmoded, had the temerity to display on its front a shameful repair, and I felt a cruel chagrin. This piece of my wardrobe would cause me to be completely despised in gallant company, and, what's more, would doubtless deprive me for ever of the sweet joys that the little house on the rue Trouvevache had promised me that very morning. What to do? Without my own money, or any money I could expect from Samson, was there any remedy to this predicament?

I was in the midst of such mental thorns and brambles when I saw a middle-aged gentleman enter the arena clad in shirt and leggings only—that is, without his doublet. He was fairly tall, but well built, youthful and vigorous, with tanned skin, grey eyes, thick eyebrows, a square face and a goatee more pepper than salt; his head was erect and he had a spring in his step even though he was walking slowly. He headed towards the queen mother, made her a deep bow, to which she responded with a nod and a smile gracious enough for me to believe that this gentleman was well received in court. This was confirmed by the applause of the courtiers and the ladies when he greeted them all with an ample and gracious gesture.

"Monsieur de Nançay," observed the scorekeeper to our mentor, "seems none the worse for his fall from his horse."

"Indeed," Rabastens replied. "The captain is built with brick and mortar. You'd need a cannonball to take him down!"

A brouhaha from the grandstand interrupted him, followed by a burst of applause, and I saw that a second gentleman, also clad only in shirt and leggings, had entered the tennis court. But this one rushed up to the stands, bowed to the queen mother and then ran over to Nançay and embraced him. After which, wishing to reach the opponent's side, he simply jumped over the rope; but, strange to tell, he went head-first as if diving into a river, and landed on the ground on his two hands and neck and did a complete somersault before coming to a standing position with incredible dexterity—an exploit that was warmly applauded by the spectators.

"Now there's a marvellous leaper!" I exclaimed to Rabastens. "Who is the gentleman?"

"But it's the king," whispered Rabastens.

"What? Did I hear you right? The king?"

"The king himself."

I was astounded, and you may well imagine that I had eyes only for the sovereign as the tennis master walked over to him, followed by two valets, one carrying the racquets and the other a basketful of balls.

Charles IX was fairly tall and well proportioned, though very thin and a bit stooped, and, despite his agility he had a generally unhealthy look about him. His eyes maintained a thoroughly distrustful look; this was coupled with an expression that suggested both a lack of self-assurance and a general nervousness. Moreover, his gestures and his behaviour betrayed a need to be seen and, at the same time, a sort of childish fear of not being seen enough, having nothing of the composure or the self-confidence of a man of twenty-two whose power, if he'd wanted to exercise it, would be practically limitless.

With the tennis master I found him both too familiar and too brusque, all smiles one minute and frowning the next. Of the racquets that were offered him, two were strung with string, one square and one oval, and a third, round one was made of stretched parchment. From what I could tell by watching him, it was this third one that the tennis master recommended, a choice the king refused outright, as if he judged this suggestion to be impertinent. He then seemed to hesitate between the two strung racquets and kept taking up the oval one, then the square one without being able to make up his mind. This oscillation threatening to last the entire morning, the tennis master, without any sign that he was intimidated, again suggested the one made of parchment, and this time the king accepted it, but with visibly bad grace and less because he was convinced it was the right choice than because he simply couldn't make up his mind between the other two.

The second valet offering him the choice of a ball from the basket, the king made a brusque and impatient gesture, rejecting the responsibility of this decision, passing it on to Monsieur de Nançay, who acquitted himself admirably in this task, bouncing each of the balls on the ground and keeping the liveliest of them.

"Nançay," said the king, "I'm wagering 100 écus on myself. How much do you wager?"

"Fifty écus on myself, sire."

"By God!" cried the king. "Fifty is very little!"

"Sire," replied Monsieur de Nançay, bowing to him, "I'd wager more if I were more assured of winning."

At this the king laughed and seemed happy, and even more so when the Medici's page stepped up to announce that the queen mother would give 100 écus to the winner and fifty to the loser. The colourful assembly applauded and buzzed with appreciation at this announcement, and, as for me, I wouldn't swear that the whole thing hadn't been arranged beforehand by the Florentine and Monsieur de Nançay so that the captain wouldn't leave any feathers on the court.

The two umpires (two gentlemen, one chosen by the king and the other by Monsieur de Nançay) immediately requested the money from each player and the whole amount was deposited in a little pile on a small velvet rug placed at the level of the cord. All the while the king was jumping up and down with impatience and giving furious racquet strokes in the air.

"Sire," said Monsieur de Nançay, "shall we play *à la bricole* and allow ricocheted shots?"

"I don't know," answered the king. "Do you want to?"

"I think not."

But since Charles IX fell silent and couldn't decide, Monsieur de Nançay, pretending the decision had been made, continued, "Sire, would you like to serve first?"

"I don't know," answered the king. "I don't see that it's to my advantage."

"Then don't, sire, since it might be to your disadvantage," smiled Nançay.

"Sire," said one of the two umpires, "may it please Your Majesty to spin your racquet? Let chance decide."

"I choose the mark," said Nançay.

"And I the blank side," said the king, quickly making this choice since there was no other.

The king placed his racquet on the ground with it's oval top down, spun it like a top and let go. It fell on the mark, so that Monsieur de Nançay had service and the king seemed quite vexed, as if, not having it, he suddenly perceived that there was some advantage to it he hadn't discerned before.

"Now, let's play!" he cried, backing up in little jumps almost all the way to our little gallery, and, seeing him take up his position, the valets who would pick up the balls ran to take their places, some to the four corners of the court and others to the sides of the rope. The tennis master threw a ball to Monsieur de Nançay from among the ones that he'd chosen. The captain caught it with his left hand and immediately set himself to serve.

"Here you go, sire!" he cried.

He served the ball over the rope with great force and, though it bounced quite a distance from him, the king rushed at it and struck it so fast and at such a low angle that Nançay couldn't reach it, even on the rebound.

"Fifteen for me!" shouted the king, greatly pleased with himself.

To which the umpire—although the two consulted on each point, only one of the two spoke—echoed the king: "Fifteen for the king!"

So the scorekeeper, with a sweeping movement of his arm, as if he were about to put his lips to a trumpet, marked "fifteen" in white chalk on his slate in exquisitely shaped and rounded characters.

"Here you go, sire!" cried Nançay, but this time the king couldn't catch up with the ball, even with the end of his racquet.

"Messieurs, you're at fifteen each!" cried the umpire.

"Now, let's play," said the king, teeth clenching and jumping with impatience and spite. However, Nançay did not serve the ball.

"What are you waiting for, Nançay?" snarled the king.

"For them to bring me more tennis balls, sire," replied Nançay with a bow.

And, indeed, from what I could gather, the rule here was that the valets' job was to pick up the balls, but instead of giving them to the players, they were to return them to the tennis master, who, alone, had the right to toss them to the server—a slow and pompous process that was unknown in the provinces. Likewise, a single ball was used here for a game of sixty points, after which they put it in the basket and took another—a good method of assuring the same bounce throughout, but one that tended to slow the game down, whereas in

Montpellier we were so refined that we used half a dozen balls despite differences in their bounce.

"Here you go, sire!" called Nançay as soon as the tennis master had supplied him.

Whether by design or not, he served this ball so softly that the king, taking it on the volley, returned it with such ferocity that Nançay couldn't touch it. A nice shot, however easy (but in truth also easy to miss) and which the audience applauded with great enthusiasm.

"Thirty to His Majesty!" cried the umpire.

"Hurry up with the ball!" cried the king, growing feverish and impatient.

The tennis master supplied Nançay with a ball and he served, and this time with force. And as the ball rebounded, the king made a very pretty leap and sent it back to the left of Nançay, who, though surprised, sent it so hard to the king's left that the king missed it.

"Messieurs, you're at thirty each!" announced the umpire.

At this, overcome with a sudden rage that completely silenced the spectators, the king threw his racquet to the ground and stomped on it, piercing the parchment. "By God!" he cried, crimson, his eyes darting flames. "Tennis master from hell! This racquet is nothing but piss and shit, God's truth! Do you want to see me lose, you knave? Bring me a string racquet and fast!"

At which the tennis master, ashamed and abashed, ran over with the two racquets that the sovereign had first rejected and that now he immediately scorned, throwing them both to the ground, though neither broke. A hush fell over the arena at this and the mood was quite dark when a pretty page, very beautifully dressed in a crimson doublet, leapt out of the grandstand and, going up to the king, made him a profound bow and said in a clear voice, "Sire, Monsieur de Nemours would be very honoured if you would consent to use his racquet."

"The honour will be mine," replied the king, recovering a courteous tone as quickly as he'd lost it. "Monsieur de Nemours," he added after a moment, "is the best player in the kingdom."

This reply was enthusiastically applauded and considerably relaxed the spectators, who went back to chattering, which included some smiles, certain of which, as far as I could tell, were quite brazen and others openly derisive. While they were going to fetch Monsieur de Nemours's racquet, I said to Rabastens: "What a smashing return the captain made to the king!"

"He let himself get carried away in the heat of the moment," smiled Rabastens. "Otherwise he wouldn't have hit it so hard."

The scorekeeper turned round and, looking at me, said, "Monsieur, do you play?"

"Daily."

"And where would that be?"

"In Montpellier."

"So you don't know Monsieur de Nemours?"

"Not at all."

"Aha!" replied the man, his sewed-up face wrinkling, and he rubbed his bald head with his right hand, which had the effect of whitewashing his skull since his hand was covered with chalk dust. "As for the captain's return, I agree that they're very, very good. But if you could see Monsieur de Nemours's returns! If you haven't seen them, you've seen nothing at all!"

"Doesn't he play against the king?"

"The king hasn't invited him to do so," said Rabastens, with a sly light in his grey eyes.

"Now, let's play!" cried Charles IX, brandishing the famous racquet that he'd just been handed.

"Here you go, sire!" said Nançay.

And taking up his position, he served the ball with so little force that it dropped no more than a quarter of the way into the king's side of the court. The king rushed madly to hit it on the first bounce and did so with the end of his racquet, sending it screaming over the rope. The ball barely cleared the rope and was hit so low that it scarcely bounced at all. Monsieur de Nançay, caught off guard, was frozen to the spot and made no attempt to field it.

"Well, sire," he laughed, "now there's a shot that reminds me of your grandfather François I, absolutely unreturnable!"

At this recollection, which was often evoked at the court, the king smiled gratefully, and the assembly broke into wild applause—as much, I thought, to acclaim the dexterity of the sovereign as to recognize the diplomacy of the courtier's response.

"Forty-five for His Majesty!" cried the umpire. "Thirty for Monsieur de Nançay!"

"Sire," said Nançay, "hold on to your racquet! I'm going to equalize!"

"For the love of God," laughed the king, "you'll do nothing of the kind! Plague on you, Nançay! 'Sblood! The game will be mine!"

"I thought," I remarked to the sergeant, "that, according to royal decree, no tennis player in the arena should tolerate blasphemy, swearing or impiety."

"The king," Rabastens, his face inscrutable, "knows the decree well. It's he who signed it!"

"Alas," said the scorekeeper, who seemed to have a very serious turn of mind, "many of our young gentlemen of the court believe that blaspheming makes a man more valiant and stronger! It's quite the opposite."

"Here you go, sire!" said Nançay, and served up a high, soft shot which the king tried to return on the volley. He didn't miss it, but aimed too low, and the ball hit the rope and fell into the netting on his side. However, its own momentum carried it under the rope and onto Nançay's side.

"It's my point!" cried the king without waiting for the decision of the umpires.

There erupted among the spectators much chatter and laughter—for good reason—and I wouldn't have liked them if I'd been the sovereign. He, however, brandished his racquet and danced about like a child.

"Umpires, the decision!" he cried in a caustic voice.

The umpires, who were conferring in hushed tones, raised their heads, and the head umpire proclaimed: "The point is disputed!"

"What!" screamed the king, suddenly looking like a brewing storm. "You're disputing the point? That's scandalous! Look! The ball's on the other side! Nançay couldn't reach it!"

"Assuredly," conceded Nançay, smiling on the other side of his face, "I was unable to reach it!"

"Sire," said the umpire with a bow, "one of us believes the ball, hitting the rope, fell back on your side and then rolled underneath but below the netting."

"It's a scandal," cried the king, "that such an opinion should be professed in here! What says Her Majesty the queen? I will bow to her wise judgement."

There followed a long silence, during which the ladies-in-waiting of Catherine de' Medici closed ranks around her like a swarm of bees around their queen; and after this swarm buzzed and hummed for a while, one of the most sparkling ladies emerged and came onto the tennis court, swaying in her gorgeous hoop skirt, her bosom ripe as fruit, her lips fresh as strawberries, her face so beautiful and altogether so splendid in her finery that my heart started beating like a bell and my jaws tightened in the terrible appetite I had to lick the whole length of her adorable body.

This beauty made such a profound and gracious bow to the king that you would have to have been a tiger not to be tamed by her. "Her Majesty the queen," she said in a clear, sweet voice, "remembers that when your august father, Henri II, was playing this noble sport and a point was disputed, like today's, he accepted, in his royal condescension, to have the point replayed."

"I shall obey the queen, my mother," said the king, who had never in his life done otherwise, and bowed politely to his beautiful messenger with a touch of timidity, which I certainly would not have displayed in his place. But, alas, how great was my loss not to be there!

The tennis master immediately provided a ball to Monsieur de Nançay, who took up his position and said, "Here you go, sire!" And he served his master and sire so well, and so low, that the ball ended up in the net.

"Point and game to His Majesty!" cried the umpire, greatly relieved.

And the spectators all vigorously applauded the king's victory— and, I'd wager, Monsieur de Nançay's skill at not being too skilful.

That particular skill was maintained throughout the two sets, the captain winning only one game in the first and two in the second, but those two came after the king had already won five, a handsome advantage that allowed Charles IX to maintain his calm and good manners even though he was in a lather and completely exhausted.

The king changed his shirt on the court and one of his gentleman gave him a rub-down, both front and back; all the while the king coughed to break your heart, yet not so much that he couldn't demand the profits from the bet he'd made. The tennis master brought him the money in a hat and I could see the coins shining from my perch above the court. Oh, heaven! How I wished that those coins were ringing in my own purse! I could have put them to such good use!

The king won fifty écus from the captain of his guards and received 100 from his mother, who must have found this an excellent occasion to reassure her son that he was more precious to her than Coligny, who, in his Huguenot stiffness, would never have agreed to do anything so frivolous as watch a tennis match—let alone place a bet on such a thing. For his part, the king seemed very happy to have acquired these 150 écus, and said out loud (a phrase that was immediately repeated throughout the Louvre) that this money was really his, since he hadn't had to request it from his treasuries. But, after all, where did the queen mother get this money from if not from the royal treasury?

"The king," said the scorekeeper, turning to speak to us and wiping his chalky hand across the scar on his cranium, "is just as supple, vigorous and lively as his royal father was, and," he added sotto voce, "just like his father, he can't tolerate losing."

"True enough," agreed Rabastens, "but Henri II enjoyed better health. His son can't keep from coughing up phlegm and destroying his chest. That's the reason he gets exhausted so quickly. Tomorrow he'll spend the entire day in bed to recover from this match."

As he was speaking, I went over to the scorekeeper and, to thank him for his kindness, put two sols in his hand. At first he refused to take them, but, at my insistence, he ended up pocketing them, but in a very brusque and surly manner, yet smiling all the while.

"Monsieur de Siorac," said Rabastens, "the captain is not busy at the moment, and is enjoying this good and worthy defeat, which has earned him so much favour. Would you like to seize the ball on the rebound? I'll take you to meet him."

"Oh, Sergeant! How much obliged I am! I could never repay you!"

"So I absolve you of all debt!" laughed Rabastens. "Are you not from the south?"

As we were descending this spiral staircase, Giacomi took my arm and said quietly, "My brother, go to see Monsieur de Nançay alone. I'll keep Samson company while you do."

I agreed, understanding all too well what he meant and that he was afraid my beloved Samson would say something that would offend the captain. And it's true that throughout the tennis match, my mind kept returning to Samson and my fears that he was ill equipped to live in this papist Babylon and constantly risked, in his simplicity, exposing himself into incredible dangers. And in the end, as much as I loved him, I regretted not having left him in Maître Béqueret's pharmacy in Montfort-l'Amaury, and all the more so since they'd so urgently requested it and he himself had so ardently wished it, having so much interest in his glass bottles and finding nothing to interest him in this city of Paris, which had already enchanted me with its beauty and brilliance.

Rabastens led us to a small room at the entrance to the tennis courts, which he entered without knocking, indicating I should follow him. Monsieur de Nançay was having a rub-down while the tennis master watched.

He was conversing with a great hippopotamus of an Englishman, clothed in scarlet, hair so blonde it looked white, and a large face as red as a ham, who was paying him compliments about his game, laughing uproariously at every third word, being of an extremely jovial and energetic complexion.

"Milord," said Monsieur de Nançay, as he gave me a nod that was all the more courteous since he had no idea who I was, "I thank you a thousand times for your generous compliments, but I'm sure that Queen Elizabeth's subjects play tennis as well as we French!"

"Not at all as well!" laughed the "milord". "I'm amazed by the great number of tennis courts I've seen in Paris. From your king to the smallest valet, anyone can get involved!" (He laughed.) "You'd think French people were born with a racquet in their hands!" (And he laughed again.)

"And do you have the same rules in England as we do, Milord?" asked Monsieur de Nançay, smiling politely.

"All the same, even the words, except that, before serving, you say '*Tenez!*' and we say 'Tenetz!'—which some of our ignoramuses who don't know French pronounce 'tennis'!"

"And do you use the same balls?"

"We use yours since ours don't bounce very well."

"You mean mine," said the tennis master, jumping shamelessly into the conversation with great self-assurance, "for I'm the one who sells them to your country, Milord, and no one else, since mine are the best in the kingdom: they're made with the best leather, and are stuffed with oakum, or with dog hair, and not with white chalk or bran, as some black marketeers do, whom I've had outlawed by the king."

"Dog hair, eh!" said the milord, and he laughed again, a laugh I was beginning to find quite tiring, especially since I resented the amazing effrontery of the tennis master, who went on and on singing his own praises and importance, to the point where one would believe he was giving orders to the king. But later, when I got to know the court better, I realized that this fellow was simply conforming to common practice, Parisians being so credulous and gossipy that they seem to accept every accomplishment at face value. Which is why they all go around trumpeting their own glory.

As this chatter went on between the sniggering Milord and the bumptious tennis master on the subject of balls, I watched Monsieur de Nançay, who seemed to be listening, but was, I guessed, a thousand leagues away, and so I was able to study the captain of the guards at my leisure, as his valet gave him his rub-down. He was a tall man, with broad shoulders, well-muscled arms and long sprightly legs, and there was not an ounce of fat on him. He had a square, tanned face with an aquiline nose and a scar on the corner of his fleshy lower lip. His hair, as I think I mentioned, was more pepper than salt, his eyebrows very black and bushy, which gave him, even at rest, a somewhat supercilious air, something that was softened by his fine, ironic but benign look, all of which seemed to me to indicate some scepticism about common beliefs. He appeared very self-assured, circumspect and courteous, and had an elegant way of expressing himself. There was something so polished about him, it brought to mind a stone become perfectly smooth by its interaction with the other stones in the court, but one that was not without its hardness under this suave exterior—not, certainly, hardness of heart, but a toughness derived from his situation and his predicament.

At length the milord and the tennis master departed, laughing and chuckling, freeing the room and its rotundity of their unceasing noise, and Rabastens told his captain who I was and then begged our leave to go off to his fencing lessons.

"What, a Siorac!" cried Monsieur de Nançay, giving me a warm embrace. "What a delight to see the son of the Baron de Mespech here in the flesh! For if anyone ever deserved to be a baron, it's your father, who so gallantly fought when we retook Calais from the English. But 'sblood! I still can't say the name of Calais without my heart beating faster! Or without remembering the bravery of our great captains beneath its walls! The Duc de Guise! D'Aumale! D'Andelot! Thermes! Bourdin! Sénarpont! How many are already dead? How tenderly I remember these names! But none more highly and clearly than Siorac! Good God! I fought elbow to elbow with him when we crossed the ditch in icy water up to our necks to storm the breach our cannon had made in the Château de Calais! And as frozen as we all were, Siorac was mocking the enemy all the way. My good companion never lost his sense of humour, making a thousand jokes and riotous comments, always funny yet fearless in the teeth of extreme peril. A lion in combat, a dove in victory! And once the city was taken, so caring and concerned about our captives that he tolerated no carnage or rapine from his soldiers. But," continued Nançay, embracing me again, and placing his hands on my shoulders to get a good look at me, "he's here! I see him! You have his laughing blue eyes, his features, his build, his carriage and his insatiable thirst for life and love that he did! Ah, my son! Don't tell me Siorac is now hoary, sad and defeated! I'd never believe it!'"

"Captain," I laughed, "he's practically as youthful and vigorous as you, despite the fact that he's ten years older than you."

"Well!" replied Nançay, a glint in his eye. "Does he still chase the petticoats?"

"Like a madman!"

"And prosperous?"

"He's very well off, yes."

"Well, you'd never guess it from your doublet!" laughed Monsieur de Nançay, and though his remark stung, I didn't let it show and laughed with him. "Heavens! An outmoded doublet and, what's worse, it's been resewn! At the Louvre! At court! 'Sblood! If we were the same size and build, I'd lend you one of mine!"

And though he laughed, I could see that he took my situation to heart and was worried about me. Of Calais and my father, he'd spoken like a soldier, but now, looking at my repaired doublet, he was speaking like a courtier. And then, in his solicitude, he offered to give me the address of his tailor so that I could immediately rejuvenate my wardrobe. I was forced to confess that my father hadn't provided me enough money to cover such an expense.

"Ah," he joked, "so Siorac is still as careful with his money! And, I'll wager, as Huguenot as ever!"

"Unshakeably."

"Alas," said Monsieur de Nançay. "In that, I must dare to say I think he's wrong. A captain should leave religion to the clerics. It's true, when you think about it a little, that ours abounds in manifest absurdities. But bah! You just have to swallow them with all the rest. As for me, I hear Mass every Sunday and go to confession once a year without thinking about it. The world doesn't ask more than that. 'To live happily,' as Ronsard said, 'simplicity is everything.'"

"That's easy," I thought to myself, "when you enjoy the favour of the king"—something that, for both Ronsard and Monsieur de Nançay, has never failed, since this great poet howls with the wolves at the heels of the reformists. But about my father's religion—in which I intend to remain (though without any zeal)—I didn't want to argue, hearing what I'd heard from the captain, and said nothing more. Seeing this, Monsieur de Nançay, whose sharp grey eyes missed nothing, asked me about the affair that brought me here. I told him everything: about my duel and my trial and the king's pardon that I'd come here to seek.

"Well," he said, "as for your access to the Louvre, you only have to ask me: it's already granted. And as for your duel, I'll speak to my friends here to ensure that the king hears of it and is favourably disposed. But that won't suffice. You'll have to be presented to the king. And although he's not as concerned about dress as the Duc d'Anjou, I couldn't possible present you dressed as you are. So we're back to your doublet, and the money you need to have a new one made."

"But," I moaned, "who would ever lend me money, and on what guarantees, since I'm a younger son?"

"I would," said Monsieur de Nançay, continuing immediately, "if I weren't already up to my neck in debt, living in the Louvre well beyond my means, my captain's salary paid only when the king's coffers are full, which is to say, never. Ah, Monsieur de Siorac," he said stroking his long, fine moustache, "what you need is for one of our gallant, generous ladies to pay for your clothes, as several I know here do for some of the pretty young men of the court. But there's the rub! How can you ever approach one of these brilliant ladies dressed as you are?"

Ah, reader! What claws his words planted in my heart, I who was already desperate at the thought that, the next day, I should have to confront Madame des Tourelles, who had already told me to come dressed in new clothes and to have my body shaved, which of course was easier to achieve than the first thing. "So," I said to myself, laughing at my predicament, "I need a fairy with a wand to transform my body hair into an elegant suit!" Sadly, it's true that you're nothing at court without the right clothes. Nobility, merit, wisdom—nothing matters at the Louvre except show. You have to make the right impression or suffer absolute suppression.

I was in the midst of these thorns and pricks, in bitter humour from my humiliation, when a gentleman of about my age entered the room without knocking. He had roughly my build except that he was much better looking than I and superbly dressed in the most marvellous doublet of blue satin I'd ever seen, even at the Louvre. He gave a quick bow to Monsieur de Nançay and, at the very instant that I was in such admiration of him, he gave me such a scornful and insolent look that I paled in my immediate anger and returned his look with a degree of hatred equal to the admiration I'd just felt, and further nourished by the realization that the fellow had seduced me by displaying exactly the image I would have most wanted to present here at the Louvre. The gentleman was greatly surprised by my look, and when his look doubled in arrogance, I matched it, my blue eyes flashing so angrily, as Monsieur de Nançay told me later, that if our eyes had been pistols, we would have laid each other out cold on the ground. In the end, sensing it was ridiculous to continue this awkward predicament, the fellow turned his back, which, from the rigidity of his posture, communicated the infinite disdain he felt. Shaking with rage, I decided to surpass his arrogance, and, making a deep bow to Monsieur de Nançay, and asking to take my leave, I stood up straight and, as the Parthians did in retreat, shot the newcomer such a murderous look as I passed that it's a miracle he didn't fall lifeless on the tiled floor.

Alas! the dart I intended for him wounded me instead, causing me such pain as I was little accustomed to, and I was thoroughly outraged that this fatuous courtier dared trample me underfoot merely because of the sorry state of my doublet. 'Sblood! It's not with the sharp look I gave him but with the sharp point of my sword in his heart that I should have taken my revenge! I quietly roared with anger, my lips pressed as tight as the string of a crossbow and my fists, in my mind's eye, gripping the handles of my weapons, while, drunk with anger, my temples throbbing, my body stiff and my muscles flexed tight, I rushed like a madman from the room where the captain of the guards had received me. It took me a long time, my vision was so troubled, my voice strangled in my throat, to be able to see, hear and converse with my good companions as we headed back through the streets of the capital to Maître Recroche's lodgings. I was so cooked, recooked and boiled in my fury that, all the way back, I said not a word, fearing to howl like a wolf if I opened my mouth. And once back at our lodgings I found myself unbearable and, so mortified that I was unable to tolerate the view of my dear brothers, I left them, telling them in barely audible tones that I felt too dirty and sweaty and was going to head to the baths, and that they should go to the restaurant without me, since I had no appetite.

A Guillaume whom I asked for directions in a severe and roguish manner—I who am normally so pleasant and courteous—was so astonished by my imperious manner that he doffed his hat immediately and said in a trembling voice, "Well, Monseigneur, if you're looking for clean baths with a good reputation, where they won't admit lepers, the pox-infected, thieves or lowlifes, you should go to the Old Baths in the grand'rue Saint-Honoré. It's quite nearby and a prince would feel very much at ease there. The barber of the baths is so expert that she can shave a woman's snatch or a man's prick in a trice. And they have so many facilities at these baths that some people eat there, and even spend the night so they don't have to walk home after dark when the streets are so dangerous."

Having said this, he insisted on accompanying me to these baths, speaking to me with his hat in his hand and in such a humble and fearful manner that I felt a pang of remorse for having so verbally assaulted him. And so, wishing to add some oil to my vinegar, I asked him very pleasantly how it happened that his lips were split.

"Oh, Monseigneur!" he cried. "Surely you jest! You know as well as I do!"

"Not at all!" I answered, quite surprised.

"Monseigneur, you're mocking me!"

"'Sblood!" I cried. "I'm telling you I'm not!"

"What?" said this Gautier, his eyes wide with disbelief. "You're swearing too! But it's for my swearing and blasphemy (a terrible habit that I'm trying to break) that I had my lips split! Alas! First a fine, then the iron collar—and now split lips! Nothing worked! I'm still swearing like a picklock!"

"Yes," I said quietly to myself, "just like the king of France at tennis."

"Monseigneur," this Guillaume continued without listening to me, "when you spoke to me so abruptly just now, my mouth was still hot after stepping in some excrement in the street. So of course I thought you'd heard me and that you were going to denounce me."

"So what would they have done this time?"

"They would have cut my tongue out!"

"Ah! What a barbarous act! Does the judge think that he's pleasing Christ by being so pitiless? And why would I denounce you, my friend?"

"For the reward, which is one-third of the fine."

"And who gets the other two-thirds?"

"One-third to the clergy, the other to the king."

"To the king!" I said. "That's justice and equity for you! And so, friend," I continued, putting a sol in his hand, "my thanks for your escort. Go in peace and by God's blood, as they say in the Louvre, don't swear any more! You're not noble enough for it."

This encounter had somewhat revived me from my mortification and the excellent condition of the baths contributed even more. They were beautiful and clean, the marble floors had been washed, the walls were covered with blue and white tiles up to a man's height, and here and there plants and flowers graced the rooms.

The mistress of the baths was a large and powerful woman whose arms were as thick as my thighs, and whose thighs, when she stood up, appeared as thick as the trunk of a century-old oak tree. Her breasts were so enormous that, supported tightly as they were by her bodice, they were practically pushed up to her nose, which forced her to tip back her head, a soft and swollen sphere in which two eyes, just visible through little slits narrower than the loopholes in a rampart, peered out at her customers, whom she espied like a cat stalking a bird. I noticed that, as we talked, she was breathing with some difficulty and I surmised that living daily in all the vapours of the baths must have upset the rhythm of her heart.

"Monsieur," she said in so restrained and breathless a voice that it seemed to have difficulty clearing its way through her massive, greasy body, "do you want the baths or the steam rooms?"

"That depends," I replied. "What are your prices?"

"To sweat: two sols. To bathe: four sols. To bathe in a private room: five sols. For a bath cloth and a peignoir, two deniers each."

"A bath cloth and a peignoir?" I asked, mystified by this Parisian jargon. "What are those?"

"They're the same thing, Monsieur, but a peignoir is what you put under your arse while bathing to protect it from the splinters in the wood and the bath cloth is to dry yourself after the bath. One of each?"

"Yes. And the private room as well."

"Monsieur," she asked with a gleam in her eye, "with a bed?"

"Yes."

"That'll be another sol. Are you spending the night?"

"I believe so."

"One sol more. Do you want a barber to take off your body hair?"

"Yes, of course."

"Two sols."

"Ah, good woman!" I cried. "Your sums are adding up too quickly! You're strangling me!"

"Not at all!" she countered, turning crimson; and her bosom swelling under the effect of her indignation, she threw back her head. "These are honest prices, set by the provost of Paris, and you can see them posted on the wall. We're authorized to raise them if wood and coal are scarce in Paris. Monsieur, please be so kind as to pay me in advance. That'll be nine sols, four deniers."

I lightened my purse by this amount and the mistress of the baths shouted at the top of her lungs "Babeau! Babeau!" and a chambermaid appeared, brown-haired and scantily clad, barefoot and bare-armed as well, and her arms were so rosy and round you wanted to take a bite out of them. "Ah," I thought, "a wench from the villages, and it doesn't matter that these villages are in the vicinity of Paris—she reminds me of Cabusse's Cathau or Coulondre's Jacotte."

The mistress of the baths took a pile of clean linen from her counter and handed it to Babeau, who took them, pressed them against her bosom as she might have done a lover, gave me a quick glance and, saying that she'd lead me to my room, set off at such a lively pace in front of me that I could scarcely keep up with her, quite disappointed that she was shortening by her vivacity my pursuit of her, an activity that I normally very much enjoyed, since I always liked watching a pretty girl while she trotted in front of me.

Babeau brought me down to a basement room whose window, set with bars, was at ground level and looked out onto a little garden. This "micro-chamber" was indeed very clean, as was the bed, which was also quite wide, and the bathtub was in a form that I'd never seen before: not a tub really but a sort of small wooden boat, except the water was inside rather than outside and was steaming hot. Having put the bath cloth on the bed, and stretched the peignoir on the bottom of the steam bath, Babeau came over to me and began to unbutton me.

"What, Babeau? You're supposed to undress me? Am I a lady, then, to deserve such a pretty chambermaid?"

"Monsieur," replied Babeau, it's the custom here to undress the client and make sure when you're naked that you don't have any buboes from the plague, or carbuncles, pox or cankers on your shaft."

"This is good," I replied, "and as a doctor I find this rule very wise."

"What?" she gasped. "You're not a nobleman?"

"I am, but I am also a doctor."

"Ah, Monseigneur," she said, blushing, "may I tell you what I need?"

"Tell me."

Standing up on tiptoe, she whispered a few words in my ear, and I laughed.

"This is not a problem, Babeau," I told her. "I'll tell you what herbs to use and where to put them."

She thanked me a thousand times for this promise and continued the work of unbuttoning me with her smooth feminine fingers, and so I joked, "Ah, Babeau! What imprudence! If you keep on undressing me as you're doing, you risk catching your arm in a mill wheel. Once that happens, everything goes with it: the arm, the shoulder, the breast, the buttocks! And then you end up on the other side all ground up and broken."

She laughed. "Ah, Monsieur! You're so funny! But alas, this cannot be! My husband is a butcher and as jealous a man as ever lived and so furious that at any hour of the day he might burst in here, his butcher's knife in hand, shouting, 'Where's Babeau? If the minx cuckolds me I'll have her guts out!' Which is why, Monseigneur," she said with a bow, "as handsome and well hung as you are, I won't be caught up in your mill wheel."

She said this so sweetly that I wasn't hurt in the least, since I'd only spoken in jest and merely wanted to see how far her tender care would take us.

Meanwhile, Babeau, having undressed me, examined me very carefully and closely over every inch of my body. After which she was happy to declare that I was as healthy and vigorous as any mother's son in France and, taking me by the hand, she led me over to the bathtub.

"Are you sure, Babeau," I asked, hesitating to step in, "that your water is as healthy and clean as I am? Does it come from the Seine?"

"Are you kidding, Monsieur?" she cried. "The Seine? And while we're at it, why not from the cesspit on the place Maubert? This water comes from our well, which is purified every year."

I stepped in and immersed myself, comforted by her assurances. Oh, reader! What a paradise to have a body when you can bathe it! How the clear water makes you feel your firm and full parts! God knows by what good fortune bathing turns out to be not just a duty but a pleasure, whereas many of the cares we must take of our bodies demand such labour and pain—like abstaining from drinking or eating too much.

Some of the idiots of our times go about prescribing the inverse of what's good for us, claiming, for example, that a gentleman should have sweaty armpits or smelly feet. Heavens! Do we have to stink to earn the right to be noble? And what glory is there in a royal princesse's bragging that she hasn't washed her hands for a week? Or in the story of the duchesse at court, about whom it was said that if she had black fingernails it was because she was in the habit of scratching her body? 'Sblood! To these very high-born and powerful ladies who spray their encrusted bodies with the most expensive perfumes in the world, I would a thousand times rather bed the rustic Babeau, with her rosy arms and her robust body washed in clear water, shining like a newly minted écu! I've heard tell that there was a papist priest, speaking *ex cathedra*, who denounced the immorality of the bathhouses and demanded their suppression, but praised St Benoît Labre for his lack of cleanliness, his vermin and his stinking breath, which was so nauseous it caused even the most abject beggars to vomit. Good God! Can mankind sink any lower in its inhuman folly? Does one have to stink to become a saint? Is there no salvation outside of garbage?

After having let me flop about and soak in the hot water, Babeau asked me to stand up and lathered me with soap in every part of my body, leaving none out, which was, as you may easily imagine, a lively and immense pleasure, in part because it reminded me of how my Barberine at Mespech used to rub me down in my bath with her sweet hands. But how much sweeter was this soaping now that I was a man, and Babeau, in the courteous practice of her art, didn't fail to praise the objects of her cleaning, adding to the caresses of her right hand the caresses of her words. "Oh, Monsieur," she would say, "what strong shoulders! And what a deep chest! How muscular your arms are and how long your legs! How thick your fleece! It's so blonde! Isn't it a pity to shave off this hair to please our refined ladies? What's the point or turning a man into a woman, and completely in vain, since in three days he'll be as prickly in bed as a hedgehog? Whereas at present your hair is as soft and woolly as a lamb!" And saying this she passed her soapy hands over this and that part of my body.

As pleasant as this was, it had to come to an end, and Babeau, having rinsed me off, asked me to step out of the tub and, wrapping me in the bath cloth—which fell all the way to my toes it was so long—gave me a vigorous rub-down.

"Monsieur," she said as I lay down on the bed, completely relaxed and stretching my arms and legs, "I have to go and I'll send you the barber. She's very dexterous and you'll be very happy with her."

"Babeau," I said, "take a sol from my purse."

"A sol, Monsieur! That's a lot!"

"It's hardly enough to repay your kindness. Take it, Babeau."

"But Monsieur, do you trust me to go through your purse with all your money in it?"

"Yes, of course!"

"Monsieur, I cannot thank you enough! Will you think about my herbs?"

"Next time. I promised and I'll keep my promise."

"Oh, Monsieur, I feel so fond of you! May I give you a goodbye kiss?"

"With all my heart."

And, as she was leaving, this good girl gave me an earnest and resounding kiss on the cheek, but delivered as she was already backing away as if she feared my arms would encircle her. I hadn't thought about it—or rather, to tell the truth, when I did think about it, the door was already closing behind her.

I had imagined the barber of the baths would be an old hag, or, as we say in *langue d'oc*, a *ménine*, all wrinkled and dried up, hard and sour. So I was very charmed to see a young blonde girl enter my micro-chamber with her shaving implements who introduced herself as Babette and gave me a sweet smile.

"What? Babette after Babeau? What's going on? Did they arrange this on purpose?"

"No! That's my name and that's her name! And though Babeau is pretty, I think Babette is even cuter."

She laughed at this, being of a very happy nature, as I saw when she began her work, for she never stopped chatting and making merry the entire time she was scything my field, using first scissors to rough out the job and then a very sharp razor to make me as smooth as a canon's cheek. Not that I liked these attentions as much as I'd enjoyed my bath, but if I had to go through this to please the baronne, it might as well be with this pretty wench, who, when she had to move her blade around my most virile member, grabbed the latter with her left hand without any shame whatsoever, leaving me entirely in doubt as to whether this was just part of her job or whether she found some amusement in it. In any case, as I could not fail to express my appreciation for her grip on me, she laughed:

"Monsieur, if that continues, I'm going to let go. He can stand up well enough all by himself!"

"Don't your dare, Babette," I returned, my voice a bit muffled, "if he's not supported, he might fall directly on the blade of your razor!" She laughed heartily but never missed a razor stroke, so lively and dexterous was she. Meanwhile these parts that I mentioned had become as smooth as when I was a baby, but when she'd done, she let go, and I said, more as a complaint than as a joke, "Ah, Babette, you shouldn't start what you don't finish!"

"Finish?" she replied, her voice suddenly serious. "Monsieur, aren't you asking for more than we can give you?"

"And why the Devil," I replied angrily, "can't you go on?"

"Because I'm only a girl," she said, batting her eyelashes.

"I see very well that you're a girl," I said gloomily.

"Monsieur, you're not understanding me. I'm a virgin and virgin I shall remain, since I made a vow to the Blessed Virgin to remain in this state until my wedding."

"Ah, Babette," I said after a moment's thought, "I believe you. But isn't shaving men's bodies an odd trade for a virgin?"

"I learnt this art from my father," replied Babette, "since he had no son, and since he lost his right arm in an accident. So I've had to take up his art to feed him now, and my mother and myself."

"But, Babette," I said while she shaved my left thigh, "aren't you exposed every day God has made to the licentiousness and brutality of your customers? Especially when you work, as you're doing tonight, alone in a room with a man? Has no one ever tried to force himself on you?"

"Do you think they would while I've got this in my hand? And since I use it so capably?"

And my blonde beauty raised her razor with a smile but also a flame in her blue eyes, and looked me right in the eye. However, what she saw there calmed her right down and, giving me another very simple smile, she took up where she'd left off and finished shaving me in a trice.

I gave a sol to her as well, disappointed as I was in my carnal weakness, but at the same time marvelling at her valour and firmness.

"Well, Monsieur," she laughed, "I thank God and I thank you for having taken it so well! Ordinarily I am treated to insults and scorn as the price for my refusal."

And she too gave me a sweet kiss on the cheek, which moved me—but only in my heart. What a strange animal man is! He is always double: in every encounter, his body pulls him one way, his soul the other.

And yet, to tell the truth (as I promised to do in these memoirs) I wasn't as relaxed as I'd hoped to be after the two visits, finding myself a bit like one of the king's tennis balls, bouncing back and forth between two racquets, for as much as a wench's rejection—if she manages it sweetly—disarms me, it also saddens me, for I end up regretting not having tasted the sweetness she doubtless would have shown me had she given in to my desire.

I was at this point in my thinking, and, moreover, quite uncertain as to whether Madame des Tourelles would also reject me on the morrow on first glancing my outmoded and patched-up doublet (in which case I'd not only be humiliated but out of pocket for my troubles), when there came a knock on my door, and the mistress of the baths came in, looking very haughty. She was even more enormous than I'd remembered, and seemed even more domineering since I was now lying down, and she was standing over me.

"Would Monsieur desire something to eat?" she snapped very nastily.

"Yes, indeed," I replied, "some meat and a flagon of wine."

"We have no meat today. Would two eggs and a slice of ham do?"

"Marvellous!"

And yet, though everything was said and done, she didn't leave, but stood there, her stomach and breasts rising over me like a cliff over the sea.

"Monsieur," she asked after remaining silent for several moments, "would you like company tonight?"

"Company? What for?" I said, astonished, and in my surprise sat up on my seat.

"You know what for."

Her words set me thinking furiously. "Ah," I said to myself, "Babeau and Babette, you prattled nicely! And what is the role that your unbreakable virtue plays in your work here? Are you unwittingly the teasers for this bordello? Aren't you, in your naivety, just getting the customers all excited so that they'll need to be satisfied by others, to the greater profit of the mistress of the baths?"

"My good woman," I said somewhat guardedly, "I'm little inclined, being a doctor, to commercial love."

"Hey, Monsieur!" snapped the mistress of the baths indignantly. "What are you saying? We're not a bordello here! We're one of the oldest, most respected bathhouses in Paris! We don't have whores and prostitutes here!"

"My good woman," I soothed, "I meant no offence."

"And so I take none," she replied with dignity. "The company I'm suggesting is that of an honest wench who works by day at her job, and by night embellishes the repose of certain gentlemen that I recommend to her."

"My good woman," I said, "that's nicely put! And how much will this 'embellishment' cost me?"

"Three sols for her, three for me."

"That seems very equitably shared," I said with a smile that was not quite genuine. "And tell me, what's this honest wench like?"

"She a lively, frisky brunette. Not necessarily the most beautiful, but she uses her charms actively."

"Might I see her, my good woman, before we shake on it?"

"Assuredly. I'm not selling a pig in a poke."

But never was a pig, in or out of a poke, more suspicious and wary than I of a trap as I waited, fearing that some streetwalker would be passed off as an honest wench. Moreover, I was dreamy and sleepy, and wasn't so interested in playing around as I was in eating and going to sleep, tired from such a long day, one that had brought me so many disappointments.

Finally there was a knock at the door, and the first one in was the mass of fat I'd met earlier, so huge that I couldn't at first see who was behind her. But the mistress of the baths turning round to take her by the hand, I saw her and, unable to believe my eyes, immediately jumped up and said quickly to the chief ogre, "It's a deal! Leave us!"

"Monseigneur, you have to pay in advance."

"Here are your three sols!" I said, searching through my purse. "'Sblood! Leave us!"

Having no idea why I was so abrupt and hurried, she hurried off, and I ran to close the door and bolt it after her. Then, turning to the wench, who was holding her hands over her face, I said gently, but with a hint of reproach, "Alizon! What's this? You're selling your body at the baths?"

She didn't make a sound, but kept her hands glued to her face, trembling from head to toe, her shoulders convulsed as she sobbed out her soul.

"So, Alizon," I said, trying to seize her wrists so I could look at her eye to eye, "what's happened? Have you become a whore?"

"A whore, Monsieur?" she cried, ripping her wrists from my grip and revealing her tear-stained face, convulsed with grief and anger. "How dare you call me a whore? Didn't you see me working my fingers to the bone for that cheapskate Recroche from dawn to dusk and from dusk to dawn? I haven't slept but three hours these last two nights and that was on the floor of the workshop, while my miser of a master was at the baronne's. Oh, Monsieur," she continued, her voice trembling with anger, "is it from being a whore that my poor back is bent and sore? That my poor eyes are red and my fingers are more peppered with needle pricks than a hanged man's face by crows? And do you think a hot whore would arrive nearly dead from sleep deprivation?"

"Alizon, calm down," I urged, moved by her tone and her story. "Sit down here on this stool. Dry your tears. Forgive me for using the word 'whore' if it offends you. But you're such an honest and industrious wench! Here! In the bathhouse! Selling your body for three sols!"

And taking her arm I tried to get her to sit down, but failed to do so as she broke loose from my grip and backed away from me, her eyes still flashing with anger through her tears.

"And how is it," she cried suddenly, leaving me astonished by her sudden reaction, "that you feel more justified buying me that I do selling myself?"

That silenced me completely, and I couldn't say a word in response, but suddenly felt ashamed (for my Huguenot conscience had scalded me, telling me she was right), and stood looking at her without a word.

"Ah!" she continued, finally sitting down. "I'd sell myself for less! I'd sell myself for a night of sleep, if I didn't need these three sols to raise my baby."

"Your baby!" I gasped, open-mouthed. "I thought you were innocent and pure, Alizon!"

"But I am!" she countered. "The gallant lad who got me pregnant swore he'd marry me. But scarcely had he noticed the swelling in my stomach before he took off like the Devil was after him without leaving me a single sol to pay a nurse!"

"A nurse!" I said. "Do you really need one?"

"What a silly question!" cried Alizon bitterly. "Am I supposed to sew with a baby in my arms?"

"But have you no mother, sister or aunt?"

"No," said Alizon, her lips squeezed in frustration. "I'm alone. The plague carried them all off."

"Oh, Alizon," I comforted, sitting down on the bed so as to face her stool, and taking her hand. "What a predicament you're in! So your salary from Recroche isn't enough to buy your daily bread and pay the nurse, so you have to come here."

"What else is there?" cried Alizon pulling her hand from mine and looking at me suddenly with anger and bitterness, her eyes flashing fire. "Do you imagine it's because I love men? You think I enjoy these pigs who have enough money to buy one of my nights and make we work in their beds like a bitch in heat when all I want to do is sleep?"

I looked silently at Alizon, all rebellious and stiff, her black eyes shining, with her small neck, her wasp-like figure—a little fly in the hell of a spiderweb created by the men who surrounded her—and her wasp-like tongue as well, which could sting, for she had a ready wit and a way with words in her sharp Parisian accent. 'Sblood! These pigs, which included me, were an awful thought. I got up and went over to my purse and, taking some money, came back to her and said with no bitterness whatsoever, but perhaps too coldly, "Alizon, I am a man, not a pig. Take these three sols and go home and sleep as much as you can."

But my words only seemed to increase her anger, for she leapt from her stool, pale with fury, her nostrils pinched, spitting like a cat on a coal, and shouted:

"What's this I hear? Are you offering me charity? Am I some beggar on the church steps? Did I ever ask you for alms? Have I fallen so low? Monsieur," she said, opening my hand, taking the three sols and stuffing them in the pocket of her dress, "I've given you nothing and I'll accept nothing from you. You've paid and you'll get what you paid for. My body is yours for the night!"

And suddenly, without another word, or looking at me, her eyes on the floor and lips tight, she undressed completely. I scarcely dared to look at her, so odious did I feel in my shame, stuck in a role that disgusted me and not knowing how to get out of it.

Good God! What should I do in such a predicament? Forcefully put her clothes back on? Call the mistress of the baths? But what would this fat bawd think except that Alizon had disappointed her client, which would probably get her chased away? I didn't know how to resolve this, and so I turned my back on my poor little wasp and walked over to the little window that looked out on the garden. It was slightly ajar; from it came a little bit of cool air on this stifling August evening and I avidly took a deep breath of it, my thoughts all confused but inclining towards sadness and self-hatred.

I turned around and looked at Alizon in her nakedness and felt the shame of having purchased this right for three sols. She was as thin as I'd imagined, but at the same time more curvaceous than I would have thought and still trembling with anger, her eyes lowered and her teeth biting her lips bloody. She was still lively and frisky enough to have whetted my appetite if the heart (hers) had been willing. But without a word, without looking at me as though I were anything more than a table or a stool, Alizon stretched out on the bed, her eyes closed, so stiff and cold it froze me. 'Sblood! How tired I was of this long day and of this misunderstanding with Alizon.

And so, in utter sadness and bad conscience, I went and lay down next to her without saying a word or touching her, not even with the tips of my fingers. What wickedness, when you think about it, to buy the body of another against the wishes of her soul! And yet with what pleasure I would have played my part if the honest wench that the mistress of the baths had provided hadn't been Alizon! I saw that the poor girl had, in her wounded pride, taken things in such a nasty way that now she would lie there, more dead than alive, like a log at my side, eyes closed and mouth shut tight. I would have lain there dead as a log as well, unable to do anything, and having no idea what to say, had it not occurred to me to ask her if her child were a boy or a girl and how old he or she was. These questions ended up unnailing the coffin and helped the dead woman out of her tomb.

"It's a boy," she replied with sudden vivacity (despite how entirely exhausted and sleep deprived she'd been an instant before), "handsome and well built and who's soon going to be a year old."

"And do you see him often, Alizon?"

"Thank God, every day that God makes, since the nurse lives in the same street where I have my room. What a joy it is to see him nursing from her breast, sometimes playing with her nipple, sometimes playing with her hair, looking at her—and at me—with such happiness, laughing and smiling."

"Is he speaking?"

"Like one of God's angels! Blessed Virgin, how he babbles! He makes up all these words and warbles with his pretty voice, letting us know with his gestures and tiny fingers what he can't tell us in words. Oh, Monsieur! He's so close to my heart that I love him even when he's upset or angry, or when he throws himself on the ground or kicks me, pouts, cries or screams at the top of his lungs, just because he's lost a walnut or some other plaything. Isn't that amazing?"

There was a knock on the door and Babeau appeared, bringing my dinner.

Alizon, still engrossed in talking about her little Henriot, without even paying attention to what she was doing, agreed to share it, and never was a serving more promptly dispatched than by her, so strident was her hunger.

However, her meal devoured, she fell silent again and went and lay down on the bed, as stiff and cold as before, her eyes closed and her hands crossed across her chest as if she were a recumbent figure on a marble tombstone. But I could tell from the softer fold of her lips that I had succeeded in pacifying her by talking about her child and that she had to apply herself to maintain her stony appearance.

Finally, I lay down next to this statue and this time took her pretty head of brown curls on my shoulder, with my arm under her neck. This done, I didn't move or speak or move for such a long time that finally she said in a sleepy little voice, "Monsieur, what are you waiting for?"

"Shush, Alizon!" I whispered in a severe tone that hardly matched my feelings at this moment. "Don't open your mouth, please, I'm meditating."

"It's just that if you wait too much longer," she said even more sleepily and softly, "I'm so dead tired that I'm likely to drift off into such a deep sleep you won't be able to wake me."

"Shush, shush, Alizon. Don't bother me any more!"

And this time, she quieted down and fell asleep almost instantly; her head, which weighed no more than a bird on my shoulder, rolled into the hollow of my neck and remained nestled there with such childish confidence in this abandoned posture that I was overcome with emotion. How could I be indifferent to her misfortune, I who believed myself poor as Job simply because I didn't have enough money to have a doublet made that I could parade at court, and who had spent in one night at the baths more money than she could expect to earn in five days working for Maître Recroche? How cruel life is for these unfortunate wenches who, in addition to the hardships that men of their condition might endure, have to suffer from a swelling in their bellies that they never wanted, a fruit that is so unwelcome outside marriage that the world points at them if they keep it and hangs them if, like my poor Fontanette, they try to get rid of it.

Remembering my unfortunate Fontanette gave me such heartache that it brought tears to my eyes, and I felt a new and more intimate concern for Alizon, as if the two wenches were but two opposite faces of the same misfortune, one selling her body in the baths to nourish her child and the other hanged for having killed hers on orders from the knave who'd fathered it. Oh, heaven! What a deep sleep she fell into in her dark and smooth nudity, abandoned against my side, the thorns and arrows of her hard life momentarily forgotten in the merciful night, but not the great love she bore her little Henriot, if I could trust the half-smile that remained in the fold of her tender lips for having been able to talk about him.

On this last thought, being, myself, thoroughly exhausted from this long day, during which I'd seen and experienced so much, I felt myself slipping into sleep as if into a warm bath, laughing gently at myself for being so happy, for once, to be chaste, and to have paid six sols to remain so.

6

WHAT A STRANGE AWAKENING I had the next morning in the little chamber-ette where I'd fallen asleep next to Alizon.

Of Alizon, however, I saw not the least trace as I blinked, trying to clear my eyes. Her clothing had disappeared as well, my sweet little fly having fled at dawn to reach Recroche's atelier and start her twelve-hour day. But I realized I wasn't alone, and when my eyes had cleared, I saw a fellow dressed entirely in black standing in my room, his back turned to me and his left hand on his hip as he gazed out of the little window at the garden. He was tall and gaunt, and looked very elegant as he stood there on one leg like a heron. I couldn't believe my eyes and quickly combed my hair with my fingers and sat up, and was about to speak to this Gautier and ask him what he was doing when, hearing me sit up, he turned round.

"'Sblood! Fogacer!" I cried in amazement, jumping up and running, naked as I was, to embrace him. "This is magic! How did you find me?"

It was a moment before he answered, returning my embrace with some embarrassment (remembering no doubt his craziness at the carnival in Montpellier), something that I secretly thought was funny, and, releasing him at last, I began immediately to get dressed.

"Well," Fogacer began, catching his breath and regaining his composure, "I know a pretty little cleric at Notre-Dame de Paris, who is as beautiful as any of God's angels."

"Except that God's angels don't have any genitals," I smiled. "But go on, Fogacer, doesn't this angel offer tours of the towers of Notre-Dame to curious visitors?"

"That's the very one, Siorac. Aymotin told me the what, the who and the lodgings."

"And from the lodgings, who brought you here?"

"Miroul. He secretly followed you yesterday evening to make sure you were safe, and when he learnt from the mistress of the baths that you were spending the night he was reassured and went home to bed. I saw him this morning at Recroche's place."

"He's the angel!" I said, very touched by the care my good valet had taken of my life.

"But this angel takes very poor care of your feeble flesh," returned Fogacer, spreading his spidery arms wide (as if to make fun of himself and of me). "For if I'm to believe what I heard, you didn't spend the night alone. Oh, Siorac, at the baths! Is this prudent? Don't you know that the Naples disease and the wenches in the baths have a natural affinity for each other?"

"Fogacer," I said, smiling somewhat bitterly, "Heaven is my witness that I'm leaving these baths as healthy as when I came in."

"May Heaven hear you!" cried Fogacer, who believed in neither God nor the Devil, as perhaps the reader will remember.

There was a knock at the door and Babette came in. "Monsieur, the milkmaid just came by. Would you and your friend like a bowl of milk, some good white Parisian bread and some fresh butter from our villages?"

"'Sblood, Babette!" I cried. "Not another word! I'm drooling at the very idea! Fogacer, a bowl of milk?"

"Wholeheartedly, but boiled, if you please."

And while our pretty blonde set off to fetch our breakfast, she was followed by two sets of eyes: one happily attracted, the other coldly suspicious.

"Is she one of the bawds of the baths?" said Fogacer disdainfully.

"Not at all!" I assured him. "She's a virgin and all locked tight for her future husband. Fogacer, you don't know everything. In the great book of nature, you skipped the feminine pages."

"It's good I did!" he said. "If my appetites didn't tend in the direction you know, I wouldn't have had to flee Montpellier in great danger of being burnt alive. And if I hadn't fled, I wouldn't have found refuge in Paris, and I wouldn't today be aide and assistant to the venerable Dr Miron, physician to His Royal Highness the Duc d'Anjou."

"What!" I cried. "Why, Fogacer, that's marvellous! You've already reached such heights in Paris? I've heard much good of the famous Miron."

"And they're mistaken. He's an ass in a skirt. And the most miserly man alive! I'm lucky to collect a few crumbs from his banquets of money." At this he laughed out loud, arching his satanic eyebrows. "What's more," he continued, "I work hard to hide from Miron that I know more than he does, for in truth, if he were a humble man and had any conscience whatsoever, he could say what St Augustine said to the Lord: *scientia nostra, scientiae tuae comparata, ignorantia est*."*

"Well, Fogacer," I said, "aren't you being a bit too proud yourself?"

"Not at all! I'm so humble I make nuns ashamed! Of the sixty-two doctors who exercise their talents in this murderous city, there are not more than five or six, including me, who understand how little they really know. The others, Miron included, are nothing but charlatans who foist their fraudulent, outmoded ideas, deceptions and fallacies on their patients, and parade their bad Latin about, deifying their nasty drugs like monks their saints' relics."

"Well, Fogacer," I laughed, "I see that you don't respect yourself enough! You're not in the least ignorant, since you laboured so diligently during all those long years of study in Montpellier!"

---

* "Our knowledge, compared to Thine, is but ignorance."

"But all I do is recite in a drone what I have to read," confessed Fogacer. "What do we really know about the geography of the human body? What do you know, Siorac?"

"The ABC."

"And who taught you?"

"Servetus, Vesalius, Ambroise Paré."

"Servetus," replied Fogacer with his long, sardonic smile, "was burnt by your Calvin in Geneva. Vesalius was condemned to death by the Inquisition of his king. And Ambroise Paré, the only one still alive, is rejected and despised by the professors in Paris because he's a surgeon and not a professor of their silly ancient medicine, which is empty meat, inane superstition and worn-out tradition…"

Babette returned at this point, carrying a tray with our hot breakfast.

"Well, here at least," I laughed, "is more substantial food! Eat, Fogacer, eat! *Vita brevis est** and our art takes so long to learn!"

And although we were both appalled by the way our own medical art seemed to flounder in the mire of ignorance, of verbal and scholastic disputations, we nevertheless downed our breakfast very happily and Fogacer told me all the details of his flight from Montpellier. When he'd done, I recounted to him the story of my duel with Fontenac, the nasty legal proceedings that ensued and the quest that brought me to Paris to seek the king's pardon and the whereabouts of my Angelina.

"So what are your impressions of this great Paris where you've been thrown?" asked Fogacer.

"Its beauties are numberless, its garbage infinite!"

"Well," laughed Fogacer as he stood up, stretching his long arms, which suddenly seemed to fill the whole micro-chamber, "you've still got a way with words, I see! Assuredly you can live better elsewhere, but in Paris you meet so many people with talent and there's so much

---

*   "Life is short."

diversity in complexion and behaviour, so many riches and so much art as well. Have you seen the nymphs that Jean Goujon made for the Fontaine des Innocents?"

"Not yet."

"Ah, Siorac, you who are so infatuated with women's bodies, you must see them! You'll be very happy you did. Even I, who see only their beautiful movements caught in stone, am moved."

But then, looking at me with his sharp and cunning hazel eyes set under those arching eyebrows, he chuckled, and, putting his foot on the stool as if he were a dancer testing the suppleness of his calf muscles, added in a suddenly serious voice, "Siorac, I have to go. Dr Miron is expecting me at the Louvre and I don't want him, in his incredible stupidity, to kill the Duc d'Anjou with his drugs *in absentia mea*, because, to tell the truth, I'm mad about His Highness…"

"What!" I gasped. "You value the life of the Duc d'Anjou? This monster who ordered Montesquiou to kill Condé when he was his prisoner?"

"Oh, you Huguenot!" laughed Fogacer. "You're not going to cry about that little muddle-headed Condé! Didn't he dare to take up arms against his king? Your Coligny—who would hang any soldier who disobeyed him—what would he do to a rebel subject if he were king? What haven't both sides done during those troubled times? Do I have to remind you of the Michelade?"

"I was there, alas!"

"In reality," Fogacer continued with a heat quite removed from his usual sarcasm, "Henri d'Anjou is a man of real intelligence: he excels in intrigue; he is firm in his endeavours, supple in their execution and, what's more, a good general."

"Well, as for that," I interrupted, "it was Tavannes who won those battles for him at Jarnac and Moncontour!"

"At least Henri d'Anjou had the finesse to listen to his wise counsel, which Charles IX, who's so impatient and childish, would doubtless have failed to do."

"'Sblood, Fogacer!" I cried. "If he's such a good friend of yours, why don't you recommend me to Anjou for the favour I'm seeking from his brother!"

"This recommendation would kill you, Siorac! The king hates his brother."

"He hates him?"

"He hates him from the depths of his guts. Other than God, the king loves no one as much as his mother, who doesn't love him, but loves Henri d'Anjou instead, whom she's been mad about from his earliest childhood. She's the one who arranged for him to have so much power in matters of state, and who's raised him to be practically the equal of the king, who is insanely jealous of him, both as his brother and as a duc, and can't bear to have him around the throne. He'd love to see him leagues away. Outside of France, if he could! Married to Elizabeth of England, or, if that didn't work out, at least elected king of Poland and exiled to Warsaw, surrounded by soldiers and his mouth frozen by their winters. 'Sblood! You know that Charles is working as hard as he can to distance Anjou from the Louvre? He's fed up with this vice-kingdom the queen mother has carved out for Anjou within his own. If he dared, he'd stab his too-brilliant brother with his own hand. But being as pious as he is limited, he'd fear losing his soul by being the Cain of this Abel!"

"This Abel!" I smiled. "Aren't you making Anjou a bit too angelic?"

"But don't we know that there are very different kinds of angel in this vale of tears?"

"Oh, heaven," I thought to myself, turning slightly away, "are these white sheep from the same pasture? Cooing doves from the same dovecote? Puppies from the same litter? What am I hearing?

The Duc d'Anjou as well? This subtle fraternity extends right into the Louvre?"

"Fogacer," I said, gulping down the last mouthful of this good white Parisian bread, which is the best anywhere in the world, "since you work in the Louvre, enlighten me and remove my doubts. What's the rhyme and reason of this marriage between Margot and our Navarre?"

"The rhyme *or* the reason?" replied Fogacer, arching his diabolical eyebrow.

"Both."

"The rhyme is to have their wedding bells sound the arrival of fraternity between Huguenots and papists by reconciling them in a princely marriage, joining Navarre and France."

"And the reason?"

"You'd have to discover it from our Machiavelli in black skirts, whom you call Jezebel. She's the one who wanted this marriage, and she will see it celebrated, come hell or high water, no matter what the objections, even from the Pope."

"And what are her reasons?"

"The state. Coligny is austere, but old and infirm. Navarre is young, insouciant, apparently crazy, a tepid Huguenot, chasing petticoats as if they were deer. If Coligny were to die for whatever reason, Navarre would become head of the reform party, but the queen mother hopes that, if he were coaxed at court by her, by Margot, his wife, and by the other ladies around him, and being the de facto hostage of his brother-in-law the king, he would convert to Catholicism; if not, your party would simply be decapitated."

"Very nicely calculated," I conceded. "And what do you think?"

"That this is very short-sighted and hasn't been properly thought through. For if Jezebel had a sharper nose, she'd have smelt in Navarre a man of infinite finesse. And finally, I think that Navarre, as the head of the reform party, would very much need its body to stay alive, and would not cut himself off from it until his power were sufficiently established in the kingdom."

"So Navarre is more Machiavellian than Jezebel?"

"Assuredly so! Navarre is deep enough to play the fool and to disarm the king by his apparent heedlessness, and to charm the court by a 'cordiality that makes people think he has heart'. So says the great tennis master and ball-maker Delay."

"Ah, you know him?"

"I know the universe!" replied Fogacer with a kind of false gravity. "Which is to say everyone who enters or leaves the Louvre, from the greatest to the smallest, who isn't really all that small."

"This 'smallest' one would be you, I would bet," I smiled, "since you've always been so attentive to what's going on around you."

"I've had to be," sighed Fogacer, "since I grew up using ruses and finesse, having been ever since my childhood in danger of being burnt for not being like other people. I must go, Siorac; I'm very sorry not to be able to help you with the favour you've asked of me. On the other hand…"

"On the other hand?"

But instead of finishing his sentence, he smiled with that slow, sardonic, sinuous smile, and, his hazel eyes looking at me maliciously, he took my right hand in his fine, firm long hands and said: "I'll do better, Siorac. Since I know, as I said, the universe, I'll help you find, in this immense Paris, Angelina de Montcalm."

"Do you know where she lives?" I cried, almost floating on air at his words.

"I'll find out."

"Fogacer!" I cried.

But without another word, and dropping my right hand, he turned on his heels like a ballerina and was already out of the room with his lively gait, looking so tall and gaunt in his black robes.

Behind her counter, presiding immutably in her fleshy mass, the mistress of the baths, when I'd paid for our breakfast, asked me if I'd been happy with the bath, the room she'd assigned me, the barber who'd shaved me and my companion for the night.

"Yes indeed!" I proclaimed. "Like a rat in straw!"

"So you'll be returning to see us?" asked this mountain of a woman, her breath coming in short gasps between each word.

"Assuredly, good woman."

"In that case, Monsieur," she wheezed, "may I ask you not to give Babeau a sol for her gratuity or that amount to Babette?"

"Why ever not?" I asked in surprise.

"Because," she panted, "you're spoiling the both of them, giving them for scarcely an hour's work half of what I give them for an entire day."

"I'll think about it," I replied coldly, and immediately turned on my heels and walked away, disgusted with this miserly gorgon.

I have to admit that the grand'rue Saint-Honoré, which was my route, was much cleaner than many others in the capital, because it was lined with so many grand mansions belonging to the nobility, the Louvre being so close by, so that the paving stones tend to be relatively free of refuse. As I left the baths that morning, the air had something very piquant and exhilarating about it that I've never breathed anywhere else but in Paris, and which made you feel as though you had wings on your feet. Which is why, I imagine, the inhabitants of the city speak so abruptly and are so lively in their affairs and so heated in their passions, as if they were inebriated by the air they breathe into their lungs. And what's more, despite the fact that at noon the air in the city could be as stifling as it was in Montpellier, the morning air was so cool and healing that you just wanted to warble like a bird, spread your wings and launch yourself into the silvery, misty light of the break of day, bursting with hope and as though drunk with life.

And so it was with me that morning, walking along the pavement with a spring in my step, forgetting for the moment my despicable doublet, which, like the poisonous tunic of Nessus, prevented any access to the king to ask his pardon. It's true that in my mind, ever since Fogacer (who was so good and beneficent in the teeth of his impieties) had promised to find my Angelina, I saw her as if in a daydream, walking beside me with her languorous step, and turning her long elegant neck to look at me with her beautiful doe's eyes, which nothing could ever equal in their tenderness.

Meanwhile, I couldn't stop thinking as I walked here and there, window shopping in the Parisian manner, that there wasn't a single shop in this street (where there are so many beautiful ones) that I wouldn't have "licked the floor" of (as they say here), enjoying the curiosities displayed in each, so much so that I finally went into one and bought a top, amusing myself by taking it between my thumb and index finger and spinning it—just the way, as a child, I'd enjoyed the many tops Faujanet had carved for me, as well as some that were activated by pulling a string wound tightly round the middle. I paid two sols for this top that so delighted me, but then, remembering the nest where I'd developed my first feathers, my Huguenot conscience began to bother me about this crazy and ultimately useless expense (after all the money I'd spent in the baths), and, to calm this inner voice, I told myself that, when I returned to Mespech, I'd give this top to my little sister Catherine, though she was now sixteen and was probably more interested in turning men's heads than spinning tops.

As I passed through the atelier of Maître Recroche, Coquillon, very focused on not working, gave me a smile from ear to ear and Baragran bid me a civil good morning, informing me that Miroul was out in the stable tending to the horses, but that my brothers, he surmised, weren't up yet since he hadn't heard them stirring. As for my little fly from hell, though she appeared refreshed and rested after the eleven hours she'd slept in my chaste arms, she was sewing, sitting very straight on her stool, looking exceptionally pretty, but kept her eyes down as I passed, not giving me a look, a smile or a word of welcome.

However, no sooner had I retired to my micro-chamber than there came a knock on my door and Alizon appeared, her face expressionless and her black eyes shining more brilliantly than a ball of jade; she looked at me without a trace of love and a very stand-offish air and said:

"Monsieur, a chambermaid, who belongs, I believe, to the household of Monsieur de L'Étoile brought this letter here for you."

She handed me the letter stiffly, and was turning to leave when I took her by her cold shoulder and exclaimed:

"Alison, what's this? Are you angry with me?"

"Monsieur," she replied, pulling away, her eyes now suddenly full of anger, "have you even looked at me? Am I so ugly and decrepit? Am I some slattern in a slum? Or an old hag on her filthy bed? Do you really think that the Baronne des Tourelles, when you take off her feathers, is more beautiful than me?"

"Not at all, Alizon," I said, seeing where this anger was leading, "you're a perfect beauty, young and smooth, clean as a new coin, comely and fresh, with breasts to die for!"

"You're making fun of me, Monsieur," she spat, her jade eyes throwing sparks at me. "I'm old, wrinkled and I stink. If I weren't so awful would you ever have slept twelve hours by my side without taking what was yours?"

"But Alizon," I protested, "how could I have done that after you made me ashamed to have bought you?"

"How could you have paid attention to me when I was angry? The wine was poured! You should have drunk it! And not offend me a second time by despising me!"

"Despise you! Quite the contrary, I respected you and didn't want to trade coins for you!"

"Blessed Virgin!" she screamed, beside herself. "I don't want that kind of respect! It cheapens my body, which, Monsieur, is more beautiful and smoother than those of your noble whores!"

"Alizon, no one knows this better that I, who saw you entirely naked!"

"Appetite comes by eating, not by looking!" cried Alizon, her claws out in her fury, and, not daring to scratch my face, she dug them into her own palms.

"Could I have awakened you, Alizon, when you were sleeping like a log?"

"A *log*!" she screamed, each of my words seeming only to increase her anger. "Am I a log? Would I have been a log when you took me? Oh, no! Here, Monsieur, take your money! I don't want it!"

And ripping the three sols from her pocket, she sent them flying across the room, and after this demonstration stood there, arms crossed, defying me, trembling from head to foot and looking at me with fire in her eyes. I walked over to the door, leant against it and said calmly, "Alizon, pick up those coins. They're not for you, they're for Henriot."

"What?" she said, all of a sudden softening. "You remember his name?"

"I remember his name and everything you told me about him: how he threw you such gracious smiles and glances while his nurse was suckling him, and how he would caress her breast with his little pink fingers."

"Those are my same words!" she said with great feeling, and from the pillar of salt that she'd become, she turned back into a woman, saying softly, "Monsieur, do you like children?"

"I love them."

"Oh, Monsieur," she said in a voice trembling with tears, "I'm so sad that the experience of the baths came between us! I dreamt it could be another way. Do you despise me? Tell me!"

"Absolutely not! You only worked there out of necessity and not for greed."

Going over to her, I took her in my arms and my little fly from hell let herself be comforted without any more buzzing or biting.

And while she quieted down like a wounded sparrow in the hollow of my hand, I held her close for a long moment, wondering whether or not I should lay her down on my bed; yet, despite the enormous desire I now felt for her, I abstained, thinking that Alizon might not be very happy about it later, having these three nasty sols between us that so wrecked everything, and that left us, whatever we did or didn't do, all confused and ashamed. Meanwhile, as we stood there quietly, holding each other, and no act following upon the words we'd had, things might have become embarrassing had I not suddenly remembered the top I'd just purchased and wondered why I hadn't thought of offering it to little Henriot.

"Oh, Monsieur," she said, pulling away and laughing out loud (in part, I think, to hide her emotion), "that's men for you! My little boy is much too young to play with a top! I'm going to keep it for him for when he's old enough to enjoy it. Oh, Monsieur, thank you so much! You have such a generous heart!"

And throwing herself back in my arms she covered my face with little kisses. She then picked up the coins and repocketed them in her skirt, gave me another quick kiss, left my room with tears welling up in her eyes and fairly danced down the stairs.

I unfolded the letter Alizon had given me, and it was, indeed, as she had believed, from Pierre de L'Étoile, who begged me to join him for dinner that same day at eleven o'clock in his lodgings in the rue Trouvevache, where I would find other guests, who, "though not of the gentler sex, will not fail to please you: the very illustrious Ambroise Paré and the very learned Petrus Ramus, assuredly the most knowledgeable man in the kingdom in philosophy and mathematics".

I could hardly contain my joy at this invitation: "Oh, the good L'Étoile!" I cried out loud, before going immediately to knock on my brothers' door to tell them I wouldn't be dining with them at midday at Gautier's restaurant in the rue de la Truanderie. I found Giacomi standing at the tiny basin, washing his face, and Samson stretched out on the bed, completely naked, half asleep but looking very sad.

"Oh, my beloved brother," he said as he got up to greet me with a hug, "I see little profit in being with you in this city that I like so little. I never see you, neither last night at dinner nor during the night you spent at the baths. And now you're off to dine with Monsieur de L'Étoile, and this evening you're invited to sup with the Baronne des Tourelles. At least promise me, Pierre, that you'll stay there tonight given how dangerous the streets are after dark."

Hearing this, Giacomi turned around and, as he towelled off his face, gave me a quick and knowing grin, having understood that my brother's recommendation was absent of any malice.

"Samson, I promise you, at least as far as that is up to me," I replied, with a wink at Giacomi. "But Samson, you have to be patient. We're not in Mespech, where we spend all our time together day and night, never leaving each other, but in Paris, where diverse affairs and obligations necessarily cause us to go our different ways."

"Well," complained Samson, as he ran the fingers of his left hand through his copper-coloured hair, "if that's the case, then, my brother, you should have left me in Montfort-l'Amaury in Maître Béqueret's pharmacy. At least there I could have earned some money working in his shop, instead of wasting it as I do here in this modern Babylon. You don't need my presence to ask for the king's pardon, and what pleasure can I find in this Paris that's so filthy and corrupted and whose inhabitants, so blind to the pure truth of Holy Scripture, worship stone idols carried through the streets? Oh, my brother, all I want is to leave as quickly as possible, like Lot, this ignominious Sodom before the Lord visits His wrath on the leprosy of its iniquities and reduces it to ashes."

Having said this, he turned away and went to wash in the little basin, leaving me speechless at this sombre sermon that predicted with apparent certainty the destruction of the capital. "Oh, my poor brother," I thought, "how can you, in your zeal, have such a cruel thought? What do you know of the world, since you're so blind? Do you flatter yourself in believing that Montpellier is less corrupt than Paris simply because it's smaller? And don't you remember that Lot himself, whom you like to call 'just' could resist neither wine nor the lascivious ardour of women?"

While Giacomi was dressing and Samson was washing, both had fallen silent, and I went to sit down on a stool, full of my thoughts, astonished at my brother's fury, yet still able to admire his smooth, polished beauty, which Babette hadn't needed to work on to make it conform to the current Parisian customs. I doubted as I looked at him that there was any connection between hair and strength, since Samson certainly possessed the latter without being able to lay claim to any of the former; Delilah, in her fatal designs, certainly wouldn't have had to cut very much of his hair since, despite its profusion of curls, it was very short. Yet as beautiful as this feminine smoothness was, it did not hide his muscles—though they were not hard and bulging like Monsieur de Nançay's, but enveloped in his pleasant rounded flesh, all of which suggested that Samson wasn't a man so much by the hardness of his flesh as by the design of his body, with his large shoulders and slender waist.

Meanwhile, Giacomi had finished dressing, and made a sign that he wanted to speak with me, so I left their room and returned to mine, where the master-at-arms soon joined me.

"My brother," he said, "why not let Samson leave for Montfort-l'Amaury, since he wants so much to go! He's not in his element here, since he's developed *il dente avvelenato** and is so set and rigid in his beliefs that it's dangerous for him to wander the streets, given how bitterly and stridently the Parisians hate the Huguenots."

"Giacomi," I agreed, "everything you've said I've been repeating to myself ever since the fanatics of the procession of Notre-Dame de la Carole nearly lynched him. And yet, I still can't make up my mind. My father gave him into my care and I hesitate to send him so far away."

"But you can't watch out for him any better here than there. You're so busy in Paris with so many different affairs," he said with a smile, "that all Samson can do is sit around and mourn his distant glass bottles. Empty hours weigh on us much more than full ones."

"But what about you, Giacomi?"

"Well," he said, "it's not the same for me! I'm going today to work in my new position as assistant to Sergeant Rabastens, which we discussed while you were with Monsieur de Nançay."

"What, Giacomi?" I cried. "Assistant to Rabastens! You, a master-at-arms? You, a person of quality?"

"I'm not ashamed," said Giacomi with a smile. "Rabastens is a good man, and I can't live without working on my art, which is as necessary as my daily bread. And, to tell you the truth, life being as expensive as it is in Paris, I wouldn't mind earning a few sols to help maintain my beloved brothers' purse."

"Oh, Giacomi," I gushed, embracing him fondly and planting kisses on both cheeks, which he returned just as enthusiastically, "everything I have is yours, you know."

"And all I have is yours," echoed Giacomi gravely, "including my labour and the few coins I might earn. Maybe in a week's work in my new position, I could squeeze out enough money to buy you a new doublet!"

---

* "A poisoned tooth."

"Ah, Giacomi," I said with such a poignant sigh it could have turned a windmill, "who could have guessed, when I had this one made back in Montpellier with Madame de Joyeuse's écus and which I went proudly to show off to her, that it would be so utterly despised in Paris! And despite this tiny repair—this repairette, as Maître Recroche would say. Good God! Am I nothing more than my clothes? Are my bravery and my knowledge worth nothing? Oh, Giacomi, the world and its customs please me so little, that if I were a papist, I'd put on a monk's habit."

"*L'abito non fa il monaco!*"* Giacomi laughed. "In any case, there are habits and there are habits and yours must be of the finest! You wouldn't rest until you were the abbot!"

At this, we both laughed. And on the promise I made him to go to watch his lessons at the Louvre that afternoon, he left me; I, taking my writing case and my paper down to the atelier, joined Baragran and Alizon at the large table there. They interrupted their work with a series of jokes as soon as they saw me carving my pen.

"Go ahead and mock me," I told them, "it won't make me write any worse!"

"Oh, Monsieur! I'd never dare!" said Alizon. "How clever you must be to put words to paper! I can't write but I can read a little," she said modestly, "but it's a challenge to be able to read even a short letter! Now I've spoken, and won't open my mouth while you're doing your writing."

"Me neither!" said Baragran.

"Nor I!" added Coquillon, giving me a wide smile with his big mouth. And this said, the apprentice went back to his labours, which consisted of annoying the cat with a ball made of rags that he waved here and here on a thread.

---

* "The clothing doesn't make the monk!"

"I thank you, all three," I replied.

But of the three, only two kept their word. For when I was at the end of the first page, Alizon said, "What a long letter, Monsieur! Are you writing to a lady?"

"No. To my father."

"And to Madame, your mother?" she asked.

"No, she died in childbirth."

"That's how we'll all die, we women," sighed Alizon, "and without ever reaching the end of our natural lives."

"Quiet, there, Alizon," said Baragran. "Can't you see you're disturbing our gentleman?"

"Quiet, yourself, you big idiot!" Alizon shot back, with her back up and hissing like a snake. "Monsieur," she said, softening her tone and sounding more like a baby lamb, "did I disturb you with my babbling?"

"Not at all."

"A thousand pardons, even so, Monsieur. In the future I'll be as mute as a *log*," she continued with a knowing smile as she pronounced this last word.

But this was, like the first one, an empty promise, for, seeing me put my seal on the first letter and immediately take up another, she said, "Ah, Monsieur, now you're writing to a lady."

"Not at all. I'm writing to an apothecary in Montfort-l'Amaury."

"In Montfort-l'Amaury! I know a Guillaume who's going there tomorrow to his farm and he could bring you back the response in two days' time."

"But would he take my letter? He doesn't know me."

"Yes, but he knows me," insisted Alizon, "and he'll do it if I ask him."

"Marvellous, Alizon! A thousand thanks!"

So I gave her a grateful look, thinking to myself that patience is a great virtue, since, having allowed the girl to chat while I was writing, I had gained a much more rapid dispatch.

When my letter to Maître Béqueret was waxed shut with my seal, I gave it to Alizon and she immediately placed it in her lap as though it were a love letter I'd written her, and sent many smiles and glances my way, just as she'd described Henriot as doing. All of this couldn't help but warm my heart in the midst of all the thorns that I'd felt concerning my doublet, though it didn't yet blunt their points.

Such is my nature, however, that from every difficulty I manage to rebound just as quickly as a ball once it hits the ground. Just as Alizon was giving me that tender glance, eleven o'clock sounded on the clock tower of the chapel of the Saints-Innocents, so I set forth from my lodgings to go to the rue Trouvevache, blessing at every step the beneficence of Monsieur de L'Étoile, and my heart beating eagerly at the thought that I was going to dine in such learned and famous company.

Whether it was his salary as Grand Audiencier or an inheritance from his parents that was the source of his wealth, the lodgings of Pierre de L'Étoile were neither miserly nor poor, and the dining room where he received us (situated on the first floor) was set off by its beautiful, well-polished oak woodwork, a fireplace so large you could have roasted an entire calf in it and a series of large windows which were furnished not with small, leaded stained-glass panes, but with large, square, transparent ones, as was currently the style in the noble houses of Paris. Pierre de L'Étoile was alone and was clothed, as usual, in black, and seemed especially melancholic when I arrived. I complimented him on this room, adding, "Ah, Monsieur, what wonderful light this series of windows gives the room!"

"Ah, yes," he replied after embracing me warmly, "but as light as my lodgings are, their inhabitant is sombre."

"In what way, Monsieur?" I answered in surprise. "Are you suffering?"

"Infinitely. This year has been a most unfortunate one for me, afflicted as I have been by divers ills of both body and mind, hit with extraordinary losses of goods, overwhelmed by lawsuits, rejected by my family, despised and hated by all, even my churlish valets and chambermaids… And, on top of all that, so worked by my sins," he added, lowering his voice and his eyes downcast, "that I fear both death and life itself equally."

"Oh, Monsieur," I cried, struck by his cruel assessment of himself, "put away your bitter thoughts and try to see the possibilities open to you. Don't go letting the hereafter ruin the here and now! Don't let the fear of death destroy your life! And for the rest, let the Sovereign Judge make His judgement when the time comes!"

"Ah, my dear Siorac," replied L'Étoile, a sudden smile lighting up his sad face, "it's you who brings light to the room, with your sing-song accent and your happy, optimistic outlook! Oh, how I envy you your happy disposition! Your sins don't appear to weigh on you any more than on a little wren on the branch of an oak tree!"

"That's because I have such faith in the beneficence of our Creator that I don't think He'll punish us for the poor little pleasures that we've gleaned along the way through our short lives."

"Alas! That's not what our Church teaches us!" lamented L'Étoile with a sigh.

"I also trust my own feelings more than the dour sermons of some angry priest, believing, as I've said, in the sweet goodness and beneficence of Christ, who pardons both the whore and the adulterous woman."

"They were wenches," sighed L'Étoile, "and as the weaker sex they are more easily pardoned than we men are."

"Weaker?" I laughed. "Aren't we every bit as weak?"

I don't know what he might have said in response to my incredulity, since we were interrupted by the arrival of the surgeon Ambroise Paré and the venerable Master of Arts Pierre de La Ramée, who was called Petrus Ramus in the Latinized French of our schools. I don't know if these two were good friends, but they came in arm in arm and had something about them that made them look related even though their faces and body types were quite different.

Ambroise Paré, who was then sixty-three years old, was of moderate height, with large shoulders, and robust without being fat; he sported some sparse grey hair on his balding head and a flowing but not very thick beard. His face was long, with hollow cheeks, a large nose, rounded at the tip, and lively, bright, yellow-brown eyes, at times serious, at other times quite jovial. Ramus, who was ten years his junior, seemed tall, mainly because he was so slim, and whereas Paré and L'Étoile dressed austerely in black velvet, Ramus wore a blue satin doublet with slashes, and a white lace collar rather than the little Huguenot ruff on which Paré's head was so stiffly perched. Ramus's clothes and the sword he wore at his side gave him the look of a nobleman, as indeed he was, though as the son of a ruined gentleman he'd had during his early years to serve as a valet at the College of Navarre, nourishing his love for letters at night.

He had dark-brown, very piercing eyes that peered out from under an irascible set of eyebrows in the form of a circumflex, an aquiline and imperious nose, and a strong and prominent jaw adorned by a salt-and-pepper beard; atop this strong face was perched like an august dome his large cranium, as polished as an egg.

Both of these men greeted me with very good grace when Pierre de L'Étoile presented us, and Ambroise Paré immediately sang the praises of the Royal College of Medicine in Montpellier, placing it well above its homologue in Paris, which he considered to be hopelessly sunk in "the rut of scholasticism". This said, Pierre de L'Étoile invited him to take his place at table, and Paré immediately set to devouring everything the little valet and a chambermaid put in his bowl, having a strident appetite, but not stupefyingly so, for before swallowing each mouthful he worked his jaws for quite some time as if he were trying to discern the good from the bad: a habit that astonished me until he explained that someone had tried to poison him at the siege of Rouen.

At the word "scholasticism" that Paré had pronounced, Ramus shuddered like a horse that feels the spur, and scarcely had he taken his seat or eaten any food before he launched into the subject, his eyes like flames, in a lively and furious diatribe, mixing French and Latin, but immediately translating the latter, since Ambroise Paré had come to his work in surgery from his profession as a barber, and had never immersed himself in the arts as Ramus had done.

"Aha! You said it, Paré," he cried. "'The rut of scholasticism' is just as pernicious in philosophy as it is in medicine, consisting in vain disputations, logical and theoretical, as if these great babblers had nothing better to do than to gloss Aristotle, this pagan being the God they worship, and they place his supposed truths above those of Moses or Christ. Heavens! I cannot tolerate that kind of idolatry, nor can I accept the kind that takes as its object Mary the Mother of Christ, or the saints."

"Monsieur de La Ramée," L'Étoile counselled, "eat your roast while it's hot. And, I beg you, don't impugn the religion of the king in here, which," he said with an ambiguous smile, "also happens to be mine."

"My host," explained Ramus in a gentler tone, "you have such a degree of open-mindedness and tolerance that I almost forget you're a papist! I beg of you a thousand pardons for my words—and of Monsieur de Siorac as well."

"As for me," I replied, "there's no offence. I'm of the reformed religion."

"Ah, that's marvellous," said Ambroise Paré, sticking a piece of his roast in the corner of his mouth so he could continue to masticate as we talked. "My dear L'Étoile, there are three of us and one of you.

So you're the heretic here. If only the reformers made up the same proportion of the kingdom!"

"If that were the case," replied L'Étoile, smiling bitterly, "then I'd be among the quarter that were persecuted."

"Alas, I'm afraid that's true," sighed Ambroise Paré.

This said, he began to chew again, his tongue and palate focused on their work, his eyes wandering off, his circumspect mind turned in, as it were, on the contents of his mouth, as if he might have suspected the good L'Étoile of wishing to poison him.

"As for me," said Ramus, "I'd not persecute anyone, not even the berobed asses in the Sorbonne who've condemned my book on Aristotle."

"Well, you have to admit that your book against Aristotle was very brutal," replied L'Étoile. "Did you not go as far as writing this sulphurous sentence: *quaecumque ab Aristotele dicta essent, commentitia esse?*"

"Translate, please!" said Paré.

"Everything Aristotle said is but falsehood."

"Oh!" exclaimed Paré.

"Admit it, Monsieur de La Ramée," continued L'Étoile, "this was like waving a red cloth in front of the Sorbonnic bulls!"

"Poor bulls!" observed Ramus with the utmost scorn.

At this we all laughed.

"What's so surprising," remarked L'Étoile, "is that, as a consequence, not content to condemn your book, some of the Sorbonnites asked the king to burn you at the stake!"

"'Sblood!" I cried. "The stake for having criticized Aristotle?"

"Didn't I tell you that they'd made a god of him?" replied Ramus, frowning.

"Alas," said Ambroise Paré, interrupting his endless mastication, "in this century we're suffering too much from the excessive authority of the ancients. This excessive attention to Aristotle in philosophy is the same with Galen and Hippocrates in medicine. As soon as any little pedant cites them, all you can do is fall to your knees and put your hands together. This century is devilishly religious, and not just in the domain of religion."

"The authority!" cried Ramus, his brown eyes now showing fire under the circumflex of his bushy eyebrows. "The supreme authority of the ancients, that's where the shoe pinches the most!"

"So do you want to destroy it?" asked Pierre de L'Étoile, as if terrified.

"Not at all," replied Ramus, "but put it in its place, which would not be on top. No authority," he continued, thrusting his jaw out in a bellicose way, "no authority should be above reason. It is reason, on the contrary, that should be the mistress of all authority."

"If I follow you," mused Pierre de L'Étoile, suddenly looking dubious, fearful and confused, "this would entirely upset all orders of thought! What's your opinion, Paré?"

Ambroise Paré swallowed the portion he'd just reduced to pap, and, bringing his cup to his lips, drank a small precautionary taste, as if he suspected his wine were laced with arsenic. After which he said in a grave voice, but as calm and quiet as Ramus's speech had been tempestuous:

"The ancients, in my art at least, said some good things, but one can't just rest on their work like a hog on its sow. The ancients didn't see everything, nor did they know everything. I would say that they built watchtowers of the ramparts of a castle and now, posted on these ramparts, we can see much farther than they could."

My heart beat faster to hear this opinion, so much did it seem to open up to our human knowledge a marvellously infinite field of understanding. But I couldn't help noting that Pierre de L'Étoile seemed very agitated, as though he found Paré's and Ramus's proposals too novel and too daring.

"Well, in any case," he said as if he wished to change the subject, "there's one sow that Parisian pigs won't go to bed with any more. The 'beautiful handmaiden' has died. I heard of it yesterday afternoon."

"What, the 'beautiful handmaiden'?" said Ramus. "But she was very young!"

"And looked strong enough to live to a hundred!" added Paré. "I took care of her last year. She was healthy and vigorous and her insides as good as her body was beautiful. What illness carried her off?"

"Appendicitis."

"Ah, there's no remedy for that," said Ambroise Paré sadly, as if he were lamenting the limits of his art.

"Might I ask," I said, "who this 'beautiful handmaiden' was, who was so famous?"

"The wife of one of the palace ushers," replied L'Étoile, "and famous in Paris not only for her beauty, but for the agility of her thighs. My friends, would you like to hear some verses that one of the palace judges wrote as an epitaph for her?"

"Gladly," said Paré, who, to be able to hear better, swallowed the mouthful he was so slowly crushing between his teeth. Ramus said nothing, but as Pierre de L'Étoile pulled a paper from his doublet, he smiled, arching his circumflexed eyebrows in amusement.

"So," said Pierre de L'Étoile, "here's the epitaph:

"Alas! she so liked cocks to suck
While she still had life and all her pluck.
Her husband never did enjoy
To have her hands on his small toy
As oft as she'd extend her reaches
To toys she found in others' breeches.
In a single morning she did play
With more slick pricks than in a day

> *Her husband cried out from his report*
> *The names of guests to Charles's court.*
> *So now all you who, 'fore she died,*
> *Caressed this lady's sweet backside,*
> *Say a prayer to God that He*
> *Might save her soul eternally."*

We four laughed uproariously at this satire, but perhaps not all four for the same reasons: L'Étoile as if he saw in it punishment for the lady's immoral ways; Ramus as a licentious gentleman; Paré with a shade of melancholy; and I in surprise that these learned gentlemen should find as much pleasure in these little verses as any bourgeois. I was more than a little surprised, too, at the light-hearted attitude taken towards the death of a young woman, but later when I got to know Paris better, I understood that everything, the tomb included, could be material for jokes, epigrams and scabrous quatrains, and in the end I had to agree that the humour of this proud city is not about feelings, but, given the tyranny of the court, tends more towards showing off one's cleverness than displaying any concern for others.

"Venerable Maître," I said, turning to Ramus, "in your opinion, is Aristotle completely mistaken, so that there is nothing at all in his thought that you can forgive?"

"No, of course not," replied Ramus, his eyes shining. "Aristotle had one great merit: he taught us about mechanics, which proves that he didn't despise the people and their common use of mathematics, the way Plato did, who preferred to see mathematics as a subject of pure contemplation rather than allowing his disciples to dirty their hands in its applications. Oh, Monsieur, what great harm this lamentable error of Plato's has inflicted on the world! For, by letting the use that might be made of mathematics decline, the very subject of mathematics declined. This is why, ever since the Greeks, mathematics has not prospered—to the point where, in France today, it is hardly taught at all and its use is limited to merchants, navigators, jewellers and the royal treasurers."

"What?" I gasped. "Mathematics is hardy taught in France? But in Germany it is flourishing! How is this possible?"

"Monsieur de Siorac," replied Ramus, his angular visage animated by both grief and anger, "the king created for me the first chair of mathematics at the Royal College, which I occupied with some distinction and usefulness for ten years, after which time, having renounced the religion of the king, I had also to renounce my chair, which was bought by some fellow who knew a little about mathematics, but, soon tired out by old age, resold it. And do you know who bought it?"

"No, I don't," I replied, astonished at Ramus's fury, which had gripped him and had made his hands, arms and head shake uncontrollably.

"A totally uneducated man!" screamed Ramus. "An idiot who knows absolutely nothing! A blank slate who's never studied or used mathematics and who publicly mocks the science that he's supposed to be professing and goes around saying that mathematics is an abstract and therefore vain and fantastical activity that has no use whatsoever in human life!"

After saying this, he seemed so strangled by his own anger that he had to stop talking, and his whole body continued to shake. And as I stared at him amazed and, truth to tell, somewhat dubious and incredulous, Pierre de L'Étoile, seeing my confusion, said gravely:

"This is true, Monsieur de Siorac, however incredible it may seem. This uneducated idiot, as Monsieur de La Ramée calls him, is named Charpentier; he knows not a whit about mathematics, and if he was able to purchase a chair in the Royal College, it's because he was supported by the powerful Duc de Guise and the Jesuits, since the man is a fanatical papist, a zealot, howling with the wolves, and, what's more, a nasty, venomous little fellow, bilious, spiteful and a mortal enemy of our friend here—who has challenged him on his abysmal ignorance."

"Ah," said Ambroise Paré, ceasing his slow mastication, "I know all too well these Sorbonnic hatreds! Each time one of the thinkers of our day has taken one step out of the scholastic rut, and stumbled on some truth, there isn't a single little pedant at the Sorbonne who, sitting on Aristotle like a crow on a church steeple, hasn't squawked a thousand insults at him! It's the same for me, for having dared to get my hands dirty and discovered with my knife things they can't see in their books. And yet it doesn't make any difference to our common practices and the public utility of our science whether some ignoramus, spouting Greek, goes about quoting Hippocrates and cackling about surgery if he's never dissected a body! It's not in the library but on the field of battle that I discovered how to tie up an artery so a man wouldn't bleed to death."

"Ah, venerable Maître," I cried with some heat, "the men wounded in our wars will be forever grateful to you, for the cauterization of their wounds with boiling oil led to unbearable suffering!"

"Which," agreed Ambroise Paré, "coming after amputation, was so piercing that it frequently caused death. So, watching this, and with the screams of pain in my ears from those soldiers who were burnt after amputation, I calculated that, given that blood is flowing from the arteries, it would be enough to pinch the arteries and tie them up to stop the bleeding."

Given how simple the solution that he discovered was, and how simply he described it, it's a wonder that no surgeon in the world had ever thought of it before he did. And yet this man who discovered it knew neither Greek nor Latin and was, consequently, not a doctor of medicine!

"Well said, Paré," agreed Ramus, growing heated. "Getting your hands dirty, that's what our impotent colleagues at the Sorbonne would never forgive you for, they who sit in their rat's nest, spouting endless inanities at each other in their false, bookish science! And so the untutored Charpentier, scorning what he doesn't know, goes around repeating that 'counting and measuring are the excrement and garbage of mathematics'. And our Platonists applaud, who place contemplation of ideas above all. And certainly," he continued (the word "certainly" betraying his Huguenot beliefs, as I'd learnt from Madame des Tourelles), "mathematical theorems are in and of themselves admirable and profound—but how much more marvellous are the fruits that can be culled from them for the use of mankind? I count speculation on the essence of mathematical entities as pure vanity and of no profit. The goal of the arts is in the use that may be made of them, in the same way that there's no point in searching for gold beneath the ground if we forget to cultivate the vegetables at its surface!"

"Ah," I exclaimed, "what an excellent apophthegm, one that would so please my father if he were listening!"

"This is the reason," Ramus continued, "that Archimedes is so great; it's not only because of his theorems, but because of the applications that he made of them: the worm drive, the pulley, denticulated wheels, machines of war and even the enormous mirrors by which he set fire to the Roman ships that were attacking his little country. Did you know, Monsieur de Siorac," he continued, turning towards me as I listened excitedly, "did you know that the Sorbonnites blamed me for having inserted in my book on arithmetic methods of calculating that are in common usage among the merchants around Saint-Denis? No one claimed that these methods were false, and, for heaven's sake, how could they have proved it? But they claimed that they were 'soiled' by the practice these mechanicals made of them! Ah!" he cried, raising his arms in anger. "The awful prejudices of the pedantified pedants!"

"Monsieur de La Ramée," queried L'Étoile, with a smile, "if you continue to be this angry, you're going to produce so much bile it will ruin your digestion! Please taste these cock's crests and kidneys, and these artichoke hearts. They're such delicacies that I'm astonished the queen mother nearly died from eating them."

"She just ate too many of them," explained Ambroise Paré, "since she's an ogress at table as, so they say, she was in Henri II's bed. L'Étoile, you who know everything that's going on in la Ville and at court, and who are a sort of living chronicler of our daily life, is it true that the bishop of Sisteron died last Monday, in Paris, and under the same cloud that he'd been under all his life?"

"Alas! It's only too true," replied L'Étoile. "Moral and morose as was his wont, this prelate was of all the epicurean pigs the dirtiest and foulest. Charitably visited on his deathbed by a beautiful and noble lady who asked what she could give him to help in his last moments, he replied shamelessly, 'Give me your snatch. You could offer me nothing that would please me more. What was dear to the living ought to be the same for the dying.'"

"And did she give it to him?" asked Ramus, his eyes lighting up. "Did she push charity as far as that?"

"What would he have done with it?" said L'Étoile. "He was at the farthest extremity and was vomiting up a thousand other profanities at the moment he met his Maker."

"And with what nasty grace this villain welcomed the good offices of this noble lady!" said Ambroise Paré, his voice quite calm and quiet, though his yellow-brown eyes looked very melancholic, as they did every time people around him talked of death, which he considered his great and personal enemy. "Isn't it marvellous," he continued, "that the lowest soldier shows more human gratitude than a bishop? I remember that in 1552—now twenty years ago—at the siege of Metz, where I was the surgeon of Monsieur de Rohan, I saw that they'd left a soldier in their company behind on the ramparts. Finding, upon examination, that he was still breathing, although a bullet had passed clean through his right lung, and that Monsieur de Rohan's doctor had decided that he was lost, I had him carried to my house, where he spent a month, and at his bedside I served alternately as his doctor, his apothecary, his surgeon and his cook. God granted that in the end he recovered, and all the soldiers in his company, amazed that I had laboured so hard to snatch one of their comrades from the jaws of death, each gave me an écu, and the guards half an écu. Certainly," he continued, "I have no complaints about the generosity of my more noble patients. I've received both money and jewels from them. But largesse is measured by the size of the purse, and is easier for a deep one. And so I'm all the more moved by the heart of these mercenaries, each one of whom pulled an écu from his poor purse, even though the wounded man was not related to any of them."

"Well!" I thought. "How to measure the generosity of Ambroise Paré himself, giving so many days of unrelenting care to this humble man of arms from whom he expected nothing other than the joy of giving him his life back?"

"Venerable Maître," I said, "what you told us about the wound to this man's lung reminds me that, when I was watching his tennis game, I heard the king coughing with a raw, villainous and uncontrollable cough, which is said to be chronic with him."

"It's true," sighed Ambroise Paré, "and I'm very distressed about it, being the king's surgeon and not his doctor. For it's my belief that a sickness of the lungs—whether it's from a natural disease or from a bullet wound—can be cured and healed only if the patient rests without coughing, without talking, without tiring himself by running around a lot and sweating. Alas, the king does exactly the opposite: he coughs to break your heart. He roars instead of speaking. He blows himself breathless into his trumpets. He sweats at his forge. And he exhausts himself in his hunting and tennis games."

"Have you told him, though?"

"Every day. But the king trusts only his physician in such matters, who is an ass of the most Sorbonnic type and who flatters the king's penchant for the most violent sports. It would be wiser to push him to seek quiet refuge among the 'learned virgins', as your Périgordian Montaigne would say."

"You mean Charles IX likes the Muses?" I asked, surprised.

"Oh, yes! He reads some poetry. He writes some as well. He loves to imitate Ronsard."

"All of the house of Valois are crazy about the arts," said the honest L'Étoile, though I couldn't tell, given his morose tone, whether he approved of this or not. "The queen mother is a patron of Bernard Palissy and Jean Goujon. Princesse Margot speaks Latin perfectly. And the Duc d'Anjou's eloquence in French is very pleasing."

This discussion was teaching me so much about so many things that I hoped it would never end. But, our repast at an end, Ramus apologized for having to leave, saying that he had a rendezvous in the grand'rue Saint-Denis with a merchant whom he was interested in, for the fellow, he believed, had a very fast and amazing way of calculating the relative value of different monies, measures and weights, since he daily did business with merchants from Italy and England.

"*Dico atque confirmo,*" he said with a smile as he stood up, "*nullum esse in Academia Paris mathematicis artibus eruditum quem non familiarem carumque habeam.*"

"Translate, please," said Ambroise Paré.

"I said and I affirm that there's not a man properly educated in mathematics in the Academy of Paris that I do not consider my familiar and my friend, were he," he added "one of these 'mechanicals' that the uneducated Charpentier despises so greatly."

Seeing Ramus leaving, Ambroise Paré, who would have delayed his departure since he was still chewing his meal, also arose, saying that he would accompany his friend, having, as he did, some business in the Saint-Denis quarter (which is called "la Ville", as the reader perhaps remembers). Indeed, he'd been asked to reconnect the bones of a broken knee, which is why, that morning, he'd been studying the skeleton of a man who'd been tortured, which he kept in his study, and had made a drawing of the knee and its adjoining parts, which he showed me and I found excellent in every minute detail.

"Of the two," said Pierre de L'Étoile, when he'd closed the door behind them, "the more celebrated is Ambroise Paré, since he's our ally against the menace of death. But in my view, Pierre de La Ramée is the greater mind, since his intelligence embraces all the arts, even mathematics which he knows better than any other man in France. This reformist, the pride of his Church, would like to reform everything where abuses exist: teaching, grammar, spelling—being, with such a vast mind, a heretic in everything, as Ambroise Paré is in medicine. Which is why attempts have been made on both their lives, so hateful and so venomous are the champions of tradition in this country."

"He seems very angry with this Charpentier," I said.

"And for good reason!" replied L'Étoile. "But the cruellest thing about this chair in mathematics that is occupied by this unworthy fellow is that Ramus, having founded the chair at the Royal College, decided to endow it, as he departed (hounded out by the persecution of his people), with a 500-livre salary for whoever would succeed him. And so not only does this uneducated Charpentier not teach the science of mathematics, but, in addition, he pockets Ramus's money according to a legacy that cannot be revoked."

"Well," I said, clenching my fists, "that would make the angels cry!"

Alas! The angels would cry much harder a few days later on the occasion that was so fatal for those of my religion: St Bartholomew's eve. Ramus hid in a cellar to escape the massacre, but the students in the Royal College whom Charpentier had set in hot pursuit of him, after having inflamed them with hatred for his genial rival, found him, demanded a ransom with no promise of his life in return and, once his money was pocketed, eviscerated him with pikes; then, with his entrails bursting from his body, they dragged him through the streets. Finally, growing weary of this monstrous game, they returned to his body and, in their abject fury, cut him to pieces.

It was already hot and the sun was shining brightly when I left Pierre de L'Étoile after a thousand thanks for the excellent meal and the amazing discussion that I'd been so happy to be present at.

"Ah, Monsieur de Siorac," he said on the threshold of his lodgings, "times are so vile, rotten and corrupted that it's a rare joy for me to converse with good and honest people who think only of the common good and the advancement of mankind. On the other hand," he said, suddenly lowering his voice and looking around him at the passers-by in the street, "there are certain people whose zeal is at such an insane pitch that they foul the very air that one breathes. If you were to go next Sunday to hear the sermon at the church of Saint-Eustache, you would be strangely edified."

"I shan't fail to do so," I promised in a respectful tone, but secretly amused since I could clearly see the drift of Pierre de L'Étoile's sympathies, despite his papism.

I headed now, however, in the sultry heat of the noonday sun, towards the rue de la Ferronnerie to meet up with my beloved brothers at Maître Recroche's lodgings. Samson was very happy to be able to spend an afternoon with me, and Giacomi was delighted at the idea of crossing swords with Rabastens at the Louvre. Seeing how happy they were, I decided to make the fourth member of our band happy as well, and invited Miroul to join us, though his presence wasn't required to guard our horses. But my good valet has always been more than a valet to me—and hadn't my father ordered him never to leave my side, so that his wisdom could, if necessary, calm my hot temper?

The Louvre gates were wide open, and a crowd of brilliantly clothed people were pouring in and out; but whereas the mass of those leaving flowed freely through the massive archway, the way in, which was through the smaller gate, was much slower, one by one, and was controlled by two gentlemen: one very corpulent, seated on a stool, and the other, standing by the first, with a red cape thrown over his shoulder. When it was my turn, I told them my father's name and the nature of my business, and the man seated on the stool studied me from head to toe with a wry smile at my doublet, and said to his companion, "Do you know a Siorac, Baron de Mespech in Périgord?"

"Not personally, no," said the other, "but I've often heard his name on the lips of d'Argence. Mespech fought under Guise at Calais."

"Ah," said the other, "Calais! Now that you mention Calais I remember that Nançay spoke to me yesterday about Siorac's son here, and about his repaired doublet."

Of course, I blushed deeply to have such a tawdry description of me circulating around the Louvre.

"Monsieur," said the seated gentleman, seeing my intense embarrassment, "don't take offence. I don't judge a man by his clothes. I heard from Nançay that your father is a very brave man, and that you follow in his footsteps, being a brave and proud young fellow."

"In any case," counselled the other gentleman, who, despite the sultry weather, was still wearing his heavy red cape, "if you want my advice, don't get in a lather when some gentlemen here, who enjoy a good joke, as we're wont to do in Paris, smile at your doublet. Neither the king, nor his brother, the Duc d'Anjou, tolerates quarrels. It's a capital crime in the Louvre, so near such august persons."

"Monsieur," I replied, bowing to him, "I shall try to follow your advice."

I passed through the gate after naming the other members of my party: my brother, *maestro* Giacomi and my valet—the last of whom, as we passed through the courtyard of the Louvre, suddenly disappeared completely. And so, when we were at the door that led to the gallery where Giacomi was to do his fencing, I had to wait for several minutes, looking anxiously around, impatient and getting more and more annoyed, my foot tapping the pavement. But when I had decided to call him, he appeared at my side, as suddenly as he'd disappeared a moment before. His brown eye looked very happy and he said to me in *langue d'oc* but speaking as fast as any urchin in the capital:

"Monsieur, I beg you, don't scold me. I only disappeared for your own good, and went to ask one of the footmen, who I thought was from our provinces, who the two men were who admitted us at the gate."

"And did you find out?"

"Yes, certainly, Monsieur," said Miroul, who was now taking his time, with his brown eye clearly indicating his pleasure.

"Well, then! Tell me!"

"Well, Monsieur, it depends," said Miroul, his eye sparkling. "Was I right to leave you or not? I could see you the entire time from across the courtyard."

"Miroul, you're making fun of me! Speak!"

"Ah, Monsieur, I see you're still angry."

"I'm going to be if you keep me waiting any longer!"

"What, Monsieur? You'd punish me for taking such pains and trouble to find out the who, the what and the why?"

"Ah, Miroul," I laughed, "How dearly you're making me pay for this little frown! What would you have done if I'd really been angry?"

"Monsieur, would you like to know what I found out?"

"Didn't I already ask you twice?"

"Ask, Monsieur? Did you ask me? *Brevis oratio penetrat caelos.** But, Monsieur," he continued, seeing me frown again, "enough joking. I don't want to exhaust your patience."

"My patience! Good God!"

"Well, Monsieur, here's what I learnt. The gentleman who was seated at the gate to take the weight of his great stomach off his feet is Monsieur de Rambouillet. He belongs to the king. As for the tall, gaunt fellow standing with his hands on his hips, looking very superior, that's Monsieur de Montesquiou. He's the captain of the guards of the Duc d'Anjou, which is why he's wearing that red cape, even in August."

"What? Montesquiou?" I whispered. "The assassin of Condé! I didn't like the look of him."

"I liked him well enough," countered Miroul. "*Bravaccio* as he is, he has an honest look."

At this I fell silent, thinking about this Montesquiou, whose very name seemed synonymous with our defeats at Moncontour and Jarnac.

Miroul continued:

"Monsieur, would you like to know why such important gentlemen are standing guard at the gate today instead of a simple sergeant?"

"Tell me."

"Because they're expecting the papal nuncio, who is supposed to visit the queen mother."

"Ah," I said sotto voce. "No good can come of this! As everyone knows, the Pope and Felipe II of Spain are working together to get the king to agree to the eradication of our people."

"But how could they get his approval," asked Miroul, "when Coligny has the king's favour?"

All of this was spoken in *langue d'oc* and in a whisper, but we could just as easily have yelled it at the top of our lungs from the middle of

---

* "A brief prayer reaches heaven."

the courtyard given how loud and resplendent the crowd of courtiers was, whose members, though they entirely surrounded us, were wholly occupied in their own affairs, however unimportant.

The gallery where the *maestro* and Rabastens had begun their fencing match, while Samson looked on amazed, was a long hall well lit by a series of tall windows overlooking the Seine, but the room was entirely unfurnished, not even with stools, so that the fencers who had no valets to hold their doublets had to simply drop them on the floor.

As there were three or four matches going on simultaneously in the gallery, the clash of steel, the heavy breathing and shouts, and the odour of sweat mingled with the smell of sawdust spread on the floor all produced a sort of excitation that I found most refreshing.

I couldn't help being amazed by the strength that emanated from Rabastens as he faced off against Giacomi, and not artlessly as far as I could tell. But Giacomi was so serene, and gave way so little, keeping his body well aligned, his long arm beautifully deployed and his blade miraculously present, ready for every lunge by Rabastens, that I felt no doubt as to the outcome of this friendly match—though Giacomi was constantly on the defensive, I'll wager, so as not to offend the Frenchman's pride with too many touches.

The combatants fought near the windows, and the spectators were grouped against the opposite wall and separated from the matches by a red rope stretched a few inches above the floor. But between the duellists there was no barrier, so that some, breaking away from a furious assault, might bump into the backs of gentlemen engaged in another match and seriously upset them. In such cases, the match was interrupted and with ceremonious excuses and bows from each side. I was astonished at such polite behaviour, no doubt introduced by the Italian teachers, for the custom of the courtiers, despite their colourful and brilliant costumes, was, whether at tennis or in the courtyard of the Louvre, much more aggressive and crude, with elbows given to women and men indifferently, feet stepped on indiscriminately, and spitting and sneezing done with little regard for the people on whom the phlegm landed. At times men would go so far as to lift a lady's mask with one finger, or administer with a wayward hand a pat on her backside. Of course it's true that these offences were more for effect than they were real affronts, since our refined ladies were, as I'd been told, padded in this place with a kind of false arse, which was made of material that made their backsides look more rounded, and must have also served as a bastion or shield against impertinent assaults.

Meanwhile, Miroul left my side again without giving me his usual warning, and I watched him as he went to mingle with some of the other valets who were holding their gentlemen's doublets. I surmised that he was going to collect some pollen of news, and indeed he was back as quick as a bee to the hive and divulged what he'd learnt.

"Monsieur," he whispered, "would you like to meet the great Silvie?"

"I don't know who Silvie is."

"An Italian, and the master-at-arms of the Duc d'Anjou, and reputed to be the best in the kingdom, though the king prefers Pompée."

"Who's Pompée?"

"An Italian."

"'Sblood! Are there no Frenchmen in this profession?"

"Yes there are: Carré, who is master-at-arms to the Prince de Navarre. And Rabastens."

"And who do you think is the best of all?" I asked, knowing that seeking his opinion was a way of complimenting him on having gleaned all this information, especially since Miroul was so interested in this sport—at which, under Giacomi's guidance, he'd made so much progress.

"Well, Monsieur," he replied, lowering his voice even further, "my heart tells me Giacomi, but if I believe my eyes, it's Silvie."

"What does he look like?"

"A beanpole of a man, so thin you'd think he'd break. But he doesn't. He's like a well-tempered blade of steel."

I laughed at this, so loving everything about my good Miroul: his French, his *langue d'oc* and also his Latin, or at least the pearls he'd gleaned that he sprinkled over his own language.

"So now," I said, taking Miroul by the arm, "let's go see this great artist *pingere cum gladio*."

"*Pingere cum gladio?*" asked Miroul. "What's that?"

"To paint with the sword."

And, since he was quiet for the time it took us to cleave a passage through the crowd to get to the other end where the great Silvie was fencing, I could hear him moving his lips to repeat and learn my Latin phrase before he forgot it.

Heavens! How I would have admired Silvie, this marvellous master swordsman, perhaps the greatest in the kingdom, had not my eyes fallen on the gentleman who was crossing swords with him. 'Sblood! My blood boiled when I saw him; I dug my nails into my palms, and my breath came so short I thought I might faint from the rage that suddenly had me trembling and shuddering like a leaf in the autumn wind. For the man I saw, directly in front of me in his brocaded silk shirt, agile and quick as a fawn in a forest, was none other than the popinjay of a courtier I'd seen the day before in the room at the tennis court, where he, an impertinent valet of Monsieur de Nançay, had overwhelmed me with his insolent and scornful looks. Oh, God! My rage awakened, hotter than ever, shaking me from head to foot and filling my throat with a bile all the more acrid because, though I hated this rascal to the absolute limit, I couldn't help but admire him, so well proportioned was he, so agile and skilled with a sword. And what added oil to my fire was that this sprig of a fellow resembled me in his age, his build, the colour of his hair and eyes, and even the thirst for life that was evident in his looks, though he was certainly more handsome than I. This resemblance only served to make matters worse. For, dear reader, imagine that you looked in a mirror and saw your earthly being at its most perfect, but that, instead of smiling back at you, this more perfect being glared at you with infinite scorn. Perhaps now you can understand my mortification.

Meanwhile, this presumptuous gallant not only fought marvellously, dissimulating his strength and his art beneath a graceful nonchalance, but also managed, while his eyes were glued to the flying blade of the great Silvie, to exchange pleasantries with two gentlemen standing near me, and it was amazing to see the way they interacted. The elder of these two lords was about forty years old. He had a noble and polished face and a piercing and sagacious eye; his body was solid but not fat, and his clothes were light brown, with yellow slashes, so that it was if he had two tones of but a single colour. His younger companion's clothes were of such diverse colours you might have said that he resembled a meadow in May. He couldn't have been more than twenty years old and his face was so handsome and resplendent that, other than my beloved Samson's, I didn't believe I'd ever seen one to equal it.

"Monsieur," said Miroul, who had followed very curiously my looks, "do you want to know the whats and whys of these two gentlemen?"

"Yes, thank you. And also the name of Silvie's opponent. Especially his."

"I understand," replied Miroul. "I could tell from looking at you that you didn't like him very much."

And in a trice he'd disappeared into the crowd, as lively and slender as an eel flowing between two rocks.

"My brother," said Samson, his eyes all lit up, "this gentleman we're watching is as skilful as he is handsome. He fences very nearly as well as his teacher."

"I hope to God," I said between clenched teeth, "he's as benign as he is pleasant to look at."

315

Meanwhile, the swordplay between the two combatants was so quick, so fine and so fluid, and their blades seemed to be touching so continually—as if each man sensed at every second what the other was going to do—that the lively interest I took in them had gradually succeeded in calming the anger that the memory of the young man's disdainful looks had reawakened.

"Monsieur," whispered Miroul, suddenly materializing at my side like the Devil arising out of the ground, "the grey-haired fellow in the brown doublet is the Marquis d'O. There's not a gentleman in the kingdom with a shorter name, or, it seems, a longer arm."

"And the lad on whose shoulder he's put his right hand?"

"This lively little fellow's Monsieur de Maugiron, a young nobleman in a well-placed family. The *tertium quid*,* that is, the arrogant sprig, whom you don't seem to like very much, is named Quéribus. As young as he is, he's already a baron. All three belong to the Duc d'Anjou, and are devoted to him to the death, and even beyond. Which is to say that they'd sell their souls for him, if they had any."

"Did a valet tell you all this?" I asked with some surprise.

"He spoke very ungraciously of them. But I don't know whether everything he said is true. He serves a gentleman who belongs to the king, and between the Duc d'Anjou and his brother the king, it seems to me that there's not much fraternal love."

At this moment, the great Silvie, who was as tall and thin as his own foil, and presented to the eye so little substance in his corporeal being that one wondered how the point of a sword could ever touch him, suddenly retreated (which he normally never did) and, standing to his full height, gave an Italian bow to the Baron de Quéribus, signalling that the lesson, if lesson it was, was over. To which Quéribus responded with a similar bow, though not as ample, since he did not

* "The third one."

have the fencing master's height to permit it. A valet ran forward to take his épée from his hands to save him the labour of resheathing it, and another handed him his doublet, which was, like mine, made of pale-blue satin, but as magnificently brocaded, pearl-studded and stylish as mine was not. Quéribus, throwing it on, headed over to the Marquis d'O and Maugiron, smiling broadly and readying some joke to tell them, but then, all of a sudden, he caught sight of me.

His face froze and his lips curled in derision; his eyebrows arching haughtily, he threw me a look of such infinite scorn that my hatred for him instantly flared up again. Suddenly I was carried away by such extraordinary anger at the odious repetition of his offensive manner that I returned his murderous look and, unthinkingly, my right hand gripped the hilt of my sword—and I would have drawn it had not Miroul put his hand on my arm. His touch awakened me, so to speak, from my trance, and I abruptly turned on my heels and, drunk with anger, pushed my way roughly through the crowd, scarcely aware of my surroundings, so blinded was I by my fury. Miroul and Samson followed behind, the first having some idea of my emotions; the second, understanding nothing of what had happened, kept repeating "Whath thith! Whath thith?" so insistently that finally I turned and snarled:

"My brother can't you stop lisping at us?"

He blushed and immediately fell silent, looking so aggrieved that I was overcome with shame at my nastiness; I slowed my precipitate pace and, as we stepped out into the courtyard of the Louvre, went to his side, slipped my arm under his, pulled him close to me without a word and walked next to him for the rest of the way, loving him more in proportion to the hurt I'd caused him.

Miroul, who was walking on my right, his face raised in concern towards mine, seeing that I was somewhat more calm, said in *langue d'oc*, "Monsieur, have you exchanged angry words with this gentleman?"

"No," I replied curtly. "Only looks."

"God be praised!" breathed Miroul gravely. "I feared for the worst."

"No words could be worse than this sort of look."

"But, Monsieur," smiled Miroul, "you returned an eye for an eye. Leave it at that! You're in Paris to ask the king to pardon you for one duel. Are you going to add another to your list? That would be madness! And all the more so since this time you could be killed. The knave is a marvellous swordsman."

"Ah, Miroul! That's just the point! If the rascal weren't so good, he wouldn't dare be so insolent to everyone. And, for me, if I give in to his insolent looks, he'll think me a faint-hearted coward."

"Monsieur, what does it matter what he thinks? You're no coward. Is this fop going to push you into a duel simply because you're afraid he'll think you're a coward? Isn't it also a kind of cowardice to let yourself be troubled by another man's scorn?"

"I need an explanation," Samson broke in, who was listening to our argument with amazement. "My brother, have you been offended?"

"Not at all," I replied impatiently. "It was just an exchange of looks."

"Monsieur," continued Miroul gravely, "may I remind you that your father ordered you to take my advice in extreme situations?"

"Miroul," I said, smiling somewhat reluctantly, "I'll take it. What do you advise me to do?"

"Monsieur, if your eyes and those of that popinjay continue to insult each other at every encounter, then words will follow. And they'll be irremediable. I advise you, then, while there's still time, to cease looking at him when he's looking at you, and simply to pretend to ignore his slights, so as not to have to answer them—as the Maréchal de Tavannes did, who turned a deaf ear when Coligny got angry and dared question his courage."

"Miroul," I said, eyes downcast, "I'm persuaded that, ultimately, your advice is good. I will follow it."

"Ah, Monsieur," warned Miroul with much alarm, "it looks like you'll have a chance to do so much sooner than I would have thought! Here comes the swordsman now, heading straight for us, accompanied by the Marquis d'O and Monsieur de Maugiron. I beg you, Monsieur, keep your eyes on the ground, or on Samson, and let's talk in *langue d'oc* as we were doing, and simply pretend not to see him!"

"You have to admit, Miroul," I said in my native tongue, my head lowered, but secretly watching the Baron de Quéribus as he advanced towards us, magnificently dressed and with his haughtiest expression, my heart beating with the hatred and the admiration he inspired, "you have to admit that these pretty little tarts are the most execrable race of vermin that ever crawled on this earth!"

"Ah, Monsieur!" said Miroul in terror. "What are you saying? Is Périgordian so little understood here?"

But he couldn't say more, for Quéribus, passing us, flanked by his two acolytes, turned to look at us, and said in a loud and clear voice:

"These rustic fellows are speaking *langue d'oc*."

Dropping Samson's arm, I turned as if I'd stepped on a thorn and, trembling with anger from head to foot, I said with subdued fury:

"Rustic, Monsieur?"

"Ah, Monsieur!" cried Miroul in despair.

"Rustic, Monsieur!" replied Quéribus with a deep bow. "Rustic, from the Latin *rus, ruris*, countryside."

"Monsieur," I said, bowing in turn, "I take offence."

"I believe that none has been given," said the Marquis d'O, who looked with astonishment from Quéribus to me; and, placing his hand with authority on Quéribus's arm, he added: "The Baron de Quéribus said, 'This rustic fellow is speaking *langue d'oc*.' He meant the valet and not the gentleman."

"I meant the two of them," corrected Quéribus, with the greatest nonchalance.

"Quéribus!" said the Marquis d'O, frowning. "What are you doing? A challenge! Here in the Louvre! Are you ignoring the orders of the king and of the Duc d'Anjou?"

"Not at all!" answered Quéribus, now speaking more softly, all the while assassinating me with his insolent looks. "As for me, I saw no offence in the word 'rustic', by which I simply meant a foot soldier who has his roots in the countryside. Monsieur de Siorac, having arrived directly from Périgord, cannot be from anywhere but the country."

"Aha!" I thought. "This gallant found out my name and origins from Monsieur de Nançay, and for what design is now obvious." And yet I made no answer, for I could tell that Quéribus, without in the least renouncing his quarrel with me, wanted to blame it on me.

"Monsieur," I said at last, "I accept your explanation. Nevertheless, would you consent to take back the word 'rustic'? Even though it means a simple soldier to you, it does not suit a gentleman."

"On the contrary," observed Quéribus in suave tones but with a murderous look, "it seems to me that it nicely fits a gentleman who was raised with pigs."

"Quéribus!" cried the Marquis d'O.

"Monsieur," I said calmly, "when you think about it, aren't we all different kinds of animal, some who are able to reason, others, as I gather, devoid of reason. So do you believe that the rustic rat is so inferior to the urban rat?"

At this, the little hanger-on Maugiron, as mad and insouciant as one often is at his age, laughed outright, which only served to goad Quéribus on.

"A rat, Monsieur?" he said, frowning.

"Urban," I replied.

"Offence taken!" cried Quéribus, in a tone less aggrieved than triumphant.

"I see none!" the Marquis d'O said quickly. "Monsieur de Siorac called himself a rustic rat."

"Monsieur de Siorac does himself justice," said Quéribus, "but not to me. Monsieur, answer! Am I a rat?"

"Urban," I explained. "From the Latin *urbs, urbis*, city."

"Ha!" cried Quéribus in the most derisive tone. "*Urbs, urbis*! Monsieur de Siorac is declining! Like his courage!"

"Quéribus!" cried the marquis.

"Monsieur," I said, "you provided the first example of this declension."

And little Maugiron laughed again.

"Ah, yes!" cried Quéribus, suddenly beside himself, and burning all his boats. "Laugh, Maugiron! Laugh! Monsieur de Siorac will laugh even harder when I add a buttonhole to the stitches in his ridiculous doublet!"

"There you have it, Monsieur d'O," I said, turning to the marquis, "there is offence, defiant, provocative and public. I beg you to give me leave to act."

"I give you leave to act," said the Marquis d'O mournfully.

"Monsieur d'O," I said, bowing deeply, "I'm lodged in Paris at the home of Maître Recroche, rue de la Ferronnerie: you're sure to find me there in the morning. Monsieur de Quéribus," I continued icily, "I am your humble servant and at your command at a time you shall designate."

"Monsieur, it is I who am manifestly your humble servant," said Quéribus calmly as he bowed to me. And as he stood straight again, I noticed that, by some magic, all the anger and haughtiness had been completely erased from his face, and he gave me a look, to my immense surprise, that wasn't the least bit unfriendly, but quite the opposite. I was even more astonished by my response, for I returned his look without a trace of bitterness. And as we stood eyeing each other, neither of us could repress a hint of a smile, as if the scene in which we'd faced off so angrily had only been a sort of mask behind which we had sealed a sudden and intimate friendship! That we were forced to cut each other's throats before getting to this point was what left me not a little perplexed.

"Ah, Monsieur," wailed Miroul, wringing his hands in despair as we walked away, "you shouldn't have taken offence at the word 'rustic'! You managed to be blind, but you couldn't remain deaf."

"How now? How now?" said Samson, his complexion taking on a deathly pallor. "A duel with a man of his calibre? Ah, my brother, he'll kill you!"

"Or, if you kill him, Monsieur, you lose your head!" choked Miroul, his throat constricted in grief. "A baron! A brilliant courtier! One of the Duc d'Anjou's gentlemen! Oh, Monsieur! It's madness!"

"What could I do?" I replied. "If I hadn't taken offence at the word 'rustic' he would simply have gone on with his persecution!"

"Alas, I think you're right," sighed Miroul.

"Ah, my brother," said Samson, "if the baron were to kill you, I'd have to take up the challenge."

"Oh, very nice!" said Miroul. "Then he could kill you as well!"

"And your death would give me great comfort up there in heaven," I laughed. "But my brother, let's say no more about this and close the book of lamentations. I suggest we tell Monsieur de Nançay about this nasty business and ask for his advice as to what to do."

Monsieur de Rambouillet, to whom I spoke to learn how best to find the captain of the foot guards, told me that he hadn't seen him yet, but that he might perhaps be found at the Five Virgins tennis court, where he usually spent his leisure time, since there would be few people there at this hour. I sent Miroul to Giacomi in his gallery to tell him where we were headed, and passed back through the gates of the Louvre and knocked at the massive oak door of the Five Virgins. The door opened slightly, and a valet asked my name and my business. I told him, and immediately the tennis master and ball-maker, Delay, appeared and very graciously greeted me, and told me that he recognized me as the Périgordian gentleman whom he'd seen with Monsieur de Nançay the day before, and that I had only to go on in, since the captain was about to start a doubles match. Saying this, he led us to the grandstand, which was empty at this early hour, and, sitting down with me, asked me, in the Parisian way, an infinite number of questions about my parentage and my province. I listened with one ear and answered only as much as necessary to avoid being impolite, my attention focused on two gentlemen who, in breeches and shirts, were hitting a ball back and forth over the rope, while a third gentleman stood by and served as umpire, seeming very impatient at not being able to join the game. At least so I surmised by his manner and by the fact that he was holding a racquet in his hand, which was of no use to him as an umpire.

"So these must be the gentlemen who are waiting for Monsieur de Nançay to make up a doubles game? What's the name of the tallest of the three? He plays very well."

"What?" said Delay almost indignantly. "You don't know him? You're kidding! Everyone in the world knows the Duc de Guise!"

"I'm afraid not. I've been in Paris only three days, though I've heard so much about him since my father, the Baron de Mespech, served under his father at Calais."

"I'll speak to Henri de Guise about you," said Delay good-naturedly. "He'll like you the better for it since he venerates the memory of his father, who was assassinated."

"And who's the gentlemen who's returning his shots?"

"Well, this is the amazing thing! This lord is the son-in-law of the man who had his father killed."

"But," I said, now on my guard, "is it certain that it was Coligny who had François de Guise killed? The king tarnished him with this infamous insinuation."

"Well," said Delay, "the king plays his own game, and his game is to keep everyone guessing."

He lowered his voice mysteriously as he said this, suffering from the same fever that afflicts everyone at court: wishing to appear well informed about everything. But other than this very Parisian weakness, I liked the master ball-maker well enough, if only for the fact that he was as round as one of the balls he produced: in his backside, his stomach and his face, with eyes that were a strange mixture of naive and sly.

"The Duc de Guise is very handsome," I observed as I watched him bound here and there on the tennis court.

"A beauty which nearly cost him his life," whispered Delay with a delicate smile. "The king nearly had him killed when he discovered his clandestine affair with Princesse Margot."

In truth, this was common knowledge, even at Mespech, thanks to the letter d'Argence had sent us, but I let him go on, since I was finding among these scraps some useful bits of information.

As we talked, I watched the Duc de Guise at tennis, and found him a vigorous, agile and dexterous player, his face an apt image for turning the heads of the ladies at court, having soft, narrow eyes, fine features and a delicate moustache that ravishingly turned up at the corners.

Unfortunately his beauty far surpassed his talents, which, according to the Brethren, were few: Guise gave a poor account of himself on the papist side in the civil wars, having inherited from his father neither military genius nor political finesse. And yet it was miraculous how his dedication to his party made up for his insufficiencies. There wasn't a Catholic church, cathedral pulpit, school, sacristy or seminary—or even confessional—which didn't daily resound with his idolatrous praises, since Guise was seen throughout the kingdom as the only steadfast defender of the Vatican faith, Charles IX being quite suspect on this account, since Coligny had his ear. Guise let it be known that, as a direct descendant of Charlemagne, he had a better right to the throne of France than Charles. Monks and priests went about whispering this with such fervour that ultimately the tall, handsome duc couldn't appear in the streets of the capital, looking so imposing on his black stallion, without the ignorant populace running up from all sides to kiss his hands, his feet and even his horse's shoes! What a strange place Paris is—indoctrinated by its priests, it created for itself another king than the king of France!

"You will notice," said Delay, "that Monsieur de Téligny doesn't have much of a backhand and that his service is shaky. Do you play, Monsieur de Siorac?"

"Much better than Téligny, a little less well than Guise."

"And your pretty brother?" asked Delay, leaning over to get a better look at Samson, who, dreamy, lost in thought and bitterly sad, was already imagining me, I suspect, with a sword through my heart.

"Very little."

"Is he always this quiet?"

"Always."

"Isn't that marvellous!" said Delay. "I never have enough hours in the day to disgorge all the words that swell up my cheeks."

I laughed at this, and he did as well, being a good-natured fellow, though proud and cunning. Turning the discussion away from my brother—so much did I fear that he would unleash some unfortunate remark about religion—I said, "So how does Guise consent to play tennis with the nephew of the man he believes killed his father?"

"The king wishes it so," replied Delay, "and is preaching reconciliation. Monsieur de Téligny served as an intermediary between Coligny and the king before the present amicable arrangement between the

Huguenots and us. And, from that point on, the king has showered benefits on this Téligny, who counts them as money in the bank."

"Do you think he shouldn't?" I asked turning to look at him.

"Good gentleman," answered Delay with a somewhat bitter smile, "at the court, you can't trust anything you hear. Everything is in constant movement: favour and disfavour. Moreover, whoever is loved by one king will find himself hated by the other."

"What?" I asked amazed. "But we have only one king!"

"We've got four of them," replied Delay, lowering his voice. "The crowned and sanctified one; the queen mother's king, the Duc d'Anjou; the king of the Huguenots, Coligny; and then there's Guise, the king of Paris."

"As I watch him play tennis," I said sotto voce, "the king of Paris is doing a lot of favours for the son-in-law of the king of the Huguenots. Look how he smiles and seems almost ashamed to have taken so many points from him."

"He smiles at him," said Delay, "but if he didn't fear the king's anger, he'd immediately slit his throat like a chicken. And Coligny's, as well. And those of all the heretics."

Thank God, Delay had said this so quietly that my brother didn't hear it. Otherwise we would have been in great danger of his giving us away, and that would have been the end of the confidences that Delay was sharing with me, as well as of his jokes, which I found quite enjoyable, especially given how much this man, who was not of the court, knew about his clients, who were.

A closer look at these tennis players allowed me to see that, indeed, Guise's smile was as false as Téligny's was candid. This latter gentleman, who had just arrived from Rouergue, was a fairly agile person with a pleasant and benign face, and visibly proud (in the simplicity of his heart) to be so well received at court and favoured by the king and the lords.

"So," I asked, "who is the gentleman acting as umpire of the match and who appears to be so impatient for Nançay to arrive for a game of doubles."

"The Chevalier d'Angoulême. But they call him 'the bâtard' since he's the fruit of fornication between Henri II and an Irishwoman."

"He's very dark," I observed. "His hair, his eyebrows, his eyes and his skin."

"And his soul," added Delay. "Look at his eyes, deep-set in their sockets and unnaturally close together, a sign of cruelty of character. In any case, the king loves this dark fellow, and always wants him near him, and entrusts to him his basest assignments."

"His basest assignments?"

"No one here is ignorant," Delay whispered in my ear, "that the king ordered him to kill Guise when the duc had the impertinence to bed Margot. If Guise hadn't got married immediately thereafter, the bâtard would have killed him."

"Well!" I thought. "What a world has Fortune thrown me into! Guise would slit Téligny's throat on a sign from the king, and, on a sign from the king, the bâtard would have dispatched Guise. But here they all are, playing tennis, with such courtesy and good grace. 'Sblood! What a royal court we have in France! All you see is fond embraces, smiles and kind words. But he who smiles at you on Monday could dagger you on Tuesday!"

The thought of daggers reminding me of my duel with Quéribus (which, however much I tried, never left my mind the entire time I was talking with Delay), I considered that my future in this treacherous city was very shaky indeed, which saddened me no little bit given how much I love our earthly life.

"Well," said Delay, "I can see that the bâtard is not a little impatient that Nançay's not here. Monsieur, perhaps you'd consent to be the fourth, if these gentlemen are willing."

I was so astonished at this that I could only agree, and straightaway Delay rose and trotted across the court, buzzing like a hornet around Guise's, then the bâtard's and then Téligny's ears. He came straight back and informed me that it was all arranged, and that I should strip to my shirt, and added, to my great shame, "I don't want these gentlemen to see you in this doublet."

After which, and having taken up a very good racquet, Delay introduced me to the bâtard, to Coligny's nephew and to Guise, partnering me with this last gentleman for the match.

"Well, Monsieur de Siorac," said the Duc de Guise, graciously, "I'm very happy to meet the son of Captain de Siorac, whom my father never failed to mention when he told us about the siege of Calais: a story I must have heard a hundred times as a boy."

"Monseigneur," I said, bowing low, "I also heard the story from my father, who had enormous veneration for the military talents and courage of yours."

This was, however true our statements were, in reality a kind of courtly balm, for Guise knew very well which religion my father embraced, and I knew that he was the sworn ally of the Pope and the Spanish king, dreaming only of acceding to the throne by means of the blood of the Huguenots: a long-standing plan that he dissimulated beneath the amiable mask of his courtesy. He could accept almost anything patiently—except not being king.

I played only a few minutes with them, enough at least for Guise to pay me some very pretty compliments on my game; he even told me, when Monsieur de Nançay arrived, that he'd happily have me as a tennis partner again should the occasion arise—a promise which seemed sincere enough, tennis being one of his passions.

Nançay didn't arrive alone. Monsieur de Montesquiou followed him in and came over to me in the grandstand where I was donning my doublet, and said gruffly that the Duc d'Anjou had ordered him to bring me straightaway to see him, along with my brother, news that I heard with prodigious amazement, as did Delay, who, seeing Montesquiou approach, came over to hear what he had to say.

"But Monsieur," I said, showing him the state of my doublet, "how can I appear before His Highness dressed as I am?"

"I have my orders," replied Montesquiou, his tanned face barred with two black stripes: his eyebrows and his moustache. "The matter can suffer no delay. Were you to refuse to come," he continued without a trace of a smile, "I would have to take you to His Highness by means of my guards."

"What a nuisance for them!" I smiled. "And what an escort for me! Monsieur de Montesquiou, you've entirely persuaded me to follow you!"

But to my smile, Monsieur de Montesquiou responded only with a most serious and angry expression, so that, when Samson and I were walking ahead of him in the courtyard of the Louvre, I turned and asked quietly, "Monsieur de Montesquiou, is this a serious matter?"

"I know not," he answered, his face inscrutable, "but His Highness looked very angry and his orders would admit of no delay."

Slowing my pace so that he could catch up to me, I looked silently at these two black stripes on his face, which, at this moment, did not look very accommodating. Ultimately, his silence so weighed on me that I said, thinking it was a joke:

"From your expression, Monsieur de Montesquiou, one would think I were being taken to a judge who was going to send me off to the Bastille this very night!"

"I'm not sure," replied Montesquiou, through his teeth. "Have you quarrelled?"

"Yes."

"In that case, it's possible."

7

MONSIEUR DE MONTESQUIOU led us to the new wing of the Louvre, and into a suite of rooms inaccessible to most of the courtiers. The ceilings of these rooms were superbly decorated with golden panels, on which were painted depictions of an ancient victory containing images of helmets, lances, cutlasses and pikes; the walls were hung with magnificent tapestries, and the parquet floors were covered with sumptuous rugs—all ornaments that I would have enjoyed, I think, had I not been so worried, both about the predicament I found myself in and about the august presence before whom I was to appear. Samson walked quietly beside me, throwing me such piteous looks that my throat knotted up. I was, moreover, horribly ashamed to appear before His Royal Highness looking so ridiculous in my doublet, and would have preferred to have been wearing a simple black velvet costume, like my brother, rather than displaying this repaired clothing to the prince.

At first I couldn't see the Duc d'Anjou, since he was surrounded by a group of brilliantly clad young courtiers, who, at our entrance, turned round to stare at us with as much curiosity as if we had been strange beasts brought that very morning from the Americas, and spoke quietly among themselves, shaking their heads, their bodies in constant movement, stroking their beards, rolling their hips, their soft hands caressing the ribbons, curls and pins in their hair, and exclaimed every other minute, "It weighs on my conscience!" or "I should have died of shame!"—phrases I'd already heard on the lips of the Baronne des Tourelles, and that they whispered with such suggestiveness you'd have thought these clichés were acquiring some new charm or authority.

I noticed that, despite the stifling heat, all of these gentlemen were wearing capes that were so short that they scarcely reached the waists of their wasp-like figures. On the other hand, some of them wore their capes attached only at the right shoulder, so that they fell lower and fluttered about when they turned on their heels, giving the impression of multi-coloured birds with red tails. I also noticed that almost all of them affected having one sleeve of their doublets unbuttoned with the other buttoned up tightly, so that each sleeve was of a different colour, as were their slashes, and so ample around the shoulders that they could have kept a purse under their armpits. They wore their leggings very tight about their thighs, almost like a woman's girdle, their stockings a different colour from the leggings, and the left a different colour from the right. Their ruffs, on which their heads were set as if on a plate, were quite wide, the plaits bleached the purest white. On their heads, atop their resplendent coiffures, they wore Italian caps surmounted by a plume that reminded me of the bonnet my mother used to wear.

Their eyebrows were trimmed into thin, delicate arcs, and their faces made up discreetly with white and red powders, and framed on only one side by a pearl or diamond earring. They all had sweetly suspicious looks on their faces, with their delicate hands posed on the hilts of their swords, which, from what I'd heard, these dangerous popinjays all wielded to perfection. All in all, despite the fact that they looked so soft and arrogant, they were a courageous lot, and valiant to the death, as many of them demonstrated during our wars.

My Samson was dumbfounded to see all of these refinements and trinkets on these dandies, the likes of which he'd never encountered, even in the Louvre, where the typical courtier, however decked out, would have looked like a worn-out rooster in the barnyard compared to these parading swans. As for me, horribly ashamed to see all these eyes on me, nearly suffocated by all the perfumes these peacocks sprayed on themselves, and struggling to understand their way of speaking, which was stuttered, mannered and lazy, their words falling almost inarticulately from their mouths, I dared not advance into their midst, but tried nevertheless to maintain my dignity as I confronted them in all their plumage.

"Messieurs, let us pass!" cried Montesquiou, whose tanned face and bushy eyebrows gave him the appearance of a crow among all these canaries, for whom, moreover, he seemed to have no liking—nor did they for him, given the lack of good grace they displayed in allowing us room to pass, some putting on faces and even holding their noses as if the captain smelt bad, and others putting their hands on their sword hilts as if they were suddenly going to pierce him through. Montesquiou scornfully refused to look at all these antics, but went straight to his prince, to whom he said, with a deep bow: "Your Highness is obeyed: here are the Messieurs de Siorac."

At these words, a complete silence fell over the gallery, all the pretty lordlings showing an almost devotional respect, ceasing their cacophony as the Duc d'Anjou, with a gesture of his hand, signalled that he was going to speak.

In fact, however, he didn't say a word, but stood, looking Samson and me over with intense curiosity, and perhaps attempting to gauge the extent of his power over us, for there are two ways of being quiet in this world: that of the subject and that of the prince. Although the Duc d'Anjou was sitting on an unadorned high-backed chair that was so low it was close to the floor, this chair looked like a throne given the majestic way he sat there—wholly different from his brother Charles IX, who, even when he was most angry, seemed childish. Nor could the duc be distinguished from the lordlings that surrounded him by his dress, for all the extravagances I'd noticed in them could be found in him as well (though his dress was clearly the origin and source of theirs), except that today he was dressed all in one colour: a white satin doublet with innumerable pearls and other jewels set in rows over his chest and shoulders. He didn't seem as handsome as I'd been told: his Valois nose was long and heavy like his father's and grandfather's—but his eyes made up for this imperfection, being very Italianate, large and black, and expressing almost simultaneously liveliness, mistrust, suspicion and a kind of gracefulness that had a way of winning you over even before he said a word, so that all he had to do was look at you to seduce you.

As for me, I wasn't immediately completely won over, for as I looked back at him with all the respect in the world, it seemed to me that his physiognomy tended less towards happiness and compliance—qualities that are always reassuring in a king—than towards bitterness and melancholy, for I could just detect in the turn of his mouth something that allowed me to see that this man, however young and favoured by the gods, was not at ease in his own skin.

I also observed that Anjou wore a thin and fine moustache, falling down at the corners of his mouth (which only emphasized the slight pout that I just mentioned), a little bunch of hairs under his lower lip that connected with a trim beard that encircled his chin, all of which were the most beautiful black, as was his hair, which emerged from under his cap, and fell in places over his forehead, which was high, wide and luminous.

"Monsieur de Siorac," he said in a deep voice, his eyes serious but not angry, "is it true that you entered into a quarrel in the courtyard of the Louvre with Monsieur de Quéribus?"

"Yes, Monseigneur," I replied, making a deep bow.

"And which of the two of you began this dispute?"

This question embarrassed me not a little, and all the more so because Quéribus, whom I'd not seen as I entered the gallery, since I had my eyes on Anjou, suddenly appeared on my right, still flanked by the Marquis d'O and Maugiron, but no longer looking the least bit haughty, but instead quite pale, ashamed and more confused than I was myself, evidently very fearful of losing the good graces of his master. And I suddenly realized that I myself had nothing of the kind to fear, being a Huguenot, and so, since I was already out of favour, I resolved to take the burden of the baron's responsibility.

"Monseigneur," I answered, "the fault lies neither with him nor with me, but with my doublet, which Monsieur de Quéribus could not look at without surprise, and his unhappy reaction produced a like reaction in me, and so looks passed to words and we exchanged a few of these that were prickly enough to cause a dispute, though the occasion hardly warranted such a difference since it derived entirely from his despising a despicable doublet."

At this, His Highness deigned to smile, since he enjoyed *giochi di parole*,* as I discovered after our conversation.

"Quéribus," said the Duc d'Anjou, "what think you of the account Monsieur de Siorac has given of your encounter?"

"That it is far too generous and absolves me of far too much blame." And saying this, he bowed graciously to me, a bow I instantly returned.

"Quéribus the Quarreller," said the duc (who seemed very happy with his own alliteration, which the courtiers greeted with a delighted murmur), "do you have any additional grievances or complaints concerning Monsieur de Siorac's person or sartorial choices?"

"None whatsoever, Your Highness."

"Do you hate him?"

---

* "Word games."

"Quite the contrary," said Quéribus with some heat. "You'd have to be very valiant to dare cross swords with me, and equally good-natured not to resent me for my insolent treatment of him. I've only known Monsieur de Siorac since yesterday, but already I like and esteem him greatly."

"And yet you were ready to cut his throat!" said Anjou with a sudden frown and raising his voice. "And not just you, but your seconds and your thirds! Oh, my friends," he continued, now addressing the entire assembly, "isn't this madness, all these quarrels that start up daily among you and in this very chateau? And near the person of the king—which is a capital crime according to the laws of the kingdom! And quarrels over what? Over things as unimportant and empty as this doublet. You'd think that killing each other were a kind of sport for you that needed no more justification than does a tennis match! Beware this monster, called a *quarrel*, which has been gaining popularity among the nobility, doesn't little by little devour you all! If you were to count up all the people in France who lose their lives every year in these duels, you'd discover that there have been battles, both in foreign and civil wars, at which there were fewer losses of such young and valiant lords—who might, with time, have attained to greatness, instead of dying uselessly in a field in the bloom of their youth. My bonny lads," continued Anjou (who was exactly our age, and was only our elder by reason of his rank), "can you imagine anything crazier than that a gentleman, with no hatred in his heart for his adversary, nay, having an obligation of friendship with him, should kill him in the name of some duty of false gallantry and false sense of honour?"

This powerful and beautiful remonstrance, eloquently delivered in fluid French, quieted our lordlings so completely that you could have heard a pin drop on a rug, each of them holding his breath in proportion to his sins, which must have been many and great judging by the expressions on many of their faces, though doubtless there were none here who'd pushed their excesses to killing a man in a private duel.

The Duc d'Anjou, meanwhile, fell silent, sitting on his high-backed chair, in his most elegant pose, his beautiful hands (which, I learnt later from Fogacer, he kept soft by applying all manner of fancy pastes and ointments) placed lightly on the arms of his chair, his beautiful, black, angry eyes fixed on Quéribus's as though he expected him to speak in a certain way but without explaining what he wanted.

"What should I do, Monseigneur?" asked Quéribus, who, pale and almost trembling, appeared to be in despair to have displeased his master. "Shall I straightaway make my peace with Monsieur de Siorac and ask his forgiveness?"

Still, His Royal Highness, head held high, looked him in the eye but said not a word, remaining majestically still as stone.

"Well, then, since I must," said Quéribus, flushing with anger at being forced to apologize to a man of inferior rank. "Monsieur de Siorac, I beg you—"

But I didn't let him finish, since things were not at all going the way I wanted. Pulling the baron suddenly to me, I embraced him warmly saying loudly: "Ah, Monsieur de Quéribus! It's not an apology I want, it's your friendship and only that!"

At this, he reddened, laughed, paled, laughed again and, suddenly dropping all his defences, embraced me in turn and kissed me several times on both cheeks, to which I responded in kind, finding this exchange infinitely more pleasurable than I would have found the clash of our swords. For, to tell the truth, he was so skilled in swordplay that, in the blink of an eye, he would have laid me out cold in the field, if our duel had taken place.

However, releasing me from his fond embrace, Quéribus, his face still red from pleasure, with tears in his eyes, and his face radiant, said to me, "Siorac, I confess here and now that you are no more rustic than I."

"Nor you more of a rat than I."

"Nor is your doublet any more shabby than mine."

"What?" cried Anjou suddenly. "Do you really believe that, Quéribus?"

"Assuredly so, Monseigneur," replied Quéribus with a bow.

"Well, I'm very glad," laughed Anjou, "for, looking at you, I see that you're the same height and build, and I had the idea that, as a gauge of your new friendship, you could exchange doublets!"

At this suggestion (which was really an order) there was a burst of laughter from the entire assembly that died down the minute Anjou looked up disapprovingly. I leave you to imagine the discomfort displayed by Quéribus as he exchanged doublets with me, and to guess how hard it was for me not to look too happy at my rich spoils, my double's displeasure touching me deeply, given the new feelings I had for him. And though the lordlings who were watching were struggling to contain their mirth, their cheeks so swelled they looked like frogs, such was the sovereign control that Anjou maintained over them that not one burst out laughing, and those whose eyes were too full of mockery immediately cast them down when they thought he was watching them.

"Well, this looks like an excellent fit," said the Duc d'Anjou, maintaining his gravity, "and also looks good on each of these sworn friends! Quéribus," he continued, "I am grateful for your compliance and would be even more so if you were to consent to spend the next hour, dressed as you are, walking about the Louvre with Monsieur de Siorac."

"Ah, Monseigneur!" cried Quéribus, turning ashen. "Must you submit me to such torment?"

"Monsieur," replied His Highness, "would you be ashamed in front of us, who order you thus, to appear in this doublet?"

"In front of you, Monseigneur, not in the least! But in front of the others!"

"The others are nothing, where we are not present," replied the Duc d'Anjou, with such majesty that I suspected that he sometimes forgot that he wasn't the king of France.

"Baron de Quéribus," he continued, "I shall see you here in an hour. Monsieur de Siorac as well."

That was our invitation to take our leave. We had to bend to it, and leave the hall, I in his splendour, he in my rags. Samson followed along behind, very glad, I'm sure, to see me safe and quieter than a log. Quéribus was also mute and blushing deeply in his excessive debasement, shaking like a leaf and looking entirely crestfallen, submitting to the despair of a punishment that for him was as cruel as death itself, so immense is the vanity of our courtiers—how different from our Huguenot sense of nobility, which prefers to be rather than to appear, and inclines more to the possession of wealth than to the display of it.

"Ah, Monsieur," I said, taking his arm and speaking quietly to him, "don't put on such a long face. People will laugh at you if they think you've been humiliated. Instead, put on a smile! Look happy! And when people look surprised to see you thus, simply say, 'Siorac and I have made a bet, and I'm going to be the winner!'"

"Heavens, Siorac," laughed Quéribus, "you've got as much wit as courage! That's excellent advice, and I'm going to follow it. It won't be said that people here who don't like me too much will have the pleasure of seeing me with my tail between my legs!"

And he stood up straight, squared his shoulders, held his head high and sallied forth into the courtyard of the Louvre, his lips opened in a smile (even if it was a bit jaundiced and forced). And I, seeing him in this disposition and hoping to fortify it, decided to recount my experience with the sorceress in Montpellier, who had fornicated with me on a grave in the cemetery because she believed I was Beelzebub, but then, seeing me in the street later, threw a curse on me which, for the next ten days, left me completely impotent. My story got Quéribus laughing out loud till he had tears in his eyes and was holding his sides.

"Ah, Siorac," he cried, "you're too funny! And when you think that Monsieur de Montaigne's sachet of herbs helped you regain your virility, but turned out to be empty—I mean the sachet not your virility."

And he laughed even louder at his own wit, and I along with him until we were bent over with mirth. Seeing this, several of the courtiers (which must come from the Old French word "*courre*"—to hunt—rather than from "court", since they seem always to be out of breath from chasing the higher-ups, begging favours), their attention attracted by our hilarity, came up to ask Quéribus the reason for his strange attire, and, obtaining no response because he was laughing so hard, decided they simply had to know the secret that had us prey to such mirth. Plus, when the crowd saw that we were followed by the dreamy Samson, by Giacomi, on his way back from his fencing, by Miroul, all amazed, and by Montesquiou (who, no doubt, had been told to follow us to ensure that we didn't hide for the hour of the punishment), their curiosity was so whetted that they fell in behind us and we soon had an impressive following, since there are as many gapers at court as there are in the city, who were bent on solving the mystery of why one of Anjou's lordlings would go about in such a decrepit costume.

Our procession, as you might imagine, put us in a very merry mood, but suddenly Quéribus, squeezing my arm, whispered in my ear, in the most sportive tones, "Siorac, I suspect you of being of the same religion as the Grand Prieur of France."

"And who is this great person?" I asked, secretly alarmed that he was talking about religion with a Huguenot.

"The bâtard—the Chevalier d'Angoulême. And thank God he has only the title and the revenues from the position, for, if he had to bless or absolve any of the ladies, the Devil knows what sprinkler he'd use, since there's no crazier petticoat-chaser in the kingdom!"

We both laughed at this, and I even harder than he, since, looking back at our sheep-like following, I saw that many of them were laughing as well, without having heard a word of our conversation, simply to give the impression that they were in on the joke.

"Ah, good God, Siorac," said Quéribus, "what a good companion you make! What a pity it would have been to kill you, since you possess all the talents it takes to make a gallant gentleman. What's more," he continued without a trace of vanity, "the more I look at you the more I think you look a bit like me."

"Quéribus," I said, pretending a sigh, "you flatter me. I have blonde hair and yours is golden. My eyes are grey-blue and yours are azure. I have pale skin and yours is white. My nose is straight enough, but yours is as though delicately chiselled and your lips as well, so that the ladies must go crazy over you. In a word, Monsieur, I think I'm the sketch and you're the finished work."

And even though my words were said a bit in jest, this beautiful speech so delighted Quéribus that he clasped me to him and gave me a dozen kisses, saying, "Ah, Siorac! Ah, my friend. I like you so well I don't ever want us to part company. I open my house, my purse and my stables to you! Good God! I'm ready to give you anything I have, and more! And if there's any lady in the court you desire, you have only to say her name and I'll do everything in my power to make her yours!"

It seemed to me that Quéribus was overdoing it and was trying to impress me with his power. I was wrong. For when I'd got to know the court better, I discovered that everything was done to excess in Paris: be it friendship or hatred. A certain gentleman that I heard about, having been left for two weeks by his intimate companion, went into such mourning that he let his beard grow and gave up eating and drinking, taking only the minimum necessary to survive until the return of his absent friend.

I expressed my deep gratitude as fervently as I could to this friend who, only a hour previously, had wanted to cut my throat: it was my turn to embrace him and plant a dozen kisses on his cheeks, and I told him that the lady had already been selected, that she'd invited me that very evening for supper—to be followed by "dessert"—and that she lived in the rue Trouvevache. When I mentioned this street, Quéribus broke out laughing uncontrollably.

"Ah, Siorac," he said, "I know the lady. It's the Baronne des T.! There's not a decent-looking gentleman at court who hasn't also been invited to her little suppers, but *caro mio*, it's very light fare! The lady is an arch-coquette: for soup you'll have sweet nothings, and the little minx gives nothing away beyond her lips; she keeps you amused with little snacks but the pot roast never gets to the table."

As he was explaining this, someone tapped him on the shoulder, and, turning round, we saw Monsieur de Montesquiou who, looking as austere as ever with the two bars, eyebrows and moustache, lining his face, told us the hour had now elapsed and that we were to return to the hall where His Highness was waiting for us.

Accordingly, we headed that way, followed, still, by our Panurgic procession, which Montesquiou halted with his raised hand at the entrance to the gallery, Quéribus and I still enjoying our various stories and witticisms, eyes shining and faces smiling, and our cheeks nearly worn out with all the kisses we'd exchanged.

I was so fascinated by the Duc d'Anjou and by the very Italian subtlety of his behaviour (but wasn't he, after all, the son of a Medici mother and the heir of all the charm, cunning and appreciation of beauty of his Florentine family?) that I was looking forward to seeing him again and hearing him speak. And yet there was a scruple that was bothering me, scarcely larger than a pebble in a boot that, though it doesn't prevent you from walking, nevertheless reminds you constantly of its presence: how could I admire the sworn enemy of my party, the victor at Jarnac and Moncontour, the man who murdered Condé by means of the hand of this very grim Montesquiou who was escorting me to him? And if, however, as Delay had pointed out, there were really four kings in this war-torn kingdom—Charles IX, Coligny, the Duc d'Anjou and Guise—why should I be surprised that each of the four, feeling threatened by the others, should plot their rivals' destruction, and that there should be a series of constantly shifting alliances in order for the four to keep each other in check? And in this present, strange and almost unnatural convergence, in which we saw Charles IX make Coligny his advisor—out of mistrust of his mother and hatred of his brother—Anjou might well enter into some understanding with Guise, though he should have worried more about Guise's unquenchable ambitions to unseat the entire Valois family, as events later proved only too well. And so the papist party presently had two heads, like Janus, under one bonnet: Anjou and Guise, each of whom was unable to keep from hoping that the other would falter and leave the terrain open to him.

In the midst of such thoughts, I found myself very disappointed that, as we re-entered the hall, Anjou was not there, and nor was the crowd of his courtiers; instead there were only five or six people, among whom I recognized Fogacer, next to a very serious-looking character with an honest face that I liked well enough, and who must have been Dr Miron (who, in truth, did not turn out to be so stupid and ignorant in his practice as Fogacer had said; indeed, quite the contrary). As we came in, a tall, well-built gentleman with a high forehead and a bold look in his eye (who I discovered later was called Du Guast) stepped over to us and said:

"Messieurs, His Highness was unable to wait for you, but was called away by the queen, his mother. Before he left, however, he dictated a letter to the Baron de Quéribus that he asked me to give him."

Whereupon Du Guast handed the letter to Quéribus, who opened it straightaway, read it and, his handsome face illuminated by the most exalted joy, said, nearly shaking with happiness:

"Oh, God! What a good, loyal and beneficent prince! And if I had a thousand lives to give, I'd offer all of them to him! Read this, Siorac! It is about you as well."

Reader, I was able to keep this letter, after pressing Quéribus so hard for it that he finally gave it to me, and here it is, sadly written by his secretary, but signed by his hand and composed in his own style:

Monsieur de Quéribus,

I do not know how to thank you for the generosity of spirit you devoted to obeying my command, by which I have appreciated your goodwill towards me, which, I assure you, I shall have occasion to repay. Monsieur du Guast will give you a doublet on my behalf, to replace the one in which you were seen in this chateau, which should be returned to Monsieur de Siorac, though he will not return the one you gave him, but keep it as a gauge of your sworn word that you will be brothers and friends for ever, like two bones that are solidly rejoined after being broken.

Monsieur de Siorac's father served my grandfather at Ceresole and my father at Calais, and though he's of the new opinion, he has never raised his sword against his king, being a loyal and faithful Huguenot, like La Noue. I am assured that his son will serve me and the king, my lord and beloved brother, with the same dedication. Having observed that his fortune does not permit him, at present, to maintain his rank in this

343

chateau as he merits, I have directed Du Guast to provide him with 200 écus from my account, so that he and his beautiful brother may clothe themselves as they see fit.

Quéribus, my gentle friend, I don't want you to quarrel any more, but, having always loved you and loving you still, your obedience can only redouble the friendship and affection I bear you. Monsieur, love me always, I beg you. Your friendship will create an unbreakable bond between us and I assure you that it will be rewarded.

Your very good friend,

Henri

My Quéribus was practically beside himself with inexpressible happiness at the doublet that His Highness had had brought to him. Du Guast handed it to him, though with what I thought was a jealous smile (due perhaps to the fact that he envied this unprecedented privilege) and the baron put it on and buttoned it, his hands trembling with joy, its splendour inundating his dazzled countenance. I believe he was more honoured with this gift than if he'd received from the king the order of Saint-Michel, or from the papal nuncio a rosary of beads blessed by the Pope.

This princely vestment was made of pale-blue satin (like the one Quéribus had given me), and though it was decorated with as many precious stones and pearls as was the white garment worn by the Duc d'Anjou during our conversation, I am quite certain that the baron counted as of little consequence the monetary value that he might have realized from the sale of these decorations, compared to the intimate and particular favour displayed by the prince and the tender words that had accompanied it in his letter.

But for my part, it hadn't escaped me that, while Du Guast was counting out one by one into my purse the shiny and tintinnabulating écus, Anjou had not so much linked Quéribus to me as he had tied the two of us to himself. He had tried, so to speak, to kill two pigeons with one shot of his arquebus, attempting both to rein in duels in his court and to attach us to him, using a combination of largesse and flattery in a letter that he well knew, as he dictated it, would be cherished in time by both of us well beyond the gifts he'd bestowed on us.

Well, certainly, I couldn't forget that that the Duc d'Anjou was the grandson of a Florentine lord, to whom Machiavelli had dedicated his famous work, *The Prince*. Of course, the duc knew very well that you command the arms and hearts of men as much by honour as by the promise of favours. But in the application of this great precept, this letter displayed such easy finesse. What an example of Italian *gentilezza*, in which nothing was missing, not even real emotion! How astonishing his passage from the formal *vous* to the intimate *tu* when, almost in the same phrase, he orders the obedience of his subject and asks for his friendship! Nevertheless, beneath these caressing words, how could one miss the expression of an authority that brooks no refusal? Anjou had once said: "Others don't exist when we are not there." Beneath this velvety paw, the claws were always ready to be bared.

I also noticed that rather than refer to the Huguenots injuriously as a "cult" as the papists did, or "the so-called reformed religion", the prince used more courtesy and grace in designating us in his letter those "of the new opinion"—more measured language, which he maintained even when, in the siege of La Rochelle, he asked his brother to intervene, calling him "Monseigneur and beloved brother", a king who was barely the first and certainly not the second of these terms of respect.

Quéribus would have wanted to remain with Samson and me and dine with us, and when I reminded him that I was expected at the rue de Trouvevache, he tried to dissuade me from visiting this "arch-coquette", arguing that if it was pleasure I wanted he knew where to send me to get "complete satisfaction". But I didn't consent, both because I didn't want to break my invitation with Madame des Tourelles, and because I didn't want Quéribus to occupy all of my time, which he seemed inclined to do in the heat of this new friendship. It wasn't that I didn't like him, quite the contrary, but I wanted to establish right away some reserve in our relationship that would allow me to be master of my own time.

I finally managed to get away, but only after a last embrace and I don't know how many kisses, pats on the back, promises of eternal friendship, affectionate regards and even a few tears of joy. I watched him as he walked away through the courtyard of the Louvre in the setting sun. And though he was only walking, his step was so lively that you would have said he was running on the tips of his toes up a steep hill, as if to take flight into the skies of happiness.

"*Heu! Quam difficilis gloriae custodia est!*"* said a sardonic voice behind me, and turning round I recognized Fogacer, his eyebrows arching and his eyes ablaze, looking like nothing so much as an enormous grasshopper; putting his hand on my shoulder, he looked at me with his slow, sinuous smile, and continued: "Siorac, *mi fili*, you know it's to me that you owe all these tender embraces from Quéribus, which are certainly preferable to his sword point in your throat—a secret move that he learnt from the great Silvie—for, seeing you a while ago cavorting in the courtyard of the Louvre with this dangerous swashbuckler, I immediately informed Anjou, which produced the result you're aware of. And now I'm wondering if it was the right or the wrong thing to do. Assuredly, it's not easy to protect your life from another threat, *mi fili*, you whom I nourished from the breasts of philosophy and logic, the two sterile mammaries of Aristotle. I didn't raise you to the heights of the Capitol, so splendidly attired as

---

* "Alas! How difficult is the custody of glory!"

you are, your purse overflowing, only to see you thrown into the void from the Tarpeian Rock. *Fortuna vitrea est. Tum cum splendet frangitur.*"*

"Fogacer, what are you telling me?" I asked, opening my eyes, while Samson, Giacomi and Miroul (who had joined me as soon as I'd left the building) stood completely silent and amazed, both at my incredible fortune and at the warning this black grasshopper had just emitted.

"Siorac," Fogacer continued, leaning closer to me (a movement that Samson, Giacomi and Miroul immediately imitated, so anxious were they to hear the rest), "within the hour, the entire court will have learnt that you received from the Duc d'Anjou these extraordinary favours. This afternoon, Pierre de L'Étoile will learn of them. Tomorrow the entire city."

"So? Is this such a bad thing?" I replied.

"The worst!" announced Fogacer growing more serious. "From this day on you will be seen as belonging to the party of the Duc d'Anjou, and hence you will be suspect to the three others. To the Huguenots, of course, who will turn their backs on someone who has earned the friendship of the victor of Jarnac and Moncontour. To the Guisards, who fear the shrewdness of Anjou much more than the king. And, of course, to the king."

"To the king? How could that be?" I cried, confused and stammering in my emotion.

"Didn't I tell you? The king hates his brother and, from first to last, he abhors all his friends. Siorac, here's the full extent of the irony of your situation: until today you wouldn't have been able to present your petition for pardon to the king because of your ripped doublet. But now, given your splendid attire, you could appear before the king, but he would never receive you."

"Ah, Fogacer," I moaned, mired in bitterness, "what are you telling

---

* "Fortune is like glass. When it shines most brightly it breaks."

me? If that's true, I've miserably failed at the enterprise that was the reason for this entire journey! For these incredible dangers, all of this wasted time, all this expense. Should I have refused Anjou's money and the doublet?"

"What are you thinking? Anjou would have hated you and your Quéribus as well. And his sharp blade would have been the messenger of his disappointment."

"So," I said, crushed with astonishment and despair, my legs trembling beneath me, "without ever having desired it, by the sole work of chance and the invisible linking of events, here I am, a Huguenot in the Duc d'Anjou's party, detested by the Guisards, suspected by the king, and in trouble with my own people."

"Wait, my beloved brother!" cried Samson all of a sudden, his azure eyes all illuminated in the purity of his zeal. "Heaven has spoken to us through the mouth of Fogacer!" (At which, Fogacer arched his diabolic eyebrow sceptically.) "Return to Anjou the corrupt money and the frivolous doublet, which sticks to your skin like the red mantle of the prostitute. What do you care about the king's pardon? Hasn't your conscience absolved you for having killed the evil Fontenac? My brother, let us flee from the villainous people of this Babylon! We'll seek asylum in the sweet fields of Mespech, far from the vices and abominations of this stinking Paris!"

This eloquent speech, exploding in our midst, left us all a bit awed, all of us except Miroul, who said sotto voce, "This red mantle is in pale-blue satin."

However, just as I was about to unleash my anger at my poor brother in the midst of such frustration, Giacomi laid his hand on my arm and said very quietly, "Samson! Weren't you listening? *È une questione di fatto e non di principio.** Pierre cannot do without the

---

*   "It's a question of fact and not of principle."

king's pardon, without which he's in danger of decapitation, even in Mespech. He cannot be presented to the king except in this doublet, and not in the one Miroul is holding. But if he refuses the largesse of Anjou, his life will also be in danger. Do you want your beloved brother to be in mortal danger from all sides?"

Of course, hearing this, Samson, tears in his eyes, fell silent, never having had any way of understanding life's setbacks other than through his biblical and pastoral vision. Certainly my beloved brother had little skill at wisely managing life in the city or at court, where I myself was now caught in a trap like a confused hare that had ventured out of its hole. Oh, how I wished Samson were a hundred leagues from there, or at least in Montfort-l'Amaury, where I'd requested in a letter to Maître Béqueret that he be allowed to stay for at least the time we'd remain here in the capital. And now I was even more eager for this distancing, since it hadn't escaped me with what favour the Duc d'Anjou had looked at him during our conversation, calling him in his letter my "beautiful brother". Heavens! All that was missing in my current predicament was for this "special favour" to be explained more precisely, and for my brother, who happily was a little slow, to end up understanding it! Oh, God! What fires, what flames, what biblical brimstone would burst from his mouth! And in what new peril would we be embroiled!

It's not that I thought everyone in the duc's retinue was, shall we say, "Fogacerian", although this custom, which in France is called "the Italian vice" and in England "the French vice", was not entirely unknown, Anjou himself seeming to swing between two passions, each with a different object. To tell the truth, I'd initially suspected that the Marquis d'O, little Maugiron and Quéribus were Fogacerians, though I quickly dismissed this thought regarding Quéribus, having observed that, as we frolicked through the courtyard of the Louvre, he'd been "hooked" by every good-looking lady we passed, regarding each and every one with the same interest, which convinced me that his appetites were entirely focused on Eve, rather than on the one who'd been created before her, as a first, primitive sketch.

But to return to my subject: I looked around me at Fogacer, Giacomi and Miroul, who weren't looking very hopeful, given our situation, and said quietly, "Well then, my friends, what should I do?"

"*Aspettate domani*,"* said Giacomi.

"*Patientes vincunt*,"† agreed Fogacer. "The court will forget about this. Favour fades away. So does disgrace."

Miroul said in *langue d'oc*, shaking his head:

> "*Samenas sezes en Brial.*
> *N'auras tot l'estiu.*"‡

"So we're all agreed," I said.

"But I didn't give my opinion," complained Samson with such a sad and disappointed tone that I took his arm and embraced him, and said as reassuringly as I could, "So speak, Samson."

"We should stay here," he said in a voice strangled by the knot in his throat. "But, my brother, I would like to request that we leave this Babylon the minute the king signs your pardon."

"I promise, Samson," I said immediately.

I made this promise lightly and kept it just as lightly, alas! For it cost me dearly and caused me a lot of pain, and tragically so, as I shall explain.

Full of hope, and now relieved of some of my worry, thanks to my friends' encouragement, I left them at the rue de la Ferronnerie, on their way to share a meal at Guillaume Gautier's restaurant, and,

---

*   "Wait until tomorrow."
†   "The patient will triumph."
‡   "Sow your peas in April. You'll be eating them all summer."

followed by Miroul, who had absolutely insisted on accompanying me, I headed towards the little house on the rue Trouvevache, where the Baronne des Tourelles had invited me to supper. Upon my knock, and after an eye had examined me from the little peephole, the door opened and the little valet, Nicotin, greeted me with a playful look.

"Is the baronne at home, Nicotin?"

"*By my conscience* I do not know!" replied Nicotin, who found it very natural to speak like his mistress or like the lordlings of the court, never hearing anything but their jargon.

"And Corinne?"

"I'll go and fetch her, Monsieur, if you like," he said with a deep bow, which seemed slightly mocking to me, but was polite enough to deny me the pretext of giving him a good boot in the backside, though the thought did cross my mind.

"Ah, Monsieur," said Miroul, "this is infuriating! These Parisians have a kind of mocking civility that turns my blood to water. And especially this little rogue who hides his impertinence behind his greeting."

"Give him two sols on my behalf. That'll sweeten him up a bit."

"Two sols? I'll give him a slap—that's what I'll give him! That's the only titbit Nicotin will get from me. And a swift kick in the arse."

I laughed.

"Ah, Monsieur," Miroul continued, "this doesn't augur well for our evening. Like valet, like mistress. They're going to have fun with us, I'll warrant."

"Yes, I was warned," I whispered. "But Miroul, how will we know unless we give it a try?"

"Ah, Monsieur, more's the pity! If you don't succeed you'll be laid out on the carpet all confused and crestfallen! And what would Barberine say if she saw you mocked like this!"

"Well, Miroul," I replied, "now it seems *you're* making fun of me!"

But he didn't have time to respond. Corinne came in, her apple-like breasts emerging from her emerald bodice, her emerald skirt brocaded with two rows of almond green. The wench looked very healthy, clean and attractive: no make-up whatsoever, her forehead washed with clear water, her eyes shining, her teeth bright as could be, her lips full, her cheeks rosy and her blonde hair arranged in two long braids.

"'Sblood, Monsieur!" whispered Miroul, his eyes popping out of his head.

"Well, my noble Monsieur!" cried Corinne, bowing to the floor with a most indiscreet reverence. After which, coming over to me, she said in her lively and abrupt Parisian accent, "Ah, good gentleman, how splendid you look! I'm so happy to see you arrayed so elegantly! *By my conscience, I could die!* This satin! And how beautifully made! What shoulders and so à la mode! These pearls and silk from the Orient! You can see straightaway that these are not imitations from Lyons! How happy Madame will be to see you all dressed up like this!"

"Is she not here?" I asked icily.

"Madame was forced to delay her return by an unforeseen problem, but she begs you to have supper here without her and promises to join you at midnight."

This said, she gave another revealing curtsey, took me by the hand and led me into a small room that was tapestried in purple velvet, and where a large table, lit by a quantity of candles, was laden with a variety of delicious-smelling meats.

"'Sblood, Corinne!" I cried. "This is all well and good. But it's sad to have to dine alone, even if it is on a tablecloth embroidered with gold and out of silver dishes. If you will please treat me as your master and obey me, keep me company, along with my Miroul."

"Well, Monseigneur!" replied Corinne, looking like nothing so much as the serpent in the Garden of Eden wrapped around the tree of knowledge, and giving me a look that would have sent me straight out of Paradise if our ancestors hadn't already been booted out. "If I will treat you as my master? Are you asking me, Monseigneur? Command me, I beg you! I'll be at your command—as docile, pliable, malleable and submissive as all the wives of the Grand Turk rolled into one!"

At this, Miroul's brown eye lit up like a candle and, as Corinne left, parading her beautiful emerald dress bordered in almond green, to ask Nicotin to add two places to the table setting, my good valet stepped over to me and said, in *langue d'oc* and in a rascally tone, "Monsieur, I don't know what the mistress will be like, but the chambermaid is all ready to be thrown in the game bag, and so hot I think she's going to pluck herself!"

"Precisely," I whispered, "and I don't like it a bit. A girl likes to be persuaded, and this one isn't putting up enough resistance. I fear they're laying a trap for us and they're going to lead me on to make an ass of me. Why would they make me take this little tower if they're ready to abandon the castle to me?"

"Well, Monsieur," said Miroul, "if I were you, I wouldn't look so hard for possible troubles. This long journey has kept us for so many interminable days in bitter chastity."

"What, you devil! How dare you speak to me of your chastity, when you had Maître Béqueret's chambermaid right under my nose!"

"Ah, Monsieur," smiled Miroul, "that's the inconvenience of being a gentleman. You don't have the easy familiarity with the servants that we valets do. But back to your Turkish slave. Enjoy her, Monsieur! Believe me, what's up for the taking is to be taken!"

Corinne, all smiles and amorous glances, was followed by Nicotin, looking very put out, who added two places to the table, very disappointed that he wasn't invited to join us, since Miroul was. Seeing this, I let myself be softened by his pouting (for he was as pretty and cute as a girl, his cheeks so smooth that the barber, Babette, wouldn't have found anything to shave) and, not wishing to make an enemy of this little hornet, I told him to bring another place setting for himself. This made him jump for joy and smile broadly, and, running over like a child, he kissed my hand and offered a thousand thanks. And then, Corinne having left the room again, I slipped a few sols into his fingers, which so completely won him over that I thought to myself that, when I wasn't attacking the castle, I could well have spent my leisure time exploring this little watchtower. But reader, you know very well that I'm neither attracted to nor repulsed by such fantasies, considering them somewhat foreign to my nature, though I accept them easily enough in others, however much they're considered cardinal sins by our Churches and severely punished by the executioner—something that, in my opinion, should be left to our Sovereign Judge to decide in the next life.

I'm not unaware that some will turn up their noses at the idea of dining with a chambermaid and two valets. But for me, who was raised in the old, rustic ways at Mespech, where servants dine with their masters, I see no malice nor lowering of myself in this, believing, moreover, that if a chambermaid is good enough to bed, then she's good enough to share your meal, where her beauty will add spice to the food. What's more, I hold that there's no meal so sumptuous that it can do without the company of our fellows, and, to tell the truth, my plate languishes when I'm forced to dine alone.

And, at the risk of displeasing certain people, I would add that I found both Nicotin and Corinne to be in full possession of their health, their eyes bright, their complexions clear and their breath quite fresh, and I'm not afraid of saying that, in this regard, I was happier dining with them than with certain noblemen (whom I shall refrain from naming), with whom I was inclined to clean my spoon with the corner of my napkin, given how little the cleanliness of my hosts inspired my confidence. How I would love it if, in this kingdom, the refined people at least copied the ways of our good, clean Swiss neighbours, who, for each meal, give a spoon to each of their guests so that none risks putting an implement in his mouth that has already been in someone else's.

The meats served at this meal were abundant and delicious, the wines as well, though I sipped the latter in moderation, knowing full well that Bacchus is an unfaithful friend to Venus, and to carouse too much with him will likely disappoint her later. Corinne appeared to know this as well, for she refrained from urging me to drink, but instead worked to attract my attention to her blonde hair, bright eyes and frisky body by inflammatory looks that would have lit up the worst dullard. Her behaviour greatly intrigued me, for I knew that her mistress planned to return at midnight, and seriously risked finding her meal already consumed by her servant. As to where all this could be leading, I didn't have the least clue, but I proceeded in this business like a cat whose whiskers are bristling, eyes watchful and paws ready to retreat.

Our delicious meal finished, Corinne rose from the table with a very determined air, but still looking most seductive, her bosom heaving, her pretty blonde braids dancing around her pink cheeks, and, in a quiet but firm voice, told Nicotin and Miroul to clear the table. This command they seemed ready to obey, Miroul's brown eye shining with delight and Nicotin with a knowing air that made me even more suspicious.

"Now, before leaving us, my dears," said Corinne, "I think we should drink a toast to Monsieur de Siorac, and wish him as much success in love as he is superb in his new clothes."

This said, she placed in the bottom of a beautiful crystal glass a small piece of grilled bread, called a *tostée* in Paris (and which the

English call *toast* since they copy us in everything), and then filled the glass with an excellent Burgundy wine. She brought the glass to her lips, took a sip and handed it to Miroul, who immediately understood the ceremony (which is, however, entirely unknown in our Périgord) and drank a generous mouthful; then Nicotin drank a larger one still, before he handed the glass to me. I took the goblet in both hands and emptied it with all the gravity that the occasion seemed to call for, and then, taking the piece of toast at the bottom—as I supposed I was meant to do—gallantly devoured it.

"Monsieur de Siorac has drunk the wine!" cried Corinne while the two valets applauded vigorously. "He has drunk the wine and eaten the toast that I brought him! And so he will be happy and satisfied in his loves, God willing! And now," she continued her eyes blazing with desire, "be gone, my lads, and hop to it! No objections and no delay! Monsieur de Siorac and I have business of our own to attend to!"

She then took me by the wrist and led me into a small chamber where, by the light of a single candle, I saw an enormous bed with purple curtains and the most prodigious pile of cushions I'd ever seen. But I hardly had time to admire it, for Corinne nimbly shut and bolted the door, threw her arms around my neck and planted her fresh lips on mine.

Oh reader! What a *tostée* that was! You can imagine how hard I had to struggle not to finish it on the cushions I'd just been admiring. Oh, heaven! How I detested the fastidious point of honour that forbade me from enjoying the servant when I had promised myself to her mistress.

But vanity has its own part to play in such matters. Pleasure isn't enough. Glory demands its due. And although in Mespech I could enjoy my little serpent Little Sissy (to whom Anjou's money would allow me to present the gold ring I'd promised her when I left), Madame de Joyeuse had taught me to place great value in the dignity of my lovers.

It's not that I'm dazzled by a title, or that I put a baronne above a chambermaid. But though they may be the same flower, they don't have the same perfume. I read several years later a passage in Michel de Montaigne's *Essais* in which he discussed the delicacies of "adorned and sophisticated ladies". I liked this phrase, whether because Montaigne had invented it by analogy with "sophism" or because he used it by analogy with wines that they try to refine by skilful combinations (a technique that's called *sophistiquerie* in our southern provinces). In regard to my own relations with women, I think I understand what Montaigne means by this: for I love a wench who's not too naive, but who knows how to make one feel, by her art and her touch, the extraordinary value of the gift she's providing. I abhor the arch-coquettes whose promises come to nothing. But on the other hand, I have to confess that, when her consent has been given, those sweet nothings, ambiguous glances and double-entendres, and the *je ne sais quoi* of teasing, all contribute to the pleasure of her ultimate gift of herself.

But, of Madame des Tourelles, I knew only what Quéribus had told me (which may have been coloured by the spite of an unhappy lover), and, believing that the proof of a deed is in the doing, I needed to know for certain whether this haughty and gallant lady really wished me so ill that she wouldn't provide what she'd promised. Indeed, how can a woman tell her lover that she wants him to shave his entire body if she isn't interested in kissing him a bit?

"Corinne," I asked, taking her hands from around my shoulders and holding her at arm's length, "what's the meaning of your caresses? What's going on? Where is all this leading?"

"Oh, heaven, Monseigneur," she cooed, "isn't it clear enough? Didn't I already tell you that I am at your service in everything? Why are you waiting to subject me to your will? Don't you desire me?"

"You know well enough that I do."

"Well then, Monsieur, let's forget the talking! Don't act like a badly trained falcon! Your prey is flying straightaway! Swoop down on it!"

"Ah, Corinne," I laughed, "it's assuredly a beautiful, tender bird I'd put beak and claws to. But unfortunately it's other game that I'm hunting."

"Well, then, my good gentleman," she cried, "can't you hunt both?" And pulling her wrists from my hands, she tried to put her fresh and comely arms around my neck again, but again I pulled away from her advances and, seizing her shoulders, forcibly separated us, so uncertain was I that I would be able to resist her if she started in again.

"Fie, then, Corinne!" I said, frowning. "Would you then steal the first fruits from your mistress and leave her only the gleanings of your harvest? This is no way to treat a noble lady who has taken you into her confidence and who treats you so well!"

At this, Corinne blushed deeply and said with some indignation:

"Ah, Monseigneur, I love my mistress deeply and am completely loyal and devoted to her! I'm only doing her bidding here!"

"What?" I gasped. "This is her bidding? Do you really dare claim it's so?"

"Yes, indeed!" she hissed angrily.

"Corinne! I'm lost! Are you telling me that Madame des Tourelles told you to offer me your body here? I can't believe it!"

"Believe or not, Monsieur," she cried, her eyes blazing, "it's true! I swear it before the Blessed Virgin and all the saints in Paradise."

"But why?" I exclaimed, raising my arms heavenward.

"In order to test you."

"To test me?" I asked, amazed. "And why?"

"To find out whether you're good enough for Madame to admit you to the familiarities she desires."

"My God!" I shouted, suddenly drunk with rage. "Is this what happens in Paris? Are these the refinements of the court? Test me? I've never heard of such impertinence! Am I a stallion that I should need to be tested before I can be taken to the stud farm? Are you going to put a ring through my nose like a bull? 'Sblood! This is insufferable! Who does this lady think she is that she can parade herself with such royal self-esteem that I should be confined to the outskirts of her good pleasure?"

"Monsieur," countered Corinne harshly (good wench though she was), "I don't understand you at all! Our handsome gentlemen of the court don't put on such airs and seem to like me well enough!"

"That's not the point, Corinne," I said, softening my approach. "You have enough all by your pretty self to damn all the saints you just evoked! I don't disdain your attractions, quite the opposite! But I can't help refusing the presumption that would make you my judge. My friend," I added, pulling back the bolt, opening the door and crossing into the room where we'd supped, "bring me pen and paper. I want to explain myself to your mistress, and don't want to wait here until midnight."

Miroul and Nicotin were still clearing the table, and were amazed to see us reappear so soon, Corinne blushing deeply and me looking very cross. But neither of our valets made a peep, so obvious were my anger and the chambermaid's embarrassment.

The good wench would doubtless have wished to refuse me the writing materials, as she could divine easily enough that my letter to her mistress was not going to be very pleasant, but she didn't dare, and, eyes downcast, she brought me what I'd requested. And so, having taken the time to decide what to write, I sharpened my quill, and, having scribbled a quick draft that I could keep for myself, I wrote the following to the baronne des Tourelles.

Madame,

I spared no effort in following each and every one of the commandments you gave me yesterday in your carriage, and if you had done me the courtesy of being at home when I visited this evening at your invitation, you would have seen me as you wished: shaved as cleanly as Nicotin, and as beautifully clothed as one of Anjou's lordlings.

I could not, however, extend my obligingness as far as you would have wished to push it, as it seems to me, upon reflection, that you displayed too little consideration of me in using your chambermaid to put my talents to the test.

Having too much deference for you and for your rank to dare suggest that my valet, Miroul, assay the merits you might yourself possess, I see no other way out of this predicament than to abandon the intoxicating beauties you had encouraged me to claim, and to renounce henceforth the honour of being able to say, Madame, that I am

Your humble, obedient and respectful servant,

Pierre de Siorac

I folded and sealed this billet-doux and gave it to Corinne, who looked quite crestfallen, her cheeks red with spite under her blonde braids.

"Well, Monsieur," she said, "I don't know what you've scribbled there, but Madame will be very angry that you've dared confront her in this way, and as for me, I've missed out on an evening I was very much looking forward to, being made in such a way that the first Gautier to come along can send me to Paradise, and given your gallant and lively air, you all the more so!"

To tell the truth, I did not take my leave of this sweet wench without it costing me something, for I put several sols in her hand as I departed.

We unsheathed our swords, Miroul and I, as soon as we set out, and were careful to walk in the middle of the street, amid all the sewage and offal, so that we wouldn't be surprised if someone rushed us from a darkened doorway.

"Ah, Monsieur," lamented Miroul, as he moved to my left, since, being left-handed, he could better protect me there, "you have to admit that it was madness to have sacrificed your pleasure and comfort for a point of honour, while at the same time making a sworn enemy of this proud baronne! Couldn't you have just let things go their way, which wouldn't have done you any harm, instead of provoking this noble lady? You can be assured that she will try to get her revenge!"

"Ah, Miroul," I said, "I understand! But should I have abjectly submitted to having this lady stomp me underfoot in order to be admitted to her bed afterwards? Madame de Joyeuse, though a lofty vicomtesse, would never have dared play such an impertinent trick on me, however imperious she could be when moody. Why should I allow Madame des Tourelles such nasty tomfoolery?"

"But, Monsieur," Miroul countered, "she's a lady of the court, and at court, from the little I've seen, you can't take things as lightly as you can in our southern provinces without some serious result, as we saw earlier today with Monsieur de Quéribus. Monsieur, we have to bend more to the customs of the capital or I fear we're going to lose everything."

But Alizon, who was still at work with Baragran and Coquillon when we returned, though the evening was well advanced, had a different reaction when she saw me looking for my candle, and smiled broadly to have me returned so quickly to our lodgings, having learnt from Miroul where we were going and why.

"Well, my good gentleman," she laughed, "you did the right thing! You wouldn't have got anything in any case. The baronne is closely directed by her confessor and would never allow herself to commit adultery on her husband, though she likes to give the impression that she would, in order to keep up with Parisian fashion. And if I'm to believe Corinne, nothing ever actually happens at the little house in the rue Trouvevache except some familiarities between herself and Nicotin."

"But," I said, amazed, "aren't these 'familiarities', as you call them, sins as well?"

"Don't be silly, Monsieur!" laughed Alizon bitterly. "A chamber-maid and a valet? They're too low to matter."

Maître Recroche came to tell me the next morning that, since hay and oats had become so much scarcer due to the masses of people arriving in Paris for the royal wedding, the price of these staples had been driven way up, and that, instead of one sol per horse per day, he was very vexed to have to raise the price to two per horse, and for the water it would be four sols per day instead of two.

"What?" I cried. "Maître Recroche, water shouldn't go up with the price of grain! Don't you draw yours from your well?"

"Which, Monseigneur," he said with a deep bow, in which, as usual, one could detect a hint of disdain, "has gone down so fast that I fear it's going to dry up completely! So, as the water level goes down, the price must go up!"

"Maître Recroche," I observed, "ten sols for my four saddle horses and my packhorse. And four sols more for the water they drink: that makes fourteen sols a day just to stable them here. That's unreasonably exorbitant!"

"Monseigneur," countered Maître Recroche, making a second bow, one so low that the sleeves of his spidery arms dragged on the ground, "it's not as exorbitant as it seems. If you were to sell one of the little jewels on your superb doublet, you'd have enough money to nourish your cavalry with me for an entire year!"

"Ah, Maître Recroche," I sighed, "now I understand you! You're setting prices by the pearl, not by the cost of your hay! But, let's shake on it and not discuss it further. You'll have your fourteen sols."

"May I, however, Monseigneur," Recroche continued, bowing a third time (all these bows being, I surmised, the reason for the hump in the middle of his shoulders), "may I presume to give you my opinion?"

"Presume and speak, Maître Recroche!"

"Since you have no carriage to take you about in Paris, but must go on foot, these pearls you're wearing put you in danger of being robbed. Why not sell them at a good price to a jeweller I know and replace them with false ones, which are so well imitated that no one will ever know the difference."

"But," I pointed out to him, "the robbers will believe they're real and will rob me anyway!"

"Oh, no they won't!" said Maître Recroche. "Parisian thieves never make a mistake like that!"

I laughed, of course, and assured Maître Recroche that I'd consider his sage counsel, secretly suspecting that the jeweller he'd recommended would involve him to some degree in the sale. As I watched him depart, I thought how right Alizon had been. This cheapskate would shave an egg and squeezed money out of everything, even stone.

Alizon, whom I found busily working away in the atelier the next morning, looking happy and lively, though her eyes were red from her short night, asked me if I was still angry that Madame des Tourelles had disappointed me, and complimented me on my new doublet, which she'd forgotten to do the night before, she'd been so glad that I'd returned so quickly to our lodgings. She blushed as she did so, despite her dark complexion, adding that, truly to succeed at court, I'd need thirty more like it, since our dandies at the Louvre considered it a requirement to change their doublets every day.

"Well, Alizon," I replied, "as for the lady in question, if you must know, I can't feel much attachment where there's no tenderness. These arch-coquettes are like tortoises: one never knows where to caress them. And if you ever try turning them on their backs, all you find is more shell and nothing that pleases your fingers or touches your heart."

Alizon burst out laughing at this and wished me good luck and happiness in my quest at the Louvre; but alas! I went there only half-heartedly, remembering what Fogacer had told me, having little hope the king would receive me after the favours the Duc d'Anjou had bestowed on me. And indeed, scarcely had I said good morning to Monsieur de Nançay (whom I found, as usual, at the tennis court of the Five Virgins, waiting for the Bâtard d'Angoulême to join him for a game) when the captain told me not to think about my petition for the moment, since the king had heard that I had signed on with his brother, Huguenot though I was, and thought that if I loved Anjou so much, I should follow him to Poland when he is elected king of that country, which he prayed every day that God would accomplish.

"But Monsieur de Nançay," I said, "couldn't you explain to the king how fortuitous this all was, due to an accident of fate, a meaningless quarrel with Monsieur de Quéribus?"

"Yes, of course I did! But when the king is angry he closes up like an oyster, and won't listen to anything."

"Then there's nothing for me to do," I replied, wholly crestfallen, "but return to Périgord, where my head will lie just as unsteadily on my shoulders as when I came here."

"Now don't give up so quickly!" counselled Nançay, lowering his voice. "The man we're talking about," he continued, not without some bitterness, "flies into fits of anger, grows obstinate, emits fire and brimstone, and then, suddenly changes tack and does exactly the opposite of what he'd just sworn to do. He's a toy top that the same hand turns this way and that but always makes the same whirr."

"And what hand is that?" I asked, amazed that the captain should speak so openly of his king.

"Female and Florentine."

"So we'll have to pass through her."

"Not on your life! He doesn't listen to her much now since Coligny alone has the ear of the king. He's seduced Charles with his plan of waging war in Flanders, where papists and Huguenots will throw themselves together into the struggle of the Flemish against the Spanish monarch. The king likes to imagine himself in the clash of war—he who can't spend more than an hour on horseback without coughing himself to death and vomiting up blood from his lungs."

Nançay couldn't say any more, because the Bâtard d'Angoulême strode up, his eyes, skin and hair jet black, followed by Téligny, the amiable and candid son-in-law of Coligny, who looked, as he followed along behind the Grand Prieur of France, like nothing so much as a white dove following a black crow.

"Well now!" said the bâtard in an unsociable voice, without bothering to greet anyone, "since Nançay and Siorac are here, let's play doubles and not hang about!"

And without further ado, he put me, in his usual abrupt way, with Téligny, taking Nançay with him, which he thought would surely assure him an easy victory, and a few equally easy écus, which he'd win from betting on the outcome. But Nançay objected immediately, not wishing to wipe out the Huguenot camp so easily, since Téligny was our Achilles heel.

While Delay was testing the balls, one by one, with Nançay, I approached Téligny and asked whether he might arrange for me to meet Coligny to ask his help in presenting my petition to the king, who seemed not to want to receive me since he believed I was under Anjou's sway.

"Whether you are or not," replied Téligny, with great courtesy, "won't make any difference in the matter. Admiral de Coligny has made an irrevocable vow not to present to the sovereign any personal requests, since he wants to use the influence he has on the king uniquely in service of the great affairs of the kingdom."

"Ah, well," I thought to myself, "that's our Huguenots for you! Duty first! Only duty! People don't matter! Oh, how I fear for this sense of duty in the midst of the court, where perfidy reigns every bit as much as honour!"

Our tennis match was rather disappointing, since the Grand Prieur showed so much displeasure at not winning as well as he wanted to that he became rude, angry and scolding, throwing down his racquet as his half-brother, the king, had done, with dreadful imprecations (which caused poor Téligny to tremble with fear), disputing lost points furiously and throwing us nasty looks when we won a game, which happened more than once, Monsieur de Nançay, unhappy with the bâtard's failure to consult him on the sides, playing only half-heartedly and using his formidable backhand only sparingly.

I'm unable to remember the Bâtard d'Angoulême as he was that day, on that peaceful tennis court, without two other memories barging into my mind: I saw him in the torchlight of that sinister night, the eve of St Bartholomew's day, his unsheathed sword in hand, pushing with his booted foot the body of Coligny, whom his assassins had thrown from the window of his house on the rue de Béthisy; and again, one last time, on the day of his death, fourteen years later, in June of 1586, at Aix-en-Provence, where I happened to encounter him by chance. He'd started a quarrel with Altoviti, the captain of the galleys of Marseilles, whom he'd accused of having written nasty letters to the court about him. Altoviti denied this accusation, which put the Grand Prieur into such a fury that, with no regard for the dignity of his accusation, without witnesses to support it, without a challenge, without honour, he drew his sword and thrust it through the body of Altoviti, who fell to his knees, but, mortally wounded as he was, still had the strength to draw a dagger from his doublet and plunge it into the Grand Prieur's stomach. After this, Altoviti died, as did the Grand Prieur eight hours later, following his victim to the tribunal of the Sovereign Judge, exhaling up to his last breath frightful blasphemies against Altoviti.

Without Quéribus, I think I would have had the feeling that I was spending my days in this brief life in a vain quest. But the baron was mad about fencing, and practised morning and night, and since, for my part, all I could do was to wait for the king to soften his position regarding my petition, I followed him to the fencing gallery that I have already described, and faced off, at times with Giacomi, at other times with Silvie, who'd become great friends with his Italian counterpart, being men who would not allow their characters to interfere with their talents. So, rather than fear Giacomi as a rival, as a lesser man might have done, he had recommended him to other gentlemen, whom Giacomi had taken on as his students.

You had to get up very early to see the two of them face off against each other, which they did daily, but in secret, for nothing erodes a fencing master's skills faster than to spend his days crossing swords with incompetent opponents. I was unable to determine whether they were equal in skill, and, contrary to what my gentle Miroul had said, it's my opinion that it was impossible to do so, for, in their assaults, neither was able to avoid the other's hits, nor able to count his own. But that was not the point of their work. Rather, they worked tirelessly to outdo each other in certain moves that they taught each other (without, however, going as far as to reveal their most secret tricks). Silvie, famous for a thrust that struck the throat, which he'd taught to Anjou and Quéribus only after making them swear that they'd only use it in the most desperate defence of their lives, was a thin giant of a man, as supple and spare as a wire, possessing, as Giacomi did, a marvellous affability, caring for his neighbour more than any pastor or priest, beneficent and courteous to all, loving his art only for itself, and very much opposed to cartels and blood. And yet, if he had a fault, he seemed to me a bit vain; in this he was the opposite of Giacomi, who pushed his denial of any talent to the point of humility. Indeed, he'd never confided to anyone but me that he was the only one in the world to possess the famous calf thrust called "Jarnac's thrust", because the baron of this name had used it twenty-five years previously in a fair duel against La Châtaigneraie, having learnt it from a famous Italian *maestro*.

The 10th of August being a Sunday, Pierre de L'Étoile had his valet deliver a note to tell me that he'd come to collect me as he'd proposed, to take me to Saint-Eustache (which was quite nearby, situated at the bottom of the rue des Prouvelles) to hear the sermon of the priest Maillard, who was loved by his congregation for his tumultuous eloquence.

And so, at the stroke of ten, Coquillon came up to tell me that Monsieur de L'Étoile was waiting for me in the atelier, where I found him, stiffly clad in black, with his usual scowl, and yet in his babbling, both ribald and indignant about the immorality of our times.

"Well," he said, with his bitter smile, "so here's the doublet I've been hearing so much about! My dear Siorac, what's going on? You've quarrelled! Anjou loves you! The king hates you! And the Baronne des Tourelles is looking for someone to assassinate you!"

"What?" I replied, as we emerged onto the rue de la Ferronnerie. "Are Parisian women so nasty?"

"It's not just Paris, it's everywhere in the kingdom!" sneered Monsieur de L'Étoile. "There's no more malicious animal in the world than woman and no animal more lubricious than man."

"Ha! Ha!" I laughed. "Can you prove it?"

"A thousand times over!" said L'Étoile, shaking his head. "Listen to this! Monsieur de Neuville, a councillor in the parliament here, a confused young man, with little learning and less wisdom, so small a brain that he probably couldn't cook a roast, goes around bragging about the size of his member. Now, in an alley opposite his house, there lives a merchant, whose beautiful wife can often be seen at her window. So he decided this August to go parading naked at his window, trying to show off his advantages, and the lady, getting an eyeful of these, went to tell her husband about it. The husband then hid in his window with a small crossbow, and shot a tiny dart at this proud target, so wounding it that the councillor had to take to his bed. This happened yesterday, Siorac, in this very street where we're walking."

"Ah, that's marvellous, my dear L'Étoile! How did you hear of it?"

"Well, I have a reputation for knowing everything," said L'Étoile, "so that an egg doesn't get laid in Paris without some vain Gautier rushing to tell me about it, asking me if I know about it."

I noticed, as we neared the church of Saint-Eustache, that a great crowd of people was arriving from all of the surrounding streets. "Is this Maillard so learned?"

"Not at all. He's just one of the thousands of priests and monks who shape the opinions of the Parisians."

"Thousands?" I asked, amazed. "Are there really that many?"

"Ah, Siorac," whispered L'Étoile, "the place is crawling with them. There are at least ten in every street, and there are 413 streets in the capital. Siorac, be very careful not to smile or laugh at what Maillard says in Saint-Eustache, no matter how absurd: his parishioners would tear you to pieces."

"Trust me," I replied, elbowing him playfully, "I shall be as prayerful and humble as the Devil himself!"

Oh reader! You should have seen Maillard when he appeared in the pulpit! What a low and ugly face he had, with his large and oily nose, big, bloodthirsty mouth, blazing eyes, shaggy eyebrows, reddish and pimply skin, and butcher's hands more suited to cutting throats in an abattoir than to making the sign of the cross in absolution.

"Today," he said, eyes lowered in feigned humility and speaking quietly in his deep voice, which would follow a steady crescendo throughout his sermon and ultimately explode like thunder, "I'm going to speak about women and heretics."

Having said this, he paused and appeared to be praying, and though the church was full of people there was such silence you could have heard a nun breaking wind.

"Oh, you women! Oh, you girls! Oh, you maidens!" said Maillard, hammering his lectern with his fist. "You who live in vanity and lubricity, take heed! You who know only how to lead men into temptation! You who make up your faces to attract your customers! You who cover your heads with vainglorious wigs and hairpieces whose blonde hair waves over your pearled foreheads! Oh, you women! What are you doing? The Lord gave you a face and you invent another one! He gave you a body and you invent another one! You squeeze and press your breasts into close bodices! You swell your thighs with hoop skirts! You increase your backsides with false arses! You raise yourselves on high heels! You pout! You flirt! You give inviting glances! You sway when you walk and one has only to look at you to know you're deep in sin!"

And here Maillard closed his eyes and moved his lips as though he were praying again, while his congregation, awaiting his next words, held their breath.

"Oh, you women! Oh, you girls! Oh, you maidens!" continued Maillard in a menacing voice, banging his enormous fists on his lectern again. "Do you ever think about what you're doing? You who claim to be so modest that you don't even show yourselves naked to your husbands, but shamelessly parade your bodies in the street, have you thought about what's going to happen when you stand before the Lord's tribunal after you die?"

And, after another pause, Maillard continued in a thunderous voice: "Well, I'll tell you here and now! As punishment for your vanities and excesses, the devils in hell will strip you naked; these devils will drag you thousands of times across the entire length of hell, not before one man, but before 100,000 men, who will shout at you and laugh at you, seeing your shame and degradation. And how embarrassed you'll be then, when you're dragged naked before men, showing them all your shameful places, dragged throughout hell a thousand thousand times in a great fanfare of trumpets, with devils laughing and mocking you and shouting, 'Look! Look! See this whore! Look at this lewd bawd! This is Mademoiselle so-and-so who lives in such and such a street in Paris!'—naming you and naming your street—'who has so often lain with such and such a man and so many others!'

"And then 100,000 and another 100,000 people who, during your life, you women, you've know well, your dead parents, your friends, your neighbours, all furious with you, vowing mortal hatred, will run up to make fun of you, saying to each other, 'There she is, naked! The bawd! There she is, the fat bitch! After her, devils! Attack her, you demons! Get her, you furies! All together, now, leap on these shameless whores!' And they will give you back double in torments and torture all the pleasures you stole in this life!"

Having screamed these words at the top of his lungs, Maillard fell silent again, his face crimson, his fists clenched on his lectern, his eyes half-closed, watching his flock as if spying on them to see the effects of his words, which, as far as I could tell, appealed much more to the men than to the women, for, to hear him, you'd think it was only the latter who were sinners and not the former. And as I looked around, I observed among the women signs of both fear and anger, and sensed that it was dawning on them how unjust he'd been to them, a feeling they could express only through the furtive looks they exchanged. Whether Maillard could feel these mutinous reactions, or whether he was carried away by the voluptuousness of his images of hell, I know not, but, regaining his breath and his voice, he launched again into descriptions of the tortures and torments the devils would inflict on these naked women, and in such horrible and repulsive detail that I could not possibly repeat them here without offending my readers.

In any case, he succeeded in casting such fear into the hearts of these women for the crime of being women that it seemed to me that he was seeking revenge on them for his having been denied access to their bodies by his vows.

What's more, this sermon, for all its mad cruelty, struck me as particularly useless, because I don't believe the terrors of the afterlife have ever prevailed in men's hearts over the pleasures of the moment, especially since, in the papist religion, it was enough for these sinning women to go to have their confession heard to wash them of all their sins and wipe their slates clean. The most one could hope to gain from such depraved eloquence was that it might increase the number of penitents and the sums of money they'd have to pay the priests for their absolution.

But when Maillard had finally reached the end of his list of the frightful torments awaiting the sweeter half of humanity when they arrived in hell, in retribution for the activities they'd carried on with the other half, he again fell silent and prayed for a long time, and then started up again in a hushed voice:

"However great the excesses of you women and however just the punishments that will be visited upon you in hell, these are nothing in comparison with the frightful and ongoing crimes against our Holy Mother the Church, against the Blessed Virgin, Mother of God, against all our saints, against God Himself, by the bloodthirsty adherents of the so-called reformed religion. Oh, my brothers! For a month, we've seen these damned Huguenots flood by the hundreds and hundreds into our city of Paris, laughing and sneering like devils hiding in adulterous alcoves, to attend the infamous wedding—and I say *infamous* wedding!—that is to unite (God Himself has veiled His eyes) a great Catholic princesse, the sister of our sovereign, with the false and sly reformed fox, Navarre. Oh, heaven! Can one really unite fire and water in an unnatural, and, I dare to say, prostituted union? Will they be able to find a single renegade bishop in this entire kingdom willing to celebrate this union, when our Holy Father the Pope opposes it with all his might? And if misfortune should prevail and this marriage take place in the teeth of his opposition, will it not be the work and fruit of Satan, who allowed the sinister leader of the Huguenots to get the ear of our poor king, who has been incited by this perfidious and corrupting counsellor to send help to the outlawed Huguenots in Flanders against the armies of the Rex Catholicissimus, Felipe II of Spain, who today stands on the ramparts of our Roman faith in Christianity?... Oh, my brothers! Will we continue to tolerate being poisoned in our city by these undesirable guests, who, swarming like maggots in a corpse, have infiltrated our houses to corrupt our beliefs and, failing that, dream only of destroying us completely, body and soul? Oh, my brothers! Believe me! All we need is a little heart and a little courage to rid ourselves for ever of this swarm of vermin and set about the holy extermination that has been recommended by our Holy Father, and that will forever assure your safety and your repose—yours, your wives' and your children's. Oh, my beloved brothers! If you will join in this good work, that of seizing the most sacred of swords, to extirpate the human roots of this evil heresy, condemned by God, then, I tell you, in the name of God the Father, Christ and the Holy Ghost, your salvation shall be assured and you will enter directly into Paradise with His most happy saints, and not pass through Purgatory. The blood of a single heretic, I mean a single one, will purify you of all the sins you've ever committed.

"Yes, my beloved brothers, verily I say unto you, had you committed up to this very minute the most heinous crimes, offences, lewdness or atrocities, even had you killed your father, mother, brother, sister and cousin, all these sins would be forgiven when you arm yourself to avenge God of these miscreants and save the Holy Catholic and Apostolic Church from these stinking heretics who are trying to destroy her."

Having bellowed these hideous words, while hammering away at the lectern with his fists, Maillard fell silent again for a few moments, before continuing in a smoother, more soft-spoken manner:

"This is the most profound grace, my brothers, that I could ever wish for you here, and now bid you pray to God that in His bountiful mercy, He assist you in the success of the just and laudable enterprise that I've just explained. My brothers, let us commune in the edifying and comforting thought that we will soon have extirpated all heresy in this kingdom *ad maximam Dei gloriam*,* and recite together a pater-noster and an Ave."

"For the love of Heaven, Siorac," L'Étoile whispered, "stop shaking like a decapitated duck and, for goodness' sake, pray! Pray out loud! Everyone in here is spying on everyone else, and it would be your death, and mine as well, if anyone suspected that you oppose what you just heard."

Casting a quick glance around me at all the eyes burning with zeal, anger and hatred, I hastened to obey the good L'Étoile, and, my heart breaking, I joined my voice to those around me who were devoutly invoking God's help in giving them the courage to kill a significant swath of Christendom. And so I managed to recite the prayer out loud, though with some difficulties here and there in remembering the Ave

---

* "To the greatest glory of God."

Maria, despite the fact that Barberine had taught it to me as a child, and that I'd all the more happily recited it twice a day since I mixed together the Virgin Mary and Barberine in my childish imagination.

It would have been mere lip service to recite it now, among these misguided souls, had I not given it a particular inflection, praying instead for the fraternal reconciliation between the papists and ourselves so that neither of these parties should ever repeat on one another the massacre of the Michelade, which had marked my youth with such unforgettable horror.

"Siorac," hissed L'Étoile as we finally left Saint-Eustache, "not a word, I beg you, until we reach your lodgings: someone might overhear."

And so I had to hold myself back and swallow my anger until we were back in Maître Recroche's atelier, which was empty, since all work was forbidden on Sundays and saints' days, these latter having become way too numerous to suit Maître Recroche, who had little love for priests, because, he said, "every time they preach, they invent another saint and we lose another day of work: a benefit for the collection box and a disaster for us artisans".

"My dear L'Étoile," I said, my throat all knotted up from what I'd just heard, "are they preaching this infernal message in all the churches, chapels and abbeys of Paris?"

"The truth is that there are priests who are less rabid than Maillard, but there are also some who are worse."

"Well," I said, full of fear and confusion, "my good, honest friend, what was that? What was that if not an incitement to massacre?"

"Clear and obvious. The reason you're surprised is that in the provinces you don't go to hear Mass. But I hear this kind of language every Sunday, and if it appals me each time, it hardly surprises me any more. Oh, my dear Siorac, believe me! Don't remain here a minute longer than you need to for your petition. Leave as soon as you can! You'd be safer in the hands of the Grand Turk than in Paris as it is now!"

As he was speaking, there came a knock on the door, and since there was no one else at home at this hour, I went to open it and, distracted as I was by the sad conversation we'd been having, I saw in front of me a tall, well-dressed woman, whom I should have recognized despite her mask, but I greeted her with reserve and asked quite coldly who it was she wished to see in our lodgings.

"But, you, my gentle brother!" she gushed, lowering her mask. "You first of all, and then, you-know-who!"

"What?" I cried. "Dame Gertrude du Luc! Well, I'm happy to see you!"

"Well, my beloved brother," said the blonde Norman, throwing her arms around my neck and hugging me so hard I could hardly breathe, "what a comfort to have you here after so many months!"

As she said this, she pressed me even harder against her bosom, and I wouldn't have known how to avoid her hot lips, which were peppering my face with kisses, had I not spied over her shoulder, just in the nick of time, my good L'Étoile, looking very disapproving of these goings-on, and on his way out the door. Indeed, he slammed the door shut behind him, since he detested extramarital affairs, despite—or because?—of the fact that he'd found so little love in his own marriage.

"Madame," I said as I took her by the hand and seated her on a stool, since, seated, she seemed less dangerous to me, "what are you doing here? You've appeared miraculously, like a *dea ex machina*,* at the very moment I need you the most!"

"It's no miracle," she explained. "Like everyone else, I've come to see the marriage of Princesse Margot to that infamous heretic, though my heart bleeds at the idea of this unnatural union. And when I was passing through Montfort-l'Amaury, Dame Béqueret, who'd

---

* "A goddess from the machinery [i.e. from heaven]."

just received a letter from you, told me where you are staying. But is it really true, my pretty brother," she said, batting an eye and attempting to rise—a movement I arrested with a hand on her shoulder, "is it true that you have such an urgent need for me?"

"What, Madame? Didn't Dame Béqueret tell you what request I'd made of her?"

"She told me she'd agreed to your request, but didn't tell me what the nature of the request was."

"And you, yourself, Madame—"

"Oh, Pierre," she cried, "don't call me Madame! Do you love me so little?" she cooed, feigning such affliction that I was worried she was going to renew her assaults on me.

"My gentle sister," I soothed, increasing the pressure of my hand on her shoulder, but this only made her turn her head and bury her face in the back of my hand, on which she planted hot kisses (and, oh heavens! such feminine wiles are sure to make me weak at the knees and break down my resistance!), "if I asked you, would you consent to lodge with Dame Béqueret in Montfort? Would she welcome you back?"

"Assuredly so! But what would I do there? Why would I want to be so far away from my Samson, and from you, and Paris, and all these festivities surrounding the marriage of the princesse?"

"Ah, Madame," I cried, "for Samson's sake, you must! Here in Paris, because of his religion and his candour, he risks such cruel dangers."

And I quickly recounted our nasty dust-up with the religious procession, where my beloved brother, for failing to doff his cap before the mutilated statue of Notre-Dame de la Carole, nearly lost his life.

"Ah," she gasped, "I feared as much! He's so pure and noble and is as innocent as an angel, my gentle little Huguenot!" ("Ah," I thought, "at least you didn't call him an 'infamous' Huguenot!") "But by the Blessed Virgin, my vengeance would be swift and terrible if they killed him," she cried, placing her hand on a little dagger she wore in her sash, by which I could tell that our beautiful Norman had only just arrived from her journey, and yet she looked as fresh and vigorous as if she'd just got out of bed.

"Your vengeance wouldn't impress me much," I said, "or you either, if Samson were no longer alive. My sister, we must decide and decide immediately. Samson cannot remain here, announcing on every street corner that he's of the reformed religion and that he abominates idols and saints!"

"But what can we do? What can we do?" cried Dame Gertrude, very alarmed.

"I'll tell you what we'll do: forget all the wedding festivities, which you have so little taste for. Take my Samson and carry him on your lap to Montfort-l'Amaury. By day, put him in the druggist's shop among the glass bottles in the office; by night, where you know; on Sunday, at Mass. And by God's will, he'll be safe. I fear the worst, if he remain here."

At this, Dame Gertrude fell silent, her eyelids half-closed over her green eyes (in this she reminded me of the beautiful cat we have in Mespech), and as she was biting her lips I could see that she was hesitating between the joys she'd promised herself at the splendid princely wedding festivities and, on the other side, the great love she bore my pretty Samson—though she was hardly a faithful lover. Moreover, seeing her all bedecked like a queen, and almost as resplendent in all her finery as Madame des Tourelles, I imagined that she had as much desire to be seen in the capital as to see—that she would have wished to go shopping at her leisure along the grand'rue Saint-Honoré and around the Pont Saint-Michel, to stick her head in at the court where her beauty might lead to some gallant encounters, and not just to observe the royal marriage ceremony, but to be able to tell her friends and relatives back in Normandy all about it. Instead of that, I was inviting her to go isolate herself in the deserted countryside, where she would even be unable to see my pretty brother by day (buried as he would be among his jars), and have nothing to do but lie around in bed, like a marmot underground, harbouring her strength for the coming night.

"My sister," I said somewhat icily, "whatever you decide, since Maître Béqueret wishes to have Samson there, and Samson wishes to be there and continue his work as an apothecary, and since he's dying of boredom here, I'm resolved to take him to Montfort-l'Amaury tomorrow, whether you join us or not."

"Ah, my brother!" she cried as she stood up, an opportune teardrop lighting up her green eyes. "You're so stiff, mean and abrupt with me! Fie, then! Is this any way to recognize the great and fraternal love I bear you? Scarcely have I arrived in Paris before you take Samson away from me—or, if I agree to follow him, you keep me from these beautiful festivities!"

"Well, Gertrude," I laughed, "this is what I expected: you want it all! Both Samson and the festivities! And what else I know not. But my sister," I continued, "why don't you leave for Montfort-l'Amaury tomorrow with Samson. Stay one week with him. After which you can return alone—and I mean *alone*!—for the princely festivities. Once the wedding is over, you can go straight back to Montfort."

"Oh, my brother! What a saint you are!" she cried. "You've found the only happy way out of my predicament!"

This said, the little teardrops in her eyes evaporated in the rush of pleasure she felt, and she planted two or three kisses on my face and spun round, her skirts ballooning around her, crying: "It's all decided! I'm leaving! I'm leaving! Oh, my brother! I've got wings! Where is this angel of God that I can carry him off?"

I looked back at her as I bounded down the staircase, and saw her lift her skirts to go faster, her beautiful, pale complexion reddening with happiness, her green eyes as intense as those of a cat who has just caught a sparrow in its little teeth.

When she entered his room, she saw nothing of the tiny chamberette where Samson was still sleeping—Giacomi being, I thought, still at his devotions. Neither the badly laid flooring, nor the dirty walls, nor the miserable furnishings, nor the open window overlooking the Cimetière des Innocents, nothing except my pretty brother lying naked on his mat in the stifling heat of August. He lay there, resplendent in his virile symmetry, white skin, copper-coloured hair and azure eyes—though of his eyes, since he was still asleep, nothing could be seen.

"Oh, Blessed Virgin!" cried Dame Gertrude, joining her hands together. "Doesn't he just look like Jesus! And aren't I right to claim that he's divinely beautiful?"

"Divine, Madame?" I smiled.

"Oh, my brother," she cried, giving me a little tap on my hand, "what an evil man you are, making me remember my sins when I'm trying to forget them as soon as I commit them, hoping to put off my repentance till later!"

"My sister," I said, kissing the hand that had tapped me, which was warm, sleek and perfumed, "I ask your pardon a thousand times for having been such a spoilsport—I who place such joys above all the others! But, my sister," I continued, "not a word more. I'll leave you to your beautiful sins. I'll come and fetch you for supper. And tomorrow we'll leave for Montfort at daybreak."

And placing two kisses on her sweet cheeks, I left, closing the door on her—or rather on them, not without a bitter sigh and a quarrelsome ache in my heart.

The solitude of my little room was too horrible, so I went downstairs into the atelier, feeling all dreamy and immersed in my thoughts. I didn't think that anyone was there, since Miroul was out tending to the horses, but then I saw Fogacer, who, dressed all in black, walking back and forth on his long legs, his long arms behind his back, when he saw me, arched his diabolical eyebrows and said with a sinuous smile:

"Well, you've come back down rather quickly from your little perch, *mi fili*. So the Delilah I saw in front of me as I walked along the rue de la Ferronnerie was not directing her fatal charms to you, but to Samson. But perhaps, *mi fili*, if I may believe what I've heard, the noble ladies who have their gallants' hair removed are not unknown to you either. Women are so like grasshoppers in a field! *Causa mali tanti femina sola fuit.*"*

"Heavens!" I objected. "Is one example sufficient to determine the lot? *Parcite paucarum diffundere crimen in omnes,*† said Ovid."

"What?" gasped Fogacer. "Ovid! Why, everyone knows he was a petticoat-chaser! What kind of authority is that? Trust rather my Plautus: *qui potest mulieres vitare vitet.*"‡

"Ah, but Fogacer," I laughed, "listen instead to wise Seneca, *multum interest utrum peccare aliquis nolit an nesciat.*"§

"Ah, how well I know!" groaned Fogacer. "I know all too well! But I'm not so inclined! *Trahit sua quemque voluptas.*"¶

Having thus pedantically traded Latin maxims in the spirit of morning courtesy and fun, we gave each other a big hug. This kind of jargon exists in every social group: venerable medical doctors exchange Ciceronian phrases in Latin, while the lordlings of the court exclaim "by my conscience!" and "I could just die!" which are certainly less profound and substantial than our beautiful Latin, since these gentlemen's memories are not garnished with such gems.

---

* "The sole cause of all this evil was woman."
† "Do not censure the many for the crimes of the few."
‡ "Who can avoid women, should do so."
§ "There's a difference between someone who does not wish to sin and someone who does not know how to."
¶ "To each his pleasure."

"I saw you at Maillard's sermon yesterday," said Fogacer, "looking superb in your new pearly doublet, but seeming very disgruntled at having to listen to his calls for carnage, which I found, quite to the contrary, most pleasing and a comfort to my philosophy."

"What? Pleasing? A comfort?" I gasped. "Isn't this precisely the opposite of God's teachings?"

"But which God are you referring to, *mi fili*?" asked Fogacer, arching his diabolical eyebrows. "The God of the Evangelists, who is sweet and beneficent? Or the God of the Old Testament?"

"But it's the same God!"

"Oh, no, it's not! The God of the Old Testament strikes down Onan for having sown his seed on the ground, and burns Sodom, destroys the Sodomites, massacres untold numbers of honest idolaters by the hand of Israel and tortures sinners in hell. Isn't it obvious that, far from having created us, it's man who created Him in his own sad, cruel and spiteful image?"

"Please, Fogacer!" I cried. "Enough! As much as I love you I hate your blasphemies!"

"What?" said Fogacer with his slow, sinuous smile. "My blasphemies! No, no! I'm a person of infinite tolerance, and would never demand the death, in the name of religion, of any Guillaume or Gautier, were he papist or reformist! Siorac, did you hear Maillard? A Huguenot lends me 100 écus. I meet him in the street. He asks for what is owed him. So I kill him. My dagger thereby becomes 'the most sacred of swords'. And I'm automatically spared the noose, absolved, promised salvation without Purgatory and sent to heaven with the happy few! Do you think Maillard is the only one preaching this doctrine? In truth, the Huguenot has replaced the Jew as the object of hatred of our Holy Church. 'Kill! Kill! Kill!' That's what's being said—no, shouted!—in every church in the kingdom, and your side isn't any better!"

"My side!"

"Oh, come, Siorac! The Michelade massacre! And I don't know how many other Huguenot atrocities! Listen to this, *mi fili*: each religion can't help being tyrannical, and, as a result, cruel, since each pretends to speak in the name of an absolute truth, which cannot be rejected without capital offence."

"Now, Fogacer," I objected, "you're talking only of the fanatics and not the good and honest people!"

"But who are these good and honest people?" asked Fogacer, his eyes suddenly narrowing. "The late La Boétie, Montaigne, Ambroise Paré, Ramus, our poor Maître Rondelet, Pierre de L'Étoile, Michael Servetus, who was burnt by Calvin in Geneva, you, me—all of us people who want to inject a little bit of reason into men's minds and advance secular knowledge. *Mi fili*, answer! Would you sacrifice the life of a single papist to help your Church triumph?"

"Of course not!" I cried without hesitating, as if my answer were already waiting inside me, and, without my having been aware of it, deliberated at length.

At this Fogacer looked at me, his eyes shining, and a smile on his sinuous lips, but this time not sardonic, but friendly, and he said in a quiet and almost muffled voice: "Then you are less of a believer than you thought, Siorac, since you reject the victory of your faith bought at the price of a single human life."

"But I believe!" I said, as though shaken by his explanation, which suddenly entered my understanding with a novelty that greatly magnified its power.

"I'm not sure," replied Fogacer. "I'm not sure whether you believe, or only believe you believe. Or rather, if you aren't a member of a party much more than of a Church, that is, of the party of your father, whom you cherish with such great love."

To this, which moved me greatly and set me thinking, I had no answer, but decided to consider it at my leisure—a leisure I didn't have and, indeed, we never seem to have, since existence rides us and spurs us along so constantly and with such appetites, an appetite for love, another for ambition, that we arrive at the end of our path without ever having resolved, in our intimate struggles, where truth lies. And this is true today, as I write this, the ribbon of my life having been unwound so far, still as uncertain and confused as I was on that day, back in 1572, when I debated with Fogacer the connection between cruelty and our beliefs.

"Fogacer," I answered after a moment, "I am, as you know, very beset with this question of my petition to the king for a pardon. Do you think that, through Anjou, I could get to the queen mother and, through her, dispose the king in my favour?"

"Ah! The queen mother!" said Fogacer. "The queen mother thinks only of herself and fears only for herself. Imagine, Siorac, the humiliations of her reign, given that she played second to Diane de Poitiers in Henri II's bed. When he died, she dressed herself in black so as never to leave him. And she dressed herself in power as well. Now Catherine is regent, first under François II and now under Charles IX, dominating her sons through her manipulations, her cajolery and her tears. She reigns, but must share her power perilously, since she's threatened on the right by Guise, and on the left by the Huguenots. She's a strong woman, but for the last thirteen years of her power, she's never ceased trembling, and trembles today more than ever."

"What does she fear?"

"She fears losing her great love: the sceptre. Your Coligny has confused the king with this dream of conducting an expedition into Flanders. Charles IX wants it, then doesn't want it five minutes later. And if Coligny wins on this matter, Catherine imagines she'll be sent off into exile in Florence. Now, Catherine, who is a woman of infinite cunning, but narrow views, has only one idea: to stay in power. So do you really think that, in the predicament she's in, she'll dare confront

Charles with some favour for a Huguenot whom he already hates because he thinks he's his brother's man?"

"Ah, Fogacer!" I said, shaking my head sadly, "I understand that I don't count more than a speck of dust in the great winds that are rising across France, but, my friend, from what you're telling me, Coligny is in the greatest peril."

"My son, do you think he doesn't know it?"

And, pivoting on his heels, Fogacer began to stride back and forth across the atelier on his long spidery legs, casting his glance now at the fireplace, but keeping an eye on the window, now at the staircase that led up to the floor above, and then, stopping suddenly, he crossed his arms and gave me a knowing and happy smile.

"*Mi fili*," he laughed, "if, as they claim, *amare est gaudere felicitate alterius*,* then I love you a lot, for I'm very happy that I can flood your soul with joy."

"Oh, Fogacer," I exclaimed, "if there's any happiness in my situation, tell me! I could use a dose of merriment! Ever since I arrived in Paris, I've encountered nothing but misadventures and difficulties. Nothing is working out for me, not even my women!"

"Siorac," he answered, his cheeks swollen with his good news as with a good wine that he didn't want to swallow too quickly, "do you remember the judge who was my friend in Montpellier, thanks to whom I could warn you to flee before the tribunal could put you in prison?"

"Of course! I'm infinitely grateful to him! And to you as well!"

"You will be now! My friend, who left Montpellier when I did, is presently living in the capital, and though he's given up his official position, is a good friend of a judge here in Paris. *Asinus asinum fricat.*† Though I really shouldn't call them asses since they're both very intelligent."

---

*   "To love is to rejoice in the other's happiness."

†   "One donkey scratches another."

"Monsieur," broke in Miroul, who had rushed into the room and was unaware of Fogacer's presence, "shall I saddle your horse or will we go on foot?"

"Saddle it, Miroul!" cried Fogacer, gesturing with his long arms. "And yours as well, and put wings on them too, like Pegasus, to run with the wind! You'll need them straightaway!"

"What about this judge?" I asked, amazed that Fogacer was giving orders to my valet, who didn't move a muscle, but just stood there, eyes wide in surprise, as though nailed to the spot.

"This judge has just delivered his verdict in a case involving a mill where a certain lord was the plaintiff, and the verdict went in his favour. But, the Devil take me, I can't remember the name of this gentleman! Please, Siorac, help me!"

"How can I, when I don't know what you're talking about!"

"Well, perhaps you've heard tell of this mill, which is situated in a village just to the north of Paris, very famous for its good flour and the excellent breads that are baked there and that are sold in the capital. But, the Devil take me, I can't remember the name of this village!"

"You're teasing me, Fogacer," I cried, becoming increasingly impatient with his delays. "Why should I know anything about this mill? How does this relate to me?"

"Very closely, my friend! Especially since this gentleman I was mentioning, and who, I believe, has a chateau in the southern provinces, inherited this mill from a cousin, an inheritance that was hotly contested by the cousin, hence this interminable suit—and now it's a happy outcome for your friend."

"My friend! What friend? Ah, Fogacer, you're driving me mad! Are you just playing with me?"

"Wait!" muttered Fogacer. "It's coming back to me little by little: the village where this mill turns its beautiful sails, such apt symbols of your own hopes, is named Gonesse."

"Gonesse?" I gasped. "Gonesse? I know that name!"

"Monsieur," said Miroul, "I believe that was the mill you told me someone was trying to sue Monsieur de Montcalm for."

"Montcalm!" I cried, suddenly beside myself. "Fogacer! You know where he lives in Paris! And you're not telling me!"

"I knew it once," smiled Fogacer, arching his diabolical eyebrows, "but the Devil take me if I can remember the name of the street! My memory just isn't what it used to be!"

"Dammit, Fogacer!" I yelled, throwing myself at him and grabbing him by the shoulders. "You're toying with me! Tell me, for God's sake! Speak!"

"'Sblood! What kind of behaviour is this?" And seizing my wrists, he laughingly broke my grip on him with a suppleness and force I wouldn't have expected in him. "Lovers can be so ungrateful! *Ingratis servire nefas!*"*

"Their lodgings! Fogacer, where do they live?"

"But how, my ungrateful Pollux, can I fill up the gaps in my memory, which is more riddled with holes than a cheese full of mice? All I can remember," he laughed, keeping the table between us for protection, "is that the door knocker of their lodgings is in the figure of a giant Atlas bearing the world on his shoulders."

"The street, Fogacer, the street!"

"Miroul," cried Fogacer, "saddle the horses! And make it snappy, my son! Let's be off!"

"The street, Fogacer!"

"Ah, yes! The street bears the name of those bronze figurines that are used as door knockers and that we call here *marmousets*."

"The rue des Marmousets!" I shouted. "On the Île de la Cité? In l'Université?"

---

* "It is an offence to serve the ungrateful."

"On the Île de la Cité! But where are you running to, Siorac?"

"To help Miroul!"

"I'm right behind you, Siorac!" he cried, on my heels. "A horse! A horse for me as well! By all the good devils in the impossible hell," he shouted, his voice sounding loud and clear behind me, "I insist on showing you the shortest route to your Eden, which should be all the dearer to you, since there isn't any other! On this I'd wager my perishable soul!"

8

O H HEAVEN! What happiness filled my heart as I trotted down
the grand'rue Saint-Denis on Pompée, with Fogacer leading the
way and Miroul on my right. On this Sunday, every shop was closed
and not a cart did we see as we crossed the deserted Pont Notre-Dame
to the Île de la Cité and found ourselves in the rue des Marmousets.
Given the oppressive heat, most of the Parisians had withdrawn into
their homes, but as clear as our passage was, it nevertheless seemed
to take for ever, given the sting of my impatience.

"Fogacer," I stuttered, trying vainly to control the terrible beating
of my heart in my chest, "have you spied the house yet whose door
has the knocker you described?"

He turned to me, his mouth wide open, but as I heard no word
issue from it, I galloped up to his side and repeated my question.

"I was just there, before visiting you, and it's precisely this house
where you spy that coach onto which the group of valets you see is
loading all manner of trunks and packages."

At the sight of this I thought I would faint from my sudden
apprehension. I dismounted and, tossing my reins to Miroul, staggered towards the open door on legs that trembled so violently I
thought I would fall. The group of valets passed busily in and out,
under the watchful eyes of a major-domo, who commanded them
gruffly in Provençal. I approached this fellow, who looked familiar

to me, and asked him to announce my arrival to the master of the lodgings.

"Ah, Monsieur de Siorac!" he replied. "I remember you well from having seen you once or twice at Barbentane five years ago, and am well aware of what infinite obligations we all owe you, having heard Madame often exclaim that, without you, not a soul, animal or stone would still be standing today! I'll go and tell Monsieur de Montcalm you're here."

"But," I replied as courteously as I could through my knotted throat, "will I not be a bother? Are you not preparing your departure?"

"Indeed we are," he replied, raising his hands heavenward, "and God knows how happily! For this Paris," he continued in *langue d'oc*, "is a dreadful place and its people are even worse. We would have been gone by eight o'clock if this coach had arrived on time. But you can't trust anything these rascals tell you! But wait a bit, I beg you. I'll let the master know you're here."

"Lord," I thought, "I've found my Angelina only to lose her! But I shouldn't bewail my fortune completely, since, without the impertinence of this coachman, I would have missed her entirely." As I attempted to console myself thus, the major-domo reappeared, but with less warmth, it seemed, than before, and, begging me politely to follow him, led me inside to a small cabinet, where he left me, quite unhappy with the change in his manner, which did not bode well. And, indeed, when the door opened, Monsieur de Montcalm approached me with a smile on his lips but a cold look in his eye, his manner hurried and brusque.

"Well, well, Monsieur de Siorac, how happy I am to see you!" (But he bloody well didn't look it!) "I haven't forgotten how very much obliged we are to you" (but never was gratitude less gratefully expressed), "and had you not arrived just as I was leaving, having won my lawsuit, I would have loved to invite you to dine with me and to spend more time with you than I'm able to at this moment."

"Monsieur," I replied, "I'd be most unhappy to delay you, but having just had the good fortune to learn of your whereabouts, I wanted to present my respects, having come to Paris only a month ago to ask for the king's pardon."

"Yes, I learnt of your arrival from Nançay the first day I was at the Louvre, and, of course, communicated my sincere wishes that you be successful in your quest."

"Aha," I thought, "these 'sincere wishes' didn't go as far as making any attempt to find the lodgings of the man who, five years previously, had snatched him from the hands of the bloodthirsty brigands of the Barbentane woods, and saved the honour of his wife and daughter." This thought so froze my tongue that all I could do was stand there and look at him in silence. He seemed to me to be extremely ill at ease, visibly torn by the manifest contradiction between his outward appearance, which was quite imposing, as he was a large man with bushy eyebrows, piercing eyes and a severe face, and his inward feelings, which must have been a good deal less assured than he would have wished—his conscience no doubt painfully pricked to have so badly recognized the obligations that he so loudly proclaimed he owed me. And thus, as he was unable to dismiss me outright—however much he must have wanted to do so—and since I did not take my leave, being determined to see his daughter—a desire I gathered he did not intend to satisfy, since it was so contrary to his designs—we stood there, facing each other, mute but polite, each waiting for the other to make his move. And we would have remained standing there face to face like two statues if we'd not been interrupted by a richly clothed, somewhat portly young gentleman, smiling broadly, who entered the cabinet and proclaimed, "Good my father, it's time to leave! Madame de Montcalm and Angelina have taken their places in the coach and are waiting for you."

"Monsieur de Siorac," said Monsieur de Montcalm, "this gentleman is Monsieur de La Condomine, who will accompany us to Barbentane where he intends to marry my daughter."

I was speechless at this frightful news, so calmly announced, and felt myself so near to fainting from the shock that I bowed more deeply than would have been appropriate, just to get the blood flowing back to my face.

"Monsieur," I said, finally, trying to keep my voice steady, "I am at your service."

At that, Monsieur de La Condomine, who looked like a complete fop, and who doubtless knew of my connections to Angelina, said not a word, but made a deep bow of his own. And at this, looking Monsieur de Montcalm straight in the eye, I decided to burn my bridges, since it was obvious that I was being cast into the outer darkness, and said loudly but with such exaggerated courtesy that it was obviously a challenge:

"Monsieur de Montcalm, I would be infinitely obliged if you would consent to allow me to present my respects to Madame de Montcalm and to your daughter before you leave."

Monsieur de Montcalm, who was of a naturally choleric complexion, reddened with rage at the idea that I would thus hold a knife to his throat, since he could not honourably refuse to grant to the man who had saved his life the courtesy of saying goodbye. But intending nevertheless to deny this courtesy, he behaved exactly as his future son-in-law had done, and refused to say another word. Instead, he simply turned away, took Monsieur de La Condomine by the arm and left me standing there in the cabinet.

I followed them, and, emerging onto the rue des Marmousets, I saw that the window curtains of the coach had been lowered, despite the crushing heat of the midday sun. I had no doubt that this was done at Monsieur de Montcalm's orders, to keep Angelina from catching sight of me and to prevent me from speaking to her. Indignant at this odious violence practised upon my beloved, and taking courage from the realization that Monsieur de Montcalm, who was not an inherently bad man, would never have inflicted this harm on his daughter (whom he doted on) if she'd consented to his wishes, I rushed up to the coach, hoping to find a way to let her know of my presence. Seeing this, Monsieur de Montcalm murmured a few words to the coachman, who leapt quickly onto his seat and seemed ready to whip his horses into motion as soon as his master and Monsieur de La Condomine had taken their places opposite the women. But this could not be accomplished, of course, without raising the window curtains and revealing my presence.

My decision was made in the blink of an eye. Unafraid of displeasing a man who'd so cast me aside, I rushed to the other side of the coach, raised the curtain that was shrouding the window and, greeting mother and daughter, looked Angelina in the eye and cried hastily, "Angelina, I will always love you!"

I couldn't say more since the coach was shaking, Monsieur de Montcalm was shouting like a madman "Whip them on! Whip them on!" and the coachman began lashing his four steeds mercilessly into a gallop. In all the din of the whip lashes, the ironclad wheels grinding on the pavement and the horses' hooves clattering noisily away, I couldn't have been heard anyway, nor could I have heard any response from my beloved (though I saw her opening her mouth), so I ran alongside the door as the coach pulled away. Holding the raised curtain with my left hand, I unsheathed my sword with my right and managed to strike with the flat of the blade a horse that one of Montcalm's valets wanted to trample me under. As I did so, I received a longing look from Angelina's beautiful eyes (since words were of no help to us now), which glowed with a marvellous light, despite the darkness of the coach where her father, mother and suitor were moving about confusedly like creatures of the underworld. And in this glance I believed I could read the confirmation of the vows she'd made me, and a promise to hold out for ever in the teeth of this paternal tyranny.

With a bitterly wounded heart, all desire to live extinguished and a knot in my throat so tight I thought I would faint, I watched the coach bearing my Angelina away turn the corner and disappear. Sadly, I sheathed my sword, remounted my horse and set off towards our lodgings, still breathless and bathed in sweat from my pursuit, my legs shaking still and my voice so choked in my throat that I couldn't possibly have spoken a word had my life depended on it—but what words would I have found? My very thoughts abandoned me in my despair; the world become as black as ink, my whole life suddenly deprived of the bright star that had lit my path these past five years.

"Ah!" I thought. "Angelina can but weaken when she marries this fat idiot and I'll never see her again."

The apprehension I felt at this unspeakable misfortune was so painful that it now appeared inevitable. Giving no thought to the faces I passed in the street as I rode slowly along on Pompée, I gave way to the tears that now flowed freely down my cheeks and fell in large drops on my hands, which held her reins with such abandon that she would not have known which direction to take had not Fogacer's horse preceded us. Whichever way I turned my inner thoughts, blurred as they were by these storms of tears, all I could imagine in a world without Angelina was an immense, harsh, stony, sterile and meaningless desert. Certainly I did not doubt that she still loved me! And I could only imagine the valour that had spurred her on these past five years against her father's will. But his resolve had finally hardened into a pitiless inhumanity and had fallen into the violence that I'd just witnessed. And if Monsieur de Montcalm dared to do that, wouldn't he do worse to make her bend to his will? And how far could the poor girl push her rebellion before he decided to imprison her, as he had so often threatened to do, in a papist convent, killing off any hope of either marriage or motherhood, which were so deeply imprinted in her character that even the promise of my love could not overcome them? I couldn't help imagining my adorable girl buried in some cloister where everything was as cold and hard as the stones from which it was built. There, the rules were barbaric, the cell incommodious, the food repulsive, the nuns tyrannical, and I could imagine her, still so beautiful despite her funereal veils, slowly abandoning her will to live. I supposed I must face the awful truth that, no matter how much trust I had in her vows and in that last look that confirmed them, the time would come when the daily torments she faced would end up wearing down her constancy, and that anything, even the fatuous La Condomine, would seem preferable to such a fate.

How can absence be endured when it is without remedy? What? Would I never see her again? How could I pronounce the word "never" without perishing, even though loss is part of our everyday lives, like a little death, a shred torn from our hearts, a pleasure ravished from our sight, delights that have fallen through our fingers? Oh, heaven! How can it be that in the fortress of our joys a wall can collapse without the entire edifice completely crashing to earth?

As soon as we'd returned to our lodgings, I threw Pompée's reins to Miroul, nodded a sad adieu to Fogacer, who looked on mutely, ran to my tiny room and locked myself in so as not to be seen in the state I was in. My tears had dried up. All I could feel now was a kind of grief-stricken daze, a terror of what was to come, a degree of despair that would have led me to kill myself had I not been revived by my bitter anger towards Monsieur de Montcalm for having thus treated this girl whose tenderness, mildness and goodness had never seen their like on this earth.

In his letters to my father, Monsieur de Montcalm had given as a reason for his refusal the impecunious situation that befell me as a younger son. However, when my father and Uncle Sauveterre assured him that they would grant me a proper living when I married, Monsieur de Montcalm changed his tune, or rather revealed the real reasons, which he'd hidden till then and were, as you will agree, of an overwhelming magnitude. He revealed that when he told his confessor about the alliance he was contemplating, the priest threw his arms heavenward and imposed an absolute barrier to such a union: a Huguenot could not marry a Catholic! If Monsieur de Montcalm had the weakness to accept such an infamous marriage, such an unnatural union, one so obviously inspired by Beelzebub, his salvation would be immediately forfeited.

I now saw to what depths zeal could bring the heart of an honest man when it was inspired by the absolutes of religion. It had been sufficient for this stupid priest to brandish his lightning, and Monsieur de Montcalm, by submitting to it, had banished from his breast all the gratitude he owed me for having saved his life in the Barbentane woods, as well as all courtesy, honour and friendship, and even the simple, rough connection that exists between men when they have shared the same perils—and did he not remember that it was in the act of blocking the shot that would have killed him that I had been so severely wounded at Barbentane? But a priest had got hold of him and nothing merely human counted any more.

Like Monsieur de Montcalm, I worshipped Christ, but not in the same way: therefore I was a wicked man! An outlaw! A gallows bird! And if his daughter persisted in loving me, then death in the cloister would be her lot! Full of a deep selfishness that was so limitless its roots could not be seen, Monsieur de Montcalm sacrificed everything for his own salvation, trampling underfoot our young lives for his little part of Paradise, as if death were the goal and not simply the end of his life!

As for me, 'tis certain that for my Angelina I could have accepted the idols, the saints, the adoration of Mary (even if it were only lip service) and even the practice of heard confession (to which, you will remember, I had been constrained at peril of my life by the monks of the Baron de Caudebec), but could I have ever resigned myself to so deeply wound my father and Sauveterre by making such a public renunciation? Ah, Fogacer had it right when he said I was more a member of a party than one of a Church: the zeal of the Churches did not inflame me in the least, for everywhere I looked I saw only too well how inhuman were its results. How could I ever rip from my heart, without devastating it completely and making me hateful to my own self, my fidelity to the father I loved so much, to Uncle Sauveterre, to Samson and to Mespech, whose very stones would have cried out against this betrayal?

Suffering has a way of enduring. And how slowly time passes when we are aggrieved. The worst is the kind that leaves your eyes dry, your heart wounded and your understanding so unhinged that you're only half alive, or more than half dead: the future rises up like a wall you have neither the power nor the will to scale, and you have no strength to desire anything but the one who is gone.

Seeing her already entombed in a cloister amid a cadre of nuns embittered by the vinegar of chastity and seeking revenge on her for being so young and beautiful—as though it were a sin to have enjoyed the glories of the flesh, theirs having stayed so sterile—I wondered whether I ought not to wish for her a less terrible evil and, rather than the convent, a husband, even if he were a simpleton, and children, who might at least console her even if they were his offspring as well. Oh, heaven! This thought lasted only a moment: I couldn't continue to think this way, aspiring to heights that were at odds with my every fibre! It would have been hypocritical of me to hold such a sublime position for more than a quarter of a minute—to wish her other children than mine. Such thoughts only made my wound more painful.

I don't know how many hours I spent beating my head against a wall of despair, at times stretched out on my stomach on my bed, my head in my arms, at other times pacing back and forth in my tiny chamber, oblivious to the setting sun, so great was the darkness in my heart, casting glances out of my window at the Cimetière des Innocents, as if I aspired, in the bloom of my youth, to the stench of this annihilation.

There was a knock at the door. I staggered over to open it. It was my beautiful brother, Samson, who hugged me to him, having learnt from Fogacer, while looking for me to go to dinner with him, that I'd found my Angelina only to lose her. Gertrude du Luc, following him into the room, asked why I was crying, so I sat down, and in a dull, lifeless voice recounted what had happened in a most jumbled and incoherent way. Seeing me so deep in melancholy, Samson could not keep from shedding his own tears and Gertrude added hers as well. She slipped down before me on her knees and, taking my hands in hers, tried to console me, as she would have done a child, with a tenderness so sweet and feminine that I was surprised to see such compassion after her many excesses had led me to doubt she was capable of such feeling. I was thus distracted from my grief by a sense of the injustice that I'd done her, and in the blink of an eye I regained the esteem for her that I'd lost when she betrayed Samson with Cossolat. She immediately guessed this change of heart from my expression, and I could sense her happiness that this dark cloud had finally been swept away. I understood that I must henceforth embrace her as a true friend, free of any of the resentment caused by her troubles (which she couldn't help) or by the very seductive way she treated every man she met—even her brother (as she was wont to call me). And I now believed that she was indeed my sister, absent of any hypocrisy or ulterior motives, seeing how sincerely and affectionately she expressed her pity at my present sadness.

There was another knock on the door and, with Miroul at his heels, Fogacer came in. Seeing Samson by my side and Gertrude at my feet, he smiled his slow, sinuous smile and, sitting down on my left, said, "*Mi fili*, anyone who seeks to avoid suffering should never get involved with another, and should shun, like the serpent in the apple tree, this passionate appetite for another person that is called love. This is what the wise men teach us from the pulpit. But, alas, anyone who loves not women loves men, and anyone who loves neither one loves himself and spends his evenings totting up his sins and indulgences, subtracting the second from the first and trying to calculate if he'll make it into Paradise. *Mi fili*, don't trust this sort of fellow. If he's so self-absorbed and so pettily sweet to himself, he can't help being hard on other people. *Crede mihi experto Roberto*:* 'tis better to have loved and lost than never to have loved at all."

"Ah, Fogacer," I moaned, "no doubt you're right, but this is little comfort to me!"

"Well," replied Fogacer raising his eyebrow, "that's because I used the word 'lost', which is abhorrent to lovers. But have you really lost her? Miroul thinks otherwise."

"What?" I gasped, sitting up. "What do you know that I don't… and how did you discover it?"

"Shall I tell you, Monsieur?" he temporized.

"'Sblood!" I cried. "The impertinence! He sees me in the throes of misery and dares to tease me!"

"There, there, Monsieur," smiled Miroul, his brown eye twinkling, "I'm not so impertinent as to fail to serve my master. Will you have the patience to hear me out?"

---

* "Trust me, for I have the requisite experience."

"Good God!" I shouted, now really angry. "Have patience? When have I ever lacked patience with you?"

"Why, every day, my master, unlike your 'impertinent' valet!"

"Well, then, Miroul," I conceded, "I withdraw the word 'impertinent' if it upsets you."

"Monsieur," countered Miroul, half in jest and half serious, "I thank you. So here is my story without any further delay. Are you listening?"

"I'm all ears, dammit! Do I have to keep repeating it?"

"Monsieur, when I saw that great knave of a major-domo come back to see you with such a long face after having spoken with his master, I doubted seriously that there was any chance he'd let you see our young mistress; so, leaving our horses with Fogacer, I walked very boldly and nonchalantly up to the front door and leant against the door frame where I could watch the servants going back and forth bringing cases to the coach, and I began trimming my nails with a pair of little scissors as if I were a hundred leagues from there. Of course they looked at me very haughtily and I returned their looks with utter disdain. Finally, the major-domo, coming over to me, snarled, 'What are you doing here, knave?'

"'Monsieur,' I replied, admiring my nails, 'the first time anyone calls me a knave, nothing happens, since I am, by nature, very benign. But the second time, my sword leaps from its sheath, and this sword,' I said, suddenly raising my voice, 'should not be a stranger to you people from Barbentane, since it, along with those of my master and the monks from the abbey, saved your master and his household from being massacred. But given the way they're treating Monsieur de Siorac in there, I believe that this good deed seems to have slipped from everyone's memory here!'

"'Monsieur,' whined the major-domo in a very aggrieved voice, looking somewhat ashamed, 'I'm only obeying orders.'

"'From which I must conclude,' I rejoined, 'that given how coldly he was received, my master will not ever be able to see the ladies whom he saved from rape and death.'

"'Monsieur, I fear 'tis true,' replied the major-domo in an embarrassed voice; and, making a little bow, he left me standing there.

"I'd won the day, since this rascal was not without some shred of conscience and dared not confront me. And so when the Montcalm ladies came out to take their places in the coach—"

"What! You saw them?" I cried.

"And spoke to them," Miroul laughed, "while Monsieur de Montcalm was inside amusing you."

"And it's only now you're telling me this!"

"Monsieur, you've told me a hundred times never to bother you when you're deep in thought."

"Ah, Miroul, what patience…"

"Anyway, I saw them and immediately, stepping up in front of them, I made a series of deep bows as I backed up all the way to the coach, so that finally Madame Angelina cried, 'But it's Miroul! Where is your master, Miroul?'

"'Inside, Madame,' I answered, bowing again, 'with Monsieur de Montcalm, but given his cold greeting, I doubt he will allow my master to greet you.'

"'Mother!' cried our young lady, her beautiful black eyes flashing such fire and brimstone in their anger that it was marvellous to behold. 'So that's what all the whispering was about when you were preparing our departure and the great hurry with which we left the house. This is beyond shame! We are fleeing the presence of the very man who saved us!'

"'Picot!' hissed Madame de Montcalm to her valet. 'Open the door! In you get, my daughter!'

"'Madame my mother,' answered Angelina, making a small bow,

401

but her voice and look full of fury, 'I am your servant. Miroul,' she continued, turning to me, 'be so kind as to tell your master that I want no part in the ingratitude that he's been shown, and as for me, my feelings have not changed.'

"'Daughter!' cried Madame de Montcalm with a severity that seemed forced and feigned. 'What are you doing? You are betrothed to Monsieur de La Condomine!'

"'I owe nothing to that gentleman,' countered Madame Angelina, her foot on the coach's step. And pulling herself up to her full height with all the pride she possessed, she proclaimed, 'He will have nothing from me, neither my hand, nor a word, nor even the grace of a single look from Paris to Barbentane.'

"So saying, and boiling with her unleashed anger, she threw herself into the coach, but, her hem having caught in the door latch, she pulled it towards her with such fury that she put a three-inch rip in her petticoat.

"'Look what you've done!' cried Madame de Montcalm. 'You've ruined your dress!'

"'I wish I'd destroyed it completely,' cried Angelina, fixing her mother with a look of rage, her eyes blazing. 'And along with it this entire coach that I might be spared making the trip with you-know-who!'

"'Ah, Madame!' gasped Madame de Montcalm. 'Now you've gone too far! Your father will send you off to the convent!'

"'I can't wait!' cried Angelina. 'And there I'll starve to death, far from some people I could name whose ingratitude I abhor.'

"'My daughter!' screamed Madame de Montcalm.

"But, throwing herself into the coach (while pulling her skirts to her to avoid catching them on the latch), she disappeared from view as Picot, the valet, dropped the window curtains behind her, and if the dispute continued inside the vehicle, as I suspect it did, I heard nothing more. I saddled my horse and remained stationed there quietly until I saw you emerge from the house and struggle with the rascal in the escort who attempted to trample you with his horse. I unsheathed immediately, and had at him, and what the flat side of your blade had so well begun, I finished, putting half an inch of steel into the horse's crupper and sending it galloping off to the moon.

"And that's my story," Miroul concluded quite simply. But with his mismatching eyes lowered with an air of immoderate modesty, he added, "But as for the pertinence or impertinence of my story, I cannot judge."

"Ah, Miroul!" I cried, leaping from my couch, half-laughing, half-weeping, and giving him an enormous hug. "You're the most pertinent of valets, the most well informed, and the best teaser too, and you have comforted me marvellously!"

"But my brother," objected Samson, his blue eyes askance and full of tears, "will Madame Angelina let herself die of hunger? It would be a great sin against our Creator!"

"Don't worry." soothed Miroul. "Who threatens to do it, never does. Madame our mistress loves life much too well. It's a ruse of war to make her father suffer and give in, that's all."

Yet another knock was heard at the door, and into my little room, which was already as full as an egg, squeezed Giacomi, very surprised to discover us all gathered there, some in tears, others full of laughter and all in each other's arms. Dame Gertrude, seeing me rise from my ashes, was busy wiping away Samson's tears and couldn't help but add to the confusion with the immensity of her hoop skirt, which easily took up as much space as three of Fogacer. This last I introduced to Giacomi, admiring the harmony of their physical presences—they were the same height, with long legs and interminable arms; but their faces differed entirely: the doctor's so Luciferian, the *maestro*'s so joyous. They exchanged a quick and lively look—from the one of medical attentiveness and from the other of a very Italian finesse—each judging and gauging the other, and immediately accepting him for what he was—a very rare thing in this zealous century.

"My good friends!" I cried. "This business has so dried me out and famished me, and I cannot doubt that you, too, suffer from a very strident hunger, as late as it is! Will you all join me for a good repast at Guillaume Gautier's place?"

"Well," said Gertrude, rising from the couch where she'd been comforting Samson, her hoop skirts propelling us all towards the edges of the chamber, "I have to confess that I'm not alone. While passing through Montpellier on my return from Rome, where I'd gone to seek indulgences for my many sins" (and here she sighed and batted her eyelashes) "and where my own chambermaid abandoned me to take up service with a rich and luxury-loving bishop, I learnt that a famous doctor had just died—that is, in Montpellier—leaving his beautiful young servant without employment. I'd heard very good things about her and went to see her immediately…"

"And who was this doctor?" asked Fogacer.

"Dr Salomon d'Assas."

"What?" I cried. "You mean Zara is your new chambermaid?"

At this very moment there came yet another knock on the door and before I could respond with "Enter!" Zara appeared (proving that she wasn't out of earshot of our conversation), long and supple in her Italian grace, balancing her angelic head on her long, languid neck, her large green eyes examining each of us in turn, weighing the effect she had on each of us with such assurance that you would have thought she were a royal princesse and not a chambermaid.

"Madame," she began, with but a hint of a curtsey since there was so little space, "did you require my presence?" And as she pushed farther into the tiny chamber we were squeezed together even more, though her dress was hardly as expansive as that of her mistress. And whether it was the effect of this enforced (though pleasant) proximity or that of her captivatingly brilliant beauty, we all fell silent (except for Fogacer), as though dumbstruck or lovestruck—Giacomi more so than any, his eyes nearly popping out of their orbits in his excitement at this vision of loveliness.

"Well, Zara," I said at length, "I'm very happy to see you! But this is very sad news that the good Dr d'Assas has died! Were you aware of this, Fogacer?"

"I knew of it, yes," replied Fogacer, who knew everything, "but I didn't tell you, *mi fili*, knowing that d'Assas was to you what Rondelet had been for my early years: a mentor and a friend."

"Oh," sighed Zara, her marvellous eyes brimming with tears, "that's exactly what he was for me. But how suddenly he made his departure! The venerable doctor was strolling through his vineyard in Frontignan one evening as healthy and happy as you please, with his arm around me. 'Ah Zara,' he said, 'I have my three loves now: my students, my vineyard and my Zara.'

"'How now, Monsieur!' I answered. 'What's this? I'm last on the list?'

"'Because you'll leave me someday, Zara, to take a husband on the porch of a church.'

"'Fie then, Monsieur!' I cried. 'I'll never get married, and have got no taste for men.'

"'But what about me?' he laughed.

"'Oh, Monsieur,' said I, 'that's another thing altogether. You're so sweet, tender and affectionate that there's great comfort in being with you.'

"At which he laughed again, but then suddenly he clasped his hand to his heart and gave a little cry like a wounded bird, faltered, turned deathly pale and would have fallen to the ground had I not held him up. Alas, if only I could have kept him alive with these weak arms!"

"Zara, my sweet child, don't cry!" soothed Gertrude, who seemed so very fond of her chambermaid. And, taking the latter's fine little hands in her strong Norman ones, she continued, "Zara! Dry your tears or they'll make your eyes all swollen! After all, didn't you find a mistress and a friend in me right away?"

"Oh, Madame," cooed Zara, her long, gracious body undulating with pleasure, "I'm all yours and you know it very well."

But saying this, she glanced, eyes still misty with tears, at Giacomi, at whom, she could see all too well, her beauty had performed a secret sword thrust, one that, despite all of the *maestro*'s great art, he'd been unable to parry. And that Zara was able to do so many things at once—shed sincere copious tears over the poor d'Assas, cosy up to her mistress while ensnaring Giacomi—astonished me less and less the better I got to know her, cat-woman that she was, despite her very good heart.

And so Zara joined our company at supper, which brought our number to seven. Gertrude du Luc decided to accompany us on our walk to stretch her legs after the long ride from Montpellier, and ordered her coach to follow us, so Zara decided to ride rather than walk, claiming she'd injured her foot. This was a powerful disappointment to Giacomi, who couldn't join her in the carriage since, night having fallen, his protection was needed to help ensure the safety of the lady, and indeed we all drew our swords as we emerged from the rue de la Ferronnerie.

"Oh!" exclaimed Gertrude at the sound of our swords unsheathing. "How lucky I am to have all these huge blades assuring the defence of my little body!"

Little body? Not likely! She was tall, strongly built and well rounded but, knowing my Gertrude, I knew all too well what happiness she derived from being surrounded by the profusion of our sharpened protrusions. The lady gradually fell silent, clearly enjoying her pretty dreams, and remained so for quite a while, until I said, "My friend, if this coach is yours, as I believe, I would like to escort you with all your horses to Montfort-l'Amaury, to entrust them to someone who can pasture them in his fields and spare us from the fleecing Maître Recroche will inflict on us for feeding them here."

"But how will you get back to Paris?" asked Gertrude, suddenly grasping my right arm as her high heels caused her to stumble on the paving stones.

"With you, in your coach, when you come back for the marriage celebrations. We can leave Samson at Montfort, since I've made up my mind: we'll be leaving the capital for good straight after the wedding, pardon or no pardon, and I'll accompany you back to Montfort, if that's agreeable to you."

"My brother," she said, softly pressing my arm (unable, as she was, to keep from flirting with any man within range of her artillery), "I'd be delighted to have such a strong escort of handsome and brave lads around me!"

Everything happened as we had arranged it, but so ambiguous are the ways and byways of fortune that, to this day, I cannot decide if it was the right thing or not to leave my horses in Montfort (influenced as I was by my good Huguenot parsimony). My decision was to have the effect of leaving me without any mount in Paris on the night of 23rd–24th August, when we heard the tolling of the bells that launched the massacre of our brothers by the people of the capital. Of course, it would have been a great help to have my Pompée, but only if I'd been lucky enough to mount her and get through the gates of the city before they were closed, imprisoning the unfortunate Protestants within—a fate that was happily avoided by Geoffroy de Caumont, lord of Castelnau and Milandes, who galloped away full tilt, reaching Montfort, and from there, Chartres, where the vidame offered him protection. But once the Paris gates were closed and locked and chains stretched across every bridge, more than one Huguenot, caught in this net, would have been well advised to melt into the population and reach the outskirts on foot, for the guards watching the bridges and gates were mainly on the lookout for men on horseback, not for the poorer folk on foot.

Before leaving Paris with Dame Gertrude on the morning of the 12th—Maître Recroche looking very put out to have lost the fourteen sols a day that we'd been paying for stabling our horses—I asked Alizon to take me to see an honest moneylender, where I traded my real pearls for an equal number of false ones (which were extremely well crafted and which Alizon quickly sewed onto my doublet in place of the ones she'd removed). This arrangement, which necessitated much bargaining, provided me with 300 écus, which, added to the 200 that the Duc d'Anjou had given me, provided us with a nice little purse, the greater part of which I entrusted to Samson in Montfort, knowing that it would be easier to get the Lord to part the waters of the Red Sea a second time than to get my beloved brother to undo the strings of his purse.

As for me, I was relieved that he agreed to safeguard our little treasure, having much more confidence in him in this matter than in myself, being of a much less conservative nature than he, in terms of both expenses and my carnal pursuits—though I congratulated myself that I'd been much more chaste, though not necessarily happily so, since coming to Paris. And this thought reminded me to purchase a small ring for Little Sissy, which I'd so offhandedly promised her when leaving Mespech. I sent Miroul off to our lodgings to help Samson do his packing, knowing full well that he'd tease me relentlessly for my excessive largesse for this wench, who was so little inclined to do her housework that he considered her unworthy of any reward whatsoever. Instead Alizon accompanied me, taking me to a jeweller's shop she'd recommended, but I only succeeded in going from Scylla to

Charybdis in this choice, for she peppered me with questions about my gift and then became very upset that I wanted to make such an expensive and "superfluous" present to a simple chambermaid.

"Fifteen écus!" she sputtered as we left the shop, the jewel safely in my purse. "Fifteen écus for a wench whose only labour is to spread her legs for a gentleman! Fifteen écus, by my faith! That's about what I give each *year* to the woman who feeds my little Henriot, and you know how hard it is for me to have to go to the baths after my work at the atelier to lie with gentlemen who please me not at all and take up my nights! Fifteen écus! Blessed Virgin, is this fair?"

"Calm down, Alizon!" I countered. "I owe some kindness to a wench who is no doubt preparing to deliver my baby."

"What?" she gasped. "Venerable doctor of medicine! And the herbs you gave me and that you promised to Babeau wouldn't do for her as well?"

"Of course they would, but she wants to be pregnant so she won't have to do any work at Mespech other than feed her baby."

"What?" she snapped angrily. "That one would also be raised in your chateau?"

"Like my brother, Samson, yes. Would you want him thrown outside the walls along with his mother, when he shares our blood?"

"Of course not, no!" she confessed. "That's the honourable thing to do. But I can't help thinking bitterly about her lot and mine, I who am so dead-tired from work and loss of sleep, and this Gypsy girl, happy as a cow in the Périgordian sun with grass up to her udder! Blessed Virgin! I say my rosary every day that God makes, asking Him to brighten my days, but I don't see anything shining at the year's end but these needles and more needles still, the meagre salary of this cheapskate and the baths. Baba!—as Recroche says! Everything goes to the few and the rest get nothing. And if what I'm saying is heresy, then may the Lord pardon me, and my curate as well, but I can't help thinking that Heaven has forgotten me in my poor earthy jail!"

Giacomi didn't come with us to Montfort, not wishing to leave the position that Silvie had obtained for him at the Louvre simply to escort our beautiful Gertrude in her carriage, so there were only three of us to take our five horses to that town, where Maître Béqueret immediately found us a labourer who put them out to pasture for two sols a day and without charging us so much as a sol to drink from his stream.

Our gentle lady was very sorry to have to leave Samson behind on the 16th to return to Paris to attend the royal wedding, but how could she miss it, when every nobleman worth his salt in France had rushed to this spectacle? And how could she forgo the chance to deck herself out in all the splendid finery and jewellery she'd had fashioned for this great ceremony, which would doubtless be a unique event in her life, and where she'd find at court so many people to see and so many occasions to be seen?

Miroul offered to climb up next to the coachman, but Gertrude, understanding that he was much more to me than just a valet, invited him to sit in the coach next to Zara and opposite herself and me. Miroul was so delighted to be travelling in such gracious company that I would have imagined he'd take full advantage of the situation, but whether he was so exhausted from the superhuman efforts required by three days spent with Dame Béqueret's chambermaid, with whom he'd carried on amorous relations during our first stay here, or whether he was intimidated by the overwhelming beauty of Zara, or whether, seeing my own lively interest in her, he decided to yield the field to me, he behaved like a saint in a stained-glass window for the entire journey, his hands folded meekly, his tongue quite tied, and his varicoloured eyes discreetly lowered in respect.

As for me, I felt almost too much at ease in the semi-darkness of the coach's interior (the curtains lowered to protect against the August sun), feeling next to my thigh the sweetness of Gertrude's body and seeing before my eyes the remarkable charms of Zara, who, it must be said, noting the interest that both her mistress and I took in her, was careful to enhance them by every means at her disposal: chattering sweetly away in her sing-song voice; making numerous little flirtatious expressions and glances; turning her long, graceful neck this way and that; impatiently pulling her handkerchief away from her bosom with her fine white hands, and then replacing it with feigned displeasure; or playing with her hair, pulling it down and then rearranging it on top of her head in a gesture that must have required great skill, but whose art was masked by the apparent disorder it produced, if one were to judge by the emotion I felt watching her. But I was careful, nevertheless, not to look too often at this bewitching figure, not wishing, as happens far too often, to pass from the comfort of watching to the discomfort of desire. I decided, instead, to close my eyes, and, feigning sleep, began—as I had done often—to pursue sweet daydreams of my Angelina, which my reborn hope now encouraged.

Despite the splendour of its monuments, Paris now seemed dirty and foul-smelling in the suffocating heat of August after the clean, country air I'd breathed in Montfort! On our arrival, Gertrude invited me to dine in the lodgings she'd rented for three months in the rue Brisemiche, but to tell the truth, I didn't feel certain enough of my virtue to accept, given how much this journey had already put me to the test. I begged her to drop me off at the rue de la Ferronnerie, which she agreed to most reluctantly, and we parted amid such embraces, inviting glances and warm kisses that only the thought of my poor Samson surrounded by his pharmaceutical vials in Montfort gave me the strength to resist her enticements and stop myself from sliding down the slippery slope. Feeling nearly dizzy with the fury of her assaults, and still dirty and sweaty from the long trip, I decided to head towards the public Old Baths in the grand'rue Saint-Honoré, with

Miroul for protection, who left me at the door of this establishment after the assurance I gave him I'd spend the night there.

"Well, my handsome young gentleman," cooed the mistress of the baths, her massive, greasy bulk ensconced behind the counter, her eyes, however, sparkling through the thousand folds of her eyelids, "I recognize you from your shining countenance, though you are dressed much more splendidly in your Parisian finery and in the latest fashion than you were before! So what will you have? A bath in a private room as before, and sup and stay the night as well?"

"Yes, indeed, my good woman!"

"Babeau! A robe and a towel for the young gent! And would Monseigneur also like Babette to shave your body hair?"

"Thanks, but no. I'll keep it the way it is from now on!"

"Well," said my hostess, "it's all a matter of taste among our gallant ladies. Some want their popinjays to be as smooth as their chambermaids, while others prefer them all hairy as the style used to be. And do you," she added, lowering her voice, "require some company for the night so the hours will pass more quickly, if you have trouble sleeping?"

"Thank you, no, good woman!" I replied shaking my head. "I've no taste for it since my head is so full of dreams!"

"Well," whispered the mistress of the baths, "appetite grows, you know, by what nourishes it!"

And certainly, to see her massive heap sitting there on her stool, one could not doubt she spoke the truth!

"No doubt you're right. But some nourishment must come first," I smiled, "and tonight I have too much to dream about to be tempted by other food."

"Well, come to think of it," said my hostess with a wink, "it's better this way, Monseigneur, since Alizon, whom you like so much, is engaged with another gentleman tonight."

"What?" I said, as if stung by a honey bee. "Is she here?"

"Not yet. She's due to arrive at eight."

"Then, good woman, disengage her from this fellow, and send her straight to me!"

"I'm afraid I can't do that," she said with a foxy smile emerging from the folds of her visage, "since the gentleman isn't French and must pay double the usual price."

"Then I'll pay triple," I snapped coldly, well aware of the extremities to which this disputation might lead.

"Triple?" said my hostess. "That would hardly do!"

"Good woman," I frowned, "don't go flying too high. I might not follow!"

"There, there, my good man," she countered, "don't get your dander up! This gentleman finds great satisfaction in his commerce with your pretty Alizon, and I'd lose his business if I didn't satisfy him!"

"You'll lose mine if you ask too much of me!"

"I doubt it!" she hissed, her eyes disappearing within the folds of her eyelids. "You care about Alizon, and Alizon needs me, in order to pay for the care of her little Henriot. Moreover, I'm not without a conscience! I promised Alizon to another gentleman and I always keep my promises. That's my rule. I wouldn't break it for less than an écu."

"An écu!" I stammered, open-mouthed. "An écu to assuage your conscience! An écu instead of six sols! That's usury! And of this écu, how much will go to Alizon?"

"Three sols!" replied my hostess as if it went without saying.

"'Sblood!" I fumed. "Is that justice? Believe me when I tell you that for so meanly wishing to win everything, you risk losing everything—this gentleman's business, mine too and Alizon's services. I'm going to see to this right now!"

Having said this, I angrily turned on my heels and had reached the door of the baths when I heard her whistling, raspy voice croak, "Thirty sols, then!"

So distressed was I by this ugly and sordid business that I threw the thirty sols on the counter and, without a word, followed Babeau, who was waiting for me with the towel and robe pressed to her bosom. I needed, moreover, to wash and enjoy Alizon's company for as long as possible before leaving Paris, which I expected to do soon, though it would be under circumstances I could never have imagined.

I was, in my unappeasable anger, more mute than a carp in a torrent while Babeau undressed me and led me to the bath, where she soaped me down, as I've described before.

"Ah, Monsieur," she counselled, "there's no pleasure or solace to bathe in such a state as you're in, all embroiled in your anger! There's no use getting so upset at the way the world is, where the fat cats gobble up the little mice. What can you do? In my village there's a saying that goes: 'There are no good masters, just some who are less wicked than others. You just have to take 'em as the Good Lord made 'em.'"

"Did you know, Babeau," I frowned, "that I was accused of spoiling you last time by giving you a sol."

"Blessed Virgin, do I know it? God knows I heard an earful about it! And what a fool I was to go crowing about it in front of you-know-who!"

"So don't go crowing about this one," I cautioned, when she'd pulled my robe about me as I stepped from the bath. "And you'll find the herbs you need stuffed in my stockings."

"Oh, Monseigneur! A thousand thanks for what you've done for me!" gushed Babeau as she slipped the coin in her pocket and stood before me, her strong red arms crossed over her large breasts and gazing at me with great fondness. The poor wench earned but two sols a day and yet she was strong and dedicated in her work and happy to be alive. "Alizon was right," she added, "when she said that, nobleman that you are, you're as good and generous as an angel."

"She said that?" I laughed, realizing that my thoughts at this moment, as I appreciated her womanly charms, made me feel more like a devil than an angel.

"She said that and a lot more," replied Babeau, "she's so fond of you. But Monsieur, may I take my leave, I've got my work to do?"

"Be off with you, then, Babeau."

And off she went, after depositing a quick kiss on my cheek. Comforted by her kindness, I threw myself onto the cot in my little room, remembering how my father had observed, after the plague in Sarlat, that the poor possessed a kind of rough, courageous thirst for life that astonished him. 'Tis true enough of all the Babeaus, Alizons and Babettes, and of so many other wenches whose ranks fill our kingdom but whom we scarcely see, so focused are we on the those who parade themselves across the centre of the world's stage shining like foam and yet who consist of the same empty brilliance.

Babeau having taken her leave, and although I felt quite relaxed and refreshed by the bath, I couldn't help feeling a little apprehensive as I waited for Alizon to arrive, unable to guess how she might feel about my having bought another night with her, as she was so quick to take offence with me. And fleeing the thought that she might be upset with me, I fell into a deep study, no less painful, reflecting on poor Dr d'Assas, who had drifted into the other world just as he had lived in this one, very sweetly and without taking any pains over the transition, being happy and easy about everything, even in death. But this thought was of little comfort when I considered that the grim reaper makes no exceptions for those we love, be it d'Assas, Uncle Sauveterre or my father, who, at more than fifty years, though still happy and vigorous, I never thought of without some apprehension about the day of his departure, when he would leave me alone on this earth entirely cut off from him.

But then, to relieve my chagrin, I administered to myself some of that mental medicine that never failed to cure me of my melancholy, at least for a while, and which consisted of thinking about the wenches who had shown me such kindness from time to time, about the way their eyes shone and about their comely bodies. And, soothed by these memories, I never failed to find marvellous comfort in them, and finally, my anger and sadness assuaged, I drifted off into sleep. And into the dreams that awaited me there, dreams of holding Alizon naked in my arms, a joy that, had I been awake, I would have banished from my thoughts—but sleep, as everyone knows, allows us to sin without sinning, since our will has no part of the visions and emotions that are born in us by the agitation of our animal spirits, our conscience itself being asleep. These delights gradually became so acute and so lively that I awoke and, blinking in the candlelight like Adam on that first dawn, I saw that Alizon herself, and not merely her ghost, was lying in my arms, as naked as I had dreamt her, an encounter in which I found such marvellous contentment. When the tumult she couldn't have failed to provoke had subsided, I discovered an ardour and a lust for life I hadn't experienced since our departure from Mespech: proof positive that my medicine and my severe Calvinist theology could never peacefully coexist.

"Ah, Monsieur," whispered Alizon when we recovered our ability to speak, "when I came and saw you here plunged into such a deep sleep, with such a smile of delight on your lips, I wanted to find my way into your dreams without waking you. I don't believe I succeeded."

"Ah, but you're mistaken, my sweet," I replied, holding her close, "for it was you I was dreaming of!"

"Oh, Monsieur, are you making sport with me? Would you swear 'tis so by the Blessed Virgin whose medallion you wear on the chain around your neck?"

"Absolutely!" I replied, happy to be able to swear without blasphemy, since I do not consider Mary to be the idol that papists have made of Her.

"Oh, Pierre," she laughed, her black eyes shining, "it makes me so happy to hear you say it, since I've doubted you had the same appetite for me that I've felt for you—which is why, when I saw you sleeping naked on the bed, I undressed and lay with you so that you'd be too sleepy not to caress me."

"Alizon," I laughed aloud, "is this the latest style in Paris, that the women have their way with their men by force?"

"Oh, Monsieur!" she replied, her smile radiant with candour, "I would have done so when first we met if I'd had the means to best you!"

Her witty retort seemed so Parisian in its effrontery that I nearly split my gut laughing, but I also felt deeply moved by the great tenderness Alizon had felt for me and that she'd concealed so artfully all this time.

But having laughed with me, Alizon suddenly fell silent, and since all I could see was her hair, with her pretty face buried in my shoulder and neck (where I felt her breath), I thought that she must have fallen asleep after the hard work she'd put in at Recroche's atelier. But suddenly she exclaimed, "What a beautiful medallion you have here. Pure gold! And so finely worked, and so old!"

"My mother gave it to me on her deathbed, and asked me to wear it always."

"Oh, Monsieur," she continued, "I'm so happy to discover your pious zeal! And also to have caught sight of you in your bejewelled doublet at the good priest Maillard's sermon, since that hypocrite Recroche, who has no love for you, told Baragran and me that he thought you were a heretic in disguise, you and your pretty brother."

"But wait, Alizon!" I gasped, trying to laugh. "You mean that you'd love me less if I were a Huguenot?"

"Oh, Monsieur," she groaned, grinding her teeth, "if that were the case, I would not only refuse to touch you with the tips of my fingers, but I'd consider you more horrible and disgusting than a leper, so much do I abhor these offspring of the Devil!"

Hearing this, I was glad she was nestled into my neck and couldn't see my face and the horrible grimace I couldn't repress, feeling devastated to be so suddenly the object of such violent hatred.

"You really detest them so much, Alizon?" I said when I'd regained control of my voice.

"Oh, Monsieur," she wailed in fury, "I consider them the most abominable monsters in all creation, and I'd toss them alive into the most cruel torments and from there into hell, to be slowly roasted for the rest of eternity."

"What?" I gasped. "You really hate them so much? What have they done to you? Aren't they human beings after all?"

"What they've done to me," replied Alizon, with such fury that I felt her body trembling against mine, "is to want to take away our saints!"

"Our saints?" I replied. "But many people even in the Catholic Church believe that there are too many saints."

"Oh, Monsieur," she cried, "believe me! There will never be enough of them!"

"And why would that be?" I said, bewildered.

"Because we don't have to work on saints' days! Because these good saints (whom God the Father and the Blessed Virgin will bless for ever in their goodness) lighten our workload by fifty-five days a year, giving us every month four Sundays more. So, for example, this August, we have three—not counting the Assumption: St Lawrence, St Peter and St Bartholomew. Unfortunately, St Bartholomew's day falls on a Sunday this year."

"Which means one less day off, my poor dear!"

"Well, not really," she explained, "since the custom is that if a saint's day falls on a Sunday, we get to quit work at noon on the day before. And this custom is so established and so supported by our priests that even Maître Recroche wouldn't dare oppose it."

Having said this, she fell silent, and, being so exhausted from her long day in the atelier and the tumult I've described, as well as from the fury that had just shaken her, she instantly fell into a deep sleep like a child, her head in the hollow of my shoulder, and her light breath on my neck. And as I thought about what she'd just said—which had so shaken me—I realized that if Fortune had so arranged it that I'd been born into her condition, I wouldn't have thought any differently, exhausted as she was by her fourteen hours of labour every day, not counting the nights she had to spend here. At which point, I reflected that the Catholic Church, as tyrannical and occasionally cruel as it was in the application of its power, as excessive as its complacency was about popular superstition, was perhaps more attuned to the needs of the poor than was our Church, providing them, in all the feast days of its innumerable saints, both the pleasure and repose without which their days would have been an endless and unbearable Calvary. So one can understand that, in addition to the bloodthirsty sermons they heard from the priests on Sundays, the hardworking Parisians had their own reasons for feeling for the Huguenots a great and strident detestation: a Calvinist victory would have extended their living hell by fifty-five days a year. I remembered how our miller Coulondre had made the same observation when my father had, on his own authority, converted all the servants of Mespech to the Protestant faith.

"Alizon," I thought—saddened by her words, yet moved so deeply by the fact that her head on my shoulder weighed no more than a sparrow, "it's by an accident of birth that I'm a Huguenot, and isn't it a pity that you love me for my person, but hate me for my Church, to the point that I must hide who I am to preserve your friendship.

Poor girl! And poor kingdom as well, that we cannot hold a tender young wench in our arms without having our hearts at war over the way we worship God!"

The next morning, I was overwhelmed with joy at the reception I received in the fencing room from the Baron de Quéribus, who did not share the zeal of his Church and didn't give a fig whether or not I was a Protestant.

"Ah, Siorac!" he cried, embracing me warmly. "How happy I am to see you! It feels like for ever that you've been away! I don't know what I'll do when you leave Paris, as I understand you're intending to do. Giacomi tells me you've given up on obtaining your pardon."

"Quéribus," I answered, taking him by the arm and strolling up and down the room, "I'm no baron but a younger son, so I have to get started on my practice of medicine without further delay."

"But why don't you establish your practice here in Paris?" cried Quéribus, pulling me to a halt and entreating me with his azure eyes. "I'm sure I could get the Duc d'Anjou to set you up with Dr Miron and your friend Fogacer!"

"Quéribus, I'm deeply touched by your friendship and concern, and offer you a thousand thanks. But my heart is in Provence and I couldn't live anywhere else."

"You mean to say that you've been bewitched by a beautiful lady from your region to the point that you want to marry her?"

"Precisely."

"Well, then, why don't you marry her?"

"Her father fears his own damnation if he takes a heretic for his son-in-law."

"This kills me!" laughed Quéribus. "God's truth! Such stinking superstition! Do you think the king of France has condemned himself to hellfire by choosing a Huguenot brother-in-law against the advice of the Pope? But, to come back to your immediate problem, what can we do to solve it? Shall we carry the girl off by force and have you marry her afterwards? 'Sblood! I'll help you with all my heart and all my strength! Your wish is my command and my fortune and all my men are at your service!"

"Oh, my brother!" I said, embracing him. "I cannot express my gratitude for your exceeding generosity, but Angelina is the sort of girl who would never consent to be carried off. She respects Monsieur de Montcalm too much, however much she disagrees with him in this."

"Montcalm!" said Quéribus, raising his eyebrows. "The Montcalm from Nîmes? That's her father? I know him well, though I've never met him. We are even distantly related. Listen, Siorac, I'm going to write him," Quéribus continued with a smile, "to tell him in what extraordinary esteem Anjou holds you—you and your brother. But, by my faith, what have you done with your beautiful Samson? He who never leaves your side, like Castor and Pollux? The Duc d'Anjou saw him only once but is quite taken with him and often speaks of him."

"I left him in Montfort-l'Amaury with an apothecary."

"Well, perhaps that's best," replied Quéribus with a sly smile and a wink. "This court is perhaps too dangerous for such good and upstanding types. Siorac, I'm going to write Montcalm a letter, which, I dare hope, will soften his position. After all," he continued, lowering his voice and casting a careful look around, "Montcalm cannot fail to realize that the duc is our future sovereign, with Charles being so ill and having no heir. From what I've heard, Montcalm is tired of being a magistrate and aspires to be the seneschal of Nîmes. Perhaps," Quéribus laughed, "hell will seem less hot and its flames less intense if he can be brought to understand that his future son-in-law, heretic though he may be, is so well placed at court that he can advance his earthly fortunes."

At this point, a salute from Silvie signalled that he was ready to begin their bout, so Quéribus took his leave of me with a warm embrace,

ROBERT MERLE

numerous kisses and pats on my shoulder. His sword unsheathed and his doublet removed, he returned to my side once more to make me swear to take all of my meals with him, since, he said, he didn't want to lose sight of me that day. And, as I watched him fence with the supreme grace that comes from the adroit management of one's strength, I couldn't help feeling moved by his friendship—he seemed so thirsty for mine—nor help being surprised that he was, as many important personages of the court had claimed, a "sceptic" (as Montaigne would say) in matters of religion.

No doubt Quéribus would have found it extremely vulgar to be, like Fogacer, an atheist, for, in truth, he could never have come to the position through study and reflection since, other than Ronsard, he'd read nothing. And yet would a true believer ever have suggested making a bargain, so light-heartedly and in such jest, with Monsieur de Montcalm, to trump hell with his worldly advancement?

Exemplo plus quam ratione vivimus.* Catherine, the true sovereign of the kingdom since the death of her husband, Henri II, appeared to have no religious zeal whatsoever. Niece of a Pope who was so blatantly dishonest that no one believed him even when he spoke the truth, you would have said that this Machiavelli in skirts had developed a disorder that could best be defined as "indifference" and that spread from her to those around her until the entire court was infected with it. Catholicism, the reformed religion—it was all the same to Catherine. To convince the Cardinal de Bourbon to preside over the marriage of Margot and Henri de Navarre, she produced a letter from the papal ambassador that falsely proclaimed that the Holy Father had given his authorization to this marriage "against nature". It was so widely known that Catherine didn't care about the heresy of her future son-in-law that the priests and people of

---

*   "We live more by example than by reason."

Paris hated her for having arranged this "infamous" union, calling her "Jezebel" and throwing all sorts of accusations at her, condemning her to public obloquy. It was not to defend a religion, which she cared about as much as a fish cares about an apple, but by political calculation that, in order to maintain her personal power against that of Coligny, she stumbled, through an unpredictable concatenation of events, from the murder of a man to the most vile massacre in our history. When Navarre was forced to recant his Huguenot faith after the St Bartholomew massacre and went to hear Mass for the first time, Catherine, turning to the foreign ambassadors, laughed out loud, as if the horrible apocalypse that the kingdom had experienced during the night of 23rd–24th August had, in her eyes, merely been a farce, and the conversion of a prince, accomplished by holding a knife to his throat, a cause for unbridled mirth.

My good Quéribus was, thank God, no party to these horrors, but, as a member of this court, he shared its indifference, and thought nothing of Monsieur de Montcalm's trading of eternal damnation for his appointment as seneschal of Nîmes, which he also considered a joke. Moreover, because of his fortune in belonging to the court, he knew a great deal about many people, including the appetites of Monsieur de Montcalm, whom he'd never seen! Well, I thought, so this is the advantage that accrues to the lords who occupy the Louvre and enjoy proximity to the king. They decry what the common man believes and know what he doesn't know. And what infinite resources accrue to them through their daily actions, both from this disbelief and this knowledge I leave to your imagination.

My Quéribus was merely an elegant young man, as well as, if one wished to be censorious, vainglorious and chatty, and enjoyed, I believe, an almost infinite degree of luxury. But he had more heart, and was of a much less heady and light-hearted nature than he first appeared, for the letter he'd promised to write to Monsieur de Montcalm, which

I assumed was merely an empty promise, a compliment paid in the morning and forgotten by evening, my good baron actually wrote (though he struggled to do it and made copious spelling mistakes) and sent off to the chateau in Barbentane—the effect it had on Monsieur de Montcalm I shall relate later in these memoirs.

Maestro Giacomi's greeting was less uproarious, but was very touching in its quiet dignity, for he'd been worried about me, having heard from Fogacer that the Baronne des Tourelles had reacted hysterically to the letter I'd sent her, mocking her, and that she sought to hire some assassins to effect her revenge on me. I begged him to cross swords with me, wishing to get some exercise after my trip, and, after our combat, while still breathing hard and sweating from our exertions, he pulled me into a window embrasure and said softly, his eyes watchful:

"My brother, listen carefully. I've decided to teach you my secret sword thrust."

"What?" I gasped, shuddering and barely able to believe my ears. "Your calf strike?" Jarnac's move? Giacomi, you'd do that for me?"

"My brother," he said gravely, "I must do so, given the danger you run with these hired assassins, who know everything there is to know about ambushing a man at night and who are as much to be feared as tigers. They won't engage you in a duel, but will have at you en masse."

"But I'll have Miroul with me."

"There will be only the two of you and, most likely, four or more of them. And that's how my trick will get you out of trouble. For it works so quickly and so irremediably that in two seconds you'll have two men on the ground, not dead, but mutilated and screaming in anguish, which will so terrify the others that they'll flee the scene."

I looked at Giacomi, unable to find my voice to answer him, my eyes wide, my whole being paralysed in disbelief at the notion that, to protect me, he would share with me this secret of swordplay that he'd inherited from his teacher, that he was the only one in the world to have mastered (other than Jarnac, but Jarnac was now old and infirm) and that he valued more than all the treasures of the Grand Turk. I can well imagine that it was not without much bitter inner debate and out of the deepest friendship that Giacomi had decided to divulge his famous trick. Only after asking me to swear on the Bible never to reveal his secret to anyone and to employ it myself only if my life depended on it in a manifestly unequal combat did Giacomi teach it to me, which he did over the next few days, in a private room protected from the view of any onlookers, which Quéribus offered us in his house in the grand'rue Saint-Honoré. Not even Miroul was allowed to watch.

On 17th August Princesse Margot was officially engaged to Henri de Navarre and the wedding was set for the next day. Quéribus told me that, if I wished, he could arrange for me to be admitted to the platform, erected outside Notre-Dame, where the benediction would be given, Navarre having refused to enter the cathedral to hear the Mass.

"My good friend," I replied, "might it be possible for me to be accompanied by a noblewoman from Normandy and her chambermaid?"

"What?" laughed Quéribus. "So now you're the lover of a noblewoman just you were in Montpellier! You've been keeping secrets from me!"

"Not at all! She belongs to my brother Samson and not to me, and while he's in Montfort, I'm her chaperone."

"You're killing me!" cried Quéribus, laughing all the harder. "What kind of a chaperone is this? Good God! I'd have more trust asking a fox to protect my henhouse!"

Dame Gertrude and Zara nearly suffocated me beneath all the kisses, hugs and caresses they bestowed on me when I arrived at their lodgings in the rue Brisemiche to announce the good news. They'd despaired of getting to see the ceremony and were thrilled that they'd be able to see up close the dresses and finery of Margot and the queen mother, as well as all the royal princes and handsome gentlemen that would be attending.

I left them to tend to their preparations and headed off to see Alizon in her lodgings, since the king had decreed that no one should be required to work on the day before the royal wedding, so that they could decorate all the streets and intersections of Paris for the wedding festivities.

Her lodgings, which consisted of one tiny little room, were on the rue Tirechappe, under the roof, which made them exceptionally hot on this August afternoon; the only air came from a small dormer window, next to which my beautiful companion was sitting, her sewing needle working as rapidly as a spider spins her web.

I entered straightaway without knocking, the door being ajar to let some air circulate through the room.

"So Alizon," I greeted her, bending as I approached her so as not to bang my head on the low ceiling, "you're sewing! On your day off!"

"Ah, Monsieur," she replied without getting up, her manner at once busy, agitated and happy, "I have to! I'm making a new petticoat that I want to wear tomorrow for the marriage of Princesse Margot, since the king requested all the inhabitants of Paris to wear their finest clothes to honour his sister!"

"What, Alizon!" I said, a bit piqued that she kept at her task without stopping to give me a kiss, "you're going to this marriage that you think is so shameful?"

"Well, Monsieur," she replied without missing a stitch, her tongue as lively as her fingers, "'tis infamous for sure and entirely against nature. It's truly a union of air and fire—the air of Paradise and the fire of hell."

"So why attend in that case?" I asked, secretly amused at the notion that Margot could be compared to the air of Paradise since everyone knew about her profligate carryings-on with Guise.

"Blessed Virgin!" cried Alizon. "Do you expect me to sit at home when everyone else is going? A wedding is a wedding! Am I going to miss seeing the most beautiful ceremony of the reign just because the groom is a heretical dog? But Monsieur," she continued with a sigh, "I'm desperate! Dusk is falling and I have no candle that would allow me to finish before going to bed, I'm so exhausted!"

"What about little Henriot?" I asked, seeing the empty cradle next to her bed.

"My neighbour is looking after him. He's been so noisy that I can't keep him in here when I'm working."

"I'm going to see him," I said, turning on my heels, disappointed (frankly) that this damned petticoat prevented me from taking her in my arms as I wanted after my three days in Montfort.

Little Henriot was laughing like an angel (which he strongly resembled) so that I didn't have any trouble finding the right door; nor did I have to knock, since all the doors were open to allow a bit of fresh air to circulate through the rooms.

And what a pretty little fellow he was, so round and pink and, as I said, so jolly! As soon as I laid eyes on him I thought what a marvel it was that in Paris, despite the stench in the air, there could be children as beautiful as the ones at Mespech, since it's milk and love that make them so—I mean the great love that surrounds them and is a form of nourishment every bit as necessary as the other, one that clearly wasn't lacking here, from what I could tell, as much from the mother as from the neighbour, who was carrying the child in her arms and who was prattling and humming to him as if he were her own son. I was delighted with this pretty tableau—both the child and the comely and welcoming lass who was caring for him and who didn't need any introduction, since she already knew who I was and was happy to entrust me with the child while she went off, at my request, to buy two candles, an errand for which I paid her a sol.

I returned to Alizon's little room with the child in my arms, who neither whimpered nor cried, and was quite happy to let an unknown man carry him around, fascinated as he was by my doublet and the rows of pearls that he tried to grab with his tiny hands.

"Oh, Monsieur," gasped Alizon, who breathed two deep sighs (but without dropping a stitch), the first an expression of pure joy, the second a mix of joy and sadness, "how happy I am to see little Henriot in your arms. It's obvious you love children. Whether your Little Sissy bears you a son or a daughter, you'll be a good father, and she'll never have to worry about her child, as I do, fearing to fall sick with some disease that would keep me from working for Maître Recroche and at the baths at night. And if my health fails, exhausted as I already am both by the work and by the lack of sleep, what will become of my little Henriot?"

"Alizon," I said, "I've already thought of that."

Then, with little Henriot in my arms, I went to close the door of the tiny room, and, returning to her side, I whispered so softly that none of her neighbours might hear:

"My sweet, I will always honour you with my friendship, and your little man as well, and want you to stop selling your body at the baths, which I know brings you great shame, not to mention the Italian malady that you might contract there. And so I'm going to give you fifteen écus to pay your nursemaid for a year."

"What?" she whispered, following my lead. "Fifteen écus!" But she couldn't say another word because there was a knock at the door, and her neighbour came in carrying the two candles, which Henriot immediately reached for; and when he couldn't grab them he began to howl to wake the deaf, which made me very glad to hand him back to her, who carried him back to her room with a saucy look at the two of us as I closed the door behind her.

I counted out the fifteen écus into Alizon's lap, as she sat there open-mouthed and mute (having never seen so much money before in her life), looking at me without breathing a word, almost forgetting the new petticoat she had begun, and which she cared so much about, as if this princely marriage had replaced the one little Henriot's father had fallaciously promised her.

However, once her treasure was tied up in a sack, and the sack placed in a hole in the wall covered by a brick, I could see that she was torn between finishing her sewing project and the gratitude she would have liked to express to me; but, however much my male instincts were pressing me, I could see that her dressmaking was of so great a consequence to her that our love-making necessarily came second, and so I left her under the pretext that Giacomi was waiting for me outside in the street. As I left, I could see her black eyes fix mine with such a great love that, to this day, I have only to close my eyes to remember that look and to experience her love again with all the emotion I felt at that moment.

I was very surprised as I stepped out into the rue Tirechappe to see so many people out and about, given that it is the Parisians' wont, as soon as evening falls, to lock themselves in their houses, abandoning the streets to the bad boys of the night. But tonight, they were all occupied in building, by the light of their torches, a wooden triumphal arch, which they were decorating with branches and garlands of flowers, as if the royal procession were going to go by—which surely was not the case, since the procession was to go from the Louvre to Notre-Dame.

"That's beautiful work and well built!" I observed to a heavyset fellow in his shirtsleeves, all sweaty from nailing the various pieces of wood together. "But isn't it a lot of work for an arch that will only be standing for a day?"

As I said this, I tried to imitate the lively, clipped speech of the Parisians, since they seem all too ready to suspect anyone from the *langue d'oc* of being Huguenots.

"Not a bit of it, Monsieur," replied the fellow in a fairly civil tone. "We're going to leave it up for a good week, until St Bartholomew's day, to honour both Princesse Margot and the saint. As for the labour and the expense, they're shared: the bourgeois of our street pay for the wood and iron and the labourers do the construction."

As I walked from the rue Tirechappe to the rue de la Ferronnerie, I counted no fewer than three arches that were being built and decorated in the same manner, none of them on the route of the royal procession, but all of them interesting to see, given the numbers of people working on them, their enjoyment of the work, the torches and candles that were shining in all the windows (none of whose shutters had been closed, despite the lateness of the hour), and the way all the people were chatting and calling out to each other from one house to the next, while the wenches and chambermaids were out throwing pails of water into the street to wash away the refuse and mud, a daily cleansing prescribed by royal ordinance but respected only on great occasions like this one—Parisians being by nature the least law-abiding of any citizenry in the world.

When Quéribus arrived to pick me up in his carriage on the morning of 18th August, I was very surprised to see the streets decorated with a large number of large, beautiful tapestries, with brilliant designs and colours, which the nobles and bourgeois had removed from their walls and hung on their balconies—as was their custom, I learnt, when processions were scheduled to pass by their houses. What was curious, however, was that it wasn't just the streets where the royal procession was to pass that were so decorated, but every street in the capital that housed noble and well-to-do families.

During the night, triumphal arches, like the three I'd seen the night before, had sprung up everywhere, and I couldn't help admiring the marvellous work that had been done so rapidly on these structures, which were not only finely crafted, but also magnificently painted in floral and bucolic designs, and in a style that I've never seen anywhere but in Paris, whose inhabitants, for all their ferocity, rebelliousness and insurgencies, seem nevertheless to possess a high degree of artistic sensitivity. Under the bright August sun, which was not yet too intemperate, all of these tapestries, as well as the flowerpots blooming with bright colours on the balconies, the paving stones, which were, for once, freshly washed, and the streets inundated with festive, well-dressed crowds, all contributed to a sense of amazement at the city's splendour, its beauty and its wealth that I'd never experienced before. "Ah," I thought, "so this is what makes Paris the envy of all the other nations! Here she is, clean and decked out in her glory the way she ought to be every day!"

We picked up Gertrude du Luc and Zara in the rue Brisemiche, and I don't need to detail with what alacrity Quéribus was set upon by the beautiful Norman and her chambermaid, who was alluringly clad in one of her mistress's dresses and looking more like a noble-woman than a servant, so much had she discovered a new sense of refinement from her close contact with her mistress. As for Quéribus, he responded in kind, and in the ensuing combat both sides launched enough darts and arrows from point-blank range to cause irreparable damage to any hearts and bodies who chanced to be in range of their bows. Nor did I escape entirely unscathed, particularly by Zara's missiles, for, however much she professed to have no taste for men, she certainly enjoyed being the object of their attentions and affections.

The flood of people flowing into the streets and alleys carried us along from the Saint-Denis quarter to the Île de la Cité, so that, other than the comfort of being seated, there was no advantage to riding in a coach, since the crowds in front and behind us were so thick that, even had they been able to, they were not at all inclined to let us pass, their numbers redoubling their natural effrontery. As for the comfort I just alluded to, it too was confiscated at the Pont aux Meuniers, which we weren't allowed to cross, a sergeant of the French guards politely informing us that no carriages could be admitted onto the Île de la Cité given the great crush of vehicles and people that were already there. So we had to get out of the coach and submit to the curious stares and ribald humour of the Parisians, who were very happy to see us reduced to the same status as themselves. Of course, as we walked along, they gawked at the women with a degree of impertinence all too easy to imagine, and began loudly praising their various attributes, the ladies feigning not to hear a word of their coarse remarks. Quéribus and I walked on either side of them to keep the rabble from enacting their taunts, and Miroul and the coachman protected them from behind, without which they doubtless would have been in danger of being groped by the crowd, so great was the insolence and lubricity of this mob. Nor could we do anything to rein them in, since Quéribus and I were so pressed on either side that we would have had no room to draw our swords to answer and correct their manners.

Eventually, in the midst of all this heat and these sweating bodies, whose odour was nearly nauseating, we came up to the huge platform that had been erected in front of the porch of Notre-Dame, where Henri de Navarre and Princesse Margot would receive their nuptial benediction. This platform was raised to the usual height that would allow the populace to watch a public spectacle, be it a circus, a public execution or, in this case, a royal wedding, for which occasion it had been covered with thick tapestries that must have been brought from the Louvre at daybreak.

A thick cordon of Swiss guards and French guards, some belonging to the king and some belonging to the Duc d'Anjou, the latter recognizable by their red jackets, surrounded the platform. Heading towards them, we were delighted to come upon Captain de Montesquiou, who looked at us with but a hint of a smile.

"If you please, Captain," said Quéribus, "get us out of this crush. The smell alone will kill us!"

"I know you well, Monsieur," replied Montesquiou sternly, "and I know Monsieur de Siorac, but these ladies are unknown to me."

"They're both noblewomen from Normandy," answered Quéribus without batting an eye, "and I answer for them as for myself."

This lie led me to think that in his mind he'd already made his choice and that he'd selected Zara, since a chambermaid would never have been admitted onto the platform, where already a number of brilliant courtiers and ladies were taking their places on the benches. It was certainly a relief to be seated, but, under the terrible, leaden heat of the sun, a number of ladies had already begun to complain, fearing it would ruin their complexions, but also because they were suffocating under the tight bodices that they'd worn to appear more comely. I have to admit that even without such a constraint I was cooking like a loaf of bread in an oven. All buttoned up as I was, and sporting a high collar, I could feel the perspiration dripping from my face, and yet I felt fortunate to be there with these two women and to have the chance to see up close the characters in this great drama.

In a great flurry of pages and officers, and a loud fanfare of trumpets, church bells tolling wildly and an explosion of cannon shots, the king appeared, and on his arm the queen mother, followed by his queen. He was dressed in pale-yellow satin, on which a sun with its rays was figured by a series of golden threads and precious stones. Catherine de' Medici, having for once abandoned the black mourning clothes she'd worn since the death of Henri II, appeared in a sumptuous blue silk gown, covered—and I mean *covered*—from head to toe with her celebrated Florentine jewels, the most beautiful in the world, radiating beams from their thousands of facets to such a degree that they seemed to rob the very sunlight from her son, just as, in truth, she had, from the very day of his coronation, robbed him of the real power of the throne.

Behind the king came his brothers, the Duc d'Anjou and the Duc d'Alençon, clothed as he was in pale-yellow satin, as was also Henri de Navarre, who followed them. I doubted, however, that any of the three could be seen by the populace, since the queen mother's many officers and her twelve ladies-in-waiting (of the twenty-four in her squadron) so crowded the front of the platform as to render the rest of the company invisible.

The king and queen mother were half-heartedly greeted by the people, who, like Alizon, seemed half scolding and half happy, and, on the whole, divided between the pleasure this royal ceremony afforded them and the bitter resentment they felt about this "infamous" marriage that had been forced down their throats.

These meagre acclamations were stifled when Margot made her appearance, splendidly adorned, arriving from the archbishop's palace, where, according to the rumours that were flying about, she'd spent the night tortured by bad dreams (since she still loved Guise). She was presented by the Cardinal de Bourbon, who'd been fooled, or pretended to be, by the dispatch from Rome that Catherine de' Medici had fabricated.

Margot, properly Marguerite de France, was clothed in a dress of deep-red velvet, decorated with fleurs-de-lis embroidered in gold, her shoulders weighed down beneath a magnificent velvet mantle, with a train that was four yards long, held by three princesses. On her head, an imperial crown, shining with pearls, diamonds and rubies, jewels that also decorated the ermine bodice that she wore over her dress and that must have added to the unbearable heat of the sun, as I imagined from the way perspiration was flowing down her cheeks. She stood there, immobile in her triumph, enthusiastically applauded by the populace, wearing a very unhappy expression to signify *urbi et orbi* that this marriage gave her little pleasure. It got to the point that the poor Cardinal de Bourbon, to get her to move forward, had to take her by the hand and more or less drag her behind him like Iphiginia going to her death. Seeing this, the populace, believing that Margot refused to marry a heretic, and believing that it was zeal rather than physical repugnance, redoubled its cheers, both sympathizing with the sad fate of the princesse and at the same time admiring her magnificent finery.

Not that she was, to speak the unvarnished truth, as beautiful as Pierre de Bourdeille, lord of Brantôme, has described her, calling her on this occasion "the marvel of heaven on earth". As everyone knows, for our good Périgordian neighbour Brantôme, it's enough for one to be of royal blood for him to label one as unique and without equal. I found the princesse pleasant to look at: her face was round, her eyes were large—but they protruded like her mother's, and her expression was set in a perpetual pout, so that, if it hadn't been for all the finery, the only thing I would have admired in her was the extreme appetite for life that emanated from her lively and eloquent eyes—a feature that gave her what I might call a devilish beauty, and, in my view, quite justly so, as the rest of my story will illustrate.

"See how bored Charles is!" whispered Quéribus in my ear. "I'll wager he'd like to be a thousand leagues from here. Hunting, playing tennis, working in his forge, playing his trumpets or running through the streets at night with the Bâtard d'Angoulême and Guise, playing a thousand tricks on passers-by."

"What? He does that?" I whispered back.

"He's done worse," hissed Quéribus. "He's so childish. The Duc d'Anjou once found him in his apartments on all fours, with a saddle on his back, whinnying like a horse."

I laughed at this.

"Monsieur my brother," said Dame Gertrude du Luc, tapping me on the hand with her fan, "you and the baron are sharing secrets."

"Which are all about you, my friend," I whispered in her ear. "He told me he finds you very beautiful."

"Ha!" said Gertrude out loud, fanning herself and leaning over to smile at him. "Then why doesn't he sit next to me?"

"But I'd be delighted to!" gushed Quéribus, and, getting right to his feet, he changed places with me so that I had Zara on my left and the baron on my right, who wanted to remain seated next to me so he could continue to share his witty observations about the royal family in his very unguarded way.

At this point, the king, who, though dressed as the sun, looked very gloomy indeed, suddenly burst out roguishly:

"Now then! Let's get on with it! Where's Navarre?"

Whereupon Navarre moved forward, along with the Duc d'Anjou, who was holding his hand and was, so to speak, leading him over to his sister to give her to him in marriage.

The sight of Navarre immediately raised the hackles of the crowd, who emitted something like a groan, which immediately died in their throats when they spied Anjou, who was second only to Guise in the hearts of the Parisians, because he'd defeated the Huguenots at Jarnac and at Moncontour. So, in the end, unsure whether to boo Navarre or cheer for the Duc d'Anjou, the populace fell silent, very bewildered that it should be Anjou himself who was throwing his sister into the clutches of the Devil.

I was able to inspect Navarre at my leisure as he made his bows and compliments to the king, to Catherine de' Medici and to his future spouse (who remained as stony as marble and made no reply whatsoever). He was clothed in pale-yellow satin like the king and his brothers, and though at his late mother's request he had made a great effort for this marriage to hide his rustic origins, I had to admit that his bearing had something unpolished about it that suggested more a labourer or a soldier than a courtier.

But though his face, with his long nose, was hardly handsome, there was in his expression an air of false naivety, of finesse and of sarcasm, that gave me food for thought.

"So, what do you think of the groom?" whispered Quéribus in my ear.

"Monsieur," I replied with a smile, "although the bumpkin speaks *langue d'oc*, I think he's got more finesse than buffoonery about him."

"Clever he most assuredly is," laughed Quéribus, "and even more so than Catherine, who thinks she can chain him to his throne and thus attach him to France by giving him her daughter, whose thighs, Catherine believes, will take him prisoner. But, God's truth! Those thighs are too light to put lead in Navarre's shoes!"

"Monsieur," I observed, "your metaphor is like the Princesse de Montpensier: she's beautiful but she limps."

He laughed out loud at this and threw his arm around my shoulder, but gave a quick look around to see if anyone had been able to hear our damnable words. But in truth, the ladies and lords seated around us, and seated so close together that their knees were touching the backs of those in front of them, were all, like us, too occupied in their gossip to hear us, so true is it that slander, no matter how politely expressed, is the daily sustenance of every heart.

Seeing us laughing, our ladies took us to task for being more caught up with our own conversation than with them; of the two, the more imperious by far was Zara, who, from the minute she had clothed herself in an aristocrat's clothes, had adopted aristocratic manners and now commanded me in a whisper to explain exactly who this Montpensier woman was whom we were laughing about.

"You mean you don't know, Zara?" I replied, giving her a little kiss on her neck, under the pretext of speaking in her pretty little ear. "It's Guise's sister and the most zealous papist in the entire kingdom!"

"Monsieur," said Zara, batting her eyelashes and bending her long neck towards me—little gestures that she knew delighted me, "don't speak ill of the papists!"

"Don't tell me," I hissed, "that you're a turncoat!"

"Monsieur," she explained, "I'm of the religion of the person who loves me: Huguenot with d'Assas, Catholic with Dame Gertrude. But Monsieur, where is the Duc de Guise? I'm told he's very handsome."

I was unable to answer her, for at that moment there was a great stir on the platform, since the king, having stood up, was heading towards the porch of the cathedral to go to hear Mass, while Navarre, who refused to hear it, was heading towards the cloister of the archbishop's palace (which stood to the left of Notre-Dame), and was immediately followed by the Prince de Condé, Admiral de Coligny, his son-in-law Téligny, the Comte de La Rochefoucauld and a number of other great Protestant lords. As for the future wife of Navarre, she had taken the arm of the Duc d'Anjou, who was to play the role of husband during the Mass.

The platform was suddenly all flux and reflux: the flux of the papists entering the nave and the reflux of the Huguenots heading to the cloister to stroll about during the Mass, waiting for it to end and for the return of Margot to the platform, where, outside the church, the nuptial benediction would be bestowed on this strange couple who had separated into their respective religions before being united before God.

"Assuredly," Quéribus whispered to me as we followed Margot on Anjou's arm, "the lady, rather than marry her bumpkin Navarre, would prefer, given Guise's unavailability, to marry her brother as the Pharaohs did. You've no doubt heard, even out in the provinces, about how crazy she was about him when she was younger?"

"What?" I gulped. "Isn't that just a nasty rumour? Where did you get it from?"

"From an excellent source—Margot herself!"

"And the Duc d'Anjou?"

"Well, Anjou has been pursuing her with a hateful love ever since she opened herself to Guise. The king as well. And Alençon. The Florentine ways don't change. Margot is loved by her three brothers, but in the Italian way: jealously."

Terrified by these licentious words, I threw a quick look around us and saw that the fraternal couple, as they walked up the nave, were watched by the entire court with smiles, sneers and whispers, which said a very great amount about the very small amount of respect that these bowing and scraping courtiers accorded their prince. "Well," I thought, "now I understand why the people of Paris are so rebellious and insolent, like their Maillotin forebears. The example comes from above."

Huguenot though I was, I'd never had such great scruples about entering a Catholic church that I couldn't overcome them out of respect for others, and could not in good conscience abandon my brother Quéribus and the ladies at the door. But without meaning to offend anyone who shares the king's religion, I found this Mass interminable despite its pageantry. It lasted four deadly hours and one would have thought that the canons of the cathedral had extended it simply to annoy Navarre and the reformists, who were forced to walk back and forth in the cloister of the archbishop's palace all that time, subjected to the threats and hoots of the crowd outside, who, however noble they believed themselves, would doubtless have stormed the cloister and torn them limb from limb with their bare hands had the Swiss and French guards not kept them from doing so. But from what I heard later, their dirty and offensive words did what their hands could not, and there was no insult or threat that wasn't thrown from without, such as, "Hey, you heretical dogs! Wicked devils! Satan's henchmen! You don't want to hear the Mass? We'll force it on you sooner or later!" Of course, from our side, the insults were no more respectful or thoughtful, and from within the cloister came nasty jokes about Mary and all the saints, which they would have done much better to stifle given the flames of strident hatred that they fanned that afternoon, and that ultimately burst forth from these hot paving stones into a full-fledged massacre.

But I saw nothing of all that, for I was hearing Mass for the second time in my life, but in the cathedral of Notre-Dame, where mitred priests, decked out in resplendent chasubles, presented a ceremony that outdid in its splendour the very pomp of the royal court. I'd never seen such a gaudy spectacle; and certainly, if I considered only what I could see and hear (for the music and chants were very melodious), I would have been swept away by the marvellous beauty of this rite, if I hadn't found in it—raised as I had been in the spartan cult of the Huguenots—such a vainglorious display, so worldly and so superfluous that it couldn't fail to irritate me every bit as much as I enjoyed it. And what pleasure there was diminished to nothing as the interminable ceremony dragged on.

On the concluding words of the Mass, "*ite missa est*", we emerged from the cool vaults of the cathedral and took our places once more on the platform in front of the porch. The sun was at its zenith, and the heat was unbearable. The king and the queen mother took their places at the centre of the platform on two fauteuils, and Margot knelt before the king on one of the two prayer stools that had been brought out during the Mass. The Duc d'Anjou stood aside, his face inscrutable, and sent Montmorency to bring Navarre, who, returning from the cloister, followed by his Huguenots, came and knelt down beside Margot, facing the Cardinal de Bourbon, the bishop of Digne and two Italian priests who'd been found God knows where, and who were placed there to convince the people that the Pope had indeed given his blessing.

Margot was extremely pale, her lips set in a pout, her face sullen; and at the moment the cardinal asked her if she consented to take Henri de Bourbon, king of Navarre for her husband, she didn't say a word or even make a sound, but remained kneeling, head held high, her face stony, her eyes staring straight ahead, more mute and immobile than a log—perhaps merely to express her repugnance, or perhaps in the hope that the Church would later annul the marriage. You can imagine the stupor and scandal that spread throughout the assembly and caused all of us to fall silent, our breath suspended—though not for long. For the queen mother, unfazed, leant over and said a few words to the king, who, rising to his feet in anger, grabbed Margot by the back of the neck with the rough hands that had so cruelly beaten her when her business with Guise had been discovered, and forced her head forward, bending her neck and violently pushing down into an attitude that, however forced it was, the Cardinal de Bourbon was able to interpret as a sign of assent. Pursuing the benediction in its majestic Latin, he pronounced the sacramental words that united the happy couple "for better or for worse"—the "worse" having just been brutally illustrated for us.

It took us an entire hour to get back to our carriage because the crush of the crowd on Île de la Cité was even greater now than when we arrived. We couldn't help hearing what the people around us were saying, and it appeared that, even though they were quite ready to celebrate the event now that it was accomplished, they were not in the least reconciled to this union. Nor were they dissuaded from this opinion by all the zealous priests who were fulminating against "Jezebel" and "Ahab", both from the pulpit and out here in the street, referring, of course, to Catherine and the king, who were suspected of secretly being in league with the reformers. Proof that everyone in this zealous century appears to be a heretic to everyone else! The name "Jezebel" had already been given to Catherine after her unsuccessful attempt at Bayonne to get Felipe II of Spain to agree to eradicate the Huguenots if she'd consent to a Spanish wedding.

For four days and four long nights after the marriage of Margot, there were constant banquets, balls and galas at the Louvre. I attended all of them, and would have been happy enough had there not been nasty jabs and thorny remarks about those of my religion. No one seemed to trust this feigned reconciliation, quite the contrary. The papists had nothing but grimaces, digs, nasty jokes and malicious snubs to share with us.

On 20th August, an enormous platform was constructed outside the Hôtel du Petit-Bourbon, and members of the royal family gave a pantomime, one that stuck in our throats. A small group of evil horsemen—representing Navarre, Condé and La Rochefoucauld—could be seen attacking Paradise, which was made up of twelve nymphs, including Margot and Marie de Clèves (Condé's wife), whom the Duc d'Anjou was desperately in love with. Some angels—played by the king, Anjou and Alençon themselves—intervened, defeated the wicked horsemen and drove them back into hell on the left-hand side of the stage, where there was a bonfire and some sulphurous vapour. This done, the angels danced with the nymphs for a long time while some devils tortured the captured knights, who were ultimately pardoned and delivered, thanks, primarily, to the intercession of the nymphs, and not by their own means—an ending which merely added to the outrage of the allegory.

On 21st August it was worse. Some Turks, dressed to look like grotesque versions of Navarre and Condé, attacked some bare-breasted Amazons, who were played by the king and his two brothers—who, women though they were, defeated them in a trice.

That same day, Gertrude du Luc asked me to accompany her to a sermon given by Father Victor, whose fame had reached Normandy. He was a tall man, whose height and powerful voice seemed better suited to bearing arms than to the frock that he wore. Banging his fists on the lectern, he spoke for two long hours on the princely marriage, calling it an impious act whose punishment would be visited not just on "those who had made it" but on an entire people. At the conclusion, he crossed his muscular arms over his chest, threw his head back and stared heavenward, as if he were drawing from there, as from a well, some sacred inspiration, and then cried in a voice that shook the vaults of his church:

"God will not suffer this execrable coupling!"

At this, the faithful who'd heard him, gaping and short of breath, responded with a murmur of assent, which gradually swelled to a kind of growling so savage and terrible that I could only compare it to a pack of mastiffs pulling violently on their leashes, their maws gaping wide and their huge teeth bared in violent lust.

9

IN THE EVENING of that same 21st August, Quéribus invited me to share his country house in Saint-Cloud, where he wanted to escape the heat of the city in the company of Dame Gertrude du Luc and Zara, but, though I was tempted by the peacefulness of the countryside after all the commotion of the festivities, I didn't want to make the trip. When I left the church where Father Victor had delivered his sermon, I ran into the tennis master and ball-maker Delay, who was very fond of me because I was always happy to listen to his court rumours, being so new at the Louvre, and so unused to the ways of the capital, and he told me that another month in Paris would turn me into a perfect gallant, so stylish did I appear.

Delay, learning of my approaching departure, wanted to know—being such an inquisitive fellow—whether I was happy to be returning to the provinces.

"Alas, no," I sighed, "I came to seek the king's pardon for having killed a gentleman in Sarlat, though in a loyal duel. But since the king thinks I'm attached to the Duc d'Anjou because of the affair of the doublet, he's closed his door to me."

"What's this?" said Delay frowning deeply. "Charles has refused you an audience? By my faith, I'll get him to change his mind! You can count on it! It's as good as done: you'll speak to the king tomorrow. Be at my tennis court at ten o'clock, and I'll put you into a doubles match that Charles is supposed to play against Guise, Téligny and the Bâtard d'Angoulême. But I've just learnt that the bâtard is sick in bed with a high fever and a terrible headache, so I'll arrange for you to take his place."

I couldn't believe my ears to hear him speak so decisively, as though he could dispose of the king as he pleased. How could a tennis master succeed where Monsieur de Nançay had failed? However, since I'd seen Delay address the king with extraordinary effrontery, and since I'd observed that at court it's not necessarily the most powerful who have the ear of the king but often the opposite, I decided to run the risk, which wasn't so great anyway since in truth I had little appetite to travel to Saint-Cloud.

I reasoned that to hold Zara in my arms would be of little comfort to me if I knew that Gertrude was holding Quéribus in hers. My heart would bleed if I had to witness the infidelity she'd inflict on my brother and virtually on me. Since I'd had such trouble resisting her advances myself, I hoped that she wouldn't then offer them to another.

So I headed to the Louvre at ten o'clock on 22nd August and, just as I was approaching the entrance, I saw the king, surrounded by his courtiers, leave the chapel of the Hôtel du Petit-Bourbon, where he'd gone, I supposed, to hear Mass. At the same moment, Admiral de Coligny, followed by several Protestant gentlemen, was leaving the Louvre, and, as the two groups met in the middle of the little square in front of the chateau—the one clad in brilliant colours, the other clothed all in black—their leaders greeted, embraced and congratulated each other with a degree of friendly effusion for which the king himself set the tone by calling Coligny "my father" and kissing him on both cheeks. After which the king took his arm, and I heard him invite the admiral to come and watch him play tennis at the Five Virgins, to which Coligny acquiesced out of pure civility, saying that he would attend "for a few moments", doubtless secretly believing that such games, balls, suppers and pantomimes as had succeeded each other since the wedding were excessively frivolous.

As for me, who'd never seen Coligny up so close—the king of the Huguenots being just as difficult of access as the king of France, though the former displayed no pomp whatsoever and was not accompanied by any escort—I observed him all the while with great curiosity and found him to be of a very serious disposition, with just a hint of inflexibility in his light-grey eyes, which struck me as very imposing. The strands of hair that protruded from his dark-red velvet cap were more white than brown, and his face was quite wrinkled, but his body was still robust, no doubt thanks to his frugal and austere nature. He was dressed in a black velvet doublet, and wore appended to a black ribbon round his neck the order of Saint-Michel, which he never removed. He wore a pair of old-fashioned baggy hose of the same colour, and slippers which seemed to fall off his feet too often, as happened at least twice that I observed, for he had to back up and tap his heel to get them back on—an activity that seemed very ill-matched to the dignity of such a great man, but one that was, as insignificant as it seemed, of great consequence in the terrible chain of events that were to lead to so much bloodshed.

Among the gentlemen accompanying Coligny, I spied Geoffroy de Caumont, lord of Castelnau and Milandes, my cousin on my mother's side, and came up to greet him. He appeared very glad to see me, embraced me warmly and presented me to the others of his company: to Téligny, whom I'd seen playing tennis; to the Comte de Montgomery, an old greybeard who'd fallen into disfavour at court after a splinter from his unfortunate lance caused the death of Henri II; to Monsieur de Ferrières, the Vidame de Chartres, without doubt the wisest of the Protestant leaders; to Monsieur de Briquemaut, who'd fought at Calais fourteen years earlier; to the Comte de La Rochefoucauld, still in the flower of his youth; and finally to Monsieur de La Force, a relative of Caumont, who was flanked by his two sons. Alas! Of all of these valiant lords, who seemed so self-assured that sunny August morning, how many were enjoying the penultimate day of their lives!

I followed along behind them as Coligny and the king continued to speak in the affectionate way I'd observed, and was just going into the Five Virgins tennis courts when I felt a tap on my shoulder. I spun around.

"*Mi fili*," Fogacer whispered, "I've come to take my leave of you, very sad that I will be deprived of the light of your beautiful visage. I'm quitting Paris."

"But where will you go?" I asked in surprise.

"Where? I know not," said Fogacer, arching his diabolical eyebrow, "though I've told the Duc d'Anjou I'll be visiting my aged mother in Provence, who, in fact, died when I was a child. I must depart like a leaf in the wind."

"What? With no destination?"

"Well, not quite," he said, lowering his voice even further. "On a stage on the Pont aux Meuniers yesterday I met a little acrobat who enchanted me with his thousand and one tricks, so gracious and cute he would have seduced St Jerome while he was meditating on death and the sins of the world. You know what mine is. *Trahit sua quemque voluptas.** The show is leaving tomorrow for the provinces and I'm going with them."

"Oh, Fogacer," I said, worried, "is this reasonable?"

"Is it reasonable to while away my days uselessly here when all I can do is dream of him?"

There was really nothing I could say, knowing all too well how powerful such dreams are, however different the object may be that inspires them.

---

* "To each his pleasure."

"Fogacer," I said simply, "I wish you all the happiness in the world."

He laughed, but I think his laughter was meant to hide his emotion, and he assured me, still laughing, that if he could pray, he would pray that I obtain a pardon from the king; then he gave me a strong, but very brief, almost furtive hug, and hurried away like a black insect, leaving me feeling very astonished that his absence should create such a void in me. I felt suddenly very alone there, with Samson in Montfort and Quéribus in Saint-Cloud. And while I stood there in a daze, as if nailed to the spot, someone seized me very familiarly by the arm, and I heard Maître Delay scolding me in his brazen Parisian way:

"Monsieur de Siorac! What are you doing hanging about out here, staring at the pigeons? The thing is arranged, just as I promised! The king has agreed to take you as his partner, on the assurance I gave him that with you he couldn't help winning—not just the match, but the 200 écus that Guise and Téligny have just bet on it. Hurry, my friend! The king is as impatient as a devil in a font!"

And indeed he was! He was so anxious to see me in shirtsleeves and ready to play, as he stood there jumping up and down, brandishing his racquet, that he hardly responded to my deep bow. Never in my life did my doublet come off faster than it did on that day, Delay grabbing it and thrusting a racquet into my hand.

"So now! Let's play!" shouted Charles IX ferociously. "By God, we'll grind them to powder, the both of them. And what's your name?"

"Pierre de Siorac, sire. I'm the younger son of the Baron de Mespech, in Périgord."

"Siorac," muttered the king, who entirely lacked in his manners and his speech the exquisite politeness of the Duc d'Anjou, "how's your backhand? Good enough?"

"Sire, that's what I've been told."

"Then play to Téligny's backhand, which is weak."

And so I followed his command with every shot I took—a relentlessness I would have found discourteous in a singles match—so effectively that we won the first set without allowing our adversaries to take a single game. Téligny failed to return a single one of my backhand shots and the duc himself played less well than he was accustomed to, seeming at times lost in his thoughts, and at other times looking around to see if he could spy Coligny, as if he were impatient to see him there. Meanwhile, the admiral was seated in the stands, as calm and composed as I'd heard was his usual manner, and civilly applauded the winning shots, though he privately considered this sport—and all the games and jousts he'd had to swallow since the 18th—entirely frivolous. But the king had proclaimed that he wanted to enjoy himself to the hilt as long as the festivities lasted, and refused to discuss any matters of state, no matter how urgent, until the gala was over.

At this point, the king cried out that he needed to change his shirt, which was drenched, given the incredible heat that had built up between the four walls of the pavilion, and the admiral rose and asked to take his leave and departed, surrounded by his gentlemen (and Guise seemed to me to be quite relieved to see him go). While the king was being vigorously rubbed down by his valet, Delay went up to him and said, with his usual bluntness:

"Sire, Monsieur de Siorac is seeking your pardon for having killed a gentleman in a loyal duel."

"Have I not proclaimed that all duels are to cease?" replied the king sullenly and with a grimace, yet with clear indifference.

"Sire," I dared to reply, "I was ambushed while returning to my home and the traitor, before provoking me, had hidden a coat of mail until his doublet."

"'Sblood!" cried the king, his face lighting up with interest. "So then how did you kill him?"

"With two inches of steel in his right eye."

"Two inches!" said the king approvingly, with a cruel light in his eyes. "Two inches! What a majestic blow! Siorac, you'll have my pardon!"

"Sire," broke in Delay, who knew the value of such promises, "why not sign it on the spot? Here's paper and pen. You can write on my valet's back."

"How tiresome you are, Delay!" snapped the king, who now had a fresh shirt on and was ready to recommence the game.

"Sire," insisted Delay, not the least bit discouraged, and doubtless knowing as well as the queen mother did how importunity could overcome the king's will. "Sire, you always say, 'Strike while the iron—'"

"Enough, Delay. Enough! I want to play!"

"Sire," Delay objected. "You're too good a blacksmith to fail to strike while the iron's hot."

"All right!" growled the king, defeated as much by Delay's insistence as by his cajolery. "My pen, dammit!"

And he scribbled my pardon on the back of the valet, to whom, as soon as he'd signed it, he delivered a big kick in the backside as if to get revenge for the violence he'd suffered. And when the poor lackey fell to the ground, Charles burst out laughing uproariously, and, his good humour restored, brandishing his racquet and leaping like an acrobat, he cried:

"Back to work, partner! By God, were going to grind them into powder! The 200 écus are mine!"

I didn't need to be coaxed! My pardon in my pocket, and without time to thank Delay, but beaming with pleasure at having finally obtained it after so long a wait and so many trials and tribulations at the court, I played like a madman, ready to deliver so many blows to the unfortunate Téligny that he wouldn't know where to hide! And I remember that after this he didn't score a single point; nor did Guise, who, ever since Coligny's departure, seemed so absent that you would have guessed that he wasn't even following the ball and that he was swinging at it blindly. At any rate, we quickly won four games in a row and would soon have made a clean sweep of it, but suddenly there was a great commotion at the door, and we saw Yolet, Coligny's valet, burst onto the court, panting, tears gushing from his eyes and so terrified that when he opened his mouth all he could do was shout "Oh, sire! Oh, sire" as he threw himself on his knees before the king.

"For the love of God," cried the king, "what's happened? How dare you interrupt the king when he's playing!"

"Oh, sire!" wept Yolet, who in his despair was tearing out his hair and scratching his cheeks. "There's been an attempt to kill the admiral!"

"What?" said Guise, stiffening. "An attempt?"

And to the end of my days I shall remember the immense disappointment in his voice when he said these words, "An attempt?" and the way he immediately fell silent, his body immobile, his face inscrutable and his eyes staring blankly at the ground.

"Ah!" said the king, open-mouthed. Looking at Yolet, Guise and the ball he was holding, he suddenly became childishly petulant, upset that his tennis game should have been interrupted, and, throwing down his racquet, he screamed:

"Won't they ever leave me in peace?"

And glaring bitterly at each one of us as though we'd been the cause of this interruption, he stormed off, his valet running after him, without ever thinking to enquire whether the admiral had been killed or only wounded. Finally, Téligny, shaking Yolet with both hands as he knelt there on the ground crying and moaning, asked about Coligny in a voice that was barely audible, whereupon Yolet answered:

"Wounded."

"Monsieur de Téligny," said Delay in the officious way he adopted as owner of the tennis court, "might I remind you that Monsieur de Siorac is a physician?"

At which, without another word, I threw on my doublet and followed Téligny, who was running at full speed up the rue des Fossés-Saint-Germain, across the rue de l'Arbre Sec, and finally reached the rue de Béthisy, where the admiral had rented a house that belonged to the Du Bourg family, descendants of a Huguenot martyr who'd been tortured to death by Henri II.

There was a great crowd of gentlemen of our party in front of the house, loudly expressing their indignation and fury at this attempt on Coligny's life—most of them from the south and speaking in *langue d'oc*—swearing to take their revenge on the assassins. Téligny had a very hard time attempting to get through this angry crowd, and I was stopped by one fellow, who furiously demanded who I was and what I wanted. When I explained that I was a doctor, he shouted at me: "The admiral doesn't want any papist doctors!"

"But," I explained, "I'm one of you!"

On which Téligny turned back to confirm this, so the fellow let go of me, but continued to grumble.

Still forging ahead, with me at his heels, Téligny rushed upstairs to the admiral's room on the first floor. Coligny, looking very pale, was seated in an armchair, holding his right arm up in the air, and you could see his right index finger had been badly slashed. His left arm had a bloody wound just above the elbow. I asked the people there if they would bring me some spirits as quickly as possible, along with some bandages, and, as I waited, someone else thrust a pair of scissors into my hand and I began cutting back his left sleeve, having removed my doublet so as not to stain it with all of this blood. Even though I went very slowly with my cutting, I couldn't help shaking his arm a bit, and with each movement the admiral blinked, but continued looking at me, his lips pressed firmly together with sweat flowing down his face, and said not a word.

I'd just finished cutting off the left sleeve when, to my immense relief, Ambroise Paré arrived, accompanied by Monsieur de Mazille, who was one of the king's physicians. Just as they entered, someone—I think it was Coligny's orderly, Cornaton—handed me the bandages and spirits. Ambroise Paré poured some of this into a goblet he'd appropriated and applied some to the wounded index finger, and some to the scissors.

"Monsieur," he said, "this is going to hurt."

"I shall be patient," said Coligny. And with his face pale and sweating but marvellously calm, he watched Ambroise Paré while the surgeon, working with this pair of bad scissors as adroitly as if he had the finest scalpel in his hand, removed the first two joints of the index finger. This done, he bandaged up what remained, while Madame de Téligny, on her knees in front of her father, sobbed miserably.

"And now for the arm!" said Coligny in a firm voice.

"What, Monsieur?" said Paré. "You want us to cut it off too?"

"Of course!"

"What do you think, Monsieur de Mazille?" Paré said.

"I think we should cut at the elbow," replied Mazille. "The wound is very extensive and the bones have been damaged."

"But wounds can heal and bones as well," said Paré, shaking his head. "The problem is the risk of infection. I see an entrance to the wound but no exit. So I believe the ball is inside. What's your opinion, Monsieur de Siorac?"

"That we should first try to extract the bullet," I concurred, very surprised that the famous surgeon would ask for my opinion. I added, "We shouldn't amputate so as to avoid infection and gangrene."

Monsieur de Mazille acquiesced without further arguing the point, so widely respected was Paré's experience and talent in the matter of bullet wounds—and this despite the fact that he wasn't a doctor, and had only recently been awarded a master's degree in medicine. Paré then asked if anyone there could recount the attempted murder so that he could get an idea of the trajectory of the bullet before making any attempt to extract it.

"I can," said Monsieur de Guerchy, who had only recently benefitted from the admiral's intervention in a dispute with Monsieur de Thiange.

"Speak, Guerchy," said the admiral, who was watching Madame de Téligny on her knees, sobbing, in front of him; he added in a gentle voice, "Madame, my daughter, why are you crying? Not even a passing sparrow dies except that God wills it, and isn't it marvellous that God judges me worthy of suffering for His faith?"

"Monsieur surgeon of the king," stammered Guerchy, who was crying hot tears, like everyone else who was there, and simply couldn't find his voice to continue.

So, calmly and firmly, and despite the fact that he was now pale as wax, the admiral repeated:

"Speak, Guerchy."

And so great was the authority of the admiral over his gentle-men—who venerated him as their guide sent by God to lead their side to victory—that these two words were enough to make Guerchy get a hold on himself and stop sobbing.

"I saw the attempt from very close," he reported in a firm voice. "I was walking on the admiral's right and, to show him my respect, was a little way behind him. Which was a mistake," he groaned, "since if I'd been right next to him I could have covered him with my body."

"Go on, Guerchy," urged Coligny.

"As he walked, the admiral was reading a letter, and one of his shoes kept slipping off his foot, so every once in a while he'd push it with his heel to make it go back on, taking a step backwards each time, and this movement saved his life, for the shot was fired from his right a few yards from a house that stands next to the cloister of Saint-Germain l'Auxerrois."

"From where was the shot fired?" said Paré.

"From a lattice window that was covered by a curtain. After the shot, we saw the smoke and rushed in, but found the room empty and the arquebus still hot, leaning up against the window."

"And where was the window?"

"On the first floor."

"So," deduced the surgeon, "the shot was fired from above and obliquely, since the assassin wouldn't have waited until the admiral presented his profile before shooting. The admiral had his two hands out in front of him to read his letter, and since he suddenly took a step backwards to adjust his shoes, the ball struck the index of his right hand and subsequently, lower down and obliquely, the base of the left forearm. So it is my opinion, taking account of the position of the wound, that the ball must be situated between the radius and the cubitus, just above the elbow."

I must confess that in the very teeth of the misfortune that was striking our leader, and devastated as I was, as much as the others, I heard this diagnosis with delight, the doctor in me carrying the day over the Huguenot. Not that I didn't understand the importance Ambroise Paré attached to the position of the body in his research on projectiles, having diligently read his famous treatise on arquebus wounds, wherein he wrote that, at the siege of Perpignan, when Marshal de Brissac was suffering from a ball lodged in his shoulder blade, only one of the doctors present thought of placing the patient in the position in which he'd received the wound, and could then infer the trajectory of the bullet, and, by palpation, discover it. I saw here another example of this marvellous method, which allowed him to make a very limited incision, sparing the wounded man great pain and loss of blood.

"Operate, Monsieur Paré," said Coligny through clenched teeth, but with the same heroic serenity he'd displayed thus far, doubtless derived in part from the faith he had that his present trials were divinely ordained and thus constituted a badge of honour. He later communicated this certainty to his minister, Merlin, who confirmed his idea—one that virtually all of those surrounding him here shared. I admired his faith, though I didn't share it, and was convinced that it was at the root of the admirable strength and constancy he displayed as he was dying.

"Monsieur," Paré explained, "I've sent my aide to fetch my surgical instruments, since I cannot operate with sufficient delicacy with these wretched scissors."

And scarcely had he said this before his aide arrived, panting like a pair of bellows, having dashed like a madman to the surgeon's lodgings in the rue de Béthisy and back.

Paré asked Captain de Monins to place himself behind the admiral and to hold him firmly by the shoulders; then he requested the orderly, Cornaton, to elevate his left arm, and ordered me to hold his left hand. He then palpated the place he'd indicated, and opened it with his scalpel with the help of a small clip, the tips of whose branches were shaped like spatulas. He got hold of the bullet, but had to make three tries before he could extract it completely, because it had so tightly lodged between the radius and cubitus. The admiral underwent all of this without a sound and without fainting, though his face was very pale and dripping with sweat. The bullet having been removed with marvellous dexterity, Ambroise Paré bandaged the wound, and the admiral, having solemnly thanked us, asked in a feeble voice that he be undressed and placed in his bed, which we did.

I'd observed that, before he bandaged the patient, Paré had spread some quicksilver ointment on the wound, which Monsieur de Mazille had handed him without saying a word. As soon as the admiral was comfortably established behind his bed curtains, I asked them in a whisper why they'd done this. They looked at each other for a moment in silence, and then Mazille whispered:

"It's an antidote. We have to assume that they poisoned the bullet."

As softly as he'd whispered this, Cornaton, the orderly, heard it, something that would have serious consequences, as we shall see. Not that Cornaton bore any malice whatsoever—quite the contrary. A young and very good-looking fellow, with black eyes and hair, an aquiline nose and beautiful mouth, he was a member of Coligny's elite corps, and had already distinguished himself for his bravery, his staunch Huguenot faith and his devotion to the admiral. Which is to say that he was quite reserved, much as Samson was, and, like my brother, disposed to a dove-like simplicity, something that was not without its perils.

As the admiral was now comfortably settled, Ambroise Paré told me that I could go to dine, and that he'd stay with Coligny until I returned. Of course, I acquiesced, realizing that my care and presence were now required even though I'd never been consulted as to my availability, so obvious was it to all of them that, being a Huguenot, I could not but devote my days and nights to my admiral. So in this, my Church—despite my lack of zeal—had engaged me more deeply than I would have wished.

As I went downstairs to the lower room, I found a much larger group gathered there than before, and their grief and anger ten times as vehement. As Gascons, which most of them were, they tended to exaggerate things and so they were engaged in making terrible threats, not only against the Guise family—a nest of vipers that should be completely exterminated—but against the court, the queen mother, Anjou, Alençon and even the king. Their behaviour terrified me since I didn't doubt that among this crowd mingled eyes and ears that belonged to the Medicis—a fear that later proved all too true.

Miroul was waiting for me outside, and as soon as we entered the rue des Fossés-Saint-Germain (since I'd decided to return to the Five Virgins to thank Maître Delay), he whispered urgently:

"Monsieur, this attempted murder has a very bad odour. You have your pardon in your pocket. Let's get out of this stinking city right now!"

"Ah, Miroul," I sighed, "I'd love to, but I cannot. I promised Ambroise Paré that I'd watch over the admiral, and how could I not fulfil this promise, since I'm a doctor?"

"Ah, Monsieur," he insisted, his eyes clouded with apprehension, "please remember, I beg you, that your father made you promise to follow my advice in dangerous situations. This is as dangerous as it gets! These Parisians have tasted blood and they're going to fall on us. All you have to do is walk the streets today to see how the papists confront and insult everyone they believe to be of the religion. Monsieur, we are caught in this web and completely exposed to our enemies. We must save ourselves while there's still time!"

"Without our horses, Miroul? And without Dame Gertrude's carriage, which is in Saint-Cloud, as you know."

"Monsieur, we can rent horses. We can be in Montfort in a day and from there we can head home."

"Well, Miroul," I said after a moment's thought, "I believe your advice is sound, but I cannot follow it. My honour forbids it."

To this my good Miroul had no answer, but looked extremely unhappy, and I could see that he was not worried about himself, but about protecting my life, for which he felt himself to be the sole guarantor.

As soon as he saw me appear at the tennis courts, Delay came over to meet me, and before I had the chance to thank him for what he'd done, he pulled me over to one side and asked anxiously about Coligny's condition. And, doubting whether his concern was entirely benevolent, I answered with extreme prudence, telling him that, while the wound was not in itself mortal, Coligny's advanced years made him extremely susceptible to gangrene, so he was not out of danger.

"Well," said Delay, in a whisper and as if he were distracted, but giving me a sharp look out of the corner of his eye, "it might have been better for him and his people if he'd been killed outright. Now his Huguenots are all buzzing and angry like a swarm of furious bees, and have been seditiously threatening the court, forgetting the respect they owe their princes. I wish to God," he added with a sly smile, "that they could be as careful as you, Monsieur de Siorac, who never speak unguardedly, display little of the zealotry of your party and even go to hear Mass, from what I've heard."

"Well, Maître Delay!" I laughed to hide my confusion. "What a nice drop shot and how beautifully you placed the ball! I was crazy to think that you wouldn't know which side I was on, you, who know everything."

"I knew it the first time I saw you," confessed Delay with immense pride, "not so much from your comportment, but from your brother's, who's way too rigid, though he's as beautiful as an angel. And Monsieur de Nançay told me the rest."

"And yet," I observed, "however little you sympathize with my side, you've nevertheless rendered me an enormous favour."

He looked at me in silence for a moment, which surprised me in someone who was as loquacious as a roaring river, and then said gravely:

"I love your humanity, Monsieur de Siorac. I love the way that, despite your noble status, you don't treat a commoner like me with disdain. And I am impressed that you studied to become a doctor, nobleman that you are."

"Well," I laughed, "I inherited from my father the belief that it's study that makes a man, not birth."

"Well said! Well said!" smiled Delay, whom my aphorism had pleased enormously. "It's by study and hard work that I was able to manufacture the best tennis balls in Christendom, and to create the finest tennis courts in Paris, which our princes love to frequent."

Delay's pride in the Five Virgins made him swell up like a chickpea that's been stewing for a week. And yet, as vainglorious as he was, I liked him well enough, preferring him and his kind, and the zeal that they devoted to their business, to the gallant lords who strutted around the Louvre, wasting on vain superfluities the money that their people sweated to produce back in their provinces.

Furthermore, I couldn't help noticing that having made me beholden to him for the favour he'd done increased his affection for me, and so, since he believed I was less calculating than he, I decided to take his pulse to see how high this fever had risen that I could feel mounting around me.

"So, Delay," I whispered, looking about me nervously, "help me understand something. Did the king of Paris do this thing all by himself?"

"He never would have dared do it alone," replied Delay, casting in his turn a look about us. "More important men than he, including Charles, had a hand in it. And you can't expect them to let it go at this. If necessary, they'll go much further."

"But when the king learnt of the attempt during our game, he seemed genuinely angry."

"He's angry today," replied Delay, who, after having hesitated a little, took my arm and, whispering into my ear, added, "A child can wind up his top and spin it from left to right, but it can also be set spinning in the other direction by a different hand. Monsieur de Siorac, are you leaving today for the provinces?"

"Alas! I cannot. Ambroise Paré committed me to help him take care of the patient."

"This is most unfortunate," said Delay, giving me a brief but meaningful look. "I predict this story is going to turn out badly, after having read the preface."

And at this, having said enough, or perhaps more than he'd wanted to or judged prudent, he took his leave of me, though not before I thanked him profusely for having obtained my pardon. But this compliment caused him to change his expression completely, and he listened to my thanks with a frigid expression, as if to let me know that, since things were taking the turn he'd intimated, he wouldn't be able to offer me his good offices again, should I need them.

Miroul and I went off to dinner in the rue de la Truanderie at Guillaume Gautier's tavern, and there we met Giacomi, who'd been waiting for us for a full hour, unable to take a bite he was so frightfully worried about our safety. When he caught sight of me, he reddened with pleasure and embraced me tightly, posing a hundred questions, which I answered in whispers by recounting the events we'd just experienced, including my discussions with Miroul and Maître Delay.

Giacomi agreed that I couldn't honourably abandon the patient who'd been placed in my care, but that this was a most grievous turn of events, given how much the danger was increasing hourly. He told us that, as he'd walked through the streets, he'd seen groups of men confronting Huguenots or anyone they took to be of the religion, and that some were shouting, "To the cause! To Madame la Cause!"—injurious words by which the people designated our Church; he added that, because he was dressed in black, he himself had been stopped by a dozen ruffians, who would have torn him to pieces had it not been for his Italian accent, Italy being known to the Parisians for having crushed the embryo of heretical reformism while it was still in its shell. In short, everywhere he went he saw nasty looks, hushed conversations, comings and goings, the bourgeoisie armed to the teeth, bloodthirsty threats—all of which were signs of a growing wave of violent feelings we were sure to be prey to. For a moment, all we could do was look at each other in silence, thinking about what awaited us.

Despite the delicious fare our dinner was an exceedingly sad affair and none of us had much appetite. Giacomi insisted on accompanying me back to the rue de Béthisy, where the admiral lived, and during our lengthy walk there, we could see the increasing agitation and aggression of the Parisians. Their growing rumble of angry voices brought to mind an anthill that a hunter has just accidentally decapitated.

When I reached Coligny's bedside, I was told that he was sleeping, so I went downstairs to the great hall, where an ever-increasing number of Huguenots had gathered to express their outrage. Needing some time to reflect on the dark cloud that was rapidly forming over our heads, I stepped outside onto the little square in front of the house. Pacing up and down, I consulted my watch and discovered it was just two o'clock, and, remembered that Ambroise Paré had promised to return during the afternoon to relieve me, and so I watched anxiously for any sign of him. In the midst of my reflections, I heard a loud noise coming from the rue des Fossés-Saint-Germain and saw a detachment of the king's guards emerge from that street into the rue de Béthisy, wearing white ceremonial jerseys, known as gambesons, decorated with silver frills. They were preceded by trumpeters, walking in closed ranks and sounding their instruments at full blast to announce the king. On all sides, windows were thrown open, despite the August heat, and the occupants leant out to watch, but no one came out into the street because of their fear of the guards. In the middle of the procession, flanked by two guards who never left his side, marched the king—tall, thin and bent, his face so drawn by worry that he seemed twice as old as his years. Following him came the queen mother, all in black but resplendent in her pearls and glittering jewellery, looking younger than her son. On her right marched the Duc d'Anjou, his handsome, pale face looking especially inscrutable, and on her left came the Duc d'Alençon, her third son, who looked like the runt of the litter, and whose face wore a false, mean and fearful look that did him no honour.

The guards lined up in double rows in front of the admiral's house, and the king walked up, graciously greeting the gentlemen gathered there. They answered his greeting, bowing respectfully enough in response, but took no more notice of the queen mother and her two other sons than a fish would an apple. It was clear that, if they suspected that the king had had no hand in this murderous attack, as his visit to the wounded man was meant to prove, they could not be assured of the same degree of innocence for Catherine and the Duc d'Anjou. These last were known to mightily detest the Huguenot leader, the queen mother because he wanted to steal the authority she held over her son and Anjou because Coligny, fearing his power, had attempted to have him effectively banished by making him king of Poland.

Once upstairs, the king asked if there were a doctor present, so I stepped forward, explaining that I was filling in for Mazille and Paré and that the wounded man was resting, but could receive him if he wished, but only for a moment. The king stepped up to the bed curtains, which one of his guards raised so he could see the admiral, and Coligny, hearing their approach, opened his eyes.

"Ah, my father!" said the king (for this is indeed what he called him). "I'm very sorry to see you wounded and brought so low."

"'Tis true, sire," replied the admiral, who appeared to be quite comforted by the honour bestowed on him by this royal visit, "but the only affliction I feel is that I am prevented by my wound from showing my king how much I desire to do him service."

"You will recover, my father," the king assured him. "And by God, I tell you, I'll bring your enemies to justice. In the house from which they fired on you, we found an old woman and a lackey, who've been thrown in jail and will be tortured. Do you approve of the judges I've named to investigate this case?"

"Of course, sire," said the admiral, "if you believe in them. Only, I beg you to add one of your masters, Cavagnes, to the list."

"It will be done," said the king.

463

"Sire," whispered the admiral, signalling to me to withdraw, "I would like you to remember…"

But I didn't hear the rest, and as I turned away, I caught Anjou's eye and decided to greet him, along with the queen mother and his brother. This was not easy, since they were surrounded—almost imprisoned—by a wall of Huguenot gentlemen, who, grumbling and complaining audibly, walked back and forth around them, clearly refusing to pay them the respect they were owed. Albert de Gondi, Catherine's confidant, who normally looked so sly and disdainful, was visibly shaken by this demonstration. I could see the Duc d'Alençon's lips trembling and that he was rolling his eyes wildly like a rabbit. Catherine and the Duc d'Anjou put on better faces, but I could see that they, too, were looking very pale and that Catherine was pouting furiously. It was easy to see that they would have preferred to be a thousand leagues from there.

Just as I was bowing to the queen mother and to Anjou and Alençon, I was joined by Monsieur de Mazille and the orderly Cornaton. The queen mother appeared very relieved to have finally encountered in this den of Huguenots people who would treat her with respect, and asked Mazille if Paré had extracted the bullet, to which Mazille replied that he had, and she was shown the ball, which was made of copper.

Turning it over and over in her fingers, which were adorned with rings set with the finest jewels in the world, the queen said, with visibly false concern:

"It's very large! Did the admiral suffer much when it was extracted?"

"Very much," answered Mazille, "but he neither groaned nor fainted."

"Yes, I can well imagine!" replied Catherine. "I know of no man in the world more magnanimous than Monsieur de Coligny."

Such praise brought Mazille and me up short, so surprised were we to hear such hypocritical flattery directed at this man from those fleshy lips.

"I'm very glad," Catherine continued, looking at us with those protuberant eyes that didn't really see us, "that the bullet didn't remain lodged in the wound, since it may have been poisoned."

I was dumbfounded by these sinister words, since pubic opinion had so frequently associated Catherine with the word poison, especially after the deaths of Coligny's two brothers, Odet de Châtillon and d'Andelot, not to mention Jeanne d'Albret, queen of Navarre, who'd died so suddenly and mysteriously at the Louvre after having signed the marriage contract between Henri and Margot. Coligny himself had nearly been assassinated two years previously by means of a white powder the would-be assassin had almost succeeded in administering to him. Monsieur de Mazille, though a papist, was an honest man and was as shocked and ashamed by Catherine's impudent words as I, and, lowering his eyes, said nothing. And those words would have been left hanging awkwardly in the air had not Cornaton, obsequious as ever, cried in his dove-like simplicity:

"Ah, Madame! But we were on the lookout for that! We treated the wound with an elixir to combat the poison, in case the bullet had been coated with it!"

The queen mother visibly bit her lip at this news, and her heavy eyelids closed over her eyes for a moment. I wanted to kill poor Cornaton for his stupid indiscretion, certain as I was that it was not in the admiral's interest for his enemies to believe he was out of danger—in which case, God only knew, there'd be a second attempt on his life by the very people who had inflicted the first.

At this, Albert de Gondi (a Florentine himself, who'd been assigned to Charles IX in his youth and had wholly corrupted him), looked knowingly at the queen mother and, understanding better than anyone else what she was plotting (having so long been her confidant), said in very suave tones, his sly eyes shining:

"It's my opinion, Madame, that it would be better to transport the admiral to the Louvre where the king can at least protect him from popular sentiment, given how inflamed the Parisians have become against him."

"Nay, Madame," Monsieur de Mazille interjected immediately, perhaps because he understood what Gondi was up to, or perhaps because he was simply speaking his conscience as a good doctor, "we mustn't consider it! It would be extremely dangerous to move the admiral now, and expose him to the contagion of the air."

The queen mother, who had, for several minutes already, been growing increasingly anxious at the private conversation that was taking place between the king and the admiral behind his bed curtains, said that she wished to ask Coligny herself, and approached the bed, making a sign to the guards to raise the curtains; but, truth to tell, I got there first, and was happily surprised to see the admiral looking much better than I feared, given his age, the blow he'd received, the terrible pain he'd endured from the amputation of his finger and the operation on his elbow. Such was the enormous influence his powerful soul exercised over his body.

As I reached Coligny's bedside, preceding the queen mother, ostensibly to open a path for her through the press of gentlemen in the room, I heard the admiral warn the king about "the deadly designs of certain people" (he meant the Guise family) "against his person and his crown"—a sentence he interrupted as soon as he saw the queen mother, suspecting, no doubt, that she would not soon be warning her son about this threat.

It seemed to me that the admiral spoke to the queen mother with some stiffness, as if he suspected her of not being as afflicted as she wished to appear. In any case, he declined absolutely to be transported to the Louvre—though the king begged him to reconsider—arguing that here he was very well looked after by the king's doctors and surgeons, for which he thanked His Majesty most profusely. When the king answered that he would punish the perpetrators of this cowardly attack, the queen mother went further, proclaiming that the attack did not merely affect the admiral but was "a great outrage against the king", and:

"If today we tolerate this, tomorrow, they'll be bold enough to strike inside the Louvre itself." To which she added with great conviction: "Although I'm only a woman, I believe we should put an end to this!"

The admiral thanked her for these sentiments, but, deeply honest man that he was, and wholly unaccustomed to pretence, his expression of gratitude had a very icy feel to it. Of course it's true that the queen mother had laid it on a bit thick, and that it was very difficult to be taken in by such honeyed words that so reeked of hypocrisy.

The king and royal family had scarcely departed the admiral's lodgings, preceded and followed by their cadre of guards and trumpets, before the Prince de Condé and Henri, king of Navarre arrived. However, Coligny, overcome with fatigue from the previous visit, had drifted off to sleep, and Mazille refused to let them see him, especially since he was now trembling somewhat with fever from his wound, and they had just administered some theriacal water to calm the effects of the poison.

As a consequence, the princes came back downstairs to the large hall and sequestered themselves in Cornaton's room, where they held *ex abrupto* a council of war among the principal Protestant leaders. I recognized among this group Geoffroy de Caumont, La Force and his two sons, the Comte de La Rochefoucauld, Montgomery, Briquemaut, Guerchy and Ferrières, whose clear and incisive mind greatly impressed me as soon as he began to speak.

"I believe," he began in a loud and grave voice, which astonished me since he seemed so small and frail, "that the attempt on the admiral's

467

life is the first act in a tragedy, which, from all appearances, will end with the mass murder of all his followers. Ever since the wedding of Navarre, we've been getting information from all sides that is so clear and so manifest that all you have to do is open your eyes and ears to see it. 'This marriage,' said one of the most important people in the country scarcely a week ago, 'will cause much more blood to flow than wine.' And I have it on good authority that a president of the parliament advised a Protestant gentleman to quit Paris with his family and withdraw for the present to his house in the country. Moreover, Monsieur de La Rochefoucauld can tell you the warning he received from Monsieur de Monluc before his departure for Poland."

"What did he tell you, Foucauld?" asked Navarre, who'd been listening with great interest to Monsieur de Ferrières.

"Well," said La Rochefoucauld, "I remember only too well what Monluc whispered to me: 'No matter what caresses the court lavishes on you, be careful not to fall for them. Too much confidence will cast you into great peril. Flee while it's still possible.'"

"All we have to do is look around us," continued Jean de Ferrières, "and what do we see? Paris is armed to the teeth, and if the populace falls on us, we'll be outnumbered a hundred to one, with chains blocking all the bridges, the city gates locked tight and the public squares occupied by the bourgeois militias."

"So what do you conclude, Ferrières?" asked Condé.

"That we must escape from this trap!" replied Monsieur de Ferrières with great vehemence. "Without another moment's delay! We must put Coligny on a litter, get on our horses, swords in hand, and get out of Paris!"

"Move the admiral?" cried Téligny. "It's unthinkable! Monsieur de Mazille, who can't join us in here because he's a papist, believes that it's very dangerous to move the patient and expose him to the contagion of the air!"

"The admiral has seen worse than this," argued Monsieur de Guerchy. "After Moncontour, he ordered the entire retreat from his litter, since he'd been wounded in the cheek by a pistol shot."

"The wound wasn't so serious," countered Téligny.

"Well!" I broke in. "I've never seen a face wound that wasn't serious!"

My intervention reminded the lords present that I was a doctor, and one of them said, "And what do you think, Monsieur de Siorac, of this idea of transporting the admiral?"

"That it's dangerous and uncomfortable, to be sure, but that it's a risk worth taking if there's greater danger in staying here."

"But wait!" cried Téligny with some heat. "Who can believe the admiral is in danger when you see what great favour he enjoys with the king, who condescended to come and visit him in his lodgings?"

"I'm not a very suspicious man by nature," said my cousin, Caumont, "but I found something very sinister in this display of courtesy. The entire scene had a false ring to it. And I remember all too well what a pleasant face François de Guise put on with my older brother only two hours before he had him killed."

"Come now, Caumont," countered Téligny, "the king is not Guise. I know his heart far too well."

Téligny's naivety made everyone in the room uneasy, not just because of his manifest simplicity, but because no one dared to contradict him, at least in public, except by silence. And what a long and uncomfortable silence followed, in which the only thing that mattered was precisely what was not said.

"I nevertheless believe that we should all flee without delay," said Jean de Ferrières finally in a low but firm voice.

I could see that all of those present were inclined to agree with this, with the exception, alas, of the most important among them: the admiral's son-in-law and the two royal princes, Condé and

Navarre—especially Navarre, who, as the king's brother-in-law would need to be very careful, which he didn't fail to demonstrate.

"Leaving Paris," he said with his Béarnaise accent, which lent such a mellifluous sound to his every word that they sounded like waves lapping at pebbles on a beach, "would not be easy for the admiral. If he asked the king's leave to do so, he wouldn't obtain it. But if he didn't ask, he would insult the king, and we'd have to fear the consequences both for the admiral and for the possibility of peace."

"And, of course, for Navarre himself," I thought to myself. If the Huguenots disobeyed the king, his position at court, where he was practically a hostage, would be very uncomfortable at best.

Both because of Navarre's position in the kingdom and because of his own reputation, his opinion had a considerable effect on those present, though it failed to persuade them entirely, given the way the rock that was threatening our lives seemed to shake and sway uncertainly right over our heads.

"Well then," proposed Téligny, "why don't we go and ask for the admiral's opinion rather than continue to argue? Isn't he still our leader?"

At this, Jean de Ferrières threw his arms up in frustration, given how convinced he was that the admiral, in his inflexible and heroic firmness, would decide against leaving, since he lacked in political acumen the enviable flexibility he'd always displayed in war, where he was never so great as when, after an apparent defeat, he would slip away from the enemy only to return to sting him quickly and flee again.

"But the admiral is asleep," observed Guerchy, "and Mazille did not even allow the royal princes to disturb him."

"Let's send Monsieur de Siorac to talk to him," suggested Téligny. "Since he's a doctor, he'll know whether he can ask him the question we've been debating without tiring him too much."

I agreed immediately, left the room and went up to the first floor to ask Monsieur de Mazille if I could speak to the patient.

"He's not as poorly as we'd believed," said Mazille. "He is by nature so robust and so firm in his resolve that it's a marvel to watch him struggle against his infirmity."

"Is he sleeping?"

"No. He's lying there with his eyes open, doubtless planning great things."

This moved me more than I can say. Monsieur de Mazille, papist that he was, was honest enough to understand that Coligny was not a man who thought only about himself, but one who, quite the contrary, considered only the interests of the people.

Stepping over to his bedside, I gently lifted the curtain and the admiral looked at me with eyes that, even in the shadows of the bed, seemed to me as clear and luminous as ever. I told him what we'd been debating in Cornaton's chambers downstairs.

He responded immediately in a muffled voice as though musing to himself, "Ah! What about my war in Flanders? Can I abandon it?" Certainly, he could claim it as *his* war! For no one else at court had any appetite for it, except, fitfully, the king, who at one moment was persuaded to it by Coligny, and the next moment was convinced by the queen mother to abandon it.

Assuredly, it was a serious and grand project to redirect all the rebellious feeling of the Huguenots towards an external conflict—lining them up side by side with the papists—instead of allowing them to continue cutting each other's throats. But on the other hand, wasn't it an empty dream to attempt to persuade the court to take up arms against Felipe II of Spain (the most solid rampart of the papacy) to protect the Protestant farmers of Flanders? And wasn't it even more unrealistic to believe that one could separate this weak and flighty king from his mother, to whose skirts he'd been attached since childhood, both by her and by the counsellors with whom she'd surrounded him?

Coligny continued to lie their silently, and I understood completely that, for him, leaving Paris meant confronting the king, thereby losing his favour and forever forgoing his greatest plan: to reconcile the subjects of the kingdom in a war that would bring down Felipe II. But I nevertheless impressed on him the dangers that were accumulating over our heads, the trap that was now set for us in this great city whose jaws were already closing on us, and the possibility that we could lose everything—not just our cause, but our very lives—if we remained here. What a temptation for our enemies! All of our leaders found themselves conveniently imprisoned within the walls of the capital and could be taken by surprise without any serious resistance, and slaughtered.

"I'm well aware of all that you say," Coligny replied. "Let everyone leave who wishes to ensure his safety. As for me, I'm ready to leave this life. I've lived long enough."

Looking at him, I realized that a man should never consent in advance to his own death, whether because of setbacks or sickness. At length, he added, to emphasize his repugnance at the solution that Monsieur de Ferrières was proposing:

"My friend, I cannot leave Paris without reigniting the civil war, and I'd rather die than do that. But I am certain of one thing: I will not be betrayed. I have confidence in my king."

Noble words, assuredly, but ones in which I found—God forgive me!—a grain of absurdity, since it was obvious to anyone with a head for politics that the murder of the admiral and his cohort would not extinguish the civil war but, on the contrary, provide a new match with which to ignite it and cause the kingdom to burn like a bonfire in its flames. And as for Charles, how could a man of Admiral de Coligny's honesty and character possibly understand the complexion of this wriggling earthworm?

I understood, as I returned to deliver his message to the council being held downstairs, that this man of religion sought comfort in a quasi-religious faith in the word of the king. The crown concealed the man, who was so childish, inconstant and unstable that you could no more place your trust in him than you could in quicksand. He was a top, as Delay had said, a mere form of a man without content or will; he was an empty goblet that could equally well be filled with any wine—the best or the worst, or a weathercock spinning this way and that, according to the direction the wind was blowing.

Monsieur de Ferrières and the others who shared his views, even if they dared not say so out loud, were extremely disappointed by Coligny's decision, even though they expected it, knowing him as well as they did. And yet, even though the admiral had given them leave to quit Paris, I could see that they were ashamed to choose this option, so strong were their scruples about abandoning their leader in the middle of these perils to assure their own safety. As for Monsieur de Téligny, whose advice had been accepted, he had little cause for joy, since, no matter what we'd chosen, things looked exceedingly dark and stormy. I also noticed that Navarre, who now took his leave, agreed with the decision, though he had little to fear, being the brother-in-law of the king and under the protection of Margot, despite her little regard for him. In short, we dispersed without having resolved anything, except to remain in the capital.

The next morning, which was Saturday, 23rd August, I was very surprised, as I came downstairs from my tiny room, to see that the atelier was empty and that the heavy oak shutters hadn't been taken down from the windows. There was no trace of Alizon, Baragran or Coquillon. In attempting to leave the house, I found the door bolted and barred. With Miroul at my heels, we headed over to Maître Recroche's wing of the house and found him in his kitchen, sitting down, not to enjoy a meal, but instead with several weapons, which he was polishing with an old rag.

"Good day, Maître Recroche," I greeted him. "What's this? Are the helmet and halberd yours? Are you leaving for war?"

"No," he growled. He refused to rise to greet us or look us in the eye, but stared straight ahead, although he kept us in the corner of his right eye, like a vulture. "No," he repeated, "but you have to polish things up when they get dirty."

"And how does it happen," I asked, doubting as I did the veracity of his explanation, "that you're not working today?"

"Don't you know?" he snarled coldly. "Tomorrow is St Bartholomew's day, and when a saint's day falls on a Sunday, we get the day before off."

"Yes, you have the afternoon off," I agreed, "but not the morning, if I'm to believe what Alizon told me."

"Alizon is a silly idiot," shot back Recroche, "who talks too much about what she doesn't know. She's the most unpleasant wench in creation."

"Ah, but she must be a good worker, Maître Recroche," I parried, "otherwise you wouldn't employ her. Are these weapons yours?"

"Most assuredly so!" said Recroche proudly. "I'm a Parisian bourgeois," he said with as much vanity as if he were announcing that he was a duc, "and every bourgeois in Paris must be armed and ready to defend his city and his king against his enemies."

"Ah, so you believe that your city and your king are going to be attacked?" I said, feigning surprise.

"They already have been," he said curtly, alluding, I surmised, to the siege of Paris by our party five years previously.

After this, he said no more, but, studiously ignoring my presence in his kitchen, began to whistle and returned to his polishing. I was flabbergasted by his impertinence, even given how used I'd become to his usual incivility. The Parisians, when their backs are up, can be so disdainful of the aristocracy, especially if they're from the provinces.

"Maître Recroche," I said archly but remaining calm, "I request that you open the door of the atelier so that I can remove my belongings."

"Nay, not so fast!" countered Recroche. "You must pay me for the water you've used."

"Now?" I said. "But I'm not leaving today."

"How do you know?" grinned Recroche with the utmost insolence. "Sometimes a man leaves sooner than he wants to. What's more, I need my two rooms vacated by noon tomorrow."

"What?" I cried. "You rented them to us for the month!"

"I changed my mind," said Recroche stiffly.

"Thief!" shouted Miroul, grabbing his halberd. "Do I need to run the handle of my spoon through your ribs to teach you to be civil with my master?"

At this, Maître Recroche rose to his feet, very pale, and, his hands trembling at the end of his long arms, suddenly changed his tune and said:

"I meant no offence, Monsieur. I'm only requesting my due."

"Your due!" I cried. "I paid you 180 écus for these two tiny rooms!"

"Whether you remain till the end of the month or not," he said, his eyes icy, "you must remember our little agreements."

"Certainly," I said, "if we'd left willingly. But it's just the opposite."

"Monsieur," said Recroche, little by little regaining his colour, as Miroul lowered the halberd, "do you really want to go to court for thirty sols that you owe me? Isn't that a lot of bother for a man in your predicament? You have the king's pardon in your pocket. Why don't you take your rings and packages, including your Bible, and get out of here while you can? I will be in grave danger of being killed and pillaged if you remain here."

"Well," I thought as I looked him in the eye, "my goodness! My Bible! The man knows who and what I am and now he wants to squeeze thirty sols out of me before throwing me out in the street and slamming the door behind me. He must feel pretty certain that Paris has turned against us and that everywhere people are polishing their weapons to cut our throats today! Otherwise he never would have treated me with such scorn." If I were bloodthirsty enough I would have laid the scoundrel out at my feet, but given my father and my upbringing at Mespech I drank too deeply of the milk of human kindness to desire the death of a man, even such a wicked one as this, except when in mortal danger myself.

"Monsieur," I said calmly and coldly, throwing thirty sols on the table, "here's your money. Open the doors. We'll be gone tomorrow."

Recroche was very happy to pocket my money, and breathed a sigh of relief when Miroul placed the halberd on the table; and, taking his keys from a chain on his belt, he went to unbolt and unbar the door, just as Giacomi, whom I hadn't wanted to waken, came downstairs and accompanied us into the street, intending to head to the Louvre.

Having agreed to meet the *maestro* at noon at Guillaume Gautier's tavern, I took my leave of him and set off to see Alizon in her tiny lodgings in the rue Tirechappe. As we walked through the streets, my good Miroul on my left, I noticed that, though it was a Saturday morning, all the shops were closed, their oak shutters firmly in place. I couldn't help imagining that all the shopkeepers behind these locked and bolted doors were, like Maître Recroche, ferociously polishing their armour and weapons, in anticipation of a murderous attack on the Huguenots and the juicy pillaging of their goods, their jewels, their clothes and their horses, for many of our party had not come to the royal marriage without their finery and accoutrements, wishing thereby to honour the king and display their rank and status to all. "Ah," I thought, "what a godsend, when pillaging and murder become—thanks to the papist preachers—shining badges guaranteeing one's entry into heaven!"

"Monsieur," observed Miroul, who'd been watching my eyes and guessed my thoughts, "it looks like everything is being readied for the slaughter! We have to sound the retreat! It would be madness and pure stupidity to remain here with the entire city at our heels!"

"Miroul," I answered quietly, "Ambroise Paré is counting on me to watch over the admiral tonight. But tomorrow at daybreak, we'll shake the dust from our shoes onto this atrocious city!"

"Tomorrow!" said Miroul, his eyes full of fear. "Tomorrow? Put off our departure till tomorrow? When I can see the storm so near!"

But we'd arrived, and I told him to wait outside while I went up to see Alizon, who, when she saw me, threw her arms around my neck with a little cry, closing the door behind me with a kick, and kissed my face repeatedly, pressing me to her. I felt so comforted by her feminine sweetness in the misfortune I was facing! After we'd taken our pleasure in each other, I recounted my conversation with Maître Recroche.

"Me, talk about what I don't know? That's a lie! On the eve of a saint's day that falls on a Sunday, we get the afternoon off, not the morning. If the merchants refused to open their shops at dawn this morning it's because they fear a popular uprising and the looting that always follows it. Which is why the miser Recroche kicked you out on the street: he believes you're heretics and fears they'll murder you in his house and then loot the place, taking his things with yours."

"My sweet," I said, frowning, "do you believe the uprising is going to break out today?"

"Who doesn't think so?" she answered. Then, leaning on her elbow, the better to look at me in a mixture of tenderness and derision, she continued in her brisk and abrupt Parisian accent, "Oh, Pierre, I'm amazed at your simplicity! You may be a nobleman and a venerable doctor, but you don't understand this city. Here, at the slightest provocation, the paving stones jump out of the streets by themselves, given how rebellious and mutinous the Parisians are whenever anyone tries to make them eat soup they don't like. Now, listen to me! This is not a breeze, it's a tempest. Our good priests have been telling us since yesterday: these heretic dogs want to take out their revenge for Coligny's wounds on the house of Guise, whom we love and venerate because he, and he alone, is the only sure bastion of Christendom. And this is why everyone in the city is preparing to arm themselves to defend Guise and chase down these demons! Blessed Virgin! When the clock strikes one, we're going to crush this vermin!"

"What? Even the peaceable workers and inhabitants of the city?"

"Them too! They're vipers, even if all they do is walk down the streets with their noses in their coats."

"What, your neighbours as well?"

"Our neighbours?" she cried, shuddering as if to shake them off her like fleas. "Who would want such vipers for neighbours? Do you know, Pierre, I just saw something that made me very happy. About six o'clock, as I was running through the streets looking for my milk vendor, I saw the coal vendor marking with a white cross the doors of certain houses in the rue Tirechappe where these fiends live. The *dizeniers* were reading the numbers from a piece of paper."

"*Dizeniers?*" I asked to hide my terror. "What's that? What sort of jargon is that?"

"Silly boy!" she laughed as if it were a wonderful jest. "Don't you have them in the provinces? They're the officers of the city. The *quarteniers* command the *quartiers*, the districts—of which there are sixteen in Paris. Each *quartier* is divided into ten *dizaines*, whose commanders are called *dizeniers*, and in each *dizaine* there are fifty streets and alleyways, each one commanded by a *cinquantenier*. In this way we have our leaders who will call us together and give orders when we take up arms."

"And all this without orders from the king?"

"Well," said Alizon, smiling slyly, "this time we'll have to do without him, if this little shit of a kinglet insists on supporting the admiral."

I felt such alarm at hearing this that, fearing that it might show on my face, I began laughing to hide my terror.

"My sweet, if this is the situation, how does it happen that Maître Recroche has become so valiant as to be taking up arms with the rest?"

"Valiant? That little hypocrite?" Alizon hissed with an air of profound contempt. "He's only getting ready for the looting! He was never seen during the siege when there was fighting to do! And you can be sure of this, my Pierre: if there's a general uprising today or tomorrow, he'll fill his pockets and won't strike a blow! Except against the women and children of these Huguenot dogs."

"What?" I cried, shaken by what I'd just heard. And getting up from the bed, my face so contorted with disgust that I could hardly speak (and my throat so constricted it hurt), I stammered, "Alizon, I can't believe you're saying this. Women? Children? Are they going to be massacred as well? Is that not infamous and pitiless?"

"I would have thought so, too," she admitted, not without some shame, "but the good priest Maillard said no, and that it would be cruel under the circumstances not to be inhuman, because God Himself has commanded us to wipe this wicked brood from the face of the earth once and for all, bitches and puppies along with them."

"Oh, Alizon!" I burst out, giving full vent to my indignation. "These bitches are women like you, and their puppies, as you call them, are just like your little Henriot, except that he happens to be a Catholic by accident of birth and the other little infants happen, by another accident of birth, to be Huguenots. If they have to be murdered on that account, then the Bible is wrong and Herod was right to commit the massacre of the innocents!"

"But Pierre," Alizon cried, clearly very upset to have ignited such an outburst of anger and chagrin over something she doubtless repeated daily with all her neighbours without ever thinking about it, "if we don't kill them, they'll kill us!"

"Really? How could they, you silly goose, when there are so few of them? And when the king is against them and all the king's regiments? And the great majority of the people?"

"But that's exactly what they're doing to our children in the provinces! They kill them when they're the stronger party!"

"Oh, Alizon," I sighed, "maybe a ferocious animal like the Baron des Adrets could commit such horrors, but I don't believe they were very widespread, given what I witnessed at the Michelade in Nîmes; and though they cruelly shed a lot of Catholic blood, they at least spared the women and children!"

"What?" hissed Alizon indignantly. "You're not defending these wicked heretics now, are you Pierre?"

"I have very good reasons for doing so!" I cried, my anger becoming suddenly so intense that I completely lost control of myself. "I've hidden this from you till now, Alizon, so as not to interfere with your zeal, but, if you must know, I am one of these dogs you've been talking about, and you must have suspected as much, given how dog-like I've behaved with you and your little Henriot. You should know that my mother raised me as a Catholic until I was ten but that my father ordered me to convert to his faith or be banished for ever from his house. So this is why I must now appear to you to be a heretical dog, a demon from hell, a viper, butcher's meat, and I don't know what else!"

"Ah, Pierre," she cried, "don't shout so loud! The walls have ears, and if anyone heard you, you'd be immediately torn to pieces by the neighbours!"

"Why don't you do it yourself?" I rasped hoarsely, now completely beside myself with grief and anger, and, pulling my dagger, I offered it to her. "What are you waiting for? It'll just be one less heretical dog and you'd go straight to heaven for this single blow without passing through Purgatory, like your priest Maillard told you in his sermon!"

But she backed away from the knife, step by step, speechless, her black eyes practically popping out of their sockets, so great was her terror, so I resheathed my weapon, turned on my heels and, without a word of adieu or a look behind me, left her, so drunk with rage and grief that I could scarcely see the stairs as I stumbled down them like a madman. Emerging onto the rue de Tirechappe, I walked so quickly in my despair—the surrounding world having become black as ink to my grief-stricken eyes—that Miroul had almost to run to keep up with me. "Well," I thought to myself, "if Alizon, who is fundamentally a good wench, can have such bloodthirsty ideas, and believe they're legitimate, what about all the knaves and rascals in this immense population?"

"Monsieur, what's the matter?" panted Miroul behind me, seeing me so undone with grief and tears flowing down my cheeks. "Did you quarrel with Alizon?"

For a long while, I couldn't manage to answer him, since the passers-by looked at me suspiciously because of my distress, but finally we reached the rue de Béthisy, where, because of the numbers of Huguenots who were milling about, entering and leaving the admiral's lodgings, you would have thought you were in a little Geneva, and, feeling myself to be among my people and more safe than before, I explained to Miroul what had happened.

"Ah, Monsieur!" moaned Miroul. "You're too quick to anger! You made a terrible mistake revealing your identity to this sweet wench! If the uprising starts and Maître Recroche, knowing what he knows, bars us from his house, where can we seek refuge until the end of the storm? Dame du Luc and Monsieur de Quéribus are in Saint-Cloud and Fogacer is off chasing his little acrobat. You've now eliminated our last refuge: Alizon is lost to us."

There was nothing I could say in my defence, so I contented myself with frowning, giving Miroul a proud and disdainful look that expressed righteous anger in direct proportion to his reasonable assessment of our situation. Such is our human folly: even in the extremity of our situation, I needed to appear superior to my valet.

I found the admiral's lodgings exactly as Delay had so aptly described them: as buzzing, furious and agitated as a beehive that some good-for-nothing had tossed a stone at. But it was all agitation, commotion, furious debate without any decision, absent of any will or action, our leader still stuck on the idea of remaining in Paris, confident in the good faith of the king.

Monsieur de Mazille told me the admiral had rested well and that his fever had abated somewhat. He said he was waiting for Ambroise Paré to arrive to change his dressing, and that, with three of us, the task would be much easier. It was an enormous relief for me to look at Monsieur de Mazille's grave and benign face as he talked; it reminded me a great deal of that of Pierre de L'Étoile, a papist with no zeal whatever, for whom, as Montaigne had said, his fellow man was his fellow man, whether or not he was of the same religion.

Bowing to the assembled group, I went to kiss the hand of Madame de Téligny, a pretty young blonde, who had her father's light-blue eyes, though hers were softer, leaning a bit more to green than to blue. I told her how happy I was that her father's wound was well on its way to healing: words that caused her to tilt her head to one side and thank me with her smooth, somewhat plaintive, flute-like voice.

Besides Madame de Téligny, those present included Yolet, the admiral's valet, Nicolas Muss, his German interpreter, the orderly Cornaton, the minister Merlin and Monsieur de Ferrières. To the last of these, having pulled him into a corner, I recounted everything I'd learnt that morning from my conversations with Recroche and Alizon: about the way the papist priests had stirred up the Parisians with stories of how we were going to attack the house of Guise; and about how, in consequence, the entire city had begun arming itself behind closed shutters, and the *quarteniers* and *dizeniers* had been marking the doors of the houses of Huguenots.

"Well, Monsieur de Siorac!" boomed Monsieur de Ferrières with his grave bass voice, which was always a surprise, given his frail little body. "It's very obvious now that this evil city is going to attack us.

But what can we do? There are 3,000 of us and 300,000 of them! Signs of the approaching storm are multiplying by the hour. Did you know that Montmorency, who, in his position as governor of Paris should be keeping order, has just left the city to pay a very opportune visit to his mother?"

"But I thought he was Coligny's cousin and good friend."

"He is, but he's also a papist, very concerned about maintaining the king's favour, and not wholly uninterested in his own advancement. Seeing the wind turning, he's fled before the tempest, washing his hands, like Pilate, of the admiral."

"And us," I said, through clenched teeth.

"Well," said Jean de Ferrières, "God willing, I'll get out before it starts! It's madness to stay here, placing all our hope in the king's goodwill, which doesn't exist. Charles has never flipped an egg in the Louvre without his mother knowing about it. And he never puts meat on the fire without her taking it and cooking it in her own sauce."

Ambroise Paré came up at these words, and as the admiral opened his eyes, Paré asked him whether he'd like to get up and sit in a chair, which would greatly facilitate dressing his wounds. Coligny agreed in a much firmer voice than we'd heard before, and, without any help, rose and sat down on a nearby stool. His face was pale from the loss of all that blood, but his expression was full of resolve. His wounds were beautifully clean and free of any pus or odour, so there was nothing to do except to extract a few splinters of bone from the elbow so that they wouldn't infect the flesh around them, procedures that Paré executed with admirable dexterity. After which, having washed the wound with spirits, they rebandaged it, and Paré announced that he was very happy with the state of his patient, whose complexion was regaining its colour, signalling good progress against the injury, the pain and the lost blood.

The admiral got back into bed, and the curtains were drawn, so the king's surgeon invited me to go and get some refreshment, and said that he'd wait by the bedside for my return before going to his own lodgings.

"Well, Monsieur," said Miroul, once we were in the rue de Béthisy, "I heard what Ferrières told you about Montmorency's departure. That stinks to high heaven of the blood of our people. The only one here who can pick up a scent, can smell the hounds and hunters coming, and he's going to head into his burrow while there's still time. For pity's sake, Monsieur! I beg you in the name of your father, do what he's doing and don't delay any longer!"

"I'll think about it Miroul," I replied, now very shaken, but unable, still, to leave the admiral, for the reasons I've stated.

We headed towards the rue de la Truanderie, where we were supposed to meet up with Giacomi to join him for dinner at Gautier's tavern. He was already there, waiting for us, but the door was closed and the windows were shuttered. We rang the bell, but the only response was from a window on the first floor, where one of Gautier's chambermaids told us that her master would not be serving dinner today, having, as she laughingly put it, other fish to fry—and what fish those were, she thought we must know! We could but laugh along with her at this wickedness, since our lives were in the balance and all we could do was to pretend to enjoy the game.

Our stomachs growling with hunger, our morale at a low ebb, there was no other solution than to find an itinerant pastry-seller, and we finally met one in the grand-rue Saint-Denis, who sold his pork pies for twice the price I'd paid my first morning in Paris. I tried bargaining with him, but he refused to bring the price down, knowing full well that all the taverns in Paris were boarded up tight. I didn't dare insist for fear of putting ideas in his head, since Huguenots are reputed to be able bargainers in Paris. I was also careful to speak with something as close to a Parisian accent as I could manage and for the same reason.

We each ate three pies and they were so thick-crusted and succulent that we enjoyed the memory of the taste after swallowing them. It struck me as passing strange that one could find such solace in food when under the threat of imminent death. I even thought of purchasing some as provisions, but my Huguenot austerity got the better of me, something I was to regret bitterly over the next twenty-four hours.

"Well, Giacomi, my brother," I said quietly when we'd finished eating, "we're going to have to separate eventually. Miroul and I are going to try to get out of Paris, and we would never drag you into our uncertain fortunes, since you're a papist. We'll have time to be reunited, if we escape, back in Mespech."

"My brother," he said gravely, but with that twinkle in his eye that never left him, "surely you cannot think me so low as to abandon you in your hour of peril! Oh, no! My sword would never be unfaithful to a friend in distress. Moreover, I swore to your father to protect you on the right, with Miroul doing the same on your left. I'm going off to the Louvre for my fencing practice. But if the bell signals the beginning of this conflagration that now seems inevitable, let's agree to meet at the place de Grève, since Recroche's door is now barred to us."

And so it was decided, and, our faces streaming with tears, we embraced each other with the urgency of brothers who may never see each other again in this cruel world. Giacomi set off then, and I watched him walk away with a heavy heart, yet consoled by the thought that our hearts were attached in this hour of torment by bonds of steel.

We headed once again for the rue de Béthisy, and, to distract me from my worries, Miroul named all of the streets we passed, displaying his extensive knowledge of the city, which he'd explored every day while I was off enjoying the Louvre with Quéribus. But when we drew near the admiral's lodgings he again pressed me urgently to take my leave as soon as possible. But I said nothing in reply, since I hadn't yet decided what I would do.

Scarcely had I arrived before the orderly Cornaton told me that I was awaited in the admiral's chambers, where the principal Protestant leaders were gathered. As I approached the room, I heard a loud argument going on between Monsieur de Téligny and Jean de Ferrières, the latter arguing, with a degree of vehemence I'd never witnessed from him before, that at any hour now the populace was going to rise up against us and that we could not count on the king. As he saw me come in, he interrupted his speech to ask me to reveal what I'd learnt in the rue de la Ferronnerie from Maître Recroche and in the rue Tirechappe from Alizon. And so I reported what I'd heard.

"And yet," said the gentle Téligny, "it's just been announced that the attempt on the life of the admiral was not planned at court. The judges that have been gathered to study the matter arrested the man who was holding the assassin's horse after the dastardly attack, and this man has confessed he was working for Guise."

"Despite that evidence," said my cousin Geoffroy de Caumont, "it's still possible that there was more than one hand responsible for this murderous attempt. Did you know, Téligny, that the smoking arquebus that was found next to the lattice window belonged to one of the Duc d'Anjou's guards? Would this guard have loaned it to another without his master's consent?"

A long silence followed.

"The Duc d'Anjou is not the king," said Téligny finally, "and you know very well in what disdain the sovereign holds his brother. In truth, I can't understand what could possibly make us doubt Charles's good disposition towards us. I have it from a reliable source that the Duc de Guise and his uncle, the Duc d'Aumale, complaining that they'd been wrongly accused of the attack, went to the king and asked him for permission to leave Paris, which he granted very stiffly and icily."

"Ha!" said Jean de Ferrières. "The ducs just pretended to be leaving! They left by the Porte Saint-Antoine, and sneaked back in by the

Porte Saint-Denis. Would they have behaved this way if they weren't assured of the connivance of people at the court who are close to the king? And why would they remain here, if not in the hope that they could preside over the massacre of our people as soon as the court drops the leashes of its hunting dogs? I ask you: is the court really beyond suspicion? At noon today a number of porters were seen carrying cases of weapons from the arsenal to the Louvre, which is now surrounded by several regiments of the king's guards. What's the meaning of such a deployment?"

"No doubt," replied Téligny, "the king fears that the bourgeois of Paris will attack the Louvre."

"Are they arming themselves against him or against us?" cried Jean de Ferrières, raising his hands heavenward in exasperation at Téligny's insistence on reassuring everyone of the king's moderation.

To this, Téligny, deaf to all views that contradicted his own, said, not without some severity, though still as outwardly courteous and benign as was his wont:

"In truth, we're making a mistake by multiplying our reasons for distrusting the king in the unfortunate circumstances in which we're meeting. I beg you to speak no further of this to the admiral."

"Do you think you can make the danger vanish by refusing to announce its coming?" cried Jean de Ferrières angrily. "Do we see more clearly by blindfolding ourselves?"

He then fell silent, but seeing that Téligny's resistance to his views was too obdurate to permit a change of position, and that he would continue to fall back on the admiral's refusal to quit Paris—an enterprise that would now be infinitely more difficult given how few hours separated us from nightfall—he rose and said in a stentorian voice:

"I see that I'm wasting my time and I'm infinitely disappointed, for I am entirely persuaded the populace will attack us tonight." Whereupon, taking a deep breath, and looking at each one of us in turn, he cried: "Messieurs, I'm leaving right now! Anyone who wants to perish at the hands of these Parisian butchers may do so! As for me, I will try to preserve my life to continue the fight elsewhere, for in my view, it's madness to sit here and wait to be attacked when we know it's coming!"

At this, Jean de Ferrières left, with my cousin Caumont and two or three others whose names I've forgotten. I saw that young La Rochefoucauld was considering joining them, deeply shaken by their reasons, but in the end, he decided not to, believing ultimately in the friendship the king had shown him since his arrival at the court. But he was grievously mistaken, for when he awoke the next day he discovered this same king had ordered him to be killed in his bed by the gentlemen of his house.

After Jean de Ferrières departed, I went to check on the admiral and discovered him resting easily in his bed, his eyes closed and feeling no pain. I left his lodgings and set out down the rue de Béthisy, Miroul at my heels, who didn't dare ask me where I was headed, but instead quietly followed me to the rue des Fossés-Saint-Germain, and thence to the Louvre. I didn't go in, but instead entered the Five Virgins tennis courts. I was very disappointed not to find Delay there, and was about to leave when I caught sight of the bald-headed and very scarred scorekeeper who'd admitted Samson and me, at our first visit to the Five Virgins, to his little grandstand on the day that my brother had almost been killed during a religious procession.

"Monsieur," I greeted him, "do you remember me? I'm a friend of Sergeant Rabastens."

"I do, Monsieur," he replied, doffing his plumed hat, revealing his scarred pate, and bowed deeply.

"Monsieur," I continued, "knowing that you're a veteran of the king's guards, I thought perhaps you might know where in the capital I might rent a horse."

I noticed that Miroul was now smiling broadly at me, but didn't make a sound.

"I know all the stables," said the scorekeeper very self-importantly. "There are exactly four of them and not one more. And I'm guessing that, as you're about to depart, you'll need to know where they're located. But Monsieur, you'll have very little chance of finding a horse today, since there are so many bourgeois—Catholics and otherwise—who, since yesterday, have been leaving Paris to avoid being caught up in the popular uprising."

I felt very caught off guard, but I asked for the addresses of the stables anyway, which the fellow happily provided, seeming to have guessed why I was impatient—Catholic or otherwise—to leave. Indeed, he displayed no malice or churlishness, which I appreciated. I was so comforted to have discovered a papist who didn't hate us or want to spill our blood that I thanked him with especial warmth for his help and wanted to add a few coins to my thanks, but he refused them, wishing me, with an air of profound understanding, a good ride and a safe return to my home in the provinces. And, in gratitude, I told him that if I ever returned to Paris, I would not fail to pay him a visit, never suspecting that I would see him again twenty-four hours later in such an incredible predicament that I wouldn't have believed it if the Holy Spirit had announced it from on high!

Sadly, the scorekeeper was right, and I was unable to find even the most broken-down nag at any of the first three addresses he'd provided… But Fortune appeared to smile on me a little more with the fourth, a stable in the rue des Lavandières, not far from the rue de la Ferronnerie. And when the fellow showed me three very passable mares in his stable, my heart leapt for joy and I could already see us safe and sound outside the terrible net in which we been snared.

"Monsieur," said the scowling stable master, a tall, portly fellow with black hair that crept halfway down his forehead, two bushy eyebrows that met above his large nose, an enormous weeping-willow moustache that virtually hid his lips and a copious beard that climbed up to his cheekbones, producing the impression that his nose was the only hairless part of his face—if one excepted the tuft that decorated the end of it and the hairs that emerged from his nostrils, "I can let you have these three mares as far as Montfort-l'Amaury for only thirty écus."

"Thirty écus!" I cried. "'Sblood! That's a pretty fat price!"

"The fact is, these are dangerous times," said the stable master, his little black eyes shining like a weasel's through the shrubbery of his hair. "If I don't rent them out to you, I'll easily find others. I'm not going to lack for customers, given the turn events are taking."

"Shake on it then!" I said, understanding how useless it would be to try to bargain, and thinking that thirty écus wasn't so much if it saved our lives.

"Hold on, good gentleman," temporized my crafty adversary, "that's not all. You must deposit money as a guarantee, which I'll refund to you when the smith in Montfort-l'Amaury returns my horses to my stable."

"A guarantee? But why?"

"Well, as I said, these are troubled times. The riders could be killed and their horses stolen."

He said this with a suspicious air, which led me to think that, because of my haste, he had smelt the Huguenot in me, despite my pearl-studded doublet, which suggested more a gallant of the Louvre than a dour Calvinist.

"And how much would this guarantee be?"

"Three hundred écus."

"Three hundred écus! God in heaven! That's very portly money indeed! Your three mares didn't cost you half that!"

"That's as may be," he said frostily, "but I won't rent them for a sol less."

I looked at Miroul, and he returned my look sadly, for he well knew that I no longer had that sum in my purse, having left most of my money with Samson so he could keep it safe in Montfort-l'Amaury, sheltered from my Parisian temptations. "Well," I thought, "damn my Huguenot parsimony! First for having advised me to leave our horses in Montfort to save fourteen sols a day. And second for leading me to make Samson my treasurer in Montfort when I need the money in Paris!"

"My friend," I said, "give me an hour to come up with the money."

"Sorry," replied this bear with a nasty look, "can't do it. If someone comes along who will pay me my price for the horses, I'll have to let him have them."

"All right then, I'll give you ten écus more if you'll give me one hour."

"Twenty!" he said pitilessly.

"Shake on it!" I said, and left this bearded strangler who was so talented at profiting from others' misfortunes.

"Monsieur, where are we going?" Miroul queried as soon as we'd regained the street.

"To see Pierre de L'Étoile," I whispered. "He's a good man, despite being a papist, and he'll accommodate me if he can."

But when we reached the rue Trouvevache we found his door locked and barricaded. After I'd banged on the door for some time, the neighbour's door opened and, without passing her threshold, she asked:

"Who are you looking for, making such a racket?"

"Monsieur Pierre de L'Étoile."

"He's gone."

"When did he leave?"

"This morning, with all his servants, to go to his house in the country."

And she closed her door, killing all hope.

"Well, Miroul!" I said. "I don't have a single friend here. Pierre de L'Étoile, Quéribus, Dame Gertrude, Fogacer—all have managed to get outside the walls and we're still inside! Caught in the snare, like rabbits."

"Monsieur, there's Ambroise Paré! He's wealthy and likes you a lot."

"But I don't know where he lives."

"Rue de l'Hirondelle. I heard his assistant saying so."

"Miroul!" I cried. "You're priceless!"

We headed to his lodgings at a run but found there only a chambermaid, who reported that he'd gone off to the Louvre at the request of the king. I realized later how pretty this girl was, but at the time I wasn't aware of it given how worried I was.

At the Louvre, leaving Miroul to wait for me at the Five Virgins, I presented myself at the guardhouse, where I found, in addition to the guard, Monsieur de Rambouillet sitting on a stool, resting his paunch on his fat thighs.

"What?" he gasped sitting up. "You, here? Why have you come? You've got your pardon! Why haven't you left?"

At this he lowered his eyes and fell silent, as if embarrassed to have said too much.

"I'm looking for Ambroise Paré."

"Well," said Rambouillet, "the Louvre is vast. But you might find him with the king of Navarre. But hurry, we're closing the gates in an hour."

I thanked him and grabbed a little page in the courtyard, giving him a coin to lead me to Navarre's chambers. Which he did, skipping along like a young kid, the natural alacrity of his youth and his devil-may-care attitude setting the pace. He wore the colours of the queen mother, and he most assuredly knew nothing of what was now being plotted in his mistress's cave.

The antechamber of the king of Navarre—separated from his apartments by a simple tapestry—was full of some thirty Protestant gentlemen, among whom I recognized Piles, Pardaillan and Soubise, who was the object of much curiosity at court, since his wife was divorcing him, arguing that he was impotent. This was surprising given how vigorous, hairy and deep-voiced he was.

These thirty gentlemen were crowded together, many seated on stools, their knees touching, some chatting among themselves, others playing dice and tric-trac (a game Calvin had condemned), and were preparing to spend the night in such gaiety and insouciance.

I went to speak to Monsieur de Piles, whom I knew, having taken shooting lessons with him, since he, too, was a pupil of Giacomi, to ask if he knew where I could find Ambroise Paré.

"Alas," he said, "you won't see him tonight. He was here a minute ago, but he has retired to the king's apartments and will spend the night there. Just as we are, here, but for different reasons."

"Different reasons?" I asked civilly, despite feeling such despair at the loss of my last hope.

"There are usually not so many of us here," explained Piles with a certain knowing air, "but His Majesty warned the king of Navarre to summon to the Louvre all of his people, and especially those who'd be able to defend him." And here he gave a knowing smile, because his own bravery was quite well known after having defended Saint-Jean-d'Angély against the royal army.

"And why are so many of you here?"

"In order, according to His Majesty, to prevent Guise's insolence, who, given the agitation of the Parisians, might incite them to attempt some nasty coup."

"What?" I said, my eyes widening, so incredible did the thing seem, and so naive those who'd believed it. "A nasty coup? Against the Louvre! Which has such stout ramparts and large numbers of men and cannon!"

"Well, that's at least what the king says he fears," replied Piles, to whom it wouldn't have occurred that the king might be capable of lying.

As he was saying this, the tapestry enclosing the antechamber opened and Monsieur de Nançay appeared, armed to the teeth and looking very chagrined.

The captain of the king's guards stood silently for a moment, looking at each of the men gathered there, and, at each one, made a nod of his head, as though he were counting them. When he'd finished, he said, with the same sad expression and in a tone I'll never forget to my dying day, as if he were trying to communicate some message, or an opinion, or a warning that wasn't evident in the words themselves:

"Messieurs, if any of you wish to leave, there's still time before the gates close."

"Not on your life!" responded one of the gentlemen (to which the others expressed their approval, some with laughter). "We're having such fun at cards, we intend to spend the night here."

"And so it shall be as you've decided," said Nançay in a tired voice.

But he didn't leave, and stood there, holding the tapestry open with his left hand and looking at each of the men present as if he wanted to make a second count, and when his grey eyes met mine, they seemed full of a mute insistence, so that, obeying some obscure feeling, I said:

"Monsieur de Nançay, I must depart!"

"No, no!" said Monsieur de Piles, taking my arm. "Stay, Siorac, we'll deal you a hand at cards!"

"I'm afraid that's not possible," I persisted, "since Ambroise Paré is sleeping here in the Louvre, I must return to the admiral's bedside for the night."

"Well," said Piles, "in that case, you're doing the right thing." And he gave me a powerful hug while the other gentlemen present looked up from their games and smiled at me or bade me goodnight.

Ah, what good and valiant men they were! And how dastardly was their demise!…

As soon as Charles had given the signal for the massacre by having the great bell of Saint-Germain l'Auxerrois tolled, Monsieur de Nançay returned to Navarre's antechamber and told the men that the king had ordered them to assemble in the courtyard of the Louvre. Which they did, suspecting nothing, but believing that the chateau was under attack by the people outside and that the sovereign required their help in its defence. But scarcely had they stepped into the courtyard before, suddenly surrounded by the king's guards, they were disarmed, pushed outside the walls and assassinated. When it was Monsieur de Piles's turn, seeing the heap of bodies to which he was to add his own, he cried:

"So this is the king's word? This is his hospitality? Oh, just Judge, avenge this odious perfidy someday!" Then, unhooking a very beautiful coat that hung from his shoulder, he handed it to a papist gentleman he knew, saying, "Take my coat. I bequeath it to you, my friend. Keep it in remembrance of the heinous death inflicted here."

But, whatever he may have thought of this massacre, the papist gentleman refused the gift, since Piles was inviting him to make of it a memorial to the king's betrayal.

All of these gentlemen having been murdered in this way, the soldiers stripped them of their clothes—as was done at Golgotha to the divine victim—and noisily fought over them. After this, they ran off, panting, to murder and pillage other victims, leaving the poor cadavers naked in the street, promising to come back in the morning to throw them in the Seine, which, in these sinister hours, became the cemetery of the massacred Huguenots.

No sooner had the soldiers departed than the queen mother and her ladies emerged from the chateau, cackling and laughing, to enjoy the view of the martyrs by the light of torches carried by their valets. Jezebel took a particular interest in the body of Soubise, whom she looked at with great curiosity, as did her ladies, since he'd been reputed to be impotent by his wife. Can such actions have been taken by a queen of France, or was she an infernal succubus wearing a crown? Agrippa d'Aubigné was not wrong when he said of Catherine de' Medici: "She is the soul of the state, she who has no soul." Neither a soul nor, alas, a heart—and of remorse, this viper never had the least bit, right up to the end of her detestable days, she who, by her wiles, induced her son to hunt down his own people.

But I'm getting ahead of myself. Scarcely had I left Navarre's antechamber with Monsieur de Nançay, walking side by side, before he whispered in a severe voice:

"'Sblood! What are you doing here? The king gave you your pardon yesterday morning. Why didn't you leave?"

This question troubled me deeply, since it repeated, word for word, what Monsieur de Rambouillet had said as I entered the Louvre. I told him of my attempts to find horses, a story that the captain of the guards listened to with a most unhappy expression. When I was finished, he would only say in very muffled tones:

"In any case, it's too late now. The city gates are closed. Chains have been stretched across the bridges, which are guarded by bourgeois militia."

The implications of these words terrified me, especially since, as we descended the great staircase which led to the courtyard of the Louvre, I could see all the companies of the king's guards, who, in the short time I'd been in Navarre's antechamber, had been armed for war and deployed for battle.

As I approached the gates, to my considerable surprise I saw and heard the king of Navarre, whom I thought had retired to his apartments, talking with the captain of the gate, Monsieur de Rambouillet.

"But sire," said the latter, "you're preparing to leave when I'm preparing to close!"

"But the usual closing hour is ten o'clock!"

"I have orders from the king to lock up at eight tonight."

"Well, Monsieur de Rambouillet," said Navarre with that pleasant geniality that made him so popular with everyone, "if you please, let me pass! I pledge my faith that I'll come back quickly!"

"Well, sire," rejoined Rambouillet, "Your Majesty is too good: you ask where you could command."

"Command?" laughed Navarre. "I command no one here, not even Margot!"

And at this, laughing uproariously and giving Rambouillet a little pat on his stomach, he passed through the gate, followed by his Swiss guards, who were wearing uniforms of red and yellow (red for Navarre and yellow for Béarn) and, except for a couple of them, were not Swiss at all, but from Béarn.

I presented myself in turn to the captain of the gate, who, to my considerable surprise, since he'd never been so friendly to me, extended his hand, and, as I shook it, pressed my hand tightly and said, lowering his eyes:

"Adieu, Monsieur de Siorac! May you return safely to your provinces!"

This wish was very banal, to be sure, and yet it surprised me all the more since I'd never told Monsieur de Rambouillet that I was going to leave—which, moreover, was now impossible, for lack of money and horses, and because, of course, the city gates were now irrevocably closed.

Miroul, who was just outside, came up and could see immediately by my expression that I'd failed in my quest. I hurried forward and, as night was beginning to fall, I joined Navarre and his escort, who, as I'd thought, were heading towards the admiral's lodgings, since they were taking the rue des Fossés-Saint-Germain.

As soon as Navarre caught sight of me, he turned around and, looking at me intently with his long face, said jovially:

"Aren't you the doctor who believed that the admiral could be carried in a litter despite his wounds?"

"Indeed, sire," I said, making a deep bow. "My name is Pierre de Siorac, and I'm the younger son of the Baron de Mespech in Périgord."

"Well!" said Navarre. "A doctor and the son of a baron: I like that! What do you think of our present predicament?"

"Sire, I agree with Monsieur de Ferrières."

"And yet," said Navarre, whose manner always seemed a bit light-hearted, "you didn't leave with him."

"For lack of horses, sire, and of money to rent them."

"This is honest talk, and brave!" said Navarre. "Only a brave man wouldn't be afraid to say that he wished to flee from an ambush."

To which I made him another bow, feeling more affection for him than I had, since I'd never been much attracted by his physical presence, nor his provincial manners. But he definitely had something princely about him, however light-hearted he appeared, and however much he loved a good laugh and preferred cajolery to giving commands, understanding very well that you catch more flies with a spoonful of honey than with ten barrels of vinegar.

"All this civil discord is a great pity," he continued, but now with some gravity, "and I'm very disturbed at all the bloodshed between Frenchmen over religion. I don't know whether the admiral will get his war in Flanders. They seem to want to stop him at all costs—even that of his life. May God take Monsieur de Coligny by the hand and lead him to safety on this earth!"

Just then, he heard one of the guards behind him quietly complaining of his empty stomach, and turned round; then, returning to his more jocular tone, he joked:

"Well, me too, my good Fröhlich, I'm starving! And I'd love a crust of black bread, a garlic clove and a goblet of wine!"

"Sire," returned Fröhlich in the same familiar tone, "in the Louvre you've got other kinds of meat, *Herrgott*!"

"To be sure! But I lack the appetite that the Pyrenees gave me as a child!"

"*Ach!*" agreed Fröhlich with a huge sigh. "I miss my mountains of Berne as well!"

This Swiss, who was Swiss in name only, was himself a mountain of a man, big and fat, with arms like thighs, legs as big as another man's trunk and a large, crimson face.

"I have to say," said another of the escort, a native of Béarn, in his dialect, "I like my hills more than this shitty city, which stinks with corruption and hatred."

"Speak French, Cadieu," cried Navarre in a mocking tone, "so that our Swiss friend can understand you!"

And in response, Cadieu, who was only slight less massive than Fröhlich and seemed to enjoy a great friendship with him, repeated his thought in a French so badly pronounced that Navarre had to laugh out loud as he threw me knowing glances.

But Navarre's mood soured dramatically when we turned into the rue de Béthisy and saw that the street in front of the admiral's lodgings was occupied by about forty arquebusiers, who had taken over the two shops opposite and lit bonfires in the street, setting up camp as though they intended to spend the night there.

"By the belly of Christ!" he said between clenched teeth. "I don't like the look of this!" Then, calling to a guard who was serving as sentinel at the corner of the street, and heavily armed for combat, as were all the others there, he said, "Guard, who's in charge here?"

"Camp-master Cossain," said the arquebusier.

"Cossain!" repeated Navarre, and he frowned even more deeply.

Hurrying their pace, Navarre's Swiss guards closed ranks around him and tensely cast sidelong glances at the king's guards with little trust or amity, especially since they themselves were in simple uniforms, armed only with halberds and short swords at their belts. Navarre reached the door of the house at the moment a violent argument was taking place between Monsieur de Guerchy and a great lump of a man, armoured head to foot, as arrogant and swaggering as they come. As soon as I saw him, I knew he must be the camp-master, given the common expression around the Louvre, "swaggering like Cossain".

"What's going on?" asked Navarre, with his usual easy-going manner and a wide smile on his face—the admirable pliability with which he governed his humour never ceasing to amaze me.

"Sire," said Monsieur de Guerchy in the most inflamed tone, "Cossain wants to prevent the page, here, from bringing two arque-buses belonging to Monsieur de Téligny into the house."

This seemed to bring Navarre up short, but he immediately took control of himself and, addressing the camp-master with amiable and enviable good humour, and raising his eyebrows in feigned astonish-ment and naivety, said:

"What's the matter, Cossain? Is there some problem with that? Is Monsieur de Téligny supposed to be the only one in there who doesn't have a weapon?"

"Sire," Cossain replied, clearly crestfallen, "I'm acting under the king's orders that no firearms be allowed in the house, but," he added, playing the good servant, "if Your Majesty wishes the page to bring in some arquebuses, I'm happy with that."

"That's very good of you!" Navarre smiled, and, giving the page a little tap on the neck, he added, "Go on in, my boy!"

After which, he took Guerchy, still visibly fuming, by the arm and dragged him into the house, with Miroul and me at his heels, but the Swiss guards remained outside. They looked imperturbable enough, but I imagined that they were pretty ill at ease to be confronted with forty well-armed soldiers who were staring at their red and yellow uniforms with undisguised contempt.

"Guerchy," asked Navarre as soon as we were out of earshot, "what's going on? What's Cossain doing here?"

"He's here to protect the admiral from the uprising. It was Coligny who, during the afternoon, sent word to the Louvre asking the king for protection, believing that the sight of a few guards in the street would dissuade the populace from attacking his lodgings."

"Ah," said Navarre sotto voce, and in an ambiguous tone, somewhere between ironic and respectful, "so it was the admiral himself who requested this protection?"

And then, throwing his head back, his long nose seeming to breathe in the scents in the air, but not liking what he smelt, he added in a deep voice, through his clenched teeth, "But who's going to protect the admiral from Cossain?"

"That's exactly the problem," said Guerchy, still red-faced from his quarrel with the camp-master.

Navarre sighed, and, giving Monsieur de Guerchy a little tap on his shoulder, turned on his heels and quickly mounted the stairs to the admiral's chambers, but came down again immediately saying that Monsieur de Coligny was sleeping, but that he appeared to be recovering well, and that, at least from that perspective, he could be content. However, he remained standing there, eyes half-closed, appearing to stare at something on the floor, and seemed to be mulling something over in his mind, his expression no longer light-hearted and gay, but rather very grave. Quitting his silence and his immobility, he ordered six of his Swiss guards to remain for the night in the admiral's lodgings, commanding them to lock and bolt the door, close the shutters and keep a vigilant watch. After which, recovering his more light-hearted manner, he said goodnight to Guerchy, to me and to La Bonne (the admiral's major-domo), and left with his escort diminished by half, leaving behind, besides four others of lesser girth, both Fröhlich and Cadieu, whose combined bulk seemed suddenly to fill the house to capacity. But what could these giants do with their swords and halberds against forty arquebuses?

The major-domo, La Bonne, was, true to his name, a gentle, good fellow, as round as a top, with a suave, benevolent expression and a voice as soft as a stream in April. He set up our Swiss in the lower hall with a bottle of wine, and some bread and cheese, and then retired with me to the admiral's chambers. Miroul, his varicoloured eyes so worried they both looked black, stayed as close to me as my shadow, his hand constantly checking the hilts of his sword, his dagger and the two knives he concealed in his breeches for throwing. With us upstairs were the valet Yolet, the German interpreter Nicolas Muss, the minister Merlin, the orderly Cornaton and Madame de Téligny, but the admiral, upon awakening, asked that she be escorted to her lodgings in the grand'rue Saint-Honoré. A dozen men who were still there volunteered to take her, and were flanked by two lackeys bearing torches, but she insisted on turning back twice to say goodbye to her father, her beautiful blue eyes drowned in tears and her face wracked with grief. The admiral tried to comfort her by repeating that he felt much better, but she couldn't bear to pull herself away, prey, as she must have been, to a deep presentiment that she would never see him again.

La Bonne extinguished all the candles except one, and each of us arranged himself as best he could on the various stools, leaving the one armchair for Merlin, the minister, who was old and tired. None of us expected to get any sleep, despite the profound silence that reigned both throughout the house, which is not so surprising, and throughout this immense city, which surrounded us on all sides, holding us ensnared in its trap with no possibility of escape.

It wasn't the fear of dying that touched me in this funereal vigil—and funereal it was, well before the first Protestant had been massacred—but rather the despair we felt at being so thoroughly hated by such a large number of our fellow men, nay compatriots, subjects of the same sovereign, who endured the same human condition as us, were made glad by the same joys, suffered the same illnesses, were terrified by the same indignities of ageing on our perishable bodies—in short, they were our brothers and sisters, as we were theirs, without any doubt, and not some "rotten branch of the tree of France" that had to be cut off by force, as Jezebel was, at this very instant, explaining to her son in the Louvre in order to assuage his doubt about the death warrant he'd signed. Yes, and I'll say it again: in every way we are their brothers and sisters, and not the beings the priests in their pulpits have dismissed from the human community, calling us "dogs", "vipers", and "vermin" that God has told them to eradicate.

And as my thoughts ran in the silence of the night, my eyes barely open, fixed on the candle whose yellow flame seemed to want to go out, without ever going out—very much like the persecuted faith of the Huguenots—I began to think about Alizon, and these thoughts were very painful to me, not that I felt anything more than friendship for her, but because that good girl's very hateful words—an echo of an entire people's—were lodged in my very soul, so much so that in this silence, in this solitude, in this interminable waiting, my suffering was so intense and so great that, covering my eyes with my left hand so as not to be seen, I began to cry.

I know all too well, alas, that religious zeal has also had inhuman and pitiless consequences in our party, that the blood of the Michelade of Nîmes cries out against us and that it was Calvin himself who ordered the great physician Michael Servetus to be burnt in Geneva. Oh, God of love! When will we see the end of this chain and concatenation of hatreds that break out in both religions and are used to justify the murders that are consciously committed in the name of Truth—which itself varies and changes so much that the heretic who burns at the stake thinks only of denouncing the heresy of his tormentor?

Twice during the night, I got up from my stool and lifted the curtain enclosing the admiral's bed and listened to his breathing. It was so even and peaceful that he could have been sleeping in his sweet country retreat in Châtillon-sur-Loing, and not on a barrel of gunpowder. Indeed, poor Merlin, the minister, who was, in fact, younger than Coligny, seemed to have a much harder time of it, his uneven and difficult breathing causing him a lot of agitation as he slept. Miroul, as far as I could determine from the light of the one candle, was not asleep, but was watching over me, though he lowered his eyes when I looked his way so as not to disturb me with the care he was taking of me—which had quite the opposite effect since it comforted me more than I can say to feel loved precisely at the moment I felt myself to be the target of widespread detestation.

I heard the cry of the nightwatchman at ten as he made his rounds. I heard it again at eleven and also at midnight. But I must have dozed off after that, for a loud knocking at the door woke me with a start, and, jumping to my feet, Miroul already dressed at my side, his hand on the pommel of his sword, I saw the major-domo, La Bonne, groping about on the table for his keys, since his sight was less than perfect.

"What's that, La Bonne?" cried Merlin, sitting up on his chair, looking terrified.

"It's Cossain, who demands that we open the door," answered La Bonne calmly.

"Don't open the door, La Bonne!" said Merlin, rising from his chair, his eyes wide with terror.

"What is it?" came the voice of the admiral from behind his bed curtains, which Yolet immediately opened so that his master could hear the others.

At this moment, from downstairs came the sound of the door knocker banging loudly and the voice of Cossain shouting:

"Open up, it's Cossain!"

"Don't open the door, La Bonne!" yelled Merlin, putting his trembling hands over his ears.

"La Bonne," said the admiral, in a calm and composed voice, "open the door. It's Cossain. Maybe the king has been attacked in his Louvre. Open up, La Bonne, and bring me the news."

La Bonne took the candelabrum to light his way, and went downstairs.

I was right behind him with Miroul, Yolet, Cornaton and Muss, all five of us unsheathing our swords on the way, and we were met downstairs by Fröhlich, Cadieu and the other Swiss guards, who had their short swords at the ready. La Bonne pulled the two large bolts, and took some time finding the right key on his chain, since he was so nearsighted, and had to manage the candelabrum in his left hand. At length, however, he found the key he needed, put it in the lock, turned it and, pulling the door open, found himself face to face with Cossain, who, without saying a word, immediately stabbed him.

"*Ach!* Traitor!" cried Fröhlich, delivering a powerful thrust of his sword into the chest of the assassin without penetrating his breastplate, but knocking him backwards. Seeing this, Cadieu pushed the door closed against the rush of the king's soldiers, and, buttressing the door with his large shoulders, held it closed long enough for Fröhlich and another Swiss to push a heavy iron chest against it. This done, Cadieu fell heavily to the ground beside La Bonne, having been shot between the shoulder blades by an arquebus that had been fired at point-blank range through the peephole while he was blocking the door.

"*Ach!* Poor Cadieu!" cried Fröhlich, while Cossain's guards began hacking at the door with their axes, splintering the oak planks. Cornaton and Muss fired two shots at them, but didn't have time to reload before the guards were inside. There followed a ferocious sword fight on the stairs in which no one could be sure who was who in the semi-darkness, lit only by our assailants' torch, La Bonne's candelabrum having gone out when he fell. In the midst of this confusion, as I aimed my blows at our assailants' faces rather than their breastplates—a manoeuvre aided by their position below us on the stairs—I saw poor Yolet run through in the stomach. He pitched forward, groaning, but was immediately avenged by Muss, who drove his short sword into the face of Yolet's assassin.

As we flailed blindly at each other, I heard a shout from above to quit our positions and come up to reinforce the door on the landing. The Swiss guards, except for Fröhlich, did not understand, but he followed as we scampered up the remaining stairs like cats and closed the door behind us, bolstering it with a couple of heavy chests.

Breathing hard, we looked at each other in silence, death now being close upon us, and, hearing a noise behind me, I turned and saw the admiral, standing, a candelabrum in his hand, wearing his dressing gown, which (as incredible as it may be that I noticed this in the furious confusion) was of red velvet with an ermine collar. He'd risen, I thought, in order to die standing up, and was leaning against the wall, doubtless in pain from his wound, but looking serene despite the furious blows of the guards' axes on the door.

"My sons," he said at last, "you've fought enough. You must try to escape if it's still possible."

"No, I won't leave, Monsieur!" said Cornaton. "Begging your pardon!"

"Nor I," said Muss.

"Nor I," I said.

"*Herrgott!*" said Fröhlich in his gibberish. "*Schelme* on anyone who flees! And I've broken my sword and any Swiss who's lost his weapon must die!"

The door, broken by so many axe blows, collapsed, and a king's guard stuck his head through and tried to step over the two oak chests, but Fröhlich rushed to the mantelpiece, screaming like a devil in a font, grabbed a heavy andiron and threw it at the man's head, knocking off his helmet. The guard fell in a heap.

"Flee, my sons, I order you to flee!" shouted the admiral, pointing to the door that led to the turret.

Cornaton was the first to obey, then Muss, then Miroul and I, and finally Fröhlich, who was still complaining about losing his sword, but whom I told to be quiet since the door to the turret was the only thing separating us from the guards who were streaming into the room through the splintered door. As I hesitated as to whether I should go up to the next storey or head downstairs, I stopped in front of a little window that opened onto the admiral's bedroom and I saw Monsieur de Coligny standing, leaning against the wall, the candelabrum in his hand, which did not tremble in the slightest, facing his assassins, his face calm and composed. Cossain was among the five or six guards present, but, although he had his sword in his hand and had directed the assault ordered by the king, he didn't seem to want to be the admiral's assassin, for he allowed a soldier to go ahead of him (the man who always had such swagger). Pike in hand, the soldier shouted:

"Are you the admiral?"

"I am," said Coligny, raising the candelabrum and holding it in front of his face.

"Ah, traitor!" said the man as he drove his pike into his stomach.

The candelabrum dropped from the right hand of the admiral, who, however, did not fall; and, looking his murderer in the eye, he said with infinite scorn:

"What a shame it wasn't a man, but only a churl."

At this, wrenching his pike from the admiral's entrails, the churl delivered a ferocious blow to his head that knocked him to the ground. I didn't want to see any more and ran headlong down the stairs, with Fröhlich behind me. Miroul had preceded me and it was lucky he did, for, having unlocked the little door that opened onto the rue de Béthisy, he closed it almost all the way so that he and I could see, a mere yard or so away, a large troop of soldiers, and behind them the Bâtard d'Angoulême and the Duc de Guise, who, looking up at the window on the first floor, called:

"Is it done, Besme?"

"It's done," said the voice of the churl whom I'd just seen at work in the room above.

"Monsieur d'Angoulême here," replied Guise, "won't believe it until he's seen the corpse at his feet."

So the corpse was immediately thrown from the window by the soldier he'd been talking to, who was, as we later learnt, a German from Bohemia (which is why they called him Besme) and a servant in Guise's household. As Coligny's head was already bloody from the blow of the pike administered by this fellow, the Bâtard d'Angoulême couldn't immediately recognize him, and so he leant over and wiped some of the blood from his face with his handkerchief, saying, finally:

"It's really him."

He then stood up and, in keeping with his natural baseness, delivered a kick to the dead body. Seeing this, the Duc de Guise put his hand on the bâtard's arm, as if to signify that the insult could no longer reach a man who could not feel it; then he looked around him with pride, as if this were the most glorious day of his life, and said to the king's guards and the other gentlemen who were standing several yards away, all armed to the teeth, bearing torches, their eyes lit up in anticipation of the coming carnage:

"My friends, let's go out and finish the work we've so handsomely begun here!"

Hearing this, Miroul quietly closed the little door and, having bolted it, said in my ear:

"Monsieur, the only way out of here leads right into the mouth of the wolf. Let's go up and try the rooftops."

Which we did, and you can bet we were on tiptoe going by the window to the admiral's bedroom, but we needn't have worried. When I peeked inside, I could see the guards so furiously occupied in pillaging the chests that a pack of horses could have stampeded down the staircase without distracting them from their pilfering.

At the top of the stairs, a small window opened out onto the roof, through which Miroul slipped like a ferret, I with some effort and Fröhlich only by dint of a struggle as protracted as if he'd been a camel trying to pass through the eye of the proverbial needle. At length, after much breathing, panting and gasping, he made it through, and, the three of us holding on to the top of the turret from which we'd emerged, we could see below us in the rue de Béthisy the torches and the sinister shadows they threw of the assembled swarm of cuirasses and halberds.

On our right the moon had come out from behind a cloud, and we could see the towers of Saint-Germain l'Auxerrois, and behind them the sombre mass of the Louvre, whence had come our death warrant. As the night began to wane, we realized that the dawn would greatly increase our peril, and that we would doubtless be spied up here and hunted down. But as we were debating how we might get out of this predicament, an explosion of sound hit us as if it were solid and shook the air all around us: the great bell of Saint-Germain l'Auxerrois began to toll, and this terrible din was taken up by all the churches in this immense metropolis, and the doors of all the houses in the rue de Béthisy flew open and those of all the neighbouring streets as well, vomiting by the hundreds hoards of Parisians, armed to the teeth, brandishing pikes and swords, torches held high so as to identify the doors that the *dizeniers* had marked that morning with a white cross. And above them the church bells continued to ring in every quarter of the capital as if to call the faithful to celebrate this strange nocturnal Mass, whose martyrs, too, worshipped Christ.

10

"HURRY, MY MASTER," Miroul urged, shaking me from the momentary paralysis the bells had cast on me, "we've got to get off this roof or they'll start shooting at us like pigeons."

'Sblood! He was right! We had to act quickly and wisely, though so often in perilous situations it turns out to be blind luck that turns stupidity into genius or wisdom into folly.

I saw, as I cast a glance behind me, that there was a building attached to this one that looked like a stable, and that overlooked a courtyard that contained a number of small gardens. Indeed, one of the surprises of Paris is that, in the street, you see only the urban facade, but behind it there is a little rural landscape, complete with wells, fruit trees and all the greenery a housekeeper would need.

Thinking we'd be better hidden in these gardens, away from the massacre, I began to climb down the roof on that side. Miroul quickly passed me, of course, and leapt, with his usual agility, onto the roof of the stable and from there onto the ground. But having landed on the ground, he made a sign to me not to follow, since the fall would be too hard for me, and, running to grab a rickety ladder that he'd spied in the garden, he brought it over and leant it up against the stable wall for us. As much of a help as it was to me, it was absolutely necessary for Fröhlich, who weighed so much that the last three rungs broke under his weight and he reached the ground much faster than he would have wished, though without injury. Miroul couldn't help laughing, though quietly, so irrepressible was his natural gaiety, even in the most desperate situations.

There wasn't so much as a cat in these gardens, our beautiful papist angels being wholly caught up in the pillaging of the house behind us. In all of the windows, which were lit up by the torches that were passing to and fro within, we could see the guards moving about in their frantic search for money, clothes, weapons, boots and silverware—such being the worldly rewards God was providing for their murder of the heretics, not to mention the heavenly reward of bypassing Purgatory on their way to Paradise. So taken were they by this glorious quest that not one of them thought, thank God, to cast a glance out of the window, otherwise they surely would have seen us by the light of the full moon.

"My friends," I whispered, "let's head for the gardens! Better trees than men!"

So we leapt into the first garden we came to, and from that to the next, and to the one after that, Miroul leaping over the fences like a rabbit, I clearing them with some effort and Fröhlich simply trampling them before him like an elephant. Seeing this, I invited him to go before me, since his work greatly eased my way. 'Tis true that he made an infernal racket as he crushed or ripped up everything in his path, but none of this noise could be heard over the deafening tolling of the bells, the echoes of arquebus shots in the streets and the general noise of the crowds that came from all sides.

Eventually, moving from garden to garden, we came out onto a street, which, as we learnt from Miroul, who now knew Paris like the back of his hand, was the rue Tirechappe.

"Monsieur," said my gentle valet as we hid in the shadows of a doorway to get our bearings, "we're but fifty yards from Alizon's lodgings. Let's ask for her help!"

"Not on your life!" I growled through clenched teeth. "We can't. She's been blinded by the sermons she's heard, and considers me her mortal enemy."

"But, Monsieur, she's a good wench, who's enjoyed your generosity and your caresses! There must be some love yet from what you've shared!"

"There is none, I tell you! Let's move on!"

"Where?"

"Wherever fate takes us."

This fate seemed to fall out of the sky on us in the form of a poor fellow who landed in the mud a few yards from us, having been defenestrated after his assailants had ripped his stomach open. Above us several women were screaming, and I hesitated, wondering whether we should rush to their aid. But suddenly I saw a man rushing towards us, pursued by half a dozen bourgeois armed with pikes. As he reached us, he suddenly turned to face them, sword in hand, wrapped his left arm in his cloak, and stood with his back to a house, clearly resolved to die fighting since he had no chance against his attackers, being clothed only in his doublet while they were in helmets and breastplates. One of his assailants raised his torch in order better to see his victim, and I couldn't help yelling as I recognized Monsieur de Guerchy. He looked our way at this, and seeing the red and yellow colours of Fröhlich, yelled:

"Help me, Navarre!"

You can easily imagine that, hearing this appeal, we all drew our swords and had at these cowards, taking the wind out of their sails and managing to inflict enough wounds that they fled, shouting, "To arms! To the cause! To Madame la Cause!"

One of them dropped his sword in his panic, and Fröhlich immediately seized it, saying "*Herrgott!* This is a good!" for he'd been without a sword since the melee at the admiral's house and had been feeling very vulnerable.

Poor Guerchy was staggering, and Miroul and I held him up, but blood was flowing from all parts of his body, especially a nasty wound in his chest. When I told him I'd examine his wounds, he replied in a very weak voice:

"Don't waste your time, Siorac, I'm done for! But if you succeed in getting away, I beg you to tell others that my death was worthy of my life."

"I promise."

"And watch out for these scoundrels! They're all wearing a white cloth on their arms and a cross on their caps to recognize each other."

Then, his heart full of gall, he opened his mouth wide in a last attempt to breathe but could not, and gave up the ghost, honourably, as he had wanted, his face full of resolve and his sword in hand.

"Monsieur! We can't stay here!" hissed Miroul as we withdrew into the shadow of a doorway, realizing that even there the moon was so bright that we could easily be seen. "Those scoundrels may return! Let's keep moving!"

"All right, but not before Fröhlich removes his red and yellow colours that will give us away."

"*Ach! Mein Herr!*" said Fröhlich, his voice constricted with emotion. "Ask one of Navarre's Swiss to hide his uniform! *Schelme! Schelme!*"

"You have to, Fröhlich," I said stiffly. "You put all three of us at risk!"

"*Ach!*" he objected. "Taking off my uniform would break my oath as a Swiss guard!"

"Then break it, Fröhlich," I said, "or by God you must leave us!"

"*Was?*" he cried, tears streaming down his large red face. "Leave you? Where would I go without you, Monsieur? What would I do? Who would command me?"

"I command you, for the present, Fröhlich, and my orders are to disrobe this second and leave your uniform here."

Which, finally, he did, amid copious tears and great sighs, and not without carefully folding his tunic and placing it lovingly on a windowsill nearby, as if he thought he'd come back to collect it after the massacre. Then, he sheathed his sword in his belt, which seemed to comfort him a bit. As for me, all lathered from our encounter with these rascals, I felt so sweaty that I unbuttoned by doublet and my chemise, which, as it turned out, was a very good thing.

"Now!" I said. "Let's head towards the Seine! Maybe we can get across despite the chains!"

But we hadn't gone more than twenty yards before we met a large band of papists, who, seeing us, began shouting "To the cause!" and looked as though they'd surround us, a manoeuvre we frustrated by standing with our backs to a wall and drawing our swords, which seemed to slow their charge.

"Brothers!" I shouted, trying to affect as Parisian an accent as I could. "What's going on? Did you take us for heretical dogs?"

"Assuredly so!" said a tall, fat man, whom the others called "captain", and who must have been the *quartenier* or the *dizenier*. He looked, from his clothes, to be a master artisan, and was now, by choice, a master assassin and pillager, but one who I supposed was happier pillaging than fighting. "You're heretical scum," he yelled, brandishing a pistol, "and we're going to crush you without further ado!"

"Blessed Virgin!" I cried, and, seizing the medallion of Mary I wore around my neck, I brought it to my lips, crying: "Blessed Virgin, protect me from this terrible mistake! I'm a good Catholic, my brother, and as zealous and assiduous in my obedience to the good priest Maillard's teaching as any man, and I can recite the Ave Maria as well as any man, forwards *and* backwards, as I've heard His Holiness the Pope do!"

"Backwards!" said one of the scoundrels, visibly impressed.

"Torchbearer!" snarled the *quartenier* stiffly, without taking a step nearer. "Go and see what's with this medallion!"

"It's really the Blessed Virgin," said the man without daring to get too close, seeing my sword and dagger at the ready. "The medallion's made of gold, Captain!"

"Gold!" said the captain with a greedy air, raising his pistol, a movement that made Miroul, on my left, coil like a snake and slip his right hand down to the dagger that was hidden in his boot.

"It's only bronze, my brother," I corrected quickly. "I'm not well heeled enough to afford a gold one."

"It's my opinion," said one of these knaves, putting on airs, "that this is one of those Genevans who wants to throw us off the scent with his lies! He's a nobleman, he is! Look at his fancy doublet and all his pearls!"

"My good man!" I laughed (though somewhat hollowly, knowing how the people of Paris hold the nobility in low esteem). "You've just ennobled me! I'm just an honest man of the people, like you, an apothecary from Montfort-l'Amaury, and I just acquired this doublet from my pillaging, though it was hardly worth it. These stones are plaster copies from Lyons, that's all."

"Knave," shouted the captain, "if you're one of us, how come you're not wearing a white armband?"

"My serving girl sewed it on so badly it came undone during the first brawl."

"And who are these two?"

"They're my assistants in the shop," said I, taking this tack to amuse them. "This one" (pointing to Fröhlich, whom I wanted to silence because his German accent would have been a certain sign of his reformist views) "is as mute as a carp. The other one's got mismatched eyes."

"Why, so he does!" said the torchbearer in surprise.

And these Parisians, who think they know everything, were in fact so credulous that they immediately thought that Miroul's eyes were some sort of divine miracle from the Blessed Virgin, since they'd never heard of anything like this.

"What's more," I continued, "he can throw a knife better than any mother's son in France! If you please, Captain, step back a few paces and he'll sink his knife into the ring of that door knocker that you see over there."

"Torchbearer," cried Miroul, "shine some light on that door!"

And scarcely had the captain taken a step backwards before Miroul launched his knife and planted it quivering in the board of the door, exactly in the centre of the ring of the knocker. The *quartenier* appeared quite discomposed to feel the wind of the blade as it whistled by his fat nose, and seemed to have visibly lost his swagger, no longer assured that, even with their pistols, they held an advantage over us—and especially when he saw Miroul bend quickly and seize a second knife from his other boot.

"That's enough, my brother," said the *quartenier*, softening his tone considerably, "you've persuaded me. I'm now convinced of your zeal to perform pious works on this holy feast day of St Bartholomew! But take my advice! Get your brassard sewn back on quickly. Who can see a grey cat at night? My lads! Let's be off, we have better things to do elsewhere!"

And off they went, quitting the field, perhaps convinced, perhaps not wishing to risk their tender skin for the slim profit of a few pearls and a medallion. Whether or not he believed it was bronze, I now valued it as worth much more than its weight in gold, not just because it had been given to me by my late mother, but because it had just saved my life—after having nearly cost me it during the Michelade in Nîmes five years previously. But isn't it a terrible thing than men can play "heads or tails" for a man's life using an image? Oh, Lord! What a strange power over men is wielded by the very idols they have fashioned with their own hands!

As we watched them run off towards other exploits, we were conscious that the church bells had stopped tolling, but all around us we could hear the repeated explosions of arquebuses, the thuds of battering rams splintering wooden doors, the panting of fleeing victims, the battle cries of the assassins and the screams of martyrs who had been surprised in their homes and had then fled in their nightclothes, but who were then caught, their throats slashed pitilessly, stripped, mutilated and dragged through the filth of the street.

"Monsieur," said Miroul, "you did an amazing job of out-talking those rogues, but I don't think your medallion is going to save you a second time. We have to find a way to have some white armbands sewn on our sleeves, and the only one who do that is Alizon. Outside of Alizon, no salvation!"

"*Ach*, good Monsieur," said Fröhlich, "do I have to stay mute or may I say something?"

"Speak, Fröhlich."

"It's a great *Schelme*, in my opinion, to wear the white brassards of these killers!"

"Ah, no, Fröhlich, quite the contrary!" I said. "It's a legitimate strategy to imitate your enemy when it's a matter of life and death! Miroul, in the end, I think you're right. Go and see if the priest's sermons haven't entirely corrupted Alizon's good heart."

But once we got to Alizon's lodgings, the door was locked and barred from within, and even though I dared knock, no one came to the windows.

"But look, Monsieur," observed Miroul, "the upstairs window is open and there's candlelight within. If you please, Monsieur, let me climb up to her room and test the waters."

"*Was?* My little friend," said Fröhlich, "are you a fly that you can scale that facade?"

"He's done better than that," I said. "Bend over and lend him your strong back, Fröhlich, so he can get past the corbel, and by the time you stand up straight, he'll be through the window."

Miroul managed this feat with his incredible agility and the grace of a cat—and, like a cat, without appearing to be in any hurry but, with total calm, choosing each step. I watched him from below, illuminated in the moonlight, while, in the shadows, I agonized, my heart beating frantically with his every step, anxious and uncertain about the success of his mission. But I needn't have been. Scarcely two minutes passed before the door was unbolted and thrown open and my Alizon fell into my arms, sighing and planting a thousand kisses on my face and neck.

"Who's that?" she whispered, seeing the great mountain of a man behind me.

"A good Swiss from Berne."

"May God keep him!" she murmured. (But which God, I wondered, the God of the assassins or the God of the assassinated?) "Come up to my room," she continued, "but don't make a sound! The men of our lodgings have all gone out, but the women are here and I'm not sure they're sleeping since the sound of the arquebuses is so near. Monsieur," she said over her shoulder to Fröhlich, "the stairs are creaking, make yourself light!"

This can't have been very easy for him, but at last we reached her room and closed the door, and each of us found a place to sit down. I told Alizon in hushed tones what I hoped she could do for us.

"They're not brassards," she said without hesitating, "but shirt-sleeves cut and sewn into the shoulder of one's doublet. I have the needle and thread, but I don't have the sleeves, and certainly not enough for three."

"Four," corrected Miroul, quietly, "since *maestro* Giacomi is waiting for us on the place de Grève."

His words pricked me with shame, because I'd completely forgotten, in the heat of our escape, our rendezvous.

"Here's my shirt," I said, removing my doublet. "Cut away, Alizon! A shirt without sleeves is perfectly adequate in the August heat."

"And here's mine," said Miroul. "With two sleeves a shirt, we've got four."

Without a word, Alizon set to work by candlelight, cutting and sewing, beginning with my shirt—not without a tear in her eye, however, for I had no doubt that, by helping, nay, saving us, she was risking her life, and not just hers, but that of her little Henriot, who was so prettily asleep in his cradle, his fist under his tiny cheek.

I would have liked to take the pretty little child in my arms, so comforted would I have felt by that tiny warm body of one who knew nothing of the cruelty of this world, since he was not yet a man, but still so close to heaven. But I didn't pick him up. Not only did I fear waking him from his starry dreams, I felt too blood-soaked and sweaty after my two battles to dare to touch him with my finger. I shall never forget to my dying day, however, the silence of that little room as Alizon went about her sewing by candlelight, her eyes misty with tears, her breath coming short, and, in his cradle, little Henriot smiling angelically, as if he were gambolling about in the garden of Eden.

Since none of us was wearing a hat that we could attach a cross to, we had to be content with the armbands. Miroul slipped into his doublet the armband Alizon had made for Giacomi, with pins to attach it to his shoulder, should Fortune be kind enough to favour our meeting at the place de Grève. We then went—or rather slid—downstairs, as silent as weasels in a meadow, and, after Alizon had unbolted the door, she dared, as she threw herself into my arms, to whisper in my ear, since the noise in the street was so loud:

"Oh, Pierre! This is hell in all its fury! In the lodgings you see there, they slashed the throats of an entire family—father, mother and a child who was Henriot's age! Then these pitiless monsters tore their clothes off and dragged their bodies out into the street and through the filth down to the Seine, some still groaning, and then the lot was thrown on a cart. Oh, Pierre! Between the promising of what they were going to do and the doing of it, what an abyss! I cannot believe the Blessed Virgin, who is so sweet, could ever have called for so much bloodshed!"

There was nothing I could say, since my heart was so heavy, but I kissed her dearly, and held her so close to me that our bodies were as one. Finally, recovering my voice, I whispered my thanks and promised to come back to see her if we escaped this terrible night. Then she pulled me to her and wrapped her arms around my neck with a strange force, as if to offer me her breast like her infant. Her fear for my life led this good wench to engulf her lover with as much maternal care as if he were her child. But ultimately I had to force myself to leave her, my eyes so blinded with tears I could scarcely see my way back into the evil world of men.

Luckily, Miroul was able to guide me through a labyrinth of muddy streets to the Hôtel de Ville, and from there to the place de Grève, where we encountered a huge crowd of people carrying torches and very excited by the spectacle that the pillory offered: it was a sort of octagonal wooden cage painted blood-red, which was turning slowly on a pivot, exposing as it did its collection of unfortunates, whose heads were visible through holes in the wood and thus exposed to the harangues, mud, filth and stones of the good-for-nothings who surrounded them. An onlooker whom I dared ask the identity of the Devil's fiends who were thus exposed, shamed, mocked and tortured, laughed and happily explained that they were three ministers of the reformed religion who had just been captured and who were going to provide the crowd some amusement before being stabbed and thrown in the river.

My heart ached with sorrow and pity as I watched the slow revolution of this cage—a remarkable example of man's ingenuity when he's looking to torment his brothers—and, examining these martyrs carefully, I was afraid I'd see Monsieur Merlin among them, but I doubted I'd now be able to recognize him, since the faces of these poor victims were so swollen and covered with blood, mud and excrement, and their eyes were mere empty sockets from the stoning.

"Well," laughed the fellow I'd just been talking to, "what a dirty and nasty look these heretic dogs have! We can already guess what they'll look like when they reach hell!"

I turned on my heel and walked away, with Miroul on my left and Fröhlich behind me, our swords unsheathed and tucked under our arms in case we needed suddenly to use them, but not held at the ready, since we didn't want anyone to get ideas about us and start a ruckus, given how bloodthirsty and murderous the night's business had made the people.

I walked around the outside of the square, past the houses, hoping to catch sight of Giacomi, knowing he'd prefer to meet in the shadows of some doorway, rather than in the full light of the moon and the torches. We made it around the entire square without any trouble other than the appearance of a thief, who nearly stole my purse, and who nearly lost his fingers when Miroul crossed knives with him and sent him scuttling into the crowd like a snake in a bush—all of this happening so quickly that I wondered whether I'd dreamt it. But thank God I wasn't dreaming when I saw Giacomi emerge from a doorway, and then felt him embrace me fondly and plaster a hundred kisses on my cheeks—a greeting I generously answered. I was overwhelmed by his incredible fidelity in this valley of death in which we found ourselves, stranger as he was to our civil discord, being Italian—not to mention a papist.

"Well, my brother!" he exclaimed with his charming lisp and in the elegant language he always used even in the face of such mortal danger. "I ran here at the firtht thound of the church bellth, and I've been waiting for you ever thinth, hoping againtht hope!"

"Giacomi, my brother," I whispered, "I'll tell you of our adventures later, but first step into this doorway so Miroul can pin a white brassard on your sleeve to identity you as one of their party. When that's done, we'll try to cross the river and get beyond the city walls."

There was no need to ask which way the river was! People were heading there from all directions, talking about the "beautiful spectacle" of all the bodies—dead and alive—of the Huguenots that were floating in it, some dragged there, naked, by ropes under their armpits, others escorted there, then beaten, undressed and thrown in the water.

From the place de Grève to the part of the bank of the Seine called the Port-au-Foin (a dilapidated quay for boats bringing hay for the 100,000 horses stabled in the capital) there's a very slight slope, but the way is very muddy, since the paving stones give way to earthworks, now slippery with the blood of all the martyrs dragged there by there assailants to defile them further, since the custom in Paris is to bring condemned prisoners here for their execution (by water, in this case, rather than by fire) and drown them the way one would drown puppies. And since some of our people were only wounded and had been thrown in the water without being finished off, so hurried were their assailants in their dastardly work, they would try to swim or call for help; in response, some of these monstrous assassins unchained the boats that were there and, floating along with the current, amused themselves by ending the lives of those who were still moving with blows of their oars.

It wasn't easy to get near the Port-au-Foin, so great was the press of men and wenches, who, I'm ashamed to say, were screaming and shouting like hell's Furies. We were so chilled by this horrific spectacle, despite the sweat that was running down our bodies in the insufferable heat of this August night, that we had no appetite for watching it—or for listening to it, for the hoots, howls and whistles of the populace made us wonder if they might not be wolves or vipers. So we headed downriver in the hope of reaching one of the two bridges that remained, the Pont Notre-Dame being closed for repairs. Below the Port-au-Foin, the riverbank was more grassy and open, and so we were able to move along more quickly, but a little farther on we saw a large number of naked bodies, which the current had pushed into the bank, where the river grass had entangled them and held them fast.

As horrible as this sight was, we were to witness something much worse a few yards farther still, where we encountered a large group of people shouting obscenities, in whose direction we headed, driven by a kind of morbid curiosity. I told Fröhlich to push through the crowd, which he did effortlessly, simply by ploughing forward, using his bulk to separate the mob as easily as a knife cutting through butter, with me behind him like a rowing boat in tow, and Giacomi and Miroul in our wake. And there we saw a large semicircle, kept open by the king's guards, who held off the crowd with their halberds while three of them pulled from the water a corpse that, as far as I could tell, when they'd brought it up to the bank, had been decapitated, and had its genitalia mutilated.

The guard who came up to me had more than he could manage with the noisy rascals pushing up against him, despite the weapon that he brandished, so I told Fröhlich to create a little space for him, which this great hulk from the mountains did simply by turning away from them and backing up, the pygmies behind him falling like dominoes in his path. The guard, much relieved, laughed and thanked me, saying to Fröhlich:

"Haven't I seen you around the Louvre?"

"Guard," I said, stepping between them, "my valet is a deaf mute and can't answer you, but perhaps you can answer me something: whose body is that they've just taken such pains to pull out of the river?"

"That's the brigand Coligny!" said the guard, and, hearing his name, the populace began to shout and whistle like all the devils in hell.

"Well," I managed to say through the knot in my throat, and as casually as I could manage, "and who ordered him to be beheaded?"

"Guise, so he could send his head to the Pope."

"And who mutilated him?"

"This stupid crowd here. They dragged him here and threw him in the Seine."

"But why pull him out now?" I said frowning.

"King's orders. We're going to hang him at Montfaucon."

"Guard, how are you going to hang him without a head?"

"By the feet."

"And we're going to set a fire underneath the gibbet!" shouted a knave, who from his habit looked like a sort of mendicant friar, but with a low and mean look about him. "So," he shouted over the noise of the crowd, "we'll have killed this demon by the four elements God gave us: the earth we dragged him on, the water we threw him in, the air where he'll dangle and the fire that'll roast him!"

These mean-spirited and barbarous words were cheered by those within earshot, and then repeated from mouth to mouth by the multitude. But our guard only shrugged and said:

"Who's dead is dead. Don't matter much the manner nor the means of it."

As for me, I'd heard more than enough, and we fought our way back out of this angry mob and headed to the Grand Châtelet in the hope of crossing the Pont au Change and reaching the Île de la Cité, and from there the Pont Saint-Michel, which would take us to l'Université. Once there, we hoped to be able to get through one of the drawbridges and to safety outside the walls. So we still had two bridges and a gate, and all three guarded by the bourgeois militias or the guards of the Louvre! And everywhere we went we were surrounded by hordes of assassins, by any one of whom I might suddenly be recognized. How many incredible obstacles had we to negotiate before we'd be out of this enormous trap where we were thrown together with our enemies, without any lodgings in which we might seek shelter, nor friends we could trust?

In order to reach the Pont au Change, we walked along the quai de la Mégisserie, which Parisians call "the Valley of Misery", since the Seine floods the area frequently, but which now was earning its name from the hundreds of drowned or dying bodies that the moon and the dawn's early light revealed floating along, while on both banks you could see the torches and hear the cries of the victims, which mingled with the bloodthirsty howls of their assailants and the sound of firearms coming from every direction, along with the dull thuds of battering rams against oak doors, and an occasional church bell that recommenced its tolling, as if to reawaken, if it needed any encouragement, this enormous appetite for killing.

Meanwhile, we weren't making much progress, since, behind the chains at the bridge, we spied a detachment of the king's guards bristling with pikes and arquebuses.

"My brother," said Giacomi in hushed tones, taking me by the arm, "I think it would be madness to try to cross the bridge now. The guards will surely ask us for passes, which we'd be unable to present."

"Not to mention," added Miroul, "the fact that our Swiss, who's no needle in a haystack, will be recognized as one of Navarre's men by anyone who's seen him at the Louvre. And on this particular morning, the name Navarre spells death, for all four of us."

"As for me," announced Fröhlich, "I don't mind passing from life to death, but I wouldn't like to pass those guards without my uniform!"

Giacomi had to turn away to hide his smile and Miroul as well, which proved how irrepressible these worthies' gaiety was, even in the worst of times.

"My brothers," I said (and observed despite my terrible fatigue how Miroul blushed with happiness at being treated this way), "I believe you're both right. And daybreak is only going to multiply our perils. The best thing would be to find some hiding place where we can lie low until nightfall."

"But where?" shrugged Miroul.

"*Mein Herr*," suggested Fröhlich, "I twice carried messages from my king" (he meant Navarre, of course) "to Monsieur de Taverny, who is a lieutenant in the provost's guards."

"I'm not sure it would be safe, since Taverny is a Huguenot."

"If he weren't he wouldn't let us in," observed Miroul, "and if his house hasn't been attacked, at least he could provide us with some nourishment. My stomach is down in my heels and I have such an appetite I could eat the shells off the oysters. Those three pastries we ate yesterday are only a memory."

"Ah, my friend," sighed Fröhlich, "don't make my mouth water talking about pastries!"

Isn't it amazing that, in the midst of such incredible dangers, we were all four as famished as a pack of wolves in a blizzard, so much so that, ironically, in order to find nourishment, we were prepared to leap from the frying pan into the fire?

"Fröhlich, can you lead us to Monsieur de Taverny's lodgings?"

"Of course I can! They're just past the rue Leuffroy, in a house called the Black Head."

So, leaving the Pont au Change and any hope of immediate escape, we retraced our steps and headed back towards the city, very unhappy with all these detours we'd had to make in our dizzying flight.

Once past the rue Leuffroy, Fröhlich diverted us through a very filthy and muddy alleyway, which at least had the merit of being sparsely travelled, for we saw only one fellow coming towards us— but he immediately got our attention since he was carrying a baby without cloth or blanket of any kind, who was happily laughing and playing, his chubby little fingers enmeshed in the man's abundant, curly black beard.

"Friend," I said, stopping, moved by this sweet sight, "this child seems to like you!"

"Maybe, but I don't like him," he growled rudely, glaring at me out of small black eyes. "He's the pup of a heretic. I'm heading down to the Seine to stab him and drown him."

"What?" I gasped. "Kill him? Even though he's so young he can't speak or understand anything? What does he know of religion?"

"He's the seed of a heretic," frowned the man. "Monsieur," he said, looking towards the rue Leuffroy, where we could see bands of murderers running wildly, "will you let me pass or do I have to call 'to arms and to the cause'?"

"You're mistaken, friend," I said. "We're good Catholics. I'm only interested in this infant since I could take him to my sister in the country, who could raise him in the true religion."

"Impossible," replied the man, refusing to bend, even while the baby continued to coo and laugh, caressing his beard with his little fingers. "Like I said," he continued, his eyes shining, "I'm going to stab him and throw him in the river. And I'm so eager to do it, my hands are itching!"

"Friend," I said, "I'll pay you whatever you ask for him."

"Well, then," said the knave, looking at the child and then at my purse, as if he were torn between two equal pleasures.

"Ten écus," I said.

"It's a deal," agreed the bearded man, though with some reluctance, I thought.

I counted out the coins for him and he put them one by one into his pocket. But then, strangely, as he went to hand me the baby, he suddenly turned away from me; and as he turned to face me again, he thrust the child into my arms and took off running as fast as he could.

"Monsieur," cried Miroul, "he stabbed him! That's why he turned around! Look at the blood gushing from his little heart!"

"Your knife, Miroul!" I cried, drunk with rage.

But Miroul had already seized his dagger and had taken off like a hare in pursuit of the rogue, and hurled it at him. The knife hit him between the shoulder blades, dropping him flat in the alley's filth and ordure, which, as it was, was worth more than him.

A group of men now entered the alleyway and headed towards us, and, seeing Miroul still bent over the body, I shouted:

"Hurry, Miroul! What are you waiting for?"

"Taking back your money, Monsieur!"

"Just grab the purse! It'll be faster!"

This Miroul did, and got back to us before the band of papists reached us, who, when they saw the bloody child, assumed I had killed this offspring of a heretic and made merry with us, some congratulating us on our exploit and others joking that it was a shame we hadn't been able to get any money from it.

"My brother, what will you do with him?" said Giacomi, seeing me in tears.

"We'll bury him in this garden, so that the dogs won't devour him, the very thought of which makes me shudder. Fröhlich, break down this fence!"

He did so in a trice, and quickly dug a small grave with his short sword to bury the little corpse, covering it with earth and a large stone so that it couldn't be dug up.

All this while, the house behind which we carried out this sad labour remained dark, its inhabitants no doubt running through the streets, committing more of the mayhem we'd already witnessed—or else asleep, dead tired from all that killing.

We arrived too late at Taverny's lodgings. They had already been turned inside out and half burnt, the furniture outside in the street; on the staircase inside was the body of Taverny, his sword fallen from his hand, and three or four rogues lying dead around him, proof that the lieutenant had valiantly defended himself.

On the ground floor, we discovered a dozen pillagers at work, who were, from what I could tell, porters and butchers from the nearby Écorcherie quarter. These good-for-nothings, seeing that there were only four of us, and thinking we wanted to take their booty, hurled themselves at us, but, without helmets or any armour, they had no time to repent of their folly. Giacomi laid three of them out on the tiles with his sword; Fröhlich wreaked such carnage with his short sword that he broke the hilt; and Miroul and I dispatched the others, all except one who had the presence of mind to flee.

"Well, Fröhlich," I laughed, "now you've got no sword!"

"My friend, this will suffice," countered the good Swiss, grabbing a huge mace that one of the butchers had dropped, the kind that is normally used for slaughtering cattle. And balancing this heavy weapon on his outstretched hand as if it were a feather, he began flourishing it with amazing agility.

We found some bread and cheese in the kitchen that the pillagers had disdained in their search for more durable goods, and after I'd divided this meagre booty into four shares, we gobbled it up like hungry dogs without taking a breath or uttering a word. After which, Miroul went scrabbling about like a weasel in a henhouse, and found a flagon of wine that had miraculously escaped the pillagers' notice.

We made quick work of that miracle, being so dry after our long nocturnal wanderings. Meanwhile, Giacomi suddenly noticed that the fellow who'd escaped was coming back with about forty of his fellows, all carrying picks and spikes, and all looking very determined to exact justice from us for the murder of their friends. We escaped up a small spiral staircase, Fröhlich going first, which was lucky for us because the tower was dark and, in his haste, he banged his head on the trapdoor at the top, which burst open without hurting him in the least, so hard-headed are these Swiss from Berne. Using his mace, he broke through the door and we all burst onto the roof, while, beneath us, the rascals were screaming "To the cause!" loud enough to wake the dead. Meanwhile we traversed the half-burnt roof at great risk of breaking our necks or being fired at from below, and eventually reached a dormer window, which Fröhlich smashed with his mace and, risking life and limb, leapt through… landing in a loft piled high with sweet-smelling hay! We decided to hide out there for the rest of the day and busily hollowed out a nest for ourselves in the thickest part of the hay, where we stretched out our tired legs on this soft (but prickly) bed, and were almost asleep when suddenly we felt our bed giving way beneath us. Fröhlich gave a shout of surprise and disappeared. We hardly had time to gather our wits before we, too, slipped through the funnel he'd created, landing on top of him and the hay he'd dragged with him in the manger of a mule that was stabled there. She was so surprised to see us that she lost both her bray and her appetite, and backed to the rear of her stall—her soft eyes a thousand times more benevolent than those of any man we'd seen since the bells of Saint-Germain l'Auxerrois had begun tolling those many hours ago.

Would you believe it? We began laughing! It would seem that joy is so deeply rooted in us and is so connected to our will to live that it cannot help but burst out of us at the slightest provocation, no matter how horrible the situation we believe we're in.

"Well," I suggested, "let's use this old ladder to climb back up into the loft."

"My brother," said Giacomi, who was delicately removing hay from his hair, "I think we'd be better off here in the stable, hidden behind these barrels, which, being empty, won't attract those flies, any more than a flagon of vinegar would."

"But why here rather than up there?"

"Well, Pierre, if you were those rascals from the Écorcherie, where would you look for fugitives? In the hay, surely? This hiding place is better simply because it's less obvious."

"'Sblood, you're right," I conceded, and, gathering up the hay that had fallen, we stuffed it behind the barrels to make a bed that would cushion us against the stone floor. Fröhlich was no help to us now, since he was whispering sweet words in the mule's ears in his patois, while caressing them with his huge hands, no doubt because she reminded him of the mountains in Switzerland. We called him over when we'd finished his bed and he stretched out to his full length—which was considerable, not to mention his girth—with his mace by his side, and, looking very much like Hercules, he fell asleep in the blink of an eye, as peaceful as if he'd lain down on some grassy hillside in Berne.

Meanwhile, we undertook to place some barrels in front of a little door that opened into this part of the stable, so as not to be taken by surprise from the rear, the larger door to the stable being off to our right, beyond the manger where the mule had gone back to feeding. We agreed that each one of us would keep watch in turn, me first, then Miroul, Giacomi and finally the Swiss, our weapons unsheathed and tucked in the crooks of our arms like tender wenches.

Although I was comfortably stretched out and exhausted, I had no inclination to fall asleep, my mind rattled by all the horror I'd witnessed since Cossain had knocked on Coligny's door and killed the poor La Bonne. I tried not to think about it so as not to suffer, and, fleeing the present, went back to thinking about all that had happened since I'd arrived in Paris, wondering about the rhyme or reason of all the joys and sorrows I'd experienced and if it would soon be my turn to be thrown into the Seine, naked and drowning—a thought that brought me back to my present predicament, from which I so desperately wanted to escape.

At least I could take some comfort from the idea that my beloved Samson was safe and sound in Montfort. But even this idea wasn't without its thorns, for I then began to fear that he might jeopardize his own safety if he learnt of the massacre in Paris, knowing that I was here. This fear made me angry at Dame Gertrude, since she'd gone off to Saint-Cloud to flirt with Quéribus, rather than returning to Montfort to be with my brother, where she could prevent him from any excesses to which his zeal exposed him.

I don't know how long I was afflicted with these worries about Samson, which simply wouldn't leave me but kept coming back to haunt me. In any case, such fears kept me feverishly awake, as did the image of the little child whom the bearded rogue had thrown into my arms after stabbing. But as these sad thoughts turned round and round like a top, the sun having now risen, as I could see through a crack in the stable walls, I heard some footsteps and some voices in the courtyard, and then someone rattled the little door that we'd barricaded. I woke my companions up, one by one, Fröhlich being the hardest to stir since he was so sound asleep, and, swords in hand, and all ready to spring, we gathered behind the barrels, our hearts beating madly.

Peeking out between two of the barrels, I saw the door on the side of the mangers open and admit forty knaves armed with pikes, spears and firearms, who found the presence of the mule very comical. Two of them untied her and led her away to sell her, they said, and then stand a round of drinks for all to celebrate this bargain at the Golden Horse tavern. However, the rascal who appeared to be the leader of these thugs—a tall braggart who wore a butcher's knife in his belt—told them that before heading to the tavern he wanted to search through the hay barn for the "Huguenot dogs" who'd killed his brothers; and, climbing up the ladder, the gang proceeded to thrust their swords into various parts of the hay loft, swearing by God and Mary that they'd have their "justice" with the heretics, severely disappointed that none of these thrusts emerged bloody from the hay.

I thought with a shudder, as they came down the ladder, that these rogues wouldn't be content until they searched for us among the barrels and that, when they did, we'd be done for, since some of them had pistols and arquebuses. My eyes met Giacomi's and we both understood that the next sixty seconds would decide whether or not we'd die and be thrown unceremoniously in the river. At that moment I discovered how ashamed I felt to be, at the hour of my demise, so sweaty, filthy and covered with blood, and so heartsick; I clenched my fingers in fury around the hilt of my sword, telling myself that if I had to die, I wouldn't go without taking with me a goodly number of these rogues. They were now coming down the ladder, the fat butcher ahead of the rest, who I swore would be the first to die by my sword, so vile was his demeanour. My heart nearly burst from my chest as I watched one of the rascals, thin as a fish bone, approach our barrels.

"What the Devil are you doing?" growled the butcher.

"Just takin' a look, Cap'n," said the fellow.

"'Struth!" spat the butcher with a sneer. "Can't you see? Those barrels are as empty as the head of an idiot!"

At which, of course, his entire band burst out laughing like a swarm of flies.

"Didn't mean no disrespect, Cap'n," he apologized, as he followed the butcher out of the stables, the butt of the others' humour, who all jostled each other in their haste to get to the Golden Horse tavern to drink up the profits from the mule.

Thank Heaven! We all gave a sigh of relief that would knock a windmill's wings off their axle! After which we just sat there in silence, looking at each other, astonished still to be alive.

The rest of the day we passed in fitful sleep (all except Fröhlich, who snored like a bellows in a forge), our eyes more open than closed, on the alert for any sound, like rabbits in a bush, our thirst so violent we thought our tongues were going to stick to the roofs of our mouths. Worst of all was the gnawing hunger, which was so tormenting that we would have accepted a crust of bread from a leper or a thief. All I remember is that, towards the end of the day, my head nodding off, I had a dream in which the child who had died in my arms suddenly became little Henriot, and Alizon was running after me with a huge knife, because she believed it was I who had killed him.

At nightfall on Sunday, luckily not as luminous as the preceding one, we resolved to leave our hiding place like owls and accept the risks of trying to cross the bridges.

We followed the rue de la Grande Joaillerie down to the Pont au Change, but, once there, decided not to cross all four together, so I sent Miroul to reconnoitre, to establish how well the bridge was guarded. Which he did, disappearing so completely into the shadows of the cantilevers of the bridge that I lost sight of him after a few yards and was completely surprised when he suddenly reappeared with the news that the bourgeois militiamen, who were supposed to be guarding the chains, had gone down to the riverbank to drag to shore any corpses they thought they could pillage.

So it was that we crossed the bridge without striking a blow or meeting a single soul, except for a foul-smelling, hideously thin and twisted fellow in rags, who was lurking in the shadows of the ravaged houses, a huge sack on his back, which he dropped when he saw us, falling on his knees and begging us to spare his life. He said that he was only pilfering the remains of what hadn't already been pillaged, and that there was really nothing left to take, since the workers of the Écorcherie had got there first, and, after them, the nightwatchmen.

"Friend," I said to this poor fellow, who was so wretched that I couldn't help feeling pity for him, "we want neither your sack nor your life. But, by my faith, tell us why there are so many sacked houses on the Pont au Change. I thought I'd heard that there weren't many heretics here."

"Well, now," said the fellow, "of heretics there may be none, but *jewellers*, now, that's another story! Lots of 'em, and well heeled too, reason enough to baptize 'em, kill 'em and toss 'em out the windows into the Seine! The pillaging was very lucrative!"

"What about the night watch?"

"Oh, them!" laughed the fellow. "They don't have the heart to fight to maintain order since they enjoy pillaging as much as the next man!"

We continued on our way, since Miroul was pulling on my sleeve, worried to see me delaying, as was my wont, even in dangerous situations, to satisfy my curiosity.

At the end of the Pont au Change, the shortest route to reach the Pont Saint-Michel was along the rue de la Barillerie, but as we headed that way we saw, some distance ahead of us, a group of torches, and could hear the clicking and clashing of swordplay, a sure sign there was a large detachment of the king's guards in our path. So we quickly turned left down the rue de la Vieille Pelleterie, which is the darkest, most foul-smelling sewer of any street in Paris, and from there into a labyrinth of streets and alleyways, and some dead ends that forced us to retrace our steps in this night that was so dark you wouldn't have been able to see a white cat. We had a difficult time of it, wading through the offal and excrement, tripping over the occasional corpse that had been left there after the massacre by assassins too lazy to drag it to the river. We lost a lot of time wandering around this maze like rats in a cage, and when we finally emerged we were so exhausted, hungry and thirsty that all we could do, despite the urgency of our situation, was fall onto a stone bench outside a very run-down dwelling and remain sitting there silent and haggard, trying to catch our breath.

The sound of firearms had greatly diminished since the night before, the papists having killed off so many of our side on the first night, and most of the rest having fled or gone into hiding, but this street where we'd stopped (which I learnt later was the rue de la Licorne) seemed dead, all of the houses locked and boarded up. But after a few minutes we were surprised to see an unusually bright torch coming towards us along this street, although we were not alarmed since we heard no more than a single pair of footsteps on the paving stones, which, here, were clear of filth. We were somewhat surprised, however, to hear the sound of three steps rather than two, and, as the person drew nearer, we saw that the fellow was limping along on a wooden leg and using a halberd as a cane. He appeared to be quite old, but was still vigorous, his face tanned and scarred, and he was sporting a hat with more feathers than a cock's tail. Holding his torch out ahead of him, he stopped about a yard from us, looking at us with surprise but without a trace of fear, though we were all armed, and he was old and alone.

"On your feet, my children!" he cried in an abrupt and yet cordial voice. "You'd best be on your way! This is a bad place to be stopping!"

And, raising his torch even farther, he showed us, hanging from the door of the lodging behind us, a black crêpe ribbon and a small basket, both of which indicated that within, sequestered with his family and prohibited from leaving, was a victim of the plague, who was hoping for some charitable nourishment to be left in the basket. These signs struck my companions with terror and they leapt up as if the flames of hell had suddenly scorched their backsides.

I, however, rose slowly from the bench and said as calmly as I could:

"Don't be afraid, my friends. The plague can only be spread by contact with those already infected, or their clothes. It isn't carried through the air as some have claimed."

At these words, which revealed my medical training, the fellow raised his torch again and looked at me, and when I returned his look, I realized that I knew him, but didn't say a word, since his expression begged for my discretion.

"In any case," he said, "this is a pretty shabby resting place for honest men who look like they're exhausted."

"*Ach!*" cried Fröhlich. "It's not so much the fatigue—it's the hunger that's eating at us!"

"My good friends, if you're all suffering from the same complaint as this fellow, who reminds me of myself when I was younger, I'd like to invite you to come to my humble lodgings to enjoy a meal with me. It won't be a banquet since my wife's not there and I'm not very competent in the kitchen when she's not around."

The four of us were all too happy to follow him with a lively step and our mouths watering, and were not ashamed, once we reached his poor but respectable lodgings, to sit down at his table and take a crust of bread, a few slices of ham and a goblet of claret, all trying hard not to wolf down our food, to make it last as long as possible. While we ate, our good host watched us with beneficence, leaning his halberd against the wall and removing his feathered hat, revealing a head as bald as a tennis ball and furrowed by a long white scar.

"My friends," he announced, "the king has proclaimed with great pomp a ban that prohibits the inhabitants of his good city of Paris from hiding, feeding or giving any kind of assistance to the fleeing heretics, on pain of death. That's why I was so happy to see your white armbands, which tell me you're good Christians—like myself— without which I would have found it impossible to comfort you, not wishing to risk my neck in such a dangerous act of charity. As for me, as a veteran of the king's guards"—at which words Fröhlich suddenly pricked up his ears—"I have no desire to stick a white ribbon on my arm and go running around killing unarmed people in their beds, doubting there's much glory in such sport, and, frankly, lacking sufficient religious zeal or appetite for others' possessions, since the little that I have is quite enough for me."

"Monsieur," I replied (avoiding referring to him as "scorekeeper", since I could see he didn't wish to reveal that he knew who I was so that he could claim ignorance of my religion if he was accused of disobeying the royal ban), "you're a good man and I admire your beneficence, which I find all too rare in these troubled times. As for me and my men, we're not very happy wearing these brassards."

"I suspected as much," he said with a smile and looking me in the eye. "Didn't I hear you say," he continued in his clever and jocular way, "that you were hoping to return to your native Périgord?"

To this I nodded "yes", matching his smile and looking him in the eye in return, never having said any such thing.

"So you know the Caumonts?" said the scorekeeper.

"They're my cousins and allies."

"Well, Monsieur," he replied, now quite serious, "you'll be very happy to hear from me, good Catholic that you are, that Jacques Nompar de La Force is safe."

"What about his father and older brother?" I cried.

"Alas!" he said, and, sitting down on a stool, his eyes riveted to the ground in sorrow, he added, "Yesterday afternoon in the rue des Petits Champs, Monsieur de La Force and his two sons, all three on the run, were stabbed by good Christians. But it happened that the younger son wasn't actually wounded, but had the marvellous presence of mind to scream 'I'm killed!' and to fall between his father and brother, who bathed him in their blood. After which, their assassins stripped them of all their possessions, and, with clear consciences, departed. In the evening, one of my friends happened to be passing by, and, coveting the stockings that were still on the boy, took them off him. But while he was thus engaged, he took pity on this handsome youth and said quietly, 'Alas! What a pity! So young! What could this child have done to merit such a death?' Whereupon the lad raised his head and whispered, 'Good man, I'm not dead yet! Can you help me?' 'Yes,' said my friend. 'Be patient. Don't move. I'll come back tonight.' So he returned with a ragged old coat in which he wrapped the boy, and was taking him to the arsenal, to give him to Biron, the captain of the artillery, who is the boy's relative, when he met some of the assassins, who, seeing the boy all wrapped like that, asked: 'Who's this? Why's he all bloody?' So my friend replied: 'He's my nephew. He got drunk. Look how he ended up. Isn't it awful? I'm taking him home for a whipping!' So they let him pass, and Biron welcomed his cousin and was able to guarantee his safety behind all his walls and cannon."

"Well, Monsieur!" I cried. "I hope that Biron rewarded your friend handsomely!"

"My friend didn't do it for that," said the scorekeeper, blushing deeply, while the long scar on his pate whitened considerably. Then, observing that we'd finished our repast and that not a crumb of bread remained on the table, or a drop of wine in our goblets, he shook his head and said, "My wife's not here because she had to take a medallion of Notre-Dame de Chartres to her friend Colarde, who's lying in. This blessed medal, as you know"—and he smiled knowingly—"is renowned for easing labour; in fact it is so potent that all you have to do is place it on the mother's stomach and the baby pops out, squealing and vigorous. But perhaps you should be happy she's not here! She'd be very suspicious of your white armbands, given how zealous she is for the Church. By St Denis, she hates heretics and would gladly strangle them all herself with her bare hands, or—at the very least—set all the hounds in our neighbourhood on them. As for me, as I said, I'm not so zealous: I treat as Catholic anyone who says he's Catholic, since I keep my nose out of people's business and don't tend to see the harm in anything."

Reading between the lines of his speech, I understood that we were welcome to stay as long as we wanted without discomfiting the good fellow. I stood up, after having slipped an écu under my goblet, and thanked our host profusely for his good offices.

"If you try to cross the Pont Saint-Michel," he whispered, brushing aside my compliment, "be aware that they request a pass, so the best time to go is at dawn, when the guards are likely to have fallen asleep from the rigours of the night; and when you get to l'Université, the Buccy gate is the best place to get beyond the city walls. That's the gate that they've opened for the villagers to bring provisions into the city, so there's always a lot of crowds and confusion there."

The scorekeeper wanted to show us our way, and, even after we'd left him, he stood there holding his torch as high as he could to light our way. Just before turning off to the right as he'd indicated, I took one last look back at his lantern, which, though it was but one little flame in the darkness of the shadows of the city, comforted me as much as the beneficence of the man who held it high. As we turned the corner, the light disappeared, but not the hope that it had provided me. "Well," I thought, "that's an example of real faith and there's really no other kind! May all the inhabitants of this vale of tears someday come to understand, as my scorekeeper does, that zeal in the Church without love for one's fellow man is the ruin of the soul!"

We followed the rue de la Calandre as far as the rue de la Barillerie, and there I sent Miroul to investigate the situation at the Pont Saint-Michel, as he had done at the Pont au Change. This done, like a grass snake in a bush, my gentle valet slithered up to my side.

"Monsieur," he said, "there's half a dozen bourgeois militiamen down there who are soaking up their drink like pierced soles. If we rushed them it would be all too easy."

"Not so fast," said Giacomi. "Do they have firearms?"

"Two."

"That's two too many," observed Giacomi. "We can't put our lives in danger. Especially since the large troop we saw near the palace might be sweeping the city, as the night is so calm."

"That's true, *Herrgott*, it's much too calm!" said Fröhlich.

"But, my good Swiss," noted Miroul, "even executioners must sleep!"

"Your advice is golden, Giacomi," I said. "Let's wait until these heroes drown the little bit of sense they still have in their flagons."

We four gathered under a corbel, sitting down on a stone bench and leaning against the wall of the house, without saying a word, and saw no one, except for an emaciated dog that was prowling around a cadaver that the assassins had left a few yards from us in the street. In truth, we didn't see the corpse at first, the night was so dark, only the dog, which was white. But as our eyes grew accustomed to the shadows, we saw the poor martyr and Miroul, getting up, went to chase away the animal, which was getting ready to bite into the body since it was perishing from hunger.

We decided to rest farther on, but farther on there were more bodies and these smelt so putrid given the heat of the last twenty-four hours that we had to come back to the stone bench, with the dog at our heels, who went after its original feast, its tail between its legs and whimpering lugubriously. Miroul tried to chase it away twice, but failed and gave up. We would have killed it, but none of us had the appetite for that, finding that the dog was a good deal less cruel than those who'd slain the man in the first place and were hunting us.

Finally, as the day began to dawn, we decided to wait at the entrance to the bridge. So, with our weapons at the ready, we started out, single file, our eyes peeled and ears pricked up to catch the slightest sound.

Once we'd crossed the chains onto the bridge, we saw a lantern some distance away, and, continuing, we saw that it was lighting a game of cards, which some soldiers were playing on a drum. The men were excitedly gambling their part of the booty, each against the others, which created an enormous brouhaha of threats, insults and cheers from the group, who were staggering around drunk and bleary-eyed. One of their number, however, was less inebriated than the others and decided to bar our way, pistol in hand, and shouting, "Who goes there?"

"Good Catholics, my brother," I replied, "and from the Écorcherie."

"You rascal! I'm not your brother! Show me your pass! And make haste with it!"

"Here it is," I answered, and, searching in my purse, I put an écu in his palm.

"What's this?" he cried as if my coin had burnt him. "'Sblood! You trying to bribe me?"

This was not, I suspect, inspired by virtue so much as by the sight of my purse, for he immediately thrust his pistol in my ribs. But he couldn't do more. Miroul raised his arm, let fly with his dagger and laid him out on the pavement. Unfortunately, as he fell, his pistol went off, thankfully wounding no one, but inciting this drunken hornet's nest to have at us, shouting, "To arms! To arms! To the cause!" and firing two arquebus shots that went wildly astray.

We ran off at full speed, hurdling the chain at the far end of the Pont Saint-Michel, and veered left into a labyrinth of little streets, stopping after a while, breathless, to listen for any pursuit. But there was not a sound; our heroes had gone back to their cards and their flagons, which doubtless came from some wine cellar they'd pillaged.

We thus found ourselves in the rue de la Parcheminerie, which runs parallel between the rue Saint-Séverin and the rue de la Huchette. This would have been a pretty spectacle, with the sun just rising and illuminating all the little towers, bartizans, gables and finials of the quarter, if, in the shadows below, there hadn't been so many despoiled shops and houses, their windows smashed and doors ripped from their hinges, and, amid the filth of the street, a pitiful pile of clothes, broken chests and tapestries, all covered with dirt—not to mention here and there a poor naked body of a man or a woman, sniffed by the starving dogs and by armies of bold rats. At six in the morning, however, the bells began ringing on high and shamelessly calling all the faithful to matins.

Miroul, who knew this quarter well, named each of the churches according to the sound of their bells: Saint-Étienne-des-Grès, Jacobins, Saint-Séverin, Carmes, Saint-Blaise, Saint-Jean-de-Beauvais and Saint-Julien-le-Pauvre. Oh, what a joyful sound they would have made on this bright August morning if they had been calling the faithful to reconciliation, instead of repeating the call for murder, and this in the name of a "miracle" that God had done, as I will explain shortly.

We stayed where we were for a while, sweating, thirsty, out of breath, our indecent bodies whinnying for their provender, the scorekeeper's modest repast being now but a memory. Already the housewives were busy, the younger ones heading out for their shopping, or, as they say in Paris, for their "mustard", the older ones opening their windows to the first rays of the sun, chatting with their neighbours from window to window, exchanging the latest news, which seemed as exhilarating to them as it did sad and calamitous to us.

A waffle-maker began opening up his shop a few yards away; he was lighting his fire and preparing his mix, and toasting his golden waffles. We stepped forward as if drawn by a magnet.

"All right, step right up!" said the waffle-maker, whose weaselly, dishonest face wasn't very reassuring. "What will you have?"

"Your tastiest!"

"That'll be two sols each!"

"Well, my friend," I observed, "St Bartholomew's day has fattened up your prices!"

"Well, flour's gone up since the gates of Paris have been closed."

"Really? That's not true!" shouted one of the housewives, who was returning from her shopping, her basket under her arm. "The Buccy gate's not closed, you rogue! They're admitting all the villagers now, and at the market this morning I saw all the usual poultry-sellers, dairy farmers and greengrocers."

"Well, look at that feisty hen, who wants to crow louder than the rooster!" said the waffle-maker, careful not to let her hear him, since doubtless he feared alienating the entire population of this henhouse.

"Here you are then! Four golden waffles done to perfection! Lay out your money and let these tasty beauties melt in your mouth!"

I paid him in small coins to prevent him from seeing that I had any écus.

"Monsieur waffle-seller," said Miroul, his mouth full, "you forgot the salt!"

At this reproach, the merchant calmly reached into a pot and pretended to take a pinch of salt, which he threw into the air in the direction of our food.

"*Commediante*," growled Giacomi. "You don't consume roasted meat by breathing its smoke! That salt's still in the sea!"

Just then a malmsey-seller passed by, wearing a yoke on his shoulders from which two vats of wine were suspended, and crying:

> "*Drink up, my friends, drink up*
> *This heavenly wine as I pass by;*
> *It's Greek ambrosia in a cup*
> *'Twill keep your throats from getting dry!*"

"Friend," said our waffle-maker, "ambrosia or not, pour me my morning cup of wine! All that blood last night made me thirsty!"

"Ah, good fellow! Were you out on a spree last night, like all good Christians?"

"I think I did my part," said our cook, his eyes lowered in false modesty.

"As for me," said the malmsey man, "with my own eyes I saw them burn Spire Niquet alive, who sells Bibles from Geneva. We piled his Bibles in the middle of the rue Judas, put Niquet on the top of the pile and kept him up there with our pikes so he could roast in the flames of the pyre. You could hear him screaming from Notre-Dame to the Louvre!"

"Ah, good work! So he died in the flames?"

"Oh, no! We threw water on him when he was half cooked, so he could enjoy the two torments together!"

Both men had a good laugh at this and we were all very glad our mouths were so full of food that we couldn't open them to protest.

"Well," said our waffle-maker, not to be outdone in epic tales by the wine merchant, "yesterday I was on the Pont Notre-Dame when we broke down the door of the Pearl, which is owned by Maître Mathieu, the jeweller from Geneva, as everyone knows. Well, my friend! What a celebration we had! The men, the wenches, the children and chambermaids, all were disembowelled and thrown out of the windows into the Seine! It's so convenient to live on a bridge when you're a heretic!"

At this the malmsey-seller nearly split his sides laughing; and then he proposed a round of wine for all, but we declined, despite our terrible thirst, for the fellow inspired such disgust we could never have swallowed his drink. The waffle-maker threw him a few coins, and off he went in search of other clients, carrying his yoke on his shoulders and crying his wares with his rasping voice.

Meanwhile, the younger housewives having gone off to do their marketing, the older women were chattering like magpies from one window to the next.

"Crestine!" cried one of them with yellowing jowls and a triple chin. "Have you heard about the miracle?"

"What miracle?" said Crestine eagerly, from the opposite side of the street. "What was it, my dear, and where?"

"What! You mean you haven't heard, Crestine! All Paris is talking about it. The mayflower in the Cimetière des Innocents suddenly bloomed yesterday!"

"A mayflower bloomed in August! Blessed Virgin! It's a miracle!"

"Jesus God!" said another hag from her window, anxious to add her two sols to the story, though she could hardly be understood since she'd lost all her front teeth, save one. "How could you not know it, Crestine? That's all anyone is talking about! And so many people are rushing to see it that the priests have had to post guards there to keep people from getting too close and damaging the flower!"

"I was suffering from the vapours yesterday," explained Crestine, who was feeling very ashamed to be so ignorant.

"My goodness!" said the toothless one. "A mayflower blooming in August! Our good priest at Saint-Séverin said that this is a clear sign from God that the Church will suddenly be renewed by the death of the heretics."

"Well, my God, that's the veritable truth!" cried the jowly one. "And it's Jesus's way of telling us we haven't killed enough of 'em! Right, my boys?" she continued, recognizing our white brassards and assuming that we were heroes of the massacre.

"You going to the Saints-Innocents, Crestine?" said the toothless one.

"Well, I just don't know," said Crestine. "My left leg swells up when I walk too far."

"But it will be so beautiful!" said the toothless one, hissing out such gobs of spittle that it was itself miraculous. "All the confraternities in the city are processing there this morning, beating drums and singing the Gloria, carrying crosses and banners!"

At my request, the waffle-maker had gone back to work, since a single waffle was hardly enough to fill the empty spaces in our stomachs, but we'd turned our backs on him because his face was so insufferable, and were listening to the chattering hags, while giving each other knowing looks, since our tiny rooms on the rue de la Ferronnerie looked out on the Cimetière des Innocents, and we knew all too well that no blooms had appeared on its branches the day before, so that, if they now saw one, without allowing anyone to inspect it too closely, it had to be that they'd tied it on there, though by what false and dishonest means God only knew—along with the sly clergy of the (badly named) Saints-Innocents parish, which would profit enormously from this miracle, not just in 1572, but for years to come, right up to the end of the century.

As we stood there listening to this cacophony of zealotry, a nun dressed in black passed us, who caught our attention because she had such a beautiful face and a more voluptuous body than such vestments usually cloaked. She was walking very quickly and looked quite terrified, but the most surprising thing was that she was wearing a pair of bright-crimson slippers.

Everyone in the street fell silent as she passed, but this silence was suddenly broken by the jowly housewife, who cried at the top of her lungs:

"Look, my lads! Look at those red slippers! She's a false nun! She's a Genevan snake on the run, sacrilegiously disguised!"

At this, the unfortunate woman began to run down the street, and the old hag redoubled her cries: "To arms! To the cause! To Madame la Cause!"

And leaning far out of her window, the hag shouted to burst her lungs: "Look, boys!"—meaning us—"Look at her red shoes! Kill! Kill!"

"Monsieur," whispered Miroul in *langue d'oc*, "if I had a taste for killing right now I know who to kill!"

"Quiet!" I hissed, and, as Fröhlich was opening his large mouth, I tapped his hand, which was clenching his mace, and whispered, "Don't forget, you're as mute as a carp in a pond."

"Well, what are you waiting for, boys?" shouted the toothless one. "Are you going to let the viper get away? Kill her, for God's sake, kill her!"

"My good woman," I replied calmly "there's a time for everything. A time to kill and a time to eat waffles. What's more, dressed as she is, she won't get far.*

"What a loss and what a lack of zeal!" shouted the hag nastily and with a very suspicious air. "How do I know your armbands aren't counterfeit as well?"

"'Sblood!" I laughed. "Come down here in the street and put your twitching nose on our swords and you can tell us what they smell like!"

"Well now," answered the toothless one, "that's sensible talk! 'Tis true that a heretic's blood, when it flows, stinks like the pus of a man with the plague, since his heresy rots him from within."

I was quite surprised the this strange bit of medical lore came to my aid from that quarter, the jowly one not wishing to contradict her comrade, despite her nasty looks at us; and doubtless she didn't want to press her luck since the four of us were robust and well armed.

So of course she directed her wrath at the nearest object: an honest-looking house that stood nearby and that they'd stoned the

---

* Alas, I was only too right. The nun with the red shoes, as I learnt later, was named Mademoiselle d'Yverni. She was a Huguenot, though the niece of a cardinal. Arrested nearby, they promised her life if she'd relinquish her religion, and when she refused, she was stabbed and thrown in the Seine. [Note by Pierre de Siorac.]

night before, smashing all the windows but not breaking down the door. I was amazed that the neighbours hadn't stripped the house of its possessions once they'd started the attack. The mystery was explained once the chatter started up again among the parish witches, who, though they never drew blood themselves, we're fanatically driven to see it spilt, and incited their neighbours to the worst atrocities.

So it was that I learnt that the house belonged to Monsieur Pierre de La Place, the president of the Court of Aids, a Huguenot and benefactor, to whom Coligny had entrusted the treasury of our cause. For this reason, Senneçay, the provost of the Grand Châtelet, had set up a guard in front of his house at the beginning of the massacre, on the pretext of saving him from assassination, but in fact to prevent him from fleeing before the king had decided his fate—some members of the court having an interest in inspecting the finances of the cause before he was dispatched.

"There's a nest of vipers, for you!" snarled the hag with the yellow jowls, making the sign of the Devil over the house. "This dog of a heretic thinks he's safe just because they gave him four guards and a captain! But just wait! We'll see what a joke that is!"

"Indeed!" croaked the toothless one. "It's not over till it's over! You can count on the people to finish the festivities."

"But are they going to kill them as well?" asked Crestine, of the three the most ignorant and perhaps the most to be pitied.

"Silly bird!" cried the jowly one furiously. "The more important the Huguenots are, the more diabolical! And you can count on the fact that, presidents or otherwise, they're not going to leave a single one of 'em alive in the parish of Saint-Séverin!"

"You're so right!" said the toothless one. "Before this day is over they'll all be sent off to Chaillot."

They all laughed at this, Chaillot being a village that lay downstream of Paris, where, because of the thick grass in the river, all the bodies of those who had been stabbed, denuded and thrown in the water had created a human dam, flooding the banks around them.

While our hags were chattering away, a young milkmaid, carrying her shop on her shoulder, appeared in the rue de la Parcheminerie, crying her wares; it was the same cry I'd heard in the grand'rue Saint-Denis the first morning I'd spent in the capital, so happy to be walking around the city, with Miroul by my side, since it was all yet unknown.

> *"Every morn, when light comes streaming,*
> *I cry out 'Milk!' for all the nurses*
> *Whose babes are now awake and screaming,*
> *Saying: 'Quick! Give 'em a pot, you nurses!'"*

It wasn't the same blonde milkmaid, this one being dark-haired and not very pretty, I thought, but it was the same cry, which, I know not why, filled me with emotion, as if it had brought me a promise of life, after all the bloodthirsty words I'd been listening to. The women's ugly chatter ceased, moreover, as the doors in all the houses opened one by one and the housewives appeared on their thresholds, holding pitchers, pots or goblets according to the quantity they wished to purchase from the milkmaid. There was a serene and ordinary peacefulness about this distribution, our Furies themselves quieting their cackling to take part in it (as is said of wild beasts themselves: that they'll make peace in order to drink, savage as they are). So peaceful was it, indeed, that I was not surprised to see a little door in the stoned house open and the head of a girl appear, her blonde curls escaping from her night bonnet. She had a pretty, though sad face, and with her eyes, since she didn't dare trust her voice, she beckoned the milkmaid, who came over and filled her two pitchers with milk, without any of the neighbouring women making the slightest objection, so calmed were they by the magic of this daily routine.

I don't know why I suddenly had such a thirst for this warm white milk flowing into the pitchers, and so much compassion for this poor blonde wench, who was besieged with her masters in this wreck of a house, that I forgot all my prudence, crossed the street and asked the milkmaid for a goblet of milk.

"Not possible," she replied harshly, "I don't have a goblet. No goblet, no milk: that's clear enough!"

"Oh, but I have one, Monsieur," said the girl, giving me a friendly look with her sky-blue eyes. And, withdrawing, she went immediately to her kitchen, and I was daring enough to follow her, whispering to her not to believe my brassard, that I was in flight and that she could easily guess why.

"Well, Monsieur," she replied softly, "I was sure you were pretending. I was watching you from behind the curtains and when you refused to chase down the poor nun, I could tell that neither you nor your companions had any taste for the blood of the poor wench. But since there are four of you," she continued, "wouldn't it be better for you to take a pitcher? That way you can all drink your fill in turns."

She took down a pitcher, and the two of us returned to the door, where the milkmaid, looking very unhappy, begrudgingly poured me some milk, accepted my payment without a smile and turned away coldly. I called to my companions, who came running from the other side of the street, and, as stupefied as they were by my incredible lack of caution—a bit of craziness which turned out to be quite wise, as we shall see—they drank like parched earth in August, so desperate were they, having refused the malmsey from the wine merchant.

We were just going to return the pitcher to the sad-looking young woman, when a band of five or six rogues rounded the corner, and, seeing the door of the house open and hoping to take advantage of it, rushed at us with so little warning that we hadn't time to unsheathe our swords and had to resort to our fists. Miroul turned out to be very adept at this, and, more agile than an acrobat, decked two of them straightaway. I managed to break the pitcher over the head of a third; Fröhlich delivered a powerful blow of his mace into the midriff of another; and Giacomi, anxious not to reveal his secret sword thrust to such ruffians, simply stuck out his foot and tripped the last of them, saying, "What's this? What's this?"

But now a new group of assailants arrived, much greater in number and armed with pikes, and, seeing the odds shift so quickly, I yelled, "Brothers! We'll never hold on! Get back into the house!"

And so we did, slamming the door in a trice and bolting and barring it. We were safe, yes, but now trapped. Imprisoned in this house of shame and one with its fate.

"Well, Monsieur," said the blonde chambermaid (who, I soon learnt, was named Florine, after a local saint in her native Auvergne), "that was valiantly done! But what about the guards and their captain upstairs? Are they going to attack you now?"

"How many are there here?" I asked.

"Five in all."

"Well, that's not very many," observed Giacomi, unsheathing his sword.

I did the same, but, on reflection, after listening to what was happening up there, I said:

"I think we'd better try to make our peace with them. I can hear the captain haranguing the crowd outside, warning them that he'll send for reinforcements from the Grand Châtelet if they try to batter down the door. So, in a sense, he's our ally, however precarious. Florine, go and tell him we're waiting for him down here in peace and friendship."

But the captain, who was assuredly not a very brave fellow, refused to come down, since he'd watched the dance we'd performed on the rogues outside and feared being taken in the same way. Consequently, he demanded that I come upstairs alone and unarmed, but I decided against this, certain as I was that he'd simply take me hostage. In the end, it was decided, after Florine exhausted herself going up and down the stairs several times, that we four would go up without disarming, and would wait outside their door, so that we were within earshot but not visible to them. When we'd arrived at their door, I called:

"Captain! I urge you not to misunderstand who we are! We're four good Catholics, masters and servants. But as we were having breakfast at a shop nearby, our valet noticed that your chambermaid had opened the door downstairs to buy some milk. And since my valet had met the girl at a dance recently, he decided to ask her for a pitcher so we could buy some milk as well. You saw what happened, and how those rogues attacked us to try to get in the door and how we had to retreat into the house. You can understand how unhappy we feel about this, since we don't want to be taken for heretic dogs who live here."

"The problem is," the captain replied in a voice that sounded like it had been marinated in wine, "that it would seem that you are! Else why would you have fought to prevent them from coming in?"

"Because," I explained, "we knew you were in here to protect the house, on orders from the provost, and we thought we were doing the king's bidding to come to your defence."

"Indeed, my friend!" said the captain. "You certainly have a ready tongue and don't fear anyone in a debate!"

"That's because I'm a clergyman," I replied, "and though I'm not yet tonsured, I can recite you the four Gospels of Jesus Christ the Lord in Greek!"

The Greek was conclusive, though I suspected the captain was less persuaded by my words than swept away by my eloquence, since his mind seemed so clouded with wine.

"And so, my friend," he said in a trembling voice, "what do you want?"

"We want to be free to pillage the house."

"By the love of God, good clergyman," laughed the captain, "what do you hope to find after we've been through it?"

"We'll see."

There then took place within the room a confused council in the hushed and slurred voices of men who've been doing more drinking than sleeping, our heroes appearing reluctant to fight us since they had the advantage of neither numbers nor weapons—they being without firearms or armour, from what Florine told me, but dressed only in their livery and armed with short swords. It was a miracle that these uniforms of the Grand Châtelet had so terrified the population—with the threat of jail and the gibbet that they implied—that no one had made any attempt to break into a house that was so inadequately defended by five drunk soldiers!

"My friend," said the captain finally, "for the liberty you're requesting, I'll have to charge you one écu per archer and two for me. And," he added, "you are forbidden, on pain of death, to enter this chamber."

"Well," I replied, "that's a lot! I'll have lost a lot of money if I don't find anything worthwhile in my pillaging."

"It's that or nothing!" declared the captain, though I doubt he knew what "or nothing" meant since he neither wanted nor was able to throw us out.

But we'd gone back and forth enough and there was no point in bargaining any further, especially since it was obvious that our agreement confined these drunkards to their room, and that they were as much our prisoners as we were theirs. Truly, what a strange farce! And how incredible to encounter such a bizarre situation in the middle of such a storm!

Florine brought my money to these scoundrels, but they must have attempted some unwanted advances on her while she was fulfilling her mission, for we heard a loud slap on a cheek, and then she burst back through the door, blushing and angry. Her blouse had been badly torn, revealing her full, white breasts, which were a vision of loveliness, as I realized from watching Miroul's eyes, which were shining like lighthouses on a stormy shore. My valet immediately came to her aid, but very respectfully, since the girl was a Huguenot and therefore most likely unbendable.

I made a sign to Florine to close the door on those rogues, which she did, and then, taking her by the arm, I asked what had become of the owners of the house and why they had not appeared in all this noise and confusion.

"Well, Monsieur," she explained, "they've barricaded themselves in the library on the second floor, so horrified are they by the excesses that have been committed by these guards ever since they entered the house—opening chests, pillaging, beating the servants, who've all run away except me. And it's a miracle I've still got my virginity, the way they came after me, but, thank God, they've been so drunk that they couldn't manage to do me any real harm."

I told Florine who I was, and asked her to give this information to her masters and request that they receive me. But before she did that, I asked her to unstitch the brassard that was dishonouring my shoulder, and allow me to clean up a bit—at least my face and hands, as well as my trousers, which were so covered with mud and grime from our night's journey though hell. She wanted to clean up my doublet, but couldn't entirely remove the blood of the child who'd been stabbed in my arms, although she did manage to lighten the stain a bit.

Miroul insisted on accompanying me up to the second floor, fearing some foul play from our friends the guards, bloated with drink as they were, and, with Florine introducing me, I entered a room that was admittedly smaller than Michel de Montaigne's library (the most beautiful I had ever seen), but very pleasant, with its oak woodwork, and well lit by a series of windows that ran the length of the house, which had been stoned and broken, but the glass and stones had been cleared away, so one could scarcely tell there'd been any damage.

Monsieur de La Place was seated, a book in his hand, in a great armchair, set some distance away from the windows, doubtless to protect him from any further stones, and, despite the noise and shouts in the street, he appeared as tranquil as if he were seated in the great blue room of the Louvre.

He rose as I came in, and approached me courteously, as I entered and bowed, and took my hand with a grave and somewhat sad, yet serene smile. He was a fairly tall man, whose thin face reminded me a bit of Uncle Sauveterre, except that he hadn't been so hostile to human weakness that he hadn't married, but, as I would see, displayed great tenderness to his wife.

"Well, Monsieur de Siorac," he said, after I'd given him, at his request, a brief account of the horrors of our night, from the moment Cossain had knocked on Coligny's door to the present, "perhaps you could inform me what's happening with this popular uprising, whether it's run its course or whether it's still aflame?"

"Alas, Monsieur," I lamented "it's not just a popular uprising but the mass murder of all our people, without pity or mercy, commanded by the king."

"What?" gasped Monsieur de La Place, paling at my words. "Would the king really order the murder of all the Huguenots, including La Noue, Taverny and me, who have served him so loyally?"

"Alas, Monsieur de La Place," I sighed, seeing under what illusions he still laboured, "the king does not look upon Taverny with such favour…"

"What, killed?"

"By the people, swords in hand, who stormed his lodgings, accompanied by the king's guards."

"God in heaven! The king's officer!" And, grief-stricken, not just as a man and a future victim, but as a magistrate, he said: "What are you telling me? It's the end of the rule of law when the sovereign sets one half of his subjects up against the other half! How can such a fratricidal murder be lawful in a kingdom?"

To this cry of despair, I could make no answer, as much because I had no response as because I believed that this wasn't the moment to debate the question.

"Monsieur," I said, "if you have any friend in l'Université who might hide you for a while, tell me and I'll try to get a message to him."

"Well, Monsieur de Siorac," said Monsieur de La Place, "I myself tried that at midnight last night while all my jailers were insensible with wine, and was heading out of my secret door—"

"What?" I cried, amazed that he wouldn't have used it to escape. "You have a secret door here?"

"It's right here!" said Monsieur de La Place, and, pushing an oak panel with his finger, he revealed a staircase leading down into the darkness. "This passageway, which I had built simply for convenience, leads down to the stables, and there a door hidden behind the hay storage leads out onto the rue Boutebrie. However, when I crept out alone the other night, without my valet, I knocked on the doors of several of my friends, but they were slammed in my face once I was recognized, since the royal decree banned giving aid to Huguenots on pain of death."

"Do I understand, Monsieur, that you came back here of your own free will to be caught in this trap?"

"But Monsieur de Siorac," he replied with great feeling, "surely you can understand that I would never abandon my family and household! The mob would have taken its revenge on them!"

"So it's true," I thought, "he who takes a wife and children gives hostages to fortune. But who could forgo these tender cares even when he knows they limit and hobble him!"

As I was thinking about the sad plight of my host and how my own condition seemed so full of possibilities by comparison, the library door opened and La Place's cherished family came in, looking, as one would expect, quite desolate. My host introduced me to his wife, a woman of about forty, who had blonde but greying hair protruding from beneath a black bonnet, and was dressed in a modest black gown with a bunch of keys hanging from her waist. She was followed by her daughter, whose beauty was so striking that I had to lower my eyes to avoid looking at her too avidly in this house of mourning; her son-in-law, Monsieur Desmarets, a counsellor of inquiries, who had an open and honest face, but couldn't help looking terrified given the situation; and her two young sons, who were of an age at which one never imagines one can die, and so were clearly more afflicted by their parents' plight than their own.

They all gathered sadly around the head of the household, some taking his arms, others kissing his hands and others still kneeling next to him.

"Ah, my love," said Monsieur de La Place to his wife, raising her from her knees, "I beg you not to despair. Never forget that nothing happens in this world, not even the death of a sparrow, but that God wills it. And so, may God's will be done and His name forever blessed!"

Seeing me discreetly heading for the door to allow them to enjoy their final prayers together, Monsieur de La Place said:

"No, my friend, we share too many concerns here to allow you to leave the room. Indeed, you are one of us, since, without you, our door would have been stormed and our house completely destroyed. No, no, rather than leaving, I beg you to summon your friends, and the faithful Florine, that we may all pray together."

So I invited the others into the room and they all lined up in front of the bookshelves, Florine next to Miroul, who, I sensed, was trying to offer her some comfort in her despair. Monsieur de La Place seated himself in the large armchair and read in a grave and vibrant voice the first chapter of the book of Job. Now, I ask the reader's forgiveness, in case this story appear frivolous or profane; and it may sometimes scandalize innocent hearts (given how excessive the actions of this period may seem). But I want to quote from the Scriptures, because none of us, in this terrible predicament in which we found ourselves, trapped in this house by a screaming mob and betrayed by our king's hatred of us, could hear this text without shedding copious tears.

And it came to pass that one day the sons and daughters of Job were taking food and wine in the house of Job's eldest brother. And a messenger came to Job and told him: "Your bulls were working the plough and your donkeys grazing by their side when suddenly a band of Sabeans burst in and seized them and put all of your servants to the sword…"

And even as he was speaking, another servant ran up and said: "Fire from the All Powerful One has fallen from the skies. It burned up all your sheep and the shepherds with them…"

And before he could finish, yet another arrived, who said: "The Chaldeans have rounded up your camels and taken them and killed all of your servants…"

And while he was still speaking, another of his servants came running up and cried: "Your sons and daughters were enjoying a meal in the house of the eldest brother, and a great wind came out of the desert and so shook the house that it collapsed on them and killed them all…"

And Job rose up and tore his coat. And then he shaved his head, fell to the ground and said: "Naked came I from the womb of my mother and naked will I return there. The Lord has provided and the Lord has taken away. Blessed be the name of the Lord."

And, closing his Bible, Monsieur de La Place quietly explained to us, with great composure, that suffering is necessary so that Christians can exercise their virtue, and that it is not so much that the Devil makes us suffer, but that God permits it. "My children," he concluded, "pray to the Lord for me as I pray for you. If, as I fear, a great wind strike down my house and disperse my family, pray, I beseech you, pray that we will all be joined again in the life hereafter since our only hope is in God and in God alone!"

Monsieur de La Place's homily was longer than I've been able to tell it here, but I will only add that at the end I began to feel some impatience begin to mingle with my emotions, believing as I do that the Lord does not wish to abandon His creatures to the storm, but wishes us to struggle tooth and claw to hold on to life, because He granted us that life to begin with. Listening to Monsieur de La Place as he confronted the last hours of his life, it seemed to me that he had some appetite for martyrdom that inclined him to submit rather than to act. I do not share this attitude, but incline more to the one displayed by another famous Huguenot, Monsieur de Briquemaut, who, at more than seventy years of age, while he was being pursued by the mob, undressed and threw himself into the mass of cadavers in the street, escaping by night and disguising himself as one of the grooms of the English ambassador. Unfortunately, in the end he was seized and hanged, but at least we can laud the struggles of this brave desperado.

I couldn't help thinking, as I listened to Monsieur de La Place with all the reverence his deep faith couldn't help but inspire in me, that if I had been he, I wouldn't have forgone the use of my hidden staircase, and my horses, to flee, being more resolved to live and less inclined to die than he was, more active and less prayerful. Not that I think prayer is superfluous, but I believe it is the sister to action and not a form of resignation.

Monsieur de La Place had scarcely finished his sermon when there was a loud knock at the door, which was immediately shaken, though it didn't open, since it was bolted from within.

"Who is it?" demanded Monsieur de La Place.

"The captain from the Grand Châtelet!" cried the brutal and guttural voice that I knew well.

"Unbolt the door, Florine," commanded Monsieur de La Place.

"Monsieur," I whispered, moving quickly to his side, "before Florine unlocks the door, I beg you to permit us to withdraw. We'll serve you better if we're not seen with you by this brigand, who takes us for a bunch of pillagers."

"Then you must hide in the secret stairway," agreed my host.

The four of us disappeared in a trice, and I remained on the top step with the door slightly ajar so that I could watch what was to happen.

God knows, the rogue wasn't pleasant to look at, with his large moustache and heavy eyebrows, which were pressed into a terrible grimace when he burst through the open door, his large hands gripping the hilt of his sword. He stood there glaring at the two peaceable legal men, their wives and the two young boys.

"Now then!" he growled in a voice more thick from drink than arrogant. "Are you still at your prayers? Enough hypocrisy! We know what those sad faces are worth after the excesses of the Genevans! Stand at attention, Monsieur de La Place! President Charron wants a word with you!"

No sooner had he said this than the provost of the merchants crossed the threshold, holding a pike in his hand and gallantly decked out in full battle dress, with a jacket of chain mail, and a captain's field helmet with a gold neck-protector. He was a fairly tall man with broad shoulders, a red face and an air of immense self-importance, as befitted the First Bourgeois of Paris. And yet, for all the violence we'd experienced from men of his ilk, I didn't find that

562

his countenance evoked such evil cruelty. On the contrary, I was not surprised to learn, much later, that, when the king had ordered him to launch the massacre of the Huguenots that previous Saturday, he'd spent the day weeping and begging the king not to proceed, and had only given in to Charles's orders when they threatened to send him to the gibbet.

Behind President Charron, serving as his escort, entered two soldiers, who wore blue helmets decorated with fleurs-de-lis, and immediately eyed the white jacket of the captain of the Grand Châtelet suspiciously, since there'd always been deep antipathy between the two squadrons. For his part, the captain, who received his orders from the provost of the Grand Châtelet, was scarcely able to hide, behind a mask of apparent respect, the utter disdain he felt for the provost of the merchants and his blue acolytes, all decked out with fleurs-de-lis. And so, standing there obstinately in the library, he make it clear that he was in charge of this dwelling, and cast mistrustful looks at both Monsieur Charron and Monsieur de la Place, listening in on their conversation with a most suspicious air.

"Well, Monsieur de La Place," said Monsieur Charron, stepping forward with his hand held out as an expression of his peaceful intentions, "I want you to know that I am here to ensure that you have what you need and to render you any service you might require."

Monsieur de La Place was too moved to reply to these generous words, but his wife, his daughter, his son-in-law and the two young boys rushed up to President Charron and pleaded tearfully, "Save us, Monsieur! Save us! And save our father!"

The good and beneficent Charron could not help showing how moved he was by this supplication, in part no doubt because this family reminded him of his own, and he could imagine what distress they would have experienced had he not, against his conscience, obeyed the king.

"Please! Save us, Monsieur!" begged Madame de La Place. "And save my husband!"

"And so I will, Madame," said Charron finally, "if it is God's will… and the king's," he added, seeing the glowering looks of the captain.

But whether he immediately reproached himself for such prudence, or whether he became suddenly angry at the captain's insolence, I know not, but he began pacing back and forth in the library, biting his lip and appearing to reflect on the matter.

"Monsieur de La Place," he said, finally, "if you please, ask your family to leave us for a moment. I want to speak with you eye to eye."

On these words and at a sign from Monsieur de La Place, his wife and children retreated into a little room that was adjacent to the library, but the captain remained, his right hand grasping the hilt of his sword, his left on the handle of his pistol. He had such an arrogant and defiant air about him, strutting and prancing like a peacock, that I thought what a shame it was he didn't have a third hand with which to stroke his prominent moustache.

"Well, Captain, what are you waiting for?" said Charron imperiously.

"Monsieur provost," said the captain with a hint of disrespect, "I must stay. The prisoner is in my charge."

"And I'm ordering you to leave the room!" said Charron, baring his teeth.

"Monsieur," said the captain, "I take my orders from the provost of the Grand Châtelet."

"And did he order you," shouted Charron furiously, his eyes ablaze, "to spy on the provost of the merchants? You little fly," he continued, stepping up to him and brandishing his pike, "I have twenty guards stationed outside and if you delay one second more in obeying me, I'll have them give you a spanking in the kitchen like a little brat! Now get out of here, or you'll regret it, my little friend!"

At these words, since the captain still hesitated, Charron's two blue helmets stepped forward, so eagerly intent on throwing him downstairs that the captain reversed his position and, visibly crestfallen, fled like a rabbit into a bush.

"Ah, Monsieur!" gushed Monsieur de La Place. "I am so indebted to you for teaching that little coxcomb a lesson. His men have committed every excess imaginable here, beating my servants and pillaging the entire house."

"What! They pillaged the place?" said Charron, amazed. "I'll put things right before leaving. My friend," he continued, "I wish I could now guarantee your safety, but I cannot: to do so would be to disobey the king, who wants you kept here, perhaps so you can be interrogated about the finances of the Huguenots. On the other hand, I am able to give sanctuary to your entire family, either with me at the Hôtel de Ville, or with Biron at the arsenal."

"Ah, Monsieur," said Monsieur de La Place, taking his hands in gratitude, "I cannot thank you enough and will continue to express my gratitude in the next world when I leave this one. And, once my family is safe, I promise to remain here awaiting orders from my king and I give you my word that I will make no attempt to flee."

Charron seemed somewhat taken aback by this pledge, as though he weren't asking for so much, but after a sideways glance at his blue helmets, who seemed uncomfortable with such displays of friendship for a Huguenot, he decided to remain silent. And when La Place's family returned to the library, he hurried the anguished adieux of these poor people, who naturally feared the worst for their father despite Charron's assurances that the king had ordered the cessation of all executions that morning. I later learnt that he was speaking the truth, and that the orders had indeed come from the Louvre that morning, but were almost immediately rescinded.

Before leaving, Charron ordered his blue helmets to expel the four Grand Châtelet guards and their captain from the house, which they did with admirable alacrity and not without some bruises and cuts administered to the departing troops. We watched their expulsion through the broken windows of the library, I in delight, Monsieur de La Place in tears at the departure of his family.

I heard Charron order Florine to rebolt and rebar the door. This done, he stationed six of his guards in front of (not within) the house, and with the rest—about fifteen or so—he surrounded the group of prisoners (as he affected to call them), and, taking the lead, set off with his men in tight formation and with brandished pikes, since the mob that had surrounded the house began hooting, shaking their fists and spitting at the "prisoners", all the while chanting, "To the cause! To Madame la Cause! Kill! Kill!"

"Monsieur de La Place," I urged, as soon as they turned the corner, "now your family is safe. But time is of the essence! We must look to your safety and get you out of here as quickly as possible. Those guards will be back soon to put the blue helmets to flight. Do you think you can count on the provost of the Grand Châtelet as you did on Charron?"

"Not at all! Senneçay is a viper and hates me, I'm certain. But, Monsieur de Siorac, I cannot leave this house. I gave my word to the provost of the merchants."

"But he didn't ask for your word and he seemed to regret that you'd given it!"

"Nevertheless, I did so," replied Monsieur, his head held high and the Ten Commandments imprinted on his face. "I'll wait here for the orders of the king, who knows me as his loyal subject and would never hand me over to my secret enemies."

"What? You know who they are?"

"One of them is, like me, a magistrate at the palace, and would be delighted by my assassination, coveting as he has done for so long my bonnet of office as president of the Court of Aids."

"Well," I thought, "so you can engineer the murder of a colleague simply in order to wear his black velvet, gold-braided president's hat?"

"And what's the name of this good friend?" I asked.

"Nully," laughed Monsieur de La Place, "the dative of the Latin *nullus*, and that he is null and void I wouldn't doubt."

"So you're saying that Senneçay would, for money, do Nully's dirty work?"

"Yes, alas, it could happen, since Senneçay is accustomed, from what I've heard, to take money from any hand that proffers it."

"Well then," I cried, "it's pure folly, Monsieur de La Place, to remain here!"

But I was wasting my breath. From the fidelity he'd sworn to Charron there was no turning back, no matter how much I (and Giacomi, who added his voice to mine) insisted, and this from the conviction, I believe, that, once they'd taken his life, they'd spare those of his loved ones.

"But Monsieur," he said with a smile that, though sad, also displayed a sweet serenity that was not of this world, "you must take the advice you've so liberally offered me, and secure your own safety without delay. Take the secret staircase, saddle my horses and be gone! But may I ask you to take Florine to the rue des Grands-Augustins, to the home of her cousin, who may be able to take her in?"

As he was saying this, we heard a loud noise in the street, and, leaning out of the windows, saw a group of forty guards from the Grand Châtelet putting Charron's men to flight, not without a few parting caresses from their axe handles. This done, there came a tremendous blow on the front door.

"That's Senneçay," sighed Monsieur de La Place, paling, yet calm, "and he's got three or four of the most unruly *quarteniers* with him.

Florine, go and open the door, and come upstairs ahead of them so that you can quickly slip into the little room there until these men can lead you to safety."

Saying this, he pointed to the secret staircase, and, after embracing him a final time, I headed there, followed by my companions, our heads bowed and our hearts beating heavily in our chests at the prospect that awaited our friend. Once in the staircase, I watched through a crack in the door as Senneçay burst into the room, armed for war, sword in hand and small shield on his arm as if he were just about to plunge valiantly into battle in the midst of a great clatter of pikes rather than entering into the quiet library of a magistrate who was alone and unarmed.

From having been for most of his life a man of exceedingly supple spine, the doer of the foulest deeds required by the Louvre, Senneçay had acquired a sly mixture of cruelty and deceit in his expression. His eyes were as shifty as a pair of servile, nervous little weasels, and his thin, colourless lips seemed to have been pulled inside his mouth and masticated by his various appetites. His face was entirely covered by red and purulent sores, as if his conscience were trying to push out the pus that it secreted.

Behind him, wearing the gold-embroidered collars of the captains, entered the three fellows whom Monsieur de La Place had described as the most unruly *quarteniers*, and who seemed to me to be more beasts than men, having the bearing, the muzzle and the smell of wild animals, one of them displaying his blood-spattered bare arms like a badge of honour, as if to remind us of the part he'd played in the butchery of the Huguenots over the last two days.

"Monsieur," said Senneçay, without honouring Monsieur de La Place by using his title of president, and without even looking in his direction, his mendacious eyes flitting about the library without settling on any one thing, "I have express orders from the king to bring you to the Louvre."

"To the Louvre, Monsieur!" cried Monsieur de La Place. "To the Louvre in the middle of this tumult! With the people on all sides screaming for death! Even in the middle of your guards, pikes at the ready, I'll never make it there alive!"

"I guarantee you the opposite," said Senneçay, without however being able—or wishing to?—look him in the eye, his gaze wandering all over the library. "I will give you for your security a captain from Paris who is well known to the citizenry and who will accompany you."

"Who would that be?" asked La Place.

"Monsieur Pezou, here present."

At which, Monsieur Pezou, who was a sort of red-haired giant with watery eyes, stuck out his enormous stomach and put his hands on his hips with an air of ostentation.

"Pezou!" cried Monsieur de La Place, looking at him with horror. "I will say this to his face: Pezou is reputed to be the most violently cruel of all the *quarteniers*! Monsieur, you couldn't have made a worse choice! Do you not see how Pezou, even at this moment, is parading the blood of my countrymen on his arms?"

"Of course I'm parading it," sneered Pezou, his watery eyes glinting with bloodthirstiness. "I swore to the Blessed Virgin that I wouldn't wash my arms—but would eat and drink with all this crusty blood on them—until every last heretic has been eradicated."

"Monsieur," laughed another *quartenier*, "it's always for his own good that we bleed a body that suffers from any disorder. And the body of the state is no different, which has suffered too terribly from your pestilential heresy. Moreover, that's what we heard from Monsieur de Tavannes, at dawn on St Bartholomew's morning: 'Bleed 'em! Bleed 'em, my friends. A good bleeding is as beneficial in August as in May!'"

Hearing this, Pezou winked his pale eyes and, shaking his head with pleasure, repeated, "A good bleeding is as beneficial in August as in May!"

And whether or not it was the charm of this particular phrase, the three *quarteniers* looked at each other and burst out laughing uncontrollably, though their mirth seemed to embarrass Sençeçay, who, though a devil through and through, was hypocritical enough to wish to hide his delight at this.

"Monsieur," cried Monsieur de La Place, "you heard him! Are you going to deliver me into such evil hands? Monsieur, I demand and beg you to deliver me personally to the Louvre under your responsibility."

"Monsieur," soothed Sençeçay, his voice dripping with sanctimoniousness, "you must excuse me. I regret that I have other business I must attend to. I cannot remain with you more than fifty paces. Pezou will do the rest."

"So you see, Monsieur, that you're now married to me!" laughed Pezou. "And by God, you won't regret it!"

"Well then, Monsieur," said Monsieur de La Place to Sençeçay, his voice as ashen as his face, "this is treason! It's a felony! I will not accompany this assassin. I refuse!"

Sençeçay frowned deeply at these words, and immediately, without a word, walked over to the door of the library, opened it and called for half a dozen of his guards.

"Monsieur," he hissed to Monsieur de La Place, coming back to him but, again, without looking him in the eye, "that's enough rebelliousness and insurrection! When I speak in the name of the king I intend to be obeyed. If you do not willingly surrender to the king, I will have to have you bound hand and foot and carted to the Louvre."

After a few moments of reflection, Monsieur de La Place conceded, "I will spare you this ultimate infamy. It would clearly be too great a burden on your conscience."

This said, he took up his cape (without which no one of his nobility would have thought of going out into the street in Paris, even in this August heat), threw it over his shoulders and, his face ashen but calm and full of determination, stepped towards the door. However, at the moment of crossing the threshold, he turned, without deigning to look at either Senneçay or the three *quarteniers*, and gazed one last time at his armchair, his writing table and his books.

His escort, as I learnt later, took him by way of the Petit Pont, which Senneçay did not cross, withdrawing as he said he would; Pezou took the lead of the troop, whom the mob accompanied, shouting "Kill! Kill!" but not daring to attack the guards. They continued through the Île de la Cité, but as they arrived at the corner of the rue de la Verrerie, Pezou ordered the guards to stop. A handful of assassins who had been posted there on purpose threw themselves on Monsieur de La Place and stabbed him to death without the guards preventing them in any wise.

As for me, I believe that, while the king did nothing to protect La Place, he had not specifically ordered his death either. Otherwise, his name would have been included on a list and he would have been murdered in his lodgings like so many others on Sunday, 24th August at dawn. In my view it was Senneçay who plotted this murder with Pezou and Nully, who'd had to give up his role as president of the Court of Aids during the Peace of Saint-Germain, and had never forgiven his rival. Pezou's help was purchased with a few coins and Senneçay's for a few écus, and so Nully managed to keep his reputation stainless by absenting himself from the murder.

And so it went in these sinister hours. It became acceptable for anyone who so desired to murder his heretic, one in order to usurp his place, another in order to inherit his money, another simply to exact his revenge and another still to win a lawsuit. Thus, for example, the famous Bussy d'Amboise, who'd sued the Huguenot Antoine de Clermont over the marquisate of Renel, went after him on the morning of the 24th and put an end to their legal proceedings by stabbing him to death.

As soon as Monsieur de La Place had left with his executioners, I ran to close and lock the library door, convinced that the minute they saw the door of the house unguarded, the mob would swarm inside to pillage it. Florine emerged from the little cabinet in tears, and I had to prevent her from going to gather her affairs from her room since we could already hear the marauders downstairs, who were swarming through the house like rats through a block of cheese.

So I pulled the wench into the secret staircase, drew the wooden panel closed and down we went into the darkness, Fröhlich leading the way while I brought up the rear. Our Swiss giant would have simply knocked down the door at the bottom if I hadn't stopped him and asked Miroul to find the latch, which he did and immediately provided us access to the stables. Once there, Florine showed us, hidden behind the stacks of hay, the door that led out onto the rue Boutebrie, which appeared, when we peeked out, to be calm and deserted. You can imagine that we lost no time in saddling our horses for fear that the pillagers would decide that they wanted them as well, and, Florine mounting up behind Miroul, we burst out into the street and turned right, then right again and took the rue de la Harpe down to the Pont Saint-Michel, and from there the left quay along to the rue des Grands-Augustins, where one of Florine's cousins was living at the home of her aunt, who was a very beneficent lady.

Alas, the cousin was not so tolerant. As soon as he opened the door and saw Florine, he slammed it in her face, despite her pleas not to leave her out in the street alone and abandoned. In response to her cries, this zealous papist opened an upstairs window and showered her with insults and threats. It wasn't long before other windows were thrown open and housewives began screaming "Kill! Kill!" and I realized that we couldn't linger here for long without having the entire parish after us.

We left, urging our horses into a trot, winding our way through a series of unfamiliar streets until we reached the rue Hautefeuille, which was completely quiet, so we stopped there. Florine was pressed into Miroul's back, crying hot tears, her arms clasped tightly around his chest.

"Florine," I asked, coming up beside them, "have you no other relative you can stay with?"

"Alas, no, Monsieur!" she sobbed. "The Lord called my parents and my aunt. Oh, Monsieur, what will I do now? Where will I go? Monsieur and Madame de La Place were the only family I had."

"Monsieur," said Miroul, "we can't leave the poor wench alone in the streets of this hateful city to be killed—or worse—by these fanatics! I beg you to let her come with us, and cast her lot with ours."

"Oh, Miroul," sighed Florine, her tears ceasing immediately, and she held him so tightly you couldn't have slipped a pin between them.

"Miroul," I cautioned, "this is no casual thing, to try to save a wench when we're trying to escape ourselves!"

But Miroul had such an urgent and beseeching look in his eyes— he who was ordinarily so light-hearted—that I understood that this was indeed not a casual request at all, but a wholehearted and honest one. Glancing at Giacomi, I could see from his smile that he'd sensed between these two a tender attachment and not just a passing attraction. "And yet," I thought, "can we really take along a wench when we're on the run? In the midst of such dangers?" And what a risk she was for us, since she was the weak link in our chain, knowing neither how to ride, how to run nor how to fight—a tender burden for Miroul, but a burden nonetheless, one who would certainly slow us down. On the other hand, how could I refuse Miroul, who'd so many times saved my life? And, what's more, hadn't I promised Monsieur de La Place that I'd make sure his chambermaid was safe? Where else could she possibly go if we refused to take her?

Unable to make up my mind in the urgency of the moment, I decided not to decide immediately, and so I said, smiling at my gentle valet:

"Let's get through the city gates first. Then we'll see."

Miroul returned my smile with such immense gratitude and joy that I couldn't help feeling very moved.

"Let's be off!" I cried. "Let's see if we can get through the walls of this cruel city and out of this trap!"

But this time, Miroul failed to guide us in the right direction, and we ended up back in the rue Hautefeuille, heading towards the Cordeliers convent, where we suddenly found ourselves in the midst of a great procession of women, who were yelling and shouting and leading a group of Huguenot women to the church so that they could convert them on the spot. Since our horses couldn't take a step in this melee, we were forced to watch this strange scene. The great doors of the Cordeliers were wide open, and on the high altar, illuminated by hundreds of candles, was the idol that papists call the Holy Sacrament, before which these Furies wanted the unhappy women to throw themselves on the ground and abjure their faith. Some of these, in particular those who were holding small children in their arms, consented to renounce their faith, no doubt, I believe, to protect their offspring from pain and death. Others, however, stubbornly refused, and were thrown onto carts, stripped and dragged to the statue of the former king St Louis (which stands at the entrance to the convent gates), where they were beaten, scratched and trampled underfoot by bunches of the parish witches, who made such hideous cries, whistles and ululations as to curdle your blood, and, from what I could tell, abandoned their victims to their heresy only after they thought they were dead.

I don't need to describe the terror with which poor Florine watched this scene, imagining herself in the place of these poor martyrs and dismembered by these hags, and pressed her face into Miroul's back as a chick might seek comfort under a hen's feathers. My gentle valet was grinding his teeth, and for once his brown eye was more angry than his blue one.

"Easy does it, Miroul," I cautioned. "Get hold of yourself! Let's get out of this buzzing swarm!"

So the four of us began to move backwards on our horses, their large hindquarters opening the way through the crowd, until we succeeded in emerging from these screaming harpies and reached the rue du Paon. From there we made our way to the rue de l'Éperon, where we found calm again, and then to the rue des Arcs,* which wasn't so peaceful: just as we reached it we heard the noise of carriage wheels on the pavement, and a travelling coach passed by, whose curtains were closed tightly, and which was escorted by thirty horsemen in battle dress, all of them with swords or pistols in their hands. And though all of these horsemen displayed the Lorraine cross on their caps and the coat of arms of the Guise family on their caparisons, they were having a hard time maintaining the respect of the mob, who suspected that this was some prominent Huguenot who was disguised as a member of the Guise household, and were swarming around the coach shouting "To arms! To arms! To Madame la Cause!" Some of them ran right in front of the horses and seemed not to be discouraged by the blows bestowed on their backs by the horsemen.

I immediately realized that this was our chance to escape! Having no doubt that this procession would be passing under the drawbridge at the Buccy gate, I galloped up to its rear, crying "Long live Guise!" I was even able to come to the aid of the valet who was driving a cartful of travel cases at the tail of the procession, arriving just in time to fend off a couple of rogues who would otherwise have knocked him

---

* Today the rue Saint-André-des-Arts. [Author's note.]

from his saddle. Finding himself safely surrounded by four fellows, the driver, who was an older man with a pleasant and open face, thanked me, but couldn't say more, because we were now assailed by the mob, who began throwing stones, and by the housewives in their windows, who were launching all manner of missiles in our direction: garbage, tiles and even flowerpots—projectiles we had great trouble dodging, the old valet being so badly hit by a frying pan that it was all I could do to maintain him in his saddle.

Thank God, the carriage was now passing onto the drawbridge, though still fiercely beset by the mob, and the bridge guard, luckily seeming less suspicious of the Guise coat of arms than the crowd had been, allowed the coach to pass; but when it was our turn, an archer lowered his pike and demanded:

"Whose trunks are these?"

"They're the Dame de Belesbat's," affirmed the old valet. "We're going as far as Étampes."

"Well, by God, these fellows aren't! They're not in livery!"

"Oh, yes they are!" yelled the valet. "They're our men, and we hired them yesterday, since they're strong and good swordsmen!"

"Of that I have no doubt!" said the archer, seeing how fierce we looked, and raised the bar to let us pass, being more concerned with controlling the mob, who wished to "escort" us all the way to the Faubourg Saint-Germain. 'Sblood! We managed to leave these bloodthirsty villains behind as they argued with the gatekeepers, and galloped off, rejoining the procession quickly, and were very glad to be included in their party when we passed the customs house at the Croix Rouge, whose officers were more interested in interrogating the villagers and merchants who were accustomed to bringing their provender into Paris.

I thanked our ancient valet profusely, who was glad to have been of service given the help we'd provided him, and he refused my pourboire, saying that, without me, he would have been lying on the pavement in the rue des Arcs, his throat slit by the mob, and stripped of his earthly possessions. He added that he suspected we had our own reasons for leaving Paris, but he believed we were too honest for any enquiry about them to be necessary.

"My friend," I said, "may I ask who this Dame de Belesbat is that you're following to Étampes?"

"You mean you don't know?" he said. "She's the only daughter of Michel de L'Hospital, and though he's Catholic, the people hate him as much as if he were a heretic because he supported the heretics when he was chancellor. And you, Monsieur," he asked as delicately as he could, "will you follow us as far as Étampes?"

"I'm afraid not. We are stopping at Saint-Cloud, where we have some friends."

Our valet looked very much relieved that we would be leaving him so soon; he must have been worried, I supposed, that some of the horsemen, who had turned around in their saddles to give us suspicious looks, might have asked us to identify ourselves if they'd had the leisure to stop and did not have to provide escort for the coach.

Finally, the first windmills of Saint-Cloud came into view, turning their blue blades in the evening breeze, and, crossing the Seine again, which I couldn't look at without shuddering, the coach slowed down to a walk to climb the steep hill that led up to the village, where, extending a warm right hand to my old valet and smiling broadly—a smile he returned without a word but with great feeling—I dismounted in front of the church. Looking around, I saw one of those little good-for-nothings whom in Paris they call "go tell 'ems" since their masters send them back and forth bearing messages, and said:

"A sol for you, young man, if you can lead us to the house of Monsieur de Quéribus."

The boy reflected a moment, looking at each of us in turn with great curiosity. After which, finding, no doubt, that our clothes were too dirty and dusty and our cheeks too unshaven, he leapt up onto the porch of the church and, with a foot on the railing to put him out of reach, he said:

"Monsieur, I'm not sure. I wouldn't want to get beaten for my imprudence. Why are you looking for Monsieur de Quéribus?"

"I am Pierre de Siorac."

"Pierre de Siorac!" cried the boy, his freckled face breaking into a smile. "Rue de la Ferronnerie! Lodged with Maître Recroche? Well, Monsieur! I brought you a message! Good gentleman, give me a hand and the use of your stirrup: we'll go faster with me behind you on your horse than running in front of you!"

The lad had only to show himself: his livery was the shibboleth that opened the heavily barricaded portal of the lodgings—a sort of small chateau with unusually thick walls, the thick door doubled by a portcullis, which I heard with enormous relief close behind us with a crash of iron. Normally one might feel imprisoned by such bars, but for me in my predicament this was a sure and safe haven, one that already had the promise of Mespech, my beautiful crenellated nest, Barberine's capacious lap! So perilous was our flight through Paris, harassed from one street to the next by the cruel mob, that I would have taken refuge in a lion's cage! I'm not saying that the wild beast would have welcomed me, but the bars of his cage would have at least protected me from the world of men.

"Good gentleman," said the little freckled valet, wrinkling his nose, "please wait here. I will let my master know you're here."

And this said, he flew up the stairs more airily than a bird and disappeared. I looked at my companions, but they just stood there staring at me, unable and unwilling to say a word, so drained were we by hunger, thirst and fatigue, our present understanding blunted by the horrors we'd seen our fill of. Nor could we quite believe that we were really safe, fearful that the hunting cries might be heard again at any moment, putting us to flight.

Suddenly the door burst open behind us and Quéribus bounded up the steps towards us, perfumed, rings on his fingers, a pearl dangling from his right ear, shimmering in his yellow satin doublet, his smooth face beaming with friendship—though, when he saw how awful I looked, he wouldn't embrace me for all the world.

"Well, Pierre," he exclaimed, "my brother, myself! What have you done to yourself, all dirtied, disgusting and bloody! But you're alive, thank God, you're alive!" But when he went to embrace me, the stench of my clothes so repulsed him that he stopped in his tracks. "*Maestro* Giacomi," he said, stepping imperceptibly backwards, "I am your servant. Miroul, good day to you, gentle servant. But Pierre, are these two in your company?"

"Yes indeed, they are!"

"Welcome, then, to the giant and the blonde wench!" he said with a gracious gesture of his bejewelled hand. "Well, Pierre," he laughed as he backed away "by my faith, you stink! I could die! Would you like to bathe?"

"And eat, if you please! Eat and drink!"

"'Sblood! You'll have all that and more!" cried Quéribus, his voice ascending to the highest notes. "Call the chambermaids! Let's get water on to boil! Let's pamper our guests! And prepare the blue room for Monsieur de Siorac!"

"Ah, Monsieur!" I said. "A thousand thanks! But we can't stay. As soon as I've caught my breath I must gallop to Montfort! I've been so worried about Samson!"

"Well, you can stop worrying! Gertrude has already seen to that!"

"What! She's not here?"

"Ah, my friend, you misjudge her!" laughed Quéribus. "As smelly as you are, she would already have embraced you with arms as large as her heart if she'd been here! As soon as she heard about the massacre in Paris, she rushed off to Montfort to prevent your pretty Samson from heading to the capital to save you!"

"Which he certainly would have done!" I cried. "And how did she dissuade him from this?"

"By assuring him that you were safe here with me!"

"Well, good for Gertrude! There's one white lie that'll be worth more in heaven that the indulgences from ten trips to Rome!"

"As long as the Lord belongs to the reformed religion!" said Quéribus merrily, which confirmed that for him the Churches were of as little consequence as the pearl that dangled from his pretty ear. And, all in all, though I found his scepticism a wee bit scandalous according to the strictest Huguenot standards, it was, after all, a minor sin compared with the fanaticism I'd seen and experienced in Paris.

I wanted to leave the next day, but Quéribus wouldn't hear of it, since he first wanted to make enquiries about the perils we might expect to encounter on the road to Périgord. He rode off to Paris, accompanied by a strong escort, since the mob continued to commit excesses of all kinds, and visited the Louvre to discover whatever he could that might be of use to us. He returned very alarmed for me. The carnage continued in the capital, although it was less apparent since there were now fewer people to kill. As for Navarre and Condé, they'd been called on by the king to choose between Mass and death, and were effectively prisoners in their apartments, their future precarious and their guard dissolved. But it was especially the king's messages to the provinces that, though at times self-contradictory, were worrisome: he had ordered that the faithful massacre all heretics, sparing no one, though his orders were obeyed or disobeyed according to the complexion of the governors and seneschals.

Quéribus returned from the Louvre, furnished with a safe-conduct pass (which he showed me) in his name and his younger brother's name that allowed them free passage on the highways and through the cities and towns of the kingdom as far as Carcassonne.

"You have a younger brother?" I asked, astonished that he'd never spoken of him.

"He's standing right here!" he said, putting his hands on my shoulders. "Aren't you struck by the close resemblance between him and me? He's the sketch, as you once said, and I'm the finished drawing!"

"Except that, if I'm your younger brother, the sketch seems to have followed rather than preceded the drawing!"

"Ah, Siorac!" he laughed. "The sketch has more wit than the drawing, for sure!"

"I don't know if it has as much heart," I said with a tear in my eye. "My friend, you'd go to all the trouble, expense and danger of escorting me to Périgord?"

"My Pierre! I need to go to take a look at my lands to keep the money flowing. Otherwise they'd be robbing me blind. And when I go through the Sarlat region, I can visit my cousin, Puymartin, who, as you've told me, though Catholic, is a good friend of your father's."

On hearing from my mouth, that same evening, that Navarre's guard had been disbanded, Fröhlich nearly fainted, for he'd continued to nourish the hope that, once the massacre had ended, he might return to the company.

"*Ach!*" he said. "Why didn't the Lord just kill me instead of leaving me like this, useless and unoccupied? Who'd hire a Huguenot soldier now?"

"My father," I said, "who's Baron de Mespech and was a captain in the king's armies in the battles of Ceresole and Calais."

"*Ach!* A captain!" smiled Fröhlich, who would never have signed up under a baron who'd not achieved his title by service in the army.

"Monsieur," said Miroul, when our Swiss from Berne had left my room so comforted, "I hope you didn't go too far in assuring him of work at Mespech! The Brethren are so careful with their money!"

"I'm not worried in the least that there'll be a place for this young giant of the mountains. I've often heard them say that our servants are getting old and soft."

"Well, it's true that our people are getting old," he replied with an air that made me prick up my ears. "Especially the women. La Maligou no longer does anything but the cooking. Barberine spends her time cooing over your little sister Catherine. And as for the younger ones, Franchou is nursing her baby and Little Sissy is expecting. That leaves Alazaïs, who has the strength of two men, but she can't do all the housework by herself!"

"Ah, Miroul," I said in mock surprise, "I never would have thought you paid so much attention to the household, which is not really a man's concern, that I know of!"

"Monsieur," said Miroul with a look of complete innocence, "how can I not be concerned with the interests of Mespech since I've been so well treated there? And how can I be sure that the work will always be done by the women if there aren't enough of them to do it?"

"Ah, Miroul!" I laughed. "If I were as much of a teaser as you, I'd pretend not to understand the what, the why and the how of this beautiful speech!"

"But Monsieur, you do understand!" said Miroul with a smile that was half jest, half uncertainty.

"And yet," I continued, pushing him a bit, "what will we do if the Brethren refuse to hire another chambermaid?"

"Monsieur," exclaimed Miroul triumphantly, "you can hire her yourself! You're rich enough!"

"Don't make fun of me, Miroul!"

"I'm not!" he laughed, and, unhitching from his saddlebag a very fat purse, my gentle valet said with enormous pride: "Here, my master, is the purse of that bearded monster who stabbed the poor child after you'd bought him. In truth, it was so heavy that there were times in our flight that I thought of ditching it but I didn't, and luckily so! Look!" And having said this, he untied the straps of this pouch, brought it to the table and, with enormous care, emptied the contents. The several écus that fell out were merely cheap lead compared to the diamonds, pearls, rubies, emeralds and other gems that sparkled before me on the darkened oak of the table, some of which—the diamonds, I mean—were of a size I'd never seen before, and beautifully cut. It was obvious that this cruel fiend had pillaged an exceptionally wealthy jeweller, but which one? All of those on the Pont au Change, despite being papists, had been murdered and defenestrated.

Oh heaven! I stepped up to the table, and, after having admired and caressed with my fingers some of the most beautiful gems, which reminded me of the stones that Maître Sanche, the apothecary in Montpellier, had ground into a fine powder and mixed with an equal amount of honey to create a remedy that's called an *electuary*, which cures any number of illnesses, I removed ten écus, the amount I'd paid the bearded monster for the child, and put them in my purse.

"Monsieur, what are you doing?" asked Miroul.

"I'm taking back my due, Miroul; the rest is yours, being your legitimate bounty from battle, since you killed the fiend who had it on him."

"But Monsieur, 'twas you who ordered me to kill him and take his purse. I was only the means."

"Not at all! Whoever killed him should keep the profits from it. That's the rule of war. What captain would ever go and take a soldier's portion? What's more, you'll have children someday, and you wouldn't want them brought up in a wretched hut as you were!"

I watched him reflect on this last remark and become all dreamy and thoughtful. "But what would I do with the money?" he asked after a moment.

"Do what Cabusse did with his booty from Calais: buy some land, live off the fruit of your labour, marry a good wench and be master of your house."

"Well," mused Miroul, "I'd never enjoy the monotony of farming! As your valet, I've seen the world and now have an appetite for that!"

"Miroul," I replied, deeply moved by his attempt to disguise his affection for me as mere thirst for adventure, "don't you understand that you are much more worthy than your condition as valet?"

"Is there any dishonour in the word 'valet'?" asked Miroul, his brown eye lighting up. "If so, Monsieur, make me your major-domo and I'll be happy."

"You're being silly, Miroul!" I smiled, throwing my arm around his shoulder. "Major-domo of a gentleman without a *domus*!"

"*Domus*, Monsieur?"

"*Domus, domi*: house."

He laughed, repeated the word, and pocketed it in his memory, and in this conversation that which was unresolvable remained unresolved, for I could see clearly enough that Miroul enjoyed embracing such subtle contradictions: on the one hand, his desire to change his condition, marry and have a family; on the other hand, his wish never to be separated from me.

Since Quéribus couldn't stand to see me in clothes that were stained with blood, he gave me a light-brown doublet with yellow slashes, which, though very handsome, was less attractive than his yellow satin one, as befitted the younger son of a baron. He dressed Fröhlich in the black and gold of his livery, and dressed Miroul as handsomely as if he were his own major-domo—a figure Quéribus was certainly used to, given his houses in Paris and Saint-Cloud and his chateau in

Carcassonne. To Giacomi, he loaned a dark-blue velvet suit that the *maestro* felt quite at ease wearing, since he was not disdainful of his earthly appearance—which I do not criticize, not wishing to behold the mote in my brother's eye while neglecting the beam in my own.

And so, Quéribus and I, riding side by side, our horses groomed and shining, were first to enter Montfort on Wednesday, 27th August at sundown, followed by a dozen brave men in livery, all armed with swords and pistols. You can imagine the awe we inspired in the Béqueret family when they saw such a large troop swooping down on them! Quéribus sent the squadron off to the inn and I was immediately overwhelmed with hugs and kisses from my beloved Samson, who simply couldn't let go of me; nor could I of him, though I felt that I hadn't suffered as much from our separation as he had, which somewhat pricked my conscience. But I had no time to consider these feelings, since I was snatched from his arms by Dame Gertrude, who took me in hers, from which I escaped only to be swept up in her chambermaid's, falling from the gentle Charybdis towards the smoother Scylla.

The beautiful Norman had no sooner heard that the Baron de Quéribus was going to escort us to Périgord than she insisted on joining our party. So I invited her to Mespech, certain that my father (if not Uncle Sauveterre) would be delighted to see her brighten our walls with her blonde hair, her lively colours and all her finery—not to mention her Zara, who was dressed as splendidly as her mistress, conceding nothing to her in terms of beauty but carrying the day with her youthful coquettishness.

There was no danger that we'd be taken for Huguenots, since we were travelling with such elegance, stayed in such luxurious inns and enjoyed such expensive meals and drinks. Gertrude couldn't pass a village without making the rounds of all the shops and purchasing lace, brocades and baubles, and Quéribus surpassed even her most sumptuous tendencies, being one of those papist dandies who consume their fortunes in superfluities and have no thought for their expenses, believing the princes will replenish any lacunae in their fortunes. And so we rode along, escorting Dame Gertrude's carriage, scattering gold behind us, and at each stop gorging ourselves with excellent cuisine. At night Gertrude displayed a fiery fidelity to Samson, but, in this, was not imitated by Zara—but I shall not elaborate on that, not wishing to offend anyone.

It was just before we reached Bordeaux, I believe, that Gertrude invited me to join her in the carriage, saying that she wished to enjoy a tête-à-tête with me. To make space for me, Florine got out and mounted my Pompée, Miroul immediately riding up beside her to protect her from any foolishness from my horse, but also, I imagined, in order to cast amorous looks at her.

"My brother," said Gertrude, "don't take that little seat! Do you like our company so little? Come here and sit between my Zara and me! You'll not feel the bumps when you're cushioned on both sides this way. Give me your hand, and the other to Zara. Are we not the best of friends?"

"To be sure!" I agreed. "Such good friends my head is spinning!"

"Oh, Pierre! You're so diverting! Do you know," she said, moving with no warning from her jocular tone to a most serious one, "I found Dame Béqueret to be quite tired, looking forward to retirement. Maître Béqueret is nearly resolved to sell his apothecary's practice and would do so, I believe, if he found a replacement who was as honest as our pretty Samson."

"Well, that's all well and good," I agreed, "but Samson doesn't have a sol to his name!"

"I'm rich enough for both of us," said Gertrude sweetly, giving me a sidelong glance.

"Beautiful Gertrude," I replied, "if I understand what you're proposing, I have to say that I see a few obstacles to it."

"What?" she frowned, suddenly angry, or pretending to be so. "Surely you're not going to tell me, my brother, that the few paltry years I have on your brother would—"

"Oh, Madame!" cried Zara, who immediately understood how wounding this was to her mistress. "It's appearances that count and you're as youthful looking as any mother's daughter in France! What's more, I think your physical beauty is completely indestructible!"

"Beautiful, beautiful Gertrude," I cooed, bringing her hand to my lips, "Zara took the words right out of my mouth. What man would not be proud to have you on his arm as you walk down the aisle of the church? But since there must be a church, and you're Catholic while he's an inflexible Huguenot, what can be done?"

"Well, not so inflexible that he wasn't willing to go to Mass in Montfort with me."

"'Strue!" said Zara, whom the Parisian jargon had quickly conquered. "You should have seen your Samson, Monsieur, trembling at our priest's sermons. Ah, me! He was boiling! But all Madame had to do was to take his hand and he calmed down."

Hearing that, and knowing the great power women hold over us from the moment we fall in love with them, and noticing that Gertrude was caressing my hand with hers in a very subtle way, I withdrew my hand and fell silent.

"My Pierre," said Gertrude, her voice trembling, "is there any other obstacle?"

"Yes, there is!" I confessed. "Once you're joined in matrimony to my Samson, I wouldn't like you to, as it were, 'Saint-Cloud' him."

"My brother," she said, lowering her beautiful eyes modestly, "there is, for widows, a certain licence that one may close one's eyes to, but which in a wife would be wholly unacceptable. I will be faithful to your brother."

"Is that a promise?"

587

"Yes," she said, taking my hand again and squeezing it hard. "My brother, tell me, may I have your consent?"

"Do you have Samson's?"

"If I have yours, I'll have his. And your father's as well, given your amazing gift and power of persuasion."

"Well then, Gertrude," I laughed, "you're not so bad at choosing your ambassadors! I'm going to think about it a bit."

And since the coachman, having just climbed a long, steep hill, was stopping to let his horses breathe, I got out, giving my seat to Florine, and remounted Pompée. I quickly caught up with Quéribus.

"I was getting bored!" he said with a smile.

"I wasn't," I rejoined with a smile. "Now I've got a lot to think about."

And despite knowing that the baron behaved like a dandy in the Louvre, I considered him a man of good sense, whose opinions carried some weight, so I told him what had just transpired. He thought about it for a while before responding.

"The lady is of *la noblesse de robe* and her dowry is not insignificant. I've heard that an apothecary's trade can be more lucrative than a landowner's—except in the Beauce region."

"She's a person of such changeable complexion."

"Well, I wouldn't know about that!" replied Quéribus with a sidelong glance. "If she doesn't go off on pilgrimages, she can remain faithful, living continuously with him."

"But he'll be in Montfort and I'll be in Mespech!" I sighed.

"Or else in Paris," smiled Quéribus.

"What!" I exclaimed, taken aback. "Me in Paris!"

"Although you hate the place at present, Paris is a Circe," said Quéribus, "and once you've put your lips to her cup, you can't stay away. What's more, you're not without ambition and the only road to success in this kingdom lies through Paris."

From Bordeaux, we headed to Bergerac, and, finally, by the tortuously curving roads of Périgord we neared Les Eyzies. Quéribus, riding in front with me, said: "Pierre, if you'll follow my advice, don't tell anyone here about your flight from Paris except your father and Monsieur de Sauveterre. Through Puymartin, I'll have the ear of the Catholic nobility of Sarlat, and I'll circulate the news that you were spared from the massacre by the favour of the Duc d'Anjou and the grace of the king."

"And why would we need to spread this rumour?" I asked in surprise.

"As a Huguenot you'll be much better protected in these troubled times, you and your family, by this news of the king's favour than by your walls and ramparts."

"Well, Quéribus," I said, "you must have read Machiavelli; you have such a head for politics!"

"I haven't read him," answered Quéribus, "but I'm familiar with his thinking since I live at court."

We found all of Mespech out harvesting the grapes in a vineyard that was a stone's throw from the chateau, the women picking the fruit and putting it in baskets and the men spread around them to protect them, armed for war, on horseback and with loaded pistols, though, since I'd killed Fontenac in a duel, there wasn't so much to fear as before, even in these times that were so perilous for Huguenots.

Indeed, our cortège was discovered about a league from Mespech by the Siorac cousins, who, unbeknownst to us, spied us from the cover of some nearby chestnut trees, and, not recognizing me, galloped off to tell my father that "two men, richly attired, followed by a coach and numerous servants" were heading towards the chateau. Hearing this news, my father, surprised by such an unexpected visit, sent Cabusse ahead, who, hidden in a thicket, saw me, recognized me and came galloping back, stuttering like crazy in his emotion. The Baron de Mespech, blushing with joy since he'd given us up for dead, was incredulous, and headed off to meet us, with Sauveterre at his heels; and he could scarcely believe his eyes when he saw me leaping from my saddle and rushing towards him, followed by Samson, while he dismounted, tears flowing down his cheeks, which were quickly mingled with ours.

It took another full hour for all the kissing, hugging, tears, sighs, questions and blessings to be exchanged with all our household, who, abandoning the grape harvest, rushed up and embraced us in their turn, squeezing us to make sure they weren't dreaming, and slapping us on the back, all the while gushing in their beautiful *langue d'oc*, which I hadn't heard for two months and which now sounded so strange and enchanting. Quéribus watched all this from astride his horse, his two hands on the pommel of his saddle, smiling broadly, while Dame Gertrude remained secluded in her coach, wishing, no doubt, to assure the Brethren of her modesty.

After a thousand thanks and compliments, my father immediately invited Quéribus and his servants to be our guests at Mespech, while Sauveterre, without a word, cast a long look at the newcomer's numerous party, quietly fearing the inroads their collective hunger would make into our pantry. Luckily for our Huguenot sense of economy, Quéribus refused:

"I cannot," he explained, "until I have paid a visit to my cousin Puymartin: he would otherwise be offended."

But on the invitation we'd made him, he promised to return the next day with Puymartin and to spend a day at Mespech. Once he'd gone, it was finally time to approach the carriage, which stood immobile and closed in the road, and towards which my father's curious blue eyes had been turning from time to time; you can easily guess how they shone when Dame Gertrude du Luc got out, with all her grace, beauty and modesty, and, following her, Zara, whom Gertrude presented not as her chambermaid but as her lady-in-waiting. Zara immediately bewitched my father with such unabashed enticements that I could not doubt he would succumb to them, given his affinity for the fair sex, and age having so little cooled his appetites, as evidenced by the children Franchou continued to bear him. "Aha!" I thought. "These clever women have distributed their roles beautifully: one raising my father's spirits, the other seducing him. Oh, heaven! How can one not admire the marvellous skills nature has given the fair sex to compensate them for being weaker than men?"

My father, after having courteously offered room and board to our Calypsos, insisted on taking me, without further delay, into the library in order that he might hear an account of our adventures, which I provided as briefly as I could, so as not to dampen our private joys with the public calamities we'd witnessed. The Brethren could not keep, when they heard my story, from shedding burning tears at the traitorous assassinations of Coligny and so many other worthy young leaders of the Protestant nobility. And yet I understood how comforted they were by their Huguenot faith and how much they put their hope in the support of the Lord.

"Although the Pope," said Sauveterre, "when he received Coligny's head, ordered a *Te Deum* sung in St Peter's and joyous bonfires lit throughout Rome, his happiness will be of short duration. The reformed Church in France has not been destroyed. Already it is reorganizing and reconstituting itself. Already in numerous towns throughout the south of France, enclosed within their walls, people are dedicating the nails in their doors to the destruction of the royal garrisons, and this little turd of a kinglet will have gained nothing from his felonies other than a third civil war and his just defeat!"

My father, who, I thought, had not appreciated Charles IX's being called "this little turd of a kinglet" (since for him the king is the king, no matter what he may have done), contented himself with nodding approvingly at this fervent speech, and then asked me what was happening between Gertrude du Luc and Samson. So I answered straightaway:

"She wants to marry him and give him as dowry a very good apothecary's business in Montfort-l'Amaury."

To which the two brothers' responses, though articulated in the heat of the moment, were very different:

"What?" said my father. "So far from Mespech!"

"What?" bellowed Sauveterre. "Another papist!"

This latter remark could not but rub me up the wrong way, given my feelings for Angelina, so I remained silent, faced with the closed and proud way my father expressed his disappointment (without actually saying so) with what he'd just heard. At my silence, my father looked at me and, observing that I was imitating him, began to laugh.

"Well, my son," he said, "don't take it to heart. Monsieur de Sauveterre wasn't referring to you."

"Although, my nephew," Sauveterre interjected, "on reflection, what I said also applies to you."

At this my father burst out laughing even louder; he then began to explain all the ins and outs of their current situation, to which Sauveterre had just alluded. It seems that, the morning after my departure for Paris, the Sieur de Malvézie rendered up to God a soul that had come from the Devil in the first place, and that one can only imagine was sent back to the latter, dying of a very opportune *miserere*, or appendicitis. Madame de Fontenac immediately forced Pincers, the priest, to withdraw the testimony he'd given that incriminated me, and withdrew the accusation Malvézie had levelled at me. I was thus safe and my entire trip to Paris became unnecessary. My father sent word to Montaigne, but I'd already left, two days earlier. He wrote to d'Argence in Paris, but, as we learnt later, he was holed up in his house in the country and didn't receive the message.

"Do you mean," I gasped, "that I ran all those risks and experienced all those misadventures and incredible dangers for nothing? To ask the king for a pardon that I didn't need? Do you mean that I was safe, and Samson as well, without knowing it?"

"I had no way of telling you! I had no idea where you'd found lodgings in the capital. And remember, it can take a month, sometimes two, before a letter can get from Sarlat to Paris! But let me continue," said my father. "If Madame de Fontenac acted so promptly it was, no doubt, out of gratitude for the cure I'd administered to her daughter, Diane, when she had the plague, but also because the lady was pressed very hard by Puymartin, who has loved her madly for a long time and wishes to marry her as soon as the law will permit."

"But," I observed, "though Diane seems not to respond to my older brother's feelings for her, it nevertheless seems to arrange things very well for him!"

"And for us as well," said my father. "An alliance with Fontenac and Puymartin would be an immense advantage for us, since it's understood that, once François is married, he'll share the management of the Fontenac lands with Puymartin."

"So it's done?" I asked.

"Not yet. The Sarlat clergy don't approve of this marriage, since François is a Huguenot and his bride-to-be is a papist, but Puymartin believes that, in time, persuasion and a few greased palms will do the job."

I then told the Brethren how Quéribus had advised me to spread the word about my great favour with Anjou and the king, and how it would considerably advance this affair. My father was delighted to hear this, and Sauveterre as well, although the latter affected to be reluctant about this marriage, the amelioration of Mespech's fortunes seeming to be little consolation for the fact that François, like his father (and perhaps his two younger brothers as well), would be united with an idolater.

Just then we heard a knock at the door, and Barberine came in to announce that the baths were now heated and steaming, and ready in the west tower to receive Samson, Giacomi and me; so, taking my leave of the Brethren, I headed to the west tower with her, giving her a thousand kisses and hugs on the way, since without my Barberine Mespech would never have been what it is for me, my old nurse being like a warm feathery nest into which I snuggled so securely. Of course, there were ramparts and walls for our defence and safety, but, for my head, a softer pillow was necessary, and that feminine tenderness without which a man's life would be hollow and empty.

"Well now, Pierre," objected Barberine, blushing both from shame and joy, "you're caressing me like a sparrow his mate. Have you forgotten that I'm practically your mother, or do I have to remind you of it?"

"Now, now," I cooed, "there's no danger! Just let yourself enjoy my great friendship for you!"

When we got to the baths, however, I let go of her, because I knew that Alazaïs would be there, who stood as stiff as a cliff against the sea of all human weaknesses, as would Little Sissy, who was, indeed, that sea itself, but who wasn't easy to face when her jealousy started causing waves.

"What?" I exclaimed. "What's this? Just three bathtubs? Fill all five immediately! I want Miroul and Fröhlich to bathe with us since they shared our perils."

Little Sissy, who claimed to be two months pregnant by me, but was not showing at all, gave me lots of little glances and uttered many sweet nothings as she washed me, but she dared not make them too bold, since Alazaïs kept her eye on her. Barberine groomed Samson with her strong, soft hands, but Giacomi was the worst off of the three of us, since Alazaïs cleaned him as if she were plucking the feathers from a chicken before putting it on a spit.

As comforting and enjoyable as this sweet moment was, I needed to cut it short and sent the three women away as soon as they'd soaped us. Once the door was closed behind them, I told the *maestro*, Miroul and our Swiss giant to be careful not to tell any of the heroic stories of our flight from Paris to anyone hereabouts, but to keep quiet, and I explained why.

"Well," said Samson, whose head scarcely emerged from the tub in which he was immersed, "I'm very happy for François that he's marrying his Diane."

When I didn't hear him express any reservations about her being a papist, I realized that it was an excellent time to ask why he wouldn't get married himself instead of living in sin with his lady.

"Because I'm not sure she would want me," he said in his exquisite simplicity.

"Oh, but she does!" I said. "All she does is dream about it and also about offering you, as her dowry, the apothecary practice of Maître Béqueret, which he wants to sell, as perhaps you are aware."

At this, he opened his eyes very wide; he then closed them, then opened them, then grew very pale, then blushed, unable to say a word, not knowing how to take in these two great joys that I was offering him all at once.

"Ah," he said at last, having sped through all the impediments he'd imagined to his dreams, "but I'll be in Montfort, my brother, and you'll be in Mespech!"

"Or maybe in Paris," I said with a smile, very moved that his first thought had been for me, even before he'd thought of our father.

"In Paris!" he gasped. "You'd be in Paris! But you hate the filthy place!"

"I'm not so sure," I laughed. "Quéribus thinks that Paris is an illness that is contracted by breathing in its air, and he thinks I'm already infected."

I waited for nightfall, and for Little Sissy to slip into my bed like a little snake, to offer her the ring I'd bought for her in Paris. She was overjoyed, breathing "Ooh" and "Aah" several times and hugging me furiously; and, between kisses, she kept holding her hand up to the candle to admire the glitter of the gold. And after we had each enjoyed our caresses to the fullest, she assured me that she'd present me with the most beautiful baby in Périgord and that, for sure, I'd be happy.

Having said this, she fell asleep like a snuffed candle, and you can imagine how she strutted around the next day, showing off her ring until the walls of Mespech seemed to echo with her excitement. La Maligou, in her vainglorious maternity, relayed the news, which grew more extravagant with every retelling until it reached the nearby villages. Sauveterre was clearly unhappy, and I had to explain to my father, who felt more rueful than joyful, how I'd been caught in the girl's web and forced to make an imprudent promise.

"You did well to keep it," he acknowledged, "since a promise was made, but in the future, take one prudent step at a time when you're advancing along the paths where captivating beauties may lead you. It's a very gentle slope, which leads from a ribbon to a bauble, from the bauble to silver and from silver to gold."

"Father," I said, "your counsel obviously comes from a lot of experience and, now that I'm thinking about it, I seem to remember a silver thimble that you offered Franchou, when, before the plague broke out, she was sent to Sarlat."

"Touché!" laughed my father, and, throwing his arms around me, he embraced me warmly. "Well, Pierre, no one's going to catch you off guard!"

Meanwhile, my little sister, Catherine, who, in the three months we'd been away, had bloomed into a beautiful flower, majestic in her new height, did not take it well that, while in Paris, I'd bought her nothing but a top, and then given that away to Alizon's little Henriot.

"My brother," she said, pulling me aside when she saw Little Sissy parading around with her new gold ring as if her entire hand had suddenly been transformed into gold, "did you not consider what an outrage it would be to give this little Gypsy wench a chance to put on airs with me?"

"But Catherine, my beauty," I said, taking her hands in mine—but she immediately withdrew them without letting me continue.

"Your beautiful Catherine," she said with a haughty air that reminded me of my mother, "is not so beautiful that her beauty couldn't be embellished by a gift from you! Monsieur, you place your affections where you should not and you forget people you should remember."

And, turning on her heels, with a flourish of her hoop skirt, she stomped off, leaving me very unhappy about the hurt I'd caused her, especially since I was very fond of her, though for the moment I was quite put off by her superior manner.

I knew not what to do about this unexpected setback. My father, having learnt what had transpired from Franchou, who'd been eavesdropping, pulled me aside after dinner.

"My son, at the rate things are going, you're not going to set things straight for less than a necklace."

"A necklace!" I gasped.

"Made of gold. Catherine is your sister: you can't allow her to be outdone by your mistress."

"But, Father, a necklace!"

"You stuck your finger into the gears," laughed my father, "and you risk having your arm go after it. That's how it is dealing with women. Or else practise being miserly like Samson, and never give anything to anybody, in which case no one can take offence since they expect nothing from you."

I ran to buy a necklace from an honest Jew in Sarlat whom my father knew, and thus made peace with my little sister Catherine, who wasn't little any more, since she'd got me to capitulate just by using her wiles.

Meanwhile, with Catherine pacified, the war flared up elsewhere, and I fell from the frying pan into the fire.

"Monsieur," said Little Sissy, whose normally rosy cheeks were ashen and whose dark eyes had turned obsidian when she saw the necklace shining on Catherine's white skin, "since you're so well off that you can buy me a gold ring the way I might buy a waffle from a shop in Sarlat, you shouldn't have given in and put me so far beneath your sister as you've done."

But at this, I was so angry that I began shouting at her like a dog in a pack, and in my wrath I might have slapped the impudent wench if she hadn't been carrying my child; and I could only turn round, walk away and avoid her for three days, so furious was I that she should compare my gold ring to a waffle.

During those three days that I deprived Little Sissy, as it says in the Holy Bible, of the "light of my countenance", I have to admit that my face wasn't very luminous, worked as I was by thoughts that were far more bitter than sweet. I'd heard Coligny say, and two days later Monsieur de La Place affirm, and then the Brethren repeat again here, that nothing happens on earth, not even the death of a sparrow, that God hasn't decreed. But when I tried to connect this principle with my personal predicament, I couldn't help perceiving that it posed a real problem for my theology: how, indeed, could I imagine that God, in His infinite goodness, could put me to a test which wasn't even useful in the moment I was undergoing it? Should I believe that it was God's express will that my father's letter should be received by Montaigne two days after I'd left, so that, continuing to believe that I was in danger for my life, I should go to Paris to ask the king for a pardon that I didn't need at all, only to encounter, while in the capital, among those of my party, the incredible perils that I've recounted?

These very perils, these assassinations, these drownings, these horrors, which were so awful and immense that my pen nearly falls from my hand as I try to describe them—must I believe that the Lord inflicted them on the Huguenots to test them, increasing, however, the wealth and power of the papists in the process, and thus fortifying the papists' belief that their corrupted cult is the good one and that their errors are truths?

But on the other hand, what if the St Bartholomew massacre were the work of the Devil and not God, complete with felonies so repugnant and cruelties so abject that they bore the mark and seal of the Prince of Darkness? How could we admit that the all-powerful Lord should not have brought His wrath down on the henchmen of this prince, instead of allowing the death of the just and the triumph of Satan, as if Satan were more powerful than He in this world that He made with His hands?

I ask a thousand pardons if these reflections seem sacrilegious. I state them in all innocence and simplicity, not wishing to seek answers from the clerics among us who can explain these mysteries. But observing that all too often the explanations they provide only make things more obscure, and since I wouldn't want these obscurities to influence the clarity I seek, nor allow them to constrict my judgement, I have decided to offer my own feelings, however infirm they seem, but truthfully, just as I conceived them in the nights and days that followed my return to the sweetness of my paternal retreat; for, after having survived the perils of the St Bartholomew massacre, I couldn't help meditating on this terrible event, which God, or perhaps I should say Fortune, wished me to experience.

At the beginning as at the conclusion of these reflections, I decided that it was dangerous to believe that the misfortune that befell us was desired by the Lord, seeing in this belief the beginnings of a limp resignation; in my judgement, in contrast, we must parry the blows of our adversary instead of treating the wounds he inflicts as if they were a test sent by Heaven. If it is a test, then I dare believe that we need to stand up to it before it destroys us.

After having so often cogitated on these ambiguous points, both back then, in the bloom of my youth, and now, when I'm an old greybeard writing these lines, I still can't decide whether it was God, or fate, that led me there—where, unwittingly, I had no business being, seeking every which way for a pardon I did not need. But I am persuaded of one thing and will hold on to this belief as firmly as a barnacle sticks to a rock, despite the waves and the tides. Having seen in this hateful city of Paris to its full extent the detestable effects of religious zeal, I made a promise never to permit my Church's zeal to cause me to raise my sword, believing that disputes over this or that form of worship should be decided only by clerics, and without knives ever being drawn, "since knives never decide anything", as the Duc d'Anjou, besieging one year later the Huguenot city of La Rochelle, dared write to "his beloved brother and sovereign", the same man whom I accuse before men, before history and before God, of bearing responsibility for the massacre of St Bartholomew.

Quéribus accomplished miracles with the Catholic nobility of the Sarlat region, having enough of his native Carcassonne in him to cover his courtly, dandyish side, and playing up the friendship he enjoyed with the Duc d'Anjou, which was, in fact, of some consequence, since Charles IX had no male heir and was quite sickly. The upshot was that people listened to him, and he used the authority he had to paint a portrait of my own connections to the future king that was so favourable you would have thought that, on the morning of the 24th, His Highness had dispatched a company to protect me in my lodgings against the fury of the mob.

I handed the copy of my pardon to Monsieur de La Porte, however useless it had become, to give additional credibility to the stories that

Quéribus was circulating. In short, the baron was so successful, and the balance of opinion leant so strongly in my favour, that even had Madame de Fontenac not withdrawn her complaint you wouldn't have found a single judge in the Sarlat region who would have condemned me, the most unforgiving among them contenting himself with repeating privately to the seneschal of Sarlat the witticism of Catherine de' Medici: "I see that your Huguenots are all cats, since they always seem to land on their feet."

The king's brother, in the Louvre, having given his doublet to Quéribus, since Quéribus had been forced to give me his, it happened that, after Quéribus left Sarlat, rumours had spread that it was I who had been the recipient of Anjou's doublet. And you wouldn't believe the prestige that accrued to me due to that satin article. The good side of my character was suddenly praised to the skies, as were all the laudable actions I'd taken, such as the part I'd played at my father's side in the defeat of the butcher-baron of la Lendrevie, and the rescue of the bishop of Nîmes, not to mention the rescue of Monsieur de Montcalm, whose story was less well known here. All of this led to a situation in which I, Huguenot that I was, could have married, on the basis of my new reputation, any of a number of gentlewomen of the region, whose mothers had begun to argue that the marriage of Margot de Navarre, however detestable it seemed at the time, had set a precedent.

But I had no thought of marrying anyone but Angelina, to whom I'd written from Saint-Cloud—without, on the advice of Quéribus, mentioning any details of my adventures, since it went without saying that in that quarter as well it was better if they believed I was protected by the king. I didn't believe this letter had much chance of arriving, since I was sure that the paternal tyranny wouldn't allow it to reach its destination; but, luckily, it was placed directly in her hands, which immediately wrote to me in reply and gave the response to the messenger. I've copied it here in all its feminine valour and sweetness:

Monsieur,

I was extremely comforted to learn from your hand that you'd succeeded in escaping healthy and strong from the terrible massacre in Paris, but, to speak openly, if I'd thought you were in mortal peril, my heart would have told me, and I don't know why, but it led me to believe that you were safe within the walls of Mespech.

Since the messenger cannot tarry here, I'm writing this in great haste, and can only give you a very short version of events from the minute I saw you running alongside our carriage, which was carrying me away from you, to the present moment.

My engagement to Monsieur de La Condomine is over. By means of grim silences, the cold shoulder, frowns and despising looks, I created a hell for him during the journey— a hell so hot that it must have burnt the moustache of that big idiot, who got out in Lyons and doubtless had to go for a swim in the Rhône after we left. And may the Blessed Virgin make him drown, for in truth I couldn't look at him without feeling nauseated, he was so disgusting.

I leave to your imagination the fury of Monsieur de Montcalm, who again threatened to send me to a convent, but it won't happen. I thank God that my father loves me too much for that. And, despite his opposition to my fondest wishes, I still love him as well because of his affection for me. And even though no one is allowed to say your name in our household, I don't want you to judge him badly; he is a man of goodwill, however zealous God made him.

Baron de Quéribus's letter described your success at the Louvre and succeeded in winning over my mother's good graces, but my father is still unshakeable, since his confessor paints such terrible images of the hell that awaits him if his daughter marries a heretic. My mother thinks my father should change confessors or that Heaven should call this one home, which may yet happen given his excessive zeal and his advanced age. My mother believes Father Anselm is very fond of you after he fought with you against the highwaymen of Barbentane, so he would certainly be more flexible.

The messenger is getting impatient and I must close. I beg you, do not judge me for the rude and rebellious behaviour I directed at that ridiculous suitor, because I was forced to be cruel out of love for you. As for that word—now I've written it. I would have preferred not to write it but there it is, and since I've expressed it I will not deny it.

Monsieur de Montcalm, in his fury, led me to believe that when you were in Montpellier you had a reputation for chasing women, and in particular that you had an affair with a woman of quality. But in truth, if the woman is the one he named, then I cannot believe it. She's almost old enough to be my mother and you would be a very strange young man if, loving me as you do, you had any appetite for such carrying-on.

But to come back to my father and his opposition to our plans, he is so firmly against them that all I can do is put my faith in God's grace and pray for our union, in the hope of which, I beg you to believe, Monsieur, in your faithful and affectionate servant,

Angelina

This letter made my Angelina so present to me that I dreamt, as I held it, that I was holding her in my loving arms. Alas, her suitor gone, nothing had been resolved! She was still in Barbentane, still as inaccessible as the wife of the Grand Turk, and still under the watchful eye of an inflexible father whom I'd rescued from the attack of the brigands but whose confessor led him by the end of his nose.

Comparing my fate with those of my brothers, I felt some cause for bitterness, which I had to combat in order to avoid being eaten up by it. I certainly didn't resent Samson's marriage to Gertrude, and had even helped to arrange it, albeit half-heartedly. But there was not much to envy there, however, since I felt that they might have trouble adjusting to their life together. But François! He didn't have to travel the highways and byways of France or overcome any dangerous threats to enjoy his dinner! Quite the contrary! Sitting around the house, being spoon-fed! By killing the Baron de Fontenac, I simply roasted his chestnuts for him, and now he gets to marry his Diane and manage Fontenac! And, what's more, although may God keep him from it for as long as possible, he'll be Baron de Mespech! But I, who have galloped, sought out adventure, suffered—I'm still the younger brother without any estate and my great love now out of reach.

But I'm not writing this to cry and lament my condition. That's just not who I am and it's not my philosophy. If the wise man claims that every test makes him wiser but sadder, I don't feel, after what happened in Paris, any great melancholy, or, for that matter, very much wiser. But when Barberine comes to wake me at dawn—my lazy Little Sissy hoping to sleep till noon—I let her encompass me in her care and warmth as I open my eyes to the new day. And I love the world I open them to! How can I moan and complain? Isn't it enough to be alive? I thank the Lord every day for having kept me safe and well in Paris so that I can sink my teeth once more into life. 'Sblood! My brother may be Baron de Mespech and half-Baron de Fontenac, but may I say without appearing too proud that I much prefer my life to his, and my experiences to his possessions? I have in my wallet (minus the ring and the necklace) the 200 écus that Anjou gave me, and the 300 I got for the pearls. So I don't have much money—or much baggage, other than my physician's bonnet and "Jarnac's thrust", the secret sword thrust Giacomi taught me. But Giacomi and Miroul are no mean companions, nor is my good Swiss from Berne, though I don't know whether he wants to spend his life in Mespech, since he loves his battles. And, to speak frankly, there are days when I can't see myself settling down as a doctor in Périgueux, and even less so in Sarlat, since I have too great an itch to urge my Pompée forward onto the great highways of France.

These are only dreams, and what becomes of dreams is "another pair of sleeves", as my friend and ally Pierre de Bourdeille, lord of Brantôme, would say: a bizarre expression that I have never actually heard anyone use but him; nor have I read it except from his pen. The Devil only knows what that "other pair" is doing there, the first pair not being mentioned. In any case, if sleeves there are, as our cousin Bourdeille intends, perhaps I'll sew them on gradually with age, if God consent to lend me a hand and keep me hearty and healthy enough to do so.

Next in the
Fortunes of France series

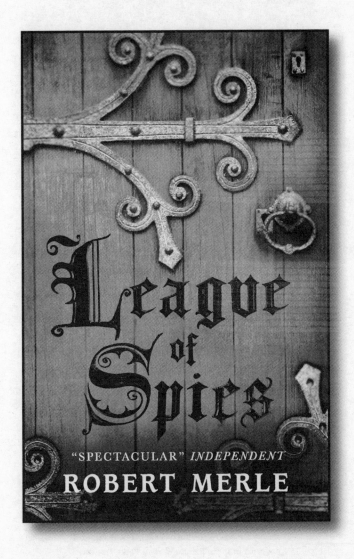

League
of
Spies

"SPECTACULAR" *INDEPENDENT*

ROBERT MERLE